James Hadley Chase and The Murder Room

〉〉 This title is part of The Murder Room, our series dedicated to making available out-of-print or hard-to-find titles by classic crime writers.

Crime fiction has always held up a mirror to society. The Victorians were fascinated by sensational murder and the emerging science of detection; now we are obsessed with the forensic detail of violent death. And no other genre has so captivated and enthralled readers.

Vast troves of classic crime writing have for a long time been unavailable to all but the most dedicated frequenters of second-hand bookshops. The advent of digital publishing means that we are now able to bring you the backlists of a huge range of titles by classic and contemporary crime writers, some of which have been out of print for decades.

From the genteel amateur private eyes of the Golden Age and the femmes fatales of pulp fiction, to the morally ambiguous hard-boiled detectives of mid twentieth-century America and their descendants who walk our twenty-first century streets, The Murder Room has it all. 〉〉

The Murder Room
Where Criminal Minds Meet

themurderroom.com

T0345487

James Hadley Chase (1906–1985)

Born René Brabazon Raymond in London, the son of a British colonel in the Indian Army, James Hadley Chase was educated at King's School in Rochester, Kent, and left home at the age of 18. He initially worked in book sales until, inspired by the rise of gangster culture during the Depression and by reading James M. Cain's *The Postman Always Rings Twice*, he wrote his first novel, *No Orchids for Miss Blandish*. Despite the American setting of many of his novels, Chase (like Peter Cheyney, another hugely successful British noir writer) never lived there, writing with the aid of maps and a slang dictionary. He had phenomenal success with the novel, which continued unabated throughout his entire career, spanning 45 years and nearly 90 novels. His work was published in dozens of languages and over thirty titles were adapted for film. He served in the RAF during World War II, where he also edited the RAF Journal. In 1956 he moved to France with his wife and son; they later moved to Switzerland, where Chase lived until his death in 1985.

By James Hadley Chase
(published in The Murder Room)

So What Happens to Me?

James Hadley Chase

An Orion book

Copyright © Hervey Raymond 1974

The right of James Hadley Chase to be identified as the author of this work has been asserted in accordance with the Copyright, Designs and Patents Act 1988.

This edition published by
The Orion Publishing Group Ltd
Orion House
5 Upper St Martin's Lane
London WC2H 9EA

An Hachette UK company

A CIP catalogue record for this book is available from the British Library

ISBN 978 1 4719 0386 1

www.orionbooks.co.uk

CHAPTER ONE

THE SOUND OF THE TELEPHONE BELL brought me awake. I looked at the bedside clock. The time was 09.05. I threw off the sheet and swung my legs to the floor. Through the thin ceiling I could hear my old man answering the telephone. The call had to be for me. He scarcely ever had calls. I struggled into my dressing gown, and by the time I had reached the landing, he was calling for me.

'Someone wants you, Jack,' he said. 'Polson . . . Bolson . . . I didn't get his name.'

I took the stairs in three jumps, aware my old man was looking sadly at me.

'I'm just off,' he said. 'I wish you'd get up a little earlier. We could have had breakfast together.'

'Yeah.'

I swept into the tiny, drab living-room and grabbed up the receiver.

'This is Jack Crane,' I said as I watched my old man walk down the path to his five-year-old Chevvy for another stint at the bank.

'Hi! Jack!'

Thirteen months rolled away. I would know that voice anywhere and I stiffened to attention.

'Colonel Olson!'

'That's me, Jack! How are you, you old sonofabitch?'

'I'm fine. How are you, sir?'

'Cut the "sir" crap. We're not in the army now, thank God! I've had one hell of a time locating you.'

The snap in that voice seemed to me to be missing. Here was the greatest bomber pilot ever with enough decorations to plaster a wall actually telling me he had been trying to locate *me*! Colonel Bernie Olson! My Vietnam boss! The marvellous guy I had kept in the air come rain, sun and snot while he beat the hell out of the Viets. For three years I had been his chief mechanic before he got a bullet in his groin that fixed him. Our parting was the worst moment in my life. He went home and I was detailed to look after

1

another pilot and what a slob he turned out to be! I had hero worshipped Olson. I had never expected to hear from him again, but here he was, speaking to me after thirteen months.

'Listen, Jack,' he was saying, 'I'm rushed. Have to get off to Paris. How are you fixed? I can steer you to a job, working with me, if you're interested.'

'I'll say! Nothing would please me more.'

'Okay. It's worth fifteen grand. I'll send you your air ticket and expenses and we'll talk about it.' Just why did this great guy sound so flat? I wondered. 'I want you down here. I'm calling from Paradise City: it's around sixty miles from Miami. The job's a toughie, but you can make it. Anyway, unless you have something else lined up . . . what have you to lose?'

'Did you say fifteen thousand dollars, Colonel?'

'That's it, but you'll earn it.'

'That's fine with me.'

'You'll be hearing from me. I've got to rush. See you Jack,' and the connection was broken.

Slowly, I replaced the receiver, then stared up at the ceiling, a surge of excitement going through me. I had been discharged from the army now for the past six months. I had come home because there was nowhere else for me to go. I had lived these months in a small-time town, spending my army pay-out on girls, booze and generally fooling around. It hadn't been a happy time for either myself or for my old man who managed the local bank. I had told him I'd find a job sooner or later and not to worry. He wanted to part with his savings to set me up as a garage owner, but that was the last thing I wanted to do. I wasn't going to be just another small-timer as he was. I wanted Big Time.

This was a nice little town and the girls were willing. I had had lots of fun as well as boredom and I told myself that when my money began to run out I would look for something but not in this town. Now, out of the blue, came Colonel Bernie Olson, the man I admired the most in the world, offering me a job that paid off fifteen thousand! Had I really heard aright? Fifteen thousand! And in the most opulent city on the Florida coast! I slammed my fist into my hand. I was so excited I wanted to stand on my head!

So I waited to hear from Olson. I didn't tell my old man, but he was a wise old guy and he knew something was cooking. When he came back from the bank for lunch, he regarded me as he cooked two steaks. My mother had died while I was in Vietnam. I knew better than to interfere with his routine. He liked to buy the food on his way back from the bank and cook it while I stood around.

'Something good for you, Jack?' he asked as he pushed the steaks around in the pan.

'I don't know yet. Could be. A friend of mine wants me to go down to Paradise City, Florida, about a possible job.'

'Paradise City?'

'Yeah . . . near Miami.'

He served the steaks on plates.

'That's a long way from here.'

'Could be further.'

We took our plates into the living-room and we ate for a while, then he said, 'Johnson wants to sell his garage. It could be a great opportunity for you. I would put up the capital.'

I looked at him: a lonely old man, desperately trying to hold on to me. It would be more than depressing for him to live in this box of a house on his own, but what kind of life would it be for me? He had had his life. I wanted to have mine.

'It's an idea, dad.' I didn't look at him but concentrated on the steak, 'but I'll see what this job is first.'

He nodded. 'Of course.'

We left it like that. He went off to the bank for the afternoon stint and I lay on my bed, thinking. Fifteen thousand dollars! Maybe it was a toughie, but no job could be too tough that paid that kind of money.

As I lay there, I thought back on the past. I was now twenty-nine years of age. I was a qualified aero-engineer. There was nothing I didn't know about the guts of an aircraft. I had had a good paying job with Lockheed until I got drafted into the Army. I had spent three years keeping Colonel Olson in the air and now back in this small-time town, I knew sooner or later I would have to pick up my career. The trouble with me, I told myself, was that the Army had spoilt me. I was reluctant to begin life again where I had to think for myself and to compete. The Army had suited me fine. The money was good, the girls were willing and I went along with the discipline. But fifteen grand a year sounded like the rise of the curtain to the way I hoped to live. A toughie? Well, I told myself as I reached for a cigarette, it would have to be damned tough before I quit on that kind of money.

3

Two days dragged by, then I got a bulky envelope from Olson. It arrived as my old man was taking off for the bank. He came up to my room, tapped on the door and came in. I had just come awake and I felt like hell. I had had a really thick night. I had taken Suzy Dawson to the Taverna nightclub and we had got stinking drunk. Later we had rolled around on a piece of waste ground until 03.00, then somehow I had got her home and some-how I had got myself home and into bed.

I blinked at my old man, feeling my head expanding and con-tracting. I was getting double vision that told me how stinking I had been. He looked very tall, very thin and very tired, but what really killed me was there were two of him.

'Hi, Dad!' I said and forced myself to sit up.

'Here's a letter for you, Jack,' he said. 'I hope it's what you want. I have to get off. See you lunch time.'

I took the bulky envelope.

'Thanks . . . have a good morning.' That was the least I could say.

'The usual.'

I lay still until I heard the front door close, then I ripped open the envelope. It contained a first-class ticket to Paradise City, five hundred dollars in cash and a brief note that ran:

I'll meet your plane, Bernie.

I looked at the money. I checked the air ticket. Fifteen thousand dollars a year! In spite of my aching head and feeling drained empty, I punched the air and yelled 'Yip-eeee!'

As I came through the barrier that led into the opulent lobby of Paradise City's airport, I spotted him before he spotted me.

That tall, lean figure was unmistakable, but there were changes.

Then he saw me and his lean face lit up with a smile. It wasn't that wide, friendly grin he kept especially for me out in Vietnam. It was a cynical smile of a man full of disillusions, but anyway a smile.

'Hi! Jack!'

We shook hands. His hand was hot and sweaty: so sweaty I surreptitiously wiped my hand on the seat of my pants.

'Hi! Colonel! It's been a long time. . . .'

'Sure has.' He regarded me. 'Cut out the Colonel, Jack. Call me Bernie. You look fine.'

'And you too.'

His grey eyes moved over me.

'That's good news. Well, come on. Let's get out of here.'

We crossed the crowded lobby into the hot sunshine. As we walked I looked him over. He was wearing a dark blue blouse shirt, white linen slacks and expensive-looking sandals. He made my seersucker brown suit and scuffed shoes shabby.

In the shade stood a white E-type Jag. He slid under the driving wheel and I got in beside him, shoving my bag at the back.

'Some car.'

'Yeah. It's all right.' He shot me a quick look. 'It's not mine. It belongs to the boss.'

He drove on to the highway. The time was 10.00 and the traffic was light.

'What have you been doing since you got out?' he asked as he steered the car past a truck loaded with crates of oranges.

'Nothing. Just getting the feel of being out. I'm shacked up with my old man. I've been spending Army money. It's running low now. You caught me at the right moment. Next week I was going to write to Lockheed to see if they could find a place for me.'

'You wouldn't want that, would you?'

'I guess not, but I have to eat.'

Olson nodded. 'That's right . . . don't we all.'

'You look as if you eat and then some.'

'Yeah.'

He swung the Jag off the highway and on to a dirt road that led down to the sea. A hundred yards or so down the road we came to a wooden built café-bar with a veranda that looked out on to the expanse of beach and beyond the sea. He pulled up.

'We can talk here, Jack,' he said and got out.

I followed him up the creaky steps and on to the veranda. The place was empty. We sat down at a table and a girl came out and smiled at us.

'What'll you have?' Olson asked.

'A coke,' I said although I wanted whisky.

'Two cokes.'

The girl went away.

'You quit drinking, Jack?' Olson asked. 'I remember you were hitting the hard stuff pretty often.'

'I start after six.'

5

'Sound idea. I don't touch the stuff now.'

He produced a pack of cigarettes and we lit up. The girl came with the cokes, then went away.

'I haven't a lot of time, Jack, so let me give you the photo,' Olson said. 'I have a job for you . . . if you want it.'

'You said fifteen grand. I'm still getting over the shock.' I grinned at him. 'Anyone but you who offered me that kind of money, I would have thought crazy, but coming from you, Colonel, I'm sort of excited.'

He sipped his coke and stared out across the beach.

'I'm working for Lane Essex,' he said and paused.

I stared at him, startled. There could be few people who hadn't heard of Lane Essex. He was one of those colourful men like *Playboy's* Hefner, although a lot richer than Hefner. Essex ran nightclubs, owned hotels in every major city in the world, ran Casinos, built blocks of apartments, owned a couple of oil fields, had a big stake in the Detroit car world and was reputed to be worth two billion dollars.

'That's something!' I exclaimed. 'Lane Essex! You mean you're offering me a job to work for him?'

'That's the idea, Jack, if you want it.'

'Want it? This is terrific! Lane Essex!'

'Sounds fine, doesn't it? But I told you . . . it's a toughie. Look, Jack, working for Essex is like getting tangled with a buzz-saw.' He stared at me. 'I'm thirty-five and I have grey hair. Why? Because I work for Lane Essex.'

I looked directly at him and I remembered him thirteen months ago. He had aged ten years. That snap in his voice had gone. There was a shifty, worried expression in his eyes. His hands were never still. He fiddled with his glass. He kept flicking at his cigarette. He kept running his fingers through his greying hair. This wasn't Colonel Bernie Olson I used to know.

'Is it that tough?'

'Essex has a saying,' Olson said quietly. 'He says nothing in this world is impossible. He called a meeting a couple of months ago and had all his staff gathered together in some goddamn hall. He delivered a pep talk. The theme was that if you wanted to remain with him you had to accept the impossible was possible. He has a staff of over eight hundred men and women: that's his personal staff; people working in Paradise City; executives,

P.R.O.s, lawyers, accountants, right down to people like myself. He told us if we couldn't accept this requirement that nothing on this earth is impossible, then to see Jackson, his second-in-command, and check out. Not one of the eight hundred dummies, including myself, saw Jackson. So now we're stuck with this slogan that nothing is impossible.' He flicked away the butt of his cigarette and lit another. 'Now I come to you, Jack. Essex has ordered a new plane: a four jet job I'm going to fly. It's a very special job with accommodation for a big conference, ten sleeping cabins, all the works: bar, restaurant and so on and so on, plus Essex's suite with a circular bed. This job will be delivered in three months' time, but Essex's runway which takes the kite I'm flying now isn't long enough to take the new kite. I have the job of lengthening the runway. While I'm doing this, I also have to fly him all over the goddamn world. It just can't be done, but nothing is impossible.' He drank some of his coke. 'So I thought of you. I'm putting the cards face up on the table, Jack. I get paid forty-five thousand a year. I want you to take care of the runway and see for certain it is ready within three months from today. We get delivery of the new kite on November 1st and I expect to fly her in. I'm offering you fifteen thousand out of my pay. I tried to talk to Essex, but he wouldn't play. "It's your job, Olson," he said. "How you do it doesn't interest me, but do it!" I knew better than to ask him for extra help. He doesn't go along with that sort of talk. You don't have to worry about expenses. I've got the operation started, but I want you to be there to see it keeps moving.'

'What's the additional length of the runway?'

'A half a mile will do it.'

'What's the ground like?'

'Pretty hellish. There's a forest, slopes and even rocks.'

'I'd like to take a look at it.'

'I expected you to say that.'

We regarded each other. This wasn't the exciting job I had been hoping for. Some instinct told me that there was something odd about it.

'At the end of three months, providing I get the runway built, what happens to me?'

'A good question.' He fiddled with his glass and stared out across the beach. 'I'll have a talking point with Essex. He'll be

7

pleased. I can talk him into giving you the job as airport supervisor and you'll earn at least thirty thousand.'

I finished my coke while I thought.

'Suppose Essex isn't pleased . . . then how do I stand?'

'You mean if you don't complete the job in three months?'

'That's what I mean.'

Olson lit another cigarette. I noticed his hands were unsteady.

'Then I guess you and I are washed up. I told him it could be done. If you don't fix it, then we both are out.' He dragged smoke into his lungs. 'I was lucky to get this job, Jack. Top-class pilots are a dime a dozen these days. Essex has only to snap his fingers to have a load of them in his lap.'

'You talked about fifteen thousand a year. What it really comes down to is you will pay me $3,750 for three months' work and then it depends on how pleased Essex will be whether I get on the permanent staff—right?'

Olson stared at the tip of his cigarette.

'That's about it.' He looked at me, then away. 'After all, Jack, as you have nothing to do right now it isn't so bad, is it?'

'No, it isn't bad.'

We sat in silence for a long moment, then he said, 'Let's go over to the airfield. You take a look and tell me what you think. I have to take him to New York in three hours so I haven't a lot of time.'

'I'd like some money paid into my bank before I start work, Bernie,' I said. 'I'm short.'

'No problem. I'll fix that.' He got to his feet. 'Let's look at it.'

There's something wrong about this set-up, I told myself as he drove back on to the highway. But what can I lose? $3,750 for a three months' stint wasn't bad money. If it didn't finally jell, I still had Lockheed to fall back on. All the same my mind was uneasy. This man at my side wasn't the great Colonel Olson I used to know. That man I would have trusted with my last cent. I would have given my life for him, but not this man. There was an odd change in him that bothered me. I couldn't put my finger on what the change was, but I felt wary of him and that's a bad thing.

The Lane Essex airport was located about ten miles behind the City. Above the big wired entrance gates was a sign that read:
ESSEX ENTERPRISES

The two guards in bottle-green uniforms with revolvers on their hips, saluted Olson as he drove in.

The usual airport buildings looked bright, new and modern. I could see people moving around in the control tower. They also wore this bottle-green uniform.

Olson drove on to the runway, sending the Jag surging forward. About half a mile down the runway, I saw a big cloud of dust and Olson slowed.

'Here we are,' he said and pulled up. 'Look, Jack, let me put you further in the photo. I've organized everything as I told you. Your job is to see that it is kept organized. I'm scared of labour trouble. We have a gang of around sixteen hundred men: most of them coloured. They sleep in tents and they are supposed to work from 07.00 to 18.00 with a two-hour break for lunch. Make no mistake about this: it's goddamn hot in the afternoon. The man in charge is Tim O'Brien. You'll be his boss. I've told him you're coming. He's okay, but I don't trust the Irish over much. Your job is to supervise him while he supervises the gang. Keep clear of them. I don't want trouble. They like O'Brien. Do you get all this?'

I stared at him. 'So what the hell do I do?'

'Like I said. Watch O'Brien. Move around the site. If you spot anyone lying down on the job, tell O'Brien. Make certain no one knocks off until 18.00.'

He got out of the car and walked fast towards the cloud of dust. Bewildered, I followed him. When we had got beyond the cloud of dust, I saw the work going on and it shook me. There seemed to be around twenty bulldozers levelling the ground. An army of men sweated with shovels, heaving rocks, cutting up fallen trees with electric saws. There was a road-making machine and the stink of tar was strong.

From somewhere a short, fat man wearing baggy, dirty khaki trousers and a sweat-stained shirt appeared before us.

'Hi! Colonel!' he said.

'How's it going, Tim?' Olson asked.

The man grinned.

'Like a dream. The boys have cut down thirty firs this morning. we're just clearing them.'

Olson turned to me.

'Jack . . . meet Tim O'Brien. You two are going to work together. Tim . . . this is Jack Crane.'

While he was speaking, I was looking at O'Brien. He was a solid hunk of bone, fat and muscle, around forty-five years of age, balding, with a blunt featured face, steady blue eyes and a firm mouth. This was a man no one could dislike: a worker, a man you could trust and I thrust out my hand which he gripped, shook and then released.

'Tim . . . wise Crane up, I've got to get moving.' Olson looked uneasily at his strap watch. 'Get him a cabin and a jeep.'

A violent, too close explosion went off with a bang that made me jump.

O'Brien grinned.

'We're blasting,' he said. 'Got a lot of rock down there.'

Olson tapped my arm.

'I've got to move, Jack. I'll be seeing you in three days' time. Tim will look after you.'

He turned and started back to where he had left the Jag.

O'Brien looked at his watch.

'Give me ten minutes, Mr Crane, and we'll go back to the airport. I just want to see the boys get their lunch,' and he walked off, leaving me standing there like a goddamn dummy.

I watched. The operation of clearing the land was going like clockwork. Already the road-building machine had completed two hundred yards of runway. There was another bang as more explosives tore into the rocks ahead and ten bulldozers roared into action.

What the hell am I doing here? I asked myself. This couldn't be better organized. At the rate these men were working the runway would be completed in two months let alone three.

I stood waiting in the hot sunshine until someone blew a whistle. The machines cut and the noise died down. Men dropped their shovels and there was a general movement towards three big trucks where negroes started to hand out drinks and food containers.

O'Brien drove up to me in an open jeep.

'Hop in, Mr Crane,' he said. 'I'll take you to your cabin. You could do with a shower. I know I could!' He grinned. 'Then suppose you and me have a snack together in my cabin. It's right next door.'

'Fine.' I got in beside him. 'Look, Tim, suppose you call me Jack?'

He glanced at me, then nodded. 'Why not?'

He drove fast down the runway, sheered off and headed towards a long row of cabins that stood near the control tower. He pulled up outside the row, got out and walked over to cabin 5.

'This is yours. Make yourself at home. Suppose you come to cabin 6 in half an hour? Okay?'

'Fine with me.'

Carrying my bag, I opened the cabin door and walked into a blessed air conditioned atmosphere. I shut the door and looked around. Everything in the big living room was luxe. Four lounging chairs, a fully stocked refrigerated cocktail cabinet, a colour TV, a bookshelf stuffed with books, a fitted carpet that felt like I was walking on grass and a stereo and radio set against the far wall. Beyond the living room was a small bedroom with a double bed, closets, night table with a lamp and beyond that a bathroom with all the equipment you could wish for.

I stripped off, took a shower, shaved, put on a short-sleeved shirt and a pair of linen slacks, then returned to the living-room. I was tempted to have a drink, but decided against it. Checking my watch, I had five minutes to wait, so I lit a cigarette and waited. At 12.30 I went to cabin 6 and tapped.

O'Brien, looking a lot less sweaty but still in the same clothes, opened the door and waved me in. I entered a facsimile of the cabin I had just left. There was a smell of onions frying that made my mouth water.

'Lunch is just about ready,' he said. 'What'll you drink?'

'Nothing, thanks.' I sat down in one of the lounging chairs.

A girl wearing a bottle-green blouse and tight bottle-green pants came in with a tray. Quickly she set the table, put down two plates, then left.

'Let's eat,' O'Brien said and sat at the table.

I joined him.

My plate contained a thick steak, lima beans and french fried potatoes.

'You eat well here,' I said as I cut into the steak.

'Everything is top class here,' O'Brien said. 'We're working for Essex.'

We ate for a minute or so, then O'Brien said, 'I understand you and Olson were buddies in Vietnam.'

'He was my boss. I kept him in the air.'

11

'How did you like it in Vietnam?'

I cut another piece of steak, put mustard on it and stared at it.

'It was fine with me, but then I wasn't getting shot at.' I conveyed the steak into my mouth and chewed.

'Makes a difference.'

'You can say that again.'

We ate for some moments, then O'Brien said, 'You have had a lot of experience in laying runways?'

I paused in my eating and looked directly at him. He was looking directly at me. We stared at each other and I just couldn't help liking this heavy, fat man as he chewed his steak, his frank blue eyes looking into mine.

'I'm an aero-engineer,' I said. 'I know the guts of most kites, but I have no idea how to build a runway.'

He gave a little nod, then plastered a piece of his steak with mustard.

'Yeah. Well, Jack, thanks for being frank. Let's take it from here. Olson told me he wanted me supervised. He's scared the runway won't be completed in three months. He said he was getting an expert to watch me. I go along with him because the money is fine. He's scared silly of Essex. When a man is scared of another man because he's worried about keeping his job, then I'm sorry for him and am willing to play along.'

I hesitated, then said, 'I knew him thirteen months ago. This is the first time I've seen him since then. There's been a hell of a change.'

'Is that right? I've only been on the job for a couple of weeks, but I know a scared man when I see him.' O'Brien finished his meal, then sat back. 'Well, Jack, what do you suggest you do? I can assure you the runway will be completed within the next six weeks. I've a fine gang working with me and I know I can rely on them.'

'Olson said something about labour trouble.'

O'Brien shook his head. 'Not a chance. Everyone's well paid and I know how to handle them.'

I shrugged.

'Then I'm damned if I know what I'm going to do. As soon as I saw your set-up I knew there was nothing in it for me. You know, Tim, there's something goofy about this. Olson is paying me good money out of his own pocket for what seems to be for nothing.'

O'Brien smiled. 'Well, if you're getting paid and it'll make you happy, you'd better supervise me, hadn't you?'

'Can I come with you and take a look around?' I felt awkward.

'Of course.' He looked at his watch. 'Time I got moving anyway.' He drove me back to the site and slid out of the jeep.

'You take her, Jack. I won't need her this afternoon. Take a look around. I'm open to any suggestions.'

Feeling stupid, I drove by the men who had already begun working, got beyond the level ground and down into the forest. There I left the jeep and walked.

Fifty or so negroes were felling trees with electric saws. They glanced indifferently at me, then one of them, a big good-looking buck, waved me away.

'Ain't safe to wander around, brother,' he said. 'Trees are falling like rain.'

I moved away and leaving the forest, I walked into the hot sun to where they were blasting. Again I was told to keep away. As O'Brien had said, the work was going ahead at a fast clip. He had enough machines, enough men and enough explosives to make the runway in six weeks.

I turned down a sloping path that led to a running stream, well away from the site, and I sat on a rock, lit a cigarette and did some thinking.

One thing I was now certain of: there was nothing here for me to do with O'Brien in charge. So why had Olson sent for me? Why was he paying me $3,750 out of his own pocket just to stooge around when he must know that O'Brien would deliver? What was behind this business? He had gone now to New York. He had said he would be back in three days. In the meantime what was I going to do? My first inclination was to go back home, leaving a letter for him, saying I couldn't see how I could be of help, but I quickly killed that idea. I didn't want to go back to that little drab house: back into small time again. I decided I would wait here until Olson returned and then have it out with him. In the meantime, I decided to write a report on the progress of the runway just to show him that I had been trying to earn his money.

I returned to the site and found O'Brien working on a stalled bulldozer. When he saw me, he came over.

'Look, Tim,' I said. I had to shout to get above the noise of the other bulldozers, 'it looks fine to me. Of course the runway will be finished in six weeks. At the rate you're going it could be finished in five.'

He nodded.

'But I've got to do something to earn my money. I need it. Could I look at your records so I can get out some kind of report for Olson? Would you mind that?'

'Sure, Jack. That's no problem. Go to my cabin. In the top left-hand drawer of my desk, you'll find everything you want. I won't come back with you. I have this machine to fix.'

'I appreciate that.' I paused, then went on. 'My report will probably lose me my job, but that's my luck. I'm going to say there's nothing I can do better than what you're doing right now.'

He regarded me, smiled, then lightly punched me on my arm.

'You've said it. I've been constructing runways now for the past twenty years. See you tonight,' and leaving me, he returned to the stalled bulldozer.

I got in the jeep and drove back to the cabins. I was sweating. The afternoon sun was fierce and it was a relief to walk into O'Brien's air-conditioned cabin. I paused in the doorway, startled.

A blonde girl was lolling in one of the lounging chairs. She was wearing red stretch pants and a white blouse that was open to her navel, just containing her heavy breasts. Her hair fell to her shoulders in a cascade of gold silk. She was around twenty-five years of age with a narrow, high cheek-boned face with large green eyes. She was about the sexiest looking woman I had seen for more years than I cared to remember.

She regarded me coolly and then smiled. Her teeth were as white as orange pith and her lips glistening and sensual.

'Hi!' she said. 'Looking for Tim?'

I moved into the room and closed the door.

'He's out on the site.'

'Oh!' She made a little face, then stirred her lush body. 'I was hoping to catch him. How that man works!'

'I guess that's right.'

All right, I admit it, she turned me on. The girls in my small-time town had nothing on her.

'Who are you?' she asked, smiling.

'Jack Crane. I'm the new runway supervisor. Who are you?'

'Pam Osborn. I'm deputy air hostess when Jean wants time off.'

We regarded each other.

14

'Well, that's fine.' I went over to the desk and sat down. 'Anything I can do for you, Miss Osborn?'

'Maybe . . . it's a lonely life sticking around this airport.' She shifted a little in her chair. One of her heavy breasts nearly escaped but she pushed it back in time. 'I looked in to chat up Tim.'

That I didn't believe. I was sure at this hour—it was just after 16.oo—she would know O'Brien would be on the site. Again I felt wary. I was sure she had been waiting for me. Why?

'You have no luck.' I opened the top left-hand drawer of the desk. There was a heavy black leather folder there. I took it out. 'I too have work to do.'

She laughed. 'The brush-off, Jack?'

'Well. . . .'

We looked at each other.

'Well . . . what?'

I hesitated, but she had me going now.

'My cabin is next door,' I said.

'So shall we go next door?'

Again I hesitated, but women like her do things to me. I put the folder back in the drawer.

'Why not?'

She slid out of the chair as I came around the desk.

'There's something about you . . .'

'I know, and there's something about you too.'

I slid my arms around her as she slammed her body against mine. Her lips crushed mine and her tongue darted into my mouth.

All caution, all wariness went from my mind. I practically dragged her out of O'Brien's cabin and into mine.

'You're some man,' she said lazily.

The loving, if you can call it that, was over and she lay like a beautiful, sleek cat on the big bed beside me.

She had been the best lay I had had since the little Vietnamese way back in Saigon who had been a little more violent, a little more intense, but not much.

I reached for a cigarette, lit it and stretched. My mind became wary again.

'Sort of sudden, wasn't it?' I said, not looking at her.

She laughed.

15

'I suppose. I heard you had arrived. I hoped you would want a little loving. I guessed you would come to Tim's cabin or your own. I'm a girl who needs it and Man! are there creeps on this camp: creeps who are scared of their own shadows. They would no more screw than cut their throats: that's how scared they are of losing their jobs.'

'So that talk about waiting to chat up Tim was so much crap?'

'What do you think? Can you imagine a girl like me taking on a sweaty, husky like Tim? I've nothing against him. He's okay, but not my type.' She raised her arms above her head and released a contented sigh. 'I was hoping to find new blood . . . I've found it.'

I half turned and looked at her. She was a beautiful, lush, hard piece of corruption, but she fascinated me.

'Does Olson get it from you?'

'Bernie?' She shook her head and her face darkened a little. 'Don't you know what happened to him? He got a bullet where it does the most damage. Poor Bernie is no longer operative.'

This shocked me. I knew Olson had been hit in the groin while completing his last mission, but I hadn't thought just what that could mean. Was that Olson's trouble, apart from being scared he would lose his job? Judas! I thought, if that had happened to me!

'I didn't know.'

'He's a marvellous man,' Pam said. 'He talked to me about you. He thinks you're marvellous too. He's a big admirer of yours.'

'Is that right?'

'He needs you, Jack. He's lonely. He doesn't get along with these other creeps. He kept asking me if I thought you would take this job. He was scared you would turn him down.'

Okay, it was well done, but there was a ring about it that warned me she had been rehearsed.

'I wouldn't turn Bernie down no matter what the job was.'

She raised one leg and regarded it. 'Well, you're here . . . that proves it, doesn't it?' She lowered her leg and smiled at me.

'But how long do I stay? There's no job here for me, baby. Tim is taking care of the runway.'

'Bernie wants you to watch him.'

'I know. He told me. Tim doesn't need watching.' I crushed out my cigarette. 'What else did he tell you?'

She gave me that blank look women give when they are not talking.

16

'Just he wanted you with him: that's all.'

'You sound as if you have his confidence.'

'You could say that. There are times when there is no flying. Essex isn't always in the air. Bernie and I get together. He doesn't like Jean. He's lonely.'

'You don't mean he's offering to pay me out of his own pocket because he wants my company?'

'That's about it, Jack. I hope you'll go along with him.'

'I think I'd better talk to him. He seems rather scared of losing his job.'

'Everyone is. Essex is hard to get along with and so is Mrs Essex.'

'Is there a Mrs Essex?'

Pam wrinkled her nose.

'You're lucky Bernie is employing you. Yes, there is a Mrs Essex . . . dear Victoria. I hope you never run into her. She's a blueprint for the biggest bitch in the world. Everyone is terrified of her.'

'Like that?'

'Yes. You put a foot wrong just once and Mrs Essex gets you the gate. She has her husband in the palm of her hand. Okay, Essex is a bastard, full of conceit, but then he has something to be conceited about. But Victoria! She's a jumped up nothing: just a beautiful face and body: a spoilt pampered bitch who plays hell with anyone who depends on Essex for a living.'

'She sounds nice.'

'That's the word.' Pam laughed. 'Keep clear of her. What are you doing tonight? Like to take me out to dinner? I have a Mini Austin. We could go to a seafood restaurant in the City. Fancy it?'

'Fine,' I said. 'Now move this beautiful body out of here. I have work to do.'

'Not on your first day, Jack. That's always fatal,' and she twined her arms around me.

CHAPTER TWO

L'ESPADON RESTAURANT, a straight steal from the Paris Ritz's décor, was built out on a pier. Four plaster, painted swordfish plus some fish-nets decorated the walls. The tables, lit by electric candles, were set wide enough for people to talk secrets and not be overheard.

Pam was wearing one of those long things, down to her heels, caught at the waist with a silver belt with a snake's head. She looked pretty gorgeous. The maître d'hôtel came sliding over to her, giving her his teeth with that wide, friendly smile that maître d's reserve only for their favourites. She said something to him I didn't catch and with a wave of his hand he conducted us to a table at the far end of the restaurant with lush, plush seats for two and a view of the whole restaurant.

'A pleasure, Miss Osborn,' he said as he drew out her chair. 'A champagne cocktail?' He didn't even look at me.

She sat down and smiled at him.

'That would be lovely, Henri.'

'May I arrange what you eat?' He was leaning over her and I could smell his after-shave.

'Let's have the menu,' I said, 'and a Scotch on the rocks for me.'

Slowly his head came around and he regarded me. His eyes moved over my slightly worn lightweight suit and a pained look came into his eyes. His expression told me as nothing else could that I was Mr Nobody.

'Let's leave it to Henri,' Pam said firmly. 'He knows.'

I was tempted to start something but the opulence of this place and the hostile expression in this fat man's eyes intimidated me. I gave up. 'Sure . . . let's leave it to Henri.'

There was a pause, then Henri drifted away to receive a party of six.

'You screw him too?' I asked.

She giggled. 'Just once. It's made a lasting impression. This is the only restaurant in this City where I eat free . . . and that includes you.'

I relaxed. From the look of the place I was sure I wouldn't have had enough money to settle the check. I regarded her not without admiration.

'You get around, baby.'

'You can say that again.' Leaning forward, resting her cool hand on mine, she went on, 'Henri is terrified of me. He has a jealous wife and he imagines I'm going to blackmail him.'

'Nice for you.'

The drinks arrived. There were little hot hors d'œuvres to keep them company. Two waiters hovered over us. The restaurant was filling up.

18

'Some place.' I looked around. 'This must cost plenty without Henri picking up the tab.'

'Oh, it does.'

The wine waiter arrived with a bottle of Sancerre in an ice bucket. He bowed to Pam, who gave him a sexy smile. I wondered if she were screwing him too.

Then a sole in shrimp sauce with slices of thick lobster meat arrived.

'You've certainly caught the knack of living,' I said as I forked fish into my mouth.

'Men!' Pam shook her head, her large green eyes wide with wonderment. 'What they will do for a girl like me. The trick, of course, is to give a little and take a lot. Men are either grateful or they get scared, but it still pays off.'

'What am I supposed to be: grateful or scared?'

She chased a piece of lobster with her fork as she said, 'Just be your exciting self.'

'I'll remember that.'

She shot me a quick glance.

'It's gorgeous, isn't it?'

'Sure is.' We ate in silence for a moment or so, then I said, 'Bernie won't be back for a couple of days?'

'Look, Jack, let's forget Bernie. Let's enjoy ourselves. Right?'

But I was uneasy. Before leaving the airport, I had had a word with Tim. Pam had said she would pick me up at 20.00 so I had had time for a shave, a shower and a drink. Tim had returned to his cabin at 19.25. He had looked in.

'Got what you want?' he asked. He looked dead tired, sweaty and dirty.

I felt a twinge of conscience.

'I had a visitor. She didn't leave me any time.'

'You mean Pam?'

'That's who I mean.'

He grinned. 'That girl! I knew she would make for you, but not this fast.'

'I'm going out with her tonight.'

Tim eyed the drink in my hand.

'I could use one of those.'

'Come on in: she's certain to be late.'

I mixed him a long Scotch and soda with plenty of ice.

19

'What is she?' I asked as I handed him the glass. 'The local hooker?'

'She's Olson's girl friend.'

That shook me.

'You know Bernie . . . ?'

'Oh, sure. He doesn't care about her sleeping around. They have a thing for each other. The only thing they don't do is go to bed together.'

'For Pete's sake! If I'd known I wouldn't have touched her! I'm not going out with her tonight if she's Bernie's girl.'

Tim drank greedily, paused to wipe his mouth with the back of his hand.

'If you don't, some other guy will. Just don't think it's anything but a lay, Jack. She's Bernie's girl. She has to have it. Olson can't give it to her, so he lets her play around. This is no secret: the staff here and I guess half Paradise City knows about it, but just don't take her seriously.' He finished his drink, set down his glass and moved to the door. 'Me for a shower and TV.' He regarded me, then smiled. 'Life's damn odd, isn't it?'

But I now had Bernie on my conscience.

'Look, Pam,' I said, then paused while the waiter took our plates away. 'Tim tells me you're Bernie's girl. He's my best friend. This bothers me.'

'Oh, for God's sake! I told you: I need it! Bernie doesn't mind. Will you stop talking about it. I tell you: Bernie knows how I am. He doesn't mind.'

The waiter brought a Tournedo Rossini with fronds d'arti-chauts and princess potatoes. He served while I thought.

'Looks marvellous, doesn't it?' Pam said. 'Mmmm! I adore eating here!'

'He must mind,' I said. 'You mean he's in love with you and you with him?'

'Oh, shut up!' Her voice was low and suddenly vicious. 'Take what you get and be thankful!'

I gave up. I told myself from now on, I wouldn't touch her. This was a hell of a situation! Bernie . . . the man I admired most and I had screwed his girl!

I lost my appetite. As good as the steak was, I now found it hard to eat. I looked around the restaurant while I played with the food on my plate. There was a sudden commotion with Henri

20

flying down the aisle to the entrance. I saw a tall, massively built man, around sixty years of age, come out of the shadows and into the diffused light. I have never seen such a man. By the way he walked he was obviously a queer. His fat face with its snout of a nose made me think of a disagreeable dolphin. He wore an outrageous orange wig that rested a little sideways on what was obviously a completely bald head. He had on a buttercup-yellow linen suit and a frilled, purple shirt. As a show-off, he was in a class of his own.

'Look at that freak,' I said, glad to change the conversation. 'Who can he be?'

Pam glanced down the aisle.

'That's Claude Kendrick. He owns the most fashionable, the most expensive and the most profitable art gallery here.'

I watched the fat man waddle to a table, three tables from where we were sitting. Behind him came a thin, willowy man who could be any age from twenty-five to forty. His long, thick hair was the colour of sable and his lean face, narrow eyes and almost lipless mouth made him look like a suspicious, vicious rat.

'That's Louis de Marncy, who runs the gallery,' Pam told me. She cut into her steak and ate.

The fuss Henri was making of these two told me that Henri considered them V.I.P. people. Interested, I watched them settle at their table. A vodka martini appeared as if by magic and was placed before the fat man. His companion refused a drink. There was a brief discussion with Henri about what they would eat, then Henri, darting away, snapped his fingers at a waiter to follow him.

Claude Kendrick looked around, like a king surveying his court. He waggled his fingers at people he appeared to know, then he looked our way. His little eyes dwelt on my face for a brief moment, then they shifted to Pam. His eyebrows crawled upwards and his mouth pursed into a smile. Then he did the damnedest thing. He bowed to her and, using the orange wig as you might use a hat, he lifted it high off his egg bald head, bowed again and replaced it, then he shifted a little in his chair and began to talk to his companion.

Pam giggled.

'He's marvellous, isn't he?' she said. 'He does that to all his women friends.'

'You a friend of his?'

'I used to model some of his special jewellery. I've known him for some years.' She finished her steak. 'Excuse me . . . I have an idea,' and, getting up, she went over to Kendrick's table. Her back screened him from me and she talked to him for about three minutes, then returned to our table.

'What was all that about?' I asked.

'He has the most marvellous motor cruiser. I thought it would be fun if we had a trip. He's delighted. You know this city is a bit dull for people who always live here. Everyone likes to meet someone new. You'll come, won't you?'

As I hesitated, she went on, 'He's really fun and very important.' The waiter came and cleared our plates. 'You'll like him.'

The motor cruiser had an appeal.

'Well, okay: what have I to lose?'

I looked across at Kendrick. He smiled and nodded to me as the waiter served him smoked salmon. I nodded back to him.

We finished the meal with coffee. Kendrick and de Marney only had the salmon and also coffee. By the time we were ready to go, they were also ready to go.

Pam pushed back her chair and led me to their table.

'Claude . . . this is Jack Crane. He's working on the runway. Jack . . . this is Mr Kendrick.'

'Call me Claude, cheri.' A hand that felt like a lump of warm dough engulfed mine. 'So glad. Welcome to this lovely city. I do hope you will be marvellously happy here.' He heaved himself to his feet. 'Let's go out into the moonlight. Louis, my pet, do take care of darling Pam. I want to get to know Jack.' He encircled my arm and led me down the aisle. Twice he paused to raise his awful wig and bow to women who smiled at him. I was sweating with embarrassment by the time Henri bowed us into the hot night air.

Here we all paused.

Kendrick said, 'Do take Pam for a little ride in the boat, Louis. You know how she loves it. Jack, will you put up with me for a few minutes? There is something I want to talk about.'

Before I could protest, Pam and Louis were walking away.

'What's there to talk about?' I hated this fat freak and hated the idea of being stranded with him.

'It's about Bernie; he is one of my bestest friends.' Kendrick mopped his face with a silk handkerchief. 'Let us get in my car. It's air-conditioned. I find this heat a little oppressive, don't you?'

I hesitated, but without Pam to drive me back to the airport, I was marooned so I followed him down the pier to where a gaudy yellow and black Cadillac stood waiting. A Jap chauffeur slid out and had the doors open as we approached.

'Just drive around, Yuko,' Kendrick said and lowered his bulk into the car. I went around the other side and got in. There was a glass partition between the chauffeur and the rear seats. It was wonderfully cool when the car doors were shut. The car slid away and Kendrick offered me a cigar which I refused.

We drove along the sea front for some minutes, then the chauffeur turned off the main boulevard and took us out into the country.

Kendrick who had got his cigar smoking evenly, said, 'I understand that you are a very close friend of Bernie.'

'That is correct.'

'I am worried about Bernie.' Kendrick heaved a sigh. 'The poor darling . . . that dreadful wound.'

I didn't say anything but waited.

'He has terrible people to work for. That man Essex! What a creature! And his wife!' Still I didn't say anything. 'Bernie feels so insecure.'

'Don't we all!' I said, watching the moon as it floated like a yellow disc in the cloudless sky.

'You feel the same?' He turned to look directly at me. 'You also feel insecure?'

'Who doesn't?'

'You're right, of course, but have you ambitions? Do you want to be rich? I'm sure you do and Bernie is the same. We often talk about money. He once said to me . . . I remember his exact words: "Claude, I would do anything to fix this insecurity. If I could only lay my hands on some real money I wouldn't care how I got it." '

'Bernie said that?'

'Those were his exact words.'

It was my turn to look directly at him.

'Look, Kendrick, suppose you skip this phoney build-up? To me, it stinks. I can see you want to feel your way as you don't know much about me, but your approach is as subtle as a bulldozer. What have you on your mind?'

He took off his orange wig and looked inside as if he expected to find something hiding in there, then he slapped it back on his head.

'Bernie warned me,' he said and smiled. 'He said I would have to be careful how I handled you. He told me he once had got you out of trouble. You held up a Vietnamese money changer and got away with three thousand dollars. Bernie gave you an alibi. Is that correct?'

'Vietnamese money changers were easy meat. I needed the money and he had plenty. Bernie talks too much.'

'Bernie said the money changer was killed by a bomb so everything was nicely tidied up.'

As the Caddy drifted along with the lights of Paradise City making a necklace of diamonds in the distance, my mind went back to Saigon.

My Vietnamese girl wanted money to get to Hong Kong. She was half out of her mind with terror. She had come from the North and she was sure the Viets were after her. Nothing I could tell her made an impact. She insisted she had to have money to bribe her way to safety. I was a bit crazy about her, but her stupid terror spoilt our nights. I had no money to give her. Although I knew I was losing her, I finally decided I would have to get her to Hong Kong. One evening I walked into this money changer's office, with a service revolver in my hand and forced him to give me the money. I had been drinking hard and didn't give a damn. I gave the money to her and that was the last I saw of her. Then the M.P.s had a line-up and the money changer fingered me. I thought I was in the ditch, but Olson arrived. He said he and I were working on his kite at the time of the hold-up. I'm sure the M.P.s weren't convinced, but Bernie had a lot of authority and I got away with it.

Thinking about this incident, it seemed a long way in the past. It was a lucky thing for me that the money changer's office, with him in it, caught one of the first rocket bombs the Viets threw at Saigon. He was going to take his complaint to the Commanding General, but the rocket silenced him.

I had told Bernie the facts and he had grinned at me.

'Well, don't do it again, Jack. I might not be around to bail you out,' and that was that.

At least, it was for a time, but I was always short of money. I got tied up with another Vietnamese girl; a dancer at one of the gaudy, noisy clubs American servicemen frequented. She held out for money; that's what most Vietnamese girls thought about. So one night, when I was really turned on, I walked into another money changer's shop. I wasn't taking any chances this time. There was a thunderstorm going on, plus a hail of Viet rockets and the noise drowned my shot. I thought no more of killing an old Vietnamese than I would have shooting a wild duck. I collected a thousand dollars out of his open safe. It was enough to get me a good time with the girl and have something in hand. I did this three times. Each time I knocked off the money changer and then my conscience caught up on me. I began to dream about these old men. I kept seeing their eyes, full of terror, as I shot them. These eyes followed me around even when I was servicing Olson's kite. So I dropped it. Sitting in this luxe Cadillac, the eyes came back.

Kendrick was saying. 'What have I on my mind? Bernie must tell you that. It's his operation, but there is one thing I would like to ask you. Bernie said he would do *anything* for big money. The operative word, of course, is "anything". May I ask if that is your thinking?'

'It depends on what big money means,' I said.

He nodded.

'That is the correct answer.' He released cigar smoke that was immediately taken out of the car by a small but efficient extractor fan. 'Yes . . . how big? Would a quarter of a million interest you?'

I felt a prickle run up my spine, but I kept my cool.

'It would interest anyone.'

'I'm not talking about anyone.' There was a sudden impatient snap in his voice. 'I'm asking *you*.'

'It depends.'

'It is a simple question, cheri. Do you do *anything* for a quarter of a million dollars?'

'I'll have to talk to Bernie.'

'Quite right.' Kendrick picked up a tiny microphone. 'We'll return, Yuko.'

The Cadillac stopped, turned and headed back to the City.

'Quite an operation,' I said. 'First, Bernie sells me on a phoney job. Then Pam seduces me. Now you appear on the scene, talking about a quarter of a million dollars. It's not what I call a well planned operation. It's too hurried. Suppose I go to the cops right now and tell them what is happening. Do you think they would be interested?'

Kendrick closed his eyes. He looked like an aged dolphin at rest.

'They might, cheri, but I think they would be more interested in you.' He shifted his wig, keeping his eyes closed. 'But don't let us talk about the police. It is always a depressing subject. There's money to be had and your cut would be a quarter of a million. You must talk to Bernie and you can always say no. If you say no, you can then take a plane back to your little town and spend the rest of your days trying to make some kind of living. That, of course, is your privilege, but on the other hand you can come in with us and become rich.'

I lit a cigarette.

'I'll talk to Bernie.'

We sat in silence until the Caddy pulled up outside L'Espandon where Pam and de Marney were waiting.

As I got out of the car, Kendrick said, 'I hope we can work together, cheri. I have confidence in you.'

I paused to stare at him.

'That's more than I have in you.' I joined Pam who was already moving to where she had parked the Mini.

'You in this too?' I asked as we folded ourselves into the tiny car.

'Did Claude talk to you?'

'You know he did. You threw him at me, didn't you? I'm asking you: are you in this too?'

She started the motor and began driving the little car fast back towards the airport.

'You'd better talk to Bernie.'

'That still doesn't answer my question, and I want it answered.'

She shrugged.

'Yes, I'm in it. Bernie will explain it to you.'

'If he handles the rest of the operation the way he's handled it so far, I wouldn't touch it.'

She shot me a quick, hard glance.

'What do you mean?'

'It's so phoney. This phoney excuse to get me here, then throwing you at me, then you throwing that fat horror at me. Was this all Bernie's idea?'

'Well, you're interested, aren't you?'

26

'The money interests me, but apart from the money, and it'll take a lot of convincing before I'll believe that kind of money, the operation, so far, stinks.'

'You must talk to Bernie.'

'You can say that again.'

We drove the rest of the way in silence and when she pulled up outside my cabin, she switched on her sexy smile.

'Let's spend the rest of the night together, Jack.' She began to get out of her car, but I stopped her.

'No.' I stared at her. 'You're Bernie's girl . . . remember?'

She looked as if she were going to hit me. I just continued to stare at her until she looked away, then I slid out of the car and walked over to my cabin.

I was up and sipping coffee on the porch when Tim O'Brien came out of his cabin. The time was 06.45 and he looked at me, surprised.

'You're early.'

'I thought I'd come down to the site,' I said and finished my coffee. 'If there's some job you can give me that I can do, I'll be glad.'

'Know anything about blasting?'

'Not a thing.'

He grinned. 'Know anything about bulldozers?'

'Sure.'

'Fine . . . then you look after the bulldozers and I'll look after the blasting.' We got in the Jeep. 'So you've decided you want to work?'

'When I get paid, I give value. But get this straight, Tim, you're the boss. Tell me what you want done and I'll try to do it.'

So I spent the day in the heat, the dust and the noise. Four times I was called on to repair a bulldozer and I did it. Engines were simple to me. I got along fine with the negro crew who worked well but hadn't any idea how to cope with a stalled engine. I didn't see anything of O'Brien until lunch time. From the bangs, he was doing plenty of blasting. We had lunch together under a tree: hamburgers and coffee. He asked me how I liked the job and I said it was fine. He gave me a curious stare, but didn't take it any further.

Before going to sleep that night, I thought over what had hap-

27

pened. It looked to me that Olson was planning some kind of
steal and he wanted me in on it, but wasn't sure of me. This idea,
and I told myself I could be quite wrong, startled me. I would
never have thought that Olson could be bent. I decided that I had
better work or someone might begin to wonder what I was doing
here.

It was sound thinking because around 16.00 the following day
while I was clearing a gas feed and was cursing, I saw the three
negroes who were standing around watching me, suddenly stiffen
as if they had been goosed. Their big black eyes rolled, showing
the whites and I looked over my shoulder.

There was a woman standing a few yards from me, surveying
me. What a woman! I knew at once she couldn't be anyone else
but Mrs Lane Essex. Starting from the top of her head and reading
downwards, she had Venetian red hair that hung to her shoulders
in long, natural waves: a broad forehead, big violet-coloured eyes,
a thin nose, a firm mouth. Quite an inadequate description. She
was the most gorgeous looking woman I had ever seen and she
made Pam Osborn look like a cheap hooker. Her body was something a saint would have thoughts about: long, long legged, full
breasted. She was wearing a white linen shirt tucked into white
jodhpurs and knee high, glittering black boots. Some yards behind
her, a negro in white held the bridles of two horses.

She flicked one of her boots with a riding whip and her violet
eyes continued to survey me the way a cattle dealer will survey a
prize bull he might or might not be going to buy.

I began to wipe the dirt and grease off my hands with a lump
of oily waste, aware of the tensions of the three negroes who very
carefully, very slowly, as if backing away from a puff adder, moved
out of the scene. They kept on moving until they were lost in the
dust.

'Who are you?' There was an arrogant snap in her voice that
made me remember that Pam had described this woman as the
blue-print for the biggest bitch in the world.

I decided to play this one humble.

'Jack Crane, ma'am,' I said. 'Is there something I can do for
you?'

This fazzed her a little. I could see that by her frown and the
way she shifted her elegant feet.

'I don't remember seeing you before.'

'That's right, ma'am.' I kept my expression wooden. 'I've just arrived. I'm working for Mr O'Brien.'

'Oh.' She paused but continued to examine me. 'Where's O'Brien?'

Just then there was a hell of a bang and the horses shied, nearly over-throwing the negro who began struggling with them. I could see he was in trouble and I slid past her and caught the reins of the biggest horse and by sheer brute strength brought him to a standstill. The negro had all he could do to handle the other horse.

'No place for horses, ma'am,' I said. 'We're blasting.'

She came to me, snatched the reins out of my hand and swung herself on to the saddle. The horse reared up, but she gave him a flick of her whip and brought him down to stand trembling but mastered.

The negro swung himself on to his horse.

'Take him away, Sam,' she said, 'before another bang.'

The negro rode off fast, leaving her looking down at me.

'You know something about horses?' she asked.

'No, ma'am. I don't dig anything without brakes.'

She smiled.

'You handled Borgia well enough. Thank you.'

Then the mother of all bangs went off: it sounded as if a five hundred pound aerial bomb had exploded at our feet.

She was under the impression she had the horse under control so she was relaxed. The bang shook me and shook her. What it did to the horse was nobody's business. It reared and snaked and she hadn't a chance to stay on. She was thrown heavily as the horse took off.

There was nothing I could do in that split second she hung in the air, then I started forward, but was much too late. She landed on her shoulders and her head hit the tarmac and there she remained, still gorgeous to look at, but out to the world.

As I knelt beside her, a ring of gaping negroes formed. I didn't know if she had broken her back and I was scared stupid to touch her.

'Get O'Brien!' I bawled. 'Get me a jeep!'

The snap in my voice brought action. Four or five of them ran wildly down the tarmac towards the blasting site. Two others rushed into the dust.

Gently, I touched her and she opened her eyes.

29

'Are you hurt?'

Her eyes closed.

'Mrs Essex! Can I move you?'

Again her eyes opened. She shook her head and the glassy look went out of those wonderful violet eyes. 'I'm all right.' She moved her arms, then her legs. 'God! My head!'

'Take it easy.' I looked around. A jeep skidded to a standstill. A big buck was at the wheel, his eyes rolling. 'I'll take you to hospital.' I gathered her up in my arms and she moaned a little. I carried her to the jeep and got in beside the negro, holding her across my knees. 'Get to the hospital,' I told him. 'Not fast . . . be careful.'

The negro stared at the woman, let in the clutch and began a slow drive along the tarmac. It took ten minutes to reach the airport's hospital. Someone must have phoned. Two interns, a couple of nurses and a grey-haired man in a white coat surrounded the jeep as it stopped.

There was a stretcher and everything was very efficient. They had her off my lap and on to the stretcher and inside the hospital in seconds.

I sat there wondering if by moving her I had done damage and the thought made me sweat.

A jeep came roaring up and O'Brien tumbled out. I told him what had happened.

'Hell!' He wiped his sweaty face. 'What did she want to come down there for? She's always sticking her goddamn nose into anything that doesn't concern her! This could lose me my job when Essex hears about it!'

I shoved by him and entered the air-conditioned coolness of the hospital. There was a nurse at the reception desk.

'How is she?' I asked.

'Dr Winters is examining her now.' She regarded me as if I were a bum begging a dime.

I hesitated, then seeing one of the interns who had handled her come out through a doorway, I went to him.

'How is she? Did I do wrong moving her?'

'You did dead right,' he said and smiled. 'Nothing broken, but concussion. She's asking about her horse.'

'Okay. Tell her not to worry about it. I'll take care of the horse.'

As I started towards the exit, I heard the intern say to the nurse, 'Get Mr Essex and snap it up!'

I went out into the hot sunshine, got in the jeep and started off in the direction where the horse had bolted. O'Brien had gone. It took me two long sweaty hours to come up with the horse. It was at the far end of the airport in a thicket and it was then only by luck that I spotted it. It had got over its scare and I had no trouble tying it to the jeep and I drove slowly back with the horse trotting behind.

Mrs Essex's groom appeared from nowhere as I pulled up outside the hospital. He grinned at me and took charge of the horse.

I went into the hospital and to the reception desk.

The nurse regarded me, lifting her eyebrows. 'Yes?'

'Will you arrange to tell Mrs Essex I've found her horse and it is safe and undamaged,' I said. 'It's news that might do her good.'

She inclined her head. 'And you are . . .?'

'Jack Crane. Mrs Essex knows me.'

Sudden doubt came into her eyes. Suddenly it entered her stupid, snobby mind that in spite of my sweat, filthy hands and shabby clothes, I just might be someone important in the Essex kingdom.

'I'll tell Dr Winters at once, Mr Crane. Thank you for telling us.'

I gave her a long hard stare, then nodding, I went back to the jeep and drove to the site.

As I got out of the jeep, I heard another bang from the blasting site. At least, O'Brien wasn't stopping work. He didn't give a goddamn about Mrs Lane Essex, but I did.

I remembered the feel of her body as I had held her. I remembered those violet eyes and the Venetian red hair against my face as I lifted her.

I walked across to the stalled bulldozer and began work on it again. As I worked I thought of her. I was still thinking of her when the whistle blew and we knocked off for the day.

Back in my cabin, I took a much needed shower. I was getting into a pair of slacks when there came a knock on my door. Thinking it was Tim, I shouted to come in and reached for a shirt.

The door opened and Pam Osborn slid in. She quickly shut the door and I saw her face was pale and her eyes angry.

'What do you want?' I didn't want her here. 'Run away, baby.' I tucked in my shirt. 'I made a mistake about you.'

31

I could see from the expression on her face she hadn't heard what I had said.

'Must you act like a moron?' she demanded. 'Now you're under a spotlight and that's just what Bernie didn't want.'

I moved over to the table and sat on it.

'What are you yakking about?'

'It's all over the airport. You taking that bitch to hospital and then finding her goddamn horse.'

'What's so wrong about it?'

'Everyone is asking who this Jack Crane is. Don't you see every one of the creeps here would have given their right arms to have done what you did?'

'What the hell did you expect me to do? Leave her lying there?'

'It's the horse!' She clenched her fists, then unclenched them. 'That bitch cares more about that horse than she does about herself, her husband or even her money! Couldn't you have thought of that instead of spending hours looking for the blasted brute when anyone could have found it?'

'How was I to know?'

'And another thing . . . what made you start working with O'Brien? Didn't Bernie tell you to supervise him and to keep out of sight? Didn't he tell you not to mix with any of the gang? You have to go out there and fool around with the machines! When Bernie hears about this, he'll blow his stack!'

I began to get angry.

'Oh, shove off!' I said. 'I'm not taking talk like that from you! I'll talk to Bernie. Now get the hell out of here!'

'I came to warn you, you jerk! Before long the establishment will investigate you. The grapevine here is really something. Have a story ready. This sonofabitch Wes Jackson will be descending on you. He's Essex's manager. Watch him! He's so sharp he could cut you by just looking at you. He'll want to know everything there is to know about you. What you are doing here. Who you are. Why Bernie hasn't put you on the payroll. Have a story ready or we'll be sunk. Do you understand?'

'No.' I stared at her. 'I don't understand and I don't like any of it. If you . . .'

The sound of a car pulling up outside my cabin made both of us turn fast to the window.

'He's here . . . Wes Jackson!' Pam's face was whiter than a

fresh fall of snow. 'He mustn't find me here.' She looked around wildly, then darted into the bathroom and closed the door.

That left me standing there on my own.

CHAPTER THREE

WES JACKSON stood in the doorway of my cabin like an under-sized King Kong, but not all that undersized. He was around 6ft 5ins, massively built and around thirty-two or three years of age. He had a turnip-shaped head that sat on his vast shoulders without suggesting he had any neck. His small nose, his small mouth and his small eyes struggled to survive in a sea of pink-white fat. His jet black hair was close cropped. He wore heavy black shell glasses that slightly magnified his sea-green eyes. He was immaculately dressed in a blue blazer with some fancy badge on the pocket, white linen slacks and some club tie pinned to a white shirt with a large gold tie pin.

'Mr Crane?'

The tiny mouth went through the motions of a smile: the sea-green eyes, like points of ice-picks dipped in green paint, moved over me.

I knew at once this man was a natural born sonofabitch and I would have to handle him with care.

'That's correct,' I said and waited.

He moved his bulk into the cabin and closed the door.

'I'm Wesley Jackson. I take care of Mr Essex's affairs.'

I nearly said that must be nice for him, but instead I said, 'Is that right?'

'That's right, Mr Crane. Mrs Essex asked me to come here and thank you for finding her horse.'

'How is she?'

He edged further into the room and slowly settled himself in a lounging chair. It creaked under his weight.

'She had quite a fall, but you know about that.' He shook his turnip head and his fat face expressed sorrow. 'Well, she could be worse. Slight concussion, but nothing really serious.'

'Fine. When I saw her come down I thought she had broken her back.'

He winced.

'Happily, no.'

He crossed one enormous leg over the other and seeing that he was making himself comfortable, I took a chair opposite him.

'It was very thoughtful of you, Mr Crane, to go searching for her horse,' he went on. 'No one seemed to have thought of it. Her horse is important to her.'

I let that one drift and waited.

'Mrs Essex is appreciative.'

I let that one drift too.

He studied his beautifully manicured fingernails, then shot me a sudden hard look.

'You work here, Mr Crane?'

Here it comes, I thought. This fat fink isn't wasting time on me.

'You could say that.'

He nodded.

'Yes.' A pause. 'You don't appear on our payroll, Mr Crane, yet you tell me you are working for us.'

I put a blank look on my face.

'I didn't say that, Mr Jackson. I'm working for Colonel Olson.'

He nibbled at his thumbnail while he stared at me.

'Colonel Olson engaged you?'

'Maybe I'd better explain.' I gave him my frank expression with a slight, apologetic smile. It didn't seem to make any impact on him but I couldn't imagine anything making an impact on him. 'Colonel Olson and I served together in Saigon. He flew a bomber. I kept him flying.' I was speaking very casually. 'I heard he was working for Mr Essex and as I was looking for something to do and as he and I got along fine together I wrote, asking him if he could get me a job here. He wrote back and said there was nothing at the moment but if I were free, how would I like to come here and help out on the runway. He said he could give me a cabin and food, but there would be no money. I could look on it as a vacation. He said later he would talk to the staff manager and maybe there would be a vacancy. I was bored staying at home. I have my Army gratuity and I wanted to see Paradise City and I wanted very much to see Colonel Olson again . . . he's a fine man, Mr Jackson, but I don't have to tell you that . . . so . . . here I am.'

He nodded his turnip head several times and his little eyes half closed.

'I'm afraid Colonel Olson is at fault. He had no business having you here: no business at all.'

I didn't say anything.

'This is most irregular.' He frowned. 'Perhaps you don't realize it. Everyone who works for us is insured. Suppose you met with an accident on the runway? You could sue us out of sight and we wouldn't be covered.'

'Is that right?' I gave him my humble, blank face. 'I'm sure Colonel Olson never thought of that nor did I.'

He seemed to like my humble face better than my frank face for his tight little lips lifted into what I suppose he imagined to be a smile.

'I can see that. Colonel Olson is a good pilot, but he is no business man. What exactly are you doing on the runway?'

'I'm working under O'Brien. I keep the bulldozers in operation. The crew don't know about engines.'

The smile went away. 'But isn't that O'Brien's job?'

'He's taking care of the blasting. Colonel Olson thought it would save time for me to take care of the bulldozers. I understand the runway has to be gotten ready fast.'

'I am quite aware of the need to get the runway finished.' The steel in his voice warned me I was talking too much.

'I'm sure, Mr Jackson. I was just trying to explain.'

'We must regularize this business. Please report to the staff office and they will sign you on as one of the crew. You will be paid the usual union rates and you will be insured.'

'Thank you for the suggestion, but I won't do that. You see, Mr Jackson, I am on vacation. I'm not looking for that kind of work. I like messing around with engines but not for long. I was just helping the Colonel and enjoying myself.'

This threw him. He stiffened and stared at me.

'You mean you don't want to work for us?'

'Not as a ganger. I'm a fully qualified aero-engineer.'

His eyebrows crawled almost into his black hair.

'A fully qualified aero-engineer.'

'That's correct. Before Vietnam, I was with Lockheed.'

He began nibbling at his thumbnail again.

'I see.' He paused, then went on, 'Mrs Essex is pleased with you. Crane. Perhaps we could find you a place here in your own line. Would that interest you?'

I noted he had dropped the 'mister'.

I had a sudden idea he wouldn't be wasting his busy time with me unless he had to. *Mrs Essex is pleased with you.* That gave me the clue. This fat fink had been sent by her to do something for me in return for finding her horse. It was a guess, but I felt it was a good one.

'That depends on the job and the pay.'

He recrossed his legs. I saw by the sour expression on his face he hated me the way a snake hates a mongoose.

'Could you service a Condor XJ 7?'

'I'm a fully qualified aero-engineer,' I told him. 'That means I can handle any kite, providing I have a good working crew.'

'I see.'

I had him fazzed. I could tell that by the way he again recrossed his legs and again took a nibble at his thumbnail.

'Well. . . .'

A long pause, then he got to his feet.

'I must see what I can do. You would like to work for us?'

'As I said: it would depend on the pay and the job.'

He peered at me. 'What did Lockheed pay you?'

'Twenty, but that was four years ago.'

He nodded. I was certain he would contact Lockheed and check, but that didn't worry me. I was a white-headed boy with Lockheed four years ago. I knew they would root for me.

'Oblige me by staying away from the runway,' he said as he moved to the door. 'Please make yourself quite at home. I will tell the staff manager that you can enjoy all our facilities. I must talk to Mr Essex.'

'I wouldn't want to stick around here, doing nothing for long, Mr Jackson.'

Again he peered at me as if I were a reptile behind glass.

'You will have a car at your disposal. Why not enjoy the city?' I could see he was hating this. 'Go to the staff office. Mr Macklin will provide you with funds.' His mouth pursed as if he had bitten into a quince. 'It's Mrs Essex's wish.'

I gave him my graven image face.

'That's nice of her.'

He stalked out of the cabin, climbed into a Bentley coupé, driven by a negro chauffeur in the Essex bottle-green uniform and was driven away.

Pam came out of the shower room. She stood staring at me, her eyes wide.

'I'd never have believed it!' she said breathlessly. 'I don't know what Bernie will say.'

I lit a cigarette, my mind busy.

'Jack! Bernie will be furious.'

I looked at her. She now bored me.

'Run away, baby. I have thinking to do.'

'Listen to me . . .!' she began, her eyes snapping with rage.

'You heard me. Piss off. I have thinking to do.'

'Bernie made a mistake,' she said, her voice unsteady, her face white. 'Do him a favour. Get out of here! We'll find someone else! If you really are Bernie's friend, get out and fast!'

I regarded her.

'You won't find anyone else,' I said, 'so run away baby and stop shooting off at the mouth. I'm in and now it's up to Bernie. I'm not asking you to explain the set-up, but so far, as I've told you before, it stinks. I'm getting the idea Bernie isn't the man I thought he was. He could need help.' Then putting a bark in my voice, I snapped, 'Beat it!'

She went out, slamming the door behind her.

I sat still, smoked and thought.

I thought of that lush body, the Venetian red hair and the big violet eyes—the most exciting woman, to me, in the world.

I went along to see Mr Macklin, the staff manager, and caught him just as he was about to go home. The time was 19.00, but apart from giving me a quick look up and down with eyes that had the same ice-pick quality as Wes Jackson's, his smile as he shook hands with me seemed sincere enough.

'Ah, yes, Mr Crane,' he said. 'I have had instructions about you from Mr Jackson.' He slightly lowered his voice when mentioning Jackson's name. I was surprised he didn't genuflect. 'I have an envelope for you with the compliments of Essex Enterprises.' He went to his desk and raked around and finally came up with a large white envelope. 'If you want a car, do please go to our transport department—it is open twenty-four hours a day—you can have what you like.'

I took the envelope, thanked him, said I would like a car and went with him to his office door. He pointed out the transport department, a hundred yards or so from where we stood, shook hands again and I left him.

The Transport people had also been alerted. They asked me what car I would like. I said I didn't mind so long as it was small. They fitted me up with a 2000 Alfa Romeo which suited me and I drove back to my cabin.

Inside the envelope was five one-hundred-dollar bills and passes to three movie houses, the casino, four restaurants, two clubs and three nightclubs. Each pass was stamped: *Essex Enterprises: admit two.*

I found O'Brien settling down to television. He didn't need a lot of persuading to have a night out with me.

We had a hell of a night out: doing the City in style and it only cost me tips.

Slightly drunk, and on our way back to the airport around 02.00, O'Brien said, 'From now on I'll keep my eye on Mrs E's horse. Boy! Did you play that beautifully!'

'It's a natural talent,' I said and decanted him from the car, then going into my cabin, I stripped off and rolled into bed.

Before I turned the light off, I did a little more thinking. This wouldn't last long, I told myself. Mrs Essex wasn't going to keep me in luxury for more than a week, if that. Right at this moment I was a very rich woman's whim. First, I would listen to Olson's proposition. Then I would decide, whether to play along with him or to try to turn the whim of this very rich woman into something much more substantial than a whim.

I told myself I was drunk enough to make dreams. I thought of her again: the red hair, the violet eyes, the feel of her body. Reaching for the moon? That was old hat now. Men went to the moon. Why not me?

The sound of an aircraft coming in to land brought me awake. I looked blearily at the bedside clock which registered 10.15. I rolled out of bed and was in time to see the dust as a Condor settled on the runway. This meant that Lane Essex, plus Bernie, was back.

There was Jackson's Bentley already rushing to the landing point as well as three jeeps. I decided it would be quite a while before Olson would get to me so I took a shower, shaved, put on a sweat shirt and slacks and then called room service. In spite of the heavy drinking of the previous night, I was hungry.

I ordered waffles, eggs on grilled ham and coffee.

The man taking my order sounded as if I were granting him a favour.

'In ten minutes, Mr Crane,' he said, 'not a minute more.'

I thanked him, slapped after shave on my face and sat in a lounging chair to wait. I dug for this V.I.P. treatment, but I wasn't kidding myself it would last.

The breakfast arrived in eight minutes . . . I timed it.

After eating, I read the newspaper that had been delivered with the meal. Every now and then I heard a bang that told me O'Brien was still blasting.

At midday, I got bored waiting. Olson must be tied up, so I decided I would go into the city and use one of the credit cards. As I was crossing to the door, the telephone bell rang.

I scooped up the receiver.

'Mr Crane?' A woman's voice, very cool and abrupt.

'Could be: why?'

A pause. I could imagine her change of expression.

'Mr Jackson wants you. A car is on its way for you . . . in twenty minutes.'

Playing a hunch, I said, 'In twenty minutes, I'll be in the city. Mention this to Mr Jackson,' and I hung up.

I lit a cigarette as the telephone bell rang again.

'Mr Crane?' There was now an anxious note in her voice.

'That's me. You've just caught me. What is it?'

'Would you please wait until the car arrives? Mr Jackson wants to talk to you.'

'That's a nicer approach, baby,' I said, 'but it so happens I'm not in the mood to talk to Mr J right now . . . it's too early in the morning,' and I hung up.

I waited, smoking, staring up at the ceiling, wondering if I was playing my cards right but all the time thinking of that phrase: *Mrs Essex is pleased with you.* Seconds later the telephone bell rang again.

'Yeah?'

'Mr Crane, please co-operate.' Her voice sounded frantic. 'It's Mrs Essex who wants to meet you.'

'So why didn't you say it before?'

'It's Mrs Essex who is asking for you. Could you, please, make yourself available? The car is on its way.'

'I'll wait.' I paused, then went on, 'And listen, baby, the next time you call me, get that snooty tone out of your voice. I don't like it.' I hung up.

Ten minutes later, Jackson's Bentley pulled up outside my cabin. The negro chauffeur, bowing and grinning, had the rear door open for me. I climbed in and was wafted away at high speed.

The two guards at the airport entrance saluted me. The Bentley took me along the coast road, then up behind the city into the hills. While I was being driven, I leaned back against the English leather upholstery and thought about her.

Okay . . . a pipe dream, but life must be made up, sometimes, of pipe dreams . . . how else can anyone survive in this world of violence and madness?

We arrived at the entrance gates of the Essex estate. Two guards in bottle green had the gates open. We swept through and up a quarter of a mile of drive, bordered with trees, lawns, flowering shrubs and beds of roses.

The Bentley drew up at the front door: a tricky, rich affair of wrought iron and glass. A fat, white-haired English looking butler was standing, waiting. He smiled at me: that patronizing smile only the English can produce. 'Please come this way, Mr Crane.'

I followed his fat back down a wide corridor, plastered with modern paintings that had to be genuine.

Finally, we arrived through double glass doors on to a vast patio with an ultra-violet glass roof to shield the weak and the weary, plus orchids and troughs packed with multi-coloured begonias. In the centre of this opulence a vast fountain played into a vaster basin in which tropical fish swam as if doing a favour.

In this scene of richness, I found her.

She was lying on one of those things on wheels with a head rest and yellow cushions. Wes Jackson was seated slightly away from her, nursing what looked like a dry martini.

As I came out on to the patio, Jackson heaved his bulk up and got to his feet

'Come on in, Mr Crane,' he said and his smile was like a drop of lemon juice on a live oyster. I noted the 'mister' had returned. He turned to her. 'You've met before, Mrs Essex. I don't have to make introductions.'

She looked up at me and extended her hand. I moved forward, gripped her hand that felt hot and dry, then released it.

'Are you feeling better?' I asked.

'Thank you: I'm not so bad.' The violet eyes were looking me over. I told myself there couldn't be any other woman in the world as glamorous, as sexy, as gorgeous as this one. 'It was quite a fall, wasn't it?' She smiled and waved to a chair close to where she was lying. 'Sit down, Mr Crane.'

As I sat down, a Jap in white drill materialized from nowhere.

'What will you drink, Mr Crane?' Jackson asked.

'A coke with bitter.'

That threw him and the Jap. They both stared at me. I had been rehearsing that while in the Bentley.

Mrs Essex laughed.

'That's a drink I've never heard of.'

'At this hour of the day, it suits me. I get to the hard stuff after sunset.'

There was a pause and the Jap went away.

Jackson moved to his chair, but stopped short as Mrs Essex flicked her fingers at him.

'All right, Jackson,' she said, 'I'm sure you have lots of work to do.'

'Yes, Mrs Essex.'

Without looking at me, he faded swiftly and silently from the scene.

'I don't like fat men,' she said, 'do you?'

'He has a lean and hungry look,' I said. 'I would rather settle for a fat man than a very lean one.'

She nodded.

'So you read Shakespeare?'

'I was on an airfield, ten miles outside Saigon for three years. The guy who had my hut before I arrived and who walked into a faceful of shrapnel had Shakespeare's plays and an album of blue photos. I spent my off time looking at the photos and reading the plays.'

'Which did you prefer?'

'After a while the photos lost their impact, but the old Bard lingered on.'

The Jap came back with a frosted glass of coke and set it on the table beside me as if he was setting down a bomb. He drew back and waited.

'Is that how you like it?' she asked.

'It's fine.' I didn't taste it. 'It was a gag.'

She flicked her fingers at the Jap who disappeared. This finger flicking act of hers impressed me. I wondered if a time would come when she would flick her fingers at me.

'A gag?'

'Just trying to hold my end up,' I said. 'I'm not used to this opulent scene . . . at least it fazzed Jackson.'

She stared at me, then laughed.

'I love that. It certainly did.'

I took out my crumbled pack of cigarettes.

'Could you smoke one of these or are yours gold plated?'

'I don't smoke.' A pause, then she said, 'I find you refreshing, Mr Crane.'

I lit a cigarette.

'I'm glad. While we are paying compliments, may I tell you, to me, you're the most glamorous woman I've ever seen.'

We stared at each other and she lifted an eyebrow.

'Thank you.' Another pause. 'And thank you for finding Borgia. Not one of these stupid people at the airport thought of looking for him. I don't believe you haven't ridden a horse. The way you handled Borgia: only a horseman could have done that.'

'That was another gag.' I smiled at her. 'I'm like that, Mrs Essex . . . a gag man. Out in Saigon, I spent most of my time on a horse when I wasn't working on kites.'

'And, of course, when you weren't reading Shakespeare or looking at blue photos.'

'That's it.'

'Would you be interested to work for us?' She shot the question at me the way Ali shoots a jab.

I was expecting it and had my answer ready.

'Would you qualify the word "us"?'

She frowned. 'The Essex Enterprises of course!'

'That would mean working for Mr Jackson?' I regarded her, then went on, 'Just for a moment I thought you were suggesting I should work for you.'

This threw her as I hoped it would. She tried to hold my stare, but her eyes shifted away.

'I asked Jackson if there was some interesting opening we could offer you.' She still looked away from me. 'He seems to think that might be difficult, but then he always makes difficulties.'

'I can imagine.' I saw she was back on an even keel again and I smiled at her. 'I appreciate this very much, Mrs Essex: especially you asking me here. After all, I only found your horse, but if you could find me a job here . . .' I let it drift. 'I would like to talk to Colonel Olson. Frankly, working for Mr Jackson isn't my idea of fun and I like fun.' I got to my feet. 'Thank you for your hospitality.' I was now standing over her. 'Now, if you'll do your finger-flicking act, I'll disappear as they all disappear.'

She stared up at me and there was that sudden thing in her eyes that all women get when they want a man. I've known a lot of women in my life and that look is unmistakable. I could scarcely believe it but it was there and then it went away: like a green traffic light changing to red.

'Good-bye, Mr Crane.'

'So long.' I paused and looked right into those big violet eyes. 'I know this doesn't buy me anything, but I want you to know that, right now, I'm looking at the most beautiful woman in the world.'

I made that my exit line.

There was no sign of Bernie Olson when the Bentley decanted me outside my cabin. I went in, wondering if there was a note for me but didn't find one.

The time was after 13.00 and I was now hungry. I rang room service and asked for something to eat.

'The special is excellent, Mr Crane: baby lamb with all the trimmings. Should I send that over?'

I said it would do fine and hung up.

During the drive back to the airport I had thought about Mrs Essex. Could I have been mistaken about the look that had come into her eyes? I don't think so, but it seemed fantastic that a woman in her position could have got turned on by a guy like me. So okay, accepting that fact she had been turned on, it didn't mean a thing. A woman like that wouldn't take risks when married to Lane Essex. She could have her private thoughts but putting those thoughts into action was something else beside. All the same, she had me turned on. I would have given a couple of years of my life to spend a night with her: that, I knew, would be an experience that I would never forget.

After a while, the meal arrived and I ate it. By this time it was 14.23. While I was lighting a cigarette, the telephone rang.

'Hi! Jack!' It was Olson.

'Hi!'

'Have you a car?'

'Yeah.'

'Do you think you can find your way to that café-bar?'

'No problem.'

'Suppose we meet there in half an hour?'

'Okay.'

He hung up.

Well, I thought as I crushed out my cigarette and got to my feet, I would now know what this was all about. As I left the cabin and got into the Alfa there came a distant bang of blasting. O'Brien was still at it.

It took me twenty minutes to reach the café-bar. The white Jag was parked in the shade. I parked the Alfa by it, then walked up the creaking steps to the veranda.

Olson was sitting, nursing a cup of coffee. He waved to me and I joined him.

The girl came out and smiled at me.

'Coffee.'

'Well, Jack, seems like you have been having yourself quite a ball,' Olson said as the girl went away. 'It also seems that you have forgotten the Army faster than I had imagined.'

The girl came back with the coffee and went away.

'What does that mean?'

'You've forgotten how to obey orders.' There was a snap in his voice that annoyed me.

'You said yourself we're no longer in the Army. Look, Bernie, I'm not going to make any excuses. You dumped me here on a phoney job. You didn't take me into your confidence. So I've played it the way the cards fell. If you don't like the way I've played it, say so and I'll get out of here.'

He tried to stare at me, but failed. His eyes shifted. I could see he was sweating.

'Well, maybe there's no damage done, but I wanted you to keep out of the spotlight. From what I hear, you're now in good with Mrs Essex.' He stirred his coffee, not looking at me. 'Maybe that's a good thing. I hear you were up at the house this morning.'

'Your grapevine's working well.'

He forced a smile.

'Don't let's get off on the wrong foot, Jack. This operation is too important. I'm relying on you. I need your help.'

'Look, Bernie, up to now you've handled this wrong. Why the hell didn't you tell me what you're cooking when you first brought me here instead of feeding me this crap about building a runway? If you had done that, there wouldn't have been this foul-up.'

'I couldn't. Kendrick insisted on seeing you before you joined us. He's like that . . . he wouldn't trust his mother. Then I had to fly the boss to New York: that was unexpected.'

'Kendrick? That fat queer? Where does he fit in?'

'He's financing it.'

I lit a cigarette.

'Okay, Bernie, suppose you tell it.'

He fidgeted with the spoon, put it down, picked it up, tapped it against his cup.

'Yes.' A pause, then he said, 'You remember my last mission in Saigon? You remember the airfield was bombed and your hut was destroyed?'

I stared at him. 'What's that got to do with this?'

'A lot. You remember I told you to move in with me?' Bernie put down the spoon, pushed his half-finished coffee away, then drew it towards him. 'You remember I had the bed and you the couch?'

'I remember.'

A long pause, then Bernie said quietly, 'You talked in your sleep, Jack. Three old money changers. I'll never forget that night, listening to you muttering. Then later when I got this itch to make big money and when I hatched out this plan to get it and when I realized I had to have a top-class man to help me, I thought of you.' He put down the spoon and looked directly at me. 'I figured that if you could kill three old men for around $5,000, you would do a lot more for a quarter of a million.' He ran his hand over his sweating face, then asked, 'Am I right?'

I drank some coffee.

'It depends, Bernie. A quarter of a million is nice money, but I was safe enough in Saigon . . . how safe would I be here?'

'It's safe enough. That's the least of the problem. Right now, you're my problem. I can understand what you did out there. The Viets meant nothing to any of us. Shooting an old Viet under battle conditions is something I can accept, but this thing . . . well, if it comes unstuck, then you could go away for a long time as I could. I can't see how it could come unstuck. I've thought a lot about it and I reckon we have a 95 per cent chance of getting away with it.'

'I could accept those odds,' I said.

'Yes.' He picked up the spoon and began to fidget with it again. 'What I want to know, Jack, is how you react to this offer.'

'Suppose you tell me about it? Then I can tell you.'

He shook his head.

'I can't do that unless you tell me you're in with us. If I tell you the plan and you duck out . . . where are we left?'

I stared at him. 'That's telling me you don't trust me to keep my mouth shut.'

He looked away from me.

'I'm not the only one in this. Either a quarter of a million persuades you to come in with us without being told or it's no dice.'

'You didn't talk this way to me in Saigon. I'm not walking into anything blind. You either trust me or you don't. That's my final word.'

We stared at each other, then he gave me a sudden smile and it did me good to see it. It was the kind of smile he used to give me before he took off on a bombing mission.

'I apologize, Jack. Okay . . . here it is. If you don't want it, I'll give you three thousand dollars and you go home and forget it . . . right?'

'Right.'

'I've been working for Essex now for a year. I've had enough of him and his wife. There's no future in it. Working for them has aged me. I don't have to tell you: you can see for yourself. Pilots are a dime a dozen. Essex could replace me like that.' He snapped his fingers. 'So I got thinking.' He stared down the sandy road at the distant beach. 'This brings us to Pam. When I took over the airport, she was there, as deputy air hostess. Maybe this will be hard for you to understand. She and I have a thing for each other. She can't help being over-sexed. This is something I can't do anything about, but we really mean a great deal to each other. When she has to have it, I look away.' He took out his handkerchief and wiped off his sweating hands. 'We were out one night, eating at L'Espadon where she has credit and she introduced me to Claude Kendrick. You've met him. Kendrick not only runs a profitable art

46

gallery, but he is also the biggest fence on the coast. He is in the market for any goods to be sold: no matter what. Over coffee, I got talking about Essex's new plane. This is quite a job, Jack. The final bill will work out around ten million dollars. It's . . .'

'Hey! Wait a minute!' I stared at him. 'Did you say ten million?'

'That's right.'

I don't believe it. You can buy a Viscount for two and a half. Ten! Are you sure?'

'This is a unique plane, Jack. There's no other plane like it in the world. Essex's experts have been working on it for four years. Essex has poured money into it to get it right. This is not a mass-produced job. It's like a Rolls-Royce car: nothing but the best. I won't go into details now. You'll probably see it for yourself. Two weeks after my meeting with Kendrick, Pam told me he would like to see me again. We met and he told me he had a client who would buy the plane if I flew it to Yucatan. The cut for me would be a million. I told him he was crazy. He said there was no hurry, but he would like me to think about it. So I started thinking. The plane wouldn't be ready for test flight for another three months. The more I thought about it, the more I became convinced that it could be done.' He looked up, regarding me. 'I would need the right crew. I have a co-pilot lined up. I have Pam. I need a flight mechanic—you. How do you like it so far?'

I lit a cigarette while I thought about it.

'It's an idea. Could I dig at it, shooting off the cuff?'

'That's what I want.'

'Okay. You have a ten-million-dollar aircraft. Don't let's worry about how you steal it. Let's first look at the financial end. You get a million. I get a quarter. Pam gets something and also the co-pilot!'

'That's about it.'

'Kendrick sells the kite for five million. That's half price. He takes no risk and puts three million in his pocket. Do you think that's a good proposition?'

Bernie shifted uneasily. 'You just said a quarter of a million was nice money.'

'That doesn't answer my question.'

'I don't know how much Kendrick will collect: could be a lot less than five.'

47

I shook my head. 'No. I've met him: he's all shark. He'll probably get seven. He's gypping you.'

Olson shrugged. There was again that weary, cynical look in his eyes that gave me no confidence in him.

'I'll settle for a million. With that kind of money, Jack, I could set up an air taxi service in Mexico. You could come into it too.'

I finished my lukewarm coffee.

'Suppose we talk to Kendrick. He could be squeezed. Suppose you got two and I got one. That would be better, wouldn't it?'

'Kendrick holds the cards, Jack. He has the client. I don't know who he is. Without the client we would be whistling in the wind.' He stared at me. 'And another thing, I don't think Kendrick can be squeezed.'

'Suppose I try? After all, who is taking the risk?'

'Well, maybe, but I'll have to discuss this with Pam and Harry.'

'Your co-pilot?'

He nodded.

'Tell me about him.'

'Harry Erskine: he's been my co-pilot for the past nine months. Young: around twenty-four, tough, a good pilot, not easy to get along with, but he's okay.'

'What made him come into this set-up?'

'Mrs Essex dangled herself and he fell for it and then she cut him down to size: That's her speciality: turning it on, making a guy think he's going to get into her bed, then telling him he isn't.' Olson looked hard at me. 'I don't know how far she's got with you, Jack, but watch it. She's a copper-plated bitch. Now Harry hates her and has joined us.'

I filed that bit of information away in my mind as I said, 'So how do you plan to steal a ten-million-dollar plane?'

'We have time to work out the details. The plane will be delivered on November 1st—two months from now. Harry and I will collect it and fly it down here. The plane will have to be flight tested. Essex travels a lot and often wants to be flown at night. There'll be no problem about doing a night test flight. So, you, Harry, Pam and I take off on a night flight. We fly out to sea, then I'll radio the port engines are on fire. The Air Controller then hears nothing. It'll take him some minutes to get out an alert. By that time we'll be heading for Yucatan, flying wave high to cut radar. Kendrick's client has a runway outside Merida. It's in the bush and jungle. We land there. The details have still to be worked out, but that's the plan.'

I thought about it.

'Sounds good,' I said finally. 'The theory being the plane crashed into the sea and sank without trace?'

'That's it.'

'You have no idea who the client is?'

'No.'

'He must be quite someone to construct a runway.'

'Yes.'

'So . . . we're dead people once we have radio silence.'

'That's right.'

'We get the money and we settle in Mexico?'

He nodded.

'Each one of us takes a risk if we go back?'

'We can't go back. If we go back and if any of us is spotted, the operation explodes. As you said . . . we're dead people the moment we go off the air.'

'You're sold on this, Bernie?'

'Yes. It's big money and I need big money. I want to feel secure.'

I remembered that fat queer with his ridiculous orange wig talking about security. 'With the money I can start an air taxi service. I've already got that lined up. If you would sink some of your cut into it, we could work together. There's a big demand for air taxi services in Mexico.' He regarded me. 'Well, Jack, you now know as much as I do about the set-up. What do you say? Are you in or aren't you?'

'I like it.' I got to my feet. 'But I want to meet Erskine. Let's all get together, huh?'

Bernie stared uneasily at me.

'Harry's tricky. You may not dig for him.'

'What's that mean?'

'I'm telling you: I need him as co-pilot. He does what I say. You don't have to bother with him.'

'This is a steal, Bernie. We all could go away for fifteen years if it's fouled up. This has got to be a team and I'm not working with anyone I can't get along with.'

Bernie got to his feet. 'I understand. I'll fix a meeting.'

'And Bernie . . .' I stared at him. 'Let's have Kendrick at the meeting as well.'

'We don't want Kendrick.'

'Yes we do. This is a team and Kendrick is part of it.'

He lifted his hands in a weary gesture.

'I'll see what can be arranged.'

'Do more than that, Bernie. You, Erskine, Pam, Kendrick and me around a table and let's talk this thing out.'

'Okay.'

We walked together into the sunshine and paused by our cars.

'I'm not being tricky, Bernie,' I said. 'I'm thinking of you as much as I'm thinking of myself.'

He patted my arm.

'That's why I picked on you. I'm not quite the guy I was and I need your help.'

I watched him drive away in the Jag, then I got into the Alfa.

I sat there for some minutes, thinking, then I drove back to the airport.

CHAPTER FOUR

BERNIE PHONED around 19.00 while I was watching a soap opera on TV. He said the meeting was set up for 21.00 at the café-bar.

'I'll pick you up at 20.30, Jack,' he said, 'with Pam and Harry.'

'Kendrick coming?'

'Yes.'

'Fine.'

Since I had talked to him and now knew what was cooking, I had done a lot of thinking. His plan looked good, but there were a lot of details to be ironed out. Hi-jacking a ten-million-dollar plane could put me in jail for a long time and that was something I didn't dig. This had to be foolproof and I had the idea that Bernie wasn't the man to swing it. There was something about him that didn't jell with me. Pam didn't count: she was an over-sexed neurotic. A lot depended on Erskine. If he had the same kind of guts Bernie had, then I'd duck out. I wanted to control the operation. The more I thought about it, the more I liked it, but not with Bernie handling it.

Around 20.30 I heard a car pull up outside my cabin. I went to the door. A Buick, with Bernie at the wheel, was coming to a standstill. He waved to me and I climbed in beside him. There was a man and Pam in the back. It was too dark to get a look at Erskine. He looked big, but that's all I could see of him.

As Bernie set the car moving, he said, 'Jack . . . here's Harry.'

'Hi!' I said and lifted my hand.

Erskine made no movement. After a long pause, he said, 'Hi!'

We drove in silence and fast from the airport to the café-bar. Arriving, we all got out and it was still too dark for me to see him. He was bigger than I had imagined. Three inches above me and I'm no dwarf.

Bernie and I walked together. Pam and Erskine came behind us. We climbed the steps to the veranda. It was a hot night and I could hear the waves breaking on the beach in the distance.

There was no one in the café. A dim light lit the veranda. As we settled ourselves at a table, the girl came out, smiling.

Bernie said, 'What'll we have?'

I was now looking at Erskine as he was looking at me. The dim light showed me a lean face, small eyes, a flat nose and thin lips: young, tough, a fighter with jet black hair cut close, sitting on his head like a black cap. He had on a sweat shirt and I could see his muscles: he was built like a boxer.

Pam said she would have a whisky on the rocks. I went along with that. Erskine said an orange juice with gin. Bernie settled for a coke.

When the girl had gone, Bernie said, 'Meet Harry, Jack.'

I nodded to Erskine who leant forward, staring at me.

'So what's the idea of this meeting?' he demanded aggressively. 'What's eating you?'

'Just a moment,' Bernie said sharply. 'I'll handle this. Jack doesn't think much of the pay-off. I . . .'

'You hold it, Bernie,' Erskine said. 'This guy is an aero-engineer . . . right?'

Bernie looked uneasily at him.

'You know that, Harry.'

'Yeah. So he's not important. You and I have to fly the kite . . . right? So what's he beefing about? We use him: he gets paid and keeps his snout out of our business . . . right?'

'Look, sonny,' I said quietly, 'don't act tough. You and Pam are mugs to this kind of operation. Come to that, Bernie isn't all that hot. You have a nice idea, but you're handling it like amateurs.

You have a ten-million-dollar kite and you're selling for a two-million pay-off. That tells me what a bunch of amateurs you are.'

Erskine braced himself. I saw his big muscles bulge. I had an idea he was going to take a swing at me.

'So you're a pro . . . right?'

'Compared to you three,' I said, slightly shifting my chair so I could get up if he started something. 'Yes . . . I'm a pro.'

'Harry!' Bernie's voice was pleading. 'I have confidence in Jack. That's why I've brought him in. I think we should let him handle Kendrick. Let's see what he does.'

'No!'

This was from Pam.

Bernie looked at her. 'What is it?'

'This man's dangerous.' She waved her hands at me. 'I know it. He could talk us into trouble.'

I laughed.

'You're already in trouble, baby,' I said. 'I could talk you out of it. But, okay, if you three feel like this, then it's okay with me. I'll dust, but the way you've been handling this tells me I'll be sending you all a postcard in some jail. I'm great at sending postcards.'

Kendrick's Cadillac pulled up outside the café-bar.

'Here he comes,' I said, pushing back my chair. I looked at Bernie. 'Either I handle him or I quit. What's it to be?'

He didn't look at the other two.

'You handle him.'

Before the others could react, Kendrick came puffing and blowing up the steps to join us.

'My darlings! What a dreadful place to meet!' He waddled to the table and Bernie stood up and pushed a chair towards him. 'How quite, quite frightful!' He dropped his bulk on to the chair. 'Don't offer me a drink. I'm sure germs are festering on every glass.' He lifted his orange wig and bowed to Pam. 'Dear Pam . . . lovely as ever.' He slapped the wig back on his head. 'Do tell me. What is all this about? I thought we had it all beautifully arranged.'

'Jack wants to talk to you,' Bernie said.

'Jack?' Kendrick's little eyes swivelled to me. 'What is it, cheri? Aren't you happy?'

'Let's cut the grease, Kendrick,' I said. 'First, we talk about money . . . then the operation.'

Kendrick released a theatrical sigh.

'A moment, cheri. Are you talking for these three lovely people? Am I to understand that Bernie is no longer leading this operation?'

'He doesn't talk for me,' Erskine said.

'Nor me,' Pam said.

I looked at Bernie, then got to my feet.

'Okay: so I duck out. The majority is overwhelming.'

'Wait!' Bernie looked at Kendrick. 'I brought Jack into this because he has the know-how. From now on, he talks for me. I'm running this operation and what I say goes.'

I looked at Pam then at Erskine.

'You heard the man. Now's the time for you two to get up and walk.'

Neither of them moved.

I sat down. Kendrick rubbed the end of his nose with a fat finger.

'Well . . . so what's the trouble, Jack?'

I rested my arms on the table and leaned on them, looking directly at him.

'We're stealing a ten-million-dollar aircraft,' I said. 'That's called hi-jacking. We four stand to get life sentences if we foul it up and it could get fouled. But we five are in this together—note the five—I'm including you. We want to know how much your client is paying you.'

Kendrick smiled.

'So you're worried about the money, cheri?'

'I said cut the grease. How much are you getting?'

'That is my business!' There was a sudden edge to his voice. 'Bernie and I made a deal. I pay two million . . . Bernie has accepted this . . . haven't you, Bernie?' and he looked at Olson.

'Just a moment,' I broke in. 'Let's take a look at it. The kite's worth ten: it's brand new. If you're not blind stupid, and I'm sure you're not, you will get at least six for it. That gives you four million profit after expenses for sitting on your fat butt and letting us take the risk: do you call that a deal?'

'Six!' He threw up his fat hands. 'Cheri! I'll be lucky if I get a million for myself and I'm handling the expenses. Come, come! You mustn't be greedy.'

'We want three and a half,' I said, 'or the deal's off.'

53

'Hey! Just a moment,' Erskine broke in. 'You. . . .'

'Keep out of this!' I snarled at him. 'You hear me, Kendrick? Three and a half or the deal's off!'

'Suppose we hear what the others say.' Kendrick's eyes were now like glass beads.

'No! I'm handling this,' I said. 'So suppose they go along with your offer? I'm not going along with it. So they drop me, but I now know the plan.' I smiled at him. 'The kite's insured. The kite vanishes. Someone talking on the telephone to the insurance people could start a lot of trouble for you. We want three and a half, Kendrick.'

He stared at me for a long moment, then nodded.

'You're quite a business man, cheri. Suppose we settle this sordid haggling for three million? I'll be robbing myself, but I will settle for three.'

I looked at Bernie.

'We don't want to rob him, do we? So shall we settle for three?'

Bernie, looking dazed, nodded.

I looked at the other two. Erskine was gaping at me, his eyes goggling. Pam didn't look at me.

In less than ten minutes, I had made us all an extra million.

'Okay . . . three,' I said.

Kendrick grimaced.

'Then that's settled. If that's all, I must be running away.'

'It's not all.' I turned to Bernie. 'How is the money to be paid?'

Bernie stiffened.

'Well . . . Claude is going to arrange for it to be paid into the Florida Bank here in my name and I share it out.'

It was now my turn to gape at him.

'For God's sake! Three million suddenly paid into a local bank when we are all supposed to be dead?'

Sweat beads appeared on Bernie's face.

'I—I hadn't thought of that.' He looked helplessly at me. 'What do you suggest?'

I turned to Kendrick who was watching me, his little eyes granite hard.

'You pay half the money: one million and a half into the National Bank of Mexico under Olson's name: you pay that before we take off. Then you pay the rest to the bank when we deliver.'

He shifted around on his chair, took out his handkerchief and then fanned his face.

'That could be arranged.'

'It has to be arranged. We don't fly the kite out until Bernie gets a bank receipt for half the money.'

He lifted his fat shoulders. I could see in spite of his fixed smile he was hating me.

'All right, cheri. I'll arrange that.'

A pause, then I said. 'Now there's another thing. We want to inspect the runway where we land the kite.'

That really threw him. He stiffened, his face flushed and his beady eyes turned to stone.

'The runway . . . what do you mean?'

'The runway.' I made my voice offensively patient. 'We want to inspect it.'

'There's no need. I've discussed this with Bernie.'

'So, now, discuss it with me. Where's the runway?'

'A few miles from Merida.'

'Who built it?'

'My client.'

'What's he know about making a runway?'

Kendrick shifted his orange wig, then put it straight.

'There's no problem. He knows what he is doing. He's spent a lot of money constructing the runway. If he's satisfied, so should you be.'

'You think so? Do you imagine we're going to risk a ten-million-dollar kite on a runway built by a gang of Mexicans? Do you think we're crazy?' I leaned forward and glared at him. 'What do you know about building a runway? We could crash the kite.' I turned to Bernie. 'Do you remember the foul-up we had when the Viets built a runway for us? It sagged and we crashed. Remember?'

This was a lie, but Bernie caught on quickly. 'That's right.'

I turned back to Kendrick.

'These three are tied up, working for Essex. I'm footloose. I'll check the runway . . . you fix it.'

Kendrick licked his lips. 'I'll ask my client. He may not agree.'

'Then that's too bad. We don't fly the kite in until I've checked the runway.'

'I'll see what can be arranged.' A pause, his eyes dwelling on me. 'Is there any other little problem that's bothering you, cheri?'

55

I grinned at him. 'No: my problems are your problems now.'
He got to his feet.

'Then I'll run away.' He lifted his wig and bowed to Pam. "Bye, dears,' and he moved around the table, then paused, looking at Bernie. 'You've found a smart boy, Bernie . . . watch him, he could get too smart,' and then he waddled away down the steps to his yellow and black Cadillac and was driven away.

I lit a cigarette and looked at Bernie.

'So what have we got?' I said. 'We now have an extra million to cut up between us. We're now going to find out who is buying the kite. When I go out there, I'll find him. I've fixed at least half the money comes to us, even if Fatso gyps us out of the other half and he could. How do you like it, Bernie?'

Olson smiled crookedly.

'Why else do you imagine I picked on you?'

But I could tell by his eyes that I had taken the lead out of his hands: I could see he now knew who was the better man.

I then looked at the other two.

'How do you like it?'

Erskine stared for a long moment at me, then he said, 'I apologize, Jack, for being hostile. The way you handled it was marvellous. From now on, I co-operate. What you say goes with me. Hell! I never thought of any of this stuff you fed to him. You're right. We're just goddamn amateurs.'

'Fine.' I shifted my eyes to Pam. 'And you? You happy?'

She didn't even look at me. She just shrugged.

'Baby! I'm talking to you . . . are you happy?'

'Let's leave her out of it,' Bernie said sharply.

'Oh, no! ' I leaned forward. 'She's part of the team. I want to hear her angle.'

She looked at me, her eyes snapping.

'You did very well. You are the miracle boy. Is that what you want to hear?'

I swung around and looked at Bernie. 'Do we need her?'

Olson rubbed the back of his hand across his mouth.

'Pam and I are together and we go together.'

'Fine. So . . . you take care of her. From where I'm sitting I have you and Harry. You take care of her . . . right?'

Pam got to her feet.

'I'm going, Bernie. I can't stomach this . . . this . . .' She stopped as Erskine grabbed her wrist and jerked her down on her chair again.

Bernie half started up as Erskine said quietly to her, 'Cut it out, Pam!'

She looked at him and I knew he had screwed her as I had screwed her and looking at Bernie's white, drawn face, I knew he knew it too.

She stared at Erskine, then lifted her hands helplessly.

'I'm sorry.'

There was a long pause, then I said, 'No more drama for the moment?'

No one said anything.

'So . . . here's another thing. While we're talking we may as well talk this out.'

'Sure,' Erskine said. 'Let's have another drink.' He snapped his fingers and the girl appeared. He ordered another round of drinks. It was a good idea. The atmosphere grew cooler while we waited.

'You got something else on your mind, Jack?' Erskine asked after the girl had delivered the drinks and had gone away.

'The idea is that when we have radio silence, we have accepted the fact that we are dead people. We have all gone into the sea,' I said. 'Have you thought what that means? I go along with the idea. We can't take the risk of coming back to the U.S. of A. We have to stay in Mexico, but the thing is we have to act as dead people.'

'I told you that,' Bernie said impatiently. 'Life in Mexico could work out for all of us, but if it didn't, with all this money, we could get lost in South America or even Europe.'

'You're not catching, Bernie,' I said. 'Kendrick and his client will also know we have to be dead people to get away with this. Have a think about it.'

Bernie stared at me, his eyes puzzled. He looked at Erskine who was also staring at me.

'Still doesn't jell?' I said. 'You still don't catch?'

'Just what are you talking about?' Erskine demanded, his voice angry.

'Oh, you babes in the wood! Hasn't it entered your innocent minds that when we land the kite, how convenient it would be for Kendrick and his client for us to be met by a bunch of Mexican thugs who would slit our throats, bury us in the jungle, and

Kendrick and his client pick up a ten-million-dollar kite without paying us for our services?'

Erskine shoved back his chair, his expression startled.

'I never thought of that!'

'Kendrick would never do a thing like that,' Bernie said feebly, but he looked sick.

'No? Anyone smart, and Fatso is smart, wouldn't bother about four lives if he could net six million dollars,' I said. 'We could be walking into a trap. I'm not saying we will, but we could.'

'You're right,' Erskine said. 'Goddamn it! It could happen!'

'You're a trusting bunch, aren't you?' I said. 'If ever you say your prayers, thank the Lord you picked on me to handle this.'

'So what do we do?' Erskine asked.

'We use our brains. We have two months to get this operation fixed. I'll go out there and find out who is handling the deal, then we all concentrate on the important thing . . . how we remain dead and yet still keep alive.'

I was just dropping off to sleep when I heard a tapping on my cabin door. I snapped on the bedside lamp and swung myself out of bed, looking at my strap watch. The time was 00.15.

Again the tap came on the door.

I crossed the living-room and opened up. Harry Erskine came in and I shut the door.

'I want to talk to you,' he said.

The only light came from my bedroom. He loomed before me: big, broad, like the shadow of a tree.

'I was just going to sleep.'

'Never mind about sleep.' He moved further into the cabin and dropped into a chair. 'Listen, Jack, I'm sorry I got off on the wrong foot with you. I thought you were a phoney, blown up by Bernie, but when I saw you handle that grease-ball, I knew you were my man. I want to talk to you about Bernie.'

I sat down near him and reached for a pack of cigarettes. I lit one and tossed the pack to him. He lit up and we regarded each other.

'So talk about Bernie,' I said.

'He's going down hill so fast he could be on a toboggan. This goddamn bitch has fixed him.' He flicked ash on the floor. 'He has her continually on his mind. I don't have to tell you, she screws around and this is poison to him, but he can't part with her. It's affecting his mind.' He leaned forward. 'At the speed he's failing, he can't last more than three or four months as a pilot. I know. I work with him. He's so goddamn absent-minded, he'll start to take the kite off the floor before going through the flight routine. Three times recently I've stopped him and he has given me an odd blank look and then started the routine. He's got this bug in his mind that he must have money to start an air taxi service in Mexico. The way he's sliding he couldn't handle one taxi, let alone a fleet. Now look, Jack, don't think I've got anything against Bernie. We've worked together for nine months. At first, I admired him. He was a fine pilot, but this woman has really fixed him. If you knew the number of times I've averted a certain crash you wouldn't believe it. His mind just isn't on flying.'

I listened to this with growing dismay.

'Well, for God's sake!'

'Yeah . . . and what's he going to do with the new kite? We're both going up to the Condor's works at the end of the month for a course of instruction. As he is now, the test pilots will murder him. Essex will get a report that will give Bernie the gate in seconds.'

'I can't believe this! Bernie can handle anything with wings! He's the finest pilot I've ever worked for!'

'He was . . . that I grant you, but not now. He just doesn't concentrate and you know a pilot damn well has to concentrate.' He crushed his cigarette, then went on, 'Suppose you talk to him? Suppose you try to persuade him to get rid of Pam? I can't think of any other solution. Get rid of her and he might settle down again. What do you think?'

I shied away from this suggestion. I couldn't imagine talking to Bernie about his woman.

'Why don't you talk to him?'

Erskine shook his head. 'He might start thinking I was after his job. You could do it. I can't.'

I thought for a long moment, then asked, 'If he got the heave, would you get his job?'

'No. I'm too young. Essex would find an older man . . . no problem. Look, Jack, if we're going to swing this operation, you either talk to Bernie and make him see sense or the operation is a nonstarter.'

'You're sure Pam is the trouble?'

'I know it.'

Again I paused to think. The idea of losing three million dollars because a woman had hot pants stuck in my maw.

'Maybe it would be better if I talked to her.'

Erskine grimaced.

'She's tricky.'

'That's right.' I sat back, my mind racing. 'Look, I'll think about it. Okay, Harry, thanks for wising me up.' I didn't want to talk any more this night. I now had enough to think about as it was. 'I'll see what I can do.'

'You think this operation will jell?'

'I don't know. All I know is if you want to pick up three million dollars, you have to expect a lot of headaches.' I stood up.

'You really believe these Mexicans could knock us off when we land the kite?' he asked as he climbed to his feet.

'Ask yourself. We haven't landed yet: let's take one problem at a time.'

'Yeah.' He brushed his hand over his close cut hair. 'Well, I'm leaving it up to you. I'm in Cabin 15 if you want me.'

'Where's Pam's cabin?'

'No 23: the last in the row.'

I let him out, then moved around the living-room, turning over in my mind what he had told me, then I went into my bedroom, slid out of my pyjamas, put on a shirt and slacks, shoved my feet into sandals and left my cabin.

I walked silently down the row of cabins to the last one. I checked that it was No. 23, then rapped on the door.

A light was showing around the curtains. After a pause, Pam said 'Who is it?'

'Your boy-friend.'

She opened the door and I pushed by her, closing the door behind me.

She had on a flimsy wrap and her feet were bare.

'You! What do you want?' Her voice was shrill.

'A talk about Bernie.' I moved to a lounging chair and sat down.

'I'm not talking to you about Bernie! Get out!'

'Take it easy . . . this is business. We four stand to pick up three million dollars, but it could come unstuck because of you.'

She glared at me.

'Because of me? What do you mean?'

'If you don't know, you are dumber than I think you are, but I'll spell it out to you. Because you are screwing around with anything in trousers, Bernie is flipping his lid. He's not concentrating and I'll tell you, baby, just in case you don't know, a pilot has to concentrate. Because you sleep around and imagine Bernie goes along with it, you have demoralized him.'

'That's a lie!' She clenched her fists. 'Bernie told me. . . .'

'Oh, wrap up! Bernie's soft about you. To hold on to you, he'd tell you anything. Now, listen to me. We're in this thing for three million dollars. I'm not going along with a bitch like you who thinks she has to have it and by having it, ruins a great pilot. Hear me?' I wasn't shouting, I was talking quietly. 'So tomorrow you see him and you tell him that from now on you stay with him and there's going to be no more screwing and you'll convince him.'

'Who the hell do you think you are, talking this way to me?' she yelled at me. 'Bernie and I. . . .'

'Wrap up! This is an ultimatum, baby. You either keep your legs crossed from now on until this operation is over or you get out of here. You convince him or you're out.'

'Yes? And who's going to put me out?'

I smiled at her.

'Baby, I have you over a barrel. It'd be too easy. I have only to tell Mrs Essex that you are acting like a whore for you to get tossed off the airport. I don't want to do it, but I will if you don't convince Bernie that from now on, you're going to behave.'

'You bastard!'

I got to my feet.

'That's the deal. You convince him or you're out.'

I left her.

Back in my bed, I thought about it all. I couldn't see how I could have improved on what I had said: it either worked or three million dollars went up in smoke.

Eventually, I fell asleep to be awakened by the sound of the telephone bell. I looked at my watch. The time was 10.24. The sun was coming through the drawn curtains. I had slept better than I had expected.

I went into the living-room and picked up the receiver.

'Jack, cheri.'

I knew who was calling. 'That's me.'

61

'I've talked to my client. You can inspect the runway. He tells me it isn't necessary, but if you're nervous about it, you can inspect it.'

'I'm nervous about it.'

'Yes. Well, go to the Continental hotel at Merida. I have arranged for you to be picked up around 12.30 on the morning of the 4th. That will give you three days to get organized. Will that suit you?'

'Fine.'

' 'Bye now, cheri,' and he hung up.

I showered and shaved, then taking the Alfa, I drove into Paradise City. I spent the whole day there, taking in the sights, the sun and thinking about this operation. I had three good opportunities to pick up a dolly, but I resisted that. There was too much to think about without getting into complications with one of these little pushovers.

I returned to the airport just after 19.00 and went to cabin 15. With a cordless shaver in his hand, Erskine opened the door.

'Hi!' He grinned at me. 'You're a goddamn miracle worker!' He stood aside so I could move in and then shut the door. 'Did you swing something! Bernie's a different man!'

I felt suddenly relaxed. 'You think it worked?'

'It's worked. Look, Jack, I have a heavy date and I'm late already. Go, talk to Bernie. He's in his cabin: No. 19. See for yourself.'

'I'll do that,' and leaving him I went along to No. 19.

Erskine was right. As soon as Bernie opened the door, I could see the change in him. It was as if the cloud that had been obscuring him had lifted. He stood upright and there was that grin again.

'Hi! Jack! Come on in. Have a drink?'

As I started into the cabin, I paused, seeing Pam sitting there.

'I don't want to barge in.'

I looked at her and she looked at me, then she smiled.

'Come on in: you don't have to be shy.' She leaned back. 'We have got it all straightened out . . . haven't we, Bernie?'

'Yes.' Bernie started to mix drinks. 'Pam told me about last night. You were right, Jack. She needed to be told.'

'Okay . . . so let's forget it. Let's talk business.'

'Just a moment.' Bernie gave me a whisky on the rocks. 'I want to say thank you and so does Pam.'

I couldn't believe any of this, but again looking at Pam, I saw she was smiling and completely relaxed.

'Let's skip it. It's all water under a bridge. Man! What dialogue!' I waved my drink at her. 'Here's to you and I mean it.'

We all drank. There was a pause, then she said, 'You came at the right time, Jack.'

I sat down.

'As I said, let's skip it.' I turned to Bernie. 'Kendrick has given me the green light to inspect the runway. I leave on the third.'

'You're certainly handling this,' he said. 'You know I would never have thought of checking the runway.'

'I'm sure it's okay, but it just might give me the chance of finding out who Kendrick's client is.'

'Is that so important?'

'Could be. I don't like Kendrick. He could gyp us. If we know who his client is, we would be in the position to gyp him.'

'Kendrick won't gyp us.'

'Let's hope not, but I'll be happier if I know who his client is.'

'Well, all right. How are you off for money, Jack?'

'I could do with three hundred dollars. I won't be away more than a couple of days, and there's the flight fare to Merida to take care of.'

He went to a drawer and gave me five hundred dollars.

As I put the money in my pocket, I said, 'There's another thing: have you a gun, Bernie?'

He looked startled.

'You don't need a gun, Jack. What do you mean?'

'We're playing with dynamite. Kendrick now hates me like smallpox. I could just run into an accident when inspecting the runway. With me out of the way, his life would become a lot easier.'

'You're not serious?'

'If you have a gun, I want it.'

He hesitated, then went into his bedroom and returned with a .38 automatic and a box of shells.

Silently, he handed them to me.

'Thanks,' I said.

There was an awkward pause, then he said, 'Tomorrow I'm flying Essex to L.A. Harry and I won't be back until Saturday night.'

My eyes shifted to Pam and then away from her.

63

'So suppose we four meet at the café-bar on Sunday at 18.00?' I said. 'I'll be back from Merida and could have some information.'

He nodded. 'I'll tell Harry.'

'We'll leave Kendrick out this time.'

Again he nodded.

'One more thing, Bernie, if I don't show up on Sunday, forget this operation. Don't go through with it: it won't be safe.'

While he was staring uneasily at me, I left the cabin.

After a shower and a shave, I found the time was only 20.22. I could hear the sound of TV coming from Tim's cabin. I knocked on his door.

'Want to spend some of Mr Essex's money tonight, Tim?' I asked when he opened the door.

'Sure. Where do we go?'

'On the town.'

It was while I was driving the Alfa towards Paradise City that I said casually, 'How's the runway shaping?'

'Fine,' O'Brien said. 'No problem. It'll be ready in three weeks: going like a bomb.'

'I hear there's a similar runway being built outside Merida. You wouldn't know about that?'

'Merida? Sure.' O'Brien chuckled. 'Now that was a real sonofabitch to build, but it's finished now. My side-kick, Bill O'Cassidy, is putting the finishing touches to it. I was talking to him on the phone only last night. I wanted his advice about a rock problem I've run into. Bill is about the best man in this game. He told me he can't wait to get out of Yucatan. He's had a bellyful.'

'But the runway is finished?'

'Oh, sure.'

'O'Cassidy? I knew a Frank O'Cassidy. Would that be a relation?'

'Could be. I know Bill had a brother serving in Vietnam, his name was Sean. He was killed out there in the 6th battalion, parachute. He won the Silver Star.'

'Not the same man.'

I pulled up outside the Casino. 'Let's eat.'

Later, after a top-class meal, I said casually, 'Your pal O'Cassidy. Would he be staying at the Continental hotel?'

O'Brien had had a lot to drink and thought I was just making conversation.

'He's at the Chalco.'

Just then two dolly birds moved up to us and asked if we would like some fun.

I said some other time and they smiled and went away, waving their hips at us. I signalled to the waiter, signed for the meal and pushed back my chair.

'How about bed, Tim? You have a hard day's work tomorrow.'

'Damn fine meal.' Tim got to his feet. 'Man! Did you strike it good!'

My mind was pretty active on the way back to the airport. I decided I would leave for Merida the following morning. After I had left Tim at his cabin, I called the Florida Airlines and booked a flight to Merida, leaving Paradise City at 10.27.

I would be a day's jump ahead of Kendrick and I had a feeling any jump ahead of that fat queer was a move in my favour.

CHAPTER FIVE

A BATTERED, RUSTY CHEVVY rushed me from the Merida airport to the Chalco hotel. The driver looked as if he should still be at school: his blue-black hair reached to the collar of his dirty white shirt and he continually leaned out of the car window to curse other drivers.

The heat was something and it was raining fit to drown a duck. I sat back on broken springs and sweated, and every now and then, shut my eyes as a crash seemed certain, but the boy finally got me to the hotel in one piece.

I paid him off in Mexican money I had collected at the airport and dashed through the rain into the hotel.

It was down a narrow side street, painted white and the lobby was clean with cactus plants, bamboo chairs and a tiny fountain that made a soft sound which encouraged a coolness that didn't exist. I went up to the reception desk where an old, fat Mexican sat picking his teeth with a splinter of wood.

'A room for the night with a shower,' I said.

He shoved a tattered register towards me and a police card.

I went through the motions, then a tiny, dirty boy appeared to take my bag.

65

'Mr O'Cassidy in?' I asked.

The old man showed slight interest. He said something in Spanish.

'Mr O'Cassidy,' I repeated in a slightly louder voice.

The little boy said, 'He in bar.' And he pointed. I followed the direction of his dirty finger and saw a door. I gave the kid the equivalent of a half dollar and told him to take my bag up to my room. The kid's eyes nearly fell out of his head. The old man leaned forward and stared first at the money in the kid's dirty hand and then at the kid. I doubted if the kid would stick with the money. I left them and entered the tiny bar where a radio played soft music, where a fat girl with long black plaits supported herself on the bar and where, at the far end of the bar, was a man, hidden by the *Herald Tribune*.

'Scotch on the rocks,' I said, moving down to the middle of the bar.

At the sound of my voice, the man lowered the newspaper and regarded me. I waited until the girl had given me the drink, then looked at him.

He was a man of around forty-five, big with reddish, close-cropped hair, a blunt, heavily tanned face and steady green eyes. He was the same ilk as Tim O'Brien: a man you couldn't help but like.

I raised my glass and said, 'Hi!'

His wide Irish smile was warming.

'Hi, yourself. You just moved in?'

I wandered down the bar close to him.

'Jack Crane. May I buy you a drink?'

'Thanks.' He nodded to the girl who busied herself with a Scotch and soda. 'Bill O'Cassidy.'

He offered his hand and I shook it.

'That's luck. Tim O'Brien told me to look out for you.'

He lifted his eyebrows.

'You know Tim?'

'Know him? We were out on the town last night.'

O'Cassidy glanced at the fat girl as she brought him his drink, then picking it up, he jerked his head to a table away from the bar and we went over there.

'That babe never stops listening,' he said as we sat down. 'How's Tim?'

'Fine. He's working like hell on this runway. You know about that, don't you?'

'Yeah. He's in trouble with rocks.' O'Cassidy grinned. 'He doesn't know when he is well off. I've had swamps to cope with.'

'Tim was telling me.'

'Well, that's all behind me now. I'm leaving tomorrow. Phew! I can't wait to get out of this god-forsaken country!'

'Certainly hot and this rain!'

'This is the beginning of the wet season. The sonofabitch will rain non-stop now for a couple of months. Just got the job finished in time.'

'O'Cassidy?' I said idly. 'No relation to Sean O'Cassidy who won the Silver Star?'

He sat upright.

'My kid brother! You knew him?'

'I was out there. I was with the bombers. I met him once. 6th Parachute . . . right?'

'For Pete's sake!' He leaned forward, grabbed my hand and shook it. 'Hell of a small world! You met Sean?'

'That's it. We had a drink together. I had no idea he would win the Silver Star. We just got drunk together.'

He sat back and beamed at me. 'A great little guy.'

'He certainly was.'

'What did you say your name was?'

'Jack Crane.'

'Okay, Jack, you and me are going out on the town. It's my last night here. We eat, we get goddamn drunk, but not too drunk and we get us a couple of girls . . . how's about it?'

I grinned at him. 'Fine with me.'

'Nothing gets moving in this city until around 22.00.' He looked at his strap watch. 'It's now only 20.18. I'll take a shower and suppose we meet here at 21.45 . . . okay?'

'Sure.'

We collected our keys at the desk. The old Mexican regarded us without interest. My room was five doors along the corridor from O'Cassidy's room. We parted. I found my bag on the bed. In spite of the window being open, the room was stiflingly hot. I stared down into the street, watching the rain making puddles, then I unpacked, dug out another shirt and another pair of slacks and lay on the bed.

The noise of the roaring traffic and the clanging of the church bells made a nap impossible so I did some thinking.

Later I stripped off and took a shower, changed, but it didn't help much. Life in Merida was like living in a sauna.

I went down to the bar and asked the girl with the plaits for a whisky on the rocks. At least there was a fan in the bar. I read through the *Herald Tribune* and then O'Cassidy joined me.

'That's the last drink you buy yourself tonight,' he said. 'Come on . . . let's go. I've got a car outside.'

We ran through the rain to a Buick. By the time we had scrambled in we were both pretty wet, but the heat dried us before O'Cassidy parked outside a restaurant. We ran from the car and ducked out of the rain into the entrance lobby.

A fat, grinning Mexican in a white coat shook hands with O'Cassidy and then led us into a dimly-lit room, but air-conditioned, to a table in the far corner. There were about thirty tables dotted around, occupied by sleek looking Mexicans and sleeker looking girls.

'I've been in this city now for nine months and I always eat here nights,' O'Cassidy said as he sat down. 'The food's fine.' He waved to a dark, sulky looking beauty who was at the bar and who lifted a tired hand and weary eyebrows. He shook his head, then turning to me: 'The dolls here are very willing, but let's eat first. You like Mexican food?'

'So long as it's not too hot.'

We had tamales which were hot but very good, followed by Molé de Guajolote: a fricassée of turkey seasoned with tomatoes, sesame seeds and covered with a thick chocolate sauce. The sauce startled me until I tried the dish to find it excellent.

After we had got through the Molé and had talked of Vietnam and O'Cassidy's brother, I felt O'Cassidy was relaxed enough for me to get to business.

'Can I ask you about this runway you've built, Bill?' I asked cautiously.

'Why, sure. You interested in runways?'

'I'm an aero-engineer and anything to do with flying interests me.'

'Is that right? Well, this goddamn runway was the worst I've ever had to build so far. Right in the middle of the jungle: trees, rocks, swamps, snakes . . . you name it, it was there.'

'Yet you built it.'

He grinned.

'When I get paid to do a job, I do it, but no kidding there were times when I nearly packed it in. The crew I had to work for me drove me nuts. They had an I.Q. a child of four would be ashamed of. I had around a thousand of them and they did as much work in a day as twenty good Irishmen would do. Six of the jerks during the nine months got themselves killed either by snakes or walking into blasting or a tree falling on them.'

'But you built it.'

He nodded, leaning back in his chair, a look of pride on his face.

'That's what I did.'

'I remember in Vietnam we had to build a runway fast with coolie labour,' I lied. 'The first bomber to touch down smashed it up and the kite was a write-off.'

'That's not going to happen to my runway. I guarantee a 747 could land on it and when I guarantee something, it stays guaranteed. . . .'

Then I came to the sixty-four thousand dollar question.

Casually, I said, 'Who the hell wants a runway slap in the middle of a jungle?'

'You get these nuts.' O'Cassidy shrugged. 'The one thing I've learned in my racket is not to ask questions. I get propositioned: I get paid. I do the job and then I move on. I'm going to Rio tomorrow to extend a runway for a Flying Club: that'll be an easy one. How about a brandy and coffee?'

'Why not?'

He gave the order then we lit cigarettes.

After a moment of hesitation, I said, 'It's important to me, Bill, to know who financed your runway.'

He stared at me, his green eyes probing.

'Important? Why?'

I flicked ash on the floor.

'I've got myself mixed up in something I can't talk about,' I said. 'It's to do with your runway. I smell trouble and I need as much information as I can get.'

The coffee and two brandies arrived.

He put sugar in his coffee, stirred and I could see he was thinking. I didn't hurry him. Suddenly, as if he had made up his mind, he shrugged his heavy shoulders.

'Okay, Jack, because you're a friend of Tim's and you've met my kid brother and because I'm pulling out of here and frankly, I don't give a damn now I've got my money, I'll give you my ideas about this runway, but they're ideas not facts . . . understand?'

I nodded.

He paused to look around as if to make certain no one was paying us any attention, then leaning forward and lowering his voice, he went on, 'It's on the cards there is going to be a revolution here. Listening to the jerks who work for me I get the idea something's on the boil. That's my guess. I could be wrong, but I don't think so, that's why I'm damned glad to be getting out tomorrow.' He sipped his brandy, then went on, 'The man financing the runway is Benito Orzoco. He's a nutter, Jack. A real nutter but he is a big shot around here. He leads the left wing extremists and so I hear is a blood brother of Castro of Cuba. Orzoco considers himself a second Juan Alvarez who was the first President of the Republic way back in 1855. Orzoco is stinking rich. Anything he wants he has and I mean anything. With this runway, plus a big kite, he could fly men and arms in and keep them hidden in the jungle until the green light goes up.' He finished his coffee. 'Look, Jack, I don't know a thing for certain. I'm telling you what I think could be the reason for building the runway. Maybe it's something else, but I don't think so. I'm off tomorrow and couldn't care less . . . that help you?'

'Sure does. Did you ever meet Orzoco?'

'I'll say. He came to inspect the runway every month.' O'Cassidy's nose wrinkled. 'I'd rather touch a black mamba than him.'

'Give me a better idea than that.'

O'Cassidy blew out his cheeks.

'He's a nutter. I'm sure of that. He's short, powerfully built and a dresser. He has snake's eyes. First glance he's like any other rich dago, but he has something plus. He's crazy in the head. Every now and then, it shows. He is rich and has power but wants more power. He's as deadly as generalized cancer.'

'Sounds nice,' I said soberly.

O'Cassidy sipped his brandy.

'I don't know what your racket is, Jack, and I don't want to know, but take a tip from me . . . watch out.'

Two dolly birds descended on us and we began drinking in

70

earnest. Later, they took us back to their pad. They gave out. Finally, we got back to our hotel around 03.40.

'Some night, huh?' O'Cassidy said as he shook hands. 'So long, Jack. I'm off early.'

'Some night.'

I wasn't to see him again.

I went along to my room, fell into bed and went out like a blown flame.

Around midday I checked out of the Chalco and took a taxi in the pouring rain across to the Continental hotel. This was one of the top hotels in Merida and the lobby was crammed with American tourists, wrapped in plastic macs and making a noise like a disturbed parrot house.

I edged my way to the reception desk and waited while an elderly American quarrelled with a bored-faced clerk about his check. When the argument was settled, the clerk turned to me.

'Checking in. Jack Crane,' I said.

He stiffened to attention.

'Happy to have you with us, Mr Crane. Yes . . . room 500. Top floor with a view. If there's anything you need, please ask. We are at your service, Mr Crane.'

A boy in buttons appeared and took my bag and the key the clerk gave him. He led me around the tourists to the elevator and up to the fifth floor.

Unlocking a door opposite the elevator, he bowed me into a big sitting-room, led me into a big bedroom with a king's size bed, then placing my bag, he showed me the ornate bathroom, bowed, accepted the tip I gave him, bowed again and removed himself.

I looked around, wondering how much this set-up was going to cost. Then I moved into the sitting-room and through the open french windows on to the covered terrace. The humid heat was making me sweat again.

A man leaned on the terrace rail, looking down at the slow moving traffic. He turned as I came out on to the terrace.

He was tall, thin, with thick longish jet black hair, around forty years of age, his eyes hidden behind black sun goggles: a long thin nose, an almost lipless mouth, a cleft chin. He was wearing a white suit that looked as if it had just come back from the cleaners, a yellow shirt and a blood red tie.

'Mr Crane?' He advanced towards me, smiling.

'That's right.' I took his offered hand, dry and hard, and shook it.'

'Allow me to introduce myself. I am Juan Aulestria, but call me Juan . . . it's easier.'

I got my hand back from his grip and waited.

'Welcome to Yucatan, Mr Crane,' he went on. 'I hope you will be comfortable here. I'm sure you would like a drink.'

I wasn't going to let this smoothie be sure of anything as far as I was concerned.

'No, thanks: I'm easy. Just who are you?'

This fazzed him for a brief second. The smile slipped, but it came quickly again into position.

'Ah . . . yes.' He turned and stared at the rain-swollen clouds. 'Such a pity. Sad for the tourists. If you had come two days ago you would have seen this City as it should be seen. Suppose we sit down?' He moved to a lounging chair and sank into it. 'You ask who I am, Mr Crane.' He flicked a speck of dust from his immaculate white sleeve. 'I have to do with the runway that has just been built. I am told you want to inspect it.'

I stood over him. 'That's what I want to do.'

He nodded, looking up at me.

'But do sit down: are you sure you wouldn't like a drink?'

'I like standing and I don't want a drink.' I paused to light a cigarette. 'I represent the people who are bringing you the plane. This plane costs ten million dollars. My people want to deliver it in one piece and unless I'm sure the runway is right, we don't deliver.'

He hated sitting there, looking up at me so he got casually to his feet.

'Our contact explained this to me. This shows efficiency, Mr Crane, but I assure you the runway is perfect. However . . .' He waved his thin hands, 'you are the expert. You shall see it and decide for yourself.'

I was liking him as you would a big spider in your bath.

'When do we go?'

'Would this afternoon suit you?'

'Fine.'

'Then at three I will have a car here for you. We will go by helicopter. We can survey the ground, then we will land and you can inspect it. I'm afraid you will get rather wet but I have ordered plastics for you.'

'Thank you.'

'I have also arranged for you to lunch up here. Would that please you?'

'Thank you.'

He started towards the living-room.

'So glad. Since you have already tasted our great national dish of Molé de Guajalote, may I suggest you try our Chile Jalapeno. quite excellent.' He turned and smiled at me.

Keeping my face wooden, I said, 'I'll settle for a steak.'

'Anything: then at 15.00, Mr Crane.'

We shook hands and he let himself out of the room as silently and as smoothly as a snake.

I closed the french windows and turned on the air conditioner. Then I went to the refrigerator and poured myself a stiff whisky and soda.

So he knew I had met O'Cassidy. Obviously he wasn't making any secret about it by telling me what I had eaten last night. I sat down and did some thinking.

After a while a tap came on the door and a little Mexican in white drill pushed a trolley towards me. Another little Mexican came behind him with a suitcase in his hand. He set it down as his companion took off the covers of my meal. They bowed themselves out.

The steak was fair. I ate it, left the carafe of red wine, decided against the mangoes, lit a cigarette and inspected the suitcase. It contained a short plastic coat, plastic trousers, rubber boots and a plastic hood.

I lay on the bed, smoking until 14.50, then I got up, took Bernie's .38 from my suitcase. I checked it, loaded it and stuck it in my hip pocket.

As a nearby church clock struck three, I went down to the lobby.

The reception clerk came around his desk, smiling.

'There's a car waiting for you, Mr Crane.' He led the way and handed me over to the doorman who had an open umbrella. The doorman conducted me to a sleek Cadillac, driven by a blank-faced Mexican in a smart blue uniform.

As soon as I was seated in the rear of the car, the chauffeur took off. He was a skilful, fast driver and in spite of the thick traffic, he got me to the airport in ten minutes. He by-passed the reception and departure building, drove around the back and pulled up beside a helicopter. He was out of the car with a big umbrella before I could move. I got out of the car, carrying the plastic gear and got into the helicopter without getting more than a sprinkle from the pouring rain.

Aulestria occupied one of the seats just behind the pilot. He smiled his snake's smile as I settled.

'Did you have a good lunch, Mr Crane?'

'Fine, thank you.'

The blades started to swing and in a few moments we flew away over the city.

Aulestria made small talk, pointing out the Palace of the State Government, the Cathedral and the National University. Leaving the city and heading south, I looked down at the haciendas and the many sisal factories. The rocky countryside slowly changed to dense forest land and finally to jungle.

After an hour of flying, Aulestria said, 'We are now approaching the runway, Mr Crane.'

I looked ahead but could see nothing but tree tops and jungle.

'It's well hidden.'

'Yes: very well hidden.' His voice was smug.

Then I saw it: an engineering feat de luxe. A solid ribbon of tarmac that stretched for at least two miles, bordered by the jungle on either side, painted a dullish green and unless you were hunting for it, you would never spot it.

'Some job!' I said, leaning forward as the chopper flew the length of it, circled and came back again.

'We think it is satisfactory,' Aulestria said. 'It is good that you approve.'

'Tell him to fly back a mile, then come in. I want to see the approach.'

Aulestria spoke to the pilot.

Now I was ready and as we came in again, I judged how Bernie would come in. I decided it presented no problem to a pilot of Bernie's experience.

'Fine. Now let's look at the control tower.'

We landed by the side of the tower and I put on my plastic coat. It was still pouring with rain.

74

Aulestria led me from the chopper, up steps and into the tower. I spent over an hour checking the instruments, the radar and all the gimmicks needed to bring in a kite. I couldn't fault anything.

What bothered me was the personnel in charge of the control tower. They all looked like bandits right out of a Western movie: real thugs who watched me with snake's eyes and who wore .45 revolvers on their hips.

'Do you want to walk the runway Mr Crane, or did Mr O'Cassidy convince you that he has built something to last?' Aulestria asked.

'I won't walk it.'

'Then I may take you back to your hotel?'

'That's it.'

He led the way into a small air-conditioned office.

'Shall we talk?' He sat down behind the desk and waved me to a chair. 'You are satisfied?'

'Yes. We can bring the kite in.'

'Good.' He stared at me, his eyes hidden behind the goggles. 'Now, Mr Crane, let us be practicable. This plane is highly sophisticated. We have three pilots. Naturally, they will have to be trained to handle the plane. I take it that your pilots will train them?'

'That's for them to decide.'

'It would be no use for us to accept the plane unless our people could fly it. I was under the impression our contact had arranged for this?'

'He said nothing to us about it.'

'Would you check then, Mr. Crane? My men must be trained by your people or the deal's off.'

'I'll check. How good are your pilots?'

'Excellent. One of them has been flying a 747.'

'Then I see no problem.'

'Good.' He got to his feet. 'There's a flight back to Paradise City in three hours. The sooner we get this arranged the better. When will the plane be delivered?'

'In two months: could be less.'

'Send me a cable: just the date and time of expected arrival. That's all that will be necessary.'

'I'll do that.'

As he moved to the door, he paused.

'Mr Crane, you haven't asked any questions as to why we need

75

this aircraft and I like that. I am aware that O'Cassidy has talked to you and perhaps he has given you his views. Dismiss anything he has told you from your mind. There should be no talk: is that understood?'

Keeping my face wooden, I said, 'That's okay with me.'

'I hope it is, Mr Crane,' then he led me through the rain to the helicopter.

Because of what is known as a technical hitch, my flight back to Paradise City was delayed for two hours. I didn't reach the City until 20.25. I collected the Alfa I had left in the airport garage, then drove down to the waterfront. I decided not to return to my cabin this night. I didn't want to run into Pam while Bernie was away. I parked the Alfa and booked in at a modest hotel.

After a quick shower, I wandered out to find a meal. I picked on a small, but smart looking sea-food restaurant, ordered curried prawns, then read a newspaper while I waited. I had just finished the prawns and was waiting for coffee when Mrs Victoria Essex, accompanied by Wes Jackson, came in.

She saw me at once and smiled. Jackson also went through the grimace he called a smile. She started towards me so I stood up.

She looked marvellous in a simple white dress that must have cost the earth and there was that look in the big violet eyes that immediately turned me on.

'Why, Mr Crane, I thought I had lost you,' she said. 'Where have you been?'

'Around and about,' I said. 'Glad to see you're no worse for your fall.'

'I'm fine now.' She was staring at me, then she turned around and looked at Jackson as if seeing him for the first time. She flicked her fingers at him. 'All right, Jackson, don't wait.'

'Yes, Mrs Essex,' and he took his bulk out of the restaurant.

'May I join you?' she asked.

I pulled out a chair and she sat down. I went back to my chair. The waiter came and she ordered coffee.

'I wanted you to ride with me this morning. They told me you had left.' Her big violet eyes moved over me. 'Had you?'

'That's right. I've been in Mexico for the past two days. An airline offered me a job. I thought I'd take a look at it.'

'Mexico? You wouldn't want to live in that hole, would you?'

SO WHAT HAPPENS TO ME?

'I guess not.'

'Then why did you go?'

'A free trip: I was getting bored here.'

Her coffee arrived.

'God! Yes! I can understand that! I get bored too.' She stirred her coffee. 'My husband's jealous. When he goes on a trip, I either have to stay home or if I want to go out I have to have Jackson with me. He's supposed to be my chaperon and spy.'

'Supposed to be?'

She smiled, sipped her coffee, then said, 'He's more scared of me than my husband.'

I finished my coffee.

'Have you anything to do tonight?' she asked.

'Not a thing.'

'Have you a car?'

'Just across the road.'

'I'll take you to a place. We can have fun.'

'It's only a two-seater. There would be no room for Jackson.'

She laughed. 'Don't worry about him. Let's go.'

'Don't you want to eat?'

'I only eat when I'm bored.' She looked directly at me and there was that thing again in her eyes. 'I'm not bored now.'

'Just a moment. I understand Mr Essex is due back tonight.'

'Are you scared of him?'

'I'm not scared of anyone, but I thought I'd mention it.'

'I had a telex this afternoon. He's staying over at L.A. and won't be back until tomorrow.'

I got to my feet, paid the check and smiled at her.

'So what are we waiting for?'

We went out into the moonlit night. There was a Mercedes parked under a street light with Wes Jackson at the wheel. She went over to him, spoke to him and he nodded. He drove away.

Together, we walked to the Alfa and she slid under the wheel.

'I'll take you,' she said.

I got in beside her and she drove away from the waterfront: expert, fast driving, perfect control and I sat back and enjoyed being driven.

We got on to the hill road and we drove fast for three or four miles, then she turned up a dirt road and finally pulled up outside a knotty pine cabin.

'This is my retreat,' she said, sliding out of the car, 'where I exercise my hobbies.'

As she was unlocking the door, I remembered what Bernie had said about Harry Erskine: *Mrs Essex dangled herself and he fell for it and then she cut him down to size. That's her speciality: turning it on, making a guy think he's going to get into her bed, then telling him he isn't.*

The set-up looked good, but she could just be dangling herself. I decided to play it cool. She would have to make all the advances.

I followed her into a large, comfortably furnished room and I saw a big divan across by the picture window.

'Pretty nice,' I said. 'What are your hobbies?'

'I paint: I'm not bad.' She walked over to a cocktail cabinet. 'A whisky?'

'Thanks.'

She made two drinks, handed me one and dropped down into a lounging chair. On the arm of the chair was a number of buttons. She pressed one and then sipped her drink. Soft music came from concealed speakers.

'That's neat,' I said and sat on the arm of another lounging chair. 'What it is to be rich.'

'Do you want to be rich?'

'Who doesn't?'

'It has its disadvantages.'

'Such as?'

She shrugged. 'Oh, boredom. When you have everything, you also have boredom.'

'You would know . . . I wouldn't,' I said.

She set down her glass, smiled and stood up.

'Let's dance.'

She looked very inviting as she stood there: too inviting.

I sat where I was, looking at her.

'Mrs Essex,' I said quietly, 'I have some inside information about you and I don't want to take advantage of you. You should have some inside information about me.'

Her smile slipped away and the violet eyes became hard.

'What do you mean?'

'I have been told you are a copper-plated bitch. What you don't know is I am a copper-plated bastard. It's only fair for you to know this. You see, Mrs Essex, although I think you are the most gorgeous woman I have ever seen, the most desirable, the sexiest, no matter how good you look, I don't tease. You either get out of the dress and get on the divan and give out or I get out. Is that plain enough for you?'

Her eyes opened wide.

'How dare you talk to me like that!'

'That's what I thought. Well, I'll be running along. See you,' and I started towards the door.

She sprang at me, grabbed my arm, swung me around and slapped my face.

'You devil!'

I caught her up, gave her a stinging slap on her bottom, then tossed her on to the divan.

'Get out of that dress,' I said, standing over her, 'or do you want me to tear it off?'

'You hurt me!'

'Okay, so I tear it off.'

'No! I have to have something to go home in!'

I laughed.

'So go ahead and get out of it.'

Her eyes glittering, her breasts heaving, she slid out of the dress.

I got to the café-bar twenty minutes before the others were due. I ordered a coke and sat in the shade on the veranda and waited.

While I waited, I thought about Mrs Victoria Essex. I knew she would be good, and that's what she was. She acted like a woman who had been sexually starved most of her life. But why go into details? When it was finally over, she had got off the divan and taken a shower while I lay there feeling as if I had been hit by a truck.

She had dressed while I still lay there.

'Lock up,' she said. 'I have a car. Put the key under the mat,' and she was gone.

I waited until I heard her car drive away, then I dressed, locked up, put the key under the mat and drove back to the hotel.

Well, I told myself, you have laid one of the richest women in the world: what happens next? Would she tell Wes Jackson to get rid of me or did she want another session? It was a matter of waiting and seeing.

Olson's Buick came down the sandy road and pulled up. He, Pam and Erskine got out and joined me.

'Good trip?' I asked as the girl served cokes.

'The usual.' Bernie shrugged. 'The boss got held up. We've only just got in.'

I didn't tell him I knew this.

When the girl had gone, I said, 'It looks all right. I've checked the runway. No problem. It's raining like hell out there and the fly in could be tricky.'

I went on to give them a detailed description of my reception, how I had met O'Cassidy and what he had told me.

'I think he's right: this is a political thing,' I concluded. 'Not that it matters to us. The thing that does matter is to be sure Kendrick pays up. We don't shift the kite until we get that bank receipt.'

'How do you react now about us getting knocked off once we deliver?' Erskine asked.

'I think if we do what we're told and don't make reasons for them to turn rough, we'll be okay.' I had thought about this a lot. 'You see, you two have to train their pilots. As we've delivered the kite the agreement is we get the full payment. So we'll probably have to stay at the airfield for a couple of weeks while the pilots are being trained. It seems to me once we have done that, fulfilled all obligations, there is no reason for them to get rid of us. They can't get their hands on the money once it has been paid into the bank so what's the point in knocking us off?'

Erskine thought about this, then nodded.

'But . . .' I paused to look directly at Bernie, 'Pam doesn't fly with us.'

He stiffened, but before he could say anything, Pam snapped, 'I'd like to see you stop me!'

I ignored her, looking directly at Bernie.

'The airfield is staffed with thugs, Bernie. There are no women there. With you two busy training their pilots, Pam could run into trouble. I'm not taking the responsibility of looking after her. That's strictly out. If one of those greasers makes a pass at her, we could have the trouble I want to avoid. So she doesn't come with us. She takes a flight to Merida and stays at a hotel and waits for us, but she doesn't come with us on the flight. Can you see that?'

'Bernie!' Pam's voice was shrill. 'You're not listening to this jerk, are you? I'm coming with you!'

'I guess I'd better think about this, Jack,' Bernie said uneasily.

'There's nothing to think about. She doesn't fly with us. I've seen these thugs . . . you haven't. The moment they set eyes on her, they'll come after her and then we'll have real trouble.'

'Makes sense,' Erskine said. 'Why look for trouble?'

Bernie hesitated, then reluctantly nodded.

'Yes. Okay, she doesn't come with us.'

'And what am I supposed to do? Sit in some stinking hotel and wait? Suppose you three decide to ditch me! I'd look a mug, wouldn't I?' Pam said viciously. 'I'm coming with you!'

I shoved back my chair and stood up.

'Want a lift back?' I asked Erskine.

'Sure.'

'Bernie, this is your problem: she's your woman. You fix it.'

I walked down the steps with Erskine at my side to the Alfa.

CHAPTER SIX

I WAS TRYING to make up my mind what I was going to do with myself on this Monday morning when the telephone bell rang. I was hoping the call would be from Mrs Essex suggesting a ride, but it was Bernie.

'Hi! Jack! Look, I've had a call from Mr Essex. Something's cooking. Will you stick around? From what Jackson tells me the Condor is ahead of time. As soon as I get back, I'll drop in.'

'I'll be here,' I said and he hung up.

The time was 9.47, I was feeling a little limp. Tim and I had done a movie, then some heavy drinking the previous night. I had got from him that the runway would be finished by the end of the week.

He was in a merry mood as he was five weeks ahead of schedule. He told me he would get a big bonus for getting the job done so quickly.

I ordered breakfast and when I had eaten it, I turned on the

TV and watched an old western. It passed a couple of hours, then I shaved, showered and dressed.

Bernie showed up around 13.00. He looked like a man with a load on his back. Shutting the door, he dropped into a chair.

While I was fixing him a drink, I said, 'Did you talk sense into Pam?'

'Yes.' He took the drink. 'You're right, Jack. I hadn't thought of that angle. A woman out in the jungle could really foul up this operation.' He drank, blew out his cheeks. 'I had a time. God! Women!'

'What's cooking with Essex?' I wasn't interested in his domestic problems.

'I've got instructions to fly him to Paris tomorrow. The new kite is ready for delivery. So I drop him in Paris, fly back, sell the old kite, take delivery of the new one, go on the course and be ready to collect him from Kennedy when he returns. He flies back from Paris by Pan-Am.'

'Is Mrs Essex going with him?'

'Yes.' He looked sharply at me. 'Why the interest?'

'I want to know where everyone is. And Pam?'

'The airfield closes down for four weeks. Everyone except Harry, Jean and me go off on vacation. Pam is going to stay with her married sister until the green light goes up, then she flies to Merida and waits for us.'

'So we have four weeks?'

'That's it. I've talked to Jackson about you. I've told him I need you to handle the servicing of the Condor. So he talked to Mr Essex and it's fixed. You're now on the payroll from today at thirty thousand. You'll have to see Macklin, the staff manager, who will sign you on and fix everything. Officially, we start work in four weeks' time, but while you and the rest of them are on vacation, you get paid.'

'I like that.' I paused, then went on, 'Can you give me a date when you fly in the new kite?'

'October 3rd unless the tests don't jell.'

This day was September 4th.

'When we hijack this kite, Bernie, we need to be armed. I'm not taking any chances with these greasers. Each of us should have a machine pistol and at least one automatic rifle.'

He stared uneasily at me.

'You really think there could be trouble?'

'I don't know, but I'm taking precautions. Where can we get them?'

'That's no problem. We have an armoury here and it's pretty comprehensive. All we have to do is to help ourselves.'

'Fine. Now, there's another thing, Bernie. We all have to have false passports. We all have to begin new lives. Do you think Kendrick can fix that?'

'Hell! I never thought of that. You're right.' Bernie hesitated, then nodded. 'If he can't, no one can.'

'I'll see him today. I'll want passport photos of you all.'

'No problem. We always carry spares. I'll get them for you.'

'Then another thing. I've been thinking more about the pay-out, Bernie. I suggested it should be paid in your name to the National Bank of Mexico. This was half-ass thinking. My new thinking is we form a company in Mexico. This is much the safer way. I'll fly down to Mexico City and fix it up. I thought of calling the company the Blue Ribbon Air Taxi service. Once the company's set up then Kendrick pays the money into the bank who will credit the company. What do you think?'

He blinked.

'You're way ahead of me, Jack. That's fine. I like the Blue Ribbon Air Taxi Service.' He smiled, looking happy for the first time. 'You'll be needing more money, won't you?'

'I'll get it from Kendrick. Get me the photos and leave the rest to me.'

'Okay.'

'One more thing. How is the three million to be shared.'

He looked vague.

'I haven't really thought about it.'

'Well, I have. You dreamed up the idea: so you get a million. I handle your idea so I get a million and a quarter. Harry gets three quarters. That's the way I see it.'

He moved uneasily.

'You've forgotten Pam.'

'She's your woman, Bernie. You take care of her. She's not in the operation.'

He hesitated, then shrugged. 'Yes.'

'Okay, so the pay-out is agreed?'

'I'll have to talk to Harry.'

JAMES HADLEY CHASE

'Those are my terms. Without me this operation would never get off the pad and you know it.'

He got wearily to his feet. 'Okay, Jack. It's agreed.'

When he had gone I rang room service and asked them to send their special for the day. The maître d' said in a chilly voice that he understood I was now on the staff. If I wanted to eat, I would have to go to the restaurant.

I then went over to Macklin's office. He greeted me the way a high executive greets a staff hand. He asked me to return all the credit cards he had given me, then he shoved a form at me. He told me once I had completed the form my first month's salary would be credited at the Florida Bank. After I had completed the form, he said I was no longer to use the Alfa. Wes Jackson had certainly been busy this morning.

I went over to the restaurant, had lunch and paid for it, then returned to my cabin. After a while Bernie came in. He handed me a set of passport photographs.

'Did you talk to Harry?' I asked.

'Yes. He goes along with the share-out.' He looked thoughtfully at me. 'You seem to have made quite a hit with him.'

'That's something. Look, Bernie, I'm no longer a V.I.P. here. I need a car.'

'Take mine: the Buick. I can use a staff car.' He started towards the door, then paused. 'I have a hell of a lot of work to do now, Jack. We leave tomorrow at midday. What are you going to do with yourself while I'm away?'

'See Kendrick, then fly down to Mexico City and set up the company, then go home and spend a couple of weeks with my old man.'

'You can reach me at the Avon Air Corporation, Texas, from September 10th. Harry and I will be working on the course.'

'Okay. Anyway we meet here on October 3rd?'

'Yes.'

We shook hands.

As he opened the door, he looked uneasily at me. 'You do think it will jell?'

I grinned at him. 'It's got to, hasn't it?'

Louis de Marney, Kendrick's stooge, weaved his way down the aisle of the gallery bordered with art treasures, waving his hand.

84

'Mr Crane! How nice!' he gushed. 'Claude was only talking about you this morning. We were really wondering when we would see you again.'

I looked around. The vast room was stuffed with items the rich would fall for.

'Is he around?'

'Of course. A tiny moment. I'll tell him,' and he swished his behind along the aisle and disappeared through a doorway at the end of the gallery. He reappeared in moments and beckoned to me.

I went down the aisle and entered a vast room with a picture window looking on to the sea, sumptuously furnished with what seemed to me impressive looking antiques and pictures that were probably worth a fortune, hanging on the silk-covered walls.

Kendrick was sitting in a vast chair, his feet on a footstool. He rose and offered his hand. His vast face lit up with a roguish smile.

'So glad, cheri. Do sit down. A tiny drink? Whisky? Champagne? We have everything. Do just say.'

'Nothing, thanks.' I lit a cigarette and sat down opposite him. De Marney lurked in the background. 'I want false passports.' I laid the photos on an occasional table near him. 'Can you fix that?'

'For whom?'

'Bernie, Erskine, myself and Pam.'

His little eyes studied me, then he nodded.

'You will have the new names?'

I took out my wallet and handed a slip of paper to him.

'It can be arranged, but it will cost, cheri.' He blew out his cheeks and sighed. 'Everything costs.'

'You're financing this caper,' I said. 'I'm not interested in costs.'

'Yes.' He took the photos and the slip of paper, beckoned to de Marney and handed them to him. 'Arrange it, precious.'

De Marney went away.

Kendrick shifted his awful wig, then looked inquiringly at me. 'What else, cheri?'

'I want two thousand dollars in cash.'

He grimaced. 'It will be deducted from your share.'

'No, it won't. It's for expenses and you're taking care of the expenses.'

He smiled, but his eyes were like wet stones.

'Yes.' He heaved himself to his feet, went to a desk, opened a drawer and after fumbling around for some moments, returned with a roll of bills. 'You have no doubt that this aircraft will be safely delivered?'

'Bernie delivers it. I don't. Ask him.' I put the money in my hip pocket.

'You are satisfied with the runway?'

'Yes.'

'Good. Is there anything else to discuss?'

I got to my feet. 'Not right now. When will the passports be ready?'

'Tomorrow afternoon.'

'I'll pick them up.'

As I started for the door, he said, 'You foresee no trouble?'

I stared at him. 'Not from our side. Have you the money ready? One and a half million dollars?'

'It will be ready by the end of the week.'

'I'll be giving you instructions how to deliver it. We have had a change of ideas about payment. We're forming a company in Mexico. I'll give you details later.'

He squinted at me. 'How very wise to form a company.'

'Yeah.' I again stared at him. 'The kite doesn't move until we get the advance payment.'

'I understand.' He paused, then went on, 'If you need a sound Mexican lawyer . . .'

I cut him short.

'I'll handle that end of it. Well, so long,' and left him.

I drove to the Florida Airlines and booked a 10.00 flight to Mexico City on September 6th, then with nothing else to do, I drove down to the beach and spent the rest of the afternoon chatting up a dolly bird who had a *Playboy*'s body and a mind like a hole in a wall. Still, she amused me and then, when the sun began to set, she announced she had to return home to cook her husband's dinner. We parted amicably.

I decided I would take Tim out for a last drinking spree, but I found him already packing. He apologized for not coming with me.

'I'm leaving at the crack of dawn, Jack,' he explained. 'I've got a big job waiting for me in Rhodesia.'

'You runway builders certainly get around.' We had a drink together, said good-bye and I left him. I didn't feel like going out on the town by myself, so I went along to the restaurant, had a light supper and returned to my cabin. I switched on the telly.

Around 22.00 the telephone bell rang. Lifting the receiver, I heard a woman say, 'Mr Crane?'

I felt a tingle run up my spine. I didn't have to be told who was calling. Mrs Essex had a very special kind of voice: once heard never forgotten.

'Hi,' I said.

'I will be at my cabin on September 24th for five days,' she said. 'You are invited,' and she hung up.

I replaced the receiver, lit a cigarette, turned off the telly and dropped into a lounging chair. Since she and I had got together, she had been seldom out of my mind. I had kept wondering if our explosive affair had been a 'ships that pass in the night' thing: now I knew it wasn't. Five days and I was invited! Five days with her alone in that hidden cabin! Eighteen days to wait! I drew in a long, deep breath. I didn't sleep much that night.

The following afternoon I collected the passports. Kendrick was out, but de Marney coped with me. My passport was good. I was now Jack Norton. I checked the other passports: they were all as good as mine.

'Satisfied?' de Marney asked.

'Sure. Give the fat boy my love,' I said and left him.

My old man was at the station to meet me. He looked taller and thinner and older.

We shook hands and we walked to his beat-up Chevvy.

'How's it been going, Jack?' he asked as he drove the car away from the little station towards his house.

'Pretty good, Dad. How are things with you?'

'The usual. One doesn't expect much when you have reached my age. Still, the bank is going well. I had four new accounts this week.'

A triumph! I thought, and my mind dwelt on the million and a quarter I would soon be owning.

'That's fine, Dad.'

'Well, it's not bad. I've got a good steak for your supper tonight. You been eating all right, son?'

'Sure.'

'You look fit.'

'That's what I am.'

There was a long silence while he drove. I looked at the streets, the small shops, the small time people. Some of them waved to the old man. Already I was beginning to regret coming back, but I had to. This was the last time I would see him. In another thirty days I'd be dead to him and I would have to remain dead if I was to hang on to all that money.

When we got home, I went up to my small shabby bedroom— what a contrast to the luxury cabin on the Essex's airfield! —and unpacked. Then I went down to the living-room. My old man produced a bottle of Cutty Sark.

'Go ahead, Jack. Make yourself a drink,' he said. 'Not for me. Whisky doesn't seem to agree with me any more.'

I gave him a sharp look.

'Are you all right, Dad?'

He smiled his gentle smile.

'I'm sixty-nine. For my age, as they say, I am all right. Get your drink and come and sit down.'

'When are you going to retire?'

'The bank talked about it, but I told them I wanted to carry on. My clients don't want me to go so it was decided I could keep on until I have to stop.' He smiled again. 'I don't want to stop yet.'

I made myself a stiff whisky and water, found ice, then came and sat down.

'Tell me what you have been doing,' he said.

That I wasn't going to do, but I told him that I was now working for Lane Essex, that I was on his payroll, that a new kite was expected and I had charge of its maintenance.

'Lane Essex?' My old man looked impressed. 'A clever man . . . he must be worth a billion. They say he has cut corners.' He shrugged. 'I don't suppose any man can make his kind of money without cutting corners.' He regarded me, his eyes sad. 'So you're settling in Paradise City? I won't see much of you.'

'Oh, come on, Dad! I hope you'll take your vacation down there. Anyway, when I'm on vacation, I'll come here.' I hated myself talking this way to him for I knew in a couple of weeks I'd never see him again.

'You hungry, son?' He heaved himself out of his chair. 'Do you think it would be an idea to have some fried onions with the steak?' He looked hopefully at me. 'I've bought some.'

'Why, sure.'

'Just leave it to me.' He started across the room towards the kitchen, paused and asked, 'Did you meet Mrs Essex, Jack?'

I stiffened. 'I met her.'

'I understand she is a very beautiful woman. I saw a photo of her in a magazine, but photos can be deceptive . . . is she?'

'You could say that. Yes, she's beautiful.'

He nodded and went into the kitchen. I finished my drink, lit a cigarette and thought back on the past week.

I had flown down to Mexico City and had booked in at a minor hotel overlooking the Alameda Gardens. I had gone to the National Bank of Mexico and had introduced myself as Jack Norton. I told the executive that I wanted to form a company with a starting capital of a million and a half dollars. From that moment I had no trouble. He produced forms and filled them in for me. He said there would be no problem. I gave him Bernie's new name as President of the Company and told him I was the Managing Director. I added Erskine's and Pam's new names, saying they were directors. I spent half an hour signing forms and he told me within a week the Blue Ribbon Air Taxi Service would be registered as a going concern. I told him the money would be credited to the company about the same time. We shook hands, he bowed to the floor and I left him.

It was as easy as that. Foreign money, especially dollars, was what the Mexican economy wanted.

Now here I was with that hurdle jumped, back in my old man's shabby little home. We ate the steak which was good, talked some more and then went to bed.

That was the first day. I don't know how I endured the next seven days, but somehow, because of my old man, I did. He was at the bank all day and I was on my own. I went around and met the girls but I found them so dreary, so dull and so goddamn awful after Mrs Victoria Essex that I stopped going out. I stayed home, watching the telly, smoking and counting the hours until September 24th. On the night of September 23rd, I suggested we two might go out and have a farewell dinner together.

'I could cook you something, Jack,' he said, 'but if you want to go out. . . .'

'Don't you? I bet you haven't been to a restaurant since Mum died.'

89

'That's true. Well, it will make a change. Yes, let's do that.'

We went to the best restaurant in town: nothing special, but decent enough. The restaurant was fairly full and everyone there seemed to know my old man. It was quite a procession to our table. He had to stop and shake hands, introduce me before he moved on to the next table. All small time people and they bored me rigid, but I was as pleasant as I could be.

'You're quite a personality here, Dad,' I said as we finally settled at our table. 'I had no idea you were so popular.'

He smiled happily. 'Well, son, you don't work in a town for forty-five years without making friends.'

'I guess that's right.'

The maître d' came over and shook hands. He was a tired, fat looking little man and his tuxedo was shiny and worn, but he treated my old man as if he were the President and I dug for that.

'What would you like, Dad?' I asked. 'No ... not steak!'

He laughed. He looked really happy. His reception had done him a load of good.

'Well. . . .'

'Let's have oysters and the game pie.'

His eyes lit up. 'Well ... the oysters come high, Jack.'

We had the oysters with champagne and the game pie with a decent claret. After the food I had eaten in Paradise City, this was pretty poor fare, but my old man really enjoyed it.

After the meal, a couple of old guys, fat, faded and pompous, came over and joined us. One of them was the Mayor, the other the Commissioner of Parks. My old man had a real ball. I went along, thinking of tomorrow.

When we got home, my old man said, 'Well, Jack, that was the nicest evening I've had since Mum passed away. We two could have a good time together if you took over Johnson's garage.'

'Not yet, dad,' I said, 'but maybe some time,' and I felt like a heel.

I picked up Bernie's Buick at the Paradise City airport and drove along the highway.

I thought of my old man, working at his small time bank, aged sixty-nine, and how he would react when he learned that I had died in an air crash. I thought too of the fact that I was now on Essex's payroll at thirty thousand dollars a year and could earn more. Maybe I was nuts to go ahead with this hijacking. Why couldn't I accept the job Essex had given me and not take the risk of stealing this kite? Then I thought of what a million and a quarter dollars meant. I could never hope to make a sum like that even if I remained in the Essex set-up until I was retired. One thing I was sure of: once I got paid my cut, I would leave Bernie. I had no faith in the Blue Ribbon Air Taxi Service Corp. I would take my money and go to Europe. Just where I would settle I had no idea, but I would settle somewhere and with all that money, well invested, I could lead a life that had to have interests.

I reached the secluded cabin around midday. I wondered if Mrs Essex was waiting for me. Mrs Essex? I found it hard to think of her as Victoria . . . even Vicky. There was something about her that didn't encourage familiarity even though I had slapped her behind and had screwed her. She was a very special woman.

I pulled up outside the cabin. As I got out of the car, the cabin door opened and the negro groom came out, smiling.

The sight of him really shook me. I stared at him as he came towards me. He was lean, tall with a flat nose, sparkling black eyes and he had on a white coat, green slacks and his splayed feet were in green sandals.

'Hello there, Mr Crane,' he said.

'Hi!'

What the hell is this? I was thinking.

'Mrs Essex won't be here until after lunch, Mr Crane.'

'Oh . . . well . . .' I was floundering.

'I'll get your bag.' He paused and smiled at me. 'I'm Sam Washington Jones. You call me Sam: okay?'

'Sure.'

He opened the trunk and took out my bag.

'I'll show you to your room, Mr Crane.'

He led the way into the cabin, paused at the door, nodded at it, said, 'That's Mrs Essex's bedroom.' He moved along the passage and opened a door. 'This is your room, Mr Crane.'

'Thanks.'

'May I unpack your bag, Mr Crane?'

'I can do it.'

91

He put my bag by the bed.

'Lunch in half an hour. May I get you a drink, Mr Crane?'

'A whisky on the rocks, please.'

I stood for a minute or so. Then I told myself she would have to have someone to take care of her. A woman like her wouldn't be able to cook, look after the cabin, make the beds. I wondered how she had corrupted this nice looking negro.

I unpacked, put my things in the closet, washed up in the bathroom and then went into the lounge. A double whisky on the rocks stood on an occasional table. I sat down, drank, lit a cigarette and waited.

Sam came in after twenty minutes.

'You ready to eat, Mr Crane?'

'I'm always ready to eat.'

He grinned and went away, A few minutes later, he came in wheeling a trolley. As a starter I had ten king-sized prawns. The main dish was kebab served with a curry sauce. There was coffee and brandy to finish.

'You're some cook, Sam,' I said.

'Yes, Mr Crane. Missy likes good food.'

I sat there, smoking and relaxing, then around 15.00 I heard the sound of an approaching car. I got up and went out into the open.

Mrs Essex came belting up the drive in a Porsche and she waved to me as she nailed the car a few feet from me.

'Hi! Jack!' She got out of the car.

God! She looked marvellous. She was wearing a jazzy shirt, like a Picasso painting, and white slacks that looked painted on her.

'You look terrific,' I said.

She gave me an up from under look and smiled.

'You think so?'

She came to me and linked her arm around mine.

'Did Sam take care of you?'

'Sure. He's a marvellous cook.'

We walked into the cabin and she moved away from me and dropped into a lounging chair.

'Surprised?' She smiled up at me.

'You can say that again!'

'Pleased?'

'That's to put it mildly.'

She laughed. God! She was a gorgeous looking woman!

'Right now I am spending five days with my sister in New York,' she told me. 'She has the same problem as I have so we co-operate. I lie for her and she lies for me.' Again she laughed. 'Lane is far too busy to take care of me.' She looked up at me, her eyes sparkling. 'You will, won't you?'

I held out my hand. 'Why wait?' I said.

The next five days slipped away, following a pattern. We slept together, made love, got up around 10.00, had breakfast served by Sam, then rode in the forest. She was marvellous on a horse. I kept looking at her as she rode. Then we came back to the cabin and Sam served us a meal. We went to bed after the meal and she was always wildly excited when I covered her. Then we took a long walk with the sun shining on us, through the forest, holding hands. She didn't talk much. She just seemed to want me by her, holding her hand and wandering. Then when the sun set we returned to the cabin and closed the shutters. We had drinks and watched telly, then Sam brought in a light supper, but Sam's light suppers were extra special: a lobster soufflé, trout with almonds, an egg salad with smoked salmon and so on. Neither of us attempted to talk as ordinary people will talk. This was a sexual thing. She wanted me as if I were a stallion: personal feelings didn't exist. The surroundings were wonderful. Sam's food was wonderful and she was wonderful.

On our last night, when I knew Bernie, the following day, would fly in the new kite, we had a special dinner. We started with quails, then a pheasant with all the trimmings, washed down with a Latour 1959.

'I now go back to Lane,' she said as we sniffed brandies. She smiled at me. 'Was it good?'

'For me . . . marvellous: the best. And you?'

'Mmmm!'

She got up and I watched her walk around the big lounge, watching the slow sensual move of her firm buttocks and the way she lifted her breasts.

'You're a better lover than Lane.'

'Is that right?' I stared at her. 'Only because I have time to make love to you and he hasn't.'

93

'A woman needs love. When she is unfortunate enough to get hooked up with a man who can only think of making money . . .' She shrugged. 'Money and business: a woman needs taking care of.'

Sam came in to offer more coffee.

As he poured, he said, 'Should I pack your bag, Mrs Essex?'

'Please.'

So this was the end of an experience. This woman who had given herself so freely to me seemed to me like my old man. She and he from tomorrow wouldn't exist for me. By tomorrow I would be in the Condor and I would be dead to the world. I would never see my old man again, but this I had come to accept. He had had his life, but it hurt that I would no longer see this woman again as she sat by my side, those marvellous violet eyes dwelling on my face.

When Sam had gone, she said, 'I have had a lot of men, Jack. A woman needs a man and Lane—I've said this before—is too busy to bother with me and also too tired. You wouldn't know how frustrating it is for someone like me to wait around for her man to return and then to find he's too tired. Men only think of themselves. He imagines I can just sit around and wait for him to get in the mood.' She patted my hand. 'This is our last safe night together, Jack, but if we are careful, there could be other nights.' She got to her feet. 'Let's go to bed.'

The following morning I watched her take off in the Porsche. She waved once, then was gone.

Sam came out into the sunshine.

'Your bag's packed, Mr Crane.'

I offered him a twenty-dollar bill.

'Not for me,' he said, smiling. 'This has been my pleasure.'

So I left him and drove back to the airfield.

Around 15.00, the new Condor settled on the runway. I drove out in a jeep and arrived as Bernie and Erskine came down on to the tarmac. 'Some kite,' I said as I joined them.

'You don't know the half of it. It's a real beauty,' Bernie said.

'No problems?'

'Not a thing: she flies like a bird.'

We looked at each other.

'When is the night test to be?'

'I thought Saturday.'

That gave us three clear days.

'You're sure there are no problems?'

'Not a thing,' Erskine joined in. 'She's marvellous.'

'Take a look, Jack,' Bernie said. 'I've got paper work to do and then I've got to phone Mr Essex. Harry will show you around.'

He got in one of the waiting jeeps and drove off.

Harry and I climbed into the kite. It had everything a top executive could wish for. There were six cabins, beautifully fitted out as sleeping quarters. Essex's private suite was really something in luxury. There was a narrow long conference room that could sit ten people; a small secretary's office equipped down to an I.B.M. Executive, a bar; a small beautifully equipped kitchen and at the far end were two less well equipped cabins for the staff.

'It seems to have everything but a swimming pool,' I said after the tour. 'A shame, isn't it, that this greaser will tear out all the luxury and fill the kite with Cubans and arms.'

Harry shrugged. 'That's the way the cookie crumbles. I couldn't care less as long as I get money.'

'So Saturday night?'

He nodded.

'How do you feel about it, Harry? About being dead? About never coming back to the U.S. of A.'

'Yeah: it's a tough decision, but there's no way else I could make this kind of money.'

'Are you going in with Bernie and his taxi service?'

He shook his head. 'Not me. I've no faith in it. I'll take my cut and blow. How's about you?'

'The same. Any ideas where you'll go?'

'Rio. I've connections there. And you?'

'Maybe Europe. The first thing is to get the money.'

'Think there'll be trouble about that?'

'Not the way I've fixed it.' I went on to tell him about setting up the company, about my talk with Kendrick. 'It should be okay.'

We got in the jeep and headed for the control tower. While we were drinking beer, Bernie joined us. He said he had talked to Mr Essex in Paris and told him he would night test the plane on Saturday night.

'I'd better go see Kendrick,' I said. 'If the operation is for Saturday night, I want that bank receipt. And Bernie, get the guns on board and ammo. We each have a machine pistol. What else can you dig up?'

Bernie looked at Harry. 'You know the armoury.'

'We've got three Jap Armalites: that's really a weapon and there are around four Chicago Pianos.'

'Let's have one of each. How about grenades?'

'Can do.'

'Say six.'

They both stared at me.

'Are you really expecting trouble, Jack?' Bernie asked, sweat showing on his forehead.

'I want to be sure we can stop trouble.'

'Well . . .'

'Get those weapons on board.' I got to my feet. 'I'll go talk to Kendrick. Suppose we have dinner together and tie this all up?'

'Sure,' Bernie said. 'We meet at my cabin. I'll order a meal.'

'Around 20.30?'

'Okay.'

I took Bernie's Buick and drove into Paradise City. Three hours later, I knocked on Bernie's cabin door and he opened up. Harry was drinking Scotch and he got up to make me a drink.

'How did you get on?' Bernie asked. He looked worried and there were smudges under his eyes.

I sat down, took the drink Harry offered me.

'Friday we get the bank receipt. I told that fat queer the kite doesn't move until I get it.' I grinned at Bernie. 'Relax. It's okay. This is going to work.'

But how was I to know the one thing none of us even thought of would occur? It looked fine to me. I had taken a lot of trouble to make it look fine, but there is always something, repeat something, that none of us could have imagined.

CHAPTER SEVEN

ON FRIDAY AFTERNOON I collected the bank receipt from Kendrick. I told him the kite would be delivered in the early hours on Sunday morning and there were no problems. I then sent a cable to Aulestria, giving him the same information.

Then I returned to the airfield and put a call through to the National Bank of Mexico. I asked the executive with whom I had dealt if the money had arrived. He said it had and had been credited to the Blue Ribbon Air Taxi Service Corp. I could almost hear him bowing as he spoke. I relayed the news to Bernie and Harry.

'Now it's up to you two to deliver the kite,' I said. 'I've done my stint.'

All Friday afternoon, from 15.30 to 19.00, we three worked on the kite. I familiarized myself with the jets while Bernie and Harry worked in the flight cabin. No problems came up. Saturday morning was spent in the control tower while Bernie and Harry logged our flight schedule. My crew looked a little blank when I told them I wanted full fuel capacity. They filled the tanks while I watched.

The hijack take-off was scheduled for 20.30. By that time it would be dark. In the afternoon we took the plane on a test flight around Miami and back. She behaved beautifully.

Harry had got the guns on board and I took charge of them. I concealed one of the Armalite AR 180 high velocity rifles in Essex's bedroom. I put it under the mattress. This rifle fired a .223 dum-dum bullet that would kill instantly. The second Armalite I concealed in one of the staff cabins. The Thompson sub-machine gun, known as a Chicago Piano, I hid in the flight cabin. The six hand grenades I hid in a locker by the entrance door to the kite. The machine pistols we decided we would carry on our hips. I took Bernie and Harry around, showing them where I had concealed the weapons.

'We may not need them,' I said, 'but if there's trouble, you know where to find them.'

I could see Bernie didn't like any of this and he looked pale, worried and he sweated. Harry just nodded.

Well, that seemed to be that. We had three hours to wait before we took off. I said I was going to pack my things, left them and returned to my cabin. I gave myself a drink, lit a cigarette, then after hesitating, I put a call through to my old man. This, I knew, was the last time I would speak to him. I realized as I was waiting for the connection that I would miss him and again I had doubts that I was planning the right thing for my future.

He came on the line after a delay.

97

'I was cutting the grass, Jack. I only just heard the bell.'
I asked him how he was.
'I'm all right. And you?'
'I'm fine.' I told him we were night testing the Condor.
'Is that dangerous?'
I forced a laugh.
'Nothing to it, Dad, just routine. I have a few minutes to kill
and I got thinking of you: I enjoyed my stay.' I wanted to say
something nice to him to remember me by. 'That was a great
evening we had together. We'll repeat it.'
'You're sure this night flight is going to be all right?'
'Sure, Dad.' I paused, then plunged on, 'I've got to go now. I
just wanted to hear your voice again. Take care of yourself.'
'There's nothing wrong?'
'Everything's fine. Well, see you, Dad,' and I hung up.
I sat staring at the opposite wall. I felt it had been a mistake
to call him. Now I knew he would worry. He was shrewd. I hadn't
ever called him long distance before. Well, at least I had heard
his voice for the last time.
I gave myself another drink, then my mind switched to Mrs
Essex. I had a longing to hear her voice too for the last time, but
I hesitated. This could be a dangerous call. I decided against it,
but after wandering around my cabin and having another drink,
I walked over to the telephone and dialled the number of the
Essex home. I told myself if the butler answered, I would hang
up, but she answered.
'Hi!' I said.
'Oh . . . you.'
'Yes. Can you talk?'
'He's not back until Tuesday: yes, I can talk.'
That marvellous voice! I saw that body and those violet
coloured eyes. 'I've missed you,' I said.
'Let's do something tonight, Jack.' Her voice was urgent. 'Jack-
son is taking his wife to a show. He'll be out of the way. Let's
meet somewhere.'
'I can't. We're doing a night test flight on the Condor at 20.30.
I've got to go along.'
'Oh, hell! I want you, Jack!'
'How about Sunday night?' I was now wishing I hadn't started
this and knowing on Sunday night I would be in Yucatan.

'Can't you get out of this test flight?'

'Not a chance.' I now really wished I hadn't started this. I knew how determined she could be. 'Let's make it Sunday, huh?'

'No! Jackson will be around. He'll be around Monday too. It *must* be tonight!'

'It can't be done. I'm sorry. I'll call you later,' and I hung up.

That was a mistake, I told myself. Why couldn't I keep my stupid mouth shut? I looked at the time. It was just after 19.00. As I flung my things into a suitcase, the phone bell rang. Fearing it was Mrs Essex, I ignored it. I went to the restaurant and joined Bernie and Harry for a steak dinner. Bernie looked uneasy. He scarcely ate a thing.

'Did you talk to Pam?' I asked.

'She's now on her way to Merida.'

'She okay?'

He blotted his sweating face with his handkerchief.

'I think so. She doesn't like it, of course, but she'll be all right once we join up.'

'Yeah.' To change the subject, I said, 'How do you feel about landing the kite in the dark and the jungle?'

'The Met report is good. I don't see any problem.'

I shoved my plate away and looked at my watch. The time was 20.15. 'Might as well get moving.' I stood up.

Harry said, 'Just for the hell of it, I stocked the refrig. We could get hungry.'

'That's a smart idea.'

'I don't believe in starving.' Harry grinned. 'If we get lost, a refrig. full of food is a great morale booster.'

'We won't get lost!' Bernie snapped. 'Don't talk wet!'

Harry winked at me and we followed Bernie out into the starlit night and climbed into a jeep. The three of us knew this was the last time we would be on American soil. It was a sobering thought and none of us spoke as Harry drove us to the waiting Condor.

The crew were waiting. The Chief Engineer, a guy named Thompson, gave me a thumb's up sign as we got out of the jeep.

'All correct, Mr Crane,' he said and grinned. There was something sly about that grin that made me stare at him, but when Bernie said, 'Let's go,' I thought no more about it.

Bernie and Harry went to the flight cabin. I closed the exit door and then joined them.

Bernie went through the take-off routine, then talked to Air Control.

'Okay, Fred?'

'Sure: no traffic around, Bernie. It's all yours.'

A few minutes later we were airborne. We looked at one another.

'Three million dollars, here we come!' Harry exclaimed.

I stood around until Bernie headed out to sea. I was feeling restless. I left them and wandered into the conference room, looked around, then went into the kitchen. I peered into the refrigerator. There was a good selection of canned foods. I went past Essex's suite and entered one of the guest cabins where I had left my suitcase. There was nothing for me to do for at least forty minutes. I lay on the bed, lit a cigarette and tried not to think of my future, but I didn't succeed. I kept thinking I was walking out on a top class job, paying thirty thousand a year and I was also walking out on Mrs Essex. A million and a half dollars! What the hell would I do with all that money? I asked myself. I would have to begin an entirely new life. It was all right to imagine living in Europe, but I couldn't speak any language except my own. I was cutting myself off from a way of life I had known. Was money everything? So why had I started this? This was pretty late thinking, I told myself. I was committed now. In forty minutes I would be dead to my old man, to Mrs Essex and to the various people who knew me. I had got beyond the point of no return.

I looked out of the cabin window and watched the lights of Paradise City, then Miami fading in the distance. I watched until a sea mist blotted them out and I realized I was seeing them for the last time.

Worried by my thoughts, I went back to the flight cabin.

Looking at the altimeter over Bernie's shoulder, I saw he was climbing.

'Another ten minutes,' Harry said.

When Bernie got to twenty-five thousand feet, he levelled out.

'Harry, you talk to Fred,' he said, his voice husky. 'I've got the shakes.'

Harry and I looked at each other. He raised his eyebrows.

'No, you haven't, Bernie,' I said, putting my hands on his shoulders. 'You dreamed this one up. You handle it.'

He shook off my hands and wiped his sweating face.

'Look, guys, should we do this?' he said. 'We have still time to turn around. Should we do it?'

'What the hell are you talking about?' Harry barked.

Bernie lifted his shoulders in a helpless shrug.

'Yes.' He turned his white face so he could look at me. 'Will it work out, Jack?'

I was suddenly tempted to tell him to turn around, but while I was hesitating, Harry grabbed the mike.

'Fred!' His voice was high-pitched. 'We're in trouble. The two port engines are on fire. The goddamn extinguishers aren't working!' I could hear Air Control shouting. Harry cut in on him. 'We're ditching. Our position . . .' Then he snapped off the radio. 'Put her down, Bernie.'

Like a zombie, Bernie shoved the nose down and we screamed into a dive towards the sea. Harry put down the mike.

'Here we go,' he said. 'How did it sound?'

'It almost convinced me.' I was feeling shaken. My hesitation had settled my future.

'I bet Fred is laying eggs.'

I was watching Bernie. He began to level out. We were some eight hundred feet above the sea now. He took the kite lower. Then, when we were three hundred feet and when I could see the waves, he headed for Yucatan.

'This calls for a drink.'

'Yes: get me a coke, Jack,' Bernie said huskily.

'Me too,' Harry said.

I left them and went into the kitchen, opened the refrigerator and took from it three bottles of coke. As I began to break out ice, a voice said softly, 'Hi! Jack!'

I dropped the ice container into the sink.

I would know that voice anywhere. I felt blood drain out of my face as I turned.

Smiling at me, in the doorway of the kitchen, was Mrs Victoria Essex.

I was vaguely aware that the floor was vibrating and that told me Bernie was flying at maximum.

Cold sweat broke out all over my body. My heart skipped a beat and then began to race.

'Surprised?' Mrs Essex laughed. 'You said it couldn't be done.' She laughed again. 'That's fighting talk to me; nothing is impossible . . . so here I am. How long is the test flight going to last?'

I tried to speak, but my mouth had dried up and my racing heart made me breathless.

I just gaped at her.

'Jack! What's the matter? Aren't you pleased?'

'What are you doing here?' My voice was a croak.

Her beautiful eyebrows came down in a frown.

'Doing here? This is my plane! What do you mean?'

'How did you get on board?'

'What's that to do with it? I told the Chief Engineer I intended to fly with you.'

I remembered Thompson's sly smile.

'This is a test flight.' I was now over the shock and was forcing my brain to work. 'Mr Essex would blow his stack if he knew you were on board. This could be dangerous.'

'I don't give a damn! Lane need never know.' She moved into the kitchen. 'Aren't you pleased?'

'But Thompson will rat on you!'

'Oh, skip it! He's as scared of me as Jackson. I asked you: how long will the test flight last?'

'Three hours . . . I don't know.'

'Let's christen Lane's bed. I want you.'

I wanted her right now like I wanted cancer.

'They're waiting for drinks.'

'Give them their drinks; I'll wait in the suite.' She reached out and touched my face. 'This is going to be a new experience for both of us.'

Her touch was like the kiss of death to me.

I watched her walk along the aisle and disappear into the Essex's suite. My mind worked frantically. Questions without answers crowded into my mind.

Should I tell Bernie and Harry she was with us? Should we turn back? How the hell could we when Harry had told Air Control we were ditching? We were beyond the point of return! So what did we do? I tried to imagine the reception Mrs Victoria Essex would get if those Mexican thugs caught sight of her and I flinched at the thought. I had managed to persuade Bernie to leave Pam out of the trip and she was a long way behind Mrs Essex in looks. I had a feeling that neither Bernie nor Harry would give a damn about her: both had reasons to hate her. But she had that fatal thing for me, and I knew I wouldn't stand by and see her raped by a bunch of greasers.

I decided I had to tell her what she had walked into before breaking the news to Bernie and Harry.

I took the cokes to the flight cabin.

'You've taken your time,' Harry said, grabbing the drink. 'I'm dying of thirst.'

'Sorry: the ice container was tricky.'

He grinned at me. 'We have luck, not a ship in sight.'

'No problems, Bernie?' My heart was thumping.

He finished the coke and handed me the empty glass.

'So far . . . okay.'

Harry was wearing headphones: one clamped to his right ear, the other against the side of his neck.

'Fred has called out the navy.'

'Will we get there, Bernie?' I asked.

'Sure. At this height the radar can't spot us.'

'Okay. I'll leave it to you two. I'll take a nap.'

'Going to try out the Essex bed?' Harry laughed. 'I guess that holy of holies couldn't come alive without a woman.'

I rubbed the sweat off my chin.

'See you,' I said and left them.

I walked down the aisle, then went into the Essex suite. She was lying on the big circular bed. I could see she was naked under the sheet she had drawn across her.

'Come on, Jack,' she said. 'We haven't much time,' and she held out her arms to me. 'Are the others busy?'

I closed the door and shot the bolt.

'You're in trouble,' I said. 'I'm in trouble, too.'

She stared at me. 'What does that mean?'

'Right now, this plane is being hi-jacked.'

The sexy light went out of her eyes. Now her mouth turned thin and her face became a hard mask. Mrs Victoria Essex wasn't Mrs Victoria Essex for nothing. Her brain worked fast as quicksilver.

'Are Olson and Erskine stealing this plane?'

'That's it.'

'Are you in this, too?'

'Yes.'

I had to admire her. She looked as unruffled as a bishop at a tea party.

'Where are we going?'

'Yucatan. We arrive in two and a half hours . . . with luck.'

She threw aside the sheet and slid off the bed. I watched her as she walked, naked, to where she had left her clothes. I watched her dress quickly and without fuss.

She then walked to the mirror and ran a comb through her hair. Satisfied she looked like the always glamorous Mrs Victoria Essex, she turned slowly and regarded me.

'We have time. I'll talk to Olson. Was this his bright little idea?'

'Yes.'

'Then I'll tell him to turn around and go back.'

She started towards the door, but I didn't move and she confronted me.

'Get out of my way, Jack!'

'Three million dollars are involved,' I said quietly. 'Not even you can talk Olson nor Erskine out of that.'

'Get out of my way!' Her eyes flashed. 'I'll talk to him!'

'Get wise! Olson has no use for you. Erskine hates you. If you go to the flight cabin and sound off, Erskine will knock you over the head and drop you into the sea. I'm telling you: you're in trouble.'

She stared at me for a long moment.

'Am I in trouble with you too, Jack?'

'I'll do my best for you. Why the hell did you have to come on board?'

'What does your best mean?'

'I'll do what I can to protect you.'

'That's kind of you.' She turned away and wandered over to the big, circular bed. 'I think I prefer to protect myself.'

Before I could move, she had drawn the Armalite rifle from under the mattress where I had hidden it and pointed it at me.

'Don't move!' The snap in her voice made me stiffen. 'No one is hi-jacking me! Don't imagine I can't handle this gun. Go ahead, Jack, we're going to the flight cabin.'

'This won't get you anywhere,' I said. 'I'm on your side, but we've got beyond the point of no return.'

'No, we haven't! Go ahead!'

I wondered how Bernie and Harry would react when I came into the flight cabin with her and the gun. I drew the bolt and stepped out into the aisle. I had an idea she wouldn't shoot me if I turned on her and I suddenly didn't give a damn. I opted to be neutral. If she could force Bernie to turn the plane around, I'd go along. If Bernie and Harry were smart enough to outplay her, I'd also go along. The ball was in her court.

Because I was half in love with her and because I really didn't know what I was going to do with a million and a quarter dollars, I went like a zombie into the flight cabin.

Harry turned his head as I entered.

'Short nap, Jack,' he said. 'Your conscience worrying you?'

I moved aside and Mrs Essex stood in the doorway, pointing the gun at him and Bernie. Harry stared, his jaw dropping, then he made a move to get to his feet.

'Stay still!' she snapped.

Harry relaxed back in his seat.

'For God's sake, Bernie! Look who's here!'

Bernie glanced over his shoulder, stared at her, stared at the gun and his face turned the colour of a dead, stale fish.

'You're not hi-jacking this plane!' she said. 'Turn around! We're going back to the airfield!'

Harry grinned at her.

'No, we're not. And there's nothing you can do about it, baby. That gun means nothing. You start shooting and we'll all dive into the sea.'

'I said turn around!'

Harry shrugged. 'Run away, hot pants, you bore me.' He shifted in his seat so his back was to her.

'Olson! Do you hear me!' She was a tryer. 'Turn this plane around and fly back to the airfield.'

Bernie said nothing. He stared at the instrument panels as if he hadn't heard her.

She looked at me, her eyes blazing.

'Make him turn around, Jack!'

'Yeah . . . go ahead, Jack, make us turn around,' Harry said and laughed. Then glaring at her, he snarled, 'Get out of here, you spoiled, over-rich hooker! Get out!'

She hesitated for a moment, then ran down the aisle and into Essex's suite. She slammed the door.

'Well!' Harry stared at me. 'How did she get on board?'

'Thompson let her on.'

'What are we going to do?' Bernie's voice sounded strangled.

'Let the dagoes cope with her,' Harry said. 'Why should we care?'

'No!' I said.

His eyes hardened. 'Oh, yeah? You getting it from her, Jack?'

'We can't let her fall into those thugs' hands.'

'So what? Why should we care ... or do you?'

'Yes, I care,' I said. 'Listen, Bernie, it's one thing to hi-jack this plane but another to kidnap Mrs Lane Essex! The heat will be ...'

'Oh, skip it!' Harry snapped. 'We're all dead and in the sea ... remember? Thompson will have reported she was on board. So Essex will think she went into the drink with us. There'll be no heat.'

'He's right,' Bernie said. 'We didn't ask her to come. Now she's here, she'll have to look after herself.'

'Go and hold her hand, Jack,' Harry sneered. 'We're busy.'

I left the flight cabin and going down the aisle, reached the suite. I knocked on the door.

'It's me: Jack.'

'Stay away! No one's coming in here! No one!'

'I've got to talk to you.'

'No one's coming in here! I'll shoot first!'

'You haven't a chance. Come on, be sensible. Let me in!'

The vicious crack of the gun startled me. The .233 bullet smashed through the top of the door. It missed my head by six inches: too damn close for safety. I hurriedly stepped back.

'Next time I shoot lower!'

'Okay, then you're out on your own.'

'And I'll manage!'

I went back to the flight cabin and told them. Harry laughed. 'So why should we care? We deliver the kite. It's up to the greasers to winkle her out: they'll love it.'

'Talk sense! No one's going to get near her with that gun!'

'All they have to do is to wait her out. It'll be goddamn hot when we arrive and the air conditioners will be off. Without food and drink, how long to you imagine she'll last?'

That was something I hadn't thought of.

*　　　*　　　*

We had been flying now for fifty minutes, crossing the Gulf of Mexico, still at three hundred above the sea.

I sat on a stool behind Bernie while Harry listened to the radio, headphones clamped to his ears.

I thought of the woman, alone in the Essex suite. I wondered what she was doing. She certainly had guts! What would happen to her when we landed? Was it possible to conceal her, then get her away? I knew I would get no help from Bernie nor Harry. That was for sure. We would land in the jungle surrounded by Orzoco's thugs. How could I get her away?

Harry said suddenly, 'It's on the air. The world now knows that the fabulous, glamorous Mrs Victoria Essex was on board and she, like the intrepid birdmen, crashed into the sea. It'll be front page news tomorrow. How do you like it, Bernie?'

Bernie didn't say anything. He had been flying the plane now in complete silence. I could see sweat running down the back of his neck and his greying hair looked as if it had been ducked in a bucket of water.

'I bet those greasers are smacking their chops,' Harry went on. 'Man! Will I get a bang to see them lay their paws on that bitch. She has it coming!'

'Shut up!' I said.

He looked at me, an ugly expression on his face.

'You've gone soft on her, haven't you, sucker?'

'I said shut up!' I got up and left the cabin.

'Hi! Jack!'

I turned.

Harry came out into the aisle and closed the cabin door. He joined me. His eyes were vicious.

'Let's get this straight,' he said, a snarl in his voice. 'We don't want any trouble now we've got so far. We're all in this for three million dollars. Just what is this bitch to you?'

'I'm not standing by and seeing her raped by a bunch of greasers,' I said quietly. 'We've got to get her out of this mess.'

He shook his head.

'No! To hell with her! She once played me for a sucker and that's something I don't forget. She's no better than a hooker. You start something and you won't find me on your side. Understand?'

'Is that right?' I was getting mad myself now. 'So what are you going to do?'

107

He glared at me.

'No one—including you—stands between me and my cut.' Then he did something I could never take. He began digging his forefinger into my chest to emphasize his words. 'I don't give a damn if you're horny about this hooker . . .'

I hit him solidly on the side of his jaw. It was a reflex action and the moment I had done it, I regretted it. He went down like a felled ox and his head thudded against a row of metal studs, lining the floor.

I stared down at him, then knelt and lifted his head. My hand became sticky with blood. A cold chill ran through me. Had I killed him?

'Harry!'

I could see he was breathing, but he looked bad. I laid his head down gently and stood up.

'Thieves fall out?'

She was standing in the doorway of the Essex suite, the Armalite in her hands.

I stared at her.

'Olson won't get the kite down without him,' I said breathlessly. 'There's something wrong with Olson! Do something! Get this man on his feet!'

'I wouldn't touch that sonofabitch if it cost me my life!' she said, her face like stone.

'It could do, you fool!'

I ran back to the flight cabin. Looking through the plexiglass I saw sandy beach and then jungle ahead.

'Bernie! Harry's had an accident! He's knocked out!'

He didn't say anything. He just sat there, his shirt and head soaked in sweat.

'Bernie!' I bawled at him. 'Hear me?'

'Don't touch me.' His voice was a husky croak.

'Make altitude! We're too low!'

We were now only two hundred feet above the dense jungle. He gave a shuddering sigh that chilled me as he pulled back the stick. The kite's nose lifted. We were now flying fast over the jungle.

'Higher! Get her up!'

'For God's sake, Jack, leave me alone!'

There was something about him that scared the hell out of me. His stiff, set position, the sweat and now his voice.

I ran back into the aisle and shook Harry, but he was out to the world. Rushing into the kitchen, I drew water into a bowl, rushed back and threw the water in his face: this produced no reaction.

She still stood in the doorway, watching.

'Do something!' I yelled at her. 'Olson can't make the landing! Get this man on his feet!'

She turned, entered the suite and slammed the door. I heard the bolt snap to.

For a moment I stared down at Harry, then I rushed back to the flight cabin.

I saw we had lost altitude again and now we were flying less than a hundred feet above the dense jungle.

'Bernie! Pull her up!' I shouted.

He made a feeble effort to pull back the stick, then a moan of a man in agony escaped him.

'Bernie! What's wrong? Are you ill?' I slid into the co-pilot's seat. 'Bernie!'

'My heart . . . I'm dying . . .' Then he fell forward. His body shoved the stick forward and the nose went down.

As I heard the undercarriage smashing through the tree tops. I flicked up the various switches, cutting the engines. In the split second that remained to me I saw Bernie's eyes roll back and I knew he was dead.

The crash flung me across the cabin.

Blackness came to me and I gave myself up as lost.

CHAPTER EIGHT

I SWAM OUT of a deep, black pit, feeling I was drowning, aware of water pouring on my face. The water was warm and as I returned to consciousness, I realized it was rain.

'Come on! Come on!' That voice I would know anywhere was shouting at me. 'You're not hurt!'

I opened my eyes and saw the light of dawn coming through the tree tops, then I dragged my body to a sitting position. I became aware that my head hurt and there was a nagging pain in my shoulder.

'Jack!!'

'Okay, okay! For God's sake, give me a minute!'

I wiped my face with my hand and blinked, then I saw her, standing over me. She looked like a drowned cat, her shirt and slacks plastered to her body, her hair like rat's tails: no longer the glamorous, fabulous Mrs Victoria Essex.

I looked around. I was sitting in squelchy mud: broken trees lay around me. Rain beat down and the humid, stifling heat was as if I were packed in steaming cotton wool.

'Get up!'

I looked up at her. 'Are you all right?'

'Yes: and so are you! Where are we? What happened?'

Shakily I got to my feet and leaned against a tree for support.

'Olson had a heart attack.' I turned and looked at the smash. I saw how lucky we had been. There were no big, solid trees. The plane had sheered through the jungle like a scythe. The wings with their jets had come off, but the fuselage looked intact. The tail unit was gone.

'Some smash,' I said. 'How did I get out?'

'I pulled you out.'

I stared at her. 'You're some woman, aren't you?'

'I thought it might catch fire.'

Then I remembered Harry. 'How about Erskine?'

'I don't know.' Her voice told me she didn't care. 'What are we going to do?'

I tried to think, but my mind was still groggy.

'I must find Harry.'

'To hell with him! We've got to find shelter!'

Leaving her, I walked unsteadily over to the wreck. I peered into the flight cabin that had torn away from the fuselage. I could see Bernie still sitting at the controls, his head on his chest. I hoisted myself into the cabin, opened a locker and took out a powerful electric torch. I played the beam on his dead face, then with a grimace I climbed down and into the fuselage.

Harry lay where I had left him. A pool of blood made a gruesome halo around his head. His jaw had dropped and his eyes were sightless.

I felt a chill of horror crawl up my spine. Had I killed him or had the crash killed him? He had been breathing when I had left him! I stood staring down at him.

'You killed him, didn't you?'

She had climbed up to join me.

'I don't know. If I did, it was because of you.'

We stared at each other, then she pushed by me and tried to get into the Essex suite, but the door was jammed.

'Open it! I want to change out of these wet clothes!'

'Don't waste time. We've got to get out of here pronto. You'll be wet anyway.'

She glared at me. 'I intend to stay here until I'm found!'

'We sold this kite to a Mexican revolutionary for three million dollars. If he gets his hands on you, he'll be happy with the exchange. He will ransom you for twice that sum.'

Her violet eyes opened wide.

'So what are we going to do?'

'We can't be more than fifteen miles from the coast. Once there, we'll telephone your husband and he'll have us picked up. It's going to be a long, tough haul, but that's the way it's got to be. Wait here.' I struggled up the inclining fuselage to the guest cabin where I had left my suitcase. I emptied the contents on the bed, retaining only three packs of cigarettes, then I went into the kitchen. I packed some canned foods in the suitcase and included three bottles of tonic water and three cokes, a bottle opener and a can opener.

'Come on,' I said to her and helped her down into the mud and the rain. I handed down the suitcase, then clambered into the flight cabin. I unclipped the Thompson machine gun, then searched in one of the lockers and found a pocket compass.

Flies were already settling around Bernie. I felt bad leaving him, but we had to go.

As I joined her, she said, 'I'm hating this rain.'

'That makes two of us.' I swung the gun by its strap over my shoulder, picked up the suitcase and started off into the jungle.

The next two hours were sheer hell: a lot worse for her than for me. At least I had had plenty of experience in the Viet jungles of this kind of thing and knew what to expect. Although I had been a service mechanic I had had to go through a jungle course.

The rain was ceaseless, pounding down through the trees, giving us no respite. I kept checking the compass. I knew the coast was somewhere north-east, but there were times when the jungle was so thick we had to make a detour. Without the compass, we would have been hopelessly lost.

111

She kept up with me, walking just behind me. I paced myself, knowing we had a long way to go. Finally, we came on a clearing in the jungle. Trees had been felled. There were signs of fires, long dead, that had burned unwanted wood. I stopped short at the edge of the clearing.

I looked to right and left and listened. All I could hear was the pattering rain. I turned and looked at her. Her face was drawn and blotched with mosquito bites. I could see the nipples of her breasts through the soaked shirt. I looked at her feet. She had on casuals of white calf and they showed blood stains. She had walked until her feet were beginning to bleed and yet she hadn't uttered a word of complaint.

'Your feet!' I exclaimed.

'Don't pity me.' She forced a grin. 'If you have to pity anyone, pity yourself.'

'How about some food and a drink?'

'Not yet. If I sit down, I won't be able to get up again.'

We looked at each other and I saw she meant it.

'Okay. We'll go on.' I slapped at a mosquito that had settled on my neck and we went on, crossing the clearing and into the jungle again.

I moved cautiously, worrying about the clearing. It told me there was a village nearby, and I knew we were too close to Orzoco's neck of the woods to take any risk.

It was lucky I hadn't forgotten my jungle training. Suddenly, as we walked along the sodden muddy path, I heard a sound that immediately alerted me. I caught hold of Vicky's arm—I was now thinking of her as Vicky and not as the glamorous Mrs Victoria Essex—and swung her off the path and into the undergrowth. She went with me without resisting although we dropped into a pool of muddy water and I gave her full marks for that. We crouched down and waited.

Three Yucatan Indians came down the path, all carrying broad-bladed axes. They moved swiftly and I only caught a glimpse of them before they were gone.

'We're near a village,' I whispered. 'It's too close. We must move east and then head north again.'

We left the path and struggled across swampy ground, through the thick undergrowth and the going was bad, but she kept up. Then suddenly the rain ceased and the humid mist lifted. Like a glittering sword, drawn from its scabbard, the sun came out. The heat turned into a throat-drying sweat-soaking hell.

Mosquitoes tormented us. My arms and face were swollen with bites. I stopped to look at her. What a mess she was in! The only thing I could recognize in her swollen, insect-bitten face were those dauntless violet eyes.

'What are you stopping for?' Her voice was a croak.

'Cut out the iron woman act,' I said. 'We're going to rest.'

She stared at me, then her face crumpled and she dropped on her knees in the mud and putting her filthy hands to her face she began to sob.

I put the suitcase and the gun in a bush, then kneeling, I took her in my arms. She clung to me and I held her the way I would have held a child.

We remained like that for several minutes while the mosquitoes attacked us ceaselessly, then she stopped sobbing and pushed me away.

'I'm all right now.' Her voice was steady. 'Sorry for the dramatics. Let's eat.'

'You've certainly got guts,' I said as I opened the suitcase.

'Think so?' She looked down at the red bumps on her hands. 'If I look anything like you, I must look like hell.'

I grinned at her. 'At least you're human.'

I opened a can of beans and a can of goulash. We ate the mixture with plastic spoons that were taped to the cans.

'Are you going to get me out of this mess, Jack?' she asked abruptly.

'I'm going to try.'

'Aren't you scared of going back?'

'I haven't thought of that. Right now I want to get us out.'

She eyed me. 'You're throwing away three million dollars.'

'A million: we agreed to split it three ways.'

'Doesn't that bother you?'

I shrugged.

'It's an odd thing. At first I was thirsting for all that money, then I got thinking and realized I wouldn't know what to do with it. I remember you saying with all your money you got bored. That's something I wouldn't want.'

'Would you still work for my husband if you got the chance?'

'I won't get the chance.'

113

'Yes, you will. I've been thinking about you. I could tell Lane we crashed into the sea. You and I were the only survivors. We clung to some wreckage and you got me ashore. He would believe that, coming from me, and he'd do a lot for you.'

I stared at her. 'Would you lie like that for me?'

She nodded.

'Yes. You're the first man who has ever treated me as a woman should be treated. You mean something to me.'

I tried to think clearly but my head ached. It seemed the solution: the way out. Instead of spending years in jail for air piracy, I would have a thirty-thousand-dollar-a-year job with Essex Enterprises, plus Vicky.

'I'll get you out of here,' I said. 'I . . .'

We both heard the sound of an approaching helicopter.

'Don't move!' I looked up cautiously.

We were well screened by the tree tops and I was pretty confident we couldn't be spotted.

A few moments later I saw, just above the trees, the chopper pass over. It was painted a drab green and had Mexican roundels. It went as quickly as it had come.

'They're looking for the wreck,' I said and got stiffly to my feet. 'I guess we're about twelve miles from it by now: too close for safety. Once they find you're not on board, they'll start a hunt. Let's go!'

I reached out my hand, grasped her wrist and hauled her to her feet.

She fell against me with a cry of pain.

'God! My feet!' she gasped. 'I don't think I can walk.'

'I'll carry you if I have to, but we've got to move.'

She pushed away from me, took four tottering steps forward, her face white.

'It's all right: I'll manage.'

'Good girl.'

'Don't be so damn patronizing!'

I snatched up the suitcase, slung the gun over my shoulder and started again. I walked slowly, but steadily, giving her a chance and I kept looking back. She limped along, her head down, the mosquitoes swarming around her, but she kept going.

We walked for over an hour, then the jungle ahead began to thin out.

'Rest,' I said. 'Wait here. We could be nearing a road. Looks like we're nearly out of the jungle.'

She dropped on her knees. I put the suitcase beside her.

'I'll be right back.'

She was past speaking. She just knelt there, her head in her hands.

I moved forward rapidly. In three or four minutes I came out of the jungle. I had guessed right: before me was a wide dirt road. As I stood hesitating, I heard the sound of an approaching truck. I stepped back into the shelter of the undergrowth.

A rusty, battered truck, hauling oil drums, went roaring by, driven by a young, thin Mexican. It took the curve in the road and disappeared.

Maybe with luck, I thought, we could get a ride to the coast. My compass told me the track was heading towards the sea: possibly to Progreso.

I went back fast to where I had left Vicky.

The suitcase marked the spot so I knew I hadn't made a mistake, but Vicky was gone.

As I stood there in the steamy heat with a cloud of mosquitoes buzzing around my head, my mind went back to Vietnam. I remembered the big, powerfully-built Top-sergeant who took us on the jungle course.

'Every leaf, every tree branch, every bit of ground tells a story if you know what to look for,' he had said. 'So look for it. Look for signs that men have passed. If you look carefully enough, you'll find the signs.'

I saw Vicky's knee marks in the mud. That was how I had left her: kneeling and half conscious. Then I saw a naked footprint, then another, then two more, big, splayed prints that came to the spot where Vicky had been kneeling, then reversed and went back into the jungle.

I unslung the Thompson and moved fast and silently along the path. In the thick mud the footprints were easy to follow: two men, one of them carrying Vicky. I could tell that by the deeper impression his feet made in the mud. I moved fast. Ten minutes later, I could hear them ahead of me. They were jog-trotting, smashing through the jungle and I increased my speed. I didn't care if they heard me. With the gun I felt capable of dealing with them. I was running now and ahead of me I saw them: two Yucatan Indians. The one ahead was carrying Vicky, slung over his shoulder like a sack. The other ran behind him.

They heard me. The one behind spun around. He held a glittering axe in his hand. His lips came off his teeth in a snarl and he rushed at me.

I gave him a short burst with the Thompson and his naked chest turned into a bloody mess. The other Indian dropped Vicky, turned, his hand groping for a knife as I snap-shotted him through the head.

I went to her, turned her, saw she was unconscious. I got her up across my shoulder, picked up the Thompson and began the long, plodding, hellish tramp back to the dirt road.

As I staggered along, I heard the sound of the helicopter overhead. I paused under the shade of a tree until the chopper had gone, then I went on.

I was panting, my heart thumping by the time I reached the road. Gently I laid her down.

Her eyes opened.

'It's okay,' I said. 'We'll get out of this.'

She stared sightlessly up at me, then her eyes closed.

I sat beside her by the edge of the road, the gun by my hand and I listened and waited.

After more than half an hour, I heard a truck coming. I got up and stood by the roadside. The truck came into sight, driven by a fat Mexican. The truck came roaring along the dirt road, raising a cloud of red dust.

I stepped out on to the road and waved to the driver. He took one look at me and accelerated. If I hadn't jumped aside, he would have run me down.

The truck disappeared in dust and I cursed after it, but I didn't blame the driver. Looking the way I did, he had every reason not to stop.

I went back into the jungle and found a long, broken tree branch. This I dragged across the road, blocking three-quarters of it. The next truck that went by would have to stop.

I returned to where I had left Vicky. She was sitting up, looking dazed.

'Are you all right?' I asked, bending over her.

'What happened? I must have passed out.'

I saw she didn't know she had been in the hands of two Indians. This was no time to tell her.

'I've blocked the road. The next truck will have to stop. We'll get a ride.'

'His face will be something to see when he sees us.' Vicky forced a giggle. 'Help me up.'

'You sit there and take it easy.'

She looked up at me.

'You're quite a man,' she said. 'I wouldn't have survived without you.'

I lifted my hand.

'There's a truck coming now.' I pulled her to her feet. 'Can you stand?'

'Yes.' She pushed me away and hobbled on to the grass verge.

The truck came into sight, travelling fast. The driver spotted the branch across the road and stood on his brakes. The truck came to a tyre-burning halt.

The driver, lean, middle-aged with a tattered sombrero on the back of his head, dressed in dirty whites, climbed down from the cab.

As he began to drag the branch out of the way, I made a move forward, but Vicky stopped me.

'I'll handle him. Don't let him see the gun.'

Before I could stop her, she limped on to the road. The Mexican gaped at her, then she began to talk in fluent Spanish and I realized why she had elected to go instead of me.

He stood, listening, then nodded and finally grinned. She turned and beckoned to me. I hesitated for only a moment then leaving the Thompson, I came out on to the road. The Mexican gaped at me, nodded and looked at Vicky as if for assurance, then started to drag the tree branch out of the way.

'I told him we got lost in the jungle,' Vicky said quickly. 'He's going to Sisal. He's willing to give us a ride.'

I helped the Mexican to get rid of the branch, then we all climbed into the cab. She sat next to him and as he drove, they talked in Spanish.

Around twenty minutes later, I heard the helicopter overhead and I regretted leaving the Thompson, but I knew I would have scared the wits out of the Mexican if he had seen the gun. The chopper flew away.

117

Vicky turned to me.

'He owns a coffee plantation,' she said. 'He's taking us there. He has a telephone.'

I sat back and watched the dust road unwind before me. The Mexican who told me by leaning forward and stabbing himself in his chest his name was Pedro, continued to talk to Vicky.

I marvelled at her guts to keep up a conversation with this man, knowing she was practically dead on her feet, but she seemed to draw on a hidden reserve and she kept Pedro enchanted.

Twenty more minutes later, the truck turned off the dirt road and bumped down a narrow lane to a plantation of coffee trees. Pedro pulled up outside a long, narrow building with a tin roof. I could see a number of Indians working on the plantation. A flat piece of ground before the building was covered with raw coffee beans. Two Indians were moving the beans around with rakes.

A fat, beaming Mexican woman came out of the building and into the sun.

'Maria,' Pedro said and going to her exploded into Spanish.

I half carried, half helped Vicky from the cab of the truck. As soon as her feet touched the ground, she gave a sharp cry and I picked her up.

The Mexican woman came rushing up, waving her hands and yelling in Spanish. Pedro waved me to the house and I carried Vicky in. Following the Mexican, I carried her into a small, clean room and laid her on the bed.

Maria pushed me out and shut the door.

Pedro, beaming, led me to another room.

I made signs of washing myself.

He nodded, beckoned and I followed him into a primitive bathroom.

It was only after I had changed the bath water twice and was now lying in clean tepid water that I began to think of my immediate future.

If Vicky could make the story stick that we had come down in the sea, that I had rescued her, that Bernie and Harry and the plane had gone for ever, then I would be in the clear. But could she make it stick.

There would be an inquiry: the news hounds would be after us; the pressure would be terrific. All the same, as I thought about it, I decided Vicky could swing it with Lane Essex taking off the pressure.

How about Orzoco? He couldn't squeal without showing his revolutionary hand. As I had registered the Blue Ribbon Air Taxi Service, I could assign the million and a half dollars back to him. Doing that must surely get me off his hook.

Who else did I have to worry about? Kendrick? If he ratted on me, I could rat on him. Wes Jackson? With Vicky behind me, Jackson should be an also ran.

The one weakness I could see was that Vicky and I were going to swear the plane crashed into the sea. We had to do that to make Harry's last broadcast stand up, but suppose the wreck was found in the jungle? I thought about this. I was fairly sure the Condor had come down within twenty miles of Orzoco's neck of the woods. If he had any sense, he would have the plane stripped out and destroy what was left. This was something I had to gamble on.

As I got out of the bath and began to dry myself I persuaded myself that my future didn't look too bad. Thirty thousand dollars a year, a steady job, plus Vicky . . . no, not bad.

But everything depended on her.

I should have known she could handle it. As soon as she got to the telephone, the power of Lane Essex clicked into action.

Within three hours a helicopter whisked us to the Merida airport. With only another half hour to wait, Essex's plane landed and took us back to Paradise City. The plane was piloted by a beefy, smiling man who told me his name was Hennessey and he was Essex's new pilot. I remembered poor Olson saying pilots came a dime a dozen.

The news hounds and the TV cameras were kept at bay when we landed. Wes Jackson was at the airport, plus an ambulance, plus a doctor to whisk Mrs Victoria Essex away.

That left me and Jackson.

'You must feel in need of a rest,' he said, showing his tiny teeth in what he imagined was a smile, 'but before you rest, there are a few questions.'

I shoved back my dirty sleeves and showed him the lumps made by insect bites.

'I need medical attention,' I said. 'Questions must wait.'

An Intern took charge of me. He wanted to put me on a stretcher, but I refused. I went with him to his car while Wes

Jackson stood in the hot sunshine, staring after me like a shark who has snapped at a juicy leg and missed.

I was taken to the Essex Foundation Clinic. A pretty nurse administered to me. She spoke to me in a hushed voice. I could feel the power of Mrs Essex hovering over her. If I had been the President of the U.S. of A. I couldn't have been treated with more deference.

But of course it couldn't last. Once my bites were treated—some of them had turned septic—once I had been fed and rested, Wes Jackson arrived. He didn't bring hot-house grapes nor flowers; instead, he brought a lean hatchet-faced man who he introduced as Henry Lucas, the Aero expert for the insurance company covering the Condor.

I had had time to prepare my story and I was ready for them.

I was sitting in a lounging chair by the open window that overlooked Paradise City's yacht basin. Jackson and Lucas pulled up chairs and Jackson asked me how I was.

I said I was mending.

'Mr Crane, we need as much information about the crash as you can give us,' Jackson went on. 'What happened? Take your time: just tell us from the beginning.'

'I wish I knew,' I said, my face dead pan. 'It all happened so suddenly. . . .'

Lucas said in a voice like a fall of gravel, 'You're the flight engineer. Is that correct?'

I nodded.

'And you don't know what happened?'

'Sounds goofy, doesn't it? But that's a fact. I was in the kitchen preparing a meal when we went into a nose dive. Up to then everything was working fine. I was thrown across the kitchen and my head slammed against the open door of the refrigerator and I blacked out.'

There was a long pause while both of them stared at me and I stared right back at them.

'You were preparing a meal?' Jackson leaned his bulk forward. 'But, Mr Crane, I understand you three had steak dinners before the flight.'

Be tricky, you sonofabitch, I thought, then said, 'That's correct, but Olson seemed keyed up. He didn't eat his steak.' That could be proved. 'Then he got hungry and asked me to fix him a sandwich. It was while I was in the kitchen, doing just that, that the crash came.'

'You mean until the plane went into a dive, you had no idea there was trouble?' Lucas said. 'Erskine radioed the port engines were on fire. Didn't you know?'

I gave him my stupid, puzzled expression.

'First I've heard of that. All I know was being flung across the kitchen and blacking out.' Then as neither of them said anything, I went on, 'The next thing I knew was the sea coming in. Somehow I found Mrs Essex and got her out through the port emergency. The kite had broken up. There were bits and pieces floating around. I clung to something and kept Mrs Essex afloat. I saw the kite sink.' I tried not to look brave. 'It was tricky, but we got ashore.'

There was a deadly pause. Neither of them even pretended they believed me.

Jackson said as if his mouth was full of lemon juice, 'That is what Mrs Essex said happened.'

I smiled at him. 'If Mrs Essex said that's what happened and I say that's what happened, then that's what happened.'

Again a long pause, then Lucas said, 'I have a map here, Mr Crane. Would you pinpoint where the crash occurred?'

'I'm sorry. You don't seem to have been listening to what I've been saying,' I said. 'I told you when the crash occurred I was fixing a sandwich. Didn't Olson give Air Control a fix?'

'So you can't help locate the wreck?'

'I'm sorry.'

'You can't suggest what went wrong? Erskine said the port engines were on fire and the extinguishers weren't working. Can you say why this should happen?'

I was sure they would ask this question and I was ready for it. I went into the technical mumbo-jumbo while Lucas, with a stone face, listened. I didn't convince him nor did I convince myself but Jackson listened and he was all I cared about.

'If I had been in the flight cabin when the engines caught fire, if I had been able to read the instruments, I could be a lot more helpful,' I concluded, 'but I was in the kitchen, fixing a sandwich.'

Lucas gave me a map of the Gulf of Mexico.

'Couldn't you indicate about where the crash happened?'

I looked at the map, then shrugged.

Maybe fifty miles off Presago. I wouldn't know. Mrs Essex and I were in the sea for about twelve hours and the current took us in. Could be sixty miles . . . your guess is as good as mine. I just don't know.'

He folded the map and put it in his pocket.

'We have helicopters looking for signs of the wreck. So far there is a negative report.'

'If they search long enough, they'll find it then if you get to the Black Box, you'll know how it happened.'

They got to their feet, stared at me, then Jackson said, 'Mr Crane, Mr Essex wants to meet you. I will pick you up here tomorrow morning at ten.'

'Fine.'

Neither of them offered to shake hands. Lucas gave me a long, slow stare which I returned, but Jackson screwed his face into a smile. If Lane Essex wanted to meet me, I was still, to him, the boy with the golden halo.

Wes Jackson opened a polished mahogany door, motioned me forward, then said, 'Mr Crane, sir.'

I walked into a vast room with a picture window overlooking Paradise City. Before me was a vast desk, equipped with a battery of telephones and the usual gimmicks that go to make the top executive.

Behind the desk sat Lane Essex.

I had never seen a photo of him and I had been trying to imagine what he looked like. The small, balding man of around fifty-six years of age, with heavy horn glasses, a sparrow beak of a nose and thin, hard lips told me as nothing else could why Mrs Victoria Essex shopped around for a bed companion.

'Come in, Crane.' There was a snap in his voice. 'Sit down.'

I took the chair opposite his desk. Then looking directly at him, I realized why he had made his billions. His steel grey eyes behind the glasses went through me like a welder's torch.

'Mrs Essex has told me about you. Apparently, you saved her life. Now it's my turn to do a *quid pro quo*. I have had your qualifications investigated. You have a good record with Lockheed. Will you take charge of my airfield?'

'Yes, sir.'

'I want another Condor built. Will you handle that?'

'Glad to, sir.'

A telephone buzzed and he waved to Jackson who picked up the receiver, listened and began to talk softly.

'You could be making an important career for yourself here, Crane,' Essex went on. 'I want you to remember that here the word impossible doesn't exist. You will have all the financial backing you may need, but never come to me and tell me what I want you to do can't be done. If you do, you're out.'

'I understand, sir.'

Jackson hung up.

Essex looked at him.

'Crane takes charge of the airfield and the new Condor,' he said. 'Pay him fifty.' He looked at me. 'Are you married?'

'No, sir.'

He turned back to Jackson.

'Get him one of our good bachelor apartments. Get him a good car and someone to look after his place.' He looked at me. 'Have you a banking account?'

'Not here, sir.'

He turned to Jackson.

'Open an account for him at the National Florida: credit the account right away with twenty thousand dollars: that's a bonus. Pay him monthly and pick up his tax tab.' He stared at me. 'Is that satisfactory?'

'Thank you very much, sir.' I was pretty overwhelmed.

'Take a week's vacation. Those bites look serious. Report to Jackson Monday week.' He waved to me, dismissing me.

Jackson followed me out of the room and he closed the door as if it were made of spun sugar. In silence, he took me down a corridor and into another vast room but without a picture window.

'I'll arrange everything for you, Crane,' he said. 'Just sit down.'

'Thank you, Jackson,' I said.

He stiffened and stared at me. I stared right back at him. He hesitated. I could see he wanted to tell me he was Mr Jackson to me, but my stare quelled him. Picking up the telephone he asked for Miss Byrnes.

'Miss Byrnes is our Public Relations Officer,' he explained. 'She will take care of you.'

Miss Byrnes was a willowy, sophisticated woman of around

thirty-six, blonde, with searching brown eyes and a determined chin.

I was a little embarrassed when Jackson gave her instructions about the apartment, the car, the credit at the bank. He detailed these items in a funereal voice and when he finally got through, he said, 'Then Monday week at nine o'clock, Crane.'

'Right. Well, so long, Jackson. Thanks for your help.' I saw Miss Byrnes's eyes pop open wide as I followed her out of the office. When out of Jackson's hearing, she turned and regarded me.

'What did you do? Save Essex from bankruptcy?'

'I saved Mrs V.E.'s life.'

She grimaced. 'That's something no one here is likely to do, so that makes you unique.' She led me to her office.

Four hours later, I was installed in a three-room luxury apartment overlooking the sea with a red and beige Cadillac convertible in the garage, plus twenty thousand dollars in my banking account and six days on my hands.

I had already bought myself a wardrobe without sparing expenses and apart from the wear and tear on my face I now looked presentable.

I got in the Caddy and drove to Kendrick's gallery.

Louis de Marney hurried me into Kendrick's room. The fat queer was pacing up and down and practically biting his nails.

'For heaven's sake! What happened?' he exploded as I sat down.

I give him the whole story without holding anything back. He listened, sweat on his face, and every now and then he lifted his absurd orange wig to wipe his bald head with his handkerchief.

'That's it,' I concluded. 'A flop. Did you know Bernie had a weak heart?'

'Of course not! You don't imagine, cheri, I would have let him handle an operation like that had I known. What about the money?'

'I'll return it to Orzoco. I can fix that. The point is will he keep his mouth shut? If it comes out the kite crashed in the jungle and not in the sea we'll all be in trouble—and that includes you.'

'I'll talk to him. If he gets his money back, he will accept the situation.' Kendrick eyed me. 'You owe me two thousand dollars, cheri.'

'Expenses. Write them off against tax.' I got to my feet. 'If you can smother Orzoco then we should all be in the clear. The insurance investigators are searching for the wreck so you'd better tell Orzoco to get rid of it pronto. How do I get the money to him?'

Kendrick stared at me.

'You really mean you're going to part with a million and a half dollars, cheri?'

'That's it. I don't want it. I've got a job with Essex. I'm a sucker for work. What do I do: write to the bank and tell them to pay the money to Orzoco?'

'I'll talk to him. He may not want it done that way. Give me a couple of days.'

We left it like that.

I then drove to a florist and bought thirty-six long-stemmed roses. I wrote on the card: *With my sincere wishes for your speedy recovery. Jack Crane.* That was impersonal enough as I was sure Essex's staff would quiz. I told the girl to have the roses sent to Mrs Victoria Essex right away.

Then feeling I had done a good day's work, I drove back to my new home and telephoned my old man, breaking the news that his one and only was safe and sound and was now settling down to a job of work.

Listening to my old man babbling with joy, hearing the catch in his voice that told me he was crying, I realized, as nothing else could tell me, what a heel I was.

CHAPTER NINE

I CAME AWAKE the following morning around 10.00. I was re-laxed, my face and arms were returning to normal and I felt pretty good. Room service sent up eggs on grilled ham and I made a leisurely breakfast. This was the way to live, I told myself. I looked out of the window at the sparkling sea and decided I would take a swim, then pick up a dolly bird, take her to lunch and then a drive in the Caddy. If she wasn't too stupid, I'd take her for a night on the town and bring her back here.

While I smoked my first cigarette of the day, thinking of my future, the telephone bell rang.

'Jack? I wanted to thank you for the roses.'

Hearing her voice did something extraordinary to me. It flashed into my mind that this woman—Mrs Victoria Essex—could now prove lethal to me. Right now I was Lane Essex's special pet. I was in charge of his airfield. I was going to supervise the building of a new ten-million-dollar plane. I was being paid fifty thousand dollars a year for this and he was even paying my income tax. But if he found out I was screwing his wife, all this would explode in my face.

Lying there on the bed, the telephone receiver against my ear, it came to me that this job was something I had dreamed of: to be an executive with power, working for a billionaire.

A cold sick feeling took hold of me. I knew this woman had to be handled very, very carefully. Everyone connected with Essex Enterprises had warned me she was a blue-print for a bitch. Up to now, she and I had jelled because I had wanted her and she had wanted me, but so far as I was concerned, not now.

'Vicky! How are you?' I forced my voice to sound ardent.

'I'm recovering. My feet still hurt. Lane tells me he has taken care of you. Are you satisfied, Jack? You have only to tell me: I can handle Lane.'

A drop of cold sweat ran down the side of my nose and I flicked it away.

'Satisfied? He leant over backwards, and I have you to thank.'

'Good.' A pause, then she said, 'He's just left for Moscow. I'm going to the cabin: join me at six,' and she hung up.

Slowly, I replaced the receiver.

Suddenly my planned day of fun turned grey. I knew every time she and I met, I was putting my new career into jeopardy. Should anyone see us and send word to Essex, I would have no career, and yet I knew Mrs Victoria Essex was far too dangerous to refuse.

The relaxed happy hours on the beach with a brainless dolly bird were now a pipe dream. I had to drive to the cabin, risk my future because Mrs Victoria Essex had beckoned.

I spent the morning and most of the afternoon in my room, brooding. I drank too much. I didn't feel like eating. Then around 17.00, I went to the garage, got in the Caddy and drove to the cabin.

Sam came out into the sunshine. I nodded to him as he beamed, taking my overnight bag. He could betray me, I thought. A word from him to Essex would leave me out in the very dark cold.

Vicky was lying on the divan, sipping a dry martini.

'Jack!'

'How are you?'

She still had a few tiny blemishes from the insect bites on her skin, but they had been skilfully treated. She looked marvellous in a simple red cotton dress that reached to her ankles.

She looked up at me: her big violet eyes full of desire as she finished the martini and set down the glass.

'Lock the door, Jack. I want you!'

As I turned the key, I again realized the trap I was in, but in spite of knowing this, I wanted her: no man alive wouldn't want her.

Our lovemaking was fierce. Twice she cried out wildly and I cringed, wondering if Sam was listening outside the door. When she was finally satisfied, she smiled up at me.

'You're quite a man, Jack. Let's have a drink.'

So we had martinis, then Sam brought in dinner of lobster soup, grilled salmon steaks, salad and coffee.

She talked: I listened.

'I must tell you about Lane,' she said with a laugh. 'He was really furious with me that I had taken a ride on the Condor. I've never seen him so mad. He sacked poor Thompson who let me on. If it wasn't for my feet, he would have beaten me.'

I couldn't imagine any man beating this woman.

'Do you go along with that?'

She laughed.

'Men have their kinks. I don't mind so long as it keeps him happy. I smoke a reefer before he begins.' She laughed again. 'In a way, it's quite fun.'

I suddenly felt sickened by this.

'Vicky . . . do you think I should stay the night?' I asked. 'Don't you think it's dangerous?'

Her eyes turned hard as she stared at me.

'Don't you want to stay with me, Jack?'

Did I hell! One slip and I would lose my future.

'Of course, but I'm thinking of you. It's damn dangerous. Someone . . .'

'There's no someone.' She stretched herself like a beautiful sleek cat. 'Turn on the telly. Let's watch the fights.'

So we spent the next two hours watching bums hanging on to

127

each other and hitting the air around each other, then Sam came in to clear the dishes.

'Carry me to bed, Jack,' she said. 'My feet still hurt.'

Picking her up, taking her into her bedroom, laying her on the king size bed meant nothing to me. I just wanted to get away, but that, I knew, was something I wasn't going to do.

'Undress me, Jack.'

I could hear Sam washing the dishes. Reluctantly I undressed her while she lay still, smiling at me. When I had got her into a shortie nightdress, she said. 'Take a shower, Jack.' The violet eyes had turned hungry. 'Hurry . . .'

Around 01.00, we finally fell asleep. She woke me as the dawn light came through the open window and we made love again. She seemed insatiable. I was still in loggish, exhausted sleep when she woke me again.

'Get up, Jack. It's after ten. Go into the spare bedroom. The doctor's coming.'

I dragged myself, half asleep, into the spare bedroom. I dropped on to the bed, feeling as if I had been fed through a mincer. I slept.

What seemed minutes later, a gentle hand shook me awake.

'Lunch will be ready in an hour, Mr Crane,' Sam said softly.

I staggered out of bed, took a cold shower, dressed and went into the living-room. I was feeling like hell.

Vicky was sipping a dry martini.

'Hi! Jack! Did you rest?'

I forced a grin.

'Yes. I find you marvellously exhausting.' I reached for the cocktail shaker. 'What did the quack say?'

She grimaced. 'He wanted to shoot me full of antibiotics, but I said no.'

'You're right.' I drank half the martini to give me courage, then said, 'I have to go to the city this morning. I won't be long, but I have to go.'

She put down her drink and eyed me. 'Why?'

Just looking at her, seeing those violet eyes turn glass hard, seeing her face tighten into a stone mask told me as nothing else could that I was handling dynamite.

So I told her about Claude Kendrick and Orzoco. She listened, staring at me.

'I must get Orzoco fixed,' I concluded. 'The only way is to pay back the money, then he can't beef. I have to see Kendrick and tie it up.'

She drew in a long, slow breath.

'You've certainly involved yourself in a mess, haven't you?' There was an edge to her voice.

'I can handle it. You don't have to worry.'

That was absolutely the wrong thing to have said. She picked up her cocktail glass and threw it viciously across the room. The glass exploded against the wall. She leaned forward, glaring at me.

'Worry? What the hell do you mean? If you involve me in your sordid hi-jack, you'll be sorry you're alive! Go and fix it! But don't you dare involve me!'

'Take it easy, Vicky.' I was shocked at her viciousness. 'There's no need to get angry. I'll fix it.'

'You'd better!'

Looking at her as she glared at me, her face like stone, her eyes blazing, she lost the glamour she ever had for me. For the first time I could understand why everyone had warned me that she was a blue-print of a bitch.

As I left the room, she screamed after me, 'And come back! I want you here before five o'clock!'

Claude Kendrick received me in his room with a wry smile.

'It's all fixed, cheri: no problems. I have a document for you to sign. I have talked to Orzoco. He understands. Actually, he isn't displeased. He has salvaged a lot of expensive items from the aircraft which he gets for nothing.'

'How about the wreck?'

Kendrick smiled.

'It doesn't exist any more. It's all right. There's no problem. Just sign here. This assigns your company to Orzoco.'

I signed with the name I had used to register the company: Jack Norton.

That seemed to be that.

'I understand Mr Essex is going to build another Condor?' Kendrick said, looking slyly at me. 'Maybe we could do another deal?'

'Not a hope.'

He lifted his orange wig, stared inside it and slapped it back on his head.

'Yes.' He squinted up at me. 'Mrs Essex owns a number of expensive baubles: particularly a diamond necklace. I would be in the market if you could arrange something.'

'Get stuffed, fatty.' I said and left him.

I got into the Caddy. The time by the dashboard clock was 13.30. I wasn't expected back until 17.00. I decided to return to my apartment. I needed time to think.

I ordered the special for the day and it was served on a trolley. I ate it, then lit a cigarette and sat by the open window.

I told myself that once I began working for Essex, I would be out of Vicky's clutches. I had to ride for the next four days, but once I reported for work, I would be safe. She would know this and have to accept it. I would be on the move all the time to satisfy Essex. To run the airfield and to supervise the building of the new Condor would give me no time to be in bed with Mrs Victoria Essex.

I had four more nights of risk and I sweated at the thought. Still, I tried to assure myself, her risk was as great as mine, and if she was satisfied she was safe, sleeping with me, surely I could feel safe too.

At this moment, my front door bell rang.

Without thinking it was anyone but the waiter to take away the trolley, I got up and opened the door.

There is a phrase people use: *he jumped out of his skin.* An exaggeration, of course, no one can jump out of his skin, but he can do so mentally. He can be so shocked that blood leaves his face, he turns cold, and for a long moment, he becomes breathless. That was what happened to me when I saw Pam Osborn standing in the doorway.

There she was, blonde hair falling to her shoulders in a cascade of gold with her narrow, high cheekbones and her large green eyes. She had on a buttercup-coloured blouse and white stretch pants and her smile was the smile of a panther.

'Hi! Jack!' she said. 'Surprised?'

I retreated, and she came into the room, closing the door.

Pam!

From the moment I had insisted that she shouldn't fly with us and that she had to wait in Merida, she had gone completely out of my mind. Now here she was: the one fatal link between

130

me and the hi-jack. I had believed, after talking to Kendrick, that I was clear of trouble. I also believed I could get clear of Vicky. She would soon get bored with me when I couldn't run when she beckoned. Up to this moment, my future had looked settled, but not now . . . certainly not now.

I stood watching her as she chose a chair and sat down.

'I'm so happy, Jack, that you are making such a success of your life,' she said as she opened her handbag and took out a pack of cigarettes. 'I've been talking to Dolly Byrnes: she's a special friend of mine. So you're now Essex's white-headed boy.' She stared at me: the hatred in those green eyes was chilling. 'Fifty thousand a year, tax free, this nice apartment, a Caddy and Mr Big Shot at the airfield. How marvellous!'

I sat down. I was over the shock now and my mind was beginning to work.

'Fantastic, isn't it?' I was aware my voice was a little husky. 'That's the way the cookie crumbles, Pam. A terrible thing about Bernie. I had no idea he had a dicky heart: did you?'

'No.' She lit her cigarette. 'I went to his funeral: it was the least I could do. I hoped you would have been there too.'

A chill crawled up my spine. So she could explode the story that we had crashed into the sea.

'I know you and Bernie . . .'

'Don't let's talk about Bernie,' she cut in. 'He's dead. Let's talk about me.'

'Sure.' Without any hope, I went on, 'Do you want your job back, Pam? I can fix it.'

'How nice of you, Jack. Well, no . . . I will want something rather better than that . . . now.'

So it was going to be blackmail.

An immediate thought dropped into my mind. She had come here alone. Suppose I killed her? Would that stop this nightmare that was slowly building up around me? So, okay, I killed her, but what was I going to do with her body?

I said, 'What can I do to be helpful, Pam?'

'I've been talking to Claude. He tells me you've returned all the money. Claude hasn't been helpful. He told me to talk to you.' She crossed her slim legs. 'Bernie was planning to marry me. We would have shared a million dollars. I would love to own a million dollars.'

131

JAMES HADLEY CHASE

I nodded. 'Who wouldn't?'

She flicked ash on the carpet.

'I spent five days at the Continental Hotel at Merida.' She regarded me, her green eyes stony. 'They could have been dull, lonely days, but as it happened, Juan picked me up.'

'You were always a girl to find friends,' I said.

'Come on, Jack! You're not listening: Juan Aulestria. Remember? He works—used to work—for Orzoco: remember now?'

My mind went back to the tall, thin man with thick longish hair and the smoothness of a snake and my heart skipped a beat.

'Juan was very kind to me,' Pam went on. 'He's with me now; we're staying at the Hilton. He thought it would be more tactful for me to see you first, then he will talk to you.' Her red lips parted in what could be called a smile. 'Juan has marvellous tact.'

I had had enough of this cat and mouse act. I saw now that she had me in a corner. I was thankful I hadn't done anything stupid like killing her. Aulestria was far more dangerous than she could ever be.

'Let's skip the build-up,' I said. 'Let's talk business. What do you want?'

She took from her bag an envelope and tossed it into my lap. 'Take a look, Jack.'

The envelope contained four good photographs of the Condor wreck as it lay in the jungle. There was no mistaking the plane. It's name and number were clear on the fuselage. The fourth picture made me stiffen. It was of Erskine's dead body, his head in a halo of blood.

'Just in case you miss the point of that photo,' Pam said, 'and I'm sure you don't, what was Harry doing out of the flight cabin at the time of the crash?'

I put the photos on the table.

'What else?' I asked and lit a cigarette. I was surprised to see my hands were steady.

'Isn't that enough?' She lifted her eyebrows mockingly.

'You could talk yourself into trouble. You were part of the hi-jack.'

'You prove it. I was Bernie's girl. He told me to wait for him in Merida. I had no idea what you three were planning. Juan is going to tell the insurance people: if they are to be told.'

132

'Okay. So what's the pay-off?'

'Five hundred thousand dollars: my half share of Bernie's money.'

I couldn't believe it. Staring at her, I said, 'Come on!'

'You heard, Jack.'

'And where do you imagine I could raise money like that?'

'From the Essex bitch: from where else?'

'You're crazy! She would no more give me a sum like that than fly to the moon.'

Pam smiled her hateful smile of triumph.

'She will.' She took another photograph from her bag. 'I wouldn't have thought of it, but Juan did. He arranged for a private eye to keep tabs on you the moment you returned here.' She flicked the photo into my lap. 'Five hundred thousand is nothing to her. She'll pay to keep this photo away from Mr Essex.'

I looked at the photograph. It showed me, outside the cabin, standing by the new Caddy handing my overnight bag to Sam.

She left behind her the smell of cheap scent and the five damning photographs. Just before she left she said Aulestria would be contacting me.

'From now on, Jack, he'll be in charge of the negotiations. We won't wait long. See the bitch and fix it.'

I wondered how Vicky would react. I was sunk. That I knew, but could I get her out of this mess? If Sam's loyalty stood up under pressure, that photo of me arriving at the cabin wasn't all that damaging. Vicky could tell Essex that she had lent me the cabin while I was on vacation and she had never been near it. After thinking, I realized this was a pipe dream. She must have told Essex she was going to the cabin and I was sure Sam wouldn't stand up to an Essex cross-examination.

So what was to be done?

I put the photographs back in the envelope and the envelope in my breast pocket. I lit a cigarette while I tried to find a way out. My first thought was to trap Pam and Aulestria somehow and kill them, but that, too, was a pipe dream. Aulestria was no fool. He would have taken precautions, lodging another set of photographs with an attorney with instructions: *in the event of my death.* Had Pam been handling this on her own, I was sure I could trap and kill her, but not Aulestria.

133

Again I thought of Vicky. I was wasting time, trying to find a way out. I had to discuss it with her and I cringed at the thought of her explosion. *You involve me in this and you'll be sorry you're alive!* Now, because she had had hot pants for me, she was involved. Because she couldn't give me up, she had lied about the crash not only to Essex but also to the insurance people.

I looked at my watch. The time was 14.45.

Bracing myself, I left the apartment and drove back to the cabin. It was a drive I was to remember for the rest of my days. The nearer I got to the cabin the more scared I became. I had already seen her in a rage and I flinched at the thought of how she would react once she knew how involved she was.

I also thought of the years I could spend behind bars. I couldn't hope to get out under fifteen years. I would be middle-aged by then and fit for nothing. Very late in the day, I thought of my old man. This would kill him: I was sure of that.

I pulled up outside the cabin and Sam, beaming, opened the door.

I went into the cabin, leaving him to put the Caddy out of sight, in one of the garages.

Vicky was lying on the settee, a copy of *Vogue* in her hand. I stood in the doorway, looking at her. She put down the magazine and smiled at me.

'Hi! Jack!' She laughed. 'You're nice and early.' She patted the settee. 'Come and kiss me.'

I moved into the room and shut the door. I didn't approach her, but stood still, my shoulders against the door.

She lifted her eyebrows. 'Come on, Jack! You mustn't take me seriously. I was mad. I get mad. Have you fixed it?'

'Start getting mad again,' I said. I took the envelope from my pocket and tossed it on to her lap.

Her violet eyes turned hard. The sexy, hungry smile went away like a fist when it becomes a hand.

'What is this?'

'Take a look.'

She stared at the envelope but didn't touch it.

'What is it?'

I came to the settee, picked up the envelope, took out the five photos and spread them out on her lap.

She looked at them, then slowly picked each one up and

examined it carefully. She finally came to the one of me and Sam. She stared at it for a longer moment, then she put the photos together and offered them to me.

'How much?'

Apart from the fact her face was stone hard and had lost colour and her eyes were glittering, she was fantastically calm. I could tell by the way her breasts moved under the sweat shirt that her breathing was even and that must mean her heartbeat and her pulse were normal.

'How much?' she repeated.

This was a remarkable woman. She didn't have to have it spelt out and the explosion I had expected didn't materialize.

'Five hundred thousand . . . half a million.'

She stared up at me.

'You're an expensive lover.'

'I didn't say anything.

'Well, don't look as if the end of the world has come. Sit there.' She pointed to a chair nearby. 'Tell me about it.'

I sat down.

She lay motionless, staring down at her hands as I told her about Pam and Aulestria.

'They won't stop at half a million of course,' she said as if speaking to herself. 'I pay them off and later they will come back: blackmailers always do.' She looked up and regarded me. 'You killed Erskine. Could you kill them?'

'Yes, but that won't solve this problem. Aulestria will have protected himself.'

She nodded. 'The alternative is I go to my husband and tell him I've been foolish and hope he will be kind to me.' Again it sounded as if she were talking to herself.

'You could do that,' I said nervously.

She stared at me.

'You're a little man, aren't you, Jack? You're now wondering what is going to happen to you.'

'I want to get you out of this mess.'

'Do you?' She smiled. 'Well, that's something. I have a half million. What do you suggest? Shall I pay these two? It would be no problem until they come back for more. What do you think?'

It was my turn to stare at her.

135

'You mean you can find five hundred thousand?' My voice was husky.

'Of course. That's no problem. The problem is should we do it?'
My mind raced.

If she could raise the money and if those two were satisfied with the pay-off, this could let me out. I might even be able to keep my new job with Essex Enterprises. Why shouldn't they be satisfied with half a million?

'It's a solution,' I said, trying not to sound eager.

'So it is. Yes . . . as you so rightly say, it's a solution.' She stubbed out her cigarette. 'Well, so let's pay them.' She paused to look me over. 'You've met them: I haven't. Do you think we can trust them?'

I didn't know, but I wasn't going to say so. I was too anxious to get off the hook.

'For that money, they must play,' I said. 'For God's sake! A half a million!'

'They're at the Hilton, didn't you say? See if you can reach them, Jack. Let's get it settled.'

'You really mean it, Vicky? You're going to pay then.'

'Yes. I can't land dear Lane with a ten-million-dollar bill for his stupid plane, plus the knowledge that I've been behaving like a hooker, can I?' She shrugged. 'After all, what is half a million?'

Giving her no chance to change her mind, I called the Hilton and asked for Mr Aulestria. There was a delay, then a man's voice said, 'This is Aulestria.'

'Crane. The deal's on,' I said. 'How do we fix it?'

'Here at eleven o'clock tomorrow,' Aulestria said and hung up.

'At the Hilton at eleven o'clock,' I told Vicky.

'It will take me two days to raise the money. Find out how it is to be paid.' Her violet eyes were very impersonal. 'Now run away. I must talk to my broker.' She flicked her fingers at me. 'Go home.'

I had always had a presentiment that sooner or later there would come a time when she would flick her fingers at me the way she flicked them at her other men slaves, but it didn't bother me. I was too thankful that there hadn't been a scene and that she was going to pay and my future wasn't in jeopardy to let a little thing like that cause me grief.

'I'll report back to you,' I said as I moved to the door.

She was reaching for the telephone and didn't even look at me so I went out into the fading sunshine, got the Caddy from the garage and drove back to my apartment.

I knew there was every chance that Aulestria would squeeze her again, but I told myself that she was so goddamn rich, she could afford to be squeezed.

Yes . . . my future looked bright again.

The following morning I arrived at the Hilton hotel a few minutes to eleven. As I was asking at the desk for Mr Aulestria, a man came up and lurched against me. He immediately apologized and I thought he was just another clumsy jerk who bang into people and I forgot about him, but later, I was to remember him.

Aulestria was waiting for me in a large room with a double bed and the usual Hilton fitments. Pam was sitting by the window. She didn't look around when Aulestria opened the door.

'Ah, Mr Crane,' he said, smiling his snake's smile. 'Good to see you again.' He closed the door. 'So she is going to pay?'

'That's right.'

'How wise of her. She has agreed to five hundred thousand?'

'Yes.'

'Well . . . a little unexpected. I was rather expecting her to bargain. However, that is very satisfactory. I want the money in bearer bonds.'

'That can be arranged. I want all the photos and all the negatives and an acknowledgement from you that the transaction terminates the deal.'

'Of course you get the photos and the negatives, but no acknowledgement.'

'That means you can put the squeeze on again.'

'Mr Crane! I assure you. We are perfectly satisfied with half a million, aren't we, Pam?'

Without looking around, she said, 'If you are, Juan, then I am.'

'Be assured, Mr Crane. When will the money be ready?'

'The day after tomorrow.'

'Quite satisfactory, but not later. Bring the bonds here at ten o'clock. Don't be late. We have a plane to catch.'

He conducted me to the door.

'What a fortunate man you are, Mr Crane.'

I stared at him. 'You think so?'

'Ask yourself,' and he bowed me out of the room.

I drove back to my apartment and called Vicky.

'Bonds?' There was a pause. 'All right, I'll get them. Sam will deliver them to you tomorrow night,' and she hung up.

I replaced the receiver and stared out of the open window. There was something so out of character about this set-up that it began to bother me. I had expected a vicious explosion from this woman: no explosion had come. I had been willing to bet that she wouldn't have parted with half a million dollars and yet she had meekly submitted. The only thing in character had been those flicking fingers.

I tried to convince myself that she had so much to lose that a half a million was an acceptable pay-off. Like her husband, she was stinking rich, such a sum was like a hundred dollars to me and yet somehow it didn't jell. It was so completely out of character.

As I sat staring at the sunset, my future began to fray at the edges.

I had a meal, then wandered around the city, then went to bed. I couldn't sleep. Around 02.00, I couldn't stand my thoughts any longer. I took three sleeping pills and they gave me the oblivion I had to have.

I slept until midday. The rest of the day stretched endlessly for me. I wondered what I was going to do with myself. I thought of Vicky and suddenly wanted her physically, but I knew that was finished. The finger-flicking act and those impersonal, cold violet eyes told me that as nothing else could.

I went down to the bar, had a double Scotch on the rocks and a chicken sandwich. It was all I could do to eat it. Then I drove down to the beach. The dolly birds were there, but they no longer interested me. I sat in the car, staring at the sea until dusk, my thoughts tormenting me. Then I returned to my apartment and watched the telly.

The following day was a carbon copy of the previous day. I kept telling myself to relax. By tomorrow we would have Aulestria off our backs. The day after I would report to Wes Jackson and begin work. I was sure that once I began to work, all this would fall behind me. I tried to think what I would do once I was in charge of the airfield. I even made a few notes, but my heart wasn't in it.

Around 19.00 my front door bell rang. I let Sam in. He handed me a bulky envelope.

'How is she, Sam?' I asked, taking the envelope.

'She's okay, Mr Crane. She'll always be okay.' He shuffled his feet. 'I guess I'll say good-bye. I'm moving on.'

'What do you mean?'

He smiled sadly. 'Mrs Essex doesn't need me any more.'

'You mean she's given you the gate?'

'That's it, Mr Crane.'

'What are you going to do?' I was shocked.

'I'll get by. I have my savings. I'm going home.'

'You mean she's thrown you out . . . just like that?'

'It had to happen sometime. She's a difficult lady. If things go right with her, it's fine: if they don't, it's bad.'

'I'm sorry, Sam. I feel it's my fault.'

His nice, kindly face split into a rueful grin.

'If it hadn't been you, it would be someone else.' He wiped his hand on the seat of his trousers, then offered it. 'Well, so long, Mr Crane, it's been my pleasure knowing you.'

We shook hands and he left.

Could this happen to me? I wondered. After this was over, after Aulestria had been paid off, was I too going to get the gate? I went over and sat in a chair.

Yes, I told myself. The writing was on the wall. You'll get the gate. She won't want you around as she doesn't want Sam around. You'll go: that's for sure.

I looked down at the bulky envelope I was holding in my hand. I ripped it open. It contained five bearer bonds, each worth $100,000. I could get in the Caddy and take off. These bonds were cash. I could do that, but I wasn't going to.

I sat there thinking. My future had exploded. What was going to happen to me?

I suddenly felt in need of comfort and there was only one person on earth who could give me that.

My old man answered the telephone: his voice sounded tired.

'Well, this is a surprise. How are you, Jack?'

'I'm okay. I've been thinking. This job isn't working out. Is that garage still up for sale?'

'Could be. I don't know. I'll ask. Would you be interested, Jack?'

'Maybe. Ask anyway.' I had twenty thousand dollars of Essex's money in the bank. I wouldn't have to borrow from my old man. 'How's the garden looking?'

'Wonderful. The roses have never been so good. Jack . . .' I could hear his excited breathing. His voice no longer sounded tired. 'Are you coming home?'

'Maybe, Dad. I'll let you know in a little while. Yes . . . I could be coming home.'

'All right, son. I'll wait to hear.'

'I won't keep you waiting long. 'Bye now, Dad,' and I hung up.

I didn't take any sleeping pills that night.

It occurred to me as I got into the Caddy the following morning that this would be the last time I would drive it. It was a fine car and I started the motor with regret. I drove to the Hilton and parked. A distant church clock chimed the hour. Holding the envelope containing the bonds, I walked up the hotel steps and into the imposing lobby. In a few minutes, I told myself as I entered the elevator, the pressure would slacken.

I walked along the corridor and tapped on Aulestria's door. It opened immediately and Aulestria stood aside to let me in. Then he stepped into the corridor, looked to right and left, then came back into the room.

Pam was standing by the window. She had on a light dust coat and two expensive-looking suitcases stood nearby.

'You have the bonds, Mr Crane?' Aulestria asked.

'I have them.' I took them from the envelope and showed them to him. He didn't attempt to take them from my hand, but peered at them, then nodded.

'Satisfactory.' He took from his pocket an envelope. 'Here are the photos and the negatives. Take them and I'll take the bonds.'

We made the exchange. I checked the photos and the negatives.

'How many more copies have you kept back?' I asked.

'Mr Crane . . . please. You can trust me entirely.' He smiled. 'There are no copies. I give you my word. Mrs Essex can be quite happy about that.'

'You'll be sorry if you try for another squeeze,' I said, 'but that's your funeral.'

'There won't be another squeeze, Mr Crane.'

'I'm just telling you.'

I turned and left the room, walked down the corridor to the elevator and rode down to the lobby.

I was putting the envelope containing the photos in my breast pocket when a voice said gently, 'I'll have those, Crane.'

I spun around, my heart jumping.

Wes Jackson was standing just behind me, his teeth showing in his shark's smile. He held out his fat hand.

'I'm representing Mrs Essex. She has asked me to collect the photos from you.'

'She'll get them, but from me.'

'She anticipated that would be your reaction.' He handed me a slip of paper. 'Here is an authorization.' His little eyes dwelt on my face. 'She doesn't want to see you again.'

I took the slip of paper.

Jack Crane.
Hand the blackmail photographs to Mr Jackson.
From this moment you are no longer employed by Essex Enterprises.

Lane Essex.

I stared at the signature, then at Jackson.

'So she told him?'

'Naturally. No one has ever succeeded in blackmailing the Essex people: no one ever will. Give me the photographs.'

I gave them to him.

'Thank you. Now, Crane, let's sit down for a few minutes. Let us both witness the end of this sordid little drama. It will interest you.' He laid his fat hand on my arm and guided me to two lounging chairs that faced the elevators. He sat down and glanced at the photographs, then put them in his pocket.

I sat down.

From this moment you are no longer employed by Essex Enterprises.

I had anticipated this, but all the same it came as a shock.

'You will leave Paradise City immediately,' Jackson said. 'You will be wise never to return. You can consider yourself fortunate. When discussing your case, Mr Essex took into consideration that you did save Mrs Essex's life. This weighed in your favour. I am sure you will be wise enough to say nothing to anyone of what has happened. I can tell you we have withdrawn the insurance claim for the Condor and by doing this, we have neutralized the blackmail threat. The other photo means nothing.'

'They're getting away with half a million dollars,' I said. 'You call that smart?'

He smiled, looking more like a shark than ever.

'No one gets away with anything when dealing with Mr Essex.' He stretched out his long, thick legs. 'Ah! Do look, Crane. This will interest you.'

One of the elevator doors slid open. Pam, followed by Aulestria, came out into the lobby. Behind them were two beefy looking men with cop written all over them.

Aulestria's face was ashen. Pam looked as if she were about to collapse. The two men herded them across the lobby and down to a waiting car.

Another man, again with cop written all over him, came from another elevator, carrying the two suitcases I had seen in Aulestria's room. He set them down and came over to Jackson. He dropped the heavy envelope containing the bonds into Jackson's lap.

'No problem,' he said and picking up the suitcases, he walked to the exit, got in the waiting car which drove rapidly away.

'Now, you see, how our organization works,' Jackson said smugly. 'Those three men are ex-police officers. They will escort those two petty blackmailers on to a plane to Merida: it is a chartered flight and they will have the plane entirely to themselves. Arriving at Merida they will be met by an extremely hostile reception. I need not mention that Mr Orzoco has been alerted. Aulestria stupidly took funds belonging to Mr Orzoco's party. They will know how to deal with him and with the woman. Aulestria is under the impression that the men escorting him belong to the City police. Every word you and he exchanged was taped and they have played the tape back to him. He imagines he is going to be prosecuted for blackmail. It won't be until he is put on board the plane that he will realize what is happening: then it will be too late.' He gave me his shark's smile. 'Little, stupid people, Crane, like yourself. There is an old saying: the clay pot should never go down stream with the gold pot. The clay pot invariably gets broken.' I could see he was enjoying himself. 'You perhaps didn't realize that I had arranged for a bug to be planted on you when you first called on Aulestria. You might give it to me. It's in your right coat pocket.'

Dazed, I groped in my pocket and came up with a black object no bigger than an Aspro pill. Then I remembered the man who had lurched against me.

As I gave Jackson the bug, I said, 'So what happens to me?'

'Nothing.' He heaved himself to his feet and regarded me contemptuously. 'Nothing ever will,' and he walked away, leaving me staring after him.

Perhaps he will be wrong. Ever is a long time.

I sat there thinking of my old man, the small-time town and the garage that could still be for sale.

I suddenly felt a surge of confidence.

After all, Henry Ford began small, didn't he?

BRAINRACK

Kit Pedler and Gerry Davis

'Brainrack' is published by
Souvenir Press Ltd

The Authors

Kit Pedler is a doctor of medicine and a research scientist of great distinction. He has thirty-eight original research papers on the eye and vision to his credit. He has written a number of short stories and has broadcast on radio and television about current environmental affairs.

Gerry Davis has been in practically every branch of show business, from English Provincial Repertory Theatre—putting on a play a week both as director and actor—to writing and making documentary films for the National Film Board in Canada and the U.K. He has edited and written television scripts for a number of popular British series including 'Softly-Softly' and 'United'.

Together they are the authors of some record-breaking TV dramas: the 'Doomwatch' series which explored some of the terrifying tragedies that modern science could engender, and the long-running science-fiction series, 'Dr Who', for which they created those space-age monsters the Cybermen.

CHAPTER ONE

THE HUGE BULK of Flight 697 loomed out of the industrial murk to the north-east of Paris and, as the port wing of the great jumbo jet dipped, slanting beams of bright sunlight swept like spotlights down the tightly packed passenger compartment and across the laps of Mrs Oates and her three children. The sudden brightness jerked her out of a doze and she looked up sleepily at the rows of heads in front of her and then down at the jumble of white plastic cups and knives on the seat tables folded down in front of her children. Only another hour, she thought, then I'll be able to get a good wash and a decent cup of tea. For a moment she tried to rub away the stiffness in her neck until the subdued rumble of the engines and the relaxed chatter of the other passengers gradually lulled her back into sleep. As her eyes closed, she was totally unaware that the lives of her family and the three hundred and seventy mothers and children packed into the charter plane en route from Majorca to Heathrow, London, were moving inexorably into the balance. For the next one hundred and twenty seconds her survival lay in the hands of a twenty-eight-year-old man.

The man was one of eight operators seated at a complex of multi-coloured instrument consoles in a long underground room near Deal on the south coast of England. The room, in contrast to the bright aircraft interior, was in almost total darkness except for small pools of light picking out each man and his set of console panels. Stretching along the entire wall in front of them was a curved, illuminated screen showing a bright green Mercator projection of Great Britain and the North of Europe. The outlines of the map shimmered. Criss-crossing the outlines of the land masses was a maze of curved blue lines and along each line a deep ruby spot moved slowly. There was a background hum of ventilating fans and in the air there was a faint smell of hot electrical machinery and the tarry hessian smell of new carpet.

The room housed the newly opened control room of ACE or

Air Control Europe where each and every civil aircraft movement over Britain and Northern Europe was monitored and controlled. Flight 697 was under the guidance of a computer complex controlled by twenty-eight-year-old operator number two.

Dr Alexander Mawn fingered the orange press badge on his jacket lapel uneasily and edged clear of a small knot of journalists to get a clearer view of the operation. He was entirely preoccupied with the complex patterns of red and green signals appearing and disappearing in rapid succession on the consoles in front of the operators and paid no attention to a small moving red light which had appeared on the extreme left of the screen. Neither did he particularly notice at that moment, that operator number two's behaviour was any different from the other seven. As he watched the kaleidoscope of colour patterns scurrying over the banks of indicators, he began to visualize the logical designs behind them. He concluded that of all the similar systems he had examined that year, the ACE network carried the highest potential hazard from overload.

The atmosphere in the control room was quiet and controlled and if there was any sign of strain on the face of Cartland, Deputy Air Traffic Control Officer, standing silently behind the operators, it was not due to the complexity of the multi-million dollar installation under his direction, but to the two television cameras on each side of him and the presence of Sheldon Peters, probably the most exposed television face in England. Cartland tried to listen to Peters's commentary with one ear and at the same time made an effort to keep an eye on the movements on the wall map. He was only able to pick up isolated phrases.

'. . . through that wall is one of the most advanced computers in the world and it's logging all the flight paths of every aircraft as they are transmitted from airports all over Europe. When it's sorted them out, it puts them up as those blue lines and red spots you can see on the screen. The whole system was built by the Gelder Consortium and must be the most modern and up-to-date system in the world. In fact, Mr Brian Gelder is here watching it all. . . .'

One camera swung out to a slight, dark-haired man, standing beside Cartland.

Despite the air-conditioned chill of the room, Gelder wore a lightweight shirt and a jacket slung casually around his shoulders. He smiled easily as the camera focused in on him.

'. . . so the ACE system,' Peters continued, 'has entirely dispensed with any routine voice communication between pilot and ground control and so cutting down the risk of faulty communication. . . .'

Alexander Mawn picked up the red spot now moving in over the map boundary. He quickly did some mental arithmetic. Too fast for a civil jet, much too fast, he thought, must be a military plane. . . .

Flight Lieutenant James Hodgson hunched down in the cramped cockpit of the Dassault Mirage six, trying to ease the tension in his limbs. Familiarization runs were always nerve-racking and he was already looking forward to a large scotch in the mess back at Abingdon. He looked down at the flight plan on his knee pad, checked the next procedure and pushed the twin throttle quadrants forward. Immediately the giant vacuum cleaner noise from the engines behind him swooped up in pitch and the seat pushed with massive force into the small of his back. Looking downwards he could see the Dover cliffs slide away behind him and, as he eased the controls to the right, he winced at the sickening G force as it tried to drag his body downwards to the left. He checked the Course Deviation, Turn and Bank indication and Mach reading which had already climbed to 1.8, a speed which would have enabled him to overtake a rifle bullet at more than four hundred miles an hour.

Mawn glanced anxiously at control officer Cartland, but he had already seen the intruding ruby light. He pressed a button on a small panel beside him and a light flashed on the control panel in front of operator two. The backs of the other operators were straightening.

The light on number two's panel flashed again and Mawn caught Cartland's impatient glance at the operator. There was sweat on the back of the man's neck and, as his hand came into view, Mawn saw that it had a coarse tremor more like the jerky movements of an old man. Mawn moved closer, the light had illuminated the instruction: 'Manual over-ride'. Operator two pressed a square yellow button, the instruction winked out and the remaining light signals abruptly changed into a new pattern.

On the screen the red light was visibly converging on another and Peters was directing a camera towards the screen while attempting to explain the situation, caught by the sudden tension that had gripped the room.

'. . . It's almost certainly an Air Force plane. In this situation the computer is controlled directly by the operator in charge of this sector. . . .'

In front of operator two, a row of five coloured signals had appeared—green, red, red, green, red on the computer readout screen. As Mawn watched the operator again lifted his hand, his arm seemed to move stiffly as he punched out the instruction that was to be relayed directly to the Flight 697 giving it an immediate change of course.

Green, red, green, red, red, green. Mawn caught his breath, surely that was wrong. Incredibly the simple code had been misread by the operator.

Captain Andrews on Flight 697 glanced at the incoming signal from operator two on a small screen set between the banks of dials in front of him. It stated in bright green letters: 'Starboard two four zero.' He moved the controls until the signal went out.

On the control room screen the red blips moved closer on a collision course that was now clear to everyone in the suddenly hushed room. Even Peters was silent, waiting for the red spot that was Flight 697 to break away on its new course.

Abruptly a shrill repeating tone sounded in front of both operator two and Cartland's desk and a panel flashed: 'Error function positive.' 'Error function positive.'

Operator number two was now visibly shaking, his hands tightly clenched on the console.

Again the row of colours flashed up: 'Green, red, red, green, red.' Again the operator's hand moved up to the controls, the fingers searching clumsily. 'Green, red, red,' the man hesitated, his left hand brushing away the sweat coursing down his brow. As Mawn watched incredulously, he punched up 'red, green'.

The shrill tone sounded again. With a horrified glance at the screen where the two spots were now almost together, Cartland slammed down a fluorescent orange switch and seized a microphone.

'Voice over-ride, voice over-ride.' His voice was thin, high, like a whiplash in the confined room. '697, 697, do you read, aircraft converging, starboard level—north seven five one. You should see it. Over.'

On the flight deck of Flight 697, Captain Andrews, jerked into sudden attention by the voice, peered ahead through the blue tinted screen. The co-pilot shaded his eyes against the sun. They both picked up the thin vapour trail of the Mirage streaking towards them.

'There it is, fighter, port high!' Both men simultaneously grasped their control columns and pulled them hard over.

Flight Lieutenant Hodgson looked up from the instruments. The giant wheeling shape of the jumbo almost filled the sky. Over or under, left or right?

In the last few seconds, he registered the swing of the giant plane downwards and wrenched the control column back into his stomach. As the Mirage shot upwards, he felt the anti-G air roaring into his pressure suit. His vision ebbed as blood drained from his brain like mercury, suddenly weighing six times the normal.

Flight 697 lurched into a nearly vertical bank and the scene inside the flight deck abruptly changed from relaxed anticipation to horror. A torrent of white plastic cups and trays cascaded into the aisles followed by a jumbled struggling mass of screaming women and children desperately grabbing for support as their world turned round. There was a metallic resonant grating from the grossly over-stressed air frame and for a moment the giant plane seemed suspended from one wing with its massive weight holding it in that position. There was a sudden deafening explosion from the shock wave of the Mirage as it blasted past overhead, then the cabin began slowly to right itself.

Mrs Oates, weeping and half crushed under a mass of struggling passengers, began desperately to pull herself clear and to search for her children in the screaming hysterical shambles around her. Over a bulkhead, the 'fasten your seat belts' sign lit up.

*　　*　　*

151

Flight Lieutenant Hodgson's vision gradually returned through red and then grey as he pushed the control column forwards to lessen the almost vertical climb of the Mirage and to relieve his body from the near intolerable stress.

Inside the control room, tension suddenly broke as the ruby lights converged into one and then parted again. A hubbub of voices broke out. Then, from speakers overhead, came the sudden roar of Captain Andrews's voice: 'ACE control, do you hear! What in Christ's name was that? We nearly . . .'

Abruptly Cartland cut the pilot's voice off. The journalists clustered round and Peters thrust his hand microphone towards the distraught controller. 'Exactly what happened, Mr Cartland?' Notebooks were out and ball points raised. The controller fought himself into calmness: 'It looked more dramatic than it really was—the red blips on the screen are enormously magnified—there was no danger. . . .' Gelder had joined the two men. '. . . there was a considerable safety margin between the two planes. . . .'

Peters broke in: 'The pilot didn't think so, Mr Cartland!'

Mawn was pushing his way towards Peters. Cartland glanced up at the screen, the two spots were diverging again. His voice showed visible relief: 'As you can see, Flight 697 is now cleared as far as the Kent coast and . . .'

'Just how close was it?' Peters held the microphone expectantly. 'Was it an official near-miss?'

'Can't say yet,' Cartland replied. 'We'll have to examine the tape logs first.'

'I am sure there was no danger, Mr Cartland had the situation well under control.' Heads turned to Brian Gelder. 'In fact now you've all seen the flexibility of the system—there was a need to over-ride the computer and everything functioned entirely as it should have done.'

'You can honestly claim there was no danger?' Peters persisted.

Gelder paused, but before he could speak, the tall figure of Mawn appeared in front of the camera. 'No danger! You could hear the noise of the other plane in the pilot's intercom. That wasn't a near miss—it was damn nearly a disaster!'

Cartland moved forward to usher Mawn away, but he angrily shrugged him away. Peters moved forward with the microphone: 'No, let him speak, who are you please?'

'My name's Mawn—Alexander Mawn.'

Peters glanced at Mawn's lapel press label. 'Which paper do you represent?'

Mawn ignored the question. 'I'm in computing science at Plymouth University and I'm interested in the failure rate of machines like that one.' He pointed. 'I've a lot of evidence now that the basic design is faulty and has got to fail sooner or later and it just did!'

'Why must it be the computer?' Peters demanded. 'There are eight men working it.'

'It involves both. The faults in the man-machine interface— the relationship between the computer and the operator. It's a growing threat—the Caird Oil Company and the American N.A.L.A. computers, they're all having the same problem.'

The clamour of voices from the listening journalists rose to a tumult of questions. Cartland moved forward, beckoning to security guards who had entered the long room. 'I must ask you all to go now, you're making work impossible.'

Outside in the corridor Mawn felt a touch on his arm. Peters was smiling. 'You'd better take cover for a few days.'

'How's that?'

'When that programme goes out tonight in front of X million people, they will see you accuse a multi-national company of almost killing a plane full of people. If you're right, the public will make you a super hero. If you're wrong, the Gelder people will have you in court.' He gestured not to reply as Gelder caught up with them, his face pale with anger: 'You're not going to use any of that?'

Peters smiled: 'I have to.'

'It was completely slanderous.'

'Mr Gelder,' Peters continued. 'Whether you like it or not, that whole episode is going to be in the late editions of the evening papers and all over the national dailies tomorrow, so it will go out on my programme tonight. If you'd like to come to the studios, you're welcome to oppose it.'

Gelder turned on his heels and was gone. Peters turned to Mawn: 'You know my programme "Nightstyle"?' Mawn nodded. 'I want you to come on it and say what you said today.'

Mawn paused: 'Yes, I will, it happens to be the truth.'

'Good, that's fixed.' Peters's face grew serious. 'But I'd be a bit careful if I were you.' Mawn looked puzzled. 'You've stamped on some fairly big toes today.'

Mawn looked through the side window of his car at the dark silhouettes of the trees and hedges sliding past. In his mind he compared their quiet composure with the unending stridor of the past forty-eight hours. First there had been crowds of reporters in the hotel lobby, then an urgent demand for a radio interview, followed by a two-minute interview on Sheldon Peters's 'Nightstyle' programme, where he had simply repeated what he had said at the ACE centre. The newspaper headlines had varied between the relative sobriety of *The Times* which had given one inch of column space under a headline: 'Scientist Accuses Major Consortium of Shoddy Control Systems' to the two-inch banners of the *Clarion;* alongside a picture of the passengers: 'Did these families miss death by inches?'

He looked at the dashboard clock. Tina Hale should be at home by now. He decided to ring her from a callbox in the next village to see how the experiment was going. He reflected that a few days' solid laboratory bench-work should cure his over stimulated nerves.

Tina Hale sat feet up in front of the television set and realized she was only half watching the screen. In the back of her mind there was a nagging, hollow anxious tug of something forgotten. She got up, flicked off the set, swallowed the remains of a gin and stared at the dwindling spot of light, trying to search for the cause of the anxiety. Laundry—no, phone Richard about the new ordering system at the lab—no, the lab! the experiment! —something in the experiment—something not complete.

She tried hard to recall Dr Mawn's instructions and began almost immediately to wish she worked for a more reasonable boss. He had poked his head round the laboratory door and rapped out a few terse sentences and then disappeared without even waiting for her reply. She reflected that laboratory technicians were in short supply and that there were plenty of other jobs . . . perhaps one of these days. . . .

The laboratories had been built inside the shell of an old Victorian vicarage set on the edge of the campus. A three storey grey-stone folly with a carved stone porch and garishly coloured stained glass windows, it was in almost satirical contrast to the tidy anonymity of the new University blocks. It was not Mawn's first choice for a new computing science department, but it had the one great advantage that it was a long way from the administration building and the watchful eye of the Dean of Science. In any case, he had been given no choice.

The car drew up quietly in the lane outside and a thick-set man of medium height got out. He eased the door closed and, for perhaps two minutes, stood absolutely still beside the car. Finally he walked through the open gate, treading only on the grass.

. . . Reaction temperature—the condensation columns! Tina Hale quickly opened a loose-leaf folder and started to thumb through a list of physical constants. Reaction temperature—fluor —hydro—carbons—tetrafluorethylene bromide 118 to 123° centigrade. With a dull hammer of real fear she remembered the connections Richard had made between the columns. They were polythene. Polythene softens at 80! She snapped the book shut and began to dress quickly.

The man was standing beside a large rhododendron bush holding a small case and looking up at a first floor window on the side of the house. He stood listening, sensing the air like an animal and then, began to climb up on to the flat roof of an outbuilding beneath the window. Supporting himself on the sill with one hand, with the other he pulled out a small pen-torch and ran the beam round the edge of the window. It was a sash window divided transversely into two halves and bolted by a central lever.

He attached a short thin blade of metal to the end of a threaded rod about eighteen inches long, put one end of the rod against the edge of the window frame and slid the metal blade up into the gap between the two window halves. With a short ratchet lever he began to turn a nut forcing the metal blade along the threaded rod until it moved the central lever bolt of the window. Finally it clicked over parallel with the window frame. He slid the lower half of the window silently upwards and eased himself into a small office room, then reached out for the case on the sill and pulled it in. The office door was open. He picked out the name: 'Doctor A. Mawn' printed in Dymotape on the outside.

Sweeping the thin probe of the pen-torch ahead of him and carefully keeping it below window level, he began to search through the building methodically.

After a while, he opened one file labelled: 'Barfield figures' and laid out its typed contents on separate sheets. Then, one by one, he fed the sheets through a slit in a small oblong metal box a little larger than a pencil case. After about six seconds, the sheets emerged from a slit in the opposite side of the box. Attached to each sheet was a transparent plastic film. On the film was a perfect copy of the words on the typed sheet.

As the headlights of the car picked out the signboard: 'Kramer Computing Science Laboratories', Tina saw the dark shape of the car in the lane as she turned into the forecourt. The tyres crunched loudly on the gravel.

The man jerked up at the sound, clicked off the torch and felt his way quickly to the door. He put the copies back into his case, closed it gently and retraced his way up to the first floor. . . .

Tina walked up the wide stone steps, turned the heavy dead-lock and pushed the great oak door open. The noise echoed in the front hall. . . .

The man darted quickly into a laboratory and crouched down behind a bench. He glanced up apprehensively at the equipment surrounding him. There was a maze of interconnected glassware connected to blocks of electronic apparatus. Each unit glowed softly in the darkness with a single neon eye. One tube led past a long dark green metal box. On the box was a hastily scrawled warning: 'Danger. Laser light.' From a small aperture at one end of the tube a coruscating pencil beam of light reflected an intense ruby glow from the ceiling. He could feel the warmth from the heating mantles round the flasks as he crouched down out of sight. There were faint clicking sounds as the equipment heated and cooled. A motor whined abruptly and a pen-trace recorder spewed out a length of squared paper covered in a series of irregular traces. He flicked round anxiously as a solenoid-operated tap clacked and buzzed. A large flask began to drain its contents automatically into a tall vertical condenser column.

Tina opened the door and switched on the lights. For a moment, the overhead fluorescent tubes flickered and then struck, flooding the room with light. The man screwed up his eyes in the glare and hunched down against the wall. Tina began to examine each connection between the complex leashes of glassware, turned off a glass tap isolating one segment of the condensation column and cut away a plastic tube connecting two convoluted tubes with a razor blade. From a drawer, she withdrew a coil of milky white tubing, severed a short length and reconnected the open ends of the glass tubes. She checked through the connections of the experiment and compared them with a rough flow chart scrawled on a nearby blackboard. Finally she began to realign the gas laser, altering its setting by turning heavy knurled controls on its base mounting. Then she hesitated for a moment, opened a drawer and took out a pair of heavy goggles with dark glass filters, put them on and then unscrewed a panel on the side of the laser tube. Immediately the room was flooded with a grainy red fire, which sparkled off all the metal fitments. She replaced the panel loosely.

A telephone sounded harshly, echoing through the deserted building. A red light flashed intermittently over the door. She picked up an extension attached to an amplifier.

'Kramer lab.'

'Tina! That you?' Mawn's voice boomed out on the speaker, clear and immediate. 'I tried to get you at home. All well?'

'Yes, thank you, Doctor.'

'I'm at Bacton, on my way home. I'll drop in for a few minutes.'

'All right, Doctor, I'll wait for you here, goodbye.' The man raised his head slightly. She hung up and took a mirror out of her handbag surveying her face.

The man stretched a cramped leg and moved a cable lying on the floor behind him. The cable flicked a jack plug from the side of the pen-recorder. Immediately a buzzer sounded angrily and the paper tape began to pour out of the recorder in an uncontrolled stream.

Tina whipped round gasping at the noise and saw the man's head bobbing above the bench. Stiff with fear, she inched backwards towards the door, fumbling behind her for the extension phone, her eyes fixed on the man.

'What are you doing? Who are you?' Her voice was a constricted whisper. He stood up, and they faced each other, poised.

157

Suddenly the man lurched past the apparatus making for the door, his hand struck the long green laser tube and its nozzle broke away from the optical bench and swung round towards him. The deadly red pencil of light slashed round the room like a solid red-hot bar and raked his face.

The beam lanced into one eye and, like a wounded animal, he screamed and staggered along the bench blundering through the complex of tubes, shattering flasks and sweeping electronic apparatus to the floor. Tina screamed and sprang forward trying to save the tottering remains of the experiment as the man staggered by her through the door and was gone.

Trembling and weeping, she knelt beside the shattered experiment ineffectually trying to rearrange the broken tubes. Suddenly her breath caught in her throat and she clutched her mouth and tried to scramble to her feet. Blindly she grabbed for the edge of the bench and tried to drag herself up but her head started to arch backwards then her neck and finally the whole of her body curved into a grotesque spring bow and crashed down on to the broken apparatus. Above her body the angry red pencil of the laser beam swung round in the swirling fumes and came to rest on the side of a black plastic screen.

Mawn swung the car along, sensing rather than seeing the dark winding contours of the lanes ahead. The night was clear and starlit and he drove with both windows down enjoying the bland rush of the country air over his face.

About two miles away from the laboratory, he slowed before the last turn. Abruptly, the empty lane was filled with the glare of headlights and a car bucketed round the corner, tyres squealing. Mawn jammed on the brakes and swung into the hedge. The other driver also braked and slewed sideways, offside wheels churning along the grass verge. In the beam of his headlights Mawn caught a momentary glimpse of a pale startled face with a gloved hand holding a handkerchief over one eye.

The driver double-declutched, straightened up and blasted off down the road behind him. Mawn gingerly backed his car out of the hedge and drove on. With almost clinical detachment, he felt the adrenalin surge through his body, his face turning cold.

He recognized Tina Hale's car but, as he got to the front door and put his key into the lock, it swung open. He called out, switched the stair lights on and then saw the thin white fumes curling down through the banisters into the hall. With a handkerchief against his nose, he tore up the stairs and into the laboratory.

The pen recorder was still ejecting rolled paper which had collected in a folded pile on the floor. Under the pile he saw an arm. Tearing the paper aside, he picked up Tina's body and staggered out of the room and down the stairs coughing and retching. Finally he laid her gently down on the steps outside the front door and put his ear down to her mouth. For about half a minute he knelt still, listening for any sign of respiration, then quickly pulled her jaw down and applied his mouth to hers breathing into her lungs, taking a deep breath and repeating the action rhythmically. He kept the cycle going and felt with one hand for the pulse in her neck.

Even in the light coming through the open doorway he could see her face putty white. He got up, raced into the hallway and dialled emergency then leapt up the stairs back into the laboratory. He looked quickly round through the fumes only half registering the red pencil of light from the laser, made certain there was no one else in the room and then ran back down the stairs and back to Tina.

In the laboratory, the black plastic screen was beginning to soften and run under the fiery onslaught of the laser.

Mawn was still applying mouth to mouth resuscitation when the ambulance arrived. A uniformed attendant put his hand gently on Mawn's shoulder: 'We'll take her now, sir, if you don't mind.'

The two men lifted Tina's body on to a cloth stretcher and strapped it on to a frame inside the ambulance. One of them pulled her head back and took down a mask attached to a portable respirator—putting it over her mouth—and switched on the gas flow from a cylinder. The other watched in silence. Their eyes met.

In the fume-laden laboratory, the black plastic was bubbling and running down on to the bench. Smoke began to curl up, followed by a small yellow flame. The flame caught the edge of a bunch of notes clipped on to the edge of a shelf above. The paper flared,

159

flames licked round the bottles on the shelf. A bottle cracked and broke.

Outside, the two men swung round at the muffled thump of the explosion. A window glowed bright orange, then with a succession of blasts the glass flew out and great tongues of flames billowed and licked hungrily at the eaves of the old house.

Mawn was on his feet as the glass showered down over him. He rushed back into the hall and groped his way up the stairs. Dense black clouds of smoke were pouring along the upstairs corridor and down over the hall. Pulling a foam extinguisher off the wall, he ducked down into the fumes, feeling his way along the corridor wall towards the laboratory. Gradually, as he stumbled through the murk, his movements began to weaken and he staggered, dropped the extinguisher and dropped to his knees. Somewhere behind him he could hear the discordant cry of a fire-engine. He turned and crawled painfully back along the corridor towards the head of the stairs and dragged himself over the edge and began to flop down like a fish out of water. Dimly he felt rough hands grab his legs and shoulders.

Somebody was gently slapping his cheek: 'Hello there—back with us are you?'

He felt cold air in his throat. There were flashing blue lights and men shouting, unloading ladders and paying out rolls of hose. He tried to get to his feet.

The attendant put a restraining hand on his shoulder: 'It's all under control now. Nothing you can do, sir.'

Mawn spoke hoarsely: 'We've got to get the files out—years of work—we've got to get them out.'

'The fire boys will save all they can, sir, don't you worry.'

'Tina Hale, where is she?'

'They've taken her off to the Plymouth General, sir.'

'How is she—is she all right?'

The man exchanged a glance with his companion: 'We'll get you off there now, sir, if you don't mind.'

The two men supported Mawn over to a waiting police car, eased him down into the back seat and closed the door. The uniformed deputy fire chief turned to the two men: 'Have to make a special on this one.'

'How's that?'

'Christ! You should have seen what they've got upstairs. All the flammables stacked over the electric stuff. They must have broken every regulation in the book. Could be manslaughter.'

The glow of the fire reflected on Mawn slumped back in the car, his eyes closed.

'Mild bronchitis from the fumes and a first degree burn on his forearm, nothing more. . . .' The words filtered dimly into Mawn's mind. He struggled against an overwhelming torpor and then listened again, keeping his eyes closed. Another voice with a characteristic inflexion—quiet, meticulous: 'Poor old chap—must be taking it very hard.' The Dean of Science! His nightmare was true. Tina Hale was dead. He seemed to have known for hours, as though the news had filtered through to his subconscious while he was asleep. He opened his eyes cautiously.

He saw a white hospital counterpane, sunlight streaming through a high window and a doctor with an array of pens and a chromium torch sticking out of his white coat pocket. Keith, the Dean of Science, stood at the end of the bed, his red, regency face rounded off like an avocado.

His tongue was dry and gummed to the roof of his mouth and he found it difficult to raise his head. The doctor spoke breezily: 'Good morning—you've got a visitor.' He watched Mawn struggling with his senses. 'It's almost 15.30, you've been having a splendid nap. In case you're wondering where you are, my name's Wilkinson and you're in the Plymouth General Hospital.'

Keith put both hands on the bedrail. The note of solicitude in his voice was almost perfect: 'Alex, what a ghastly business. I'm really so sorry. Miss Hale was dead on arrival here.'

Mawn took a long drink from a bedside water glass. His voice rasped: 'Is there anything left?'

'Oh, yes indeed. It was mainly confined to the central lab and your office, they managed to get it under control quite quickly. But I am afraid the roof structure is weakened, at least so they tell me.'

'What about all the files and the records?'

The Dean's face took on a well-modulated gravity. 'There's considerable loss, Alex—considerable loss I'm sorry to say . . .'

'Are they all burnt?'

'I am not sure, but your secretary's office was badly affect——'

'All that work!' Mawn cried out.

'Alex, we do have a more serious problem—I—er—want to have a word before the—the police do. . . .'

Mawn felt his heart leap: 'Police?'

'Yes, Alex. I really don't want to worry you with it now but—well the police have made a very clear suggestion.'

'What do you mean?'

'They think that you hadn't really adhered to the fire regulations properly. Of course I told them they were wrong, that the most stringent care is always taken. . . .'

Mawn met the protuberant eyes, they were saying: see where your carelessness has got us now! He gathered speed. 'To be frank, Alex, I'm worried. As you well know, we've given you a completely free hand with your department—indeed you've had a great deal of encouragement throughout. You see this is all bound to reflect very badly. I can't help. . . .'

'Just what is left?' Mawn sat up abruptly cutting the Dean off in mid-flight.

'I'm not sure.'

'Haven't you been there yet?'

'Well no, I haven't really had time, but . . .'

'Jesus!' Mawn threw back the bedclothes and got out of bed unsteadily. He put his hand out to the bedside table for support but it rolled back on castors against the wall. He almost fell.

'For goodness' sake, man!' The doctor reached forward.

Mawn brushed past him and began to take his own clothes from a chair.

'Alex, this is most unwise.' The Dean put his hand out in restraint.

'I'm all right.' He winced as he hit the back of his bandaged hand against the chair. 'I'm going to the lab.'

'What am I going to tell the police?' The Dean's voice was strained and petulant. 'I told them you were *here*.'

'Well they can find me at the lab. That's where they should be anyway, not sniffing round the fire regulations.'

'What do you mean?'

Mawn's voice was muffled as he pulled a polo-necked sweater down over his head: 'There's something bloody odd about that fire—if you want it straight I think it was started deliberately.'

'The police didn't mention anything. What are you talking about? Have you any proof?'

'Not yet.' Mawn paused by the door. 'But I tell you, when I get it I shall expect co-operation from the University. Whoever it was is a murderer. He killed Miss Hale.'

'If you want to discharge yourself you'll have to sign the waiver form.' Dr Wilkinson broke in after a glance at Keith.

'You sign it.' The door slammed and Mawn was gone.

Wilkinson spread his hands: 'I can't hold him against his will you know.'

Keith shook his head angrily: 'Really the most intemperate man. I have to put up with a great deal. The television business was bad enough . . .'

'Television?' Wilkinson looked puzzled, but Keith didn't reply and started to lead the way out of the ward.

Firemen were still working inside the gutted house, bringing out burnt and twisted laboratory equipment. Mawn quickly established his credentials with a bored police constable standing by the front door and walked in.

It was like walking into the rib-cage of a giant. One side of the building was a bare charred framework with the edges of the upper floor tilting down at an angle from the outside wall. One of the laboratory benches was perched precariously on the end ready to slide off down into the hallway below.

Mawn clambered over the charred joists and beams and found the door leading down to the basement computer room.

At the bottom of the stairs he saw that emergency lighting had already been rigged and some men were working on the units of the computer. For a moment he thought that they were there on behalf of the University, to move the machine to new premises. Then he caught sight of Duckett, the computer firm's trouble-shooter.

'Bad business, Doctor.' He said as Mawn approached. 'Still, could be worse. Fire didn't reach this computer luckily.'

'You mean it's all right?'

'This part is. I've checked as much as I can. O.K. as far as I can see.'

'Thank God for something!' Mawn's relief must have been evident and the release from tension made him sway a little.

'Here, take it easy.' Duckett caught his arm.

'I'm O.K.'

Duckett nodded and turned away a little uneasily.

'Anyway, what're you doing here?'

'Ah, well you see, Doctor,' he saw Mawn's pallor and hesitated, 'we've been asked to remove it—much as we can anyway.'

'Remove it! On whose authority?'

'Came directly from the Dean, I understand.'

Mawn understood. The return of the computer would finally draw his teeth. It would all be neatly minuted at an emergency meeting of the Academic Board. He imagined the Dean at the meeting: 'Of course the building is quite unsound—we couldn't conceivably leave all that equipment there, the whole place might collapse—I'm sure Doctor Mawn would approve if he were here.'

He looked around sadly at the twisted and blackened racks of tapes and files. Years of hard, hard work and now what?

'Mr Mawn?' A policeman was standing at the bottom of the stairs shielding his eyes against the light from the naked bulbs.

'Mr Mawn? There's a man upstairs asking for you.'

Mawn turned and slowly made his way up the stairs.

After the sour acridity of burnt wood, the fresh air outside was a benediction. He screwed his eyes against the dazzle of the sun and saw Sheldon Peters standing by his car.

CHAPTER TWO

PETERS WAVED MAWN IN through the open door. Mawn followed down a thickly carpeted corridor opening on to a living-room which blazed at him like a sun.

It had all the signs of a carefully-arranged stage set. The walls were hung with brown linen panels leading down to dimpled black leather cushions set informally around the floor. In the centre, stood a low plate-glass table, with chromium frame, and hung on the cloth walls were large abstract paintings chosen more for the current vogue of the artist than their quality. A European Television Award statue shone under its own light in a small alcove. The floor was of soft oatmeal-coloured carpet. One side of the room was hung with heavy curtain drapes, part surrounding a baby grand piano. Mawn looked about with an increasing sense of incredulity. A place to dazzle, he thought, living in it would be like trying to be comfortable in an hotel lounge.

As his eyes adjusted to the glare, he became aware of a tall, slim girl standing by a table. 'Alex, meet a friend of mine,' Peters said. 'Marcia Scott, Alex Mawn.' Her grasp was firm and he saw cool, green eyes appraising him, framed by full black hair swept evenly back. He had an immediate impression of probing intelligence. He put her age at a little over thirty.

Peters waited until they were settled into soft white leather arm-chairs, then turned to Marcia: 'You know the mess Alex has got into?' She nodded. 'Well, I've got an idea, I'll put it up—just to see what you do with it. Briefly, I think Alex is the first English victim of the environmental backlash. First there was Nader in the States when that motor corporation tried to nail him; now we've got the Japanese environmentalist Nickimodo— he has to ride about in a bullet-proof car, not because of ordinary people, but because of threats from large corporations. Now Alex goes and accuses three large consortia of incompetent production, his lab gets burnt down and an assistant dies.'

'O.K., so big business is very nasty and protective, but that doesn't make a case.' Her voice was low-pitched and she spoke with a mild Boston inflexion.

'Maybe not,' Peters continued, 'but—and here I declare myself —it'll make a tremendously powerful piece for my next "Nightstyle" programme.'

Marcia put her drink down and laughed: 'Shel—you're a real media pro, if you don't have a case—make one, is that it?'

Peters saw Mawn give a tired, wary glance at the American woman and anticipated his curiosity. 'Marcia and I have known each other for years—reason why I got you both together is that I think you've a common interest. . . .'

'Which will lead to an even better TV show!' Marcia drawled.

Peters smiled: 'Give it a rest, love.' Then to Mawn, 'Marcia is a research psychologist and she's been doing some performance tests on certain groups of workers here in England. Now I felt when you went off on TV at the air control place there might be a common thread. Alex, are you too tired to go over it again—for Marcia?'

'Don't you think maybe some other time?' Marcia looked anxiously at the large Englishman, his head sunk on his chest in near exhaustion, his coat still blackened from his search in the ruins of the laboratory.

Mawn raised his head: 'No, I asked Peters to get moving. I'd much rather talk than think right now.'

He drained his glass and watched Peters refill it before continuing: 'I'll try and explain—if it just seems too bloody obvious to you, then shut me up. I've been interested in the man-machine interface, that's just a long-winded way of describing what happens when a human being operates a machine. If you like, the interface of a typist is what goes on between her fingers and the keys she hits. Why she makes mistakes there and so on.

'Well, my work has been around human operators and complex machines like computer . . .'

'And aircraft control systems!' Peters interposed. 'By the way, how *did* you get your press badge?'

Mawn waved his drink: 'Dead simple. A reporter I go drinking with at Plymouth. He's on the local rag. I wanted to see the system at first hand. I borrowed his, that's all. Anyhow, I've been gathering a lot of data about mistakes which are made between operators and control machines—it's absolutely horrifying. There's an information jam across it. Start with the abacus. The operator slaps his beads around and does very quick arithmetic. If he makes a mistake he can see the whole guts of his machine in front of him—just beads on wires—so he can see the mistake and put it right.

'Now, we make ourselves computers and do massive sums very, very quickly. Sums which we couldn't even begin to do with our heads however long or hard we tried—interrelation of complex variables for example—if the machine goes wrong—we probably *can* put it right—but it takes a very long time. The point is we can't *see* the source of the error like the beads. . . .'

'But you can find it,' Marcia intervened.

'Yes, we can, but that was in the first and second generation machines. Now your hard technologist is a greedy bastard. He says to himself—my last machine did its sums in X seconds, now I can make it do them in half of X seconds—so he does it—not because anyone really needs it—but because it will be a very good selling point. So he has to develop more efficient and much smaller computing elements. First we had the monolith blocks, now micro-monolith and so on . . .

'. . . but that's not enough by itself. The designer's got to think up new ways of increasing his machine's performance—just to keep ahead of the field—so he takes a look at the human brain to see whether it has any little tricks he can copy and he finds it can learn. So he starts to make circuits in his machine so the machine can learn—that is improve its future performance as a result of past experience.'

'All of which is a good thing, surely?' Peters interjected.

'Yes, but there's a snag—this search for ultimate performance has a cost in reliability. Everyone's madly squeezing the last ounce of work from their circuits and so they start to take risks.'

'What kind of risks?' Peters asked.

'I've done quite a bit of work on this,' Mawn went on. 'Putting it at its simplest there are conditions where one error makes two, two makes four and so on. Sometimes it's even more severe and it can go two, six, eleven, etc.'

'A sort of mechanical brainstorm,' Marcia said.

'Yes, that's it. We're getting so incredibly lazy as a species we give more and more of our functions over to the tinware—we no longer worry about the fact that we're taking more and more materials out of the earth—things we can *never* put back—just to make computers which are so bloody smart we don't even know how they go wrong. Nobody needs the damn things except maybe hospitals—they're just an electronic phallus—a technological status symbol.'

'Oh, really, that's just polemic,' Marcia said.

Mawn continued without appearing to have heard her: '. . . So here you've got your machine wallowing in its own complexity, desperately trying to retain its efficiency in the face of its own man-built unreliability. It's a dinosaur. . . .' He gestured with the glass. 'The great lizards grew very large and they had little pea-brains. Now a small brain with slow conducting nerves can't hope to control a vast body like a dinosaur—so the poor beasts had to develop a second brain down by their backside—that still wasn't enough. They slopped about in mud and finally got extinguished, because they were uncontrollable. I've called it "the dinosaur effect".'

'That wasn't the only reason, surely?' said Peters.

167

'All right, that was simplistic, but we're making more and more complex machines and they are definitely getting more unreliable —they make faulty products and tell their human operators that the product is not faulty. . . .'

'You've no evidence of that surely?' Marcia said.

'Everything points to it, and we'll get more things like that— bound to happen—just a matter of time. Greed and opportunity that's all!'

After he had stopped speaking, there was a long silence. Peters seemed to be mentally appraising how Mawn's performance would look on his TV show, Marcia Scott was on the edge of her seat, her face flushed and excited, waiting to break in:

'Hey, that's fantastic! But excuse me, you're way off on the wrong track about the fault lying in the space *between* the operator and the machine. The fault isn't there. You see I've been working on. . . .'

Mawn, who had moodily slumped forward in his seat and did not appear to have heard a word, suddenly broke in:

'Of course!' He turned to Peters, oblivious of Marcia's annoyed stare. 'I've got it. The laser burn! We can track that bastard.' Mawn was practically hugging himself with pleasure, oblivious of the other two.

Marcia rose and Peters saw two high spots of colour on her cheeks. 'I don't think Dr Mawn is in any condition to hold a two-sided conversation right now, Shel. If you'll excuse me I'll get along.'

She walked to the door, followed by Peters. Mawn could hear him trying to soothe her down in the hall before the front door of the flat banged behind her.

'What's the matter with her?' Mawn looked up in bewilderment as Peters returned.

'She got the impression you weren't very interested in her views on the subjects.'

'Oh!' But Mawn's mind was obviously on other things. 'Can I use your phone?'

'Of course. Use the flat as your own while you're staying here. I'm seldom around anyway.'

'I'm going to phone a friend of mine, he's an eye doctor. I've an idea he can be very useful right now.'

*　　　*　　　*

To Mawn the pub exemplified all the more repellent aspects of the twentieth century. Black plastic beams complete with artificial grain ribbed the ceiling and were hung with crude brass-plated replica horse-brasses. Around the melamine-surfaced bar, groups of men in anonymous executive uniform huddled in earnest confederation around glass tankards. The walls were lined with artificially aged replicas of theatre bills and the barman himself looked theatrically Dickensian as he wheezed stertorously between customers. The smoke-hazed air smelt of hot pies, after-shave and beer.

Mawn looked down at his watch. Peter Brookman was late.

Brookman had been a last long-shot following the agony of the inquest. Mawn had spent several days trying to reconstruct the details of the laboratory layout, so he would be able to answer the coroner's questions. He had noted down the position of the experimental apparatus on the bench relative to the inflammables stored in Winchester flasks on the shelf nearby. He had also made a complete breakdown of all the wiring and electronics apparatus and talked it out with Peters at his flat. Peters had given him his spare room and was negotiating a contract with the B.B.C. on his behalf for a forthcoming television programme.

He had made his allegation about an intruder just once. The coroner—an elderly doctor—had received his statement with a stony politeness which was more insulting than a direct denial and had hinted that it was an excuse he frequently heard from people who wanted to avoid possible charges of negligence.

The police had behaved in a determined and suspicious way and had gone to considerable lengths to suggest that there might be a civil case for the University to answer.

The Dean of Science had appeared and, without overtly saying so, pointed out to the coroner that Mawn's department was separate from the main University buildings and that Mawn had been given more of the responsibility for its safety than the heads of other departments. It had been a beautifully phrased buck-passing performance, elegantly terminated by a short speech of sympathy for Mawn.

The coroner had then asked who deputized for Mawn when he was absent. He had answered that there was nobody since they all worked together as a team. The coroner then read from a copy of the University Regulations and pointed out that it clearly stated that, in the absence of a head, departments were to be officially deputized in writing.

Towards the end, it had become clear that the coroner had not been able to gather enough evidence to implicate the living so he turned to the dead.

Methodically he went through the evidence supplied by members of Mawn's department and began to construct a picture of Tina Hale as both over-worked and careless. He recalled the comments of one student who had said that she was "a sort of string and sealing wax worker" and another who called her "the artful bodger". Mawn himself knew that her slapdash methods were his own responsibility and due entirely to the overwhelming pressure he himself had created. He listened with a dull anger to the liturgy of inefficiency intoned by the coroner.

The verdict had been preceded by a long moralizing homily by the coroner about the need for increased vigilance in laboratories. The words to Mawn sounded cold and empty: 'death by misadventure'.

In the University, Mawn had suffered the full consequences of the loner. He had never troubled to keep within any particular corridors of power and had openly expressed his contempt for those who did. It was the view of many of the staff that he had been negligent with the result that the good name of the University had been tarnished. He remembered one comment overheard at the faculty club bar: '. . . nice bloke, but he's so damned erratic—too much time with his Arctic penguins I suppose—he'll catch it now: the Deanery's been looking for a chance like this for ages.'

He recalled his last conversation with Dean Keith about his personal chair which the academic board had already approved in principle. 'This sort of thing is so difficult, Alex. I really don't think we must rush things at this stage, do you?' The blue watery eyes held about as much concern as a professional assassin.

He began to think about looking for a new job. Back to the Arctic? No, never again. Television science pundit? Teaching? Medical research?

Well, first he had a job to do. He had reasoned that the man who had driven past him in the lane had held a handkerchief to one eye. Lasers burn the back of the eye and so the driver, if he was the intruder, might have retinal burns from the laser in the lab. He had contacted Peter Brookman who ran an ophthalmological department in a London teaching hospital and specialized in industrial eye injuries. He had asked whether there was any category in Brookman's records including laser burns and if so had anyone sent in any cases of laser burns to the eye within the past four weeks.

'Sorry I'm late, Alex, but one of my old ladies decided to have a bleed—lots of drama. How are you? It must be ages!'

Mawn looked up: 'Peter, good of you to come, thank you.'

'I was curious—just to see how you're doing. Saw you on the box by the way—jolly interesting—do you really believe all that rhubarb about—what was it?—your "dinosaur effect"—people not working their gadgetry properly?'

Mawn smiled: 'Yes, as a matter of fact, I do.'

'Well, all I can say is that I hope it doesn't get into my operating theatres—it's all so computerized nowadays. Can't do an ordinary common or garden cataract extraction without punching up some damn programme or other—that looks nice beer you're drinking. . . .'

'Sorry. What'll you have?'

'Half of best bitter, please.'

Mawn went over to the bar and came back with a small tankard. 'Don't want to rush you, Peter, but did you get anything out of your records?'

Brookman patted his brief-case which was lying on the bar counter between them. 'Yes, I did—three altogether. One got his burn in Edinburgh, the second is female so they're both out . . .' He opened the brief-case and took out three stiff brown envelopes labelled 'Clinical Record', '. . . and the third is—well—a possible.'

He put the envelope down on top of the brief-case. 'But we've got a little problem, Alex.'

'What's that?'

'Well you see, these are all confidential—the seventy-three Privacy Bill and all that.'

'Oh!'

Brookman put the tankard down: 'Trouble with this stuff, always puts me in mind of a piddle—where is it?'

Mawn pointed to a plush velvet curtain: 'Through there.' Brookman eased himself off the bar stool and pointed to the envelopes.

'Look after those while I'm gone, will you?' He walked towards the curtain.

Mawn scanned the notes quickly, eliminating the two Brookman had already mentioned, he opened the third envelope and read:

'TELLER, George. Age thirty-four. Heat burn to right eye. Gives only a general account of how he did it. Says he was involved in work with infra-red beam. Now he says he can't see properly and the eye is continuously watery. On examination the right eye shows some circum-limbal injection and a mild vascular reaction. *Ophthalmoscopy*: There is a small punctate lesion on the temporal side of the fovea, it extends forward into the vitreous and is typical of a coherent light (laser) burn. His story of how he got it must therefore be regarded as false. . . .'

Mawn scanned quickly through the rest of the notes and turned the page. On the back, he read: Home address: 14 Dreighton Gardens, London S.W.9. Work address: Director, Teller Intelligence Services, Pomeroy House, Edgware Road, London A41ZO.

Mawn scanned quickly down the slotted nameboard near the glass swing doors. The individually lettered titles included an accountant, a psychiatrist, a firm of insurance brokers and a dentist. He picked out 'Teller Intelligence Services'.

He looked through the glass doors at the main foyer of the building, thickly carpeted, with a long low black couch and a magazine-strewn glass table facing a long curved desk, with a small switchboard and an impersonally pretty receptionist. A medium height thick-set man in a light brown car coat was talking to her, leaning across the desk. Mawn hesitated before going in. What was he to say to this man Teller, even supposing that he was the man in question.

After leaving Brookman he had walked through the busy London streets towards the Edgware Road without a clear idea of how he would tackle him. He glanced at his watch and, almost with relief, saw that it was 17.45. Teller would surely have left his office by now.

As he glanced up the man by the desk turned for a moment and, with a shock, Mawn saw that he had a pink eye shade over one eye. His mind racing, Mawn eased back against the wall, waiting.

Finally, after what seemed to Mawn an intolerable wait, though it could hardly have been more than two minutes, the man came towards the glass doors and shouldered them open, waving back at the receptionist as he did so.

Almost involuntarily Mawn stepped forward and touched him on the arm. The man turned and, with a shock of recognition, Mawn thought he saw the face he caught sight of in his car headlights that night. Surely it was the same large, startled blue eye, the same lank strand of black hair framing a round moon face. And, to Mawn, the sense of instant recognition was mutual. The man's remaining eye seemed to register first shock then apprehension before he regained control.

'George Teller?' Mawn's voice sounded high pitched and uncertain to his ear.

'Yes?'

'My name's Doctor Mawn. I'd like to speak with you, if I may.'

'I'm sorry you've caught me on my way out—to a function. I'm late already. If you'd like to phone me.' Teller was impersonal, quick and smooth, he edged past Mawn and made for the outside doors.

'No wait!' Mawn sprang ahead of him, blocking his way. 'I must speak to you now.' He felt shaken but determined. 'It's very urgent.'

Teller looked at him coolly, almost with amusement, noting his confusion. 'Make it quick then.'

'Your eye. It looks bad. How did you damage it?'

Teller smiled: 'What is this? Professional interest, Doctor Mawn?'

'I'm not that kind of doctor. I'm a research scientist with a lab down near Plymouth,' Mawn scanned him closely, 'which was burnt down by an intruder a couple of weeks ago.'

'Really?' Teller's eye showed only a slightly puzzled impatience. 'What has this to do with me?'

'My research assistant, Tina Hale, was killed in the fire. There could be a charge of manslaughter against this intruder.'

Mawn seemed to see a slight flicker pass over the other man's face but Teller's voice was entirely steady when he replied: 'How does this concern me?'

'The intruder caught a laser beam in the eye, this leaves a very definite scar recognizable by any doctor. Attempts to pass it off as an infra-red burn won't work.'

173

Again the shadow passed over Teller's face, but he merely glanced at his watch. 'Look, I'm late. Can't we cut this short. I take it you're working up to some form of accusation?'

'Not yet. I'm just warning you to have a better story ready.' Mawn was gaining confidence, the other man seemed nervous, his hands fiddling with a bunch of car keys. 'Lasers are only found in labs.' Teller frowned: 'What exactly do you want?'

'The name of the man, or firm, who sent you.'

There was a silence for a moment, then Teller spoke abruptly: 'You don't need me, chum. You need a psychiatrist!' He gestured towards the nameboard. 'I recommend Dr Brown—you might just catch him in.' And before Mawn could stop him, he was out the doors, down the steps and walking along the street. With a sudden premonition Mawn opened the door and looked after him. Teller walked into a side road opposite, unlocked and climbed into a parked car by the long row of meters. But which car it was Mawn couldn't make out.

Then a car edged out of the line of parked vehicles and drove up to the end of the street, its side blinkers winking. Mawn shaded his eyes from the late sun and stared. There was no doubt about it now, it was a B.M.W. 2002, the same car that had so nearly driven into him in the lane.

With a new sense of purpose Mawn turned back through both sets of doors into the foyer. The pretty receptionist was standing up holding a small mirror and delicately outlining her right eye with a brown pencil.

'Sorry to trouble you but Mr Teller has asked me to make an appointment with him, this week or next.'

'Oh!' She looked slightly put out but bent down, unlocked her desk drawer and brought out an appointments book. 'Let's see.' She flicked over the pages. 'Thursday afternoon any good to you?'

'No. I'm afraid not.'

'Well, there's early Friday morning?'

'No, can't make that either.'

This time she was definitely annoyed. A buzzer sounded on the switchboard and she went over to answer it. Mawn leant over and took Teller's appointment book from the desk. He flipped back through the pages and ran his finger down the appointments between his television appearance and the fire in his lab. The first page yielded only a couple of names unfamiliar to Mawn. He turned over—there it was! Almost with a sense of incredulity he read 'Gelder—King's Head'. Brian Gelder could it be?

He flicked quickly through the pages leading up to the present date—there it was again. 'B. Gelder' this time, 'King's Head' and once more it appeared in the 13.00 column.

'Do you mind?' The girl, angry now, was back. She snatched the book out of his hands. Mawn smiled at her: 'I'm afraid Mr Teller is far too busy for me during the next couple of weeks. Perhaps you'd tell him I'll be phoning him . . . Dr Mawn's the name.'

He turned and started towards the door oblivious of the girl's irritation. As he went out he mentally dismissed Teller. Another name was recurring much too frequently—Brian Gelder.

Peters put the highly polished tray down on the glass table. Marcia noted with a wry amusement that it looked exactly like a full colour advertisement from a glossy magazine. On the tray there was a mound of hot steaming croissants, gleaming white bone-china and carefully folded blue linen napkins. It was laid for three. Peters saw the query in her expression. 'Alex Mawn's staying for a few days.' He started to pour the coffee. Marcia frowned. 'Then can I just leave the stuff I've dug out for you, I'd like to be away by the time he appears.'

Peters smiled: 'Hey, I've asked you to research a programme and work with him, that's all. Not to go to bed with the man!'

Marcia flushed slightly. 'He doesn't seem much interested in either right now. We get a ten minute monologue then wham, that's it. The great man has spoken! Sorry, I've had your provincial English academic before. It's worse than being back in grade school.'

'You don't think much of his dinosaur effect then?'

'I didn't say that. It's just his polemic I can't stomach. There certainly is something peculiar going on in the balance between man and machines—but—oh, it's just the result of years of soft student audiences—he can't see there's another side to it.'

Peters handed her a coffee cup. 'He's a pretty angry character right now. He's lost most of his records, one of his technicians is dead and his own university want to disown him as quickly as possible.'

Marcia put the cup down: 'Look, Shel, this is a tremendously real problem. You know my work. I think it very probably fits in with his, but right now he's on some private revenge kick!'

Peters got up and walked over to the door, closing it gently. 'Perhaps it will help if I tell you a little about Alex. I had one of our researchers do some digging. He's quite a man, this red-brick don of yours. To begin with he's quite a bit younger than he appears behind the beard and tweeds.' He gave a slight grimace of distaste. 'He's only just over forty.'

'You've got to be kidding!'

'Nope—forty-three he is. He runs the computing science unit at Plymouth but he's got himself obsessed with the environmental crisis. He's written dozens of articles condemning hard technology—pollution and so on. That's why he's in bad odour with his university. Apparently he spends half his time doing measurements on local pollution issues, when he should be teaching students computer logic.'

'Well, it's a good racket these days. Quickest way to grab some free publicity.'

Peters wagged his finger at her: 'That's unfair, Marcia, no, the key factor was probably his father—he was a foreman at a lead-smelting works. He got chronic lead poisoning—they were very close apparently, and poor Alex had to watch his father die in a particularly horrible way. Just to cap it all—the firm challenged that his father's condition was due to lead and paid him off—there was no worker's compensation then.'

'I see.' Marcia leant back thoughtfully. 'That does alter things. I guess it explains the chip, the need to hit big industry—O.K., Shel, but I still can't work with him. He's probably been waiting for a chance like this all of his life. I'm not going to supply data for a hatchet operation.'

'You surprise me,' Peters smiled. 'I thought I'd got through to that elusive heart of yours!'

'Really. I'd expect you to know me better by now.' Marcia looked back coolly at him.

'You still misjudge him. Apparently he also spent two years in the Antarctic. . . .' Peters broke off as Mawn appeared at the door and walked in. To Marcia his appearance had completely changed. The previous day he had appeared lumpen and awkward. Now she noticed for the first time a powerful chest under the thick pullover and heavy-set shoulders as he walked easily across and sat down by the table. He poured coffee and, with a brief nod, acknowledged Marcia's presence.

'Did you find your one-eyed burglar?' Peters asked.

Mawn helped himself to a croissant before replying: 'Yes, and he's not a burglar. He's an industrial intelligence consultant, whatever that means.'

'It can mean a great deal.' Peters went over to a line of box files on a low shelf hidden by a thick Heal's curtain and pulled one out. 'We did a programme. . . .'

'Say, a licence to break in, destroy a man's lifework and even commit murder!' Mawn's voice was not particularly loud, his face was down and he was pouring a second cup of coffee for himself with a rock steady hand but Peters and Marcia turned involuntarily towards him. For the first time Mawn took on a certain presence, the inner power of the man came through to them from the shambling provincial academic. There was a sense of strong will and an inner drive that was almost elemental.

Then the moment passed and Peters smoothly continued: 'This is research we did for a programme about a year back. There are well over twenty firms in England specializing in this particular line of business. It's a nice twentieth-century euphemism for industrial spy.'

'What, bugging, that sort of thing?' Marcia asked.

'Goes far beyond that. Nowadays they're professionals. They can plant or extract almost anything from a firm—bugs, an informer, agent-provocateurs—you name it, they'll do it—for a price.'

'Legally?'

'Oh, yes. They're completely legit—on the surface anyway. They advertise protection—"we'll help you to be secure." What they don't advertise is that they'll also do the reverse—nothing in writing and for cash. They're the technological jackals—scavenging for profit, sales figures, new processes, weaknesses in marketing structure, mistresses, kinks, the lot. People who employ them get an O.B.E. for services to industry. They occasionally get nicked.'

'Why would they want to know what I do?' Mawn asked.

Peters smiled with an effort: 'I don't know whether you're joking or not. . . .' Then, as Mawn frowned, 'Alex, you nailed three groups of industrialists in front of an audience of eight million people. You've pointed your finger at probably seven per cent of Britain's industry. You didn't give a theoretical spiel to a bunch of academics, you told some hard-headed opportunists that the way they got their bread is irresponsible and dangerous. What did you expect? Of course they're going to find out what you're doing, and how?—By putting a man on to you, what else?'

'You mean the Gelder Consortium simply held a board meeting and minuted a note to send this man Teller!' said Mawn.

There was a sudden silence. Peters's voice was quiet, almost icy: 'Who mentioned anything about Gelder?'

Mawn looked up at him. 'I was just about to. I've identified the man all right, George Teller. . . .' He described his meeting with Teller and his finding the name 'B. Gelder' in the appointments book.

'Could you substantiate any of this—in a Court of Law?' Marcia broke in.

Mawn shook his head: 'I doubt it. My word against his, the coincidence of the laser burn, the car. No. I think I've scared him pretty badly though.'

Peters, who had been pacing to and fro, turned and broke in with a new urgency in his voice: 'I think I see it now. It would be a private cash arrangement between Brian Gelder and Teller, meeting informally at that pub—what was it—the King's Head? Also I very much doubt that they meant to destroy your lab. Much more likely that they were looking to see what you had on file and how much was bluff.'

'Yes, but how could that affect Gelder?' Marcia asked.

'Depends on what Alex *has* got.' Peters looked at Alex querying. '*Had* you much?'

Mawn replied: 'It's all in ashes now.' He looked down.

'Enough, anyway, to show that he'd had a series of failures in some of his installations which would make a small business fold up altogether.'

'Gelder heads an enormous European consortium,' Peters put in. 'Their main line at the moment is building nuclear power stations. Things like the ACE control centre are relative flea-bites. He's got all the family money behind him—it's a merchant bank—so he can more or less print his own money. He's done extremely well so far, built his light-water reactors all over the world—Japan, Germany, the States, even Albania—right Alex?'

178

Mawn looked up and nodded: 'They're just taking advantage of the energy crunch and making a profit. You see—the writing is pretty much on the wall for fossil fuels—the States have run out of natural gas, the price of oil is rocketing—so every country is saying where the hell do we get power from? So they build nuclear reactors, it's obvious. What isn't obvious is that the type they're putting up is the cheapest.'

'So?' Marcia queried.

'Cheapness has got to mean reduction in safety standards,' Mawn continued. 'Nobody can successfully test the safety systems anyway, but if you cut costs—you're bound to make an untested safety system less safe. I've got information that they've had to spend so much money putting faults right in stations they have built that their profits are likely to be almost nil this year. And now they've started up this giant new station at Grim-Ness in the Orkney Islands.'

Peters was standing by the window looking out at what promised to be a fine, clear June day. He turned: 'The European Government, in their wisdom, have decided that there is going to be a chain of nuclear power stations all across Europe and that they can be contracted out to consortia like Gelder's. They are supposed to supplement our own gas-cooled reactors which, incidentally, have got a very good safety record.'

Marcia leant forward. 'So this place in—where did you say?'

'Grim-Ness—good name for it!'

'So it's a kind of test station?'

'Much more,' Mawn intervened. 'Information is that if it doesn't come in on time and they have to do the same sort of fault clearing, they may run out of cash.'

'If Mr Gelder was a poker player,' said Marcia, 'I guess it would be "go for broke", right?'

Mawn nodded. Peters slowly, almost unconsciously, began rubbing his hands together in excitement. 'So the last thing he wants is any unfavourable publicity right now, when the British Government is deciding whether or not to buy his new type of power station. It begins to make sense.' He looked over at Mawn a little ludicrously, obviously enjoying the whole situation. 'I wonder how far a thirty-five-year-old boy-wonder tycoon will go to protect his interest? Alex, we're going to have to be very, very careful with you from now on.'

179

'And we're going to carry on with the programme?' Marcia's eyes were lit up with excitement.

'Why not?'

'They're big boys, we'll have to be pretty damn sure of our facts.'

'Agreed,' said Peters. 'But a scoop like this is what makes my job bearable.'

Mawn looked from one to the other, the mercurial, very slightly effeminate commentator and the trim, almost severe New England psychologist with her hair drawn back from her handsome bony face. They both seemed to have forgotten him in the excitement of the moment and he suddenly wondered what he was getting into. The phone rang. Peters sprang to answer it.

'Hello, hello.' He was almost jocular, then his face changed as he listened, his eyebrows rose as he looked back at the other two and he sat down carefully.

'Yes, fine.' He put his hand over the receiver. 'Richard Lodge, Under-Secretary at the Ministry of Science. I've done a couple of programmes with him but he's never called here before.' He took his hand off the phone.

'Yes. Hello, Richard. Yes, I can talk, go ahead.' As Peters listened the boyish smile dwindled, his body became rigid and the others could almost feel the tension. Apart from an occasional affirmation, he did not reply. Finally, he put the receiver down and walked thoughtfully over to the window.

'Please,' said Marcia, unable to bear the suspense. 'What did he want? Was it about Alex?'

Peters nodded: 'Yes, in the nicest possible way he suggested that we didn't go on with your dinosaur effect. Apparently not only would it not be in the national interest, that's the standard Ministerial line, but,' he turned to Mawn, 'it would not be in the interest of mankind as a whole.'

CHAPTER THREE

GELDER put the lap chart down on the pit-counter. He was sitting alongside the main straight of the Brands Hatch motor-racing circuit. Behind him stood Ian Caird, Managing Director of the Caird Oil Company.

The main straight separated the two men from the packed grandstand opposite to them. Along the edge of the stand was a notice proclaiming: 'Caird Formula 5000.' The public address loudspeakers blared: 'Now we come to the main event of the day —a fifty-lap race for Formula 5000 cars, the Caird Oil Trophy. Any moment now the cars should be coming out for the warming up lap. . . .'

The echoing voice was swamped in the harsh calico-ripping snarl as the cars' engines fired up one by one in the paddock. Marshals swung back the gates and urgently beckoned. One by one, like wild beasts released from a cage, the long-snouted projectiles probed their way on to the circuit and, one after the other, howled off down the track in a haze of bright blue rubber smoke, the drivers hunched down like astronauts in fully enveloping helmets. As the last car disappeared round Paddock Bend, for a few moments there was silence, then a high-pitched whine announced the arrival of the first car as it slowed down from the warming up lap and began to nose into position on the white painted squares of the starting grid. Marshals peremptorily beckoned the remainder into position until finally an official held up both arms and signalled to the race marshal's box.

Engines snapped off as mechanics rushed on to the track surrounding their charges like bees round a queen. A man in white overalls walked out in front of the cars and held up a board with the legend: '5 minutes', a klaxon blared and the mechanics quickened their activities anxiously.

Caird turned to Gelder. He spoke with the soft rather meticulous care of the Highlander: 'How was your car this morning?'

Brian Gelder pointed to a driver leaning back in a low blue and white car in pole position on the front row of the grid: 'Mark got down to one minute two in practice.'

'Will you be winning?' Caird smiled thinly.

'Doubt it. Anderson's on good form, he did a minute dead this morning—can't do much about that.'

'You said you had a problem.' Gelder smiled and nodded. The pit Tannoy over their head crackled: 'Clear the grid—three minutes—clear the grid.' Mechanics gave a last polish to windshields, banged their drivers on the shoulder in encouragement and began reluctantly to move away towards the pit counters.

Engines crackled and banged unevenly into action, drowning

181

all conversation, as the one-minute signal went up and the starter walked to his rostrum with a furled Union Jack. The driver of the blue and white car turned briefly towards the pit where Gelder sat, nodded his helmet briefly and settled back in the safety harness twitching the steering wheel.

The starter unfurled the flag and slowly raised it. The movement was accompanied by the rising scream of the engines. Suddenly he whipped the flag down and the air exploded with a physically painful blast of sound hammering into chests, drowning all thought. The cars leaped forward as if tied together. One snaked through the pack from the rear, tyres touched. Drivers wrenched their mounts back into line.

Suddenly the whole pack was gone, thundering away down towards the bottle-neck of the first corner. Over the grid the air swirled and eddied in the wake of the cars and clouds of acrid dust and smoke blew over the crowd.

Gelder's face was alive: 'Christ, I wouldn't miss that.' He turned to Caird: 'The problem's called Dr Alexander Mawn.'

'Never heard of him.'

'I'll tell you. There's champagne laid on—let's go and get some, besides there's someone else I want you to meet.'

'What about your car?'

'It's fifty laps yet, come on.'

The marquee could have been at a motor race, a country farm show or Royal Ascot. The surroundings were similar and many of the densely-packed crowd seemed to be identi-kit copies of the bored and affluent afficionados who throng the upper reaches of spectator sports.

There were long wooden folding tables covered in white cloths. Rows of glasses, plates of tired canapes and a red-faced throng buzzing with animated conversation. Nobody reacted to the intermittent scream of the cars as they rocketed past outside the tarpaulin walls.

Gelder walked over to a short, almost completely bald man in a light Alpaca suit. He wore rimless glasses. Caird followed. 'Carl, glad you could make it.' The bald man turned and raised a glass of champagne, smiling: 'Hey, this is pretty good material for an oil company!' His face was flushed.

Gelder turned to Caird: 'Ian, this is Carl Bellamy. Carl, Ian Caird, who provides champagne and oil.' The two men shook hands, eyes moving expertly, assessing. Gelder continued: 'Carl heads N.A.L.A. computers.' Caird smiled: 'Yes, of course, glad to meet you at last.'

The bald American smiled: 'We surely ought to have met—we've done enough dealing over the years.'

Caird picked up a glass of champagne and turned to Gelder: 'Your problem, Brian?'

'Yes.' Gelder looked down at his glass. 'Dr Mawn.' Gelder turned the glass. 'Ian, you fired the mate of the *Yarmouth Pier* tanker pretty dam' quick, didn't you? After the Southend grounding.' Caird stiffened and put his glass down slowly: 'Pardon?'

'And Captain Osborne of the *Scarborough Pier*?'

'How?'

'All those people on the beach never realized how close they came to being fried did they?'

There was a long silence broken by the coughing snarl of a car in the paddock nearby. Caird's sallow face seemed to have elongated, his skin looked grey in the filtered light of the marquee. 'We've known each other a long time, Brian. Hadn't you better explain?'

'That is right, isn't it?'

'Yes.'

Gelder turned to the American: 'Carl, some of the computing elements you supplied to the Bijon coal mine were proved faulty by an independent team of investigators. And then there was the test of the control gear for the French Epourentail anti-missile missile. Ten people died in that village when it went off course didn't they?'

The American stood quite still, his eyes searching Gelder's face. His voice was silky but without inflexion: 'I'd sure like to know where you got all that, Brian. Have you changed your line of business?'

'It came from just one source, Doctor Mawn.'

'Jesus Christ!'

'What I've just told you came from his files.' Gelder continued, 'One of my employees is almost certainly involved.'

Caird nodded grimly: 'Impressive!'

Gelder picked up a champagne bottle and filled their glasses: 'You've very little need to worry, those files—are now quite safe. My point is—where do we go from here?'

'I'm not entirely with you?' Caird replied.

'This Mawn—how did he get to all that?' Bellamy asked.

'I'm not sure yet, I'm looking into it,' Gelder replied. 'But people like him automatically attract all the people with a chip, say disgruntled employees, one you may have fired. They get their own back by taking him some of your confidential material and delude themselves they're doing good to the environment at the same time. Then Mawn gets adopted by the media and we've got trouble.'

Bellamy spoke sharply: 'What use is he going to make of it?'

'Propaganda. To force more restrictive legislation on us. He's one of your zero growth people—stop using depleted resources —stop industry chasing the profit motive alone—all that.'

The American relaxed: 'We've got lots of these characters back in the States. They're always holding teach-ins, sit-ins, it's O.K. it gives the students something new to put on their placards. Soft Liberal bullshit. Why give it a thought?'

'This one's not just an econut. I've met him. He's hard-thinking, he's a scientist—he knows exactly what he's talking about and he's prepared to fight. It's not just you he's after. He's done a complete—in depth—study; economics, safety, the lot, on the nuclear reactors and control gear my consortium makes. We're three-quarters complete at my new station at Orkney. I've got to bring it in on time. If I don't—we've got so many penalty clauses against us it could jeopardize the whole deal.'

The American nodded: 'I wondered why you invited me down. We're pretty deep into that project ourselves.'

Caird spoke: 'He's taking a big risk using all that stuff. He must know it's actionable under the Privacy Bill. What does he want?'

Gelder put his glass down: 'For us all to go back to the cave. Look, consider this, ever since that man went on the media, he gave half the small investors of this country a nervous breakdown. They've been selling like the devil and buying unit trusts. You see, every investor in this country is already tremendously nervous about high technology groups like ours. You've seen the Stock Exchange Index, just one man in two days, by scare tactics, has wiped approximately four and a half-million off our stock value. Oh, we'll recover all right, but he'll do it again. Every word Mawn utters costs all of us here thousands!'

Caird smiled thinly. 'You obviously have a suggestion to make, let's hear it.'

'You agree he should be stopped?' Gelder looked at the two men. Bellamy nodded.

Caird raised his eyebrows: 'Stopped?'

'I'd like to talk to you both about it. Perhaps we could meet next week at my place in town?'

'By all means,' Caird nodded.

'Sure. I'll still be around I guess.'

Gelder looked over at Caird: 'Incidentally—did you fire those two men?'

'Nobody fires senior union men these days. But, yes—they're not with us any longer.'

'That cost you!' said Bellamy.

'I can't tolerate that sort of inefficiency,' Caird went on. 'We're plagued with it. Reliability—production standards, it's very bad.'

'You can say that again,' Bellamy went on. 'In one production line of ours we've had to make up an entirely new work force. Just inspectors. None of the products are fully operational any more . . .' He broke off, remembering he was talking to customers.

Gelder nodded: 'The most dangerous thing about the Mawns is that they're having increasing influence. They teach, they give lectures. There is the basis of a really dangerous movement here. It's almost an "invisible college" without a campus. You never know where they're going to crop up. They're getting organized, and it's time we did.'

'I'll drink to that,' Bellamy said.

Gelder looked the two men over carefully. 'But we can't publish any prospectus.' He raised his glass. 'Call it the invisible board.'

Mawn threw the papers down on the table and leaned back, realizing that he had been only half concentrating on the lists of figures he was preparing for the 'Nightstyle' programme. First of all he had been glad of the work, glad of the chance to do something, to be away from the blackened ruins of his work over the last twelve years and the hostile atmosphere of his college where he was suddenly an outcast, a loser, a man who had got the university into disrepute both by his appearances on the media and by his carelessness which caused the death of a fellow member of the staff and destroyed their only computer.

185

Campus opinion which had started out by being sympathetic to Mawn had now finally hardened, and the echoes were apparent at his club and the London college he frequented. A guarded politeness and hastily-remembered appointments were all he found when he tried to engage them in conversation.

Sitting in another man's living-room drinking his whisky and living, as he bitterly put it, on B.B.C. 'charity', Alex Mawn realized that he was for the first time in his life totally disorientated, out of touch, a spectator waiting for something to happen. He went over the previous crises in his life, the struggle to pass his finals at Cambridge, the first Antarctic expedition, the long months of privation. Then, his marriage to Gwen, the gradual drift apart, the mess of the divorce, with one harmless infidelity brought up in Court and hammered home until the girl, a former research student, was forced to leave the University. . . .

There were voices outside the main door to the flat and he quickly pulled his mind back to the present. Peters entered, followed by Marcia, shaking the rain from a folding umbrella.

Peters opened a rather damp evening paper and put it down on the table. 'Might interest you—a piece about Brian Gelder. Our friend is off on holiday with the Club Méditerranée. There's a picture of him here complete with doll on arm, taking off for Dubrovnik—looking jet-set and smooth.'

'You're kidding!' Marcia broke in. 'What's a millionaire doing with the straw hat and twenty pounds a week brigade?'

'You're wrong about that,' Peters continued. 'I went to the Cefalu place in Italy once. A lot of very well-heeled people go there. One Swiss millionaire flew his whole family down in his own plane. The food's terrific and the whole place reeks of wine and sex.'

Marcia shook her head: 'I still can't buy it. He's your sub-Onassis type. If he wanted that he'd probably buy his own island and import fifty guests by jet. There's got to be another reason. . . .'

'Just a moment!' Peters broke in excitedly. 'Do you remember that news story a few months back. There was some report of increased radiation in the air over—where was it?—yes, by God it was, over the Adriatic! Some French research vessel picked it up. I remember now, there was speculation whether the Yugo-slavs or someone had got the bomb and done a sneak test.'

'What was the result?' Marcia asked.

'Oh, nothing.' Peters went on. 'There was no confirmation—someone else denied the figures and the story died the death.'

'And there's a Gelder-built station in Albania,' Mawn said. 'Supposing they blew it up. I remember when they were building it, they gave several news stories out. Come to think of it they went very quiet about it after a bit. They're normally pretty tight but—yes they did—they cancelled a visit by some of our science people. I should think they probably wrecked it then got a rocketing from their Chinese advisers. That's their main *entente* now, at least for technical and scientific help. It also probably embarrasses them ideologically that they did a financial deal with a Western European group.'

'But if Gelder wants to visit Albania surely there's an easier way, isn't there? I mean, he'd just go,' said Marcia.

'If he is going to Albania,' Peters replied, 'presumably he doesn't want to be seen going. Maybe he's just *persona non grata* there. If they have blown the whole thing up they'd never make anything public, it was too much of a showpiece. I remember, because they told a lot of half-truths about the origin of some of the equipment.'

'Suppose they have had an accident,' Mawn said.

'We're not sure of that.'

'Right. But what would they want from Gelder if they had?'

Peters smiled: 'Their money back—with interest. And they'd search for ways of putting the screws on him, too.' He leant back thoughtfully, 'It occurs to me that I've got a way into it.'

'How's that?' Marcia asked.

'Look, I'm in Turin next week. We're doing an incredibly boring thing on the motor show there. If I go a couple of days earlier I can drop over to the Club Méditerranée and nose about a bit.'

Marcia smiled: 'Drop over! Are you taking your Walther P.P.2. in its underarm holster? It'll take you a month just to get a visa. Watch it double-o-seven.'

Peters laughed in return. 'No . . . there's a man I once helped out when I worked in the Washington office. He was a health physicist in Los Alamos. He nearly got crucified by the late, unlamented Joe McCarthy. Interesting man—Arnold Chen-wa. Would you believe?'

'No, I don't,' Marcia laughed.

'No, really,' Peters continued. 'That's his name. He was in charge of radiation checks in an isotope lab. He's a really sweet character as a matter of fact, Chinese, American-educated, a theoretical Marxist rather than a dyed-in-the-wool party man.'

'I'm not with you,' Mawn intervened.

'Well, it fits in rather nicely, I heard from him a few months back—he's in Albania. Didn't give me any details about what he was doing, but it's a reasonable shot. He's a radiation health physicist, he's in Albania and Albania puts up its first atomic reactor.'

'I don't like it,' Marcia said. 'I'll be quite frank, I think we're all building up stories. All we really know is that Teller has contacted Gelder and Teller may have broken into your lab. We can't even prove that!'

'Two days after Alex accused the Gelder concern on the air?' Peters interjected. 'Anyway, we've got the next show to put on. Alex, you're going to be on the spot—we might just as well get all the facts we can—you're going to need everything you've got to defend your "dinosaur effect".'

Mawn rose abruptly from the table. 'Marcia's right. I've stuck my neck out. Don't think I'm not grateful, you've helped me tremendously. But it's just that I've gone back over my own stuff and I'm beginning to think it may have been over the top. . . .' His voice fell away. He looked tired, sick and dispirited.

There was a silence, then Peters spoke gently: 'Alex, I don't think it is all in your head. That's just what the opposition would like you to think. They'd like to make you feel isolated. If you face them believing that, they'll stamp all over you. Look, I didn't tell you this before, but I've had a lot of very interesting reactions to the first programme from several sources. There's a very definite attitude filtering down from management. They're not actually saying "don't do the programme," but they're letting it be known very clearly that they are not in favour of it. Nothing overt—they're just making life generally difficult for my directors —no studio facilities—you know the sort of thing.'

'I'm sorry—I'd no idea,' Mawn began.

'Don't worry about it, it's part of the game. I haven't had so much attention paid to a programme of mine since a series on abortion I did in the sixties. You've really stirred them up with this theory of yours and I'd love to know why. And that phone call from Lodge. Even the Government says we should dry up.'

'It won't do you much good,' Marcia protested.

'I really don't mind. It's about time I cooked up a real block-buster. Thing is, I shall have to leave you two to get on with the preparations for the "Alex Mawn Show". My editor at BBC can help you but I want you to reassemble all your lost data and harden up a concise effective presentation.' He looked at the two of them, the slender New England spinster, her stiff stance bely-ing the promise of her attractive body and the large, bearded academic. 'You've really got to start spending some time together and ironing out any differences of approach.'

'I've been given no real opportunity to put my side of it yet.' Mawn hesitated. 'I'm sorry if I've . . .'

'Oh, forget it,' Marcia snapped. 'What really riles me is that you've got yourself fixed on this man-machine interface—this dinosaur effect of yours. It's a good dramatic title, but you've completely missed the point!'

'Oh, yes?' Mawn began to show interest at the sound of attack.

'Let's define your position,' Marcia continued. 'You say that machines are just growing too complicated for people to operate, right?'

Mawn nodded. 'More to it than that.'

'O.K., but that's basically it. You see, you're just bound up in the hardware—you can't see beyond the nuts and bolts. What about the operators?'

'Well, they're trained obviously for a particular type of machine. They pass tests, they have to. No one's going to let an untrained idiot near a million pounds' worth of equipment.'

'Right! They're trained on paper, yes,' Marcia said. 'But how do you know what happens to them once they start actual work.'

'The mistakes would show up.'

'No, they wouldn't either! First of all you know as well as I do it's quite often impossible to trace the cause of a computer fault, and second, no operator's going to admit it if he does press the wrong button. He's got his job to think about.'

'This is all amusing speculation . . .' Mawn began.

'Speculation be damned,' Marcia flushed angrily. 'Like all hard science buffs—you don't think psychology has any part to play at all, do you?'

189

'Right.' Mawn began to grin at her anger. 'Applied fantasists!'

'It so happens that I've been getting good statistically copper-bottomed evidence about a repeatable and good observation which if you can put down—I'll tear up. I've been at work on it now for nearly three years and I can show you that groups of certain types of people show a uniform loss of intelligence!'

The smile drained off Mawn's face: 'What?'

'Something like a ten per cent loss. Now look, will you come to my lab at the Institute and look at it for yourself?'

'When?'

'Tomorrow. We've an open-day happening but that shouldn't get in the way. There's a Parliamentary Secretary coming to give us the once-over, but once he's had the red-carpet treatment we can get down to work.'

Mawn nodded sombrely: 'You've just got to be wrong!'

CHAPTER FOUR

MARCIA LED THE WAY past the discreetly-lettered brass plate: 'Institute of Psychology' and on up a curved flight of stairs to the first floor. 'We're all polished and sparkling, you'll never see us so tidy again—it's open day.'

Lining the corridor there were multi-coloured sheets of peg-board on blackboard trellises supporting large black titled labels, carefully drawn graphs and tables of figures. The doors of the laboratories leading off the corridor were open and Mawn could see huddled groups of scientists in clean pressed white coats waiting anxiously inside for their first visitors. Marcia led Mawn through a door labelled: 'Ergonomic & Behavioural Studies'.

Howard Venn, Marcia's Head of Department, rushed forward, his manner excited and nervous. 'Marcia, where in heaven's name have you been? The Under-Secretary's been here for about an hour. He's on the second floor already . . .' He broke off, seeing Mawn. 'Oh, sorry. . . .'

'This is Dr Mawn, he's interested in our work,' Marcia said.

'Yes, yes, good of you to come.' Venn looked around anxiously at the array of charts and aparatus: 'It's just that we've got a visit from the Research Council—they've brought along a Minister.'

'Have to do the same myself,' Mawn replied, gesturing at the display boards. 'They never remotely seem to grasp what you're doing, do they?'

Venn smiled, shrugged, and returned to a technician who was plugging leads into a flat aluminium box covered with red and green buttons. The leads connected with a small computer terminal and a large graphic read-out screen. Blocks of figures and numerals were flickering across the screen.

Mawn looked around and, with some amusement, saw that all the lettering over the display boards was a shade more perfectly executed than in the other labs. he had passed. Venn had obviously farmed them out to a display artist. It looked more like an advertising campaign than a scientific display. Over the box with the array of buttons the legend on the label read: 'The Venn portable intelligence meter.' Again he smiled to himself as he saw that the letters were bigger than any other in the room.

There was a sudden sharp crack and a thin column of smoke drifted away from the back of a complicated block of apparatus. Venn's voice was sibilant with rage: 'You idiot. How many times have I told you not to turn the power pack on before lining up!' The technician began fumbling nervously with the leads.

Mawn turned to Marcia: 'What's all the fuss about?'

'Bread! His grant application is up for the next quinquennium. The guy who's coming round is on the board.'

A girl in a white coat stuck her head quickly round the door and spoke in a loud stage whisper: 'They're here!'

There was a brief commotion in the corridor and then a small rotund figure wearing gold-rimmed glasses bustled in followed by a tall, grey-haired man. The handkerchief protruded at exactly the right height out of the coat pocket and the suit was from the right end of Savile Row. His hands were clasped behind his back and he wore a fixed expression of intelligent interest as the Director started to describe the exhibits in the laboratory. Finally the Director turned and, almost as an afterthought, said: 'And this is Dr Venn. Dr Venn, may I present Mr Lodge, Under-Secretary of State to the Science Office.'

The tall man leant slightly forward from the hips with his hand outstretched. 'How d'you do, Dr Venn.'

Mawn reacted. Lodge! The name of the man who had phoned Peters and told him to lay off.

'. . . Now Dr Venn, I wonder if you could show the Under-Secretary your advice. . . .' He turned to Lodge, '. . . extraordinarily clever I think you'll find.' The Director tapped the top of the 'Venn portable intelligence meter' with an immaculate fingernail.

Venn spoke nervously, the words came out in staccato bursts. 'Well, it's really a very simple way of measuring some performances and skills—er—in the field.' He pointed to the box with the square array of buttons, took up a transparent slide and pushed it under a small screen set in the box to one side. He pressed a switch and the screen lit up showing a geometric pattern. 'It works by using a derivative of Karnaugh mapping with an automatic scoring logic attached to. . . .'

The Under-Secretary turned to Venn. He spoke gently: 'I'm afraid you'll have to treat me like a backward child of three.'

'Oh—yes—of course.' He paused momentarily confused, then picked up the box: 'It's a sort of electronic noughts and crosses. We show various tasks on the screen by using these transparencies then ask the subject to press the appropriate buttons. For example . . .' He pointed to the screen. 'On this one, there are different shapes which have to be matched together, so the subject presses the buttons which he thinks will show the best matching pairs. Inside, there is a small arithmetic unit which automatically scores the subject and prints out his results.'

Lodge leaned forward and dabbed at the buttons: 'So it evaluates the performance of the subject automatically?'

'Exactly.' Venn, pleased at the apparent understanding, pointed to the underside of the box: 'There are miniaturized computing chips in here, which plot error frequency using a binomial function. . . .'

'But that's invalid!' Mawn broke in suddenly.

All heads turned in Mawn's direction, noticing him for the first time. Venn flushed as Mawn continued: 'Given the sort of paired values you're comparing—you'd have to use a "Poisson" distribution, binomials simply beg the very question you're asking the machine to measure.'

Venn spoke in tight control: 'It was considered good enough to be adopted as a standard method at the last European Psychology Conference.'

The Under-Secretary's eyes moved from one to the other. There was just the hint of a smile.

'Maybe,' Mawn continued. 'But that method for that task was thrown out years ago. . . .'

'I think I've seen this down at Farnborough,' the Under-Secretary spoke deliberately as he walked over towards a screen showing an illuminated circle with a small light spot wobbling randomly inside the circle. Venn glared once at Mawn and then collected himself and followed Lodge over to the screen: 'Yes, it's a way of testing complex performance.' He pointed to a joystick control below the screen. 'The idea is that the spot is given a random movement by the machine and the subject sits here.' He pointed to a chair. 'And by moving this lever he tries to act against the machine and keep the spot in the circle.' He sat down, grasped the control in one hand and started to move it expertly back and forth gazing at the screen. After a few seconds he managed to bring the spot, still wobbling, back into the centre of the circle and keep it there.

'May I try?' Lodge asked.

'Of course.' Venn slid out of the seat and the Under-Secretary took his place. Mawn noticed that, as he reached out for the lever control, his hand overshot and his fingers had a fine tremor. He was unable to keep the spot in the circle. Mawn suddenly recalled the inept operator in the ACE control room.

Finally Lodge stood up and looked down at his outstretched fingers. His laugh was slightly embarrassed as he turned to the Director: 'Don't think I'd make a very good airline pilot, do you?' The Director smiled and looked at his watch: 'I think we ought to be moving on.' He turned to Venn: 'Perhaps we could have a quick look over the ergonomics lab.'

Venn moved towards a door. 'Yes, of course.' He turned to the Under-Secretary: 'Through here, sir, if you would.' The Director waved Lodge in front of him as they followed Venn out. Marcia wheeled on Mawn. She was furious. 'What did you have to do that for?'

'Do what?'

'Goddamnit! You made him look a complete dummy!'

'Not my intention. He's just using the wrong method. I told him.'

Marcia blazed: 'Don't be so damned British and uninvolved. You could have waited, couldn't you? You didn't have to nail him in front of the brass did you? Or was that what you wanted?'

Mawn paused for a moment: 'No, I'm sorry.'

'I told you before we began. Richard Lodge is on his committee and now you've sown the idea in his head that Howard is an incompetent. You could just have wrecked his whole grant application!'

"All I meant to say was that his maths are probably wrong.'

'So in the name of your holy truth you sent him up in public!'

'I have apologized.' Mawn turned abruptly on her and Marcia stepped back a pace. 'And I stick exactly to what I said. You can make any sort of sophisticated gadget you want and it's only as good as the theory you build into it. That thing's a typical high technology fix. You think you can just walk into a subject with a hundred and one different variables and—with what amounts to a souped-up adding machine—suddenly say you've put part of human behaviour into figures! Have you ever tested the reliability of the thing? How do you know it isn't distorting half the results you get out of it?'

Marcia frowned, suddenly anxious. 'That wouldn't invalidate the results would it? We spent months checking it out.'

'Who knows. It might only make a dent in them. Now if you don't mind.' He started towards the door.

'Alex,' Marcia's anger evaporated. 'Look, Howard's going away tonight—he's giving the Piaget memorial lecture in Paris. I've told you what I found, you said you'd take a look, God, I just can't tell you how vital it is. You can't cop out now.'

Mawn walked over to the long bow window, rain was streaming down the curved panes.

'Maybe you've too much to do?' Marcia asked.

'No, not a damn thing.' Mawn turned back to her. 'That's what riles me I suppose.' He nodded and smiled: 'O.K. Let's get to work.'

Peters lay back in the blue canvas deck chair with the white trident symbol enjoying the bite of the hot sun and ruefully compared the city pallor of his own skin with the dark brown figures lying on the beach.

Near the water's edge he could see Gelder energetically playing volley ball against a crowd of young club instructors, with apparently complete absorption. If he was using the club as a pretext, he was managing to enjoy the charade. He recalled their first meeting at the camp and Gelder's start of surprise, quickly suppressed.

It had been on the previous evening at the open-air bar, together with the half-dozen-or-so British contingent at the camp. Drink had flowed and Gelder had displayed an easy, almost insolent charm. Peters had found him difficult to categorize. Part of the time his manner had been open and laughing and then, every so often, he had caught a hint of watchfulness. There had been a crop of brainless bar games which had left Peters feeling every one of his fifty years. Gelder had been accompanied by a petite, exquisitely shaped French brunette, nicknamed Minouche, who grew more restless and spoilt as the evening wore on. He remembered that when she had started to protest, Gelder had spoken to her savagely in French and afterwards she had stayed in the corner of the bar staring petulantly at her glass. From the others, Peters had learnt that Gelder scarcely ever left his hut until late in the afternoon, missing both breakfast and lunch at the open-air, vine-covered restaurant.

The next day, the first Peters had seen of him was in a long, red speedboat with a huge outboard, screaming away into the distance across the bay.

He began to worry that their suspicions had been groundless, then remembered Marcia's objection that if Gelder had wanted a holiday in the sun he could have bought the whole camp.

He had even searched along the well-worn path to the far end of the island where nude sunbathing and swimming were permitted. He had found the beautiful bare Minouche lying unselfconsciously on a towel among a small group of girls from the camp. She behaved differently from the other limp sun-drugged figures beside her on the beach and kept glancing at her watch. A persistent young German had eventually worked up enough courage to say something and had been immediately rebuked by a hard contemptuous stare.

It took Peters several hours, a long lunch and a free supply of wine to make her unbend. He had even mentioned a coming television programme in which she might be interested. Eventually she began to talk petulantly. Gelder did not in fact rest during the mornings but took off early in the speedboat without telling her his destination. He remembered her parting words: 'please don't tell anyone, I was told not to speak of this.'

Peters settled back in the chair. For the first time in years he felt the prickle of anticipation. His mind went back to his time as a European war correspondent. Now he began to feel something of the same mixture of apprehension and excitement. He looked down at his pale arms, the muscles showing the sag of years and remembered Marcia's jibe about double-o-seven. Perhaps contentment had to be paid for by taking a risk occasionally. Tomorrow he would find out.

Venn's normally immaculate laboratory was in total disorder. Mawn sat in shirtsleeves beside a bench strewn with files, computer read-out paper and card indexes. He completed a calculation, rushed over to the computer terminal, punched in instructions then waited impatiently until the machine began to clack out its reply. Marcia was kept running as she brought fresh material from the data files. Eventually he threw down his pencil and sat back: 'Well, that's that!'

Marcia flopped into a chair beside him: 'When I asked you just to have a look, I didn't expect a marathon.' She glanced at her watch. 'You've been going for over four hours—you know that?'

'Your Venn seems to have used fairly primitive circuitry but— I'm surprised, it only makes a marginal difference. Yes . . .' Mawn nodded, '. . . it's valid enough.'

'So your attack on his maths was completely unjustified?'

Mawn smiled: 'If you insist on making me crawl, yes.'

'Fine. What are you going to do about it?'

'What am *I* going to do about it?'

'You're not just going to leave it there, are you?'

Mawn was already studying a long table of figures. 'This your American data?'

'Yes. I asked you a question!'

Mawn looked myopically at her through his glasses then laughed. 'I'd better teach you both some decent maths.' He turned back to the table. 'This is interesting, at least so far as it goes. You say you chose a particular subject and defined him?'

'Yes, we selected middle grade executives. Same age group, salaries, educational levels, responsibilities, marital status and so on.'

'So providing the details they gave you were true, they should all have had a similar I.Q.?'

196

'Well, other factors are involved, but that's about it I guess.'

'So, the first problem I've got is that your I.Q. thing is nothing whatsoever to do with intelligence! It simply measures the ability to do the I.Q. test.'

Marcia shrugged. 'That's an old one. Who's denying it? Nobody can define intelligence properly, but the tests we use are at least consistent in comparing individuals or groups.'

'Which is taking the easy way out,' said Mawn.

'No it isn't. We aren't measuring just the old I.Q. test like the Stanford-Binet, you know. We've got a little more sophisticated. . . .'

'Or complicated?'

'Maybe. But we can build in the sort of Wechsler-Jackson idea— a measure of creativity. Also we can test motor skills.' She pointed to the joystick and the spot wobbling on the screen. 'Like that thing, or the pursuit rotor. The whole idea is to get a measure of a person's total capability, not just his ability to solve paper puzzles —dominoes—matrices—that sort of thing.'

'But surely there are so many factors that can affect a person's performance—whether he's got a hangover—or he's frightened about something? Also if a person's got special gifts at expressing himself—he could use it to mask a relative dullness.'

'You've been reading the books. Yes, defects in reading ability, depression, consistency of the test itself—I admit all that. But you see Howard's test is basically non-verbal, so it should be free from that kind of error.'

Mawn persisted: 'The fact remains that your results are only as good as your observations and your figures. There's no compromise about that. You tell me that a group of subjects specially selected for the same characteristics should have shown very nearly the same intelligence, but they didn't. Well, that's no surprise to me. Statistics can either prove something's fairly obvious or merely compound stupidity, you can take your choice.'

'Bullshit!' Marcia flared again. 'You have this colossal bias against us, just because we deal with people. You've got this amazing conceit that only you—the physicists—really do any measuring. What about your "dinosaur effect"? You say machines are becoming unreliable and you say you've proved it by showing faults in one machine system. I seem to remember a pretty shirty article in *Nature* accusing you of generalizing from the particular without enough evidence.'

197

'For every thesis, there's an antithesis.'

'Oh, don't be so trite! What you have to explain in our findings is that in some groups we tested, their I.Q. level was very much lower. Not just at the low end of the normal, scattered average but very much lower. And secondly, some of the people who were in this low group showed a second decrease in I.Q. when we tested them again.'

Mawn pointed towards the Venn intelligence meter: 'Well, that thing probably had a few off days.'

'Oh, swell! Now you use your dinosaur obsession to cover every conclusion that contradicts it. You can't blame everything on machines. I've described an effect—told you how we got it—you've read your Popper—one disproof is enough—so go ahead, disprove it.'

'Have you published any of it?'

'No, it's too much of a hot one—we have to be sure.' She went over to a file of computer print-outs. 'It's all over here.' She pulled one of the files off the shelf and brought it over to him.

'You've certainly done a lot of work,' Mawn sounded cautious.

'Which you say is a load of crap!'

'Now you're arguing emotively, like a woman.'

'And leave sex out of it!'

She flung the file down on the bench and stalked away, slamming the door behind her.

Mawn opened the file and began to scan its contents. After a few minutes he reached for a pencil and started to jot down figures on a notepad beside him. He started talking to himself. . . . 'Let's see —first approximation—P point six. Stupid bastards could have saved hours using sequential analysis—point five and then . . .'

After about a quarter of an hour Marcia re-entered and started to say something, but saw he was completely oblivious of her presence. Then, with all the delicacy of a mother leaving a sleeping child, she tiptoed to the door of the lab and left, closing the door behind her.

Peters completed his inspection of the boat, primed the carburettor and pulled the starter cord. The Mercury outboard engine immediately roared into life and, while it warmed up, he began incongruously to work out a way to include the cost of its hire in his B.C.C. travel expenses. Halfway to the horizon he could just see

Gelder's boat heading south leaving a white fan of spray. He quickly cast off and headed in pursuit.

Replacing the hot clear skies of the previous two days, large black thunderheads had begun to build up over the high peaks of the mountains overlooking the bay and as he headed into open water he thought that it looked like a stage set of Götterdämmerung.

Following Gelder's boat around the spit of land limiting the bay, the straw huts of the camp standing out against the dark grey-green of the olive groves seemed almost a deliberate man-made arrogance set down to taunt the Albanians on the far side of the water. The horizon was made up by a stark, towering, half-circle of jagged peaks. It was as though the ancient gods were looking down on the presumptuous pygmies who clung to the thin green strip of land along the shoreline—looking down and waiting for a chance to shake them loose into the sea.

Peters snapped his thoughts back to reality as Gelder's boat disappeared round the point. He opened the throttle and immediately he could feel the thrust of the motor as the bows came up.

Rounding the bay into open water, he realized that he had closed too fast. He throttled back quickly, until the boat began to drift and waited until about a mile separated them; then opened up to about half throttle and settled down for the long haul.

Overhead the clouds were dense and, with a chill of anxiety, he saw whitecaps developing as the sea began to slap angrily against the sides of the hull. A distant rumble of thunder boomed menacingly off the mountains and a light warm rain began to sweep into the open cockpit.

Ahead he could just see Gelder's boat swing away from a tall craggy headland and head towards a small island about two miles off shore. In the rain he momentarily lost sight of the boat.

The island was one of many which dot the southern coast of Yugoslavia. At its centre was a ruined monastery built of great hand-cut stones lined by an orange-yellow terra-cotta rendering and topped by the remnants of a tiled roof. Protruding above the level of the surrounding olive trees was the spike of an old bell-tower.

As he closed on the shore he could just make out a dilapidated wooden landing stage partly overgrown with weeds and creepers. An old and battered fishing boat with a tall rectangular wheelhouse was moored there but he could see neither Gelder nor the crew.

He headed out to sea again and circled the island, but there was no sign of life among the stunted vegetation and crumbling walls. The fishing boat still rocked at anchor.

Spreading a map on the rear seat to pin-point the position of the island, he realized that the tall cliffs he had passed were Albanian. He remembered stories at the camp about pleasure boats whose unwary occupants had been machine-gunned for sailing too close to the Albanian coast. He opened the throttle hurriedly and headed back towards the Club.

He failed to see a man hidden in the trees near the landing stage pointing the long black snout of a telephoto lens towards his boat.

CHAPTER FIVE

IT TOOK MAWN two hours of machine time to analyse the data given to him by Marcia. He sat in front of the computer terminal in direct land line contact with a central machine complex situated over nine miles away at the National Physical Laboratory. As the machine clattered out its analysis of his data he scanned each line of closely-printed numerals comparing them with notes of his own.

Finally he punched in the 'log-out' instruction and shut down the terminal. The silence was intense after the peremptory racket of the machine. Mawn's features were pinched and drawn. He rubbed his eyes and stretched.

'I've shoved it through every routine I know and I can't put it down.'

Marcia waited without replying.

'There is one possible flaw but I can't think that it's crucial. You seem definitely to have shown that some of your groups of people confined to particular firms show a loss of intellectual performance.'

'So you believe it?'

'I wish I didn't. A general loss of intelligence seems impossible. I just can't begin to see why. But if the method—the Venn test— is right and I can't judge that—it's outside my sphere, you have a completely copper-bottomed case. Some people in some places are getting progressively more inept. Is there any precedent—anything like this known?'

'Lots of psychologists have suggested it. There used to be an idea in this country that the so-called "lower-classes" had larger families, so when they grew up they bred larger families and the net intelligence of the human race would start to fall.'

Mawn frowned: 'Which assumes working-class people are less intelligent and that their lower intelligence is transmitted to their off-spring.'

'Good old English class chauvinism.'

'And it was an American who first said black people were less intelligent than white?'

Marcia smiled: 'Ouch!'

Mawn picked up one of the files. 'These people in the firms showing the drop. You re-tested some didn't you?'

'Yes, and that's the real crunch. They showed a progressive fall.'

'What about the unaffected people? Did you re-test any of them?'

'Yes. There was hardly any change. Not so clear cut, there was a very, very slight downward trend—but it wasn't significant statistically.'

'Then you've got to test the worst affected for a third time? Three points on a graph and you've got the beginnings of a case.'

'That's under way. Two of Howard's Ph.D. students are up North now, doing it.' Mawn nodded. 'Good. Let me know the results.'

'Not so fast,' Marcia smiled. 'If you accept the conclusion then you've got a big problem!' Mawn looked up. 'Your dinosaur effect. You've been producing evidence that computing and control machinery is becoming unreliable by itself with no other added factor.'

'Right. The study I did on the N.A.L.A. system. . . .'

'But Alex, you're forgetting the interface—the man-machine-interface—what do your people call it?'

'EMMIE—short for M.M.I.'

'Well, supposing some of these less able people of mine were operating a computer and supposing the computer started to throw up mistakes. How would you know who'd done it? Man or Machine?'

201

'Obvious. Test the operator.'

'There are two things wrong with that. First of all, our sample is pretty small and, secondly, people with mental defects can often mask it. A guy who's got a good retentive memory plus a good verbal facility can cover up for a real basic inability. Like some of the old "idiot savants". They could multiply two four-figure numbers together in their head but the poor saps couldn't do their buttons up when they got dressed.'

'Why would they cover up?'

'Look, Alex, if you're a computer operator and you noticed that you couldn't do your work so well any more you'd cover up wouldn't you? There aren't so many jobs in computers any more.'

Mawn waved his hand impatiently: 'You're trying to make a case for some sort of secret army of morons running our technology.' The image struck him. 'God, it's quite a thought. Somebody in charge of a missile silo growing inept and hiding the fact from his superiors.'

'Earlier on you mentioned a flaw in our data—what is it?' Marcia asked.

'Well, I was getting a bit desperate trying to find a way round your figures and it occurred to me that the buttons on the testing box are coded red and green.' Again, as he spoke, Mawn had a mental image of the ACE control desk, the sequence of lights— green, red, green, red and the operator's, nearly fatal, mistake.

'That was part of the . . .' Marcia's voice died away. 'Oh, boy, wait a moment, I think I see . . .'

'You didn't test your subjects for colour blindness!'

'Right, dead right. We didn't.' She stared at him fascinated.

Mawn continued: 'I don't have to tell you it's pretty common. It's a point for women's lib. About eight per cent of men and only one per cent of women have some colour deficiency of some sort, most red-green-grey confusion. They're called protanopes and deuteranopes as far as I can remember.'

Marcia got up and started pacing: 'Oh, my God! This could invalidate every solitary test we've done!'

'No. If the colour defective people are spread evenly over your affected and unaffected people then it could all even out. But if it's just the affected people . . .'

'I get the question. . . . Is colour blindness more common in the groups with the falling I.Q. Right?'

Mawn nodded: 'Where was it you said you got the subjects from?'

'Oh—from a junior management personnel firm. We tried first of all going to individual firms, but they weren't too co-operative. The personnel people were quite forthcoming—in fact we did a deal with them. They supplied us with guinea-pigs and they got free tests on applicants for jobs.'

'Well, we could start testing for defective colour vision—it's not very hard—we could start with the Ishihara test and if that doesn't show it up, put them on to split field tube of some sort . . .'

The laboratory door swung open and Howard Venn bustled in carrying an airline bag: 'Marcia, hello. . . .' He glanced round the disordered room and at Mawn sitting with his feet up on the bench. His smile disappeared. 'May I ask what you're doing?'

'Marcia asked me to check through some of her figures.' Mawn slowly removed his feet from the bench.

Venn strode to the bench and snatched up a file. He shook it at Marcia. 'Who gave you permission to show these to him? They're completely confidential—you had no right, no right at all!'

Mawn gathered the computer print-outs together and stood up. Marcia stood silently between the two men. Venn reached forward and tried to grab the papers, his face white. 'You can't take them away, they're not your property.'

Mawn held them up out of his reach. 'I don't know whether you know it or not but you could have got on to a major discovery here.'

'And what does that mean?' Venn asked.

Mawn walked slowly over to the door. 'It's early days yet, but you may just have discovered a new species: *Homo non sapiens.*'

The dusty village street separated a row of dilapidated grey stone houses from a row of acacia trees alongside a shallow river. Under the trees, shaded from the bright sun, old women in black head-shawls sat impassively watching a throng of early shoppers pick over the brightly-coloured piles of vegetables on their stalls.

Peters sat nervously beside a circular metal table outside a road-side café. Passers-by seemed to regard him as an interesting speci-men and made him feel that he stood out like a sore thumb. At nearby tables, knots of men sat talking quietly around clusters of tall beer mugs. He began to imagine that they were discussing him.

Which of them were police? It was very hot and he felt out of place and unprotected.

Eventually, with a rush of relief, he saw a dumpy figure dressed in black threading its way through the crowds around the stalls. The figure resolved into a short, overweight Chinese dressed like a Methodist minister. He wore a shapeless black suit with high lapels and a silk shirt buttoned tight around his neck. On his head was a yellow straw panama with the brim turned up. Underneath the hat, there was a broad grin of recognition. The figure hurried towards Peters, hand outstretched.

'Sheldon, my friend.' Chen-wa's handshake was warm and cordial. 'What the hell you come to this place for?'

Peters laughed: 'I heard you'd become a nationalized Albanian!'

'Have to be kidding. I'm just—just—hell I haven't talked English for years. I'm just a missionary. Try to make them civilized here. So far only goddamn result is they smash up all machines we give them.'

Peters looked up at a waiter studying them. 'What are you going to drink, Arnold?'

The Chinese scientist made a face: 'No, no. Just lemon water—everything else here rots your guts.'

Peters gave the order and the waiter sniffed and drifted away with a sullen reluctance that demonstrated his indifference to both foreigners and official allies.

'Shouldn't you be a bit careful?'

Chen-wa laughed aloud. 'You ever heard them trying speak English—can't speak their own bloody language.' Peters noticed the Chinese give a long casual look around the other tables before continuing. 'Anyway—too late start licking posteriors now. Taste must be acquired when young. Now what do you want—you don't come for the holiday. You are going to make television here?'

Peters hesitated, Chen-wa continued. 'Well, I tell you, there's something bad here, so I want to talk too. Now, you start.'

'What does the name Gelder mean to you?'

'Gelder. That's the name of—Oh, shit, forget the words.'

'You remember some of them,' Peters grinned. 'Consortium—the Gelder consortium—is that it?'

'Right. That the name! They make new water reactor—package deal—sell one to these idiots. Bloody fool thing to do—can't make own electric razors work—they bugger up clockwork and blame Gelder. Sun does not shine from Gelder's arse I tell you.'

'Arnold.' Peters leaned forward. 'What's really happened to the Pukë nuclear reactor?'

'Yes, okay, we go for a walk.' Chen-wa stood up and Peters, catching on, followed suit. The waiter, who had been chatting to two men by the door, picked up Chen-wa's lemon juice and rushed forward anxiously.

They walked alongside the river until they were clear of the market and the main village square. The bank was deserted except for a chattering group of children trying to net fish from beneath the overhanging bank.

Chen-wa's manner changed: 'Sheldon. I tell you what happen —then you go home and make big crappy TV programme and their ambassador sees it in London and I get put on the next Concorde to Peking.'

'I'm not here for that, Arnold,' Peters replied. 'You've got to believe me—nothing public.'

'Then why do you come?'

Peters stopped by the bank watching green fronds of weed undulating in the flowing water. He gave Chen-wa a summary of Mawn's dinosaur theory and finally told him about the sinister aftermath of his TV programme.

The Chinese listened in silence then, as if making up his mind, began to speak in a rush:

'Now I tell you why I want to talk with you. Yes, the Pukë reactor did go up—a big smash up. These people, they keep everything secret, even from me. They ask us to come from China to give advice how to make it work and then don't tell us all information. Yes, whole reactor's gone—they had to take down station brick by brick then cover it up with thousand tons of bloody concrete—like a gravestone—be there for ever. I started radiation health department, when we begin, my job to see silly buggers don't get killed by radiation. Well I had a big worry about some of the people in the control room. I watched them during start-up before pile went critical. They make mistakes like their heads don't work properly. Then we had melt-down. Ten men killed.'

'How was that?' Peters asked.

'Some radiation—some just smashed.'

'What about the people in the control room? Couldn't they

have been exposed to radiation? I mean couldn't that have accounted for their odd behaviour?'

Chen-wa shook his head violently. 'No, no, they all have radiation check—badges I measure them myself—ordinary level, nothing dangerous.'

'Then what's the problem? I don't see.'

'Sheldon. I go to many places. Your Englishman, Mawn, is it? He's not only man to study this dinosaur effect. In Moscow, they have same. In Peking too a little, but it's not bloody machines, Sheldon. I don't think it is machines.'

'Then what is it?'

Chen-wa fished in the pocket of his suit and pulled out a small flat wooden box about two inches long, he held it up to Sheldon. 'These are microscope slides—they come from the brain of dead man at Pukë—one who made silly mistakes.'

'I still don't see.'

'These made by the pathologist in hospital. He says the man's brain all rotten.'

'So he could have had some disease—brain tumour or something?'

'No, Sheldon. Last year I went to conference in Odessa—heard a talk by a Russian about a new—don't know what you call it—brain condition.'

'There are hundreds, surely—I'm not a doctor—but there must be many different changes.'

'This Albanian pathologist—mostly bloody fool—he made a new name. I remember. This dead man from Pukë has "Betz-cell atrophy".'

'That's nothing remarkable, surely?'

'The Betz-cells are thinking cells, Sheldon.' He tapped his forehead with the box. 'The little buggers that do the thinking.' He gave the box to Peters. 'Anyway you take these to London. Take them to Dr Kingston at Institute of Pathology. He was at Odessa —he's a very big brain man—let him see.'

Peters put the box away in his pocket. Then, with a sudden change of mood, Chen-wa bent down, picked up a pebble, threw it into the river and called out excitedly: 'See, we have same fish in Canton.'

Peters became aware of two men who had appeared round the corner of the winding river path.

CHAPTER SIX

THE FLAT was in partial darkness with only a small pool of light over in one corner of the lounge where Mawn was still hard at work. Marcia entered, threw her coat over a chair, went over and put a hand on his shoulder: 'Isn't it about time you gave it a rest?'

He looked up, squinting at the light. 'What did little Venn do to you?'

'Don't be bitchy! He's getting quite co-operative, now you've told him he's got a discovery!'

Mawn smiled appreciatively at her changed attitude to Venn. 'You know I've been thinking about all this. We've found this effect—supposing it's generalized—groups of people losing intelligence—it's horrifying. Earlier on you had a go at my dinosaur effect, all right, that's not the whole answer. The two things together make an absolutely lethal mixture.'

Marcia was staring into space. Mawn tapped her gently on the arm and she jumped. 'Did you hear me?' She nodded. 'I did—·I'm thinking—go on.'

Mawn continued: 'Assuming this localized loss of I.Q. effect is more or less widespread—well we agreed, didn't we—that the people who are affected are likely to cover up their ineptitude. Now, supposing some of these people are operating machines which are faulty in terms of my theory?' He looked at Marcia waiting for her reply.

'There would be twice as much chance of a mistake, I guess.'

'Exactly. It's difficult enough already when a mistake is made by a computer to decide who made it, the machine or the man operating it.'

'Now hold on. They do have special "operator check" systems in some of them—machine checks operator, right? I remember that from one of my father's plants.'

'Yes, but that's not very general yet. In any case, who checks the check system?'

Marcia's face was pale: 'What on earth can we do?'

'Find out why!'

*　　　*　　　*

Peters awoke in a cold sweat. There had been a terror-stricken dream. He had found himself about to appear in front of a vast audience on a television programme without the slightest idea of the content. Dimly he had seen the faces of Marcia and Alex Mawn warning him not to take part. There had been danger everywhere. He opened his eyes. Above him the conical roof of the hut looked like the spokes of the wheel. Even that image held a sense of menace. He fumbled beside him on the floor mat for his cigarette pack. His fingers touched the telegram. It had read: "Essential you arrive Rome meet camera crew Friday or shall make other arrangements. David." Curt and to the point, it was an obvious "or else" warning from David Danvers, the Assistant Head of current affairs at B.B.C.

Uncharacteristically, he reached into a holdall for a small silver brandy flask and took a heavy gulp. Everything he thought about seemed to be a source of anxiety. The previous evening he had given Chen-wa's slides and a long explanatory letter to a returning holidaymaker to take back to Marcia. He had described Chen-wa's report and about Gelder.

Gelder! The previous night there had been "une spectacle"— a mixture of amateur theatricals and party games so beloved by the French on holiday. Gelder had taken part enthusiastically, organizing the English contingent in the slippery pole fight— even giving a comic version of a TV commercial. Not the picture of a man under stress. Peters imagined the pressure that the Albanians must have brought to bear on him. First contract with a western firm, then a major accident and breakdown. They were probably trying to throw everything in the book at him—to reclaim some of their money—anything. He wondered who it was that Gelder met on his daily trips to the island. Probably not technical. He guessed that it must be some sort of haggle with a political, probably a fairly senior, man responsible for finance. He began to review the evidence. It amounted to very little. A few unofficial words from a scientist—a couple of slides.

He poured a second, larger brandy. Early morning boozing at fifty—beginning of the end! David had stipulated Friday. One more day! The brandy warmed his limbs. One more day. Take the camera, the telephoto lens, get one good picture of Gelder and the man he was meeting. Then get back to London and try to identify the man.

He glanced at his watch. Six a.m., plenty of time to get out to the island first, hide the boat and wait. He began to weigh the risks, imagining a chase between his own boat and the Albanian coastal patrols. The brandy still held his courage together. He decided to use a more powerful boat belonging to Sergio.

Sergio Bracci was a minor Italian film star who had turned up at the camp in his ocean-going launch. A massively powerful craft powered by twin turbo-charged diesels, Bracci had lent him a spare set of keys as a goodwill gesture in the hope that Peters would be able to get him more English publicity. Thinking about the performance of the boat resolved Peters's last qualms.

He kept the throttles three-quarters closed as he nosed the craft through the blue-green waters of the bay. The heavy throbbing of the engines was overlain by the high-pitched whine of the exhaust turbo-chargers. He looked over at the sleeping village huts partly obscured in a light early morning mist.

Once clear of the headland, he pushed the throttle quadrant fully open. The response was immediate. The note of the engines became an aggressive thunder and the turbo-chargers' note changed to a thin strident scream. The bows lifted and the padded seat rest pushed hard against his back. He watched the speed indicator moving up. Ten, fifteen, twenty-five knots. At each side he could see a green wall of water curving away from the hull to join behind him in a boiling turbulent wake. Gradually his anxieties gave way to a sheer sensual enjoyment of speed.

The water was completely calm and it seemed only a few minutes before the familiar shape of the island appeared out of the mist. He throttled back and coasted slowly around the island twice, scanning the shoreline with binoculars. There were no boats, no people. Finally he selected a miniature bay over-hung with trees away from the jetty he had previously seen.

As he nosed the boat carefully in towards the gently-sloping shoreline, he found that the overhanging branches made an almost perfect camouflage. Finally, he had a quick look for the high water level marked by a dark line of weeds on the sand and moored the boat fore and aft to overhanging branches leaving a sufficient slack on each line to avoid grounding the boat. He looked at his watch: seven-thirty. Judging by the time of the previous meeting it gave him a minimum of two hours.

He began to explore the island.

It was bigger than it had first appeared and he probed carefully through the overgrown remains of old vegetable gardens.

The ruins of the monastery had several rooms marking the old refectory and dormitories.

In the main chapel there were bunches of old flower garlands arranged at the base of a rough stone altar. Then he found the first signs of recent occupation. Around an old stone tomb with a badly-eroded sword carved on its lid, there were several cigarette ends which showed none of the damp brown staining of age. On the top of the tomb there was one grey cylindrical fragment of ash, its shape still unaltered. He uncurled one stubbed cigarette. Its brand name was English.

He found a vantage point up worn stone steps inside the bell tower. It was a small chamber with an open window space looking down on to the landing jetty. Through a hole in the wall of the chamber on the opposite side, there was a clear view over most of the remainder of the island. Above him leading to the bell chamber, there was another series of steps, but there were several missing and one side of the wall abutting them was entirely missing and open to the air.

The sun was well up and the air was growing hot. He took off his jacket, checked the camera and settled down to wait.

The sun and the brandy began to have their effect. He dozed.

Awakening with a jerk of panic, he glanced at his watch. Nine-fifteen! He raised himself cautiously to the stone ledge of the window. A fishing boat similar to the one of the previous day was already moored about fifty yards off-shore. Alongside the jetty was Gelder's red boat.

Through the binoculars he could see two men on the fore-deck of the fishing boat. With a shock he saw that one of them was dressed in some sort of uniform. He was holding a short machine-pistol casually in one hand. Above the wheelhouse a small radar scanner was rotating slowly.

Hands trembling, he brought up the camera and rested the long telephoto lens on the sill and wound the scene into focus. He pressed the exposure button. There was no answering click and, swearing to himself, he cocked the shutter and pointed the lens for a second time. The sweat on his hands made his fingers slip on the shutter button.

A shadow moved over the sill. He spun round. Partly shutting off the bright sunlight the figure of a man stood blocking the door to the chamber. Behind him the head and shoulders of a second man were coming into view.

He felt an agonizing blow on his wrist and the camera flew out of his hand clattering against the stone wall. The man stepped out of the sun and leapt forward pulling Peters up by his hair and slamming him back against the wall. Both men were dark and one had a full moustache. Their eyes were quite impersonal.

The second man picked up the camera and the first twisted Peters's arm up behind his back and jerked him over towards the stairs.

For Peters, the next few minutes passed like the images of a silent film. He made no attempt to say anything, knowing instinctively that it was useless. The pain from his wrist made him feel sick.

Outside in the long grass surrounding the building, he caught a brief glimpse of a short neatly-dressed man in a light brown suit. One of his captors went over to the man in the suit and talked quietly for a few seconds. He returned and the two led him off down the slope towards the olive trees. Suddenly, with a surge of hope, he realized that they were taking him towards his own boat. It had been moved closer in-shore.

He realized dully that they must have known about it from the moment of his arrival. Somewhere in the back of his mind he remembered Marcia laughing about James Bond.

The second man was standing in the water near his boat. The first grabbed him by his injured wrist and flung him down the short slope leading to the water's edge. Peters screamed, stumbled and fell face downwards into the water. Gasping for breath he staggered to his feet and waded through the shallow water towards the shore almost blinded by pain. The second man was holding a short-barrelled machine-gun and with it he gestured angrily towards the boat. Peters stood swaying in the water, trying to understand through a haze of pain. The man gestured again.

Peters wearily turned round and waded back to the boat and, with one hand, clumsily dragged himself over the side, flopping down into the cockpit. Sick with pain he looked over at the two men standing on the shore. The man with the machine-gun started to walk back up the hill in the direction of the monastery and the other settled down near the water's edge putting a revolver on a stone beside him. He lit a cigarette and leaned back on one elbow squinting up at the sun.

Peters watched the man with the machine-gun disappear over the brow of the hill and then started to look around the cockpit. Clipped into a bracket beside him was a lever-operated powder-projecting fire extinguisher. The lever was locked by a split pin fitted with a ring. When the pin was pulled, the lever could be depressed releasing a high pressure stream of fire blanketing powder.

Under the protection of the cockpit side he slowly worked the pin free and then, millimetre by millimetre, eased the red cylindrical shape out of its mounting clips to avoid the click of the clips on release.

The man on the shore flicked the cigarette away and lay back on both elbows.

Peters raised the nozzle of the extinguisher on to the edge of the cockpit, aimed it and with all his force leant forwards on the lever. There was a loud explosive hiss and a cone of powder jetted out and struck the man full in the face. He screamed and clawed at his eyes. Peters flung the extinguisher overboard, jammed the ignition key over and pressed the starter. The two motors fired at once. He cast off the single rope holding the stern to a rock, slammed the gear lever forward and opened the throttle wide. The boat leapt forward as he pulled the wheel hard over to head for open sea.

The man on the beach was holding his face and writhing in agony as the boat gathered speed. Above him the man with the machine-gun ran back into view. He stopped, pulled back the cocking lever, took aim and fired a long burst.

In the boat Peters, as if in a dream, watched the instrument panel in front of him shatter into fragments. Then he felt a series of tremendous blows across his back. There was no pain.

The man on the hill let the gun fall to his side as he watched the boat curve away from the straight line of its wake. The curve became tighter and, with engines bellowing, the boat began to circle round and round like a stricken insect.

Finally there was a heavy thumping explosion and a ball of flame ballooned out of the cockpit. There was a series of smaller explosions and then clouds of black oily smoke billowed up. The motors stopped and flames licked up through the rising smoke pall. Suddenly, the flames snapped out as the hull of the boat lurched over to one side and was gone.

The smoke drifted slowly away leaving only the brightly-coloured rings of oil and a few scattered pieces of debris.

On the other side of the island Brian Gelder, deep in some of the toughest negotiations he had ever experienced, raised his head and asked the other man the cause of the explosion.

The man spread his hands: 'We have bad neighbours, they come to fish in our waters with dynamite, blow the fish to the surface, scoop them up and run for it. Sometimes they blow themselves up in the process. Is all very bad ecology, no?' The man smiled, shrugged and the meeting continued.

CHAPTER SEVEN

MARCIA SAT curled on the settee looking at the disaster area of the flat. It was two weeks since Peters's departure for Yugoslavia and in that time the whole appearance of the room had changed. The skilfully-blended colours and the chromium and glass coffee tables were still there. The spot-lighted award statuette still basked in its alcove, but the studied stage-set arrangements had totally disappeared. All the rugs had been swept to one side and the glass surface of one of the coffee tables was covered in scrawled felt-pen notes. There were papers everywhere. Hung around the neck of one of the statues there was a long perforated computer tape stretching like a clothes line halfway across the room where its other end was taped to the frame of a Hockney original. There were thick piles of computer print-out paper—one of them held down by a small Henry Moore sculpture. About a third of the floor area was covered with photo-copied off-prints from scientific journals, each one had a scrawled assessment on its front cover. One was labelled: 'good data, lousy interpretation', another 'ignore—pretentious crap'.

Marcia began to work out how she could get it back into some sort of shape before Peters's return. He was fastidious and each 'prop' had its own special position. She began to worry about him. It was ten days and, apart from one hurried phone call from Dubrovnik, there had been nothing more. She looked

213

around the disordered flat. Mawn had obviously been there all the weekend while she had been away in Kent with friends.

The doorbell rang and Marcia instinctively pulled off her headscarf and shook her hair loose before going to the door.

It was a stranger. A man in his early twenties, sandy hair, a friendly round face, grey suit and white collar setting off a recently-acquired tan.

'Miss Scott?'

Marcia nodded. The man took a thick brown envelope out of his inside pocket. 'Sheldon Peters asked me to give you this.'

'Thanks.' Marcia took the envelope. 'Say, I've just made fresh coffee, you look as if you could use some.'

He glanced at his watch. 'Thanks all the same but I'm late for the office already.' He smiled and turned to go.

'Thanks again.' She closed the door, went to the kitchen and emptied the contents of the envelope on to the table. There was a thick, tightly-folded letter and, wrapped in a wad of folded corrugated cardboard, four glass microscope slides with paper labels. She squinted at the writing on the top slide and could just read: 'Klin. Patholog. Broca area 4 H & E.' She opened the letter and began to read. About two minutes later, she heard a key in the front door.

Mawn almost sleep-walked back into the living-room and flopped into a chair. He leaned forward automatically and picked up a pile of photostats from the floor and began to read, already lost to his surroundings.

Marcia called out from the kitchen: 'There's coffee if you want it.' Mawn grunted in reply. After a few minutes Marcia appeared with a tray of coffee and the letter.

'I'm back, in case you hadn't noticed.' She put the tray down. Mawn looked up irritably at the interruption.

'Eh?'

She poured out a cup and slid it over the table towards him. 'You look half dead, come on, have some of this. Oh, by the way, there's a letter from Sheld. A little guy from the Yugoslavia place brought it by hand.'

Mawn's tiredness dropped away. 'What did he say?'

Marcia frowned: 'You'd better read it.'

The letter gave a concise account of Peters's experiences in Yugoslavia including an almost verbatim record of his conversation with Chen-wa in Albania. Mawn threw the letter down with a great shout.

'Exactly what we wanted! Where did you put them?'

'What?'

'The slides, the slides!'

'In the kitchen.'

'This could be the most important link we've got. Listen, you've a totally inexplicable I.Q. loss in your subjects here. No cause, nothing.' He picked up the letter. 'And now this man. . . .' He looked down at the letter. '. . . Chen-wa tells Sheldon. . . .' He started to read from the letter: '. . . that he watched people at the Pukë reactor make silly mistakes with their hand and . . . one of them got killed and his brain showed some physical damage . . . and the Albanian doctor gave it a name—Betz cell atrophy. Also that the Russians and the Chinese have admitted to the same sort of physical brain damage!'

'But Alex, you can't begin to prove the link between damaged brains in one place and poor mental performance in another.'

'All right. . . .' He tapped the letter. '. . . but Sheldon says here that one of the people the Chinaman actually saw make a mistake had these physical brain changes.'

'Yes, but good heavens, one case isn't a series—you can't generalize from it.'

'How many of your cases showed poor manual dexterity in the non-verbal tests?'

'A high proportion, you know that.'

'Right! The first thing we have to do is this—get those slides over to this man.' He glanced at the letter. 'Professor Kingston at the Institute of Pathology and see whether they've had any cases of this—Betz-cell atrophy—and, secondly, if they have, whether they've got a register and, thirdly, whether any of the people with your I.Q. loss are on their register.'

'That means they'd be dead.'

'Yes, yes! Can you find out whether any of the subjects you've tested have died?'

'Easily. We've got full extraction on all our data.'

'So we can find out whether any of your affected subjects have died and if they have whether they've got damaged brains!'

Marcia sat back: 'It's the other part I don't like.'

'How's that?'

'All this playing around with cameras on the Albanian border for God's sake!'

'It's obvious,' Mawn pointed to the letter. 'He didn't feel that was conclusive without identifying Gelder's associates. I agree.'

'It's easy for you—you're not there. All this talk of evidence —what for—a court case? Why hasn't there been another phone call from Sheldon?'

Mawn picked up the phone on the floor: 'Point taken. I'll ring his office at the B.B.C.'

The first call set off a long series of abortive attempts to trace Peters's whereabouts. Yes, he had got to Yugoslavia—no, he hadn't reached Rome. . . . Finally, Mawn picked up the dialling code booklet and had just started to note down the code for Dubrovnik when the phone rang. The voice was hushed, female and too carefully enunciated:

'Hello, you were asking for Mr Sheldon Peters's whereabouts?'

'Yes,' Mawn was irritated. 'Who is that, please?'

'This is Mr Danvers's secretary.' The hushed tones spaced the words carefully. 'Is that Dr Mawn?'

'Yes. Will you please get on with it. What's happened?'

He could have been speaking to a computer for all the effect he had. The voice continued: 'And is Miss Scott there?'

'Yes. Where's Peters?'

There was a pause, the voice became a little more hushed: 'I'm afraid he's been killed.'

'Killed!' Mawn looked over at Marcia. 'You're sure?'

'Quite sure. The next of kin have already been informed. It will be on the six o'clock news.'

'How, for God's sake?'

'I'm sorry, I cannot give you any more details at the moment.' The computer-like tone hesitated for a moment and then, with perfect timing, continued: 'Mr Danvers asks that you suspend your activities on the "Nightstyle" programme until he has had a chance to get in touch with you.'

Mawn slowly put the phone down. 'I suppose you got the gist of that?' he said over his shoulder. 'Sheldon's dead.'

Marcia didn't answer and he turned and saw her face. It was white and stricken. With sudden contrition he went over to her: 'I'm sorry, I didn't realize you . . .' he wanted to say 'cared so much' but couldn't get the words out.

Later, they took stock of their situation. The phone call from Danvers's secretary almost certainly meant that the TV programme was now cancelled. But what had happened? Mawn felt an increasing sense of guilt over Peters's death. First his assistant, now Peters. He, Mawn, was the only linking factor. Both had died as a result of his first statement on TV. Peters, especially, had shown great courage. How had he been killed?

Marcia shook him out of his fantasies. 'You can't take his death on yourself. Shel knew exactly what he was getting into, playing spies in sensitive areas. He wanted a scoop—a really big sensation to re-establish himself. I guess he over-reached himself, that's all.'

Mawn looked at her, troubled. She met his gaze for a moment, then looked away. 'I loved the guy, everyone who knew him did, but there's a little more than that. Sheldon was homosexual, he'd been married but it didn't stick. He had a friend, a good friend for many years, almost a marriage. He died last year.'

Mawn shook his head, confused: 'I didn't know.'

'Of course not,' Marcia's tone was sharp. 'No one outside his close friends knew. It was an entirely private thing and he kept it that way.' Her tone softened again. 'There could have been some kind of death wish tied up in this trip.' She rubbed her brow: 'Now, can we please get back to business. What do we do now?'

Mawn looked at her for a moment and then followed her lead. 'O.K. What do we do, well we lack crucial evidence. We both believe your work is right, but we must get some more hard data. We've got to re-test some of your subjects and very quickly. There's no one else down the road to get help from now. We're on our own. If we're right, then the consequences are terrifying. Men staggering about the place with a net loss of ability, we could go back to the dark ages.

'So, if we publish now, every other scientist in the field will take our stuff, rip it up and jump on the bits—that's the way it is. Their job is disproof, if we're wrong anywhere along the line, they'll crucify us.'

Marcia was giving him her full attention. Her hands folded in her lap, her eyes bright again.

'Look, it's not a nice tidy academic problem. It's messy and we're going to get more attacks. We'll get no accolades, but if we're convinced of our status as human beings, then we have to act.'

'But how?'

'We've got to get an investigation going on a global scale. We've got to look at every accident and disaster, every untoward happening where people have been in control of machinery. Train drivers, airline pilots, surgeons, tanker captains, everything. We've got to get their mental abilities measured and recorded, so that we can get some action. . . .'

Mawn was now completely oblivious of her presence. He left his chair and paced the room creating images with his hands.

'Somehow you and I have got to find a weak spot. Some danger area. We can't tackle it globally ourselves. There must be this hazard area—a piece of technology which is the least stable. Somewhere there is one potential volcano. The most obvious is the war machine but that isn't going to get off first base. There's no use going to the Pentagon or the Defence Ministry and saying, give up your missiles because the operators are stupid. We'd be laughed out into the street. Our only hope is to identify the most likely place and to use it as an example. . . .'

Marcia interrupted his torrent of words: 'Why can't we just let it happen—once—then people would see and they'd stop it.'

'We can't. It could be a major disaster involving millions of people. The third world war will almost certainly be started by accident. Just think of it, you've got one man on the D.E.W. line radar trying desperately to hide his mental inability and he makes a wrong decision. We'd never even know why we all died!

'Now take this pressurized water reactor Gelder is building up in the Orkneys,' Mawn continued. 'England's first private enterprise nuclear power station. Private enterprise means cost cutting, cost cutting means lower safety margins, lower safety margins plus incompetent operators equals an accident just waiting to happen. How many of your subjects were nuclear engineers and how many of them are working in the Orkneys already? We've got to find out.'

Catching his enthusiasm she leant forward and grasped both his hands: 'Yes, we could do it. We could maybe get it delayed and then show they had faulty people working there.' She looked at her watch suddenly. 'Look Alex, that reminds me, I've got to go and meet Sheldon's mother to see if I can help.'

'That reminds me,' Mawn said. 'I'd better move out, hadn't I?'

'No, it'll be all right, his mother's a very nice old lady, I'm sure she won't mind. I'll fix it with her.'

After she had gone, he began to think over the basis of his own dinosaur effect and set it against the evidence Marcia had accumulated about the loss of I.Q. in her experimental subjects. Why groups of people only? The puzzle fascinated him. Localized samples of middle-grade engineers, executives and professionals showing a group loss of intelligence. He began to play with ideas, inventing complex social games in office blocks where intelligence was recognized by seniors as a disadvantage.

One by one the ideas foundered and he became gradually more and more depressed. He searched his mind for the cause. Marcia's face kept on recurring. He remembered the image of her holding his hands in a curiously childlike way. In love with her? No! Like her? Yes. Attracted—definitely. He realized he had become dependent on her company, he recalled her nervous smile which almost seemed to embarrass her. She moved beautifully, a natural grace and ease. He wondered what she felt about him. For the first time for years he studied himself in a mirror. The image he saw disquieted him, almost as though an older man had taken over his psyche and was mocking him. Something would have to be done tomorrow.

At about eleven o'clock the next morning, Mawn made his way back to the flat from the University library. Stopping in front of a shop window he gazed at his reflection. Again, the long matted hair and untrimmed beard suddenly repelled him and he remembered the overheard sarcasm of a colleague: 'Must take Mawn hours each morning to get himself that untidy.'

On impulse, he turned into a nearby barber shop and mumbled something about a need for a trim. As he watched in the mirror he wondered whether a hidden Dorian Gray image would emerge, but the result was not so unpleasantly revealing as he had feared.

At the front door Marcia stood for a moment not recognizing him. Then laughed out aloud: 'You didn't tell me you had a younger brother!'

Half an hour later, Mawn put the phone down. 'That's odd. You remember we assumed they would cancel the programme?'

'Yes, of course.'

'Well, that was Danvers, they're going to do it with a new presenter.'

'I'd have thought it a great opportunity for them to cancel.'

'So would I. We must have a friend somewhere!'

'When is it?'

'Live on Sunday fortnight. He wanted me to go in and discuss it now but I said we were too busy and I'd like to think it over and let him know. Apparently they've got a new presenter—Simon Joyce. Do you know him, by the way?'

'Yes, slimy, devious and a hundred per cent on the make.'

'Anyway, the idea is for probably three people to have a go at me about the dinosaur effect. They haven't decided who yet.'

'Are you going to accept?'

'Why not? My facts are straight—nothing to worry about.'

She looked at her watch. 'We're due at "Management Personnel" in about half an hour, they said we could have free run of their data files for an hour this afternoon.'

'Very trusting of them!'

'Oh, no, they get plenty in return. I told you we did a sort of deal with them over the I.Q. tests—they get free capability assessment of their applicants and we get guinea-pigs.'

A torrent of punch cards poured down the chutes of the machine in a steady, unending blurr. Every few seconds, with a loud click, a single card jerked sideways out of the main stream and fluttered down a second chute on to a growing pile in a tray. Marcia and Mawn sat watching the controlled frenzy of activity totally fascinated by the uncanny speed of the process.

Finally, the girl operator pressed a button on the console in front of her, the flood ceased and the whirring died away. Marcia leaned forward eagerly and picked up the pile of extracted cards and began to count:

'. . . sixty-eight, sixty-nine, seventy. . . .' She put the last card down, '. . . seventy-one. Seventy-one nuclear engineers we have tested at least once.'

'That's more than I had expected,' Mawn said.

'Not really. This agency deals with a fairly narrow range of personnel, that's why we chose them in the first place. They'd already more or less selected—for their own reasons—the sort of people we were interested in.'

Mawn picked up the cards and began to study the holes punched around the edges, comparing the position of the holes with a printed list of names on the table in front of him, ticking them off on the list in turn. Finally he put the pencil down. 'You told me first of all that groups of people, in a single place, showed a high percentage of intelligence loss!'

'Right.'

'So how is it that nuclear engineers were all in one place when you tested them?'

'They weren't,' she began to tick off the points on her fingers. 'You see, we also looked at other groups—not just according to where they worked, but what they did for a living.'

'I didn't realize. . . .'

'Yes you did, you saw our analysis, back in the flat.'

'It still doesn't answer my question,' Mawn persisted.

'Yes it does. Our main problem is to explain loss of ability in groups in one place, like maybe they're all blowing their minds on pot in the basement after hours—or something like that, but if you take any other artificially selected groups, like occupation or age or salary level, they're not in one place, but you're bound to find a few of the affected people among them aren't you?'

Mawn picked up the list.

'So you've tested seventy-one nuclear engineers, and according to this,' he tapped the list, 'eighteen showed some loss of I.Q.— either on one test or two.'

'Yes.'

'So how many of the eighteen are currently working at the Grim-Ness station?' He began to gather up the papers, looking over at the sulky girl re-setting the punch-card machine. 'I think we've rather overstayed our welcome—let's get back.' Marcia looked at him, her eyes twinkling: 'I'll have you majoring in psychology yet.'

'Naylor P., Baird D., Durrell F., Elleston F., Westcott B., Haskell R., six of them.' Mawn put the list down on the coffee table. 'Six people probably concealing a loss of ability while they are commissioning England's first private enterprise reactor where the safety margins are already absolutely minimal.'

Marcia was sitting on the rug propped up on large cushions. 'Alex, are you sure we're not setting up our own private vendetta?'

221

Mawn looked up: 'If we get our facts right, does it matter what our motivations are?'

'All I meant was—it might push us too far too soon.'

'It won't do that, there are too many things we haven't got. For instance, it depends what that pathologist Kingston says when he's had a look at the slides but in the meantime, the Gelder nuclear station at Grim-Ness is the good bet. If you like, it's a microcosm of the whole situation. We won't get anyone to listen to us if we say there's a global effect and people have got to stop doing practically everything, but if we could show the presence of affected people in the nuclear station, then we'd have a case.'

'I'm not convinced,' Marcia replied. 'Just because six affected men are working up there it doesn't mean anything terrible is bound to happen. I mean—if the station starts up and nothing goes wrong we're going to look like a couple of complete goofs and then we'll have lost the chance to convince anyone how widespread the effect really is.'

'Not a bit of it. So far, the English Electricity Board have got an excellent safety record with their gas-cooled reactors—but this is as different as chalk from cheese. It's a private consortium, building a privately-funded reactor. They're already in cut-throat competition with the Japanese and the Americans. They're all chasing methods of paring down costs and so we've got a cut price reactor about to start up partly operated by people who very likely can't do their job adequately. No, we've got to bring it right out in the open—we've nothing to lose now.

'Almost a year ago I had a visit from Gelder's Chief Health Physicist—John Barfield. It was all under the counter, but the gist of it all was that the previous Gelder stations—one in Japan and the other in Dortmund—were absolutely riddled with faults, even during building. Barfield apparently tried to reason with them at the time but he just got the same old line—"it wouldn't be economic".

'But even Gelder can't ignore this double hazard. The Grim-Ness station is due to start up in December so, between now and then, we've got to stop it!'

Gelder surveyed the two men over the top of the brandy balloon. Bellamy, his round shiny head reddened from the cognac, was rolling a cigar anxiously in his fingers. Caird appeared even more sallow and repressed; he had drunk only mineral water through-out the lunch.

The noise of the traffic outside in St James's only just filtered through the drawn curtains into the dark velvet and leather atmosphere of the club morning-room.

Bellamy spoke urgently: 'I tell you, we're already getting the first results of this guy's campaign. There are a mass of rumours circulating round Wall Street—— Is our gear cheap-jack? Is it really unreliable like Mawn says? We're losing a hell of a lot of potential contracts—people are just diverting to the Japs. We've got to nail him somehow!'

'Hasn't he got any convenient skeletons?' Caird asked mildly.

'Hey, wait a minute,' Bellamy protested. 'Remember what hap-pened to that chemical firm when they tried to hobble Nader—cost them three-quarters of a million bucks.'

Gelder sniffed the glass. 'You can forget all about that, we have to do something far more effective. This man is very, very bad news and he has to be completely halted.'

The two men looked at Gelder, startled. 'And don't worry,' Gelder continued evenly, 'nothing like that. You can't get friend Mawn on women or little boys, we've got to try much harder. Now I've been doing some research. I got in touch with one of Mawn's fellow academics who isn't exactly in love with him and I've also traced the employee I told you about last time we met. Between the two of them, I think they can achieve exactly what we want.'

CHAPTER EIGHT

DURING THE TWO DAYS before the television show, Mawn and Marcia worked solidly at their data for presentation, the outlines of the flat slowly submerging in a sea of papers and files.

Mawn had made an uneasy agreement with the producer of the programme. The show was to follow on the first in which he had originally defined the dinosaur effect. He had already been told that the industries he had attacked would be given screen time to refute his allegations and Mawn had countered with the statement that he had new and important material which would help to

develop this theory. The producer had then said that the programme was not to be a further platform for his views but rather
to enable him to defend his first statements.

The programme, as usual, was to go out live on the Sunday.

Marcia leaned back in her chair and threw the pencil down.
'How did you get all this, or is that an academic secret?'

'Not at all,' Mawn said. 'Over the past few years I've had a lot of
people coming to me from various firms offering data. They're
mostly disgruntled employees with a grudge, so I ignore them.' He
pointed at the papers. 'But that stuff came from John Barfield a
couple of days back.'

'He was taking a big risk, wasn't he? What does he get out of it?'

'A clear conscience for one. You see, he used to be in medical
physics at the M.R.C. then Gelder bought him up to head his new
health physics department. It was a sort of con. Health physics is
obviously essential if you build nuclear reactors, but he was also
a public showpiece to allay Union protests about health hazards.'

'Do you trust him?'

'John? Yes, completely. The reason he came to me first of all
some months back is that basically he's a very concerned environmentalist, he didn't come for money or anything like that. He
found that most of the nuclear stations the Gelder consortium had
built kept on having breakdowns and accidents. He compiled the
history of each one and then went to the board and made suggestions about safety.'

'And they took no notice?'

'Not only that, they told him to lay off. You see, his problem is
that he burnt his boats academically by joining Gelder, he's got a
big family and so on, so finally he came round to see me with the
whole lot and said, in essence, "Do what you like with it—but
don't tell them I told you".'

'Won't they get on to him?'

'No, there are lots of people with access to those figures.'

Marcia picked up a file and pointed to a row of figures: 'That's
a bit much!'

Mawn looked up. 'What?'

'One of Barfield's estimates.' She checked with a second list on
the table in front of her. 'According to him, one of the computers
in the Dortmund reactor spent seventy per cent of its time out of
commission with faults.'

'Not unusual with the N.A.L.A. computer system. Anyhow, we checked his stuff through when we first got it. All we've got to do now is to boil it down into simple terms to convince the great viewing public. Look Marcia, if you've got any doubts at all, now's the time.'

She hesitated: 'Won't they take action for slander or something —they must have pretty big legal brains behind them?'

'They daren't. We're just pointing out the facts of what they're doing and it's up to them to answer. We've got an opportunity to reach over twelve million people. It's the best possible forum we could have. I can bring out all the stuff about your I.Q. loss and show this is not confined to this country.'

'Providing Simon Joyce doesn't try and screw you up—he's quite good with the needle.'

'That's a minor risk.'

'Oh, incidentally, I'm having some folk in to watch you. You don't mind?'

Mawn smiled.

'What, here?'

'Oh, yes, I often used to set parties up for Sheldon here.'

'I'll try and make it if I can. They want to have a final word on a late night chat show afterwards. So I'll make my way to their— entertainment suite—as they call it, and drink enough scotch to make my enemies interesting!'

Simon Joyce sat in one corner of the studio ante-room with the floor manager, tensely examining his teleprompt copy. He appeared not to notice his four guests.

Mawn sat sprawled in a plastic shell chair, suffering the attentions of a make-up girl patting away at the shine on his forehead with a powder puff. From the open door leading to the studio, there was a confused jumble of noise. Two men were sweatily pushing a new desk section into position in front of a battery of cameras; another in shirt sleeves, wearing headphones, picked up an empty water flask from the desk and shook it furiously at a harassed girl who hurried away to fill it.

Mawn listened for his own heartbeat and discovered that it was scarcely above normal. He patted his jacket pocket, feeling for his notes, and began to study his three adversaries.

Geoffrey Twining, Science Editor of the *Daily Chronicle*—

potential ally. Professor Seager, Head of Computing Science at King's University. High table manner, but a professional character assassin. William Sampson, Secretary, Nuclear Inspectorate, Department of Trade and Industry. Neutral probably. Would defend his own masters.

The man in the headphones poked his head round the door and smiled. 'Ready, gentlemen, thank you.'

Mawn settled awkwardly into his seat under the harsh glare of the spotlight. The other three were either carefully studying the dais or gazing away into the blackness beyond the lights.

Simon Joyce peered into the square aperture of the teleprompter comparing the inch-high letters with his notes on the dais in front of him.

The title music began. . . .

Marcia circulated among her guests. There were about fifteen altogether, mostly dressed in the carefully-arranged informality of the show business world. Richard Lodge stood out among the neck scarves and jeans in his Civil Service grey. His Spanish wife, Alicia, wore a dark blue velvet evening gown.

Howard Venn had just arrived straight off the plane from Lisbon and was talking to Lodge, using the special brand of authoritative enthusiasm he reserved for people who wielded power and money. His pretty, vacant, wife stood behind him carefully holding on to a fixed smile of what she hoped looked like intelligent interest. Lodge was nodding sagely as Venn expounded.

None of the guests gave any outward indication that the gathering was a posthumous tribute to Peters. No one mentioned him and kept carefully to the strident in-group gossip reserved for such occasions. During the half-hour preceding the programme, she told as many as possible the facts behind her work with Mawn since she realized that they could be helpful in various spheres of influence.

She looked at her watch with a prickling sense of anticipation and turned on the thirty-inch wall projection TV set. The guests began to settle on the floor around the screen, drinks in hand.

The title music faded and the programme began.

To Marcia's relief, Mawn spoke simply and effectively, making his points in a careful and lucid sequence with a minimum of gesture or theatricality.

As he finished, Simon Joyce came back into frame, summing up

226

the purpose of the programme and introduced the three men who were to discuss Mawn's theory.

Marcia quickly circulated, filling glasses and trying to sense the guests' reaction to the programme.

Geoffrey Twining was first. He kept strictly to the points Mawn had made and offered carefully limited challenges which Mawn was able to both put down and to expand. Although he appeared to attack, it was clear that he was only offering pawns for sacrifice.

Marcia drew a deep breath. If the other two were as easy—she crossed her fingers.

Professor Seager took off his spectacles and carefully folded them away in the breast pocket of his suit.

'I hope you'll forgive me saying so, but a great deal of what Doctor Mawn has said worries me intensely.'

'Could you say why, Professor?' Joyce said.

'Yes.' He folded both hands demurely in front of him. 'A very clear allegation has been made. Doctor Mawn says that the whole basis of our advanced technology is in some way in jeopardy from inherently faulty machines. He had moreover invented a most seductive name for the idea—the dinosaur effect! So if we deal with the more objective aspects of what I really must label as a piece of irresponsible science fiction. . . .'

'There's nothing fictional about the data I gave!' Mawn protested. 'The sources are absolutely unimpeachable I assure you. . . .'

Joyce interrupted Mawn firmly: 'I think we must give the others a chance.'

Mawn subsided and Professor Seager continued: 'Yes—ah—it has been suggested that . . .' he looked down at his notepad, '. . . the overall error rate of the N.A.L.A. computer system was seventeen per cent.' He turned to Mawn. 'That is what you said, isn't it?'

Mawn nodded.

'And that independent tests of the emergency core cooling system in the Kyoto reactor showed an irrecoverable core temperature rise of fifteen hundred degrees before operation. Is that right?'

Again Mawn nodded: 'Correct.'

'You then pointed out that X-ray tests of the pressure vessel in the Dortmund reactor showed an average two per cent failure—that is to say, two inches out of every hundred inches welded showed a fault of some kind—sealing or improper penetration of the weld, I think you said?'

'Within the limits I gave, yes.'

'And quite apart from your previous television allegations, you also seriously suggested that radiation levels in the cooling circuits were four per cent over the permitted maximum.' Seager opened a folder. 'Now I have been in touch with the Gelder consortium and they have been kind enough to open their entire research data to myself and my colleagues.' He looked down at the file. 'The overall error rate of their computer systems on test was two point four per cent whereas you allege seventeen.' He turned a page. 'Their core cooling system showed a theoretical rise of only four hundred and twenty degrees and you say fifteen hundred! As to their radiation monitoring in the primary cooling circuits—they are . . .' he looked down at the folder, '. . . in fact below the design maximum which was Oh point Oh five R. Now clearly, anyone is entitled to argue about statistical details but Doctor Mawn's figures show such a complete departure from mine that I can only assume he has been wrongly informed. . . .' He pushed his glasses back up his nose. 'And the fact that he is unable—or perhaps unwilling—to declare their origin, merely gives me further cause for anxiety.'

'My figures can be verified,' Mawn began, but his voice faltered. 'They were in fact produced by the company themselves. . . .'

Joyce turned to the fourth guest. 'Mr Sampson, you represent the Nuclear Inspectorate, would you care to comment?'

'Indeed I would. I'd like to start by pointing out that there are two forms of nuclear power station in this country. There are those operated by the Central Electricity Generating Board and those being built privately—in this case by the Gelder consortium. Now in both cases, and I really must emphasize this, the strictest control is exercised by my department over all safety measures built into these stations both State run and private. Now in this case my own department's figures agree very well with Professor Seager's. I don't know where Doctor Mawn got his figures, but as far as I can see they are completely without any foundation.'

Joyce turned: 'Doctor Mawn, any comments?'

'Well, we disagree.' Mawn's voice had dropped. 'All figures are subject to doubt, it depends on their origin. But, in fact, the situation is much more serious than I proposed. A colleague and I have been able to find evidence that not only are the new stations themselves faulty, but many of the operators are showing signs of decreasing ability. Some aspects of their behaviour and intelligence

228

are showing a definite fall. So, far from being discouraged I feel that . . .'

'Oh, really!' Seager interrupted. 'Not only have your own figures been shown to be entirely and completely wrong, but now you're trying to invent some totally new effect to cover your mistake. I really must say this; the whole economic future of our country depends on abundant—and non-polluting—energy. And instead, we have heard a completely baseless attack on the very heart of one of our most important assets—nuclear power. Doctor Mawn's data could be the result of an honest mistake, he may well have been misinformed, or he could have fabricated the entire case. The law prevents me from stating my own preference!'

Simon Joyce turned to camera; 'Well, a vexed issue! That's all we have time for tonight, so . . .' He nodded to each one in turn: 'Mr Sampson, Mr Twining, Professor Seager, Doctor Mawn, thank you very much. . . .'

It was Richard Lodge who leant over and turned off the set as Marcia sat, too stunned to move. There was a long tense silence followed by an explosive burst of loud conversation. Everyone seemed to get up at once and move towards the drink trolley.

The next hour was one of the longest in Marcia's life. They all acted as if the party itself was the reason why they were there and the programme itself was a peripheral event. Only Mrs Venn, with her usual lack of comprehension, commented that Mawn looked better with his beard trimmed.

Marcia's mind refused to think about the debacle, to reason out what had gone wrong. Gradually, as she moved around desperately trying to find small talk, she began to reassess the whole basis of their work together.

As soon as they decently could, the guests began to drift away, each pleading baby-sitting problems or an early start the next morning. Venn couldn't resist an exit line: 'Please give Doctor Mawn my condolences and tell him he's welcome to our facilities —if they're any further use to him.'

The last to leave was Richard Lodge. While his wife started to restore the flat to some resemblance of order, he gently touched Marcia on the shoulder: 'I wouldn't take it too hard if I were Mawn, main thing is to get priorities right. I'm quite sure your work has not been wasted.'

For about an hour she sat quietly in a chair without stirring. Finally she heard the front door. He stood looking down at her, she studied the glass she was holding, then slowly got up, putting the glass down. 'Alex, for God's sake what happened?'

He shook his head, his voice flat, toneless: 'I've no idea, no idea at all.'

Long after Marcia had gone home to her apartment, Mawn sat in Peters's long black armchair staring into space. Even the familiar bite of the whisky failed to blunt the edge of his pain. He felt an almost literal paralysis of the will, dangerously close to breaking point. In a few short weeks, the whole pattern of his life had been shattered, strand by strand. First, the destruction of the laboratory and now the final blow, the stripping away of his scientific reputation. And he had walked right into it, over-reached himself; committed professional suicide before an audience of millions. He had no further illusions about his chance of continuing his work—Marcia's stricken face had finally proved that. He had been shown up as a fantasist, a liar and cheat. Seager had done his task well—in a few short minutes, he had pricked the short-lived balloon of Mawn's public reputation and left nothing behind.

And what about Marcia and his fine words of a couple of weeks ago?

Mawn rose sluggishly to his feet and stumbled out of the flat, down the stairs and out into the deserted night street. Anything rather than stay surrounded by the ruins of their theory.

The night was clear and the wet streets still gleamed in the lamplight. Instinctively, his steps took him in the direction of the Embankment and the broad Thames river. Eventually, he reached the Embankment Gardens.

The attack was swift and unexpected. A shadow detached itself from one of the Victorian statues and signalled. Another appeared from behind the bushes. Together they flung themselves at him.

The fight was short. Mawn kicked out at the first figure, sending him reeling back into the bushes holding the pit of his stomach. There was a brief flash of a knife as the second lunged forward. Mawn ducked and the knife swept harmlessly across his back. Then, grabbing his assailant round the legs, he lifted him bodily, upending him on to the path. The knife clattered away on the concrete as the man fell heavily on to his back. Mawn landed on top of him jamming his shoulders back against the path. He raised his fist threateningly and the man who had been struggling violently to get free suddenly went limp under Mawn's weight. From the darkness he could hear the footsteps of the other running away.

Mawn swung the man's head round into the light and found himself looking at a youth of about seventeen. A pale frightened face stared back at him from underneath a mane of frizzy fair hair.

A wave of pity swept through him at the thin wasted face. He bent down and pulled the youth to his feet and guided him over to an all-night coffee stall underneath the railway arch.

It was a long time before Mawn managed to convince him that he was not going to call the police. Gradually, the youth began to talk:

'Yeah, well, we just wanted bread, that's all. We'd been sleeping rough for a couple of days, both bleeding starving. We thought we'd mug the first geezer that came along the path.'

'Haven't you got a job?'

'Nah. Who'd give me a bleedin' job. I can't do nothing right can I? Tried everything. Ain't got the savvy no more. Last work I had was in a garage. Couldn't even do that right could I? Couldn't work out what the guv'nor was on about. Me hands were going wrong. Lost it upstairs. Used to be good with me hands—onetime. Anyway, who bloody cares?'

Later, as he made his way back home, Mawn couldn't get the pinched unhealthy face out of his mind. He had offered the youth five pounds to come to the laboratory to be tested, but he had stopped talking at once, suspecting a trap.

'. . . ain't got the savvy, no more.' The words echoed. Where would he end up if he was affected? How many more were there? In the dark streets he saw nightmare figures of a moronic populace loping into the shadows like wolves in a forest. He thought back over the television show and no longer felt any reaction. What the hell does it matter, faced with this! There was just one thing to do; to go on. Self-pity was a luxury he couldn't afford. The streets were just beginning to lighten as he reached the front door of the flat.

Marcia woke late, feeling heavy limbed and stupid. The

slightest movement seemed to be a disproportionate effort. The humiliation and embarrassment of the party washed over her in waves; guarded comments and averted eyes. She began to long for the ease and comfort of her parents' home in the States and plotted the journey home in her mind's eye, realizing with a surge of pleasure that she could be packed and on a jet in a matter of hours. She looked around at the impersonal furnishings of the flat she had rented and began to visualize her own room at home.

He had been torn to bits, no point in trying to avoid it. All his figures had been hopelessly wrong—at least those he'd been given by Barfield. She played briefly with the notion that Barfield had been primed with false data by Gelder, but then dismissed it, remembering the data had been doubly checked.

She thought back over his whole approach to the I.Q. effect and began to suspect that he was himself faulty in his scientific approach and method. She remembered the words of one of her teachers: 'If a man wants to talk about his work before publication, the work is almost certainly incomplete and very probably wrong.' With a flush of embarrassment she remembered how Mawn's approach had originally fascinated her. A man driven by internal compulsions without any reference to his external image. She pictured Venn in the same situation. How he would have cringed: image and no substance.

He had suffered the worst attack possible for a scientist—a loss of credibility—a clear accusation of charlatanry. And in public. A public who would certainly have included many of his peers. He would never be forgiven.

There was a loud knock at the front door. She got out of bed and quickly flung on a housecoat and slippers. Fighting down a swirl of vertigo, she stumbled into the hall and opened the door. Alex Mawn stood quite still, a half-smile flickering across his face.

'Alex—I didn't know what to say last night. I just felt so bloody. Come on in.'

He followed her in and sat down. 'There was nothing to say, was there? I mean I got kicked in the balls and that's that.'

'But your figures, Alex. You were all wrong!'

'I've had time to think about that now. I got them from John Barfield, right?'

She nodded.

'Whatever else he is I think he's straight. He was desperately worried about the situation, so what advantage would there be for him to give me phoney data? To change Barfield round must have really taken some pressure!'

'What?'

'It's a bit more likely as of ten minutes ago as a matter of fact.'

She looked puzzled.

'I phoned him at home—talked to his wife. Apparently he's not available—on some sort of trip—she was most unforthcoming.'

'What will you do? Didn't last night mean anything to you at all?'

'I had a long night.' He spoke quietly, looking straight at her. 'I had this happen once before. I gave a lecture at a meeting in Milan—a perfectly ordinary mistake—it happens to everybody in research sooner or later—I made a stupid error in a paper I read and this American got up in the audience afterwards and absolutely walked all over me. He pointed out that not only was I wrong, but my work had been published before by someone else. I simply hadn't done my homework—he was right, and I was wrong. I died all the deaths.'

'But it was all wrong!'

'Last night was different. After the Milan business I came home and I literally hid. I thought I was washed up—getting stupid— all that. But last night—I don't know—I haven't worked it all out yet—but somehow I know we've been got at. All that work we did in Venn's lab.—you did it with me, after all—that was perfectly valid. . . .'

She looked puzzled. 'You don't doubt the statistical methods we used do you?'

'No, at least I don't think so.'

'I'll put it another way. You're still sure that the localized I.Q. loss is genuine, aren't you?'

'A hundred per cent—yes.'

'Well, let me tell you another thing. All my instincts at the moment are to go back to Plymouth, shut myself up in my lab. and get on with some nice pure academic problem in computer logic. I'm good at it, I enjoy it and it's fun. I tried that before and it didn't work. I've opened the laboratory door now and had a bloody good look at the stinking technological mess we're all in. I met one of the victims last night.'

233

'How's that?'

'Never mind, I'll tell you later. But listen, if what we've found is really generalized—on a global scale—it's quite irrelevant whether we've got machines which work or don't work if there is a species of man evolving who is mentally unable to operate them.'

'But, Alex—no one's going to listen now.'

'Right—my credibility's about as low as it could be. That's why we've got to get us there.'

'Where?'

'The Orkneys for God's sake! You're right, no one's going to listen until we've got cast iron evidence. So, what I suggest is this. You go round now to Venn's emporium, swipe one of those portable intelligence meters—all the other gear too—test cards—the lot. Then come back here and we'll get off. Don't forget there are six people right inside that nuclear power station who are almost certainly covering up for the fact that they're not up to their job. They start it up in December so if we can retest them in time and either show they're still affected, or better still that they've got a progressive decline in ability, then we've got just a chance of getting it put off: nothing more!'

'That won't be enough to convince anyone now.'

'Have you got any other suggestions?'

'We could find some new way of presenting the material we've already got.'

'And have it filed in the basement of a ministry? At best we'd get a reluctant Royal Commission. Then there'd be a five-year wait followed by half an hour's discussion time in the House and then nothing. Marcia, if this is as widespread as we think it is, we've got to find some immediate way of getting it recognized. I accept all your caveats—six people—one place—that's no basis for any scientific paper—I know that. In a way it's almost a piece of theatre. But we're not going to publish a paper!'

'But what action can we take?'

'Get sufficient evidence, there's no other way.'

'How?'

'Get to those six people.'

'How would we get into the station?'

'Look Marcia, you believe in your findings?'

'Of course.'

'Well, are you going to risk not doing anything. If man's brains are going addled and we fail to convince people, we'll never be able to look ourselves in the face again, never!'

'Alex, I'm not used to this sort of pressure.'

'If it's global, and it's progressive, it's the end of man, Marcia. It's a hundred per cent certain somebody will touch the wrong trigger. We have got to go up there and convince them, they've got dangerous people in their station. Will you do it, Marcia?'

For a full half-minute, she sat quite still on the edge of her chair, then looked up. 'There's nothing else we can do.'

CHAPTER NINE

MAWN SENSED the springy resilience of the compacted grass and heather under his feet. He stood near the top of a rounded hillock looking down over the huge empty expanse of Scapa Flow. The hills of Hoy just showed as dark craggy outlines over the horizon to the west. Below the water, he imagined the bulbous hulks of the scuttled warships rusting away in the gloom.

As he sat down and stretched out in the golden light of the autumn sunshine the debacle of the television show, the sophisticated backbiting of the scientific community in London dissolved away in the clear cold air of the Islands.

The plane to Orkney from London had flown through a continuous streaming overcast. And now over four hundred miles nearer to the Arctic circle, the air was scintillating and fresh. The sea was a deep Mediterranean blue and there was no sound except for the light hiss of the wind through the grass. Out of the wind the sun was hot but as he stood up in the cold air blowing straight from the ice packs to the north, he was grateful for the protection of a thick woollen sweater and overboots. The chill of the wind evoked long-buried memories of his days in the Arctic. Expeditions into howling sub-zero blizzards to set up apparatus. He thought through the long soft years at Plymouth which had followed. The easy life, two lectures a week and an occasional research project to make the annual report look sufficiently fat.

None of his critics from the faculty would have recognized him.

The incipient paunch had already begun to recede. The lines on his face had tautened and his stride was firmer.

At the top, he pulled cold air gratefully into his chest to regain his breath, and slowly scanned the great empty circle of sea, islands and sky.

To the north lay the low, bare hills of the largest Orkney Island, called by the inhabitants 'the mainland'. From the tip of the island where he stood—South Ronaldsay—stretched one of the four Churchill barriers running north and connecting all the islands together with a main road stretching across the shallows. He followed the path of the road to Burray incongruously set on a piled jumble of white sugar cube concrete blocks. A long articulated lorry had just turned off the barrier road on to the Islands and was lurching ponderously towards the main gate of the Grim-Ness nuclear power station. He could just hear the sound of its engine.

The station was totally alien to its surroundings. Set next to the coast surrounded by neatly laid out fields of pasture and kale, it looked unreal. More like a projection of a space city. Most of the buildings were low-lying and exactly rectangular. The whole complex was surrounded by a high wire fence. From his standpoint he could see the tessellated glass roof of the great turbine hall lying next to the windowless grey building housing the switching gear. On the far side of the compound, there were clusters of smaller buildings connected by a branched concrete path which stood starkly pale against the surrounding green.

Dominating the whole complex was the giant white cubical reactor hall reflecting brilliantly in the sunshine, sitting like an enormous iceberg among the low surrounding buildings, sinister and silent. There were no signs of external activity except for a thin plume of steam escaping from the top of one building.

Beyond the station he could make out the ragged line of the cliff edge and, beyond that, the white caps of the waves breaking silently on the rock-strewn coastline beneath. Just beyond the fence to the south was the large white circle of a heliport picked out in bright concentric circles of fluorescent orange like a giant archery target. A large passenger-carrying twin rotor helicopter was parked at the edge of the landing circle and Mawn noted with surprise that both the rotors and fuselage were lashed to the ground with guy-ropes.

To Mawn, the entire scene represented the harsh clash between the artifacts of high technology and the gentle outlines of the natural world.

He looked down at his watch and with a start, realized that it was almost time to meet Marcia in Dr Durrell's office at the station. They had previously agreed on the plane from Edinburgh that she would start the testing of the six men as soon as they arrived. She was to start with Philip Naylor, senior computer engineer in charge of intermediate systems control at the station.

The main control room of the Grim-Ness power station was in the shape of a drum. The circular wall was covered by a continuous array of complex instrument consoles patterned with block after block of dials, paper recorders and video screens. The floor was covered from wall to wall in a dark olive-green carpet and the panels holding the instruments were finished in a matt non-reflecting coffee-brown. Overhead, shadowless illumination was provided by an eggbox array of plastic strips hiding the glare of multiple batteries of fluorescent tubes.

In the centre of the room there were four smaller consoles shaped like slightly-enlarged executive desks. Each displayed a simpler array of instruments and on one of them four vertical telephones each of a different colour hung together in a row. There were eight men in the room, seven were standing in front of the control panels around the edge of the room and the eighth, Dr Frank Durrell, sat at the desk with the four phones. He was speaking into the blue set.

'Hello, David?—— Yes, Durrell—good—stand by.' He turned to one of the technicians. 'O.K.?' The man nodded. Durrell returned to the phone: 'Now as you plug in each thermal sensor, give us a bleep on the tone circuit—then we can start taking baselines—just a minute.' He put his hand over the mouthpiece of the phone and turned towards a man by an instrument panel to see whether he had heard. The man nodded. 'O.K.—right—thank you, David.'

David Baird had been asked during his first job interview whether he had ever suffered from claustrophobia. He had answered no. There was good reason for the question.

He was working inside one of the most heavily-enclosed spaces ever designed by man. Swaddled in enveloping set of bulky white overalls, white cotton cap and overshoes, he was kneeling on the open face of the nuclear reactor core. Over his head was the vaulting inner surface of the four-inch thick steel pressure vessel—a giant metal bottle over sixty feet in diameter and a hundred feet long. Beneath him was the flat honeycombed pattern of the reactor face. Between the surface of the pressure vessel overhead and the reactor face stretched a forest of vertical metal tubes spaced just far enough apart for him to crawl between them. Two other men also in protective oversuits crouched beside him; like animals in a metal forest.

The three worked by the harsh glare of jury-rigged spotlights clamped on to tripod frames. Temporary cables ran from the lights through a three-foot hole at the centre of the pressure vessel where a section of the steel cap had been withdrawn. Over the hole the six-ton metal plug swung gently at the end of three leashes of chains leading up through the six-foot-thick concrete floor above to a gantry crane in the roof of the reactor hall a hundred and twenty feet overhead.

The air inside the reactor sphere was hot and humid. There was a strong smell of hot metal overlain by the more pungent reek of hot electrical windings.

Surrounding the three men in the pressure vessel there were the thermal shields and then finally the solid, nine-foot-thick biological shield. A concrete cube over one hundred feet in diameter and varying between seven and nine feet in thickness totally enclosing the pressure vessel. There was only one way out of the confined space where the men knelt. Up a spidery duralumin ladder suspended across the aperture in the pressure vessel and on up a second ladder hooked to the sides of the tunnel in the concrete shield leading up through the biological shield and on to the smooth paved floor of the reactor hall above.

Hanging down through the hole in the pressure vessel alongside the long festoons of cables was a long, corrugated flexible tube capped by a square grilled box. In the box were multi-layers of sticky glass fibre filters. Through the grille came a weak supply of fresh air with all the dust and particles removed. Baird and his two colleagues were working through the long, painstaking process of instrument calibration.

Inside the lifeless reactor core, batteries of 'sensing' devices were being inserted between the uranium fuel rods, to give continuous information about the state of the core. Its temperature, how fast the process of fission was proceeding and what temperature differences existed between the cooling water at the centre of the honeycomb and the high temperature water leaving the core on its way to the steam-generating heat exchangers.

Each sensor in fact transmitted its information to the computer and to the control room by means of electrical signals. This meant that Baird and his colleagues could test each sensor by artificially injecting an electric current into the wires leading to the control room as if it were an actual signal from the sensor inside the core. The engineers in the control room could then compare the readings they received with a list of baseline values supplied by the manufacturers on instrument dials in the control room.

Baird picked up the phone beside him and punched a number into the touchtone buttons. While he waited for an answering signal from the control room, he disconnected a red wire from a terminal marked B and a green wire from a terminal marked B2 and attached two clipped leads from a small portable oscilloscope to the terminals. On a small notepad clipped to his oversuit he wrote in one box of a squared-off test chart 'B sensor matrix calibration'. A light blinked on the phone set. He picked it up and spoke: 'I've got prods on B matrix outlet—do you read?—over.'

He switched on the oscillograph which immediately displayed an illuminated shower of waveforms rushing across its light yellow screen. 'Am putting saw-tooth form at R.M.S. of four point five volts.'

An engineer in the control room watched a needle move slowly across the scale of an instrument dial. The dial was labelled: 'B, fuel pin temp.' The needle stopped at four point one. He spoke into the phone: 'It's four point one—check the level of your injection signal please.'

Inside the reactor sphere, Baird covered his eyes against the glare of the lights and studied the screen of the oscillograph. He was sweating profusely and his hands were shaking as he fumbled with a control on the face of the instrument. The peaks of the waves on the screen wobbled and then rose higher. He spoke into the phone: 'How's that now—is it up?—Yes?—O.K.' He put the phone down, unplugged the oscillograph and ticked off the

239

entry in the notepad in a column headed: 'test complete'. Finally, with clumsy shaking fingers, he reconnected the red wire to the terminal marked B2 and the green wire to the terminal B.

Marcia turned a knob on the Venn meter to 'score read-out' and a strip of paper covered in rows of printed figures silently extruded from a slot in the side of the instrument. She tore it off, looked at it, then tucked it away in a file. She looked over at Philip Naylor sitting in the archair. He was short, a dapper man of about thirty with exactly parted black hair and minimal sideburns. Although off shift, he was still wearing a rather tightly-fitting off-the-peg charcoal-grey suit, white shirt and thin tightly-knotted association tie.

'How did I do?' The surface joviality only just hid anxiety. 'Can't tell yet,' she replied.

'How does that thing work, anyhow?'

'It's a way of getting rid of any personal bias by the operator—in other words, me!' she replied. 'Means you're not influenced by any pressures I could put on you by using special words.'

'I'll never get used to that damn thing.'

She tried to speak reassuringly: 'I guess it's fairer than I'd be. Anyway, your results looked O.K. to me. It's very kind of you to give me more time—I know how busy you all are.'

Carol Naylor came in with a tray of coffee reminding her husband in an over-rehearsed tone of haste that he was on shift in an hour. The conversation gradually turned towards the vagaries of the Orkney weather and the price of food in the Kirkwall shops.

As she drove away, Marcia remembered the tension she had caught between the couple sitting poised on the edges of their chairs in the fussy overneat living-room. She began to imagine what they thought of her. An American psychologist looking inside their heads probably reporting straight back to the Station superintendent.

Their reaction had, in fact, been fairly typical of the others—a general undercurrent of suspicion. When she had first tested them in London, they had all been between jobs. They had regarded the test as a job evaluation quiz to help them realize their full employment potential. An attitude for which the personnel agency was responsible.

Now that they had a good long-term job with the prospect of

other water-reactor stations to build, the test represented a danger. Supposing they failed to measure up to scratch? There would be a secret personnel file somewhere—with all the test results. To how many people would this file be made available?

It had been only because Dr Durrell had given his approval to Marcia's request and volunteered to be retested himself that she had to get the three men to co-operate. First of all Elleston and Haskell, and now Naylor.

Marcia drove the hired car uneasily. It was an almost vintage 1974 model with a well-rusted body. Ruined shock-absorbers made the ride a continuous bouncing discomfort. She passed the featureless cubes of the homing estate built by the Gelder Consortium for its employees and drove on towards the Grim-Ness station at the north-eastern tip of the Island. She had arranged to meet Mawn at the station just before their interview with Dr Frank Durrell.

She reviewed the past forty-eight hours. For Stanley Elleston and Roger Haskell, it had been their second test. Both men had showed a slight but definitely lower figure compared with her first measurements. Only one man—Philip Naylor—had been tested three times and all three results had shown a downward trend. She reflected ruefully that two points on a curve meant practically nothing and three points as in the case of Naylor would still fail to convince a sceptical critic. Although his results were taken by themselves were impressive, his manual dexterity, pattern recognition and verbal skill levels had all shown a similar degree of loss.

She imagined trying to convince Lodge or his Minister sufficiently with this flimsy evidence to make them delay the test.

Three men still remained who had already undergone two tests: Bernard Westcott—in charge of emergency core cooling, David Baird—reactor engineer and Dr Frank Durrell—Chief Systems Designer and executive superintendent of the station. She wondered how to deal with the situation if Durrell's figures showed a progressive drop.

How do you tell a senior nuclear engineer he's getting to be incapable?

She began to work out her own reactions if someone were to tell her that her faculties were afflicted. She concluded that she would show them the door with appropriate dignity.

*   *   *

241

Mawn was already sitting in an outer office, trying uncomfortably to squeeze himself in between three secretaries clattering away at typewriters. Each one was plugged into a tape recorder. The room was overcrowded with a jumble of papers and filing cabinets.

As Marcia entered, one of the secretaries looked up, taking off her earphones: 'Miss Scott?'

Marcia smiled and nodded. The secretary spoke briefly on the desk intercom then ushered them through into Durrell's office.

Dr Frank Durrell sat behind a plain utility desk. The room was almost bare. There were neutral grey walls and a dark green tintawn carpet. On the walls there were graphs and charts held in place by masking tape. His face was thin and the skin seemed tightly drawn back, so that his nasal bones seemed to make white pressure marks underneath the skin. His high, rather square forehead had sparse sandy hair brushed over from the side to hide the fact that he was almost bald. His eyes were small and deepset and he shared the blotchy pallor peculiar to a man of middle age who has been seriously overworking for a long period.

His voice was light and precise: 'Please come in.' He turned to Marcia: 'Miss Scott, it must be—what—almost a year now isn't it?'

'Yes, over that, I think.' Marcia smiled. 'Oh, this is Doctor Mawn—he's very interested in our work.'

Durrell got up and shook Mawn's hand. 'Ah, yes—of course—I've heard of you.' He turned back to Marcia: 'I really must apologize—I don't want to rush you but we really are up to the eyes at the moment—commissioning for start-up is a very busy time—so could we perhaps get under way?'

'Yes, of course!' Marcia began to unpack the Venn meter and put it on the desk. There was a knock at the door and one of the secretaries poked her head round. 'Mr Gelder on the phone, sir.' Durrell gave them both a quick glance. 'Sorry—excuse me for a minute.' He went out closing the door. Mawn began to help Marcia arrange the pile of slides to be inserted into the meter. After a few minutes Durrell came back leaving the door open behind him. His face was flushed: 'I really am most terribly sorry but something's come up. I shan't be able to give you any time this afternoon.'

'Can we make it another time?' Marcia began.

'Well, no I don't . . . I can't really see any prospect just at the moment. Commissioning a new station runs to very tight limits.'

'Next week?'

Durrell began to move towards the door. 'Not much of a chance, I'm afraid. You see, we're under very considerable pressure—private and political—to come in on time so—as much as I'd like to—I think we'll have to call this off for the moment—so sorry—good-bye.' He held out his hand to Mawn. As Mawn put his own forward, Durrell's seemed momentarily to miss contact.

Marcia slammed the car door: 'The archetypal bum's rush!'

'The word of God came down—Gelder!'

'There are two more.'

'You've got to be kidding! Westcott's office is quite close to Durrell's—I saw it on the way in. No, we're rumbled!'

'There's still . . . ' she looked down at a list, '. . . David Baird—he lives down at the estate near Philip Naylor's home. If he's off shift maybe we can catch him before they do. Come on, we've got to get something before we go back!'

Philip Naylor sat by the side of a white polythene laundry basket watching a cascading stream of perforated blue tape curl into piles inside. The computer tape punch was shirring and clattering—spewing the blue ribbon off into the basket in an unending serpentine stream. The small discs punched out of the tape showered downwards like a continuous rain of blue confetti collecting in a square glass box clipped underneath the punch head. As the blue tape flowed into the basket it piled up on top of another length of similar tape coloured in a light green.

On a table beside him was a works check sheet on a clipboard. The sheet read: "iterative loops—error function check." Running lengths of tape through his fingers, he compared the code punched into it with the machine code on the check sheet. All around him were the tall, grey-painted units of the computer complex. The air was vibrating with a thrumming subdued thunder from air conditioning fans sucking heat away from the intricate meshes of circuitry inside the units. On one, two tape spools were stopping and starting in a jerky sequence; on another, a square panel of neon indicators was flickering in an incomprehensible fast sequence.

243

In one nine-foot length of the blue tape, the punching machine had made two errors—both of which had been spotted by Naylor. The errors consisted of two spaces where an irregular row of holes should have appeared.

Comparing the tape for a third time with the check sheet, Naylor marked the position of the error on the tape with a pencil then picked up a hand punch specially made to fit the pattern on the tape and by depressing a lever made the holes missed by the machine. At least that's what he intended.

When a computer is used to monitor information, it has to be fed with pre-set values to act as a baseline so it can compare any information coming in with the figures it has already memorized. A computer often makes mistakes, but when it does, it brings in its own internal check-system and will register an error to its human operator so the mistake can be rectified.

In a nuclear power station this procedure is not considered to be free of hazards so many of the information channels connecting the core of the reactor to the computer and the control room are nearly always duplicated and sometimes triplicated. This is known as the 'jury' system because the human operator can select any two out of three values and so get a majority verdict on any particular measurement as it comes in. The instructions on the check sheet were written on the firm assumption that each person working in a nuclear power station is fully tested for any colour blindness.

Philip Naylor had passed the test. He had intended to hand-punch the blue tape.

In fact, he picked up the green tape from the basket and punched in the correcting holes.

Agnes Baird was a warmly-attractive woman with a naturally frank and open manner.

After a second pot of tea and home-baked shortbread, concern for her husband finally broke through her reserve. Her voice had a light Welsh lilt: 'I'll have to be a bit quick, he's due back off shift in a bit.'

'What did you first notice?' Marcia asked.

'Well, I'm not sure really, like, I think it was his car. He's got this vintage bug, you see. . . .'

'Yes, I noticed,' Mawn interrupted. 'A 1961 XK 120—saw it in the garage. Must have taken years to restore—a real beauty.'

'Well, it was,' she continued. 'But he keeps on hitting things—not big bangs, mind—just scrapes here and there, you know.'

'Did you ask him about it?' Marcia asked.

'I tried to, but he almost bit my head off—left it after that, I can tell you.'

'Anything else you've noticed?' Mawn said.

She got up and walked over to the window. 'See for yourself.' She pointed to a series of black tyre scuff marks on the yellow stone wall near the front gate.

'Apart from the car, I meant.'

'Oh, yes there is. David takes this *Scientific American*. It's a magazine. They all read it up there at the station. Well, in the back of it there is a regular feature, I think it's called Mathematical Game.'

'Yes, I know it,' Mawn said. 'By Martin Gardner—very difficult, some of them.'

'Yes, that's the one. Well, he used to do those regular—used to pride himself. Now he just gets angry when he tries them, says the writer—Gardner is it?—makes mistakes all the time. Tell you the truth, he can't do them any more!'

'Anything else?' said Marcia.

Agnes Baird thought for a minute. 'Well, yes, matter of fact there is, the other morning—it was funny really—he's a bow-tie fanatic—it's a joke with all his mates—well he was standing in front of the mirror fumbling with it, cursing away he was. In the end I had to do it for him, almost like a baby.'

As David Baird wearily climbed up the duralumin ladder out of the pressure vessel, three hundred feet away from him in the computer room, the baseline values he had transmitted from the reactor core were flowing into the spinning memory drums of the computer.

As each burst of coded information finished its headlong rush into the machine, the error check circuits compared each coded figure with one already stored. By changing the levels on his oscilloscope rather than assuming that the sensor he was testing was at fault and by reconnecting the red and green cables the wrong way round, the computer had stored faulty information about a heat sensor in the B matrix of the core.

Finally, by repunching the green tape instead of the blue tape

Philip Naylor had ensured that the faulty data produced by Baird would not be picked up by the error check circuits in the computer.

The Grim-Ness pressurized water reactor was contracting a disease—before birth.

CHAPTER TEN

'DRESSING APRAXIA!'

'What the hell's that?' Mawn shouted in Marcia's ear to make himself heard over the roar of the plane's piston engines.

'If somebody's got brain damage—one of the early signs is interference with motor skills, Apraxia's one example. In the early stages the patient won't show any obvious general loss of control, they just lose specific skills. To give you an idea, if you ask a patient who's got it to touch a book lying on a table, he'd more than likely touch the table instead of the book. It's the idea of the movement that gets messed up not the actual movement of the limbs.'

Mawn tugged at his lower lip. 'So if you ask a man to operate, say, three separate controls?'

'They might not even be the right ones—exactly.'

'Try convincing the Minister of that!'

The cabin of the small Trilander aircraft tilted and there was the soft bump of the flaps as they extended. Mawn looked out of the window.

'Forth bridge, we'll be down in a few minutes.'

Marcia studied the papers on her knee: 'Alex, we haven't got much, honest to God! Naylor is the best. Three tests and a uniform progressive drop. Elleston and Haskell—well O.K.—they show a drop in level compared with the first test, but not much. All that remains is hearsay reporting from Baird's wife. We can't go to Richard Lodge with that—he'll crucify us.'

Mawn banged the armrest. 'What about all the other results you and Venn have got? I don't care how slim it looks, we've got to get them to postpone start-up till these people can be replaced. What the hell else can we do, it's too late to do anything else, much too late!'

*   *   *

November 25th

Richard Lodge closed the folder on the desk in front of him, got up and walked over to the window. Outside, the rush-hour traffic in Whitehall was beginning to build up in the November gloom and in the centre of the road, the Cenotaph reflected the sickly yellow of the street lights. There was a light fog.

'What do you think?' Mawn asked.

Lodge turned: 'This is not going to be easy.'

'Don't you accept it?' Marcia asked.

'It's not that—I'm not qualified to assess its merit scientifically.' He walked back to the desk and picked up the folder as if weighing its content. 'The gist of what you're saying is that a whole section of the population is showing a loss of intelligence and some of these—afflicted—people are staffing the station at Grim-Ness.'

'Very much more than that,' Mawn said. 'We're saying that they're mostly in key positions and the reactor is due to start up in just twelve days. We hold this to be an *impossibly* dangerous situation. Cut-price reactors are bad enough but . . .'

Lodge studied him calmly: 'But the D.T.I. records show no more than the usual run of technical faults. I checked with their Chief Inspector yesterday morning. By law they have to monitor *all* stages of commissioning.'

'But they don't know about this material of ours do they?' Marcia intervened.

Lodge put the report down. 'No, they don't. But what you've failed to show here, is that these people can't do their *job* safely. You may very well be right. It's feasible I suppose—their abilities could have been marginally affected—I don't know by what—a virus or some such. But you *haven't* proved their incompetence within the limits of their job.'

'Well, we were more or less thrown out before we'd finished . . .' Mawn began.

'That's beside the point, I'm afraid.' Lodge continued evenly, 'I think in fact this whole effect you've discovered is profoundly important but it's not enough for me to go to the Minister and say effectively: "stop the commissioning of the station." There's far too much bound up in this politically. The Government has already had its whiskers singed in the House: private enterprise taking over the public sector—you know the sort of thing. If they were to delay it now the opposition would throw the book at them,

247

and say: "why wasn't it done by a State corporation in the first place?".'

Mawn stood up: 'So you'll do nothing?' He was pale with anger.

'I didn't say so, no.' He paused for a moment. 'Doctor—forgive me—I'm going to be very direct. That business on the television —it really didn't do your credibility any good.'

'I'm well aware,' Mawn's voice was quiet, level, 'but I think I may have been set up for it!'

Lodge shrugged: 'I only know what I know. The fact of the matter is if I take this report in to the Minister—the first thing he's going to say is—throw it away. And then, if I'm lucky and he's had a good lunch, I'll get him to put it out for independent check by our own people.'

'That'll take weeks,' Marcia complained.

'No it won't. As a matter of fact I've already set it up and if all goes well. . . .' He opened a desk diary. 'I'll get you in to see the Minister on the twenty-eighth, that's just three days' time.' He pointed to the diary. 'There's a spare half-hour here—providing there's no sudden division in the House. It'll be in his room in the Commons.'

'I didn't realize. What can I say? Thanks again.' Mawn sat down again.

For several minutes Lodge sat playing with a gold propelling pencil, doodling on the blotting pad in front of him. Finally he put the pencil down and looked up. 'What I'm going to say to you must be regarded as privileged information—do you accept that?' He looked from one to the other. They both nodded slowly. 'It may sound rather vague—but the whole area is highly sensitive, particularly from the international point of view, and I can only talk in general terms at this stage.' He pointed to their report.

'What's in there bears a striking similarity to some data collected elsewhere.' He looked at Marcia. 'You mentioned some medical— er—pathological evidence?'

'Yes,' she replied. 'We shall be going to see someone at the Pathology Institute. He rang us this morning.'

Lodge rose and looked at his watch: 'I'll give the Minister a short memo on this and get it vetted as soon as possible. And we'll meet again at—er—10.30 on the twenty-eighth at the Minister's room in the Commons. Perhaps you ought to be there by 10.15.' He sighed and started to usher them towards the door. 'And now

I'm afraid I have to preside over tea and buns with some ladies from Rochdale who've been planting "trees for a green city" or some such.'

Mawn stopped at the door: 'I'm sorry we've been unable to convince you.'

Lodge spread his hands deprecatingly and smiled: 'I have masters, remember.'

Mawn persisted: 'Do you happen to remember your visit to Marcia's lab.?'

Marcia glanced up at Mawn warningly, but he looked past her.

'Indeed—yes. I enjoyed your—er—frank discussion with Dr Venn.' There was a faint edge in Lodge's voice almost as though he was anticipating Mawn's next words.

'I didn't mean that. I watched you do the joystick test. You found it extremely difficult, didn't you?' Mawn waved Marcia ahead of him and closed the door as he went out.

Lodge slumped back against the edge of the desk then raised his hands in front of his eyes, clenching and unclenching his fingers, then slowly and deliberately reached out for a gilt ashtray. Just before his fingers touched the edge, his hand suddenly overshot with a jerk upsetting an inkstand. He watched the black pool spread slowly over the walnut desk top.

At Grim-Ness, the wind had swung to the north-west, bringing with it a low scudding overcast. The colour of the water had changed to a steely grey and whitecaps showed far out on to Scapa Flow. Curtains of stinging cold rain were sweeping across the station, sending huddled workers scurrying quickly into the shelter of the low squat buildings.

In the Reactor Hall, the pressure vessel had been finally sealed off and the hexagonal concrete floor slabs replaced. The giant seventy-foot fuel loading tower had been wheeled away to one end of the cathedral-like expanse of the hall.

No one would set foot inside the reactor again for a minimum period of two-and-a-half years. In twelve days, start-up was to begin and the core would gradually heat up as the atoms of its enriched uranium fuel rods began to split. Within hours of start-up, any man left inside the sphere would die from an overwhelmingly lethal dose of radiation.

*　　　　*　　　　*

249

Professor James Kingston was in full flight along the main corridor of the Institute of Pathology. Behind him Marcia and Mawn hurried along in tow trying to keep up with his headlong rush.

James Kingston's enthusiasm meant that he never had enough time. He enjoyed his job as consultant neuro-pathologist to such a degree that a colleague once said of him: 'If that bugger ever drops dead, he'll do his own post-mortem.' A portly red-faced man of fifty-eight—his breezy extroversion while demonstrating post-mortems had got many a student over his initial revulsion for the sight of the dead.

Without slackening his pace, he pulled a gold half-hunter watch out of a grey camel-hair waistcoat stretched tightly over his paunch. 'Oh, God, Academic Board in half an hour, dear oh dear.'

He paused before double swing doors marked: 'P.M. No admittance', looked round and caught Marcia's hesitation. 'Quite all right, dear lady—nothing to be afraid of—all end up here sooner or later you know—might just as well get used to it.' Marcia had turned pale. His voice softened. 'It's all quite tidy now, everything's done you know—all sewn up as it were.' He turned and flung the doors wide open.

The post-mortem room was circular and about twenty feet in diameter. In the centre of the room there were three horizontal white porcelain tables with cast-in gullies. The floor was grey tiled and underneath the tables there were drain grilles set in the tiles. Partly surrounding the tables, there was a semi-circle of wooden tiered seats and between the tables and the wall there were glass cabinets containing shining chromium instruments and a pair of butcher's scales. On the wall a blackboard was divided into white squares labelled brains, liver, heart, kidneys. In the squares weights had been recorded in yellow chalk. There was an almost overpowering smell of disinfectant.

On one of the porcelain tables a white cloth covered a body. Kingston waved towards the tiered seats: 'Sit you down.' He turned to a small trolley. On the top was a bundle of damp white muslin about the size of a melon.

'Now here,' he slapped the bulky shape under the white cloth. 'This is the chappie I was talking about just a moment ago.' He picked up a brown file. 'These are his clinical notes—I'll read you the relevant details.' He fumbled for a pair of gold-framed half-glasses and pushed them on to the bridge of his nose. 'Aged forty-two—male—went to his local doctor complaining of headache, slight double vision, clumsiness, inability to concentrate. Doctor sent him up to our neurology bods.' He turned over a sheaf of papers in the file. 'Let me see now—yes, that's right—Romberg sign, pupils—mm mm—yes, yes, here it is—a summary.'

He read: 'The main features of this patient suggest a mild generalized cortical atrophy. His rather marked coarse tremor is more reminiscent of the toxic variety rather than the finer type usually associated with alcohol or the addictive drugs.'

He ran his finger down the sheet. 'Blah, blah—all pathological tests—normal—that's blood, urine, so on. No history of encephalitis—glandular fever. No evidence of addiction or alcohol. Recommend in-patient examination—ventriculography E.E.G. Provisional diagnosis: Cerebral Atrophy of no known origin.'

He looked up at them over his glasses: 'That's a rather elegant way of saying they hadn't got the first bloody idea what was wrong with him, but his brain was ruined.' He put the folder down. Mawn gestured at the body. 'How'd he get there?'

Kingston beamed: 'Extraordinarily obliging of him—some sort of lathe operator—turret lathe, I think they call it. Anyway, a piece flew off it—went straight through his chest. I'll show you.' He moved to withdraw the white sheet.

'Oh no, please,' Marcia gasped.

Kingston looked up in surprise: 'What? Oh!' His face fell. 'Most unusual really, came out under the right scapula—still, never mind, not essential I suppose.' He put the cloth back regretfully and moved to the muslin bundle and started to unwrap it.

'Exhibit A.' Inside the muslin was a brain cut transversely into half-inch slices and put together in sequence. Kingston began to lay the slices out in order on the stainless steel surface of the trolley. He picked up a long pair of forceps and pointed. 'First of all, it's . . .' He looked over at the blackboard. '. . . er thirty grams under weight, there was quite a lot of separation from the skull, a little dilation of the ventricles—here, and a few areas of calcification in the occipital cortex—here.' He stroked the surface of one of the smaller slices, there was a slight grating sound. He looked up at Marcia and Mawn. Marcia had surmounted her revulsion and was leaning forward on her elbows looking down, she spoke.

'So it's generalized—not any one specific area?'

'Oh, quite! We've been doing a lot of microscopy on previous cases—this one's only had frozen sections so far, but I'm sure it'll be similar. Net result is a sort of cross between senile cortical atrophy—multiple sclerosis—although there's not much demyelinization—and encephalitis. Point is though—those slides you sent me—Albania wasn't it?—they're absolutely identical, no question about it, no question at all.'

'Yes, but that's only one case,' Mawn said.

'Oh, dear me no. We've collected thirty-two already. At the last European Pathology Congress in Vienna there were over a dozen papers on the same thing. Nobody's absolutely agreed a name yet —"chronic Betz-cell atrophy" seems to be the favourite.'

'What's it due to?' Marcia asked.

Kingston shook his head. 'No idea, practically everything's already been suggested—virus—bacteria—toxins. You name it, some imbecile's written a paper on it.'

'Is there anything consistent about the clinical picture?' Mawn asked.

'You wouldn't really expect that,' Kingston continued. 'It's generalized in the brain—microscope appearances are consistent but the area of brain affected isn't. Most common sign seems to be Apraxia, thus the motor areas are involved.'

Marcia turned suddenly to Mawn. 'David Baird—you remember his wife—the bow tie?' Mawn nodded. Kingston looked up, a little irritated at the interruption to his dissertation. 'As I was saying, Apraxia and then Colour Agnosia.'

'What's that?' Mawn asked.

'It's a condition where people can't *identify* colours properly —but they can pass colour vision tests. . . .'

Mawn leant back: 'Good God almighty!'

'Quite so. Patients are quite unable to associate colours with objects—it's a known sign of brain damage—only way they can associate colours with objects is to do it by rote memory. Remember one patient I saw—fascinating—somebody showed him a colour print of a London bus—all bright red, you know. Chappie spent a long time looking at it then said it would be a sea-blue— er blood-red—tomato-orange. Typical sort of reaction apparently.'

Mawn gripped the rail in front of him: 'Could a person affected like this pass a colour vision test?'

'Oh, Lord, yes, probably a bit slow at it but they'd do it all right—in the end.'

In the road outside the Pathology Institute Marcia drew up her coat collar against the fog. Suddenly she put her arm through Mawn's and pulled close to him. Mawn looked at her in surprise.

Her face was drawn. She said: 'Alex, when Howard and I started all this, we did the test on ourselves.'

'Yes?'

'Well, we were both inside normal limits.'

He smiled. 'You probably fiddled it.'

'No, Alex. I'm serious. My results could have changed too. And what about you?'

Marcia tore the score sheet off the Venn tester, her hand shaking as she totted up the figures printed on it.

'Well?' asked Mawn.

'It's all right. Effectively the same as when I first did it.'

Mawn took the score sheet and looked at it: 'Good, so if we're both unaffected, *why* are we unaffected, that's what defeats me. We don't work among any particular group—we're not shut up in an office. Somewhere in *us* Marcia is maybe the answer. Something in our lifestyle—something we eat, some behaviour pattern. The answer's got to be in us.'

Mawn threw down the letter in disgust: 'My God—what a lot of double talk!'

'What's happened?' Marcia called out from the living-room.

He picked up the letter and walked through. 'I'll read it, it's from a Mister Tom Thorpe, Executive Secretary of the Nuclear Power Workers' Union. You remember I went to see them a couple of days ago.'

'I thought they were impressed.'

'One of them was, or he seemed to be. Listen, I'll read it to you: Dear Professor Mawn. In reference to your visit on blah blah—for which we thank etc. . . . My executive have now given the matter etc. etc. . . . and have concluded that the matter which you brought to our attention does not require any present action on behalf of our members. You will, I hope, appreciate our side of the problem. At the present time, our negotiations with the Government regarding annual wage and salary increases have reached a delicate stage and thus, if we were to suggest that some of our rank and file members were affected in the way that you have suggested, this would, of course, seriously disturb the progress of the talks.

In general terms, we are always interested to receive any information regarding potential industrial hazards to our members and we are grateful to you for bringing this matter to our attention. Your obedient servant—my arse! They're going to do absolutely bloody nothing, sit tight and screw more money out of the Government.'

'What did you expect?'

'Some sort of responsibility. It is the same old cloth cap attitude—where there's muck there's brass. For muck read danger in this case.' He looked at his watch. 'Come on, we're due in the presence in half an hour, better get moving. Have you ever met him, by the way? I don't normally mix with Ministers.'

'Campbell Baxter?' Marcia replied. 'Yes, he came to one of our do's here. Sheldon . . .' her voice broke off, '. . . talked to him on the programme. He's fortyish, very beautiful—made a million by the time he was thirty. . . .'

'As a man, I meant.'

'He's a complete pro. Only reason he does what he does is because he wants to be Prime Minister, I guess. General sort of whizz-kid reputation. He's annoyed all the scientific community by trying to resurrect the old Rothschild Report.'

'What? Putting all research on a sort of consumer-customer basis?'

'That's it. Lot of my girl friends say he's very sexy but he doesn't turn me on.'

Mawn started to pack his briefcase with papers. 'Anything else?'

'He's quick on his feet—nimble but not deep.'

Mawn closed the case. 'I'll ring for a cab.'

At Grim-Ness, the two-year process of commissioning was almost complete. Each meshwork of electrical controls, every hydraulic and steam circuit, every pipe junction, switch and warning light had received double and triple checks, and were slowly being linked together in a functional whole. First one system was run in isolation, then connected to its fellow. As a fault developed a halt was called and the particular system in which the fault occurred isolated until it was again in perfect order. Slowly, over the months, hundreds of miles of electrical cables were linked with steam valves, core controls and turbines until an inexorably growing sense of activity and life spread through the whole complex.

As if in sympathy with the growing sense of pulsing activity, the workers began to work for longer hours. Some volunteered to work double shifts, where before they were more likely to have complained about any need for overtime.

The interior of the steel pressure vessel was silent. Specially filtered, distilled and purified water had now been pumped in between the tall bundles of fuel rods to fill the primary coolant circuit. Between each rod bundle, long boron steel control rods were in the full 'down' position. Each rod was shaped like a six-pointed star in cross section and fitted between the rods absorbing neutrons and preventing any rise of temperature. The temperature in the core was an even twenty-three degrees centigrade, comfortable room temperature. Outside, the barometer was falling and a freezing wind curled off the heaving North Sea, booming and moaning around the alien shapes of the station.

The atmosphere in the Minister's corridor of the House of Commons is more than enough to inhibit the most determined of visitors. Mawn and Marcia had been conducted by a dour-faced steward past a series of uniformed police constables along stairways and softly carpeted corridors. Overhead were carved stone archways and every few yards a sombre-suited figure would pad by carrying sheaves of papers with an expression that suggested he was about to make a decision affecting millions. The names neatly painted on each door that they passed all belonged to public figures. Neither spoke during the journey.

Campbell Baxter's manner was instantly charming and relaxed. He leant back in an easy chair, one leg dangling over the arm. Mawn had just finished outlining their investigation at Grim-Ness station and Marcia had tried to give an encapsulated version of the pathological findings made by Professor Kingston. Richard Lodge sat uneasily on a hard chair holding a briefcase on his knees like a shield in front of his stomach.

Baxter got up abruptly and walked around behind his desk and sat down. For a moment he sat doodling with a pencil and then spoke: 'What you've just told me is in fact extremely important and I dare say . . .' he gestured at Lodge, '. . . that Richard's told you there is an acute international interest in this general area at the moment but my task now is relatively simple. You're asking me to take a specific course of action about a specific case. And what you've said in effect is that we should delay the start-up at Grim-Ness because some of the staff there are affected by this—I.Q. loss effect—of yours.'

'It's absolutely essential.' Mawn was vehement. 'It represents a double hazard. It's the first privately licensed reactor in this country and that means safety margins are bound to be cut because of cost. . . .'

'Oh, not at all,' Baxter replied. 'That's a problem we're well aware of. You must realize that the Department of Trade and Industry has been in there right from the start. Every single phase of construction has been independently checked by its inspectors. They're satisfied, so I must accept their findings.'

'Yes, but pressurized water reactors are more hazardous in the first place,' Mawn continued. 'And not only that, no emergency core cooling system has ever been tested in practice. . . .'

'Doctor Mawn, all this may very well be true—it's certainly a point of view. We all agonized about the whole affair in point of fact, and this must remain between these walls, more than one member of the Cabinet was totally opposed to it. But we must have energy. If your own environmental lobby is right, we're running out of fossil fuels, so what else is there to be done? Nuclear power. Of course there's a trade-off—high risk, high gain —we all admit that—at least in private, but we can't do otherwise if our economy is to be competitive. You environmentalists talk about an energy crisis—well, this is the answer, surely?'

'But we've given you evidence about a further danger,' Marcia spoke nervously.

'Miss Scott.' Baxter's smile had begun to dilute. 'What I have to make a decision about is whether or not to delay the start-up. Now, I think Mr Lodge and I have considered every single aspect of your report and I have to tell you that I simply can't do it.'

'My God!' Mawn cried. 'What else do you need?'

'Doctor, this is a crucial stage in nuclear power development in this country. My department has poured money into the project, far too much probably, the consortium which is building it is already stretched to the limit financially. If I was to delay this now, quite frankly I think it would put our nuclear programme back five years, we simply can't afford it, and, if you'll forgive me saying so, your report is not without its critics.'

'What do you mean?' Mawn demanded.

Baxter picked up a typescript. 'I submitted the whole of your material to referees for their opinion, since, of course, I'm not qualified to assess its value scientifically.'

'Could I know who they were?' Marcia asked.

'I believe it's the custom to submit scientific papers for independent and anonymous assessment before publication?'

'Of course,' Mawn said.

'Well then, I don't think it'll help matters if I tell you who they are. One is a medical statistician and the other holds a chair in psychology.' He paused for a moment looking down at the script. 'In point of fact, I find the tone of their report quite unnecessary—I—er—sometimes think that scientists are far more unpleasant to one another than even politicians, but nevertheless I am bound to act on its content.'

'But not without defence, I hope,' Mawn began.

'If I could just read it to you,' Baxter continued, and began to turn the pages. 'This is their summary, the first part is just a précis of your statistics:

'You have asked us to assess this report as to its scientific merit. We find that the presentation and methodology is in general adequate. There seem to be no important deviations from what one might regard as being the proper method for this type of study. Indeed, the phenomenon which the authors allege they have observed would—if true—be of the most extraordinary interest. However, we are bound to point out that both the premises and the interpretations given by the authors are quite misleading. There is, of course, a long and well-known literature dealing with I.Q. levels in man. From time to time reports appear alleging that mankind is becoming debased because the relatively unintelligent have larger families and thus the overall intelligence is bound to diminish in the long run.

'The factors governing the measurement of intelligence and general ability are very highly complex. Relative word skills, dyslexic factors, the bias of testers all play a highly significant role. To assert, as the authors have done, that they have pro-

257

vided evidence of group loss of intelligence on the basis of the data they provide is in our view both mischievous and irresponsible. It is well known that in any group where the individual members are related, very complex behavioural patterns emerge. In one firm where they carried out their tests, for example, we have managed to establish that the entire work force knew very well that the finances of the firm were in a highly parlous state and that many of the individuals tested were under considerable threat of redundancy. How the authors failed to take the anxiety generated by this sort of circumstances into account is quite beyond comprehension. There may very well be an interesting effect buried somewhere in this data, but we are of the opinion that the authors have entirely failed to expose its true nature.

'In conclusion, we feel bound to remark that this type of paper is a good example of contemporary pseudo-science. It is regrettably true that more and more reports appearing in journals of previously reliable status are taking on the tones of advocacy rather than properly defined argument. In our view, the contents should be set aside until such time as the observations reported can be exposed to repetition by other scientific workers.'

He put the report down. 'Well, there it is. As I said, I regret its tone but I must accept its findings.' He rose and walked towards the oak-panelled door looking at his watch. 'And now I'm afraid you must excuse me, I have a meeting. . . .'

'So you'll do nothing further?' Mawn grated.

'I'm not able to, there are insufficient grounds.' He opened the door and called over to a rather severe dark-haired woman seated at a window desk. 'Jane, I wonder if you'd find a steward. Doctor Mawn and Miss Scott are just going.' He turned, holding out his hand. 'Thank you very much for coming to see me. I'm sorry we couldn't do more.' He shook hands and went back into his room, closing the door behind him.

Lodge looked up as he re-entered. 'We'd better send a copy of their stuff to Bordheim.'

'Yes, do that, Richard, would you.' Baxter flopped down into the chair. 'One way of keeping them quiet might be to invite them up with you for start-up at Grim-Ness. Could you bear it?'

'Yes, surely. The R.A.F. have laid on transport, there's plenty of room.'

'Richard, what do you make of Mawn?'

Lodge paused for a moment. 'He seems sincere. I would wish he wasn't quite so polemic.'

'Exactly. What people like that don't seem to realize is we're on the side of the environment. They're just so completely unrealistic. If we let them do things their way, we'd have complete chaos. I suggest you keep a very tight rein on him.'

CHAPTER ELEVEN

December 3rd

AT GRIM-NESS the four-inch steel pressure vessel had been successfully tested to levels almost twice as high as its operating pressure. The one-hundred-foot-long emergency power gallery with its bubbling array of lead-acid batteries was connected to massive diesel generators for final charging and each fuel rod in the reactor was finally logged for position, temperature and zero neutron flux.

The process which every construction worker, scientist and engineer had been consistently imagining for almost four years was about to begin: 'start-up'.

High over the top of the reactor core in the neck of the bottle-shaped pressure vessel servo-motors began to turn gear trains, slowly withdrawing the long boron steel rods from the reactor core below. First the rods around the edge of the core were withdrawn, centimetre by centimetre, then others towards the centre also began to lift. Neutrons, previously absorbed by the rods in their lowered position, began to strike into the nuclei of other nearby atoms of uranium, releasing secondary neutron showers. As atomic fission accelerated, the temperature in the reactor began to rise.

Anxious engineers in the control room sat around an illuminated wall plan of the reactor face. As each rod rose so did its position appear on dials alongside its marked position on the wall plan.

The dials showed that the rods of B matrix were in correct position.

Temperatures, neutron flux levels and reactor periods were recorded as within normal and predicted limits. Finally, at the

259

end of almost three days of tense comparison and measurement, Dr Frank Durrell called a temporary halt before the final rise to operating level and criticality.

Patiently, he examined each log of events provided by each section leader. Philip Naylor was one of the last to present his data from the computer room. Durrell found in it no cause for comment and signed it and passed it back to Naylor.

Outside, the zone of low pressure which had brought the snow and wind had shifted away to the east over the North Sea towards Sweden.

To the west of the Hebrides a second region of low pressure was moving sluggishly eastwards and squeezed in between the two lay a transitory ridge of high pressure. As the air cooled, a temperature inversion developed causing a layer of still air to remain stationary overhead. A light covering of snow gave the brutal functional outlines of the station the appearance of a white demonstration model standing out against a lead-grey sky. The air was heavy and completely still and, as men walked from one building to another, the loudest sound to be heard was the dry squeaking of the snow under their feet.

December 3rd

The R.A.F. Sycamore helicopter approached from the south-west, hovered for a moment over the circular landing pad and then slowly began its ungainly descent. About twenty feet away from the ground snow began to pick up in a central vortex and then to fly away from the pad exposing the concentric orange circles on the concrete.

The turbines sang down to silence and the rotors slowed and bowed downwards. An oval door in the side of the fuselage moved inwards and sideways and a uniformed R.A.F. sergeant jumped down, hooking a short aluminium ladder over the edge of the door aperture. Marcia clambered down, the freezing air striking her face like a blow, tautening her skin into a mask and catching the breath in her throat.

As the party led by Lodge and Mawn made their way to a waiting minibus, a pale northern sun briefly appeared through a gap in the clouds. It was as though a spotlight had been turned on in a diamond mine. Every surface of the station sparkled and glittered with a million tiny points of light on the hoar frost.

Almost as quickly, the sun was eclipsed by a lowering bank of dense black cloud.

'Not exactly ideal conditions!' Mawn said.

Lodge smiled: 'You're determined something's going to happen, aren't you—even if you have to drop gelignite in the core!'

Mawn turned, his face sombre: 'I don't think it's a subject for humour.'

The aircrew of the helicopter trudged past carrying holdalls, one turned and grinned at Marcia. Lodge's manner just hid impatience: 'I'd just like to point out that we don't do this for every Jeremiah.'

'I've tried to make my point,' Mawn continued. 'I think there's a definite and measurable danger and I shall do everything I can to point it out to the people in charge.'

Lodge's voice hardened: 'I'd remind you that I'm personally accountable for you while you're here and I'd take any such move very unkindly indeed.'

Marcia stamped her feet. 'I've lost a toe already, could we get inside, please?'

Neither man heard her. Mawn's voice carried no hint of apology: 'You can have my assurance—if you like—that anything I say will be in your presence so you can take it down and use it in evidence, all right?'

Lodge stepped into the minibus, speaking over his shoulder: 'Very well.'

Inside the perimeter fence, the minibus crunched over the snow between the jumbles of contractors' huts, disassembled cranes and piles of steel scaffolding, finally drawing up alongside the entrance to the main reactor hall. There, they were met by Bernard Westcott who did his best not to react to the presence of Mawn and Marcia and instead led the party straight into a lift and then up to the nerve centre of the station on the third floor; the great circular control room.

As the lift juddered up through its shaft set in the massive concrete wall of the Reactor Hall, each one of them was awed into silence by a deep rumbling vibration of distant machinery. The building seemed to have a pulse of its own.

A group of six men in white full-length coats stood in front of the vertical plan of the reactor face. Yellow lights winked at intersections on the hexagonal pattern and instrument dials alongside each light registered the condition of each separate fuel rod assembly.

At the central desk control Dr Frank Durrell leant forward studying a cascade of coloured figures sweeping down the face of a monitor screen in front of him. Brian Gelder stood behind him looking over his shoulder. Durrell turned and spoke to a technician: 'All flux levels tally, do you confirm?'

The technician threaded a long squared paper roll through his fingers: 'Power density's inside limits. Yes, confirm.'

Durrell picked up the blue hand phone and depressed a switch. He spoke to David Baird two hundred feet away in the rod control room. Baird sat in front of a small scale version of the reactor face plan on the wall of the main control room. The pattern of lights on it were identical.

His desk was surrounded by the tall blocks of a computer. His position was thirty-five feet away from the reactor core from which he was separated by four inches of steel, two inches of stainless steel thermal shielding and the nine-foot thick concrete of the biological shields.

Durrell's voice came through on distort: 'David, leave this line open on the speakers. Will you check, please?'

Baird depressed a key on a switch panel, and spoke into a perforated grille: 'All right, can you hear?' As he spoke he attempted to hang up the 'phone but missed the receiver rest. Durrell spoke into a similar grille: 'Yes, I've got you—quite clear. Power density has been even for seventeen minutes, so we'll go on.' As he spoke, Durrell turned over the pages of an operating manual on the desk in front of him, then depressed four more switches and spoke into the grille: 'Durrell here. Are you getting me, Philip?' Naylor's voice came through clearly: 'Yes, go ahead.'

'We'll keep open now.' He looked down at the manual and read out: 'Rods five and seven A matrix, thirteen and fifteen B matrix, twenty-one twenty-three C matrix, all to positions C minus eighteen—confirm, please?' Baird's voice came back through the speaker and parroted Durrell's instruction.

In the reactor core, the rods moved up three centimetres in their narrowly fitting channels between the fuel can bundles.

In the Control Room, a soft repeating electronic chime began to sound and single red lights on four separate consoles began to flash in unison with the tone. Walking with a carefully assumed slouch, a technician detached himself from the group near the reactor plan and spoke into a microphone: 'Computer error function levels are not getting on the board.' Philip Naylor's voice crackled from an overhead speaker: 'Sorry.' There was a pause then the chime and the red flashing lights stopped abruptly. A technician turned to Durrell: 'Clearance.' Durrell nodded and turned back to his microphone: 'Move to C minus seventeen.'

In fuel can assembly four in the B matrix of the reactor core, the external temperature of the can was 610 degrees and the temperature of the uranium fuel pellets inside the can was 3,020 degrees. The instruments in the control room monitoring the B matrix registered 580 and 2,070 degrees respectively.

Read-out screens in the thrumming computer room showed no deviation from the standard values already stored and Naylor wrote neatly in a log chart on the desk beside him: "error loops clear."

Dr Durrell was the first to catch sight of the visitors as they entered the room lead by Westcott.

After the introductions were over, Gelder quickly drew Lodge aside. He spoke vehemently: 'Richard, what's that bloody man doing here?'

'He's merely a spectator,' Lodge murmured.

'I warn you, if he so much as speaks one word out of turn I'll have him slung off the station altogether.'

'I don't think you need to be so militant,' Lodge replied, evenly. 'And if I may say so, he is after all my responsibility. Just as I represent the Minister in any decision regarding the future of your stations.'

There was a silence. Finally, Gelder spoke with a sudden shift of mood: 'I'm glad you reminded me. I'll do my best to be pleasant of course—but keep in mind what I said, Richard.'

The machining of the cans which enclose the uranium fuel in a nuclear reactor is a matter of very high precision. After the long process of cutting the spiral fluting on their surface, each rod is rotated slowly around central depressions at each end. A meter with a movable foot is placed against the centre of the can and any movement of the needle as the rod is rotated indicates that the rod is not perfectly straight. All the cans in assembly four of B matrix in the core passed the test.

*　　　*　　　*

263

The air in the board room at Grim-Ness was hazy with tobacco smoke. It was built in what Durrell privately called "P.V.C. Regency". The effect was intended to convey an air of solidity and respectability couched in modern architectural terms. Rosewood wall panels were framed by extruded plastic mouldings and at intervals there were old prints of Faraday and his original apparatus set incongruously in satin aluminium frames. Bare wires protruded from the walls where wall lights were still to be fitted.

Mawn and Marcia were standing looking down through the window at the prism-shaped glass panels of the turbine hall roof far below. The corridors joining the buildings had hemispherical glass rooflights which shone through the coating of snow in the gathering northern twilight like the portholes of some immense spaceship. Underneath their feet they could just sense a faint vibration.

There was a steady buzz of conversation from a crowd of station executives each clutching a gin and tonic. Marcia saw Gelder break away from one small group and head towards them. She turned her head quickly towards the window. 'Here it comes!' As Gelder drew near, they could both see that he was smiling and that his cheeks were flushed. Marcia spoke through clenched teeth: 'Watch out . . . he's smiling.'

'Doctor, are you being looked after?' Gelder's tone was expansive. 'And Miss Scott, have we managed to calm some of your anxieties?'

'Have you seen the weather forecast?' Mawn flushed as he asked the question, wishing it didn't sound so lame. Lodge followed Durrell and Westcott over to where they were standing.

'The weather?' Gelder's expression showed an amused contempt.

'The Met. Office say a zone of low pressure's coming in from the east. There'll be some very high winds.' Gelder caught Durrell's eye and smiled as he replied: 'And what do you suppose is going to happen?'

'Well, it compounds the risk of start-up, doesn't it? You know as well as I do that these islands often get completely cut off. In point of fact the highest wind velocity ever recorded was measured just twenty miles from here. . . .'

'Thanks, Doctor. You really never give in, do you?' Gelder was smiling broadly. 'First you tell us our computers are unsafe, then our staff are below par, and now the weather's going to get us.' Durrell and Westcott were grinning. 'Surely the Minister must have told you. We did all the wind-tunnel tests at Farnborough—all these buildings are safe at up to two hundred and fifty miles per hour. Quite a wind—even for these parts.'

Mawn suppressed his irritation and replied coolly: 'So you discount all our findings on your staff?'

'Not at all. It's just that your motivation doesn't exactly lie in the field of pure science.'

'And just what do you mean by that?'

'I had quite a disturbing call from the Nuclear Power Workers' Union yesterday, apparently you went to see them?'

'Yes, I did.'

Gelder looked down at his glass for a moment. 'It's very difficult for an ordinary businessman like myself to understand your motivation. According to Thorpe, you spent about an hour trying to persuade them that their work force here is in some danger. . . .'

'We have quite enough evidence,' Marcia interrupted.

'Now, Miss Scott,' Gelder continued. 'Let me be perfectly clear about one thing, our labour relations up here have always been very carefully nurtured as Frank Durrell here will tell you. And one way of looking at what the Doctor did in London would be to call it deliberate and malicious interference. . . .'

'Really Brian, that's going too far,' Lodge said.

'Is it really?' Gelder went on, looking straight at Mawn. 'It's very hard for me to believe your motives are just purely scientific. Now I don't know what your political affiliations are, but . . .'

He stopped, Mawn was laughing in his face. 'You'd have to do better than that. I don't suppose you'd believe in any motive unconnected with straight profit and loss figures. . . .'

'And *what* about your figures?' The skin underneath Gelder's eyes had paled. 'Your scientific figures. What did your professional peers say about them? Pseudo-science, wasn't it?'

'You saw that report?' Marcia gasped.

'Of course I did! I've been in almost continuous consultation with Baxter's department right from the beginning.'

Lodge turned to Mawn: 'I think I remember telling you how the law stands. Every aspect of this station had been under the strictest supervision from our inspectors?'

Mawn swung round on him: 'And have you ever tested the emergency core cooling system? Well! Has *that* been passed by your inspectors?'

'There have been model simulation tests, yes,' Lodge replied.

'Marvellous! A simulated loss of coolant accident on a *nine-inch* model reactor!' Mawn whipped round at Gelder: 'And do you remember what they showed? You know what happened in the model. Ten per cent, I repeat, ten pert cent of the emergency cooling water reached the simulated core and that merely compounded the destruction of the pile. The rest simply blew out as steam through the original vent.'

A tone chimed from a speaker and a female voice spoke smoothly: 'Dr Durrell and Mr Gelder to main control, please. Dr Durrell and Mr Gelder to main control.'

Gelder turned to go. 'Get your beads out, Doctor. We reach criticality tomorrow. There's still time to make your escape of course, if you're frightened.'

Mawn and Lodge lay stretched out in deep soft armchairs after a plain meal of locally-killed beef and potatoes. Marcia had gone to bed and both relaxed, staring into a dying log fire which had filled the room with a sweet resinous fragrance.

The 'Earl Magnus' hotel in Kirkwall was solid and Victorian. Built from local stone, the interior was overcrowded with stuffed eagles and ospreys glaring balefully out at the world from beneath glass domes. In the corner where the two men sat, a tall marquetry-inlaid grandfather tocked disapprovingly at them.

Mawn compared the comfort and nostalgia of the scene to the huge alien shapes of the Grim-Ness station away to the south. The mixture of food, wood smoke and Drambuie had lulled him into a state of indulgent euphoria and even the tweeded figure of Lodge stretched out in his chair beside him seemed a guarantee of security.

Lodge stirred, opened his eyes and slowly got to his feet, taking a slim silver watch out of his waistcoat pocket: 'Eleven. Bed I think—what about you?' Mawn nodded. 'There'll be a car here at eleven-thirty—we shan't have to hurry. I've asked for a call about nine-thirty, if that suits you?' He started to put the watch away in his pocket, but his hand jerked and trembled and the watch bounced on the end of its chain. After two more fumbling attempts, he got it back into the pocket. Mawn followed his movements. Lodge said: 'Yes, well, see you in the morning. Goodnight.'

After Lodge had left Mawn settled back, staring without expression into the glowing embers of the fire.

During the night of December third, the Grim-Ness reactor was held at "C eight" or at a point in its operational schedule eight arbitrary stages before arriving at criticality.

From that point onwards, each man on the station began to think of the passage of time in discrete intervals which bore no relationship to hunger, the need for sleep or even the passage of night or day.

December 4th. 13.20
From his desk in the Control Room, Durrell spoke quietly into the microphone grille: 'Ready to C one please—confirm.' He scanned a panel of signal lights; there were twenty altogether in four rows of five, each separately labelled: 'rod control', 'scram auto' and 'solo rod trip'. One by one, they lit up, showing that each automatic safety control was fully operational. The last light to appear was labelled: 'Emergency diesel start'.

He leant forward to the grille: 'To C one.'

In the Rod Control Room David Baird moved a horizontal slide to position one. His hand trembled as he went back in his mind over all the test procedures he had carried out inside the core before it was finally sealed off. The responsibility weighed heavily. His body felt awkward and ungainly.

13.27
In the neck of the pressure vessel the control servo-motors working through gear trains withdrew the central rods three centimetres higher in their guide tubes.

Neutrons lanced through the high pressure water circulating between the bundles of fuel cans.

Baird studied the reactor chart in front of him, waiting for the signals on the illuminated hexagonal pattern to confirm that the control rods had moved to the position marked on the horizontal slide. A close observer would have noticed that his eyes were jerking with a slow rhythmic movement to the left and a rapid flick back to centre.

267

In the Computer Room, Philip Naylor tilted his chair and put his hands behind his head. He relaxed.

At the large wall chart of the reactor in the main control room, Bernard Westcott copied down the readings from a group of instruments next to the wall chart.

Lodge and Sampson, the Department of Trade Inspector, sat with Marcia and Mawn in front of a block of six colour television monitors each one showing a picture of a different area of the station. Each screen showed a slight picture interference like falling snow; the inevitable consequence of proximity to high voltages and stray electrical fields.

13.32
Sampson led the visitors over to the wall chart of the reactor face and pointed to a group of lights flashing in unison on an instrument panel beside the chart.

'There you are—criticality.'

'I thought that was supposed to be a big moment,' Marcia said.

'It doesn't have any real significance,' Sampson went on. 'It's a purely theoretical point—I suppose in reality it only lasts a few millionths of a second.'

'How's that?'

'What really matters is stability as they work up the power scale afterwards. The reactor's self-sustaining and controlled, now the art is to inch its power to a working level.'

13.45
The temperature inside one fuel can in assembly four of B matrix rose to 4,020 degrees and a proportion of the uranium melted and ran out of its ceramic matrix, soaking into the surrounding alloy covering of the fuel can like molten wax into blotting paper.

Heat-sensing thermocouples near the fuel can began to feed information about the local hotspot along a pair of red and green wires through the computer, where its veracity was checked, then the information passed on into the Control Room. The information was passed as true by the computer but arrived approximately nine seconds later than planned.

13.45 + 10 seconds
In the Control Room a chiming tone sounded and a light began

to flash alongside the location of can assembly four on the wall chart. Westcott looked up and called over to Durrell, 'Hot spot in four B.'

13.45 + 35 seconds
In the reactor core, the fuel can containing the molten uranium in assembly four began to bend out of line and to curve towards another adjacent bundle of fuel cans. As it did so, the local rate of atomic fission shot up and other nearby fuel cans also began to overheat.

The magnetic clutches holding the control rods of B matrix still remained energized and so the rods remained in the raised position.

13.45 + 42 seconds
Durrell whipped round in his chair: 'Why the hell hasn't it tripped—drop it!' In rod control, Baird punched the manual over-ride, magnetic clutches opened and the control rods began to fall.

13.45 + 43 seconds
The clearance between the control rod and its surrounding guide tube was designed to be 1·2 millimetres. As the rod dropped under its own weight, it had reached a point precisely halfway down its guide tube. The local area of overheating was now increasing exponentially and the guide tube was beginning to bend out of line.

13.45 + 44 seconds
The control rod jammed just over halfway down the now distorted guide tube thus failing to stop local fission. The metal of fuel can assembly four grew steadily hotter and began to melt.

13.45 + 47 seconds
Baird's voice yelled from the speaker: 'It's stuck, it's stuck!' Durrell swore and whipped round to Westcott, his face ashen pale. 'Prepare reactor scram!'

13.45 + 48 seconds
In the core, the overheated fuel can in assembly four burst, releas-

ing molten uranium into the surrounding coolant water already at a temperature of 640 degrees and a pressure of 2,050 pounds per square inch. The molten metal of the fuel can and the uranium began a violent reaction with the surrounding water.

13.45 + 49 seconds
Durrell swung round to the instrument console in front of him quickly, pulling a key out of his coat pocket. Fumbling, he unlocked a square metal flap, underneath a label; 'Boron balls' jerked open, the flap exposing a flat red button two inches in diameter.

Red lights were flashing urgently over one entire section of the vertical reactor chart and a harsh alarm bell began to clang out a warning.

13.45 + 51 seconds
The reaction of the molten metals and the high pressure water produced a series of small hydrogen gas explosions, sending out shock waves into the surrounding water and dislodging other fuel cans from their carriers. As the rods began to collapse, the rate of atomic fission again rose abruptly and rods began to melt out of their supporting frames and topple towards each other.

13.45 + 56 seconds
Durrell shouted into the microphone grille in front of him: 'Scram reactor, scram, scram!'

In Rod Control, Baird threw switch and current was abruptly shut off from the magnetic fingers holding the rods out of the reactor core. The rods fell.

13.45 + 57 seconds
In the core, the precision geometry of rod and fuel assemblies began to distort. One after another, the remaining control rods dropped down through the guide tubes and either stuck or fell out altogether.

13.45 + 58 seconds
Flashing light spread like a sparkling red tide over the whole of the reactor chart. Durrell shouted: 'E.C.C. diesels, start!' A technician stabbed a button, the lights in the Control Room dimmed suddenly and then came back up again. From somewhere outside

came a heavy rumble as the diesel engines driving the emergency core cooling pump lumbered into action.

13.45 + 60 seconds
Inside the core, the explosive reaction between the melting fuel cans and the water culminated in one long shock wave which slammed through the whole assembly, hammering against the steel shell. At a junction between the base of the pressure vessel and a four-foot diameter coolant pipe, a weld abruptly split.

13.46 + 2 seconds
In the Control Room, Westcott yelled out: 'Coolant pressure going!'

In the reactor, the super-heated water flashing into steam shrieked out through the widening gap between the coolant pipe and the pressure vessel.

Durrell, without looking up, banged down the emergency core cooling control. The noise of the diesels swelled suddenly from a muted rumble to an angry vibrating roar. The four-foot pipe blew completely off the pressure vessel and the reactor core, deprived of its coolant, began to coalesce and melt as the fuel cans collapsed in towards its centre.

Emergency cooling water driven by the high pressure diesel pumps jetted into the pressure vessel and began to well up into the incandescent core immediately, again flashing into steam and exploding.

The whole building suddenly shook and there was a deep echoing boom followed by the howling scream of gases escaping under pressure. Glass showered down from breaking fluorescent tubes in the ceiling of the Control Room. There was a second heavy explosion and an instrument panel sheared away from its wall mountings and fell massively forward striking one technician on the shoulder.

Durrell jabbed the button behind the unlocked plate and solenoids opened underneath hoppers full of boron steel spheres sending them rattling down steel ducts into the heart of the disintegrating reactor.

13.46 + 10 seconds
There was a single sustained scream of agony from a loudspeaker.

271

The horrified group standing in front of the bank of television monitors watched as one wall of the distant rod control room shook and cracked from floor to ceiling. Through the crack, a vertical curtain of steam blasted into the chamber toppling the computer blocks surrounding Baird like a row of grandfather clocks. The steam curled around the desk, picking his body up like a leaf in wind and flinging it back against the wall. For a moment, his face froze in an expression of horror, then, pinned by a six-hundred-degree blast of super-heated steam and gas, his white synthetic fibre coat began to melt down around the contours of his body then fly away in molten fragments under the deadly blast. His face first turned bright pink and then a suffused red. The heat boiled his eyes into white curdled lumps in their sockets. Finally, his cheeks began to split like an over-ripe peach. The screen went blank.

Marcia covered her face, weeping, and Gelder ran over to the bank of screen, elbowing Mawn aside.

Durrell punched one of a row of buttons underneath the screen. A picture of the Reactor Hall came into view showing the cathedral-like building with its vast hexagonal floor pattern.

He hit another button and the main coolant pumping room came into view. 'Haskell—can you hear? Haskell!' Haskell's white-coated figure came into shot on the screen together with two other men in blue overalls. All were dwarfed by the massive ducts criss-crossing the concrete chambers. Behind him were the huge green painted hulks of the coolant pumps. 'For Christ's sake get out, we've got a melt down. Get out quick, it'll blow back, get out, for God's sake, get out!'

Behind the three men the concrete floor erupted like a volcano as one of the pumps burst like a huge grenade flinging jagged cast iron fragments into the air like shrapnel. The room filled with clouds of roaring steam and fragments of the pumps careered and ricocheted off the walls. One of the men in overalls started to run for the door and fell, transfixed by a jagged length of copper tube. Haskell ran towards him, bent down and started to drag him towards the door, then suddenly both men were hurled into the air as the floor beneath their feet erupted. Under the hail of ragged metal like a volley from a machine-gun, the door itself began to disintegrate as the third man ran towards it.

Gelder screamed into the microphone: 'Get away—get back!'

As the man stumbled back the horrified group watched his body break up and fly apart in ragged pieces under the hail of metal.

White-faced and shaking, Marcia buried her face in Mawn's chest. Durrell had collapsed to the floor in a semi-kneeling position and Westcott was leaning up against a wall with his hand over his mouth retching.

Gelder leant forward and punched up the camera in the Reactor Hall. All appeared to be normal, but just as he was about to select another picture Mawn grabbed his arm and pointed at the screen. Gelder looked again and started to alter the position of the camera in the Reactor Hall by two remote control joysticks underneath the screen; it focused on the floor of the hall.

At first it seemed as if there was a fault in the picture. The hexagonal outlines of the floor appeared to be undulating. Something underneath was pushing at the steel and concrete floor. Each hexagonal segment started to break away from its neighbour moving up and down like a series of saucepan lids on boiling pans. Then, one by one, the fifteen-ton segments began to blow away into the air as a boiling mushroom of smoke and steam blasted up into the hall like a giant geyser from the reactor core beneath. At the far end of the hall the one-hundred-foot charge loading machine shaped like a metal lighthouse began to tilt as the floor collapsed. As it fell, it toppled through the east wall of the building collapsing outwards in a great cloud of glass and concrete. The control room floor under their feet shook suddenly as the massive bulk of the loader crashed to the ground.

The floor trembled as a second great cloud of steam and debris erupted through the shattered floor. Overhead they could just see through the gathering fumes that the cartwheel pattern of girders had opened outwards to the sky like gaunt fingers. On the base of the erupting clouds there was a dull flickering orange glow reflecting from beneath the floor.

Suddenly inside the Control Room there was the harsh intermittent bark of a klaxon. The silent group around the screens jumped back in alarm. Gelder whipped round: 'What the hell . . . ?'

'The doors,' Durrell explained. 'Emergency doors. They're operated automatically by radiation levels. They break up the station into a series of hermetically-sealed segments—like a submarine.'

273

Lodge wheeled and took a pace towards the double glass exit doors of the Control Room: 'You mean we're sealed in?'

'Each door can be opened by hand,' Durrell replied, shortly.

'Well come on then,' Gelder exclaimed. Durrell looked at him sombrely: 'You don't seem to understand—they're automatically operated by radiation.'

'So?'

'If they're closed—beyond some of them—and we can't tell which ones—there'll be radiation!'

For several minutes no one spoke. A thin trickle of dust fell from the ceiling. The room seemed to contract. Mawn stared at the block of monitor screens, thinking, I'll even watch my own death on television.

CHAPTER TWELVE

GELDER BROKE THE SILENCE, turning to Durrell: 'All right, what's the situation?'

Without replying, Durrell walked slowly over to his control desk, opened a drawer and pulled out a rolled-up floor plan of the reactor building. He spread it out on the desk top, weighting one end of it with an ashtray. He pointed: 'We're here and the reactor's over there. In between us, there's number one boiler here....'

'Where're these doors?' Mawn interrupted.

'They divide up the building into sealed segments,' Durrell continued.

'And they're shut automatically by radiation sensors?'

'Yes.'

'What level?'

'Can't tell. Each sensor has a filter pad wrapped round a geiger head. Air is continually drawn through the filter and any gas or particulate contamination builds up until the geiger head trips the door mechanism.'

'But we can over-ride this!'

'Yes, each door's got a local manual control.'

'So what's the way out?'

Durrell pointed to the glass doors. 'We'd have to go through there first of all and then down the stairs, but the ground floor is probably lethal by now.'

'From radiation?'

'Yes. If the base of the pressure vessel went, it presumably blew out underneath us. There's either flood water or radiation down there—it'll be no use that way, no use at all.'

'What else?'

'There's an overhead walkway on a level with this room—it leads into the Turbine Hall.'

'If it's still there!'

Gelder had moved over to the television monitors and was trying to raise pictures from elsewhere in the stricken station. The others crowded round to watch. First the Rod Control Room came dimly into view. Through thick clouds of swirling dust, they could just make out a tumbled chaos of masonry and crushed instrument controls. Every surface was covered by a thick grey deposit. Marcia gasped as an arm came into view, protruding from a pile of shattered concrete. The arm was unattached.

Gelder panned the remote controls and the camera moved and then stuck pointing at a gaping hole in the distant wall. Through the hole they could see a flickering orange glow, and jammed up against the edge of the hole by a torn metal duct was the lower half of a torso, the booted legs protruding into the gap.

Durrell was moving quickly around the banks of instruments trying to gauge the severity of the accident, but nearly all needles were set firmly back at zero. Only one bank of indicator lights showed any activity.

December 4th. 14.10 p.m.

The technician injured by the falling instrument panel was sitting huddled against the wall rocking to and fro, holding his shoulder.

Gelder quickly switched from camera to camera throughout the situation. Several gave no picture, but one set in the viewing gallery overlooking the floor of the Reactor Hall was still operating. Heavy black smoke sparkling with incandescent fragments like a giant firework still gushed through the hole over the reactor, but the flickering orange glow from the burning core was dimmer. Thick swirling snow poured in through the gaping east wall and was immediately swept into the updraught over the core. A thick

275

mushroom of billowing steam had formed above the smoke and venting out through the torn roof.

'It's getting out,' Marcia whispered.

'It won't go very far up,' Mawn replied. 'The last met. report gave us a temperature inversion overhead—there'll be a layer of still air.'

'What will that mean?'

'Depends what percentage of the core material went upwards. We can't tell. Assuming there's no wind and the temperature inversion's still in place, most particles will be carried up by the hot gases and then come down almost immediately once they're out of the updraught. We might as well assume the whole station is surrounded by a radioactive circle.' He paused suddenly aware that everyone was listening intently. 'What do you think, Durrell?'

'I've no means of knowing—assuming a thirty per cent loss of fission product inventory at a guess, it'll be already covering a circle maybe two and a half miles in diameter.'

'That's dust—what about radioactive gases—water vapour?'

'Depends entirely on the wind.'

'There wasn't any when we got in here.'

'I said it depends!' Durrell's voice was strident. 'I can't—I've nothing to measure it with—nothing's working.'

'Then what *are* the priorities?' Lodge asked quietly.

'To get out as quick as may be,' said Gelder.

'And walk straight into lethal radiation outside.' Mawn turned to Durrell. 'Could the cloud have got as far as Kirkwall?'

'I told you, I don't know!' Durrell turned away.

'He must,' Marcia spoke quietly. 'They've all got their families up there, Alex, they know they're all outside there somewhere.'

Durrell walked towards the door leading into the Computer Room. 'Naylor may be able to get a line out.' He pointed to the row of coloured phones on his own desk. 'Those've all had it.' Mawn and Lodge followed him out.

Gelder turned back to the monitor screens and began to search the remaining parts of the station covered by the cameras. Isolated groups of workers were trapped in the galleries and control rooms surrounding the shattered reactor. Some were lying in huddled groups, others retching from overwhelming lethal doses of radiation. Some cameras had sound and no vision and all that came over one line was an unbearable chaos of screams.

In the Computer Room, Naylor tried without success to contact the central telephone exchange. Lodge and Mawn stood behind him. Naylor spoke across to a technician who was checking resistance on the exposed telephone cables with a test meter.

'Any luck?' The man shook his head helplessly. He turned back to Lodge: 'The internal's working but all the outside lines are dead.'

'Where's the exchange?' Mawn asked.

'In reception block,' Naylor replied.

Mawn strode to a wall plan of the station. He pointed: 'That's here, isn't it?' Naylor nodded. 'Well, it's next to the east side of the reactor building, that's where the loading machine took the whole wall out.'

They re-entered the Control Room as Gelder finished his survey of the building on the monitor screen. He turned: 'Any good?'

'No, nothing,' Durrell answered. 'No outside lines at all.'

Gelder pointed at the screens: 'I've been round all the cameras which are working—far as I can make out there are three main groups of survivors—can't tell yet whether they've been irradiated, the first lot are. . . .'

Marcia only half listened to Gelder as he began to describe the location of the survivors. The unimaginable had really happened. She looked around at the shambles of the Control Room and shuddered as more dust sifted down from the broken light fittings. She wondered fearfully whether it was radioactive, had they already received a lethal dose from the dust hanging in the air. They might already be beyond help, their blood cells disintegrating. She saw a quick vision of the victims of Hiroshima and remembered the pathetic body scars of the survivors from the *Lucky Dragon* trawler. Rows of hospital beds. She closed her eyes against the pictures, unable to control the shaking of her legs. Gratefully she felt the comfort of Mawn's arm around her shoulders.

Three monitor screens now held steady pictures, each showing one of the three main service corridors of the reactor building.

The first, running alongside the base of the pressure vessel leading to the underground coolant pounds was completely blocked by the section of the collapsed roof. The view was almost obstructed by fumes and a torrent of water pouring in.

The second, a passageway leading from the Reactor Hall to the exterior seemed to be clear of damage.

In the third, the scene looked like the site of a mining disaster. There were about thirty men lying sprawled on the floor and propped up against the wall. It was clear that the full force of the initial explosion had fired debris in through the long row of shattered windows like a charge of grapeshot. Several bodies were almost entirely dismembered and the survivors, covered in a thick muddy layer of water and dust, huddled in a row against the wall. Several were already in the agonies of acute radiation poisoning. One, with his arms wrapped around his stomach, sat absolutely still, his mouth open, screaming. Another lay back, head lolled to one side, and watery vomit streaming from his open mouth.

They all jumped back involuntarily from the screens as the floor suddenly slapped violently at their feet. Somewhere far below there was a rumbling detonation, films of dust fell from the ceiling settling over their hair and shoulders.

'What the hell was that?' Gelder asked.

Durrell ran quickly over to the monitors and switched on the picture of the Reactor Hall. Black fumes were still belching out through the vent in the floor, but the orange glow had almost disappeared. Durrell turned slowly, walked over to a chair and slumped down. For several moments he sat staring fixedly at the floor. Gelder grabbed him by the shoulder: 'What's happened?'

'I don't . . .' Durrell began. 'I can't be sure but I think . . .'

'I'll tell you what's happened!' Mawn exclaimed. 'You've had a melt-down.'

'What?' exclaimed Marcia.

'Melt-down—the China Accident!' Mawn turned to Gelder. 'You've a little experience of this already, haven't you—remember the Pukë station in Albania?' He turned to the others. 'The glow in the fumes, it's gone! That means the whole core has melted and slumped down through the pressure vessel. Just now it'll be on its way through the biological shielding underneath the reactor —right?' Durrell sat without answering.

Lodge's voice trembled: 'You can't be certain of that.'

Mawn whipped round at him, his voice grating: 'I've no need to be sure!' He jabbed a finger at the screen. 'Somewhere down underneath that floor there's a miniature sun and it's going to go on burning down. Through the vessel—through the shielding— out through the foundations and right down into the earth and you're not going to be able to do a damn thing about it.'

278

He strode over to Durrell: 'That's right, isn't it?' Durrell nodded slowly, without looking up.

'What's to be done?' Lodge asked.

'Some of your jokers call it the "China Accident". What they mean is it might melt through to China!'

Durrell was talking to himself: 'We'll have to evacuate the station. Get my staff out.'

Mawn turned to the others: 'We'd better consider the facts!'

'What the hell makes you qualified . . .' Gelder began.

'Because this situation has been in my mind for the last month. I've anticipated this—thought it out in advance. Has anyone else done the same?' He looked around. 'I thought not.' He looked around and ticked the points off on his fingers: 'Number one, we're stuck in here, we don't know what the radiation level is, but there are no breaches in the walls and the air conditioning filters have stopped so we might just be all right. Number two, between us and the outside are any number of sealed doors. Number three, the amount of air we've got inside here is strictly limited and so we either suffocate or open one of the sealed doors and let radioactive air in. There's no point in thinking any more about the core—no one's going to go down there with a bucket of water, so let's forget it and think our way out of this place. First, before we do anything else.'

Lodge gestured towards the monitor screens: 'What about all those men—they need help?'

'Well they won't get it if we don't get out. Now . . .' He swung round to Naylor who had rushed in from the Computer Room. 'Have you got any suits?'

'Suits?'

'Protective suits, for God's sake—have you got any?'

'Oh—yes—there are some—they're in the aid room.'

'Where's that?'

Naylor pointed at the glass exit doors: 'Through there, along to the end of the corridor, turn right and it's on . . .' He paused for a moment, '. . . just down on the left.' His face clouded.

'Something the matter?'

Naylor looked at him sombrely: 'There's one of the doors just before you get to it. It'll be shut.'

Durrell had stood up. He spoke quietly: 'There are geigers there—anti-radiation injections too.'

279

'Are they any use?' Marcia asked dully.

Durrell shrugged: 'Amino acids cysteine and methionine mainly—yes, they protect mice against radiation.'

'Mice! My God!' Gelder exclaimed.

Mawn turned to Durrell: 'You said these doors can be opened by hand?'

'Yes. There's a large wheel, it over-rides the automatic solenoids.'

'Is there any indicator on this side—the safe side of the door?'

'We don't even know if it's safe this side. . . .'

'Don't be so bloody academic. Is there or isn't there any indicator showing how much radiation there is on the *far* side?'

'No, just a warning light which goes on over a certain level.'

'Right, so much for that!'

'What do you mean?' Gelder asked.

Mawn ignored him and turned to Naylor: 'How many suits are there?'

Naylor thought for a moment: 'Should be at least a dozen.'

'How heavy are they? What I mean is, could one man carry the lot?'

'No, two could, probably.'

Gelder was studying the plan of the building, his poise had returned: 'As far as I can make out from the scale of this, the aid room is about a hundred feet or so past the sealed door—shouldn't take long to get there and back.' He turned back to Mawn, there was a thin smile on his face: 'How do you rate the chances, Doctor? A forty yard dash.'

Durrell glanced at Naylor: 'I think we'd better make the first venture—we know the building pretty well.'

'No,' Gelder spoke crisply and decisively: 'This station is wholly my responsibility.'

'You'll need help,' Mawn said.

'I prefer not to risk the lives of the staff here,' Gelder said, coldly.

'Risk!' Mawn flared. 'Your own negligence has already killed more than half of them.'

There was a shocked hush then a storm of protest.

'This is not the time . . .' began Lodge, but Mawn cut in again. 'Not the time to strike attitudes, either.' He thrust a finger at Gelder: 'I'm not having our lives jeopardized by super hero here.' He grasped Naylor by the lapels: 'Take that coat off!' Naylor pulled back. 'Take it off man.' Without waiting, Mawn took hold of the white coat cover and pulled it down roughly over Naylor's arms then began to tear it into four squares about two feet across. He looked up at Durrell: 'Get yours off too, and tear it the same way—quick!'

'Will you tell us what . . .' Lodge attempted to put dignity and authority into his voice to hide the tremor. 'We must know what you're doing.'

Without looking up, Mawn went on: 'We don't know what radioactive crap there is out in the corridor and we certainly don't know what there is beyond the door. So we're going to make our own protective suits.' He began to fasten a piece of torn coat around the soles of his shoes, tying the four corners. He looked up at Gelder, gesturing at Durrell who was having difficulty tearing the white rayon cloth.

'Just copy what I do. It's the best we can hope for at the moment. Cover ourselves as completely as possible—head to foot —then go out there—get the suits—come back, dump all these bits of cloth *outside* the glass doors then come back in with the suits. O.K.?'

'Makes sense,' Gelder said.

'Go and get some more coats. For God's sake *move* some of you.'

Naylor ran back into the Computer Room and returned after a few moments with a crumpled polythene sheet and several lengths of punched computer tape. He dropped them on the floor beside Mawn. Mawn had finished tying the cloth round his shoes and was tucking his trouser legs into his socks. He looked up at Gelder: 'Cover the whole of your body surface as best you can, no gaps.' He pointed at his shoes bound with the pieces of torn coat. 'Cover your feet like that.' As he talked he tore the polythene into two ragged halves and pulled it down over his head like a hood, then around his shoulders. He pointed to the lengths of computer tape and said to Marcia: 'Now bind this sheet around me, wrap me up like a parcel.' Marcia picked up a length, hooked it round his neck and began to walk round and round him binding the sheet close to his body. Mawn pulled the edge of the sheet down round the edges of his face like the hood of an anorak. He gestured to Gelder: 'Somebody help him do the same.' Durrell and Lodge picked up the other half of the polythene and draped it over Gelder's head.

'What's this supposed to do?' Gelder asked impatiently.

Mawn replied: 'If there's radioactive dust in the air between here and the suit room it should stay on the outside of all this.'

'I'll buy that,' Gelder said. 'One thing. Why not one man—two journeys rather than two men and one journey—puts only one man at risk surely?'

'No time,' replied Mawn. 'Two may get it done quicker.'

Gelder shrugged down into the polythene without replying. Finally, each man was almost totally swathed in a baggy mass of polythene and torn workcoats wrapped incongruously in bright blue computer tape held in position with sticky tape. Each man had makeshift fingerless covers bound over his hands.

Mawn turned stiffly to Durrell: 'Two handkerchiefs.' Marcia fumbled in her handbag and brought out a small folded white triangle. Mawn brushed it aside: 'For God's sake—come on, come on—two handkerchiefs.' Durrell took one out of his trouser pocket, Lodge produced an elegant silk square from the breast pocket of his tweeds. 'Now wet them.'

'What?' Marcia said.

'*Wet* them! Then wrap them round our faces, the wet fibres should absorb most of the suspended particles in the air. I'm not getting a lungful for anyone.' He rounded on Wescott: 'Water! We need water.'

'I—there's none here. The loos are along the corridor.' He pointed to the glass doors.

Gelder smiled: 'Why not piss on them?'

Naylor held out a plastic cup: 'No need, there's some cold coffee here.'

Marcia crumpled up the handkerchiefs, poured half the coffee into each bundle and squeezed until the cloths were evenly stained brown. Then she gave one to Naylor and wrapped the other round Mawn's nose and mouth knotting it behind his neck. Mawn nodded his thanks, and had a quick last look at the building plan. He beckoned Gelder over and trudged clumsily towards the glass doors. Both men walked out into the long corridor.

As the doors swung to behind them they were both immediately aware of the chilling cold biting into the wet cloth bound round their faces. Ahead of them, two panes of a window had been blown in by the blast and snow was driving through the jagged holes forming a pool of half-melted slush on the green linoleum floor underneath. Mawn shuffled quickly ahead. His voice indistinct behind the cloth: 'Move. Don't hang about—longer we're out here, the more we're at risk.'

Both men broke into an awkward shuffling run, eventually reaching a T-junction at the end of the corridor. They turned right and saw that about twenty feet ahead the corridor expanded into a chamber about twelve feet wide and fifteen high.

Shutting off the far end of the chamber was a massive steel wall covered by parallel rows of electrical conduits and air trunking. In the centre of the wall was a thick steel door surrounded by heavy lever bar locks. To the left-hand side of the door there was a hand-wheel shaped like a cast iron version of a car steering wheel and over the wheel a single red light flashed reading: 'Danger. Radiation. Do not proceed.'

Mawn immediately started to inspect the boxes of control gear bolted to the wall by the side of the wheel. With his finger he traced electrical conduits from one unit to another. Gelder crouched beside him: 'Why the holdup?'

Mawn spoke without looking round: 'I want to make sure it doesn't slam shut behind us.' He quickly unscrewed a fly nut, pulled open the cast iron cover of one box and pulled out a fuse. There was the loud click of a relay and the red light went out.

'Be a sound way of getting rid of me wouldn't it?'

Mawn turned slowly, his eyes staring over the mask: 'I need you alive, friend.'

Gelder's eyes narrowed. It was impossible to tell whether he was smiling. 'In that case I don't mind your walking behind.' Mawn turned back and spun the wheel. The lever bolts slowly began to retract inwards towards the centre of the door. He grabbed the handle with one hand and bracing himself with the other against the surrounding steel wall, began to pull the door open until he could just peer into the gap. The two men braced themselves for what the corridor might reveal. Under their feet the floor trembled, there was a distant heavy rumble. The whole steel wall in front of them vibrated and the door swung open under its own weight.

Ahead of them the corridor was dimly lit by a string of flickering emergency lights. The linoleum floor was covered in a thick layer of white dust and one section of the wall had collapsed inwards leaving a vertical gap stretching between floor and ceiling. The debris only partially obstructed the way ahead.

283

'Is is radioactive?' Gelder demanded.

'How the hell do I know?'

'What I meant was, is it gas or dust?'

'If it's gas we've already breathed it, so we're dead. When we get moving, hold your breath as long as possible.' He stepped through and started to uncoil a fire hose, fumbling through the rough covers bound over his hands.

'If the dust is radioactive we can get rid of it like this.' He turned the polished brass valve attached to the hose. 'Hope to God there's some pressure.' He gestured at the tap. 'I'll go forward, you turn the tap wide open.' As Mawn knelt with the hose nozzle pointing ahead of him, Gelder wrenched the valve open. There was an agonizing pause, then abruptly the flattened hose coils writhed and tautened. The nozzle in Mawn's hand kicked like a gun and spat out a stream of water and air.

First, Mawn directed the nozzle at the ceiling, then along each wall and finally over the floor until the whole corridor was running with a muddy whitish paste. Mawn yelled above the noise of the water: 'Turn it off!' Gelder screwed the valve shut and the splashing jet curved downwards and stopped. Mawn flung the hose down and beckoned urgently to Gelder. 'Now move. Don't touch the walls or anything else, just keep on going like hell— never mind if your feet get wet.' He got up and began to run down the corridor. Gelder followed. They passed two doors and came to the third marked: 'Emergency Aid.' Gelder rushed forward and wrenched at the handle. It was locked. He stood back and flung himself at the door, rebounding back. Mawn pushed him away, looked at the door for a moment then raised his leg and kicked forward with all the weight of his body behind the blow. Once, twice and three times, then there was a splintering sound and the door flew open, the barrel lock clattering ahead of them into the room.

Mawn stepped in, switched on the light and pulled the door to behind them, jamming a metal chair against the handle to keep it shut.

Gelder looked around: 'No windows—no grilles, good.'

Mawn took a pistol-shaped geiger counter down from a row of similar instruments on a shelf above him and clicked a switch on its side. He swept the nozzle around the room. There was no sound. He moved a knob on the top and pointed it around the room for a second time. A speaker set inside its barrel immediately gave out a series of irregular clicks which altered in rate as he pointed the nozzle in different directions. He looked down at a swinging needle. 'Not bad—not bad.'

Gelder visibly relaxed, Mawn began to run the instrument over Gelder's protective covering. The rate of clicking shot up until it became a rising continuous note.

'Christ almighty!' Mawn exclaimed. He began to run the instrument over his own arms and legs, again the clicking rate rose to the level of a continuous note. 'We're both saturated in the bloody stuff. Get it off, come on.' He began to strip off the tape and the polythene, finally removing the cloth round his shoes.

'I thought you said we'd keep it on till we got back . . .' Gelder began.

'We've collected too much on the way here. Now—do it carefully, don't raise any dust as you get it off. Just move quietly, no jerking.' Slowly the men broke the binding tapes and eased themselves out of the makeshift covers.

Hanging along one wall, like a series of puppet dolls waiting for animation, was a row of white plastic oversuits. At the top end of each one was a transparent headpiece like a space helmet with two white gauze filters in the position of the ears. The arms and legs were closed by diagonal zips and there were gloves hanging from the wrist bands by single cords.

Mawn took one of the suits off its hook, opened the central zip and as quickly as possible eased into the shiny plastic. Gelder followed suit his voice muffled through the transparent cylindrical headpiece: 'You mentioned stuff for injection?'

Mawn searched quickly along the rows of steel shelving, finally picking out a wooden box labelled: 'Cystathone Parenteral.' He spoke without looking round: 'Get as many of the suits as you can carry.' Gelder began to unhook each one, draping it over his arm. Mawn put the box down on a table and gathered the remainder, rolling them up into as small a bundle as possible.

Gelder paused by the door: 'What about covers?'

'Not enough time,' Mawn replied. 'Just bundle them up like this, come on.'

Both men made their way cautiously back along the passage to the Control Room. Each moving awkwardly and staggering under the weight of their burden.

At the door, the occupants crowded behind the glass panels watching their lumbering approach. Mawn gestured them back then opened the door and eased himself through, Gelder following.

Marcia ran forward, but Mawn gestured fiercely: 'Get back, we almost certainly got some more dust on the outside of these things on the way back.' He threw his bundle of suits down on the floor. 'Before you get into those we might just as well take the anti-radiation stuff.'

Durrell had already opened the box and was laying out a row of small plastic tubes about the size of a cigarette. At one end of each tube there was a sheathed hypodermic needle. From the box he had also taken a small bottle of spirit and a tin full of small lint swabs. His voice sounded firmer: 'I've only seen this demonstrated once.' He removed his tie, then his shirt. 'You have to give it into a muscle—they said the safest one was this.' He pointed to the outer surface of his upper arm. 'Right here.' He described his action. 'First you shake a little spirit on to the swab like that, then rub the skin—like so—then you pull off the needle cover and then . . .' He poised the needle over his arm. 'You shove it in like—ah!' He jerked his hand down and the needle disappeared into his arm up to the end of the tube. 'Then you squeeze the tube flat until all the contents have gone in. Then pull it out and wipe your skin again with the swab. Right?'

He looked round to see all had been watching. He gestured at the box. 'You can all do the same—anyone has any trouble I'll do it for them.'

Gelder unzipped the front of his suit, pulled it down over one shoulder, picked up one of the ampoules and stabbed it straight through his shirt into his arm, squeezed the tube flat, pulled it out and threw it away into the corner of the room. Durrell started to protest, but Gelder waved him to silence: 'Just let's get out!'

Mawn had lain the suits out flat on the floor. One by one, they injected themselves and got into the suits, leaving the transparent headpieces hinged back.

Durrell beckoned them over to the station plan: it was now heavily scored in red pencil markings. He used a pencil as a pointer. 'Some of the circuits—here and here—have packed in, but we can still get the Reactor Hall ventilation control and the corridor—here.' He glanced up at Mawn and Gelder. 'Since you both went off, Elleston up on the sixth floor told us he saw about twenty or so people get away in one of the lorries from the transport pool. They went north.' He looked at his watch. 'They should be in Kirkwall by now.'

'So if we're relatively safe here,' Lodge said, 'why move?—seems to me the best thing we can do is to sit tight, surely.'

Durrell paused before continuing: 'There is one other thing, I'm afraid.'

'What?' Mawn demanded.

'Westcott, here, has brought up another possibility. You see, the core is burning down through the foundations. . . .'

'We know that, so what?' Gelder spoke impatiently.

'At a probable rate of two hundred feet in every twenty-four hours,' Mawn put in. 'At least, that was an estimate made back in 1972.'

'Yes,' Durrell continued. 'Well, the simple point is this. As Mawn says, if we say the temperature of the core is around 3,000 degrees Fahrenheit, then this figure is probably right.'

'Get to the point, for God's sake,' Gelder exclaimed.

'When the site was first prospected, the designers found a gloupy. . . .'

'A what?' Mawn asked.

'They're common on these islands,' Durrell continued. 'It's a long natural tunnel—a cave with a blow hole really. We made use of it to carry the turbine cooling water out to sea. It saved about a hundred feet of concrete ducting. . . .'

'Where is it?' Mawn's voice was flat, hard.

'That's it, you see,' Durrell went on. 'There's a tunnel from the condensers in the Turbine Hall here. . . .' He pointed to the plan. 'Which runs just to one side of the reactor building—here —and connects up with the gloupy under the cliff and then on by tunnel out to sea about three hundred feet out in the sound —here.'

'How far down is it?' Gelder demanded.

'It averages about twenty feet,' Westcott replied. 'The tunnel isn't directly below the reactor, but we can't be sure which direction the core will take as it burns down.'

'It'll be a trade-off, won't it?' Mawn interrupted. 'The core will fall under its own weight, but it'll also take the path of least resistance or lowest melting point. . . .' The floor under their feet

287

trembled, there was a distant explosion. '. . . so, if the core bursts through into the tunnel and the tunnel is full of water. . . .'

'Which it is,' Durrell put in.

'. . . then we could have a situation like an undersea volcano—Krakatoa for example.'

'God almighty!' Gelder exclaimed.

'It's pure guesswork,' Mawn continued. 'But the water could flash into steam and it depends entirely whether it can escape quickly enough back through the tunnel into the turbine condensers or out to sea through the tunnel. . . .'

'It won't do that,' Westcott intervened. 'The tunnel out to sea is already full of water—so you've got several hundred feet of tunnel blocked by a water plug. It'll go up all right, Christ! How long? Twenty feet—two hours and a bit.'

'And we're already over an hour in,' Gelder said.

'So that means we've got to get clear absolutely now,' Mawn exclaimed.

Gelder turned to Durrell.

'Frank, there's little we can do for your people now—I think they probably know it. Even if we could get them out—we'd all be irradiated. . . .'

Durrell looked at him blankly and Gelder stood silently aside as he moved over to the monitor screen. One by one he contacted the isolated groups of men trapped in different parts of the shattering building.

The men in the corridor had reached a stage of drunken euphoria. Durrell repeated his warning to them and urged them to get out and away from the building but one of them staggered towards the camera, his face distorted by its closeness to the lens. He was holding an empty whisky bottle. When he spoke his words were slurred: 'Hallo there, Dr Durrell. How are ye—bloody cold down here, I'll tell ye.' He waved the bottle unsteadily at the camera. 'Ye might bring a wee bit more of this when ye come down, the lads could do with some more—aye, it's cold.' He shivered and retched. 'You might have a few words wi' ma wife would ye—we're awful sick down here—awful sick.' He trembled and his face distorted with an impotent fury. 'Tell you laddie, when we get out of here there'll be a reckoning wi' you bastards—you got us into this.' He lurched forward and swung the bottle towards the camera. The watchers in the Control Room jumped back involuntarily and then the screen flashed once and went blank.

For several moments no one moved, then Durrell leant forward and switched through to Elleston, on the sixth floor. His face was almost invisible behind a zig-zag interference pattern on the screen. His voice was clear and urgent: 'We've just seen one of the lorries come back in again—what the hell's going on?' Durrell spoke urgently into the microphone: 'You must get out, the core's gone down and we think it may hit the turbine coolant—you've got to get out quick. . . .'

Elleston's voice was almost facetious: 'Oh, it's far too cold outside, we're quite snug in here. . . .'

Durrell shouted: 'For God's sake, listen to me, you've got to make your way out—go down by the fire stairs near the goods lift. . . .'

Elleston's voice was now totally devoid of expression: 'Dr Durrell, we've done a few measurements.' They could just see him wave a pistol-shaped radiation meter behind the swirling interference on the screen. 'We've all had over a thousand R. Leave us be—just leave us be—we've all had it—whatever you do—so don't bother—there's no use. . . .'

CHAPTER THIRTEEN

DURRELL STARED at the screen for several moments then reached forward and switched it off. Gelder broke the mood, moving towards the door and one by one, the others followed, shuffling awkwardly in the bulky restriction of the protective suits. In the corridor all they could hear was the harsh sibilance of their breathing inside the helmets.

As they turned to the left at the T-junction, the string of emergency lights dimmed and then flickered out. Westcott switched on a hand lantern and moved ahead probing the way with the cone of light. At the far end of the corridor there was a faint light from a window. They all crowded around.

A wide courtyard lay between the reactor building and the Turbine Hall and facing them was the service block, workshops and staff canteen. They could see that part of the glass roof of the service block had collapsed inwards under the cartwheel shape of the girders from the roof of the Reactor Hall. Smoke curled out of the gaping hole and from the other end of the building bright orange flames billowed out of a shattered window. From the roof of the Reactor Hall, clouds of black smoke were curling down over the courtyard and mingling with the driving snow. Durrell peered out: 'God, that's all we need, there's a wind.'

'What direction?' Mawn asked.

'Too many buildings about—can't tell, maybe south-east.'

Durrell turned to Gelder: 'Your helicopter pilot, did he say where he'd be?'

'Said something about watching from a colour set,' Gelder replied.

Durrell pointed to the service block: 'In that case, he'll probably be in the staff room over there.'

'Can we reach it?' Marcia asked.

Westcott gestured down the corridor: 'Down there's an overhead walkway across to the Turbine Hall, then we can go through the workshops and lorry pool, then there's a short bit of open ground to the service block.' Mawn and Gelder had already begun to move off as he spoke, the others followed in a shuffling jog-trot. Gelder reached the archway leading out on to the walkway, then stopped dead. The other gathering behind him.

In the deepening twilight, they could just see that the floor sagged and the girders forming its structure were twisted. All the glass had blown out of the windows and snow was pouring through the shattered structure. The ground was three storeys below.

Mawn eased forward, past Gelder and began to inch his way out on to the sloping floor. There was a sudden groaning sound and the whole sagging structure jerked downwards and then stopped abruptly flinging him off balance. Unsteady and awkward in his suit, he slowly got to his feet and, holding on to the bent and distorted girders for support, eased forward. Finally he made the far side and stood in the archway leading into the Turbine Hall. He shouted back, his voice muffled by the helmet: 'Come over one at a time, keep to the edge!'

One by one, with the care and delicacy of acrobats on a high wire, they felt their way over the roadway beneath and on into the Turbine Hall. The entire building was deserted and snow was pouring steadily through the broken roof. The galleries and giant pipes were already covered in a blanket of snow, only the massive hulks of the turbines, still hot from their previous operation, showed through like black whales in an arctic sea.

They moved on through a door leading out of the echoing cathedral-like building. Beyond it was a concrete staircase where emergency lights were still lit. After they were all safely inside, Westcott held the pistol-shaped geiger counter ahead of him. During the long walk from the Control Room they had all got accustomed to its regular clicking warning. Now the noise had almost stopped. Naylor put the counter on the floor, unzipped his helmet and hinged it back over his head. 'The level's down—we can have a breather.' Gratefully the others unzipped their helmets; their faces shiny with sweat.

Men in overalls were waiting at the bottom of the staircase. Inside the workshop the leading man, Jack Duffy, explained, above the clamour of a small generator, what had happened to them:

'We took off in some trucks from the pool. Did what we could, sealed off the heater inlets and taped up the windows. But it was bloody awful mon. It's snowing tae thick to see and the geigers went right off the scale up near the Churchill barriers.

'We were getting plastered with this wet snow, it was all grey coloured. The other trucks went on over the barriers—bloody suicide if you ask me. We turned back—put the lorry next door. I'll tell ye, we took a reading on some of the snow on the outside of the lorry when we got in. It's pumping out hard gamma—we would na' have stood a chance.'

'What about yourselves?' Durrell asked.

'Aye, we could've already copped it, our clothing's all right—canna tell how much we breathed in though. What about your people?'

Durrell began to explain the situation and Gelder turned to Mawn: 'Let's get the chopper pilot!' Naylor nodded, picked up the counter and led them across the shop floor between banks of lathes and milling machines towards the exit door. He turned: 'It'll be a quick dash across open ground, go like the devil.' He pulled his transparent helmet back over his head and Mawn and Gelder followed suit.

Naylor pulled the door ajar: 'Quick now!'

Outside, the wind plastered the swirling snow over their helmets, almost blinding them as they dashed over towards the entrance door of the service block.

Inside, the air was thick with acrid smoke which went straight through the filters on their helmets. They could hear the rapid clicking of the counter slow down as the door swung to behind them. Gelder started to undo the neck zip of his helmet, but Naylor shook his head violently, warning him not to and opened the door leading into the canteen.

The scene was like a Goya etching of war. In the dimness, the huge black girders from the Reactor Hall roof hung down through a gaping hole in the ceiling and, underneath, the rows of metal framed tables and chairs lay crushed like toys underneath a twisted mass of concrete and steel. Over every surface there was a thick layer of greyish dust.

At one end of the shattered room, the body of a middle-aged woman in pink kitchen uniform was pinned against the wall behind the serving counter, half buried in a broken pile of cups and plates which had cascaded down off the shelves behind her.

One man lay with his legs trapped beneath a large jagged piece of concrete. There was no gap between the concrete and the floor. Another had been impaled on the leg of an upturned table. He was still moving feebly, trying ineffectually to prise himself off a metal leg protruding from his groin. Other bodies were scattered around the floor and the three men silently moved from one to the other searching for signs of life. Finally, Gelder shouted and beckoned to Naylor. He pointed grimly at a pair of flying boots protruding from a pile of debris: a dark glistening pool of blood had formed around them. He shrugged hopelessly and turned away.

Mawn was bending down beside one man lying curled up against the wall. He was bleeding from a ragged wound in his thigh, his face putty-coloured in the flickering yellow light. Mawn quickly took off his belt and pulled it tight around the upper part of his thigh. The man opened his mouth to scream. The two men crouched down beside Mawn and raised the wounded man to a sitting position.

Gelder and Naylor put their hands under the man's armpits and gently raised him to a standing position holding his legs just clear of the ground. Mawn and Gelder took the weight of his body and started towards the door.

In the workshop people were beginning to filter in from other parts of the building, many of them wounded. As the three entered Durrell rushed over: 'Did you find him?'

Gelder slipped his helmet back over his head and eased the wounded man down on to the top of a steel workbench. 'Yes, we found him.'

Mawn crouched beside Marcia who was binding makeshift rags around the head of a technician lying slumped against the pillar of a drilling machine. She looked up and smiled wanly. Mawn pulled her briefly towards him, holding her head against his shoulder.

The air in the workshop was cooling down rapidly. A jury-rigged air heater had run out of fuel and the news of the melting reactor core and its proximity to the turbine cooling duct had spread a growing air of depression. Even the group from the Control Room were affected by the claustrophobic conditions. Outside, the wind thumped angrily against the walls.

Gelder was helping Durrell to carry a wounded technician over to a line of men propped against one wall. Mawn watched him. The finding of the dead helicopter pilot had seemed to alter him. At first he had been almost theatrically in command of himself, but now he moved automatically, his actions clumsy and awkward. Perhaps, he thought, he had looked forward to a quick flight over to the mainland to organize a massive rescue operation, turning defeat into a personal triumph.

Marcia had moved over to another wounded man. He felt a sudden wave of affection towards her slight, angular figure.

'Mawn!' Durrell beckoned him over to a small group standing round a small scale map of the Orkney islands spread out on a bench. Durrell pointed a screwdriver in a circle around the island of South Ronaldsay. 'Far as we can see there'll probably be a very high radiation level here. One thing we can assume, the wind is, in fact, in the south-east, so whatever solid material blew out of the reactor it will almost certainly have come down on the Churchill barriers—so we can't go that way.'

'Since we've already been irradiated,' Mawn said.

'Right. There's a small blizzard outside and if the snow is hot then it's bound to stick to these suits.'

'Is there no one else who can fly a helicopter?' It was Lodge who had spoken. He was standing on the edge of the group. He appeared withdrawn and his lips trembled as he spoke.

Gelder looked around, a small flicker of hope in his eyes, then shrugged: 'I can drive a plane, not a chopper.'

'Forget it!' Durrell snapped. 'It's doubtful if it could fly in these conditions anyway. No, we've only one way now.' He pointed with the screwdriver. 'Down here—the B9044—then south on to the A961 to Burwick.'

'South!' exclaimed Gelder. 'There's nothing down there.'

Durrell gazed at him sombrely: 'Frankly, Mr Gelder, unless we can get to expert medical help in the next forty-eight hours . . . God help us! We must have had . . . well, quite a dose already.'

'How does it show?' Marcia asked.

'Nausea, vomiting, cramps, sometimes a headache early on anyway, then . . .'

'There's no point in this,' Lodge said irritably, 'we're bound to get more radiation if we go out into the open.' His voice was high, edgy. Mawn looked at him. All the calm urbanity of the Civil Servant had cracked away. Mawn looked at his watch: 'We've maybe half an hour before the core burns down to the coolant ducts, so let's cut out the debate and get on with it. Now, Durrell, you said there's a road to the south?'

'Yes, the B9 . . .'

'Right, we take that.'

Westcott began to protest: 'You've seen what it's like outside— it's snowing like hell. I'll stay in here.'

Mawn looked across at him incredulously: 'It was *you* who told us about the gloupy wasn't it?'

Westcott just stared back at him, his lips trembling and Mawn realized he was only just under control. He turned to Durrell: 'What do you think?'

Durrell hesitated, his face a grey mask of defeat, then shook his head hopelessly: 'We've no chance here, no chance at all.'

'Then for God's sake let's move!' Mawn strode to a group of technicians clustered nervously around Jack Duffy. 'What transport have you got?'

Duffy looked up at him, his breath reeked of whisky, his eyes were watery. He gestured towards the door leading to the transport pool. 'There's a couple out there besides the one I drove back. That one's useless, be plastered in the stuff, would'na suggest you use that.'

Mawn's voice dropped a little: 'Then what?'

'We stop ourselves up in here and wait. They're bound to have heard the explosion up at Kirkwall, besides the other two lorries'll be there by now.'

Mawn's voice rose: 'Haven't you got it into your thick head. In about twenty minutes the reactor may hit the water tunnel and the whole building goes up.'

'Och, I dinna think so. I reckon this place'll stand it—remember we saw it go up brick on brick. No laddie, we'll all stay here— they'll come and get us out all right, dinna ye worry.'

Mawn looked over at the pathetic row of casualties propped against the wall. 'And what about them? We need you to get the lorries going, you're a driver, you know the road. . . .'

'And just who the hell d'ye think ye are?—giving us orders— you hav'na been out there, I *have*.' He gestured with a whisky bottle. 'I'm telling you it's plain bloody suicide.'

Mawn looked over at the others. The men behind Duffy looked apathetic, defeated. Duffy's face was clouded with drunken resentment: 'If ye want tae go you can sodding well go by yourself.' He staggered away. Mawn turned after him, and grabbed him by the shoulder, he realized he had to win the argument and win it quickly. He reached forward, snatched the whisky bottle from Duffy's grasp and flung it away to shatter against the far wall.

There was a moment's shocked silence then Duffy reacted. 'You sodding bastard. I'll bloody kill ye.' He rushed at Mawn and made a wild swing at his jaw. Mawn hit him once, heavily square in the stomach, Duffy dropped to his knees half stunned and gasping for breath. Mawn looked quickly around but the others were reluctant to come forward. He strode forward, grasped the other whisky bottle and sent it to join the first.

'Some of you give him a hand. The rest wrap up the casualties as best you can—anything you can find, rags, coats, just get them covered—it'll keep the worst of the dust off them. Move!'

The men hesitated for a moment then began to shuffle away. He called after them: 'And tie some wet rags over their faces, leave it so that they can breathe—but only through the cloth.'

Mawn walked to Marcia who was looking down helplessly at a girl of about eighteen lying motionless on the floor: 'She's dead is she?' His bluntness made her swing round. 'We can't take them all.'

'What?'

295

He gestured at the other casualties: 'Some of them are very bad, they're bleeding a hell of a lot and they're shocked, if we start mucking them around on lorries—it's going to be bloody cold outside and it'll more likely kill them than if we leave them here.'

'You can't leave them,' she blazed. 'What about the core?'

'It's one or the other.' He looked at his watch. 'Look, we may only have about twenty minutes, choose the ones who look as if they're going to make it.'

'What about the others?' she said helplessly.

Mawn held her shoulders tightly. 'Look, Marcia, there's *no* choice, *none* at all.' Her face was thin and white with the cold but her eyes were dark and outraged. She shook her head: 'I'll stay here with them.'

'Then I'll have to carry you out of here.' For a moment there was silence, then Naylor touched him on the shoulder: 'Ready to go now.' Marcia looked from one man to the other, then slowly got to her feet. She looked down at her hands covered in dirt and blood, then followed them over to the door to the transport pool.

'We've got about twenty in the lorries,' Naylor said.

In the doorway Mawn looked back for the last time. In the flickering yellow light of the emergency bulbs the row of silent figures propped against the wall looked like figures in an ancient tomb. He closed the door behind him.

The vehicle bay was a furore of activity. Lit by harsh head-lamps, two lorries and a Volkswagen minibus already had their engines running. Under Durrell's instructions each vehicle was being sealed. Polythene sheeting had been draped over the tarpaulin covers and the uninjured technicians were sticking strips of masking tape over all the apertures. One man, his head inside the bonnet of a lorry, had disconnected the corrugated heater and was stuffing rags into the open end leading to the cab.

The wounded were being carried like trussed mummies into the backs of the lorries and the air was thick with exhaust fumes. Durrell and Naylor were moving from one man to the next running geiger counters over the surface of their clothing. Duffy shuffled over to Mawn, his drunken surliness gone: 'Get aboard.'

Durrell nodded to Naylor who was standing by a large red-painted lever switch. He pulled it down. There was a shrill whine and the exterior doors began to swing upwards. Durrell shouted: 'Everyone inside, close your doors and stay there. Once we get out,

296

stay close together. Duffy in the first lorry will lead off.' Duffy swung up into the cab, a technician began to lace the rear curtain of the tarpaulin cover and as the cab door slammed the exhaust blew out a cloud of smoke and the lorry swung round and lumbered heavily out into the snow.

The second followed suit. In the back, huddled together for warmth, Westcott and Sampson sat jerking from side to side trying to brace themselves against the tarpaulin cover and hold the casualties in place on the floor with their feet. As the lorry reached the door opening, Naylor leapt into the cab.

Gelder sat waiting at the wheel of the sealed minibus with Dr Durrell by his side. Mawn, Marcia and Lodge sat in the back. Their helmets glinted in the reflected glare from the headlamps. Gelder let in the clutch and drove out into the open. Immediately thick flakes of snow began to build up on the screen. He switched on the wipers and the rhythmical whirring of the motor seemed almost reassuring. Mawn switched on the interior light and held up his watch.

'It's time!'

'Switch the bloody thing off, I can't see a thing,' Gelder rapped out impatiently peering ahead into the dark. Just ahead they could make out the red tail lights of the second lorry. As the van jerked and bounced over the piled up snow they all imagined the incandescent core forging its way down through the rock below.

Gelder stood suddenly on the brakes and the van slithered to a halt. He quickly backed away until the headlights picked out a snow-covered body lying in the centre of the roadway. Durrell moved to open the door, Gelder leant over and pulled him back violently. 'Keep the door shut!'

'It looks like Gillian, my secretary . . . I must get out. . . .'

Without replying Gelder jerked the gear lever and with its wheels spinning, the van swung around the body and straightened up. He floored the accelerator, peering furiously ahead through the screen. 'I've lost them!' He wrenched the wheel and drifted around the first bend of the exit road. The tail swung wide and there was a metallic clang as it bounced off a concrete marker post.

'For God's sake take it easy!' Lodge yelled from the rear seat.

For answer, Gelder hinged his helmet back: 'I can't see in this damn thing.'

'Look out!' Durrell yelled.

Again Gelder spun the wheel, the van skidded broadside and banged up against a great pile of masonry from the Reactor Hall. One window cracked under the impact.

Ahead they could just make out the giant bulk of the loading machine lying like a gigantic nine-pin where it had smashed out through the wall of the Reactor Hall. Lodge picked himself off the floor. He stared fixedly ahead, mouthing words to himself.

'The main gate's through there,' Durrell's voice rang out.

'No, look!' Marcia pointed towards the boundary fence.

The first two lorries had halted by the perimeter fence and the squat figure of Duffy was knotting a thick rope over the top of one of the concrete posts. To their horror they saw that he had no protective suit.

'I'll get out,' Durrell moved to open the door but Gelder stopped him and pointed.

Duffy had moved quickly round to the back of his lorry and crawled underneath to tie the other end of the rope around the rear axle casing. As they watched he slid out, feet first, and jumped back into the cab.

The engine raced and the lorry leaped forward. The rope sprang up out of the snow, jerking taut, but the post held, with the rear wheels of the lorry spinning and throwing up fans of snow. He reversed again up to the fence then lumbered forward again. Three times he repeated the manœuvre then jumped down and quickly started to unscrew the tyre valves or the rear tyres, air hissed out until the rear of the lorry began to sag.

Jumping back into the cab, he let the clutch in slowly until the flattened tyres started to grip and then, as the lorry crept forward, he suddenly gunned the engine. The rope tautened, then there was a sharp crack and the post split about a foot from the ground. The lorry careered forward, pulling down about fifteen feet of the chain link fencing.

Reversing again, Duffy turned the lorry round in a wide circle to avoid tangling in the rope, then nosed the bonnet towards the gap in the fence. Ahead of him was a long thirty-degree snow-covered slope leading down towards the Grim-Ness road running parallel with the cliffs past the station. Beyond the road, there was a ten foot border, then a low wire fence guarding the cliff edge. The lorry crunched over the remains of the fence then dipped sharply downwards on to the slope. Wheels locked, it began to toboggan down to the road. First it lurched sideways then began to swing round. As it reached the road, the rope tautened, the momentum of the lorry pulling the broken fence down over the edge of the slope behind it. The lorry lurched to a halt, its bonnet pressing up against the fence at the cliff edge. Duffy jumped out, slid on his belly under the axle and cut away the rope.

The second lorry nosed up to the edge of the slope and began to slide down. As it gathered speed the driver locked the wheels, but instead of slowing, the vehicle began to swing out of line, until it spun completely round. At the bottom it cannoned into the rear end of the stationary lorry bouncing it forwards through the cliff fence. There was a loud metallic clang as the front wheels dipped down over the edge. Duffy leapt out, but a black pool of sump oil was already welling out from underneath the engine, hissing in the snow.

Gelder put the van into gear and guided it through the gap in the torn fencing and eased the front wheels down onto the slope. Suddenly the ground seemed to jerk violently upwards.

From somewhere directly underneath them came a long deep rumbling blast of sound. The van was flung into the air and immediately began to career down the slope. There was a second booming detonation and the van gathered speed like a bobsleigh, Gelder wrestling desperately with the wheel. Totally out of control it broadsided to the bottom of the slope and slammed sideways on into the nose of the second lorry.

For a split second it remained stationary, then Gelder floored the accelerator and, weaving and twisting, the van gathered speed, swinging from side to side up the road as he fought to regain control over the ice. In the headlights the entire surface of the road in front of them began to weave and undulate as if it were made of rubber. Over the scream of the engine, apparently from the ground beneath them, came a deep juddering thunder.

'We can't leave them there. Stop!'

Durrell was pulling hysterically at the wheel but Gelder, holding on to the wheel with one hand, fought him away. Briefly Durrell gained an advantage and diverted Gelder's attention for a split second. Ahead the stalk of a concrete lamp standard appeared out of the dark.

Mawn leapt at Marcia, hurling her to the floor. There was a thumping rending crash and then silence.

299

After a few moments, Mawn painfully picked himself off the floor by grabbing the top of the front seats. The windscreen had shattered and both Gelder and Durrell had been flung forward through the glass. Durrell's body was hanging down over the front of the van, only his hips and legs were still inside. The subterranean roar had grown suddenly deeper and the whole earth was shaking.

Silhouetted against the sky, the giant outlines of the Reactor Hall began to crumble inwards. The air was full of a grinding, shuddering vibration. Then with a shrieking howl like an enormous jet engine a giant mushroom of steam and debris fountained out of the collapsing masonry. The outlines of the remaining buildings began to waver, fragment and plunge downwards. Debris started to rain down around the van. There was a deafening clang and the van roof suddenly dented inwards. The whole vehicle was shaking violently on its wheels.

A ragged crack suddenly appeared through the snow and whipped across the road, ripping it apart. The van teetered and began to slide towards the crack. The crack suddenly widened into a fissure, steam began to boil out and on the far side, they could just see the occupants of the two lorries jumping down and running like ants from a burning nest.

The ground under the lorries tilted crazily and both men and machines began to slide and tumble towards the cliff edge. One man scrabbled desperately at the tilting road, then disappeared screaming in the fissure. Both lorries locked firmly together careered towards the cliff edge, balanced for a moment and then toppled over and were gone.

Gradually, the earth tremors died away and from where the station had been, there was a roaring spouting volcano of fumes blasting hundreds of feet into the air. At the top, it was already forming into a giant mushroom cloud which was already pulling away in the wind.

Mawn switched on a hand lantern and pulled Marcia to her feet: 'Are you O.K.?'

She started to flex her limbs, feeling for injury. She nodded her head, still too shocked for speech.

Mawn bent forward over the front seat. 'Let's get these two in.' He grabbed hold of Durrell's hips and began to drag the limp body back through the crumbling edges of the broken windshield.

Marcia glanced over her shoulder. Lodge was hunched in a corner. His eyes were glazed and there was a long abrasion down one side of his face.

Mawn had got Durrell's body back into the front seat. His visor was broken and the circular air filter had been pushed inwards. A thick brown mass of blood covered the side of his head.

'Give me the light a minute,' Mawn called. 'Christ! the side of his head's right in. Help me get him in the back.' Marcia put the lantern down and between them they heaved and pulled the apparently lifeless body over the front seats and into the back.

Gelder's face was covered in a mask of blood. A long jagged flesh wound stretched over his forehead and on into the hair line. He was breathing in harsh jerking gasps. With difficulty they man-handled him into the passenger seat and strapped him in place with the seat belt.

Mawn climbed awkwardly into the driving seat and turned the ignition key. The starter whirred; nothing. He felt for the choke and was unable to find it. Again no response! Then remembering the Volkswagen automatic choke he floored the accelerator pedal, released it and turned the key. The engine fired immediately. He turned to Marcia, shouting over the noise of the engine: 'Do you remember the way?'

'It's the same road we used when we first came up. Down about two miles then on to the A road and along past the housing estate.' Mawn nodded, turned and started to back the car away from the lamp standard. Then he jumped out and walked round to the front to examine the damage. The lamp standard had made a long creased indentation in the front body panel and the beam from one headlight was pointing crazily up into the falling snow. He stood in the bitter wind trying to regain his breath, looking up at the great mushroom of fumes lying over the collapsed Reactor Hall. Instead of moving away to the north, there was a long plume directly over his head. He leaped back inside shouting to Marcia: 'The wind's changing, it's coming after us!'

He slammed the van into gear and wrenched it around back on to the road. Snow immediately began to pour in through the shat-tered windshield and every few minutes, he had to slow down and clear the perspex surface of his helmet. The skewed headlamp beam glared back off the curtain of snow so that he could only just see ahead. After a few minutes, snow began to pile up over the front of his helmet and freeze in position. Occasionally he had to stop altogether and bang the flexible plastic with his fist to crack off the impacted ice. His hands grew numb and it became acutely painful to even unbend them from the wheel. In the back, Marcia attempted to wedge the three injured men in position as the van bounced over the snow.

Gradually Mawn's senses began to dull as the cold crept in through the suit. His reactions got slower and he began to misjudge corners and twice drove off the road into drifted snow.

Lodge appeared to be asleep. His head lolled back inside the helmet, his mouth wide open. Durrell's colour had almost disappeared. All bleeding from his wounds had stopped and Gelder hung from the seat belt, his breathing rasping and irregular.

As the road unwound, Mawn managed to force the agony of the cold away. Ahead was a main road sign almost obliterated by an encrustation of snow. The sight spurred him on and, misjudging, he slewed the van round, broadsiding across the road up on to the verge. He let the clutch in slowly to give the wheels a chance to bite. They started to inch forward then the engine raced and the van spun at right angles to the road. He turned the wheel and pointed the nose down the hill.

'For God's sake what are you doing?' Marcia cried. 'We can't go back there!'

'Reverse—lower gear.' Slowly he let the clutch in and started to back the van up the hill. Gradually the wheels bit and, looking back over his shoulder through the rear window, he steered the awkward bulk of the van up towards the crest of the hill.

He shouted: 'You're in the way. I can't see!' Marcia ducked.

At the top, he turned the van around and began to coast down the other side, the engine whining in bottom gear. He peered ahead through the darkness. There was a small point of light, then another, and another. He shouted to Marcia and pointed them out and again lost his concentration for a few vital seconds. The back lashed round in a vicious spin sending them sliding off the road backwards into a snow-covered hedge. He gunned the engine, but the wheels found no grip and spun uselessly.

Wearily Mawn tore one of the rubber floor mats off the floor and clambered awkwardly down. Straining with all his remaining strength, he tore the mat into two halves and put one half down in the snow just ahead of each rear wheel.

Inside again, he let the clutch slip feeding power to the wheels slowly. Gradually the tyres moved on to the corrugated surface of the rubber and then gripped but started to slip again as the mats shot out backwards from beneath the tyres in a spray of snow and dirt.

Jamming on the handbrake he jumped down again and replaced the mats ahead of the wheels for a second time. He leant tiredly against the van for a minute, his body leaden with cold then he looked up in sudden alarm. There was no pressure of wind on his suit. Burwick lay behind him, the road was to the north and south, they were over the brow. To the west he could just make out the small peak of Cairn Hill. On the east side, a faint gleam of ice, Lake Cleat. Full of misgiving he tramped back up the hill.

At the top, the blast of air almost took him off his feet, gusting hard from the north-east. He started to race back, slipping and falling as he slithered down the icy road to the van. He ran for the door pulling himself in, shouting to Marcia: 'It's over us. Blowing like hell!'

He let in the clutch, gradually the wheels began to grip and they regained the road. The last mile was all downhill but the van seemed almost uncontrollable, swinging from side to side as if trying to escape from its driver.

Finally, through the snow pouring in through the windscreen aperture, he made out first one light, then the dark grey outlines of a row of cottages. Almost dead with fatigue he found himself bringing the van to a halt on a quayside. He switched off the engine and in the silence, all the strain and fear suddenly welled up inside him and he slumped forward over the wheel.

CHAPTER FOURTEEN

SOMEONE WAS SHAKING HIM by the shoulder. He looked up wearily, automatically wiping the snow off the face-piece of his helmet.

There were voices. A clamour of questions. He pushed himself away from the wheel and eased himself painfully out of the cab. A circle of faces drew back in alarm at the sight of the giant figure in its white plastic suit and helmet. For a moment he stood there swaying in the snow, then, realizing the situation, shouted: 'All of you get back! Get back inside. For Christ's sake get back.' Then, without warning, his body began to tremble, an intolerable nausea ballooned into his throat, the faces seemed to veer sideways and he pitched forward on to the snow.

Somewhere in the distance, there was somebody talking: 'Will you take a bit of this?' He opened his eyes warily. He was lying on a black wooden wall seat and a large elderly man with iron-grey hair and a craggy, blue-veined face was holding out a tumbler half full of whisky. He put his hand up to his face. 'My helmet, for God's sake!'

Marcia was standing beside him: 'It's all right, Alex, I used the counter—the levels are fairly low in here. We took your suit off.' He raised his head. He was in the bar of a low-ceilinged pub. A group of men in fishermen's garb stood in a semi-circle, watching. He sat up and gulped down half the whisky.

'We've got the others out.' Marcia's voice faltered. 'Dr Durrell's dead—I couldn't do anything.'

'Aye, they're in the back room, the other one's pretty bad. Dr McBurney's been in and done what he can, but they'll be needing a hospital.'

Mawn staggered to his feet. The man moved to push him back on to the couch but Mawn shrugged him aside: 'I've got to get a phone.'

'We've already done it.'

'What about the lines to the mainland? Are they working?'

'Aye, why shouldn't they be?'

'We've got to get help!'

'I think they'll be getting it in hand already.'

'In hand?' Mawn's mind was clouded with fatigue.

'What the hell happened up there? We never wanted that bloody thing on the island in the first place.'

'Why couldna you bastards leave us alone.'

The low bar-room was beginning to fill with men and women with their children all huddled in thick overcoats against the weather. After an agonizing wait Mawn finally got a line through to London. A full rescue operation was already being mounted. A county class guided missile destroyer, the *Westmoreland*, had been diverted and was pushing through heavy seas from Rosyth with all hatches sealed. A specialist medical emergency team from the atomic weapons research establishment at Aldermaston was moving north by special train. Police throughout the north of Scotland had been alerted and were touring the towns and countryside with loudhailers telling residents to stay inside under cover.

Aircraft from Coastal Command were loading up with radiation detection equipment to overfly the radiation cloud and plot its course as it swept southwards over Scotland. National radio and television announcements had already been made.

Back in the bar he suddenly recognized Mrs Naylor and Mrs Baird in the crowd. He had a momentary, horrific recall of Baird's face splitting in the jet of steam. They were all looking at him expectantly as the grey-haired man held up his hand for silence.

Mawn began hesitantly and gave a full account of the disaster as he had seen it, telling them that the station had been entirely demolished and that they must expect the casualty rate to be heavy.

Mrs Baird began to weep.

Mrs Naylor stepped forward: 'Then how did you get out? Did you just run, leaving all the others?' Her eyes blazed. Mawn hesitated: 'Some people—there were two lorries anyway—they got to Kirkwall.' He felt an intense self-disgust at the half-truth, saw the cruel false hope in the eyes of the listening women.

'Who was in them?'

'Where can we find out?'

The questions tumbled out. Mawn clapped his hands for silence: 'Please! The ones who got across to Kirkwall should be in hospital by now.' He turned to the grey-haired man: 'I'm sorry, I don't know your name. . . .'

'Furse, Jimmy Furse. I run the pub.'

'I suggest you start by ringing everyone who's got a phone and tell them to stay inside until help arrives. If they live close enough to neighbours without a phone, tell them to contact them but *without* going outside. Tell them to bang on walls, throw stones, anything. But *not* to go out and to seal up all their windows and doors.'

'Some of them live away out in the hills,' Furse growled.

'I'm sorry, that's the best we can do. You'll all have to stay inside here, you can't go back to your homes because there may be fall-

305

out from the station.' He turned to Jimmy Furse: 'What about food and heat?'

'We'll have enough food,' Furse replied grudgingly: 'There'll be compensation I suppose?'

Mawn held back a surge of anger: 'And we'll need blankets. I don't know how long we'll have to stay in here.'

A woman spoke angrily: 'You bloody scientists never do know, when it comes to it.' Mawn went on: 'There's a navy ship on its way, it should be here sometime tomorrow.' He hesitated: 'Then, I'm afraid, it's very likely you'll all have to go over to the mainland. . . .'

There was a tumult of protest. A fisherman stepped forward, his face suffused with anger: 'We're no leaving the isles. This is our home!'

Mawn held his hand up: 'It's too dangerous here. Nobody knows how long it will take to clear. . . .'

The storm of protest grew.

'You'll ruin our village!'

'Listen, please!'

'No, you listen to us!' The fisherman brandished his arms: 'We didn't want that damn power station here in the first place—you'll ruin us all, it's your doing—we'll have none of it!'

There was a chorus of assent. Mawn had to shout above the noise. 'Shut up and listen to me. Outside there's very probably a cloud of radioactive debris. The wind is now blowing from the north and it's bringing it all right down over us here. Now you can't feel it—there's no smell or anything—but it's very, very dangerous.'

'If we canna feel it, wha's the harm?' a voice demanded.

'It's radioactive.'

A woman's voice shouted: 'I dinna ken what ye mean wi' all those long words. I've a bairn staying over at Coldharbour farm. Why can I not fetch her? There's nothing but snow out there.'

Mawn pointed to the door: 'Anyone who goes out there now will almost certainly die in a very few days.' The deliberate over-statement had an immediate impact and the protesting voices slowly died away. He opened the door leading to the saloon, turning to Furse: 'They're in here, are they?' Furse nodded.

Mawn switched on the light: 'And if you want to see what you'll end up as, if you go out, come and look!'

Durrell's body was on the saloon floor covered by a blanket. Gelder lay on a wall seat, his head lolled to one side. There was vomit on his chin. The villagers crowded silently into the door opening. Mawn turned to them:

'You'll be like that.' He walked back to the door. The crowd melted back in front of him. 'Now listen, please, we've got to go round this building and seal it right up. Every single crack—anywhere where air can get in—block it up—newspaper, rags, anything you can find.'

'We'll aye suffocate,' a voice complained.

'No, no you won't. Enough air will get in.'

An old man in faded dungarees spoke: 'How long will we be awa from the isle? Can ye not at least tell us that, man!'

With a shock of pity Mawn saw that he was almost blind.

'Not for long. Just until it's safe to return.'

'Then ye'll have to leave me. I canna go, I've never been off this island. I could'na find my way.'

Marcia gently took his hand, leading him away to a corner seat. Mawn drew a deep breath: 'It's bound to get very stuffy after a while so once we've got ourselves sealed in, it'll be best if you can manage to stay as still as possible. That way you won't use up so much air.'

During the following hour, every corner of the house was searched for places where the air could get in. From the loft to the cellar door, they used everything they could find to plug gaps. One man was rolling pieces of bread and squeezing the dough into the gap between two halves of a sash window. Another drove newspaper into a door crack with a screwdriver.

One elderly woman in a black shawl had rolled up a rug and was pushing it up against a gap under the front door, another was scooping earth from an indoor plant pot and forcing it into the edge of a window frame. She jerked in alarm as the wind suddenly buffeted the panes, rattling the frame.

In the saloon, Marcia was cleaning Gelder's face, trying to move him into a more comfortable position. He groaned faintly as she tugged at his shoulder. Mawn came in and moved to help her. She turned: 'I can hardly feel his pulse.'

'What about the doctor they were talking about?'

'He's off somewhere else—anyway, he's seventy-five apparently —probably hasn't a clue what's going on.'

307

In the bar people were beginning to settle down. Some sat leaning up against the wall, the children had been taken upstairs by Mrs Furse to rest on hastily improvised beds laid out on the bare floorboards.

Gradually, over a period of about an hour, the voices died down. One small group of fishermen sat in a silent circle facing each other on the floor quietly passing a bottle.

Mrs Baird sat in a wall seat holding a crumpled handkerchief to her lips, sobbing. Mrs Naylor sat beside her, her arms round her shoulders. Someone turned out the lights and through the windows, they watched the snow swirling against the panes building into small drifts on the wooden frames. The wind howled and buffeted and there was a loud clattering sound from the roadway outside as a roof slate fell.

In the saloon, Mawn put his arm around Marcia's shoulder and led her gently back into the bar. Settling himself down on the floor up against the bar counter, he beckoned her down beside him. He took his jacket off and draped it round her shoulders. For a moment she pulled away from him, then she put her head down on his shoulder, closing her eyes. In the dim blue light from the window, Mawn could see the tears running down her cheeks. He brushed them away with his fingertips.

She opened her eyes, the tears glistening: 'All those people, Alex. . . .'

'I know. There's nothing more we can do about it now.'

'Do you think they're all dead?'

He looked down at her, stroking her hair: 'The lucky ones are!'

She shuddered.

'What about us? How much have we had?'

He pulled her head down holding her against him: 'I don't know. I think we'll be all right.'

'Does it take long to kill, radiation I mean?'

'Marcia, leave it. We're all right so far. Try and sleep.'

She pulled suddenly away from him: 'You don't even seem to care?'

He paused then reached out and pulled her down against him: 'I care. Now please, one thing at a time. We've got to rest.'

She put her arm up around his neck, pulling herself closer. Mawn sat staring at the snow building up on the window sill in front of him. Then, gradually, as if he had taken a powerful narcotic, a warm irresistible lassitude spread through his body. His eyes closed.

In the dream, he was trapped inside an enormous wooden crate. Light was streaming in from one side through gaps in the planks and someone outside was banging in heavy nails. The knocking grew louder. He opened his eyes. Through the window in front of him, a harsh dawn light was streaming into the bar through the condensation on the window panes. Someone was pounding on the front door. There was a shout:

'Anybody there—open up now!' The knocking began again and there was another shout: 'Come along—let's have you!'

Mawn scrambled to his feet and ran over to the door: 'Who is it?' he shouted.

'It's all right. It's the navy. You can open up, it's safe.' Mawn kicked away the carpet, slid the bolts and swung the door open.

Silhouetted against the bright early morning sun, stood a bulky figure in protective suit and helmet. Inside the helmet was a cheerful red face and a shock of curly ginger hair. Beyond the figure, about three hundred yards out to sea, the long grey shape of a naval vessel stood out against the sparkling water. On the quayside, its engine running, a Westland Wessex helicopter crouched nose down on sea floats, its rotors idling. The face spoke, peering in through the door.

'Many of you are there?' He stuck his head in, looking round at the prostrate figures now waking. 'Stone me, have a party, did you?'

Inside, people were getting stiffly to their feet, rubbing their eyes and stretching.

'Can I have your attention for a minute, please. My name's Petty Officer Gage. I'm off the *Westmoreland*,' he gestured over his shoulder. 'She's standing out in the bay there. Now, outside, there's a chopper and we've got to get you off a bit sharpish—there's quite a bit of radiation about.'

'Have you measured levels?' Mawn asked.

The smile behind the helmet faded a little: 'If you don't mind sir, the navy's in the atomic age now, we're quite capable of taking care of things, thank you.' He looked around again. 'Anybody hurt? We'll take them first.'

Three other men in similar suits had approached.

'Yes,' Mawn replied, gesturing at the saloon bar door. 'One in

309

there, he's got what looks like radiation sickness and a head injury. The other's dead.'

'Right then!' The figure turned to the other three in the doorway: 'Hanson, Smith and you, in there at the double. One wounded—one sleeper, leave him for last.' The three suited figures lumbered through the bar and on into the saloon. He turned to the crowd of faces surrounding him:

'Now, in a bit, we'll have you all aboard below decks, safe and sound. With a bit of naval hospitality laid on. We'll take you off ten at a time in the chopper, no time to take anything else I'm afraid, so just yourselves as you are. Get the kiddies wrapped up.'

The three men pushed their way back through the crowd, with Gelder's limp form. As they passed, the Petty Officer unhooked a pistol geiger counter from his belt and ran it quickly over Gelder's body. It clicked violently. 'Quick with this one, we'll have to put him in decontamination.'

The men struggled out towards the helicopter, their footprints showing black against the fresh carpet of snow. When they returned, Gage had already ushered nine more of the waiting islanders to the door. He spoke as if he was addressing his own men: 'Now quick as you can, double over to the chopper and get straight in, sit down and don't move.'

The islanders broke into an uneasy shambling run over the snow and crowded through the oval hatchway of the helicopter. The door slammed immediately, the aircraft stretched up on its landing struts and took off, swinging round straight out to sea towards the waiting destroyer.

Mawn and Marcia stood by the bar. They had both struggled back into their protective suits, the helmets hinged back. Next to them, Mrs Naylor and Mrs Baird had put a small month-old baby inside a protective plastic envelope supplied by one of the naval technicians. Down each side of it there were rows of press-studs and over the head portion there were a series of drawstrings around the edges of a transparent section. Both women seemed unable to understand how the fastenings worked. Marcia, seeing their difficulty, walked over to help. She had no difficulty in completing the closure. She turned back to see Mawn staring at her.

His voice rang out: 'Just a moment!'

The two women looked up nervously. He pointed at Mrs Naylor. 'Where do you come from?'

'How do you mean?'

He walked over, excitedly: 'Where do you live?'

'London, why?'

He turned to Mrs Baird: 'And you?'

'Cardiff. All my life.'

Outside, the siren of the *Westmoreland* sounded twice.

'Come on, Alex,' Marcia said urgently. Mawn remained stock still.

'Marcia, where were you brought up?'

'Alex, what is this?'

'Where were you brought up?'

'Long Island—most of the time.'

'The I.Q. loss, Marcia! I told you we had to have the answer ourselves. We're not affected are we?'

'No.'

'Why not? Don't you see? Those women are affected. They couldn't manage that simple task—you could. What's the *one* thing we couldn't understand?'

'People in one place being affected, people in another unaffected.'

'Right. Which people, Marcia?' He grabbed her by the shoulders.

'And *where* did they live?'

'I don't . . .'

'Listen, you and I have lived most of our life in the country. Those two lived in cities. Try and remember, Marcia, your groups —your affected groups—*where* were they sited?'

'I haven't got the stuff here, I can't . . .'

'Just try and give me the *location* of some of the groups that *were* affected.'

She hesitated: 'Well, there was one firm in London, another in —Birmingham, two in Manchester. . . .'

'Go on!'

'. . . one in Bristol—Plymouth yes, I think there was one there. . . .'

'O.K., now *where* were the ones which didn't show the effect?'

'There was one in the country in Breconshire, they'd moved out of Newport, another in Sussex—let's think—yes, one right out on the moors in Yorkshire. One in Devon—near Dartmoor. . . .'

'Don't you see?'

311

'What?'

'They're all in the bloody country!' He was shaking with excitement. 'Your affected groups are all in cities, the others are in the country. It's in the cities, Marcia. Whatever it is, it's in the cities. Something's rotting people's brains in the cities.'

CHAPTER FIFTEEN

'I HAVE ALREADY SPOKEN with Dr Bordheim of UNESCO and he fully confirms the conclusion reached by Mawn. There is now quite overwhelming evidence to show that there has been a loss of mental ability in both men and women and that the worst affected have lived in cities for some considerable time.' The Minister, Campbell Baxter, was speaking from a high backed Jacobean chair at the head of a long marquetry inlaid table reflecting a rich brown glow from a chandelier overhead. On his right hand a man of about thirty with alert blue eyes and slicked back fair hair was making notes. Five other men were present.

'It is also quite clearly global. No country with any large city is immune and so our most urgent task here will be to co-ordinate a plan of action as quickly as possible. I cannot possibly over-emphasise the gravity of this extraordinary effect. I have already been involved in the most delicate negotiations with the Trades Union Council. Their attitude, of course, is to demand recompense and safeguards for their workers who are affected. The military are also extremely nervous about the whole of our defence commitment. They are at the present time completing intelligence testing on all crew members of our deterrent fleet. I don't need to tell you the appalling consequences of any human error on board a missile submarine or, for that matter, in any defence installation. The only consolation seems to be that the Russians have the same problem.' He turned to a broadfaced man of about fifty on his left. 'Perhaps at this stage you would summarize the Orkney disaster, Mr Fordyce?'

'Yes. There are still eighty-four people unaccounted for. Of course no one can go near the site of the station to search for bodies since the whole island of South Ronaldsay is—er—quite uninhabitable because of the ambient radiation. Over the remainder of the Orkneys there were eighteen deaths from acute radiation and seventy-four non-lethal cases. These are being treated in various Scottish general hospitals and are probably recoverable. The Pentland Firth and Scapa Flow have been closed to shipping. In fact there is a slow eastward drift in these waters and one hopes that the radioactive content will dilute sufficiently before it reaches the west coast of Scandinavia. . . .'

'Yes.' Baxter intervened. 'The Swedes have already made some very firm claims in the United Nations General Assembly. Please continue.'

'. . . As to the Scottish mainland. It's fortunate that the north eastern tip nearest to the disaster site is fairly sparsely populated. There were nine deaths on the mainland but the fast breeder reactor at Dounreay which, as you probably remember, has been operational for nearly three years, has had to be shut down because of radioactive deposition in the area. One hopes this will not be permanent.

'As to soil contamination, this I am afraid, is going to be the most difficult and expensive operation. We estimate that altogether some four and a half million tons of top soil is seriously contaminated and will have to be removed and stored—probably at Windscale. . . .'

There was a shocked murmur.

Fordyce continued, unperturbed by the effect of his words, 'The Americans already have experience of this procedure. It is now many years since they were forced to remove many thousands of tons of top soil from Palomares in Spain after a bomber exploded and released three hydrogen bombs, so we shall be able to draw on considerable expertise there. . . .'

He looked hard at the Minister.

'. . . always providing, of course, that the operation is adequately financed. Finally, we estimate that there was probably a forty per cent serial voiding of the reactor core inventory and this had inevitably led to a widespread release and—I regret to say—ingestion of both radioactive iodine, tellurium and caesium. The Medical Research Council tells me this may well affect the local incidence of various malignant conditions—particularly thyroid cancer—over the next thirty years or so. I think that covers most of it.'

Baxter nodded to him: 'Thank you, Mr Fordyce. In point of

fact, I don't think we need detain you any more—thank you very much for giving us your time.'

Fordyce stood up and began to gather his papers into a brief-case.

The Minister continued. 'Now we come to the main issue of this meeting and I don't think I need emphasize its extreme urgency. The source of what the press have now called the "Brain-rack". Tony, if you would summarize progress to date. . . .'

The man by his side nodded, his voice had the high braying inflexion nurtured at Eton and in the guards. 'Minister, gentle-men. Thus far the field seems to be fairly open. There have been many suggestions: Dr Bordheim and his people at UNESCO seem to have got through a great deal of the more obvious investi-gations. We have their data to hand. The first thought was that there was some sort of virus about in the cities. . . .'

Baxter intervened. 'Professor Kingston, would you care to com-ment on that?'

Kingston, who had just completed a sketch of a thighbone on the pad in front of him, looked up and adjusted his gold-rimmed half-glasses: 'No. Practically no chance of an infectious agent—viral or bacterial. As I think my report shows—all the brain tissue changes are against it. In fact they are more consistent with some sort of chemical irritation.'

'Can you be more specific?' Baxter asked.

'Not at the moment, no. You see the brain has only about three main types of response to injury, very limited, very limited indeed.'

'Surely,' Baxter went on, 'if we know it's something in cities, in the air, ground or water, we should be thinking about carbon monoxide and lead. I know we have the new legislation phasing lead out of petrol but surely there would be enough still about—residual dust and so on—to produce this sort of thing?'

Kingston smiled tolerantly: 'We've looked. No—not a bit like lead encephalopathy. No basophilia—blood changes—no, not a bit like lead.'

'And carbon monoxide?'

'Again no. There were no brain petechiae—beg pardon—small haemorrhages from capillaries—no, not carbon monoxide at all, I'm afraid. By the way, I had a look at the brain of that chappie from the Orkney station—Durrell wasn't it?—extraordinarily interesting. Apparently he'd been tested by this psychologist. . . .'

'Miss Scott, yes?'

'Well, that gives us another rather pretty correlation. It's building up to the most fascinating picture. As I wrote in my report—Chronic Betz Cell Atrophy—this new condition—it really does tie up excellently with the intelligence loss.'

'Could you outline the effects you see stemming from this, Professor?' Baxter asked.

Kingston spoke gravely: 'You have to imagine a world where a considerable proportion of folk in the cities have become less able. First of all, judging by the histological changes—the affected people will never recover. Adult brain tissue doesn't regenerate once it is damaged. I honestly fear the consequences. I don't see it as the least unlikely that our life style may change really quite sharply. In many ways, you could compare its potential to that of some of the great epidemics of the past—the influenza which decimated Europe during the First World War would be one such example. Just consider—a high proportion of workers in factories may never be able to handle their machinery again. Decision makers. . . .'

He looked around the table slowly.

'. . . may have their judgement affected. We live in a densely populated world which depends almost entirely on complex and highly developed technologies. If we can't work them reliably any more then the social upset and unrest which may result quite frankly frightens me to death.'

It was Lodge who broke the silence. His face had an unhealthy pallor and he pressed his finger tips against the surface of the table to hide the tremor.

'You say this is quite irreversible?'

'Almost certainly.'

'Is it progressive?' Lodge asked.

'I can't tell—depends whether the cause—the agent, whatever it is—is still about. If it is—yes, it will progress I suppose.'

Lodge nodded slowly and looked down.

Baxter broke in: 'This brings us to the next issue. Doctor Mawn and his colleagues made considerable attempts to delay the start-up procedure on the grounds that some of the staff were affected by loss of ability. As we have just heard the post-mortem

315

findings on the technical director, Dr Durrell, have certainly confirmed this assertion.

'To be perfectly frank, my colleagues and I were intensely suspicious of Mawn's claim. On at least one occasion—on television—his views were shown to be entirely without foundation, but I'm bound to confess that his findings are now of central importance. It was he and Miss Scott in fact who spotted the relationship of the effect to cities and this has led over the past few weeks to the general acceptance of this idea. It therefore seems that we are bound to seek his help and so I have proposed to the Cabinet that he be given a temporary position to further his own and Miss Scott's work and also to prepare a report on the situation as a whole.'

He looked around for signs of reaction, but finding none, continued:

'The Cabinet approved in general but they have also made it abundantly clear that his sphere of influence is to be strictly limited by a properly worded brief.'

The fair-haired aide took up a newspaper from a pile in front of him, his drawl unmistakably hostile. The papers carried a large photograph of Mawn and a banner headline 'THE BRAINRACK —Is mankind reverting to the ape?' Underneath Mawn's picture in a smaller type was written, 'Why was this man's warning ignored?'

'It seems fairly obvious to me that we have another public guru on our hands—a saviour as it were. . . .'

Kingston's geniality disappeared: 'If you're referring to Doctor Mawn, a very large number of lives would have been saved had the government taken adequate notice in the first place.' He glared at the fair-haired aide. 'God knows how you can afford to be so self-indulgently critical of the one person who had the vision and perseverance to uncover this ghastly affair. I've come to know Alex Mawn fairly well over the last few weeks. He's a difficult and shirty person in many ways, but it seems to me he's come very well out of this affair—quite apart from being half killed in the process. . . .'

Baxter turned to the fair-haired man, his voice a shade more peremptory: 'Anything further, Tony?'

'No, sir.' The aide put the newspaper down on the table, his hand shaking noticeably.

Baxter glanced at the grandfather clock. 'He should be here by now.' He turned to Lodge: 'Richard, would you do the honours?'

The air in the ante-room was dry and overheated. A fierce black iron radiator under the high Georgian window clicked angrily and a wigged seventeenth-century incumbent glared down disapprovingly from an over-varnished oil painting. Mawn sat with his feet up on a Victorian chaise longue and Marcia poised uncomfortably on a high-backed wooden chair on the opposite side of the room. She was flipping the papers of a glossy magazine.

Mawn thought back over the three weeks which had passed since their rescue by the navy from the stricken island. Feeling for the still tender bruise in the fold of his left elbow, he remembered the blood transfusions, the regular blood counts.

With a start he realized that he would miss his appointment at the Westminster Hospital. The physician there had told him on arrival that his white blood cell count was down by over fifty per cent from exposure to radiation. Ruefully, he began to worry about his fertility, whether he would now be able to father a child.

He glanced over at Marcia and wondered whether she too had been rendered barren by exposure. With a surge of resentment he recalled her father, Harland Scott. How he had flown directly from America and whisked her away—into the rich surroundings of a private room in the Wigmore Clinic. Scott's attitude had first of all been effusively grateful, then had rapidly changed to a muted suspicion—had he really done enough? The two men had had no contact beyond carefully planned pleasantries. Without real envy, he looked at Marcia's suntan from the two weeks at the Marrakesh Hilton, still only just hiding the underlying pallor of anaemia.

He had looked forward eagerly to her return from North Africa, but soon after they had met at the airport they had found it difficult to talk. There had been an embarrassing strain and artificiality. It was as if, he thought, that she was wanting to extricate herself, to get back to the easy Long Island life. To hide from the grating realities which their work had revealed.

The door opened and Lodge came in smiling, his hand outstretched: 'Hallo again. Nice to see you, won't you come in.' He paused. 'The Minister will make you an offer. Do think about it before you accept. Most of the shots are in your locker now . . .' He paused, realizing he had transgressed and checked himself.

Mawn saw that his hand was trembling. 'Really, it's very good to see you both and looking fit again.' Before they could reply he led the way back into the Minister's room.

After the introductions, Mawn began to feel the pressure of the occasion. He wasn't at a student seminar, he was in the surroundings of power and decision. He felt a surge of anxiety. His palms were moist.

Baxter deftly gave him a precise account of their previous conversation:

'. . . and so in the circumstances, the Government thinks it right that you should be asked to head this small committee with nominees put up by yourself and our own relevant departmental heads.'

Mawn looked around the dour faces. Kingston winked at him, smiling. He remembered Lodge's comment. 'Well, thank you, Minister, but I'd like a little time to consider it if I may.'

'Of course. Oh, yes, I forgot to mention that there would be a small budget to get things started. You would be empowered to take on secretarial staff, equipment and so on. You would be in a position rather similar to a Select Committee, but in this case we can streamline matters considerably. In fact, were you to accept, we would very much like it if you could prepare a preliminary report within, say, four or five weeks. You would of course, be responsible to myself and this committee and naturally we would expect to discuss any findings you made before publication.'

A censor, Mawn thought to himself. He said: 'I'd like time to think about it.'

'Well, please let me know within perhaps two or three days,' Baxter said. 'It's very very important to get things under way.'

'Yes, I'll do that—thank you.'

'Good. Now we were talking previously about the nature of this "Brainrack" as the press have called it. Professor Kingston had reviewed the medical evidence and this seems to point against any disease process.' He turned to Kingston: 'That's so, isn't it?' Kingston nodded vigorously. 'Have you anything further to suggest, Doctor Mawn?'

Mawn immediately felt the relaxation of moving back into a purely scientific area of discussion.

'Yes, I have, yes. We've carried out some further breakdowns on the data we've already got. There's no doubt that it's city-based, but there are some affected people who live and work in the country, but so far—and this is by no means certain—all those in the country with the effect have at some time lived for a fairly prolonged period in a large town or city.'

'Have you had any further notions about the cause?'

'Not yet, no. If it's not bacterial or viral but it is in cities, then it has to be an environmental factor. Lead from cars—carbon monoxide—noise—I just don't know.'

'I think we've already disposed of the first two,' Baxter replied. 'But I can't think it will be long before we do find out. I suppose there has never been such a systematic global effect. Almost every city in the world seems to be tearing itself apart to find the cause. However, we must get on.' His charm began to withdraw. 'It was very kind of you to come, Doctor Mawn. You will let us know, won't you?'

'Yes, of course.' Mawn got to his feet, nodded to the others and was led out by Lodge.

In the ante-room Lodge's manner was hesitant: 'One thing I feel bound to say. The Minister was very anxious to clear up this business—you know—the television show. You did appear to have some facts—er—quite wrong if I may say so. Is there anything we can do about it?'

Mawn looked at him steadily: 'Yes there is. I'm going to see Brian Gelder.'

The doctor paused in front of the panelled door. 'I shouldn't stay for more than a few minutes. He's very sick. There is a depressed skull fracture as well as the aftermath of radiation sickness.'

'Is he going to be all right?' Marcia asked.

'It's very difficult to be certain at this stage, but his chances aren't as good as they might be. We were worried for a time about bone marrow aplasia but some new cells have appeared so he may recover—he just may.' He turned to go. 'Come and see me in my office before you leave.'

Mawn nodded and opened the door. The room was high and airy and Gelder lay propped up in bed. On a side table, there was a colour television set and on another a profusion of flowers, potted plants and fruit. On the table lying across the bed, there was a tape-recorder and a pile of letters. A nurse was busy adjusting an intravenous drip bottle hanging down from a vertical iron frame and an elegantly dressed woman was seated in an armchair taking shorthand notes.

The pale skin of Gelder's face seemed stretched tautly over the bones and his eyes were deeply sunken. One hand picked nervously at the bed covers.

Mawn looked at the woman in the chair. 'Could I have a word with you—in private?'

The nurse clicked disapprovingly and the secretary started to protest, but Gelder waved them to silence and he nodded them to go. 'I'll give you a buzz.'

As the door closed behind them, Mawn turned away from the window. 'I want your help.'

Gelder's eyes mocked. 'I'll buy you a drink for getting me out of there if you like. By the way, thank you.' He pointed to a pile of newspapers. 'You seem to be doing all right without me.'

'I've been asked to prepare a report on the "Brainrack" effect.'

'Congratulations.'

'And they're to provide quite considerable powers, including the power to call witnesses.'

'I'm sure you'll do very well.'

'But before I start work, I have got to put a few things right.'

'You're driving now.' Gelder lay back smiling.

'As you're aware I've lost whatever standing I had in the scientific community,' Mawn rapped suddenly.

Gelder turned away: 'Is that why you wanted the others out?'

'You don't have to worry. I doubt whether I can prove anything.'

The mocking smile was back on Gelder's face: 'What a relief.'

'But I could make a very good attempt using the powers I've got.' Mawn caught a warning glance from Marcia. He was lying and it would only take Gelder minutes on the phone after they had gone to spot it.

'I intend making a start with George Teller!'

The smile disappeared: 'Who?'

'George Teller—industrial spy and murderer.'

Gelder's face seemed to sag slightly and Marcia felt a sudden twinge of pity.

His voice faded: 'What about him?'

Mawn gripped the rail at the foot of the bed. 'You sent him to my laboratory and he caused the death of one of my assistants and the destruction of my work.'

Gelder closed his eyes and turned his head away in the pillow.

'Alex! It's not what we want,' Marcia said.

Mawn wheeled, his eyes cold: 'Leave this to me!'

'No, Alex, Barfield.'

He started to say something, then turned back to Gelder. 'She's right. This is not an emotional issue. Or I'd have broken your neck in the Power Station. How did you manage to screw up my figures on the "Nightstyle" programme?'

Gelder opened his eyes: 'Your figures! What you mean is my figures given to you illegally by one of my employees—when he was still under contract to me.'

'You got Barfield to give me false figures, either with Seager's connivance or without. It was a deliberate attempt to discredit me and hold me up to ridicule.'

Gelder shrugged weakly: 'Whatever I say or sign isn't going to make any difference with the public.'

'For God's sake. I'm not concerned with the general public!' He pointed to the pile of newspapers: 'You've seen those—according to them I'm Oppenheimer, Churchill and God rolled into one! No, that's not my concern. I've got to convince my own peers —I've got to go into Whitehall and get some sort of acute action out of the mandarins and you've got to help me. As far as I'm concerned you're guilty of manslaughter, and perhaps twice over. What do you know about Sheldon Peters's death?'

Marcia tried to pull his arm: 'Alex, that's enough, leave him.'

He pushed her away: 'From what I hear you haven't got much of a chance and frankly that doesn't really worry me at all. You're already responsible for a tremendous loss of life. Do you want to die with that on your conscience?'

Mawn's voice changed and became gentler, more pleading: 'I've got a chance of doing something about this "Brainrack" effect but I can't clear myself. I must have a statement from you before I can work effectively. Surely to God, you owe me that at least?'

Gelder lay quite still, his eyes closed. He made no response. Marcia pulled Mawn away, then bent over the bed feeling for Gelder's pulse. 'We must get the doctor.'

As they moved towards the door Gelder started to speak. His voice was weak but clear:

'I sent Teller. That was my idea. Setting up Barfield was a joint effort; two other men were involved, Ian Caird and Carl Bellamy. We made him give you false material.'

'For me to misquote in front of nine million people!' Mawn said bitterly. 'And to do the hatchet job you set up Professor Seager with the real figures.'

'He didn't need setting up. He just hates your scientific guts. We knew that, so once we'd given him the figures, that was all the ammunition he needed.'

'Wasn't he worried by them himself? Didn't he check them over?'

'I don't know.'

'Was he able to check them? Had he access to your files?'

'Yes, full access at all times.'

Mawn leaned back, his face a mask: 'Will you write this down and send it to us?'

Gelder looked up at Mawn, nodded and turned his head away: 'Now get out.'

On the way to the flat in the car, Marcia's anger boiled over: 'Did you have to do that?' Mawn shrugged and looked out of the window. He felt sick and disgusted. A small victory over the dying. Marcia started to say something, then seeing his expression drove on in silence.

CHAPTER SIXTEEN

MAWN LOOKED MOROSELY around the empty flat. He was in dressing-gown and pyjamas seated in one of the black leather arm-chairs nursing a brandy and listening to a Bach concert on the radio. He recalled Marcia's half-hearted invitation to dine with her father. The frostiness in her voice had made him decline. He felt unaccountably depressed and got up to pour another drink. Finally he forced himself to admit that he was depressed because of her recent aloofness. He realized he was afraid of losing her. He had started to feel that fear lying in the hospital bed with nothing to do except watch the dripping blood in the transfusion set.

Irritably he got up and switched off the radio. He heard the front door lock click. Marcia was standing in the doorway.

'Hi,' she flung herself down in a chair, her face flushed. Here it comes, he thought, wait for it!

She avoided his eyes, hands twisting nervously: 'Can we talk, really talk?'

He waved the brandy glass expansively: 'By all means.'

She nodded at the bottle: 'And can I have some of that before it all goes?'

He poured a full measure, her hand trembled as she took the glass.

'I'll make it easy for us, shall I?' He smiled. 'You're going to tell me it's about time I moved on. Well, O.K., it's getting on my wick as a matter of fact. And I don't somehow think father quite approved, did he?'

'Pardon me?'

'Big daddy! He's probably convinced you need more care and protection after all this. I'm sure he's got a rich executive lined up for you. Twenty feet of Cadillac and a gold-plated Loo.'

She slammed the glass down on the table. 'You arrogant self-centred bastard! You always know exactly what I'm thinking, don't you? Little rich dilettante goes running back home when the going gets hard. Just because you're a mathematical whizz-kid you know every other goddamn thing. It would never cross your mind that you're wrong, would it?'

Mawn looked up at her in surprise: 'What were you going to "really talk" about?'

'I wanted to talk about you, you great oaf. You hardly speak to me, you were incredibly rude when you picked me up at the airport. What am I supposed to have done? I was all screwed up about it. I wanted to help.'

'I thought you . . .'

Mawn's voice dropped away lamely.

'Thought what? After la dolce vita in Marrakesh I wanted the high life again. You're the most disgusting prig. Just because you're the son of a manual worker you think it gives you some special advantage. Pure working-class boy shows corrupt rich girl how to live. Christ! You give me a pain in the arse.' She turned away in disgust.

'What can I say?' Mawn began. 'I'm sorry. . . .'

'Sorry, sorry! Bump into someone—*sorry*. Completely misunderstand someone—*sorry*. Mess everything up—*sorry*. It doesn't mean a damn thing. We don't have any equivalent where I come from, thank God.'

'All right! No more apologies.' Mawn's voice rang out. 'Just the simple truth. I was shit scared of losing you.'

She halted by the bedroom door: 'You can find plenty more psychologists.'

'No, you personally. In every bloody way.' He walked over to her, standing awkwardly, his hands shaking. She turned and he had a brief glimpse of large eyes full of tears, then she was crushed against him. Mawn lifted her and carried her over to the bed and as she put her arms up around his neck and pulled him down beside her, all the tension and fear swept out of him in one single flood which he was completely unable to resist. He buried himself in the gentle sweetness of her body, giving in completely to the warmth of her touch. It was as if he had never made love in his life before. Every single feeling he possessed seemed to flow directly and easily into his movements as he entered her.

For a long while he remained absolutely still, not daring to break the perfection. She was lying with her head against his shoulder, her long dark hair spread like a fan across his chest. His pulse leapt at the thought of completely and uniquely caring for one single person. In the warmth of her body he felt protected from the days that lay ahead. The sinister pattern of the Brainrack seemed almost infinitely remote.

For a long while after she had fallen asleep he stayed awake watching the light patterns of passing cars sweeping across the ceiling. He imagined the drivers unable to control their vehicles. How would they see him? The man who said their minds were going. They would probably blame him. He would become the symbol of the whole effect. He listened for a while longer to the quiet rhythm of her breathing. Tonight nothing else seemed to matter.

Over the following days, they became totally wrapped up in the ordinary routine of the flat. He felt the years slip away from him and began to talk with a compulsive enthusiasm which he had thought had gone for ever. Ideas and concepts flowed in a continuous stream.

One morning Mawn sat in front of a jumbled pile of mail trying to sort out the serious from the insane. He had got accustomed to the venom of the mad letters, the threats, the warnings of doom, the religious fanatics who usually wrote in a heavy aggressive scrawl about the judgement of God and Sodom and Gomorrah. He had been accused of putting drugs in the water supply, of being alternatively a communist agent, a fascist lackey and a revolutionary. One correspondent had even suggested that he had invented the whole effect so he could capitalize on the serial rights.

He felt her hand on his shoulder: 'We're having lunch with my father, don't forget.'

'Today?'

'Yes. The Savoy Grill.'

'Five quid to have a waiter peel your grapes!'

'All he wants is to help.'

'Why?'

'I told him all about it, what you need. You're supposed to let the Minister have his answer today. Look, he can get you money...'

'Marcia, I can do things my way, without going round begging off rich industrialists.'

'No you can't. Remember what Richard Lodge said. All you'd get officially is just a little money—enough to keep you right under their thumbs. You'll never get good people if you can't pay them. Why does it matter where the money comes from?'

Mawn looked away uncomfortably: 'It's not that simple. There's bound to be strings attached.'

'Why, for Pete's sake? This Brainrack hits everyone from the large corporations to the corner drug store. Besides I guess he also wants to do this for me.' Marcia rose and walked to the window. 'You see, we haven't been too close. His last wife—well, we didn't get on too well. You know, classic only-daughter reaction. I was betrayed—shut out. I behaved like a spoilt kid I guess—but that's how I felt and we split up.' Mawn leant across and filled her coffee cup. 'Well, anyway, now all this, it's changed things. Now he's crazy to do things for me. He sees it as my discovery. I'm sorry, I know that's unfair to you, but he does.'

Mawn tried to explain, fully aware of his clumsiness: 'I don't mind that and I've nothing really against your father. It is just that I live here in a flat you borrowed for me. I'm using your data, now you're asking me to take your father's money. I just can't do it.'

325

Marcia put an arm round his neck: 'You've got a real life-size chip up there. What the hell, he's got far too much loot, and I can't think of a better use for it!'

Mawn stiffened, then shrugged: 'I'm not sure I take you seriously as a Marxist.' He pulled her over on his lap. 'O.K., we'll talk.'

She hugged close to him. 'I promise you that when this is all over I'll do anything you want. I'll even be tweedy British, polish your shoes and live in the country and . . .'

He pushed her away, smiling: 'And slop around in the mud in gum-boots?'

Their embrace was broken by the sound of the mail dropping through the letter box. With it was Gelder's statement confirming what he had said at the clinic. It was carefully written to minimize legal risk but the content was clear.

The Savoy Grill was in full spate. Waiters scurried between the tables with laden silver trays just managing with an almost balletic skill to avoid touching the diners. On a low stage an orchestra was playing nostalgic tunes from West Side Story. The lead violin was very slightly off key. Mawn stared around, objecting silently to the perfumed theatricality. He was brought back to himself by Harland Scott: 'You didn't answer my question!'

'Mm? Oh, I'm sorry.' Mawn collected his thoughts. 'For the moment I'm going to beg, borrow or steal every university laboratory I've got any contact with. There isn't time to get a new lab going. The Betz-cell atrophy is caused by some environmental factor in large cities and it's got to be only a matter of time before we find it. Since it isn't bacterial or viral it must be chemical—not genetic—no evidence—it's just got to be a chemical.'

Scott put his hand over Marcia's. 'And your work started it all.' Marcia smiled. 'Yes, but I didn't see the connection—he did.'

'What did you think of Gelder's statement?' Mawn asked.

Scott looked at him thoughtfully: 'It was a minor masterpiece. I doubt whether any attorney could make a charge stick—but it certainly convinced me.'

'It's careful not to mention Caird or Bellamy,' Marcia protested.

Scott smiled: 'Didn't need to. You're both witnesses, their names were mentioned. I know Bellamy, as a matter of fact. And his boss. Guess I'll have a word in their ears, then shake a collection box.'

326

'Surely they won't move?' Marcia continued.

'They will. They know they're in over their ears.'

Mawn looked more closely at the white-haired American who looked like a minister of the episcopal church with his gently smiling eyes and heavy sensitive lids.

'It's not only money,' said Mawn. 'I don't think they'd have agreed to Gelder's action unless they were worried about the Brainrack effect in their firms. I could use their full co-operation, access to their files.'

'You'll get it when I've done talking to them.'

Marcia turned to her father: 'Alex is due to see the Minister in about an hour's time.'

Scott beckoned a waiter, getting to his feet. 'And I've got to be on a plane. While I'm over, by the way, I'll jingle my box around Wall Street too.' He put notes down on a silver tray held by the waiter. 'And now good-bye kids. Oh! One more thing. I've opened a trust fund in your name, the current account reads at 200,000, as a starter.'

'In my name?' Mawn began.

Harland Scott bent down and kissed his daughter. 'Please yourself what you do with it.' He stroked her hair. 'Set her up in a chateau in France if you like, or get some work done: either way,' he raised his hands, 'no strings! So long now.'

Mawn sat in the ante-room trying to stare down the fixed glance of the figure in the oil painting. As the fair-haired aide ushered him in he looked quickly at his watch and noted wryly that the waiting time had come down to seven minutes.

In the dazzle from the chandelier it appeared first of all as though the composition of the committee was the same, then he saw that his main ally, Lodge, was absent. Instead, there was the face that had been part of his worst dreams for almost two months. His mind shot back over the debacle of the television programme. Professor Seager sat doodling with a pencil, not meeting his eye.

On the left of the Minister there was a new face. The whole of its surface seemed to be hung with folds. The deeply sunken eyes moved with an almost reptilian deliberation over Mawn as he walked to his place. He was introduced by the Minister as Doctor Max Bordheim from UNESCO. The Minister wasted no time in preamble.

327

'We have a full agenda so, may I begin by asking you Dr Mawn whether you are going to be able to accept our offer?'

'In principle, yes,' Mawn replied. 'But I would naturally like to know more about the details of operation.'

'I understand. But you do realize that time is of the essence and we must be able to establish an effective liaison between your side of things and our own efforts—mainly in the interest of accuracy.' The reference was obvious and Mawn coloured. 'So we have asked Professor Seager if he would act in this capacity. He has, as you probably know, been acting as head of one of the Rothschild groups in advising the Cabinet and I'm sure you will appreciate his expertise.'

Mawn was uncomfortably aware of all eyes turned in his direction. He was being asked to accept his public humiliator as monitor. If he accepted, he would have his hands firmly tied. If he refused, he would be judged guilty of personal chagrin and found wanting.

He felt all the bitterness and anger of the past rising like a sour bile in his throat.

'Well, Doctor?'

The Minister's tone was sharp and he realized that they had all been waiting for his reply. He forced himself to speak calmly, looking directly at Seager.

'I think I can function perfectly well without any additional assistance.'

Campbell Baxter frowned: 'To be frank, I think we have to avoid anything which interferes with the work which lies before us.'

Mawn took a copy of Gelder's statement out of his briefcase, he spoke in a flat, staccato tone, as if he were deploying a mathematical argument.

'Before I go any further, I'd like to read you this statement. . . .' He read out Gelder's words slowly, without any inflexion. '. . . and so you will see that doubts about my credibility can be answered, and I hope you will now consider this matter closed!' He threw the statement down on the table.

Baxter glanced over at Seager, trying to gauge his reaction. 'Well, you've obviously been subjected to a lot of injustice and I'm very relieved to find out the truth. But I don't see how this affects Professor Seager.'

Mawn took a slim journal out of his case. He extracted a single sheet of typed paper and cleared his throat:

'This is a copy of *Nature* dated January of this year. In it is a paper by Professor Seager and a co-author. It is an analysis of operational faults in nuclear power systems. Now, when we first gave you our findings about the Brainrack effect you subjected our report to independent scrutiny. I have got an independent report on Seager's paper by an expert whose name I am perfectly willing to supply in confidence. I will just read you the final paragraph: "The arguments presented show distinct bias towards acceptance of high-risk control systems and appear both specious and speculative in the light of the fact that the statistical support for the assertions made is lacking in strength. In many cases the authors have argued from the particular to the general without sufficient reason. In my view, the work looks as though it was assembled without due regard to accuracy . . ." and so on.'

Seager started to protest. 'I really fail to see what this has to . . .' Baxter waved him to silence.

'All I was demonstrating,' Mawn continued, 'is that for every thesis there is an anti-thesis. For every original discovery there will always be an opponent to unseat it. If you examine the opponents' work, it is amenable to exactly the same degree of intellectual destruction.'

Seager coloured.

'Professor Seager has obviously selected data which suits his case and completely ignored material which would have led to the truth. . . .'

'This is absolutely intolerable. . . .' Seager began angrily.

'. . . Had he supported my analysis of the dangers at the Grim-Ness station instead of opposing it—for what I can only call personally vindictive reasons—the whole tragedy might never have occurred!'

The Minister picked up the journal and gave it to his aide. His eyes were cold and watchful: 'Please continue. . . .'

'On the television programme I made several major points—admittedly on material sent to me by a Gelder employee—I make no secret of that. I have also been told by Gelder that Seager had complete access to their research data. He must have seen that I had a perfectly valid case. He was given a full opportunity to examine my figures before the programme and at that stage, he could easily have come to me and tried to resolve the discrepancy, but instead, he used the occasion to mount a purely personal attack.' Mawn looked down at a transcript of the programme. 'And I quote: "Doctor Mawn's data may well be the result of an honest mistake, he may well have been misinformed or he could have fabricated the entire case. The law prevents me from stating my own preference."' Mawn paused. 'You can draw your own conclusions.'

Baxter looked down at the blotting pad. 'This certainly makes matters difficult. Perhaps I can have a word with you, Professor Seager, after the meeting.'

Seager's face had now paled.

'And now, we really must continue. I was about to tell you, Doctor, that we have been able to find an initial sum of £10,000 together with temporary premises in the new wing of St Olaf's medical school. I hope you will find that acceptable?'

Mawn made an attempt at humility. 'Thanks, that will get things started.' He paused. 'But I've already been given a substantial grant from an American source.'

He watched Bordheim's smile spreading. 'So I think you'll agree this will enable me to accomplish rather more!'

Bordheim rubbed the end of his nose with a pencil, looking from one to the other. His eyes were almost closed.

'But what I most urgently need, Minister, is access to departmental reports. Mainly Department of Health—tests on school children and so on. Also data on the testing of military personnel. . . .' He handed a list to the Minister who adjusted his glasses and scanned it.

'Well, several of these are certainly outside my jurisdiction, but I'll do what I can.' He rose and, without a further glance at Mawn, hurried from the room followed by his aide and Professor Seager.

Outside in the ante-room, Mawn felt a touch on his arm. Bordheim's voice had the over emphatic use of consonants of his Swedish origin.

'Congratulations! You have made more happen than I did over two years.' The fingers tightened on his arm, drawing him away out of earshot of the others. 'We have now made over four hundred kilos of paper in Paris. Everyone argues all the time, nobody will do anything. The Americans say one thing, the Russians say nothing, the French protest, the Chinese read us little lessons; it is all impossible.

'Now, I tell you my friend, we have much data—I will give it over to you. It will be very helpful, I think. Many experiments. We started to make some ideas about the man-machine-interface, but very soon, like you, we had proved it was people. What we did not see was that it was city people. That was very good. So now must we abandon the cities? Is that what you would say?'

Mawn smiled: 'Not quite that. But we must find out exactly what it is.'

'Oh, yes, we must find out. Then maybe we find it's oxygen or water, so we all say good-bye. I have said I will send you all our information and I wish you success. And now, good-bye. I have to go back to the paper factory in Paris.' The grip on his arm relaxed, the eyelids came down and he shuffled away, chins folded against his collar.

CHAPTER SEVENTEEN

OVER THE FOLLOWING eight weeks, Mawn found himself at the centre of a rapidly spreading international octopus of communications. Max Bordheim was as good as his word and each day brought a new batch of data from the UNESCO headquarters in Paris.

One by one, the cities of the world began to turn themselves inside out to identify the cause of the brainrack. Sewers, underground tunnels and skyscraper blocks were all combed by a growing army of technical specialists. Every factory, chemical store and public institution was minutely probed for any possible source of a chemical poison.

Doctors and pathologists worked impossible hours in laboratories and post-mortem rooms slicing, examining, analysing and sifting the body tissues of people who had died from any cause in the cities.

Potential culprits were put up, examined and then discarded. No unusual levels of the heavy metals were found in the tissues of the dead. Lead, cadmium, mercury were all exonerated.

The search turned to the waterways. Already heavily polluted by the myriad of industrial effluents poured into them day by day, each river, canal and dock basin was sampled and analysed. In Europe, the Rhine—already known as Europe's majestic sewer—became a particular target for international scrutiny.

With Marcia beside him, Mawn worked at all hours wading through the mountains of data strewn around the makeshift department in St Olaf's. His students from the university at Plymouth had joined him and he had already put a dozen different departments to work investigating various possible chemicals which could have produced the brain damage.

The most horrific statistic which emerged showed that a probable thirty per cent of the total population of the world were affected. The high proportion at first seemed unlikely but demographic evidence confirmed that a probable sixty per cent of people lived in or near a major city.

The media maintained a constant barrage of questions and pressure and each day brought an article or an interview showing what the effect would be on a particular section of the populace if it proved to be irreversible: Airline pilots refused to fly with crew members who had not been tested. Drivers demanded that no one should be given a car driving licence until they had been proved free of the brainrack. Anaesthetists suspected surgeons, generals grew ulcers over the men controlling underground missile silos and policemen regularly refused point duty in areas of urban congestion on the grounds that some drivers might not be able to control their cars.

Apart from those in the cities who had actually been shown to have the effect, many others imagined that they had and doctors began to talk of the 'brainrack neurosis' as an entity quite separate from the real one. It became a major excuse for work absenteeism.

Mawn's picture always appeared beside the articles, but the policy of the papers and media had changed. Whereas they had begun by raising Mawn to the status of Messiah, now they were beginning to demand quicker results. How long is it going to be? When will this man tell us what's wrong? The questions became gradually more tense and hostile.

In the United Nations in New York, each country intimated that the brainrack had originated in one of their neighbour states. The developing countries felt they had a clear case in placing all responsibility on to the richer nations and taking no action.

As Mawn's load increased so did his capability. Having long despised the amateur politicians of his university campus, to his surprise, he began to take a chess-player's delight in battles with Civil Service mandarins reluctant to part with what they regarded as their own private material. There were innumerable protests from manufacturers as their products came up for detailed scrutiny by Mawn's growing army of chemists.

Then the inevitable happened and the public began to adapt to the situation: 'Sorry, can't come out tonight—got a touch of brainrack.' It became a stock joke for public speakers—'Well, ladies and gentlemen, speaking as one idiot to another. . . .' Slowly the syndrome was integrated into everyday life as if it was of little importance. Teachers began to hold conferences to adjust school curricula. New tests based upon the original Venn pattern were devised to sort the normal from the affected.

During the early part of the investigation, Professor Kingston had been co-opted by Mawn to correlate all chemical and pathological inquiries. Like Mawn, he had sifting data flowing in from laboratories and hospitals throughout the world and, by using facilities provided by the World Health Organization, a general international agreement had been reached concerning the nature of the brain damage underlying the brainrack effect.

There was no doubt at all that it was due to a chemical and the search had been directed towards an analysis of brain tissue to see whether any abnormal substances could be identified by analysis.

One laboratory in Geneva announced that they had isolated a substance from a series of post-mortem brains. It was present only in microgram quantities and it had proved difficult to identify specifically. Eventually a similar discovery was made in a biochemical laboratory in Los Angeles and by combining the data from each institution it was possible to name it. It was called: cyclic pentane acetylide.

The public announcement of the identity of the chemical had a shattering effect.

Kingston was sitting on the edge of Mawn's desk. He was pointing to one of a series of purple stains on a long roll of squared paper.

'There's the criminal—petrol—gasoline!'

333

'You're absolutely sure?' Mawn asked.

'We are now. Cyclic pentane acetylide. I never would have believed it you know, never.'

'Does it have any other sources?'

'Not as far as we can see. Two chemists way back in '68 first reported it in the air. They wrote a paper showing that car exhausts give off over 180 separate chemicals. It's just one of them. Many of them are actually quite simple—hydrocarbons—ethylene and so on.'

'So it's not lead or anything!'

'No. Just a product of burning ordinary common-or-garden petrol.'

'But people in cities have been breathing it for years!'

'Exactly. You see, the brain changes are very chronic, very long term. They've been developing for years. Nobody's immune. I was doing a P.-M. on a kiddy of four the other day, his brain already showed change.'

'Christ!' Mawn exclaimed.

'Quite so. Brain tissue is very sensitive—particularly in the young. Actually, we've got plenty of redundant brain cells—maybe we never use them. But this acetylide, it seems to have some sort of affinity for fat, the special fats in the brain. Probably what happens is that city folk breathe it in over the years, it dissolves in the brain fats and then starts picking off brain cells over the years, one by one. Eventually, the net reserve of cells is reduced to a level where intelligence, behaviour and so on begin to be affected.'

'Self-induced idiocy from the motor car!' Mawn spoke as he walked over to a computer terminal and began punching instructions on the keys.

'What're you doing?'

'Running a frequency scan—on jobs.' He stopped hitting the keys.

There was a moment's pause and then yellow digits began to tumble down the screen, finally settling to indicate a vertical row of numbers from one to ten. By the side of each number was the printed name of an occupation.

Mawn pointed at the names: 'Fits very well with what you've found. What I told the machine to do was to extract the occupations of affected people and then put them up in order of frequency. In other words, which jobs recur most often among the affected people.' He ran his finger down the screen.

'One—taxi drivers, two—traffic wardens, three—road sweepers, four—policemen with a long record of street work. It fits!'

Kingston continued: 'I said just now, it only comes from the combustion of petrol, but we can't in fact be a hundred per cent certain that the chemical is *only* a product of the internal combustion engine. There are so many new industrial processes—nobody has the slightest idea what half of them push out into the air. It could just be that one of them was producing it.'

'The same industrial process in *all* the cities of the world. That's unlikely, surely?' Mawn asked.

'I agree, it's unlikely. But if it *is* petrol—my God! the implications are absolutely staggering.'

Mawn began pacing: 'We've got to be sure, that's all—we've got to be damn sure!'

'Logically, the first thing to do—and I've already set this in motion—is to take blood samples from city people and try and isolate the substance from the living.'

'And if you find it in city people's blood and not in country people?'

'Then the next step,' Kingston continued, 'would be to take a sample population—say fifty or so. Measure their blood level while they're in the city and then send them into a rural area . . .'

'And see if their blood level goes down!'

'Exactly. But that still doesn't indict the motor car completely.'

'I tell you one thing that would,' Mawn continued excitedly. 'If we find this acetylide compound in the air—presuming it's a volatile. . . .'

'The petro-chemists seem to think it is.'

'. . . Right. If we find it in the air and we are not absolutely sure that it's the internal combustion engine which is producing it. Then it's perfectly obvious what we have to do!'

Kingston looked at him: 'I can't stand the suspense.'

'I've got to persuade Baxter to take cars out of London—to see if the level goes down. See if it disappears.'

'How long for?'

'I don't know yet. Several days for certain. We'll need to get baselines. There'll obviously be complications—ambulances and police cars will have to run. If there's a wind there'll be contamination from other cities—but it should give us the answer. If we keep cars out of London and the acetylide level drops and if your city people lose their blood level when they go to the country —yes, that'll be enough—just enough.'

Kingston looked at Mawn over his half glasses then he began to laugh: 'My God, laddie, you're going to be popular!'

The taxi was inextricably wedged in a dense tangle of fuming stationary traffic. Ahead, a huge articulated lorry was belching a grey-blue cloud from its exhaust. A policeman trapped on a traffic island with his arms by his side looked around helplessly. Mawn glanced at his watch, paid off the driver and guided Marcia between the shining bonnets to the pavement.

They walked quickly through Scotland Yard and on into Whitehall. Again the traffic was stationary, bumper to bumper.

In the Minister's ante-room Marcia was recovering from a helpless fit of coughing. 'It's the worst I can remember.' She coughed again. 'Good propaganda. I must remember to cough in his face.'

Lodge took them both through into the meeting room. After the formal greetings and inquiries, he turned to Mawn: 'How's the Doomsday report?'

'Two or three weeks at most,' Mawn replied.

'Splendid,' Lodge smiled. 'Poor Baxter is being hit from all sides, from the Prime Minister to the *Daily Mirror*. There's always something reassuring about a quick White Paper don't you think?'

Mawn glanced at him sharply: 'Whether it's reassuring or not depends very much on you people.'

Before Lodge could reply the Minister swept into the room followed by his aide, Bordheim and a new scientific adviser. Baxter went through the preliminaries with a terse lack of ceremony, finally turning to Mawn.

'When will your first draft be complete?'

'We've reached a problem area, I'm afraid,' Mawn replied.

'Oh!'

'We need to carry out a much more rigorous test.'

'What kind? You can hardly expect more extensive facilities than you already have!' Baxter's voice was sharp and Marcia noticed his eyes were red-rimmed, his complexion showing the uneven pallor of prolonged overwork and pressure.

'If I can just summarize our current thinking,' Mawn continued. 'Much of the evidence singles out a hydro-carbon released by . . .'

'Yes, yes, I know all about that.' The Minister cut in irritably. 'I'm not entirely unaware of what goes on. A substance from the motor car exhaust you're saying.'

'The evidence correlates very well with the medical findings, so we need to complete the logical proof. As you know . . .' Mawn continued, '. . . there are over 180 compounds released by the internal combustion engine, some only when the choke is used—I have the reference here: Sanders and Maynard in the journal of Analytical Chemistry in . . .'

Baxter gestured angrily: 'Please, if you wouldn't mind just keeping to essentials.'

Mawn controlled his irritation: 'Right. Basically, then, we need to find out whether this particular compound is directly and solely responsible and this will naturally take some months or even years of quite concentrated research.'

'Years?' Baxter frowned.

'Several years. And should we be successful it may well take as long again for the fuel industry to devise means of removing the substance from petrol.'

The Minister looked at Dr Kenny, his new scientific adviser.

'True. That sort of work can't be forced along too quickly.' Dr Kenny was young, open-faced and unafraid to speak his mind.

Baxter looked around the table, seeking support. His face was haggard: 'But this just isn't going to work. If this—material *is* the root cause, then the brain damage is going to continue. There'll be thousands of new cases. We must do something more immediate. We've already had the first reading of the Bill on exhaust converters. Lead content is seventy per cent down on the 1970 level. Surely we can develop effective new legislation.'

Mawn caught Bordheim's eyes levelled on his. The lids lowered a fraction, waiting.

'Minister, with respect, there is one way of immediately solving the problem—to stop the use of the motor car.'

Baxter smiled thinly: 'And throw the country into a complete state of economic confusion. We will have to be a lot more practical than that. To begin with, it would probably treble the unemployment rate. . . .'

Mawn persisted: 'You haven't understood what I said, sir. I am asking you to agree to a removal of all motor vehicles from London for a period of three to four days so that we can measure atmospheric levels of the acetylide.'

The silence creaked. Baxter stared at Mawn incredulously: 'Four days—London?'

'The best time would be over the Easter holiday in ten days.'

'It's completely out of the question,' Baxter exploded. 'In any case wouldn't another city—a smaller one—do?'

'No. All our previous baseline values have been carried out here, in London. Were we to start somewhere else, we would be very considerably delayed.'

Baxter jerked to his feet and walked over to the long bay window. 'We simply haven't got the powers, it's just not possible!'

Mawn drew out a paper from a file. 'As a matter of fact you have. Under the Emergency Powers Act 1975 sub-section four. . . .'

Baxter swung round: 'But that's in the event of a nuclear attack, man!'

'It also covers,' he read, 'any other contingency that is deemed to be on the scale of a national disaster.'

'For God's sake—you can't call this a national emergency!'

'With hundreds of square miles of Scotland probably uninhabitable for a generation!' Mawn rapped out. 'What else do you want? I'm sorry, but my colleagues and I see this test as crucially important. It can short circuit years of a more pedestrian inquiry. We do not feel able to publish without it.'

'Then you'll have failed to meet the brief given you by the Government,' Baxter retorted.

'I don't see it like that, and neither will the public. It could well be their view that I have been prevented from doing my job. There is, of course, another alternative. The Americans have already made it perfectly clear that they will shortly be doing a test on one of their own cities. Naturally, they haven't got my own data, but I should feel bound to let them have it, if they are able to go ahead before we do.'

Bordheim studied Mawn appreciatively.

'Of course, you realize you are now bound by the Official Secrets Act.' The fair-haired aide did his best to sound authoritative. 'Any such act would be taken very seriously, I'm afraid.'

'Good God!' Mawn burst out. 'This is nothing whatever to do

with nationalities or secrets. Secrets are simply a device for protecting the incompetent. We've got a major human tragedy staring us in the face—one which is probably going to have a permanent effect on the way we live in the future and you suggest that it should be pursued in secrecy!' He gestured angrily. 'Bordheim has already told me about the piddling bureaucratic mess he has had to contend with in Paris. He's been continually surrounded by vested interest, jealousies, deliberate attempts to suppress information. Unless I can pursue this inquiry right out in the open with no strings and no interference, I'd rather not do it at all. From your point of view, there's a chance to take an enormous swipe at one of the biggest problems we face.

'You all know perfectly well that the writing is on the wall for the motor car. Right back in the early seventies the Leach Report for O.E.C.D. showed perfectly clearly that the car's demand for oil and petrol will far outstrip supply before the end of this century. And now we find that just ordinary petrol—not lead or carbon monoxide or any other shit the things push out—just petrol, may well have changed the whole of human evolution.

'We now have a generation of the relatively incompetent. The whole of our race is now populated by an entirely new species— *homo non sapiens.* I tell you—we've got a unique opportunity to do something and we've got to use it!'

Baxter walked slowly back to his chair at the head of the table, the aide met Mawn's gaze and then dropped his eyes.

Bordheim cleared his throat. 'It will be difficult to decide how much information you will gather by such an experiment. To me, it is of great promise. I think it should be made possible even if it should prove negative. There will be no harm in it.'

Baxter had calmed: 'But Dr Bordheim, you and Doctor Mawn are in a privileged position as scientists. You only have to consider the need for experiment. If such a test happens and we take cars out of London—I shall have every lobby in the country down on my neck. Business will suffer, the tourist bureau—everyone—will find their own reason for objection. Many firms work over Easter —the Trades Unions will accuse us of all manner of sins.' He turned to Mawn. 'Should it be found possible to mount this test, you may wake up on the Tuesday to find yourself the most unpopular man in the British Isles. And that may well destroy your credibility once again.' The Minister looked across at Mawn—

there was an element of threat in his tone. 'I will raise the matter at the Cabinet meeting this afternoon, but in the meantime I urge you to re-examine the whole idea with your colleagues and decide fully and clearly whether you can find an alternative method.' He rose to go, turning to his aide: 'I believe that's all?'

Later, in the secluded bar of a basement wine house near the Embankment, Lodge spelt out the Cabinet conclusion to Mawn, Marcia and Bordheim.

'In a nutshell, the word is that they will lay on the test if you are convinced there's no alternative. Baxter's had a word with the P.M. on the phone while you were out. To be honest I don't think they dare stop you now. Not with three by-elections pending and a working majority of twelve. But, I'm afraid you've created a considerable amount of hostility. To be frank, you have them by the short hairs but they won't let you off if you're wrong.'

Mawn lowered his pint glass wearily. 'There's nothing else I can do.' Lodge looked at him speculatively: 'Perhaps not, but there are ways of doing things—a word to me first!'

Mawn looked across at the older man: 'I'm sorry, Richard.'

'Never mind, the damage is done. So—message is, go ahead if you must, but any come-back, and believe me there may well be a massive backlash, will be laid squarely at your door. Now, I must be off.' He finished a gin and tonic and rose to go. Marcia grasped his arm:

'Richard, what could we have done?'

The tall, slightly stooped man looked down at her: 'Civil servants aren't really allowed to have personal advice to give,' Lodge smiled.

'Please?'

'Well, I really can't say, it's a tremendous gamble isn't it? If it comes off and people actually enjoy walking about empty streets and you get some spectacular results out from it—then it could make your case, I suppose!'

'Or?'

'Or, if it rains all weekend, as it normally does, businesses lose money, people's pleasure is seriously disrupted, the test does not work out, then it could be as the Minister said.' He turned to Bordheim: 'What do you think, Max?'

'Well, yes I think you're right, Richard. It could be a very short way to the truth. But if it does not give us what we need, then the people will say: we gave this environmentalist full powers and look what he did. They will never again trust the environmentalist. They will just say he is an incompetent and not to be trusted.' He looked at Mawn: 'It is a big decision. I am glad it is not myself who has to make it!'

As the taxi rattled through the dark streets, Marcia put her hand over Mawn's but there was no response. He sat hunched in his overcoat on the far side of the seat staring out of the window.

She began to think out the details of her flight back to America on the following morning. The doctors had been severe, telling her that she should stop trying to meet the relentless schedule demanded by Mawn. She had an acute bronchitis, they had said, and her normal body defence mechanisms were failing to respond because of her still diminished white blood cell count. She could see her reflection in the glass partition of the cab in front of her. She decided ruefully it was quite a dramatic image. Large dark eyes set in a pale taut face.

She took her hand away. Mawn made no response. She began to long for the trip. To get away. He had long since ceased to react to her as a person. Even the research they had previously enjoyed together had taken second place to the driving need to complete his work at St Olaf's. She had simply become an adjunct as he sat in his office, drawing, calculating and planning. There had been no time for any quiet periods alone. He had become increasingly short-tempered and was already falling into the trap of being unable to delegate. Every single point raised by an already grossly overworked team around him had to be personally brought for his approval. She began to worry whether he would break under the strain and realized, with a shock, that she wasn't sure if she would mind much if he did.

She pictured the long lawns leading down to the lake at her father's Long Island home. Her room looking out over the maple copse. All the nightmare would soon be behind her and life would soon return to a relaxed and tidy predictability.

Even the flat had ceased to be a refuge. From the moment they got in, he would begin dictating an endless flow of memoranda into a tape machine, often pacing the floor into the small hours of the morning. She felt totally confused. One moment the idea

341

of a shared future seemed the most exciting thing in the world, the next made it seem too demanding and lacking in affection.

Harland Scott was waiting in the flat as they came in. He took one look at his daughter and immediately went to the phone, cancelling an arrangement he had made to attend a function at the American Embassy. Then he rang the restaurant on the ground floor and ordered a meal to be sent up.

While Marcia bathed, Mawn gave the older man a condensed account of the day's activities. Scott was friendly but non-committal and the conversation soon drifted into an uninvolved scenario session on the long-term effects of the Brainrack.

After the meal, the three sat quietly stretched out in the low armchairs. Scott toyed with a cigar.

'Frankly, I would never have believed you could have gotten so far, I really got to hand it to you. Sometimes I feel I've spent a lifetime trying to dodge the time servers—you've accomplished a hell of a lot, it certainly justifies the money.'

Mawn sensed a warning behind the praise. 'Thanks.'

'You're doing the work! It makes me feel tired just sitting around watching.'

Marcia leaned over and held her father's hand: 'You know Dad told me I was getting mellow and gracious when he came over last year; which I figured was an insult.'

Scott squeezed her hand: 'Which I guess it was in terms of the dough I blew on your education. O.K. I take it back. If you feel like moving out of this country—I guess Bordheim isn't going to last for ever. I'm convinced you could make a hell of a lot more of his job—with the backing you've got now.' He stood up, looking down at Mawn. He seemed about to place his hand on Mawn's shoulder, then drew back. Mawn could feel Marcia's body nestling in against his.

'You've a big decision and I'm glad I'm not making it, but there are maybe a few other factors you haven't thought through yet.' Mawn looked up. 'You're taking out pretty severe odds on your experiment—you're going to have to shoulder the responsibility for immobilizing this whole city.'

'Not entirely,' Mawn protested. 'Electric trains—the tube, they'll all be running.'

'O.K. But you're going to have every amateur environmentalist —all the eco-freaks—jumping on your bandwagon.' Scott poured another brandy and sniffed the glass before continuing. 'Let's assume your experiment is a good one. O.K., so all the nuts get together and say "let's completely ban the automobile", you'll get all the extremists, all the twentieth-century Luddites wandering around with sledge-hammers. Now I happen to think folks will fight like the devil to keep their autos. Take some little guy who's just saved enough money to buy his first jallopy. He's going to be mad as hell. He's going to come to you and say, what about the rich guys, they've all had their cars, now I can afford one you're going to tell me I can't have it!'

'O.K. But suppose we do prove it's the automobile, something has to be done,' Marcia interjected. 'What?'

Scott spread his arms: 'The civilized way. We live in a democracy—carefully phased legislation, time to let the industry adapt. Time to develop alternative power sources—Stirling engines, alternative fuels, that kind of thing.'

Mawn's voice tightened: 'How long will that all take?'

'I can't be sure,' Scott continued, 'but industry's got to have a reasonable chance. . . .'

'How long? Five years? Could it take less than five years?'

'I guess about that.'

'Five years while the industry finds out how to be reasonable! And meanwhile we go on producing wrecked brains!'

Marcia drew away at the tone of Mawn's voice.

'Hey, don't shoot the pianist,' Scott smiled.

Mawn sat forward: 'Can I ask you a straight question?'

'Go right ahead.'

'How much of your income comes from the car industry?'

Harland nodded easily: 'Quite a large slice, O.K.?'

'And it would take time to extract your money and invest it somewhere else?'

'I guess so.'

'So a prolonged legislation would suit your book better?'

'I've just said so.' Scott's eyes were watchful.

'And if I go too quickly, my fund dries up?'

'Alex!' Marcia drew away from him.

Scott shrugged: 'I don't recollect saying that!'

'So any decision I take won't affect the fund?'

Scott shook his head: 'Not as far as I'm concerned. I wouldn't be able to speak for any other sponsor though—especially if you start to try and force this kind of arbitrary decision on them.' He rose to his feet. 'I've got to get back—it's been a long day.' He looked over at Marcia: 'And our flight's at a God-awful hour. Don't get up, I'll find my own way out.'

At the door he turned to Marcia again: 'See you at the terminal, honey.' He nodded at Mawn: 'Be seeing you. Keep at it.' There was an ironic ring to his voice which lingered long after the door had closed. Mawn waited for the storm. But instead she wearily looked round the flat and said: 'Let's leave clearing till the morning. Mrs Best will be coming anyway.'

Later, in the darkness of the bedroom, Marcia's voice was matter-of-fact: 'You were goddamn rude to my father.'

'Yes, I suppose I was.'

'He's worked like a bat to get the fund going for you. Then you go and spit in his eye.'

'Would it help if I wrote him an apology?'

Marcia edged away from him: 'Don't be sarcastic. He was hurt a little.'

'He'll be O.K.'

'No, it's you I'm worried about.'

'Oh, yes?'

'I know you're having to push everyone to get the report out—I know all that.'

'Marcia, please, I'm tired, what are you getting at?'

'You're turning into a complete obsessional. It'll affect your judgment.'

'Do you always do your analysis in bed?'

'Please, listen to me.'

'I'm listening all right!'

She paused: 'Have you decided to go ahead with the test?'

'I've another day and a bit yet.'

'Even after all you've heard. The minister, Bordheim, Richard Lodge, my father?'

He sat up on his elbow: 'And that's making you doubt it?'

'O.K. I'm frightened,' Marcia replied. 'It's too—I don't know—extreme! You've won all the public goodwill you need, now you may be going to blow it all for one experiment.'

'Which you thought essential.'

'I'm not so sure now, Alex. Why London? It could be another city. There's time.'

'No, there isn't. We can prove the experiment in the same time, surely? But, it won't have the same impact,' Mawn said.

'Impact!' She sat up in bed abruptly. 'So Dad was right, it isn't just an experiment—you're setting up a political ploy!'

'Both, probably.'

'Alex, for God's sake, you're not a politician—you're a scientist. You could ruin everything.' She pulled him towards her but he dragged away, his voice rough: 'All right, what about you? Are you quite sure you aren't scared that some of your father's loot isn't going to get lost? You might even have to give up a few thousand dollars of your allowance.

'No, you'd better get this straight. If I decide to go on with this and if the money dries up because people like your father are scared off, so much the better! We're going to have a massive, honest experiment that people will never forget. And it's not going to be in five years when your father gets even richer at the expense of some other polluting industry—it's going to be in ten days' time. . . .'

The bedroom light glared, blinding him. She was already by the door, white faced and shaking. 'Save it! Save it for your damn lousy public.' The tears were streaming down her cheeks. 'Nothing will stop the great Alex Mawn, will it? Alexander the Great— saviour of the world. There's no point in talking to you, is there? You don't give a damn about anyone else and you never will.' The door slammed behind her.

Mawn dropped back on the pillow, his thoughts racing. First there was rage at her attack, almost immediately giving way to a shuddering sense of isolation. Each person he knew seemed to be withdrawing. He got out of bed to follow her but a sense of shame at his outburst prevented him. This time he had really gone too far. He started to feel an aching sense of loss and desolation but he pushed it to the back of his mind and climbed back into bed. It was a long time before he slept.

In one dream, he was wandering, full of anxiety, through a deserted city street. A steady driving wind blew papers along the pavement. The roadway was full of débris and curled up in the gutter a figure dressed in dirty rags looked up resentfully as he passed by. It was a grotesquely transformed Marcia. Her face was the face of an old hag and her mouth twisted in an idiot, drooling grin.

The next morning he made several clumsy attempts to break through to her but he was completely out of his depth. He felt totally inept and was almost glad when she insisted he did not take her to the air terminal. He had a vague memory of a brush of cold lips and she was gone.

CHAPTER EIGHTEEN

THE ATMOSPHERE of the empty flat pressed in on Mawn intolerably. Each sign of her presence was an ache. He forced himself to work, but as he began to arrange the detailed plans of the test, his mind began to rebel.

Just how essential was it? How much was he deluding himself. Was it just to the greater glory of Alex Mawn? Could there be other ways of measuring the necessary atmospheric levels. Gradually the idea built up in his mind that what he had done was merely an attempt to realize a fantasy of his own. To see the city emptied of cars, to see it return to dignified human occupation and to banish the ugly cacophony of the traffic for ever.

He spent hours on the telephone ringing expert colleagues to try and settle his doubts. Jimmy Kingston was at his most friendly and pompous: 'My advice, dear boy, is to go right ahead. Don't let anyone deter you. Perfectly splendid notion.' The words seemed particularly empty and non-committal.

Holden: an elderly biochemist and one of his own teachers was next. His reply was typically guarded, careful to give approval to the need for proper measurement, but equally careful not to commit himself to the scale of the enterprise. He had finished by doubting the long-term effects.

Again and again, he received only general support. Some were even openly hostile to the idea and no one seemed able to furnish him with the specific and expert support he so urgently needed. When he put the phone down for the last time, his mind was whirling and no nearer the final decision.

He began to compare the pros and cons of the test in separate columns on a sheet of paper. The result seemed ovewhelmingly in favour of the test, but the nagging self-doubt remained.

For the rest of the day he wandered morosely round the flat, picking at food. By the time the light began to fade in the big picture window of the living-room, he had drunk over half a bottle of brandy and instead of relieving his tension, it merely blunted his ability to think clearly.

When the phone rang, he violently resented its jangling intrusion. Her voice was distorted by the distance: 'Alex, it's me, yes. I'm at Kennedy. My father's waiting to ship me down to Florida.'

His depression lifted almost instantaneously. He couldn't find words: 'How are you?' Then inconsequentially: 'What's the weather like there?'

'Very cold! Alex,' her voice was hesitant: 'I flunked out, I'm sorry. I just felt I couldn't reach you.'

The brandy made his lips clumsy: 'Marcia, for God's sake. I'm the one to apologize. Everything you said was dead on target.'

'Alex, come over—I must see you. Can't you take a few days off?'

'Now?'

'Yes, come down south with me.'

'Marcia, I can't. It's all brewing up. I can't leave now, you know I can't.' He paused.

'Alex—are you still there, Alex?'

'Yes, I'm here.' He yearned to hold her. 'Put it down to this brandy if you like but I want you back. Can't you come back. I want you very badly.'

'Likewise. But you can't come over—that's final?'

'You know I can't. Not right now.'

'Alex, my father's got a whole posse of doctors waiting to check me out. I don't know yet—my chest is bad. I guess I need some sun. Have you decided yet?' Her voice changed slightly, became more distant, he had to strain to hear.

'No, I haven't.'

'What did Jimmy say?'

'Oh, he's in favour, but he doesn't really want to know. Nobody seems to be able to come right out and say, yes, go ahead, it's right.'

'Alex, honey. Believe me, I wanted to help but I didn't know how. You shut me out.'

'Hell! I'm not very easy about these things.'

'I've got to go. Take care, Alex.' Her voice faded again. 'I'll ring again when I get to Florida, I promise.'

'Yes, please ring. Look after yourself. Get well soon.'

'You bet. Good-bye, Alex.' He wondered, dully, whether he would ever see her again, poured out another measure of brandy and then, with sudden revulsion, flung it away from him.

During the night he suffered a succession of dreams. They all had to do with running, but being unable to move.

He awoke to the sound of someone shouting. Stumbling round the bedroom, his pyjamas soaked in a cold sweat, he finally convinced himself it must have been his own voice. He looked at the clock—8.30—three hours to go! Three hours to decide.

The fluctuating whine of a vacuum cleaner filtered through from the living-room. He remembered the cleaner, Mrs Best. Over the sound he could just make out the chirruping of her five-year-old-son Robert.

He slipped on a dressing-gown, had a quick disgusted look in the mirror at his pouched haggard face and went in.

She was shuffling around the living-room, thrusting the cleaner at the furniture as if it was a weapon of attack. She beamed at him over the noise.

Robert was sitting curled upon the settee trying to fit the pieces of a simple jigsaw together. Mawn sat down beside him and watched. It was an abstract concentric pattern of colours, resembling a mandela. The boy was holding one piece in his hand searching for its place in the half-completed puzzle. Mawn picked up the box and studied the picture of the completed pattern on the lid. The separate pieces were cut in simple geometric shapes and some were inter-changeable in their position. Robert had made several mistakes, particularly with colours.

He glanced up and saw Mrs Best looking at him apprehensively. She switched off the cleaner: 'Don't seem to be no good at that—can't get the hang of it, he can't. Enjoys it though, keeps him occupied.'

'Is he all right at school?'

'You mean is he like all those people you been writing about in the papers? This brainrack thing!'

'Are you going to take him along to the clinic for testing?'

'Like they said on the telly? Yes, I suppose so—don't know what good it'd do!'

'Mrs Best, where do you live?'

She looked at him blankly.

'Do you live near a main road?'

'Wouldn't call it living. Used to be nice and quiet one time. Then they built that great flyover thing. Don't never stop now. All hours it is. Bleeding great lorries come banging by. Hardly worth living but what can you do—the council don't want to know.'

'How long has the flyover been up?'

'Five years it's been now.' She turned back to the cleaner.

'Please, Mrs Best, could I ask you something? Have you—are you going to do anything about Robert?'

'What can you do? You don't think he's going to grow up backward, do you?' Her face held an expression of dumb sadness.

'Suppose there was a chance of putting things right, Mrs Best. Suppose we banned all the cars, lorries and buses. Took them off that flyover?'

'No buses? How'd I get to work? It's a mile or more to the tube!'

'Suppose we tried it over Easter. So you could have some peace and quiet for once. No fumes, no noise.'

'I work over Easter. How would I get in?'

'It wouldn't be easy. But if it helped to make Robert better? Could you get used to it?'

She pushed a straggling lock of grey hair back off her forehead: 'Get used to it in the end I suppose.'

'Would you resent it?'

'Dunno.' She jerked her thumb at Robert. 'If it would help him, wouldn't have no option would we?'

'So you think it might be necessary?'

She looked puzzled. 'I thought you said it'd make him better, stopping the traffic and all.'

'Yes.'

'Then what are you on about? You'll have to do it, won't you? Not that you'd get them politicians to agree.'

'How do you mean?'

'Well they're never in a bleeding hurry are they? I mean they never more than half do a job. Mind you, my old man's just got us an old Morris, just about goes. He'll have a few words to say to you if you stop 'im using it. But if it's for Robert he'll just have to lump it won't he? Like we all will.'

Mawn reached into his wallet and took out two notes and gave them to her: 'Look, this is for an Easter present if you like.'

'Oh, yes!' She looked startled. 'What for? Miss Scott pays me wages. You don't owe me nothing.'

Mawn got to his feet. 'Oh, yes I do. Now, will you take Robert through into the kitchen for a bit. I've got an important phone call to make.'

He gave Lodge his decision.

'What finally made up your mind, Alex?' Lodge asked.

'A lady called Mrs Best. I don't think you've met her!'

As soon as the test was publicly announced an avalanche of reaction began. Professional media experts managed to prove that it was an event for which they had been campaigning for years. Car manufacturers made perfunctory objections and one, in a fit of pique, said that the car was being pilloried for no proven cause. Business chiefs showed how it would affect transport and how many thousands of pounds they would certainly lose, even though the test was to be carried out over a public holiday.

Students held open air parties to celebrate the occasion and a 'Roast an Ox in Oxford Street' party was organized. Even the Archbishop of Canterbury blessed the occasion.

For Mawn, the ten days leading up to the test were crammed with activity. There were conferences with transport chiefs, hospital officials and the police. No one representative seemed able or willing to integrate his own activities with those of his colleagues. He was continually hounded by the media and had in the end to set up a small press office.

There were union representatives and other scientists. There were even threats. Letters accused him of being alternatively a communist saboteur and an enemy of the working man. One even described him as the alien vanguard of a Venusian invasion. A dubious ray of comfort was provided by the Lord's Day Observance Society who opined that for the first time, Easter Sunday would be properly celebrated as a day of rest.

Bicycle manufacturers organized a miniature 'Tour de France' race through the deserted city streets.

For the purposes of the test itself, the Greater London area was divided into one hundred arbitrary zones. In each, a small testing unit was assembled, where air samples were to be pumped into containers and taken by electric cars or on foot to the nearest laboratory capable of performing the analysis. From each laboratory, results were phoned to the waiting computer in Mawn's converted ward at St Olaf's Hospital.

Police had already begun to erect check points on all the major exit and entry routes to the capital and warnings appeared regularly in all media. The public were asked for their full collaboration and told that the Emergency Powers Act provided severe penalties for those who disobeyed the ban on driving. Car owners were told not to start their engines for any purpose. All garage repair shops and factories using petrol engines received a similar warning.

The public gradually accepted the idea that they were involved in a great and probably historic event which they would never forget. It was as if they were seeing for the first time, a real possibility of relief from the stresses imposed on them by city traffic. As the first day of the test approached, people began to plan their Easter holiday without the family cars. For two days beforehand, trains out of London were packed with crowds leaving the city for relatives in the country. One telecast speculated that the city population had temporarily fallen by over a quarter.

Housewives who remained behind began to stock up with food almost as if they were back in the days of wartime siege.

The managers of the London Underground sweated over route maps to provide extra trains. It was already clear that they would not be able to absorb the extra passenger load and a special appeal was made for travellers to stay away from the Tube unless their journey was essential.

On the evening of the Thursday before Easter the great exodus began. Every route out of the city gradually blocked solid with mile-long lines of traffic as tired commuters jostled each other to get out of the centre before their vehicles became immobilized.

The rush hours normally stretching between five and seven o'clock stretched on into the night. By ten o'clock jams were still present, particularly on the north-eastern exit routes leading into Essex and it was long after midnight before the streets began to fall silent. By two o'clock in the morning, a fine rain had started to fall as if nature was trying to wash the great metropolis free of the contamination.

The deadline set for the start of the test was eight a.m. on Good Friday.

351

By six a.m. Mawn's technicians had taken up their positions having arrived in specially equipped vans the day before. Now their equipment was being laid out in readiness for the collection of the first air samples.

As eight a.m. came and went, residents, long conditioned to the background roar of the early morning rush hour traffic, began to venture out into the streets, peering around fearfully, as if something essential to their feelings of security had been removed.

By eight-thirty, Mawn had completed all necessary checks on his equipment. The floor of the converted ward where he sat was covered by an interwoven network of hastily installed cables interconnecting banks of computing equipment. Along one side of the room, a temporary telephone switchboard had been installed and three operators sat ready to receive the first measurements as they were phoned in by the laboratories.

Television cameras from the three major networks had been set up in one small corner of the ward from which to scan the scene, and were already relaying minute-by-minute coverage.

Mawn sat with his staff in front of a read-out screen impatiently waiting for the first results to appear. He thought that the room looked more like a studio rigged to show the results of a general election than a scientific test. The last encounter with the media had been a nationwide flop—this one could end up in a worldwide débâcle.

There were satellite relays for viewers in countries ranging from the U.S.A. to Japan. He wondered if Marcia would be tuned in. There had been no further word from her since she had phoned from New York.

It had been arranged that samples were to be taken from each one of the selected measuring points on the hour, every hour, to enable Mawn and his colleagues to plot the atmospheric levels of the suspected acetylide on a series of graphs. The slope of the lines on the graphs would show a steady downward trend, if the acetylide came from the car.

By 20.00 on Good Friday the results were almost totally confused. In some areas, there had been a drop in the atmospheric levels of the acetylide, but in others, the level had remained the same and in six zones, measurements showed that there had been a slight but definite rise.

The effect on Mawn was catastrophic. He had in his mind allowed for the possibility that the test might prove inconclusive, but that some levels were rising was almost impossible for him to bear.

For hours on end he sat furiously discussing possible causes for the increase. Nobody seemed able to suggest feasible cause. No cars were running, there was practically no wind to bring in contaminated air from other towns near to London and yet the levels were steadily rising.

By the early hours of Saturday morning, he sat haggard and red-eyed in front of the read-out screens as the measurements continued to build up, damning his thesis.

By six a.m. there was an apparent halt in the rise, but by ten a.m. twenty-three areas showed a continuous and definite rise. The test was failing.

At eleven a.m. Campbell Baxter and Richard Lodge walked over the river from Whitehall to the St Olaf's headquarters. Mawn scarcely seemed to notice their arrival as they went slowly over to the read-out terminals and watched gravely as the digits flashed over the screens. It was Lodge who broke the embarrassed silence.

'There must be another source, Alex!'

Baxter exchanged a glance with Lodge at the sight of a three-quarters empty brandy bottle standing on a pile of papers. Mawn shook his head irritably. 'Not a chance. It's directly related to the combustion of petrol. There is no other source.'

'I don't understand it,' Baxter began. 'I don't understand it at all. I really cannot begin to describe the consequences if this goes wrong. We would become an absolute laughing stock if it fails.'

Mawn stood up. 'We've got a change—all right, I haven't got any idea what it's due to. Just give me time.'

'You've only two more days,' Lodge said calmly.

Mawn turned to Baxter: 'I may have to extend the test period.'

'It's quite out of the question,' Baxter replied. 'It would be impossible to arrange. We're under quite enough pressure already. You'll have to complete it in the allotted time.'

Mawn's hand shook as he steadied himself. 'But it may take longer to find out why it's gone up. You can't force a conclusion if we haven't got the information.'

'I'm sorry,' Baxter replied curtly, 'but you have just three days to get it. I can keep public comment at bay for that long but after that I'm afraid you'll have to answer for the consequences.'

'Couldn't there be some other factor involved?' Lodge asked. 'After all, there's been some rain.'

Baxter gestured impatiently: 'Richard, even a layman could see that rain tends to clear the air, not increase levels.'

'Well, it's considerably warmer today,' Lodge continued, lamely.

'Warmer!' Mawn gripped the edge of the desk. He appeared to be talking to himself. 'Warmer—yes it is—it's warmer.' He brushed past the two men and strode over to a man seated in front of a weather chart: 'What was the midday temperature yesterday?'

The man looked up, startled at the interruption, then picked a paper off the desk: 'It was—let's see—fifty-nine—yes fifty-nine degrees.'

'What is it now?'

The man sifted through the paper nervously: 'It's—gone up a lot—almost ten degrees. Last reading came in an hour ago—yes, sixty-eight at ten a.m.'

'That's warm for Easter,' Lodge said.

'Of course!' Mawn exclaimed excitedly. 'It could just be that the acetylide has absorbed on to surfaces—roads and buildings and so on. Now the warm air is driving it off in vapour—it's quite volatile. If it came off in vapour, then the atmospheric levels *would* rise.'

'And then if you're right about the car being the origin,' Lodge intervened, 'it should eventually come off in vapour form and . . .'

'. . . and disperse!' Mawn exclaimed. 'Yes, if that's right, and the car is producing it, then the level should rise to a peak and then begin to fall.'

He walked quickly over to the telephone switchboard. Once he was out of earshot, Baxter turned to Lodge: 'The man's in a shocking state. Can't you talk to him? He'll collapse if he goes on like that. Get him to rest.'

'He wouldn't listen for a moment,' Lodge began and then hesitated, 'matter of fact there is something I could try. I'll make a phone call back at my office.'

Over the following twenty-four hours, the levels of acetylide fluctuated unevenly. Television stations kept open with special late programmes and bookmakers raked in small fortunes by offering extended odds on the result.

By the middle of the afternoon of Easter Sunday, all levels seemed to be stabilizing, but no downward trends could be seen.

By six in the evening, Mawn gave way. In his mind he saw the whole edifice of his attempt to identify the brainrack poison crumbling around him. He took one last look at the folded pile of computer paper, desperately searching for some clue, some small indication of a change. There was none. Finally, the combined effects of two nights without sleep, little food and brandy gripped hold of him and he fell forward on the desk and slept.

There was a confused jumble of voices. Someone in the background was laughing, there was a clink of glasses. Somebody else was violently shaking his shoulder. He opened his eyes. Lodge was leaning over him brandishing a sheaf of computer readings, his face flushed. 'Extraordinary time to fall asleep!'

Mawn shook his head slowly forcing his mind to concentrate. 'What, what's happened?'

Lodge threw the paper down on the desk: 'You've been flat out for over five hours. Look at them, Alex. Look at them!' Someone forced a glass into his hand. 'They're coming down Alex—don't you see—the level's falling, every single one.' A technician pounded his back: 'You've won man, you've won!'

Mawn woke early on the Monday morning. For some time he lay back thinking over the long weeks of stress. His body felt entirely different. Even the stiffness from the hard bench he had been lying on, now seemed unimportant. The computer room was in total disorder. The floor was covered in crumpled piles of read-out paper and there were empty bottles strewn all over the metal instrument cases. Three technicians were still at work taking in the results of the night's air samples, but one glance at the numerals still flicking up on the read-out screen told him that the levels had maintained their downward trend overnight.

Quietly he told one of the technicians that he was going to walk to the sampling post in Piccadilly Circus. Once out in the street, the whole ambience of the city had altered.

The air was magically clean and the sun was already warm on

his face as he walked slowly over the bridge towards Whitehall. The waters of the Thames glinted and sparkled and there was almost complete silence. With a great surge of pleasure he realized that the loudest sound he could hear was that of his own feet on the pavement. He paused, leaning over the balustrade. Below in the water, two men were hoisting the sail of a small dinghy. He waved his hand at them and they waved back smiling.

In Parliament Square, people were already pouring up through the exit from the underground. He smiled as one old man set his dog down on the pavement and released the lead, letting the dog run yelping with excitement into the middle of the road.

In Whitehall a solitary Horseguard sat on horseback, already surrounded by tourists with cameras, his brass cuirasse reflecting brightly in the sun. A flower seller was already setting up a stall at the entrance to Trafalgar Square and, as he paused, Mawn was immediately aware of the scent of the blooms in the clear morning air. Somewhere in the distance he could hear the discordant wail of a police car speeding to an emergency. He worried vaguely about the effect its exhaust would have on the measurements and then realized it was no longer important.

The sampling van in Piccadilly was parked alongside the statue of Eros. Two men were detaching glass sample cylinders from the air pump and sealing them with paraffin film. He made a few perfunctory comments about their data but, in fact, there was nothing for him to do. He sat down on the edge of the steps at the base of the statue and gazed around in astonishment.

Even the grimy buildings with their covering network of extinguished neon signs seemed to have become brighter in the clean sunlight. People were emerging from the tube exits. For a moment they seemed to look around fearfully as if expecting a sudden release of traffic. One by one they began to step down over the edge of the pavement, treading gingerly on the surface of the road as if trespassing. Two dogs ran past, barking, one triumphantly cocking its leg against a lamp-post as though to seal his ownership of that particular territory.

A group of bearded students appeared from Shaftesbury Avenue. One was playing a guitar and as the rhythm of his tune got faster his followers broke into a dance.

For over an hour Mawn just sat and watched as people shyly filtered in. As the crowds grew, strangers began to talk to one another. Somewhere a girl burst out laughing and the sound echoed back off the surrounding buildings. The effect was instant. All conversation died away and there was a silence followed by a man's shout, trying the echo again. As the voice bounced back, there was a shout of laughter, then everyone was trying.

An old sad-faced man wobbled his bicycle unsteadily through the crowd, a hand-printed poster on his back proclaiming the second arrival of Christ. Mawn started to wander down Coventry Street to Leicester Square.

From overhead came the growing rumble of a jet. Faces turned up grimacing into anger at the sudden intrusion of the noise. The students began to chant: 'Planes out, jets out, planes out. . . .'

By St Martin-in-the-Fields a street trader wheeled his fruit barrow down from Cambridge Circus and parked in the middle of the roadway. A policeman walked ponderously over to him taking a notebook out of his pocket and began to take down his particulars, then stopped, picked an apple off the barrow, bit a large chunk out of it, nodded amiably and walked off.

The students had taken up a new position in the middle of Trafalgar Square and had lit a camping stove and were already frying sausages as Mawn arrived.

Mawn felt suddenly oppressed by the swaying movements of the crowds packed around him. He walked over to the cordoned-off sampling station and sat down on the plinth of Nelson's Column. There was nothing more to do, he felt drained.

Someone touched him on the shoulder and pointed. A police car was nosing its way up Whitehall, weaving through crowds who moved aside resentfully at the sound of its engine. It drew up alongside and Lodge and Campbell Baxter got out and walked over towards him. Reluctantly, Mawn stood up, scarcely noticing a third figure who had emerged and stood waiting by the car.

Baxter was the first to reach him, running easily up the steps and extending his hand: 'Many congratulations.' He looked around at the jostling crowd. 'Remarkable, really extraordinary. You must feel very pleased. I've just come up from number ten as a matter of fact, the PM was most complimentary.' Behind him, Lodge winked slowly at Mawn. 'Incidentally, he'd like to meet you, quite shortly I hope, to discuss all the implications . . .'

357

Mawn's attention wandered. The figure by the car. Her expression was unmistakable. He started to raise his hand. She walked towards him. Baxter caught his gaze.

'Oh, yes, Richard insisted we do a bit of taxi work for you!'

Mawn watched Marcia approach, trying to collect his thoughts. 'You talk as if it were all resolved, Minister.'

'We're well on the road, don't you think? My problems are just beginning. We shall have to decide how to deal with the industry....'

She ducked under the rope cordon and walked up to them. He searched her face. The same nervous smile.

'... they will have to completely retool, of course, if we decide to develop the Stirling engine....'

'I'm afraid you've completely missed the point, Minister.' He looked from one to the other. 'I think you all have. I don't want any of you,' he looked directly at Marcia, 'to have any illusions about my future activities.' He saw her face fall, her eyes searching his anxiously. 'That's why I don't want to meet the Prime Minister now!'

Baxter smiled: 'It would be purely explanatory....'

'But that's the whole point. We've finished all that.' He forced himself to avoid her gaze and concentrated on the youthful face of the Minister in front of him. 'We've had all the experiments and the talking.' He pointed at the waiting police car. 'You used that to cover half a mile. It wasn't an emergency, you didn't need to, you could have walked. But *you* chose to use it....'

'I think you're rather tired, Dr Mawn.' Baxter was looking at Lodge impatiently.

Mawn nodded: 'Yes I am, but my brain is still working. I'm not affected.' He pointed to the crowd. 'But you and I haven't the first idea how many of those people out there are. . . . It could just be that the use of your police car tipped one of them over the brink.'

He felt her hand grip his arm and then slip down towards his.

'Surely there can be no more doubts? We shall never be able to use cars again until the engines completely change.'

Baxter's smile had disappeared. 'I don't think they will exactly bless you if you proposed such a draconian solution.'

'I'm well aware of that and I'd get even less thanks from the

Prime Minister.' Her hand gripped his. He still forced himself to concentrate on the Minister.

Baxter spoke lightly, glancing at his watch: 'It would be his decision of course.'

'No.' Mawn's voice rang out. Faces in the crowd turned. 'It is *not* his decision. It is yours, it is theirs and . . .' he looked round at Marcia, 'and ours. Every one of us is going to make a full and final decision. From now on every car owner who starts his engine is going to be fully aware of what he's doing. There's no way for him to get out of it.' He put his arm round Marcia's shoulder and started to move away.

'Over the next forty years or so, we're going to be forced to adjust the whole of our life style—the whole of our technology to cater for millions of adults who are mentally retarded and who are never going to recover. So present my apologies to the Prime Minister and tell him that the choice is really quite simple. It's cars or the minds of our children, and God knows which we shall choose.'

THE RESIDENT

Warren Tute

'The Resident' is published by
Constable & Company Ltd

The Author

Warren Tute was born in County Durham in 1914 and was educated at the Dragon School, Oxford, and Wrekin College. He entered the Royal Navy in 1932, retiring in 1946 after serving for a time on Earl Mountbatten's staff and taking part in the North African, Sicilian and Normandy landings. After the war he wrote for radio and television, and was later concerned in film-making. He has travelled widely, especially in America and Eastern Europe. His first novel was published in 1950, and he has since written more than a dozen other successful novels, including *The Rock*, which has sold over 600,000 copies.

CHAPTER ONE

IT BEGAN IN LONDON. Now that George Mado had been reinstated in the Security Service—'plugged in again' was how he put it himself—he had become a daily commuter to the dreary little Soho building, where his branch of the outfit currently worked. It was a desk job. He had always disliked the paperwork but it meant a regular salary and his pension was secure. As you neared sixty such considerations were important.

'I'm seeing Padstow today,' he told his wife in bed, after they had listened to the usual 7.00 a.m. roll-call of bombings in Ulster. He felt her instantly stiffen, but she made no reply.

'Just routine,' he added, caressing her breasts. He found he could never be completely convincing with Anna. She removed his hand from its investigating mission and turned away.

'Don't accept it. Say you won't go.'

'Accept what? And go where?'

'Don't play the innocent with me,' Anna said sharply, 'the deal was to work in an office—and take care of your wife and child.'

'And don't I?' he pleaded, beginning to make love to her. Having a child had seemed to increase her desirability. Unkind people might—and did—call her a meaty Czech dumpling: to Mado she exactly satisfied his sexual tastes and the marriage was a success on that basis alone. But now her Middle European instincts scented danger. She was not going to be fobbed off with an early morning session.

'I don't trust that young man,' she said.

'Well, I do.'

'You promised, George. You promised you wouldn't do any more field work.'

There was a catch in her voice which moved him. It had been a new experience to George Mado at his stage in life to have an attractive young woman who actually liked him for himself, who genuinely cared about what might happen to him. Someone who knew and assessed the dangers, and who had wanted his child.

'Look, my darling, let's keep things on the ground. I've no idea why young Mr Padstow wants to see me today but you know and I know and he knows, too, that the chances of my being the slightest use in the role I once played are nil. Zero. Absolute zero. The espionage services of every country in the world have George Mado on file as a blown spy—blown as high as the dome of St Peter's. So the days of secret missions are over. They all recognize who I am and what I get up to.'

'Well, you're not getting up me,' Anna said curtly, pushing him away, 'I can make conditions, too.'

'You Czechs can be very vulgar at times. If this goes on, I might have just cause and reason to be unfaithful—sexually that is.'

'Don't make me laugh,' Anna said, getting out of bed and tantalizing him even further with her ripe nakedness. 'If I turn my back for two seconds, you're having it off with the nearest au pair you can manage to chat up.'

'Sometimes I like it better when you turn your back,' Mado said and took her as she bent down to put on her bedroom slippers. In the next room their infant daughter began to yowl for her morning feed.

Of course Anna's hunches had usually proved to be right, Mado thought, as he walked lunchwards to Pall Mall. His morning's office work had not strained his intelligence, and he had had plenty of time to think. An intuitive man himself, Mado had not reached his present age without acquiring a high respect for the instinct of others. He was also aware of the operation of 'those things unseen' of which, so the Bible said, 'faith was the evidence'.

It was a fine July day, sunny but not too hot. London had already begun absorbing into itself that tide of students, bearded, bra-less or unisexed, which Mado found more and more stimulating as the years went by. Eroticism, and every level of sexual response, had always loomed large in Mado's life. He loved women and women in fair numbers had loved him.

So such a walk on such a clear, balmy day with the smiles he gave and received from those tall, nubile girls outside American Express, should normally have filled him with contentment. Instead, as he neared the august establishment club to which young Mr Padstow had bidden him, his sense of unease grew until it was actually bobbing about in his conscious mind.

'Anna says I'm not to agree,' he remarked, once they had got over the preliminaries, 'the deal was a desk job and I'm to look after my wife and child.'

'She's a great girl, your Anna,' John Padstow said with one of his sideways smiles, 'but for once she's got it all wrong. I just wanted to have you to lunch and see how you were after—how long is it now? A year? You know me, George, there's nothing devious in me.'

Mado laughed into his Scotch. 'When I think back to Beirut . . . and the help you were to me on Operation Powder Train. . . .'

'You're not supposed to jeer openly at your host in a club of this kind. Things have changed since we terminated the Tarnham connection.'

Mado looked out of the window into the dark little garden at the back of Pall Mall into which nobody ever went. He had had to change his mind about young Mr Padstow, who was now very high up in the outfit indeed. He had once thought him as wet as a scrubber, but Padstow had proved himself in the two previous operations and willy-nilly Mado had come to like and respect him. Of course he also had the right connections, a factor conspicuously missing from Mado's life.

'I must say I never thought you of all people would end up as a pillar of Establishment . . . and my boss into the bargain.'

'And *I* never thought they'd let *you* back in,' Padstow countered dryly, 'knowing Whitehall as I now do. But here we both are.'

Mado directed on him one of his hard, calculating looks.

'Come on, sport, I'd like to enjoy this expensive lunch, so tell me what it's all about.'

'Very well. I do have a job I want you to do, but it isn't specific.'

'That tells me nothing at all. Where would it be?'

'Greece.'

Mado screwed up his puggy face into what he imagined to be a Middle Eastern expression of distaste.

'Not Marides and Elissa all over again? I thought those two were on an even keel at last.'

'They come into it,' Padstow said, 'but only indirectly—at least as I see it at present.'

'A multi-millionaire of Panayotis Marides' power comes into everything in Greece. But I thought he was turning his attention to China?'

'He is.'

'It gets him away from Elissa, I suppose.'

'Now come on, George, I know you've never liked her but Tarnham is good and dead, and she did marry Marides.'

'She's still the mother of Tarnham's children, who are very much alive.'

'Yes,' Padstow agreed, 'and that's something else. The boy's a problem on his own. The girl goes to an English school in Athens but young Master Mark is at public school here in England. He flies out to Greece for the holidays.'

'That must please Panayotis. He once told me he thought of pushing them off his yacht on a dark night. He's quite capable of that sort of mayhem when he gets in a nasty mood.'

'Well nowadays—surprising as it may seem to you, George—Madame has things much her own way. Once Marides persuaded her to marry him, he thought his troubles were over. My guess is they've only just begun.'

Mado went back in his mind over the many complicated events of the previous seven years from Paul Tarnham's defection to his death in Czechoslovakia. Since the scene was again going to be Greece, he excavated his memories of Elissa's first vist to Athens when a serious matter of diplomacy had been involved and an attempt to suborn the Counsellor of the British Embassy had been executed by Tarnham himself. The children had always been well placed pawns in the game.

'The boy wanted to follow his father to Russia,' Mado observed, 'and I used to think the sooner he did so the better for all concerned. Mark Tarnham was very much his father's boy.'

'He still is,' Padstow said, 'and the KGB consider he's ripe for recruitment, even at the age of fifteen. But that's not why I asked you here today. The Greeks have organized a Trade Fair—an Eastern European Trade Fair in Athens and up north in Salonika.'

'Those Colonels are really living it up.'

'It proves how liberal they are.'

'Look, sport, I don't know what you're going to ask me to do, but I don't have to tell you I can't exactly operate as a secret agent any more. One or two people do identify my squashed-in nose. Some of them even remember how it came to be broken. They can also recall my name.'

'Exactly. And that's why I want you in Greece. I'll get you a diplomatic passport and some sort of useless job in the commercial section of the Embassy.'

'Why?'

'Simply because everyone *does* know who you are. The Embassy may not like it very much but you'll act as a sort of magnet. You'll go to all the parties. You'll be out there in front.'

'A sort of stool-pigeon, you mean?'

'No one's going to take a pot shot at you, George. Not nowadays—not in Greece. Your very notoriety protects you. But the point is you're available. You can be trusted, you're there to be consulted should . . . should anyone feel like asking your advice.'

'I see. You think someone's ripe to do a reverse Tarnham, in effect?'

'Possibly. Someone is certainly in love with his secretary. You know how Russians are when sex gets into the act.'

'I know how most of us are, so far as that side of things is concerned.'

'Yes, well this one is an oceanographer and marine biologist with an international reputation.'

'I shouldn't have thought there was much of a defence element in that.'

'The Russian Navy wouldn't agree, George. They think he's very precious indeed.'

'And he's having it off with his secretary? Tch! tch! tch!'

'His Greek secretary—and a cousin of Panayotis Marides. I'm not sure she isn't a niece. Anyway she was born in the same village in the Pindus mountains.'

'It's an unlikely combination,' Mado said, thinking it out, 'how does he come to have a Greek secretary at all? And who is he when he's at home?'

'Dr Sergei Vassilievitch Petrov.'

'I wonder what she calls him in bed.'

Padstow gave him the sort of look a General might give a rather tiresome ADC.

'Do you ever think about anything else than sex? As a matter of fact she calls him Smootchi.'

'Oh dear!'

'Yes. It's the full sentimental bit, I'm afraid. They met at UNESCO in Paris—that Piccadilly Circus of espionage.' The upper-class disdain in Padstow's voice caused Mado to smile to himself. 'Her name is Helen Stanopoulos and she's more of a personal assistant than a secretary. She's university trained and the Russians offered her a job helping Petrov to organize the scientific section of the East European Trade Fair. They pay her well—Petrov sees to that—and everything in the garden is lovely. Only . . .' Padstow paused and shot Mado a sharp look, 'when the exhibition is over, Dr Petrov returns to Russia where his wife and family, of course, remain.'

'I see.'

For a while neither spoke. Both men tucked into the expensive meal young Mr Padstow would charge up to the firm and considered the implications from their respective points of view. At last Mado broke the silence.

'You don't need me for a possibility of that kind.' He shrugged his shoulders. 'So a Russian wants to defect—he picks his moment when the guardian apes aren't around and defects.'

'He's in Greece, George. He doesn't speak Greek.'

'I'll bet he's learnt the essentials.'

'Do you know what happened here in London to the last one who made the break? He picked on a traffic warden and addressed her in Russian.'

'That must have made her day.'

'She was writing out a ticket for a parking offence. She said she was busy and to ask someone else. Then the apes, as you call them, caught up and started to drag him away to a car.'

'Things are getting rough these days in our clean London streets. What happened?'

'The traffic warden wasn't going to have that sort of thing on her beat. So when they'd forced him into the car, she got a laundry van to block it in and then whistled up the police. But it was a near thing. Once that car had got back to Kensington Palace Gardens, it would have been Ivan's last farewell.'

'Yes,' Mado murmured, thinking back to his two experiences of the Lubyanka prison in Moscow, 'I know about that side of things.'

'Of course Dr Petrov may simply go back to the USSR nursing his bruised heart.'

'But you think it's worth the expense of sending good old reliable Mado to case up the scene in Greece? Just on the chance? I don't believe it.' Then a sudden idea struck him. 'Who's the Resident in Greece?'

'Ah! yes,' said Padstow, ordering brandy and cigars, 'I see you haven't lost your touch. I'll tell you about him in a moment or so. I think *he* may be interested in Elissa.'

'The Resident' is the senior KGB officer in any given territory. He is never the Ambassador and usually not even apparently a senior Embassy official. Inside the Russian Embassy, however, whether in New York or Kampala, everyone knows who he is. He may nominally hold down some minor post on the commercial or cultural side. This will enable him to move about the country on legitimate Embassy business and to receive each and every kind of visitor without attracting undue attention from the security services of the country concerned.

In fact he is simply the King of Spies in that particular area and he keeps an intense watch not only on his host country but also on his own staff and on the staffs of all other embassies of the communist bloc. Inevitably his power is immense since he is the one man in the area whom Moscow trusts. No one on the spot has direct control of the Resident unless and until things go wrong. Then and only then, in the manner of the medieval Roman Catholic Church, an inquisitor with plenary powers is sent.

Alexei Voznitsky, the Resident in Athens, was fully and intelligently aware of his position and of the power he enjoyed. Forty-seven years old, he had been born nearly a decade after the October Revolution. His aristocratic grandfather had been an officer in the Imperial Army of the Czar but had had the wisdom to get himself killed in obscure circumstances in 1917. By dint of a change of name and some clever footwork on the part of his father who had grasped the realities of the situation sooner than his contemporaries, the young Voznitsky had succeeded not only in staying alive through the Stalin era—a feat in itself—but also in securing a commission in Beria's outfit which later became the KGB, perhaps the most powerful private army in the history of the world. Now in Athens he was enjoying his local Czardom to the full.

'I have invited Dr Petrov and his secretary to dinner tonight,' his wife said at breakfast, 'I tried to contact you yesterday but you were out all day.'

'And I suppose you know where,' Voznitsky replied with a slight edge to his voice. He might be the local Commissar but standard KGB practice ensured that his wife kept a silent and independent watch on him as a counter-check.

'Well, Alexei, is it convenient or not?'

He nodded but exhibited no pleasure. He had been looking forward to a quiet evening at home drinking French wine and listening to an opera on his stereo equipment.

'Will you cook for them here or shall I get a table at the Karamaikis?'

Irina shrugged her shoulders.

'I don't particularly like Dr Petrov or his girl-friend,' she said, 'so unless you want to talk to him in private I'd rather not bother to have them here to dinner.'

'I'm scarcely likely to talk to Petrov in private if his girl-friend is present,' Voznitsky retorted. He was fond of his wife but for someone who also had a commission in the KGB she could be at times almost intentionally stupid and obtuse. Of course it was the little boy who worried Irina.

'But she is his personal assistant and they are sleeping together.'

'The girl is Greek,' Voznitsky said severely, 'if she had been a Russian from the Embassy staff that might be different. But no —he has to pick on a Greek. Our famous Dr Petrov may know a great deal about plankton and algae, he doesn't seem to be very aware of the world he lives in.'

'But he's loyal, isn't he, Alexei?'

There was an anxious tone in her voice. Voznitsky knew she didn't care a hoot about Petrov or his loyalty. She was thinking of Petrov's wife and family now being casually deceived, and therefore at risk. Her own little son, whom they had had to leave behind in Moscow with her mother, was also never for long out of her thoughts. Voznitsky was suddenly touched by the look on her face.

'You're pining for Boris, aren't you?' Voznitsky said. No one could describe Irina as beautiful but she had the normal attractive-ness of a healthy young mother, to which was now added the melancholy sadness of having to be parted from their only child. At seven Boris was being forced to learn the hard facts of Russian soviet life. He had been forbidden to go abroad with his distin-guished parents. He had to remain with his maternal grandmother under the watchful eye of the KGB. What made it worse was that Irina had never got on with her mother, whom she thought of as a secret church-going counter-revolutionary. It was therefore doubly depressing to have to leave Boris in her care whilst she and Alexei were on this foreign assignment.

'Of course I miss him,' she snapped, 'that's all I have, isn't it?'

'I don't know what you mean,' Voznitsky said defensively, knowing full well what she was implying.

'You men seize the first opportunity you can grab of having an affair. You go off abroad, you seduce your secretaries or your cypher clerks, anyone dazzled by your rank and your power and you leave us women to carry the whole burden of the family on our own. I wonder what Mrs Petrov thinks of it all.'

'Us women!' Voznitsky said contemptuously, 'always these clichés. I suppose you'll be taking Women's Lib back to Moscow with one or two other bourgeois ideas.'

'Why don't you go to your office?' she said, 'I have to superintend the cleaning of this apartment.'

It always ended like that, Voznitsky thought, as he drove to the Embassy. Communication grew less and less as time went by. To begin with you were in love and you sated yourself with sex. It was all a trick, an illusion. Then came the payment, the responsibilities of family, the gradual drawing apart. Yet always you were caught. If he had not been married, if he had not been able to offer a hostage in the form of a seven-year-old, much-loved son, he would never have been allowed to come abroad holding the high rank he did in the KGB.

Not that he argued with this. Some such system was essential and he accepted it. He hated capitalism. Foreign service in the KGB was looked on Jesuitically as the front line of the war which communism eternally waged on the capitalist world. Voznitsky fully concurred in this. He had an utter contempt for someone like Marides, a capitalist of capitalists, a monster of Western decadence.

Nevertheless some of the restrictions were hard to bear. Voznitsky's very success had enabled him to acquire expensive tastes in wine, music and Western literature—in all of which he was free to indulge to any degree he chose, since locally there was no one to say him nay.

Equally, of course, there was no one with whom he could share

371

these tastes. Perhaps it was his aristocratic grandfather's spirit still latent in him which gave him such a disdain of his brother officers in the KGB. Almost without exception they had the civilization of the higher apes. They drank, the rutted away at sex, they played sentimental Russian music and they lived, so it seemed to Voznitsky, almost entirely in and for their bodies.

You discussed culture, if at all, as a duty and you dealt with it in quantities, assuming that the more you took in the more educated you were. It did not matter if the art you absorbed had no meaning. Life itself had no meaning to his brother officers of the KGB except on a physical and lower mental plane. Understanding—the possibility of a soul—these were non-Marxist concepts to be treated with the contempt they deserved. It was unfortunate, therefore, that Voznitsky happened to believe that the soul existed. No one had asked him about God for many years but Voznitsky was aware of his presence too. This was not altogether a happy situation for a senior officer such as himself.

Out on the coast near Vouliagmeni, the great white house, covered with purple bougainvillæa, which Panayotis Marides had built as his main palace in Greece, had by now been gradually transformed into a home. 'Humanized,' was the word Elissa used to herself. She had come through some sort of sound barrier and was enjoying her marriage and the new life which her Greek millionaire husband took such pleasure in giving her.

'And next, I suppose, it will be a family,' Marides said, halfserious, half-aggressive in that stubborn peasant manner he always fell back on when in doubt. He was one of the richest men in the world but his roots, in spite of the British nationality he had acquired via Cyprus in the colonial days, were still firmly in the Pindus mountains of north-west Greece.

'I think that decision has already been taken,' Elissa answered, 'but I'll let you know for certain when you come back from Pekin.'

They were having a late morning ouzo on the terrace overlooking the private beach. For once no guests were expected for lunch and they had no one staying in the house.

'You're joking,' Marides said quietly, but with a hesitancy in the voice which would have been imperceptible to anyone except Elissa. He did not know how to take this news, so he probed and hedged. She studied his swarthy, intelligent face. A few years ago, when the well-bred, ascetic-looking Paul Tarnham had dominated her life, it was unthinkable even to consider an intimate life with such a man as Marides. Yet here she was now, not only agreeably married to him but also pregnant, as she now felt reasonably certain.

'You didn't think I married you for your collection of Impressionists, did you?'

'No, but I mean—are you serious or not?'

'Don't you want another son?'

'It needs thinking about. I have a son already.'

'Yes,' Elissa said grittily, 'and so far as I am concerned, you can keep him.'

'He's a good boy,' Marides said defensively.

'Some boy!'

She jeered, but not in such an unkind way that Marides could really take offence. She had learnt always to talk so that her husband never knew if she fully meant what she said. Half-truths were very much in the Greek tradition.

'He'd slit your throat if he thought he could get away with it. And he'd certainly dispose of me if he could.'

'Yach!' said Marides, who hated direct statements of that kind, 'I'm not so sure about your own son by Tarnham.'

'My own son by Tarnham, as you put it, is not quite in the same position to slit throats as your Christos. He's only fifteen. And he doesn't work in the Greek Foreign Office.'

'He's learning fast.'

'How do you know?'

Marides smiled, drawing back his head slightly and half-closing his eyes in that peculiarly Greek way of showing contempt. He gave his wife what a Victorian novelist would call 'a veiled look'. Then he shrugged his shoulders, and dropped into the Greek-American accent which he knew irritated her.

'I don't-a know a thing. He's-a your son. You know him best. You have him expensively educated in England. But I tell you— he's more his father's son than yours.'

'What do you mean by that?'

'Problems,' Marides said enigmatically, 'always a boy like that brings problems.'

'You've been talking to your Russian friends again.'

'And what's wrong with that? They charter my ships.'

'You know what I mean. That Voznitsky.'

'No, Elissa, I don't know what you mean.' There was no one better at turning a question or dodging an issue when he chose than Marides.

'But as we're talking about my Russian friends,' he went on, 'I'd be grateful if you'd keep on eye on Helen whilst I'm away. I'm not sure Dr Petrov knows what he's doing.'

'Then it's a little late, isn't it?' Elissa said crisply. 'What sort of an eye am I to keep? Is she pregnant too?'

'I hope not. Her father would wring her neck like a chicken.'

'You're so dramatic, you Greeks. What's it matter if she loves him?'

'It matters in a Greek village. Petrov has a wife and family in Russia.' He gave her an irritated look. 'I don't think you'd better go to the Pindus mountains with ideas like that. Even as my wife. They might stone you.'

She went over and put an arm round his shoulder.

'I was only joking,' she said, 'I'd forgotten the Greek mafia. I'll do what I can for Helen, but she's a headstrong girl. She's a little like you.'

'Not—very like me,' Marides said with a frown, 'not if she makes a fool of herself with that dumb Russian scientist.'

It was a small, hot room in the basement, not over clean, and outside stood the dustbins of the Royal Greek Institute of Marine Research. It was the caretaker's place and as such would not have unduly shamed a French *concierge* in a working-class district. But it was airless, especially when the curtains were drawn, and not exactly the most romantic setting for a love affair.

Anyone lying on her back, as Helen was now doing with the momentarily relaxed bulk of her beloved Smootchi on top of her, could watch the cockroaches bustling about the ceiling and occasionally falling off on to the bed. It was far from perfect. But it was all they could get. Its location provided a waterproof alibi since it was legitimate for Dr Petrov to spend as much time as he deemed necessary in the Institute where the Greek authorities had given him an office and where in turn he had installed his personal assistant. The fact that they were so rarely in the office itself aroused no comment since there were always conferences to be attended elsewhere in the building and valuable Aegean records to be studied in the vaults, amongst other places, next to the caretaker's room.

Helen had bribed the caretaker with surprisingly little difficulty. She was also under the impression that their basement *garçonnière* was known only to themselves. The caretaker had been at the Institute for years. He was a wizened, grey-haired old man with blackened teeth from the tobacco he chewed rather than smoked. He lived for the lottery and any spare drachma he acquired went straight into lottery tickets. He was a typical, uncomplicated Greek watchman.

The police, of course, had him where they wanted him and, if they asked questions, would undoubtedly get everything he knew or suspected.

But what, after all, did he know? That one of the professors wanted to have an affair with his secretary? Well, that had happened before. Nothing unusual in that. The caretaker kept out of the way, except when he felt that another tip was due. And it never occurred to either Helen Stanopoulos or Dr Sergei Petrov to look under the bed, where the Greek security forces had placed a small Japanese tape recorder; nor to examine the lapels of Dr Petrov's suit, where a pinhead microphone had been put by the Russians which picked up everything within a radius of ten metres and transmitted it to a car with CD plates outside the institute, where the love chatter emitted by two people in sexual congress was automatically and blindly recorded for possible future use.

Suddenly Petrov raised himself on his elbows and looked down on her face.

'Why are you crying?' he asked. 'Is there something wrong?'

Their common language was French since Helen spoke no Russian and Petrov only enough Greek to order a restaurant meal. Moreover they had met in Paris so French became naturally their language of love.

'I want it to go on for ever,' she said, 'and it won't.'

She turned her head as the tears poured down on to the grimy pillow. She was small and dark, with big expressive brown eyes and delicate hands. It did not seem to matter that Petrov was at least twenty-three years older than she was. She did not mind his middle-aged paunch, nor his thinning hair. In her eyes he was a highly intelligent, highly qualified man and she loved him. They separated their bodies and he traced away the tears with his finger.

'Don't cry,' he said, 'I don't like it when you cry. I love you, little Helen.'

'That's what you say. But you'll go back to Russia, to your wife and family, and forget all about me.'

It was true but he hated her saying it. 'Yes,' he said at last, 'I do have to go back. But I shan't forget about you.'

'That won't do me much good,' Helen said, getting out of bed and beginning to dress, 'I'll be here and you'll be there.'

'Then why don't you come with me? I'll get a divorce and we'll marry. Then we could go on working together. . . .'

He faltered into silence. Like Helen he wanted it to go on for ever and like her also knew that it wouldn't. He was an autocratic man by nature and resented finding himself in his present weak position.

'I don't think that's a very proper idea,' she said, tossing her head and becoming once more the brisk, businesslike secretary she had taught herself to appear. 'I'd better get back to the office, before people start wondering where we are. Call in on Records on your way back as that's where I shall say you've been if anyone asks.'

CHAPTER TWO

THE GREEK TRADE FAIR was scheduled to open early in August. This boosted the normal flow of summer tourists to Athens and overloaded travel and accommodation facilities. Even by using Marides' own airline, which went against Mado's grain since it meant more profit to someone already impossibly rich, the office could not get him the direct flight to Athens which he had wanted. Instead he was forced to change aircraft in Rome.

As he went through the departure lounge at Heathrow, however, Mado suspected that there may have been less accident than intent in this arrangement. Just ah d of him in the line of passengers boarding the aircraft was young Mark Tarnham, presumably en route to Athens for his holidays. Keeping close to the boy in that professional way Mado instantly recognized stood a tall, hard-looking man whose face was vaguely familiar to Mado although the identity escaped him.

This man and young Tarnham had not apparently made each other's acquaintance but, as if by chance, the man eased into the next seat to Mark, who was on the window side, the third seat being taken by a girl with high cheekbones and striking red hair, who was also known to Mado but whom for the moment he could not place.

Mado's years of experience had given him a chameleon quality which was invaluable. He could move fast and get where he needed to be without drawing attention to himself. He used this now, charming an elderly American widow out of the way, to secure the aisle seat in the row behind. This enabled him to keep an eye on Mr Hatchet Face and the defector's son, although he could not hear what they might say to each other.

He also had the pleasure of studying the mop of wind-swept tawny hair in front of him and of wondering what the owner of the hair would be like. Rather hard and purposeful, he concluded. Tarnham's son, who he had helped rescue from Prague in 1968, would certainly recognize him if he turned round but Mark seemed to be more of a moody introvert than ever. He at once immersed himself in a book, not even looking up when the aircraft took off.

This gave Mado more time to study the redhead in front of him, and eventually realize her identity. When they got off the plane at Rome, she was joined by a bearded young man with square metal-framed glasses and one of those student caps that made him look like a fugitive from *Dr Zhivago*. He was also carrying a disguised camera case and this signalled to Mado that he belonged to the current crop of press photographers.

'You're Andrea Eckersley, aren't you?' Mado said to the girl. He had still managed to remain unobserved by Mark Tarnham, now at the end of the transit lounge. The tall sinister man had disappeared.

'Thank you,' Andrea said coolly. She gave Mado a penetrating, keep-away look as if he were some square at a party who might ask her what sort of stuff she wrote.

'On holiday?'

'No,' Andrea said, again without warmth, 'my paper is sending us to cover the Trade Fair in Athens.'

'Ah!' said Mado, still keeping an eye on Mark Tarnham, 'I enjoy reading your column.'

'But . . . ?'

'No "buts" at all. You make me laugh. You've a very sharp eye.'

'Well, thank you again. This is Don Dowdall,' she flashed Mado a quick glint, 'whose photography you also admire.'

They nodded at each other.

'And who are you?' Andrea Eckersley inquired in a casual way. He wondered if she really knew or was simply trying him out.

'I'm George Smith, alias Brown. Sometimes known as Robinson.'

'Ah!' Andrea said, reacting with the sort of look a tart gives a difficult customer, 'you mean I ought to know who you are.'

'Not at all. My real name is Mado and I can't tell you how pleasant it is not to be recognized for a change. Especially by a lady and gent from the Press.'

'You're George Mado?' she said and allowed the hard features to break into a smile, 'Well, well, well. That's made my day.'

'You could make mine,' Mado said with a smile.

'Could I indeed?'

'I'm a pretty coarse fellow under this well-bred, elegant exterior.'

'Oh!' she said, in her own unmistakably upper-class voice which she had tried for so long to disguise for Fleet Street purposes, 'so that's what you are. . . .'

'People's ideas of breeding vary, don't they?' Mado chatted on.

'I know they breed rats for laboratory purposes.'

'Rats indeed!' Mado said, looking at her with an ironic smile, 'you can get very friendly with a rat. Especially if you meet in the right circumstances. Like a Russian prison, for instance. Rats rate above gaolers for me. But I was forgetting . . . you're a Marxist, aren't you, under that fair beautiful skin.'

'Never mind what I am,' Andrea snapped, 'I may need your help in Greece.'

'How did you know I was going to Greece?'

'I didn't. However, I just found out.'

'Where are you staying?'

'Intermittently at the Grande Bretagne. The paper likes it that way.'

He drew her slightly away from the photographer who, in any case, seemed to be absorbed by a passing Tarzan in airline uniform.

'How about standing me dinner tonight?' Mado suggested, 'I think your paper would like that, too. Or are you committed to Mr Dowdall?'

'Only for work purposes,' Andrea said with a slightly bleary expression, 'the ladies don't interest him very much.'

'Capital! Capital!' Mado went on, opting for his Edwardian *Forsyte Saga* mood, which she at once cut short.

'And you don't interest me, Mr Mado. At least not as a guest on my expense account.'

He smiled her a winning smile. 'We'll go Dutch.'

She smiled him back an equally charming negative.

'Oh! no, we won't.'

'All right,' he conceded the game, 'but don't eat too much. I work for the Government now.'

'Didn't you always?'

He looked at her and raised his eyebrows.

'I thing we've a lot of finding out about each other to do.'

'Don't build up any hopes,' she said, 'I'm not that easy to know.' Then, quickly switching the subject, she went on: 'You've had to do with the Marides, haven't you?'

'Do you mean Panayotis, his Foreign Office son or his famous wife?'

'All three.'

'Yes,' Mado agreed, lighting a cigarette, 'I know the Marides. And if you look over my left shoulder in the corner by the poster advertising Sorrento, you can see Elissa's son by the late and unlamented Tarnham.'

'Oh yes?' Andrea said, 'the one with the straw hat—or the bearded old man in a skull cap?'

Mado whipped round and stared. Mark Tarnham was no longer visible in the transit lounge. He swore softly to himself and set off for the exit.

'But don't forget me,' Mado called over his shoulder as he went, 'I'll be back.'

He checked behind all the pillars. He checked the lavatories. Mark Tarnham had definitely gone and there was no trace either of the stony-faced man who had sat next to him in the aircraft. For some reason no official appeared to be in charge of the transit passengers at that time. So Mado did a quick tour of the airline desks and of the arrival and departure lounges. But Ciampino is a large airport. It was full of summer crowds. The search was doomed. Mado decided he might as well be looking for someone in Oxford Street on a Saturday morning.

In any event Mark Tarnham was only of oblique interest. If the boy wanted to follow in his father's footsteps, that was all right by Mado. Let him get on with it. He returned to the transit lounge to find that his plane for Athens had already left. It was not an auspicious start to his new assignment.

Andrea Eckersley had only admitted to part of the truth when she had told Mado that she and Don Dowdall had been sent to Athens for the East European Trade Fair. This was her cover plan. In fact she had sold her editor the idea of a series of features on the world's richest men, and she intended to start on Panayotis Marides. Her regular column was being rested. She had worked hard for three years. There was every justification to give herself a break. Oddly enough, she had never visited Greece before.

She was an arresting-looking young woman with a determined, squarish jaw, blue eyes and that clear red hair which to Mado's surprise so often went with sexual frigidity. She looked, at first sight, like the sex symbol of all time with her slender body, well-defined waist and firm breasts. Strong white teeth, lyrical legs and thighs and that astonishing colouring—Mado had taken in all those plus factors—but experience and instinct combined to warn him that the more ravishing such a woman appeared, the less likely she was to be good in bed. It had all gone into the looks.

This was indeed the case with Andrea, who had never had a satisfactory love affair in her life. Moreover since most men reacted instantly and predictably to her attractiveness and then bent their best endeavours into getting her horizontal, she had developed a kind of brittle cynicism about the whole process. She certainly knew what to expect in France and Italy and she had no notion but that Greece would prove to be, if anything, even more exhausting.

Andrea had a further disability which she kept very quiet about in Fleet Street. She was an Earl's daughter. Being a Lady in her own right was less than no use to her in the competitive world she had chosen to enter. So when, on leaving Oxford, she had taken up with the writing, she had adopted her mother's name and had contrived, by keeping her home background and her working life completely separate, to make herself a reputation as a competent journeyman writer with the full quota of left-wing bias acceptable to her brother and sister journalists who daily sold their souls to the capitalist press. At least this was the face she showed to the world. It was also the extent of Mado's knowledge of her.

What Mado did not know was that Andrea had agreed to work in a very discreet way for John Padstow, whom she had met and liked during an off-duty weekend at her parents' house in Dorset. Padstow had taken a risk in talking to her as he had. British security was well aware of Miss Eckersley's Maoist ideas but in spite of them she was no tatty little King Street traitor. She was loyal— if not to her Queen and country—at least to her ideas of English civilization, freedom and to the general way of life which her socialist friends seemed so anxious to modify and even destroy without apparently realizing what they were really doing. She was thus a paradox to herself and, had the orthodox communists known it, something of an enigma in reverse as Philby had been.

Padstow had not told Mado anything about her at all. In fact Andrea knew considerably more about Mado than she had given away on their first encounter. She had recognized him long before he had worked out who she was. It had also been no accident that she had sat next to young Mark Tarnham in the aircraft. She had been well briefed by Padstow before setting out and she carried a very private and personal letter of introduction from him to Elissa. She also had a more formal letter from her editor to Marides. All of this she kept to herself when eventually she and Mado met up in Athens.

'You're a little late,' she remarked as they greeted each other in the bar of the Grande Bretagne Hotel. 'Forty-eight hours late.'

'I'm sorry,' Mado said, 'I should learn not to chase hares at my time of life.'

'Did you track the boy down?'

'No, and I've been at the Embassy since I arrived so I haven't checked with Elissa yet. For all I know they may have meant him to get off that plane in Rome.'

'They did not. They expected him on the same flight we arrived on—or rather that I arrived on and that you should have caught.'

'You know the Marides already? I thought you were asking me for an introduction.'

'My editor gave me a letter to Marides about the series I hope to do.'

She told him about the features she intended to write. This satisfied Mado's curiosity. It was a part of her job. She made no mention of Padstow nor of the letter she had passed on to Elissa.

'You certainly don't waste time,' Mado said, giving her an appraising look, 'how was the great man when you met him?'

'Angry. They were together when I was ushered in. To begin with I pretended I didn't know about Mark being on the same plane, but it was one of the first questions Elissa asked me. . . . "If you were on Alitalia XYZ or whatever—did you notice a young man, etc., etc., etc?" I said I sat next to him. "Where is he then?" Marides said sourly, "he should have come on to Athens on the same plane as you." Then he turned to Elissa and said something about "This is becoming a habit." At which point she got angry, too.'

'You seem to have plunged to the heart of things in record time,' Mado said, studying her face with genuine admiration. 'You're quite a girl, aren't you? We should be a team.'

She laughed.

'You like to turn everything to your immediate advantage, don't you?' she said. 'What sort of team? And for what?'

One thing was clear to Mado. Andrea Eckersley would be no easy lay.

'Well, all right,' he said, 'the way things are shaping up we'll be working together, whether we like it or not.'

'Why?'

He wondered why a sudden flash of danger seemed to light up her eyes.

'Because you've evidently got a strong sense of news.' He paused, wondering how to take it on from there, 'and I suppose I have as well.'

She gave him a steady look and smiled.

'Why have you come to Athens?'

He allowed himself the sort of mocking smile she had turned on him when first they had met.

'For the East European Trade Fair.'

'I didn't know you were interested in commerce.'

'Young lady, I used to travel in books.' A somewhat puzzled look crossed her face so he went on, 'I'd have you know that you're speaking to a properly accredited Assistant Commercial Attaché at the British Embassy in Athens.'

She could look astonishingly innocent when she chose. She was what would have been called 'scrumptious' in Mado's youth. As if reading his thoughts, she put him down with a jolt by continuing what he had just said: 'Who has an attractive young wife, a small baby and a disgustingly roving eye.'

'What's disgusting about it?'

'Has no one ever told you?'

'As a matter of fact they haven't. At least no one's complained so far.'

'Well,' Andrea said crisply, 'you may have a super understanding with your wife. I doubt you're going to have one with me.'

Such understanding as there was between Elissa and Panayotis had also been stretched to near breaking point by Mark's disappearance. Elissa had wanted to go straight to the British Embassy, but Marides had better ways of finding out what had happened and ordered her to keep the matter entirely to herself. Marides had spent the last few days in a sulky bad temper since the boy's disappearance. From his point of view it was a complication he could well have done without on the eve of an important visit to Pekin and the opening of the Trade Fair in Athens, where he intended to mature a number of tricky deals.

To celebrate this inauguration, he had arranged one of 'those sumptuous eighteenth-century extravaganzas' for some three hundred important guests—or at least guests who had some claim to importance—at the villa with its peerless view over the Aegean, where enough food and drink to keep Bangladesh going for a month would be consumed, which was to culminate in a firework display from the little island off the coast, which he also owned.

Elissa detested these exhibitions of wealth and power, but as they were an essential part of the man she loved and had married, she put up with them in such a way that Panayotis had no idea of her feelings but thought she actually enjoyed them. In a sense this was true, since Elissa was aware of the almost childish delight it gave him and relished this pleasure, so to speak, at one remove. Privately she was appalled at the vulgarity of it all.

383

About an hour before the first guests were due to arrive, Marides arrived back in a rage.

'Your son by Tarnham,' he said, waving a letter in his hand, 'is in Moscow.'

Elissa froze rigid. She felt a tightening of the solar plexus and the onset of a fear she thought she would never have to experience again.

'How do you know?'

'Voznitsky. He gave me this.'

He passed her the letter and was evidently so angry he could not keep still but marched up and down the great marble-floored drawing-room, looking as if he were quite capable of picking up the furniture and throwing it into the sea.

'Dear Mother,' she read, 'please don't be cross but I'm writing this from Moscow as I know you and my stepfather will be worried that I never arrived as I should have. But quite accidentally I was sitting next to a nice Russian diplomat who said he had known father well and would I like to go to Moscow on my way to Athens to meet some other friends of my father who was very much respected there? Mr Karai said he would fix it up there and then, so I went on from Rome and about six hours later I was standing in Red Square looking at the Kremlin. It's terrific here and I'm being very well looked after by a Russian Colonel who has a large apartment near the Kremlin. I can come on to Athens whenever I like, but I'm enjoying myself so much I'd rather stay on a few days here even though I'll miss the fireworks and all the other things stepfather is laying on for his party. Tell Lucy I'll make up for it by giving her extra tennis lessons and please don't worry—everything's OK—it was a chance I didn't want to miss. After all father *did* decide he preferred Russia to England and from what I've seen already, he was right. Things are much better here and everyone is polite and correct and I've been practising my Russian which, as you know, I'm going to take as one of my A levels. Mr Karai says he will get this letter to you "at the speed of a sputnik" and he might come on with me to Greece, as he has to look in on the Trade Fair, though he'll miss the opening as I will—but then it's only a sort of Ideal Homes exhibition, isn't it? So I don't think I'm missing much. Please tell my stepfather not to get in a tiz. They all know him here in Moscow and say they respect him very much but does he really have to go to Pekin? The people I'm with don't seem to think very much of the Chinese. They say the Chinese are a great nation but their present leaders are deviationists and not cultured. I'm being taken to the Ballet tonight. As you know the Russian ballet is the best in the world. Love—Mark.'

When she had finished reading the letter, Elissa looked out at the bluish-purple sea and thought about Paul Tarnham. It was extraordinary how things repeated themselves. She had not really understood her first husband—Panayotis was child's play to the psychology of Tarnham—and now she was ceasing to understand her own son. Perhaps, she thought, Eysenck was correct after all and a person's genes were more important than his environment. There was much more of Paul Tarnham in him than of herself. About Lucy she had no doubts. Her daughter would never light out for Moscow because some strange man chatted her up 'accidentally' on an aircraft.

'Well?' said Marides.

'Well what?'

She could be equally aggressive when she chose. There was a lot of the bully in Marides.

'What are you going to do about it?'

'I don't know. And I wish you wouldn't be so aggressive.'

'Why don't you tell him to stay in Moscow if he likes it so much?'

'You really hate him, don't you?' she walked away from him to the terrace, 'I think that's a disgusting way to behave.'

'Troubles and problems. That's all your first husband brought into the world.'

He followed her out on to the terrace where the servants were making final preparations for the party. Marides waved them away.

'You used him,' Elissa said. 'You didn't think like that when it suited your book.'

She had begun to cry in spite of herself, and this made her angry too.

'I think you can manage your rotten little party yourself. I'm going up to my room.'

He put his arm round her shoulders.

'I'm sorry,' he said, 'I didn't mean to hurt your feelings. It's just that I have enough to think about without a worry like this.'

'Damn them!' Elissa said in a low voice, 'damn the bloody Russians and their filthy KGB. Why can't they leave us alone?'

'It's all right, Lissy, I'll get him back for you.'

She got over the crying with a deep sigh.

'I don't know, Pan. Possibly you're right. If that's what he wants to do . . . only I wish they hadn't pressured him in that way. He's only fifteen.'

'I'll get him back,' Marides said, 'I'll tell Voznitsky to have him sent back tomorrow.'

'Suppose they say no?'

'They'll do as I wish,' Marides said with a grim look in his eyes.

It was a perfect setting for a party. Everything had been prepared on a Roman scale of munificence. The house, sited on the top of a low cliff, gave on to a series of terraces which had been arranged downwards to the private beach, leading in turn to the marina. This at times had the look of a private harbour. Marides' large yacht, the *Myrmydia*, lay alongside its own jetty and half a dozen smaller boats belonging to friends furnished the other bays of the marina. The effect was of a lavishly designed set and the concealed lighting, which intensified in power as evening turned into night, added to this theatrical illusion.

Marides was known throughout the eastern Mediterranean for the parties he gave, and tonight *tout Paris* or rather *tout-Athénes* was there. This naturally included a heavy 'Colonels' contingent' as Elissa called them. Now that the regime had been established for several years, Greek security men liked to imagine that they could merge invisibly into any crowd at any party, that foreign propaganda about the regime was nothing but part of an international left-wing plot headed by the British press and that life in Greece was perfectly normal and free.

Elissa knew otherwise. Now as she watched the great house filling up with her husband's friends, associates and enemies, she was able to spot the Colonels' men in their strategic and tactical positions, some with little tape recorders in their pockets, others with the oily smiles which dictators' lackeys acquire when they are not quite sure of their ground.

Although he had not been asked, Mado showed up and was now talking to Elissa. She had never much liked him nor he her, but now tonight she was glad to see him. He gave her a slight sense of security, even though his 007 days were clearly at an end.

'I don't think you'll be missing many ashtrays tonight,' Mado said, looking at a particularly unprepossessing security man standing underneath the big Renoir which dominated the hall.

'You're wrong,' she replied, 'these are the nights when the "souvenirs" go. The big stuff is safe enough and all the valuable smaller things have been put away. Ashtrays and the like are what my husband calls "consumable party trash". What brings you to Greece this time, Mr Mado? Or are you working for my husband again?'

It gave Mado a jolt to hear her talk of Marides as 'my husband' but he did not betray his feelings.

'Oh! the Trade Fair,' he said vaguely, 'I'm temporarily attached to the British Embassy. What's the news on Mark?'

'You know about that?'

'Didn't Miss Eckersley tell you? I missed my plane trying to discover where he'd gone.'

'He's in Moscow,' Elissa said, drawing Mado to one side so that they could not be overheard.

'Hijacked again? Pan must be delighted.'

'Mark says he went there at the invitation of a Mr Karai. . . .'

'Ah! yes,' Mado said, 'that's who it was. I recognized the face but I couldn't put a name to it.'

'Who is he?'

'He's one of the travelling inquisitors. A KGB troubleshooter —one of the top ones they send in when anything goes wrong in a particular territory.'

'Mark says in his letter that Mr Karai may be coming to Greece.'

'How nice for all of us! Is Mark staying in Moscow?'

'My husband says he'll get him back,' Elissa murmured, 'and no doubt he will. I'm afraid the whole thing worries me sick. Ah! Helen . . .' she went on in a normal tone of voice to a youngish attractive girl who was passing at that moment, 'I'd like you to meet Mr Mado from the British Embassy. This is a cousin of my husband's who is working with the United Nations.'

'How do you do?' Helen Stanopoulos said. She spoke English with a reasonable accent but there was no welcome in her look for Mado and the handshake was hard and insensitive. It was obvious to Mado that she also had a haughty dislike of Elissa.

'As a matter of fact Panayotis is my uncle,' she went on, 'not my cousin.'

'My husband has so many relations,' Elissa said, 'it's an achievement I got as near to it as that.'

She favoured the young woman with a chilly look. She was not going to be put in her place by a jumped-up peasant girl from the Pindus mountains.

'Where's your famous Dr Petrov?' she continued, and before Helen could answer, pressed on in a way which made Mado smile, 'Miss Stanopoulos is working on oceanography with a world-famous Russian expert. They're quite inseparable.' Then with a side glance at Helen, 'I'm surprised you let him out of your sight at a party like this.'

Helen Stanopoulos looked as if she would relish seeing Elissa carted off to Boubolina Street and given a little of the Colonels' treatment at Police Headquarters.

'Dr Petrov is a busy and important man. I'm only his personal assistant.'

The smouldering look in her dark eyes filled in the rest of the story for Mado. She gave him an impression of far greater sexuality than Andrea Eckersley, who now came up to them accompanied by the winsome Mr Dowdall. Andrea nodded at Mado and Helen Stanopoulos and spoke directly to Elissa.

'Do you think Mr Marides would object if we took some celebrity photographs at this party?'

'I should think he'd hate it,' Elissa said, 'but you could always ask him.'

'Could you do it for me?'

'No,' Elissa said, 'I think it would be better if you approached him yourself.'

'Come with me,' Helen said to Andrea with a snide glance at Elissa, 'I'll ask my uncle in Greek.'

Elissa smiled sardonically at Mado, and when they had moved away, said in a quiet voice: 'You see how it is?'

Mado saw how it was all right.

'Which is the famous Dr Petrov?'

'Talking to my husband.'

'I think I'll join them.'

'Good,' said Elissa, 'I'll take you across.'

He smiled in appreciation. 'I won't ask for any celebrity photographs, you can be sure of that.'

Although well over three hundred people were now at the party, they were dispersed over the various terraces and beaches so that there was no sense of crush and private conversations between two or three people could take place in privacy. Marides did not even know that Mado was in Athens and his face lit up when Elissa brought him across, but whether it was with pleasure or irritation it was impossible to tell. He had told Miss Eckersley and his troublesome niece that he would do something very Greek to both of them if he heard the single click of a single camera shutter, and had sent both of them away with fleas in their ears. Now he turned on Mado.

'Who asked you to this party?' he said in his most aggressive way.

'I thought I'd give you a treat.'

Marides made a sign to his personal servant who was never more than a few feet away from him, and scowled. For a moment or so Mado thought he might well be thrown out.

'Go and fetch a bottle of the Glenlivet whisky,' he said, 'and bring Mr Mado a very large glass.'

Dr Petrov watched the scene in an uncomprehending way. The man whom Mado took to be his KGB keeper edged awkwardly nearer, and found himself at the receiving end of a typical Marides broadside.

'When I want my conversation with Dr Petrov or any other guest recorded by the KGB,' Marides said angrily in Russian, 'I'll ask for somebody competent to listen in. Now you go down to the lower terrace, my friend, and leave us alone.'

The keeper gave his host a nasty grey smile but moved quickly away looking astonished and shocked. Mado, who spoke and understood Russian as well as Marides, laughed out loud.

'I see you haven't changed,' he said in English. By this time he, Dr Petrov and Marides were alone.

'Itsa one sure thing you can rely on,' Marides said, dropping into his Greek-American accent, which only added to Dr Petrov's embarrassment. He was enjoying himself.

'And what is it this time, George? You asking me for a job?'

'When I work for you, Pan, I never get paid.'

389

'Huh! You got a nerve. You never did what you were told.'

'Well, we needn't go into all that now. I'm on the government payroll again. That was part of the deal—remember?—when we liquidated the Tarnham connection.'

Marides stared at him with his enigmatic hooded eyes. No one, not even Mado, could tell what he was thinking and Mado wondered inconsequentially if Marides ever played poker. Certainly this was no time to ask.

'You visiting? or whatsa the job?'

'I'm temporarily attached to the British Embassy. Commercial duties at the Trade Fair.'

'Ah! yes, the Trade Fair, God bless it!' Marides said in his normal brisk accent. He paused very briefly and then turned to Dr Petrov, saying in Russian: 'This is an old friend of mine, Mr George Mado, who is temporarily attached to the British Embassy.'

Dr Petrov made some non-committal noise. As Mado had talked so far only in English, Petrov did not know if he understood Russian. Mado thought it politic to declare his hand.

'Dr Petrov may not have heard of me,' he said in Russian, a remark which caused Marides to splutter quietly into his drink, 'but I have heard of Dr Petrov and the distinguished work he has done and is doing for the benefit of all peace-loving peoples.' It was a long time since Mado had used the good old tarnished jargon but it came, as always, trippingly to the tongue.

'Dr Petrov works on the seabed,' Marides said, a touch caustically. The remark was easy to cap and he had given Mado the sort of opening he could not normally resist. Tonight, however, he managed to control himself.

'That's what I mean,' Mado said in such a way that his sincerity could not possibly be doubted, 'I have heard other great experts declare that the seabed may well hold the key to the future of all of us and Dr Petrov, perhaps, knows more about this subject than anyone else in the world.'

He was beginning to regret that the word 'bed' had come into the conversation, and he saw that Marides was enjoying his discomfiture to the full.

'Of course,' said Marides, 'and that's why Dr Petrov is here tonight. There are more top experts per square inch in Athens at the moment and therefore, naturally, here at my house tonight, than anywhere else in the world.'

'What a pity they can't stay in Athens,' Mado suggested, innocently raising his eyebrows at Marides. 'It would be so good for Greece.'

'I think our friend feels that way,' Marides said in English to Mado. 'The seabed is not the only one he's interested in. . . .'

'Very nicely put, if I may say so.'

He saw another man approaching. The keeper had rustled up the big red chief. On a quick look from Marides, Mado bowed slightly to Dr Petrov and said in Russian: 'I sincerely hope we may meet again. I am always available at the British Embassy and perhaps, if you can spare the time, you would do me the honour of lunching with me before going back to Russia.'

'That would be a pleasure,' Dr Petrov said, suddenly grasping his hand, and then as the stranger came into earshot, he went on in a slightly louder voice, 'I am not an expert in the commercial possibilities of the work I do—I leave that to men such as Mr Marides. But perhaps there are Anglo-Soviet links of friendship we can explore under the proper conditions.'

Mado smiled briefly and slipped away. He had not met Voznitsky before but he recognized the Resident from his London briefing. As Mado navigated an oblique route towards the unblended malt whisky, he realized that Voznitsky was only too well aware of his own identity. At this stage Mado had no wish to endanger any possibility that might mature with charges of 'provocation', a standard protective move in the diplomatic game of chess.

'I am sorry to interrupt,' he heard Voznitsky say to Marides as he moved away, 'but there is a French oceanographer I would like Dr Petrov to meet. . . .'

He did not hear the Resident add: 'Now that's an interesting face! What a collection of talent you have here tonight o kyrios Marides!'

CHAPTER THREE

BEHIND THE POLISHED EXTERIOR and the cold, diplomatic smile, Voznitsky, in fact, was very angry indeed. What was the spy, Mado, doing in Athens? And at a party such as this? It added to the many imponderables of his current life and this inner insecurity, in turn, generated an anger.

What made it worse was that there was no one upon whom he could properly vent this emotion right away. He could scarcely find reason to upbraid Dr Petrov, whom privately he thought a pompous fool, for talking to his host—and coincidentally Mado. Certainly he had at once reduced the junior 'guide and companion' to a state of quivering pulp for allowing himself to be sent away from his sentry post in action. But what could you do with a western millionaire who only played along with the double talk and the protocol when it suited him?

Marides had correctly identified the guide and companion for what he was—a junior officer in the KGB. He had been extremely outspoken and rude. But if a host chooses to be rude at his own party, a guest has only one recourse—to be rude back, if necessary, and to leave. In the case of Voznitsky and the other Russians in the front line at this stinking capitalist party, both actions were out of the question. They had to stay on and suffer.

It was true that Dr Petrov was only under normal precautionary surveillance. He had never at any time in his long and distinguished career given the slightest sign of disloyalty to his country or to the creed of communism, whatever that might happen to be at the time of asking. He did what he was told in everything except his job. In that he was king.

Petrov, so far as was known, manifested a total lack of interest in politics. He had not even bothered to join the Party, despite being invited, since he held himself interested in only one thing—oceanography and its allied subjects—and you did not need to become a member of the communist party to specialize in that.

He had signed no protest letters. He had studiously rejected western propaganda however subtly it had been planted on him. Indeed his record was unblemished and showed that he had always behaved with exemplary submissiveness as a senior member of the animal farm. In his own job he was sharp, arrogant, aggressive and, Voznitsky suspected, oversure of himself. Except for Helen Stanopoulos, he behaved as a tyrant to his subordinates who reacted with hatred and fear, but such attitudes were encouraged by the authorities, always provided that an essential loyalty was openly and continuously given to the ideas and practices of Soviet communism.

However, there were patent dangers when a knowledgeable man such as Petrov had, for reasons of state, to be sent abroad for international study or work. Inevitably he found himself something of a hothouse flower in these rough western winds. Some hothouse—some flower, Voznitsky thought sardonically. A scientist could not be trusted like a prince of the KGB and now that he was deeply and hopelessly involved with his personal assistant, Voznitsky sensed that they were all approaching a possible crisis point. The sooner Dr Petrov went back to Russia—or at any rate left his territory—the better for all of them.

When he had steered Petrov into safer hands, Voznitsky looked around to see what his wife was up to. Decked out in her best outfit, she had had her hair done by the smartest hairdresser in Athens so that she looked like a bourgeois wedding cake, and although she was as disgusted as he was by this western opulence, she seemed to be having little trouble in taking in her fair ration of champagne and smoked salmon. He strolled across.

Irina was talking to that redheaded English woman reporter who had only recently arrived in Athens. So, having nothing else to do for the moment, and telling himself that it is a first principle of war to know your enemy, he contrived as pleasant a smile as possible and decided to ask his wife to make the introductions. As he arrived on the scene, Andrea was saying: 'You Russians put us to shame—you all speak English so well. Where did you learn it?'

'In school, of course,' Irina said gruffly, 'our English schools are excellent.'

In point of fact Irina did not speak English with any fluency and Andrea knew it. It was at once obvious to Voznitsky that she was merely being polite and he wondered what information the girl was trying to prise out of his wife. Certainly the English girl was very attractive. Moreover since he had seen her talking to the spy, Mado, no doubt she was a trained security agent as well. He studied her as they talked, wondering if she would be worth pursuing sexually and what else might be got out of it that way. He became uncomfortably aware that his wife was reading his thoughts and decided to move on. He would start a file on Andrea Eckersley in the morning.

Andrea watched him go with amusement. Although this was the first time she had worked for British security, Voznitsky fitted the briefing she had been given by Padstow and, in any case, she had read most of the current output of espionage books so that she knew the scene. It surprised her to see how true to life certain matters of which she had read were proving to be. It gave her a twinge of discomfort and, possibly because she had never done this sort of thing before, she wondered in passing why it was that someone like George Mado had become so cynical about it all. Or was this merely a pose?

Mado came up now, a glass of whisky in his hand.

'Hallo, Andrea,' he said, nodding at Mrs Voznitsky who nodded back and immediately moved away, 'I'm sorry you had a bad line on the photography.' And then when the Russian was out of earshot, 'You see the effect I have on our Soviet friends?'

'I shouldn't take it to heart. Or were you going to make a pass at her as well?'

'Not even in line of duty,' Mado said, taking it on the chin. 'Passes at Rooshians add to Confooshians.'

'And the Great Spy is not a Confucian?'

'Oh! God,' Mado said, 'that's the sort of joke I make.'

He took her by the arm and led her out on to the terrace. She was nice and firm to the touch and did not stiffen and resist as he had half expected.

'You're very saucy, aren't you, on your first assignment?'

Now she did suddenly stiffen and turned to look at him in surprise. He dropped her arm and, leaning against the balustrade, studied her anew. Then she relaxed.

'Oh! you mean in Greece? Yes, I suppose I am. But that's all front. I'm dead scared underneath . . . by a man like Marides, I mean.'

Something about her manner did not ring true. She had given herself away and alarm signals were sounding in Mado's mind. Instantly the whisky fumes cleared and he lit a cigarette, watching her keenly through the smoke.

'What other first assignment are you on?'

'Look, Mr Mado, I'm purely and simply a journalist.'

'Pure and simple you may be, but only a journalist—no.'

They looked at each other. She tried to appear puzzled but only succeeded in conveying the sudden fear she felt. The intimate twinge had now turned into a tingle of panic.

'Which of your Maoist friends have you orders to meet in Athens? You don't have to tell me, sweetie, because I shall surely find out, however good your cover story may be.'

He read her like a book but was surprised at the glint of relief which crossed her face. Perhaps Maoism was the wrong tack to take. There were others he could try and he now drew one more bow at a venture.

'That's why you sat next to Mark Tarnham in the aircraft, wasn't it? You were working with Ivan Karai.'

Now she was not being devious at all, but was clearly speaking the truth.

'If I knew anyone called Ivan Karai, I certainly wouldn't be working with him. I simply don't know what you're getting at.'

'No?'

'Honest.'

He believed her. So what could it be? He racked his brains in the pause which followed. It was then that the unlikeliest possibility of all danced up to the forefront of his mind.

'Do you by any chance know anyone called Padstow?' he asked, 'John Padstow?'

She looked stunned and it was lucky they were in a comparatively underlit part of the terrace.

'How did you guess?'

He gazed out across the bay at the moonlight sparkling on the dark Aegean. Soon the fireworks would begin—perhaps in every sense of the word. Then he gave a short humourless laugh.

'The bastard!' he said in a casual voice, 'the cheeky young bastard!'

Then, to her relief, he went on: 'All right, gorgeous, we never had this conversation. OK? You never gave a thing or yourself away and I'm slightly the worse for Mr Marides' excellent Scotch.'

She touched his hand spontaneously.

'Thank you. You're great.'

'And how!' Mado said sarcastically, but letting his hand enclose hers for a moment or so. She was a nice kid for all the up front pretence.

It seemed to Helen Stanopoulos that the whole world was watching her at this party in a hostile way. However intellectually she could rationalize the relationship between Smootchi and herself, however much she could persuade herself that neither of them really cared, that it was simply a passing thing, a private and temporary arrangement—she nevertheless found herself consumed by jealousy and guilt. Jealousy of her Sergei's wife, family and position in Moscow, and guilt because she could not display openly what every girl of her age longs to do.

She was a Greek to her marrow and had an almost biological need to draw attention to the big catch on the end of her line. Her contemporaries were adept at showing off and Helen was no exception. However, not only could she not demand the attention an attractive girl of her age requires, she was forced to creep about at her uncle's party as if she were nothing more than some drab secretary who had achieved a slightly ludicrous position with the United Nations.

Sophisticates would take her as a nonentity, a person of little consequence instead of someone who could proclaim from the housetops that she had been to bed with the greatest oceanographer in the world. It was humiliating and to this had been added the totally unexpected snub she had received from Uncle Pan when she had taken over that impossible woman journalist who had wanted photographs of the party.

She had further alienated Elissa—not that she cared about that —but her *philotimo*, her pride, had been hurt. She knew that all Greeks are thought to be fixers at heart, but a fixer has to deliver. She had only asked Uncle Pan this tiny favour on the crazy English woman's behalf, and he had shut her up with a snap. It was intolerable. She felt like crying and the champagne in which she tried to drown these feelings only depressed her the more.

Mado had been watching this almost visible train of thought working in the girl as the party wore on. So picking a moment when she was alone and disconsolate, he took a second bite at the cherry.

He came up beside her as she stared unseeing at the firework display.

'A pretty girl like you has no business crying on a night like this.'

'I'm not,' she retorted. 'And anyway it's none of your business. Who are you anyway?'

She looked at him with hot, angry eyes and then answered the question herself: 'Oh! you're the man from the British Embassy my uncle introduced earlier on.'

Everyone else at the party might know who George Mado was, Helen Stanopoulos neither knew nor cared.

'That's right,' Mado said, offering a cigarette and lighting it,

'I shouldn't be upset because your uncle bit your head off just now. He'll have forgotten it all.'

'Oh! I don't care about *that*,' she said, 'my uncle can go screw himself.'

'That's a big statement in dictator land.'

'I'm not interested in politics.'

'I dare say you aren't. Unfortunately Big Brother gets interested in *us*. You're too young and attractive to get hung up like this.'

'How do you know I'm hung up?'

'I don't. But there's obviously something wrong. I'm just trying to help. Really I am. I think you're a smashing girl.'

She glanced at him suspiciously before returning her gaze to the distance, lost in her own perspective.

'Are you making a pass at me?' she asked in a disinterested voice.

'No,' Mado said, 'for once I'm not, though I might get around to it later on. Like I said before, I'm just trying to help.'

For all the occasional vulgarity of approach, Mado was at heart a sympathetic and affectionate man. He had a warm heart and a magnetic hold over women. Although now there were other more sinister motives in his approach to Helen Stanopoulos, they were secondary—as they had been throughout his life—to a sincere urge to help, comfort and restore any woman in genuine distress. Women on whom he concentrated knew and appreciated this warmth. They responded instinctively by trusting him and very often later on by giving themselves to him.

Helen Stanopoulos was no exception to the early part of this process. Under his skilful questioning, which she did not even notice, she began to talk about herself, about her childhood in the Pindus mountains, about the effect on the family which Marides' enormous success had had, about her own brilliance at school so that with minimum help from her uncle, she too had left the village, gone to Athens and had started climbing the scholastic ladder to her present position.

'How many boy-friends did you leave by the wayside?'

'There was only one who really mattered.'

She was obviously caught in her memories and disinclined to go on, so Mado said: 'Why isn't he around any more?'

'Oh! he is. He failed his exams and he's now part of the drug scene . . . and of something else. He thinks I'm unbearably square because I never have been and never will be a dope head. I don't drop and I don't smoke—except straights.'

'You mean ordinary cigarettes?'

'Yes.'

There was a pause as both thought about what she had just been saying.

'But what Nikos really can't stand is ambition. He has no respect for the great things and the great people.'

'And you have?'

'Oh! yes,' she said, a little solemnly like a child, 'that's what brought Sergei and me together.'

Mado glanced over to where Dr Petrov was holding court. A paunchy, middle-aged man with a high opinion of himself—but a great person to her. . . . The Russians could prevent Petrov talking to anyone not of their choice, they could not apply the same technique to a Greek girl on Greek soil. But it surprised Mado, nevertheless, that they had left her so much alone. The fact that he and she were now having this conversation would be noted in all the KGB reports the following day. However, the conversation was taking place. He decided to press on to the heart of the matter.

'Does he want to marry you?' he asked.

'I think he might like to. But he already has a wife and family in Moscow.'

'I see.'

It was better not to ask any more detailed questions. She smiled at him wanly. The vibrations were highly sexual and Mado wondered in passing whether the great Dr Petrov could really handle the passion he sensed in the little Greek girl beside him. He felt sad for them both.

'You know a great deal about Dr Petrov's work, don't you?' Mado said, and then in order not to let her think he was about to question her on the matter, went on quickly: 'I need hardly remind you that when Dr Petrov goes back to Russia, you may be at some personal risk—however unpolitical you may think you are.'

She stared at him silently with her big dark eyes. She held her head very erect in an almost regal posture which showed off her slender neck. Mado thought grimly of all they could do to her pliant young body if they once decided to go to work.

'I don't think my uncle would let them harm me,' she said after a pause.

'I wouldn't rely on it, if I were you. And anyway he's off to Pekin in a couple of days.'

'I still think you're being alarmist.'

He shrugged his shoulders. She had never seen the inside of a Russian prison as he had.

'Well, don't eat any apples if you want to stay in the Garden of Eden.'

'Huh!' she said with a break in her voice so that he suddenly realized she was crying, 'is that where you think I am?'

He put his arm round her shoulders, half expecting to be shaken off but instead she snuggled into the shelter of his bulk. That would be in all the reports tomorrow as well.

'I don't know what I can do but you know where to get me.'

'No . . . oh! yes, you're at the British Embassy, aren't you?'

How could she possibly have worked at the United Nations and still be so innocent?

'And the name is Mado. George Mado. Just in case.'

'I'd like to die,' she said in a small voice, 'only I haven't the courage.'

'I shouldn't do that, if I were you. An attractive girl like you . . . oh! no, there must be better things in store.'

'Are there?' she said, the tears streaming down her cheeks, 'not from where I see the scene.'

He had the sudden feeling that the weepy might get out of hand. 'Don't let it go completely,' he said, 'I'm with you, sweetie, but this is no time for a complete breakdown. Where are you going after this?'

'Home. I share a flat in Vassilissis Sophia with two other girls.'

'I have a room in the Grande Bretagne which you can always use if you want.' And then, seeing that she misunderstood, went on: 'It's all right, doll, this is not a backhand way of getting you into bed with me. It's there if you need it. Now, put that hard, snappish look back on your face and circulate some more at this elegant party. You and I have been together long enough.'

She did as he told her, tidied her face and mopped away the tears, 'I'm sorry,' she said coldly, 'it won't happen again.'

'Oh! by the way,' he said as they separated, 'what is Nikos' other name? His surname?'

She gave him a look he could not at the time interpret, 'Nikolaides. Nikos Nikolaides. It's easy to remember.' She stopped dead in suspicion. 'Why?'

'You never know.'

'Leave him alone. He has enough trouble in his life.'

'You still care a little?'

'I hate him. And I hate his friends. But I don't want him hurt.'

'Now there's a fine macrobiotic statement,' Mado said as they moved away from each other, 'I even have friends who don't kill flies any more.'

It was four in the morning before Mado 'crashed out' in his bed at the Grande Bretagne and dawn was breaking just over an hour later when the telephone rang at his bedside.

'Mr Mado?'

'Yes.'

'British Embassy Duty Officer here. The Ambassador would like to see you in the Embassy right away. I'm sending a car to fetch you.'

'Right away!' Mado said sourly, 'that's all I need.'

The Ambassador had not given him a warm welcome when he had first arrived in Greece. Now His Excellency, who had himself been got up in the middle of the night, seemed to be coldly furious.

'I don't know what you were doing at the Marides' party last night, but we've now got a first-class crisis on our hands. Dr Petrov has asked for asylum—and for good measure the Russians have smacked in a charge of "provocation", naming you.'

'I don't think we need pay much attention to that.'

'Don't you, Mr Mado? I wish I could agree. Unfortunately you are not the Ambassador and I am. I knew things would flare up when I first heard you were being sent out here. It's always the same with you people. You're always stirring the pot.'

It was a bureaucratic attitude Mado had had to deal with before. All the Ambassador wanted was peace and quiet—and now patently he was not going to get it. Mado kept his temper and let the insulting words go over his head.

'Presumably the Greeks will grant Dr Petrov his asylum?'

'He hasn't asked the Greeks. He came here—to see you. He's in the military attaché's room.'

'Surely the defection of someone as eminent as Dr Petrov is welcome, isn't it? That's one of the reasons I was sent out here to Greece. Or does it mean too much trouble for the Embassy staff?'

'I find that remark offensive, Mr Mado.'

'Oh! dear me, Ambassador, I'm very sorry indeed.' Mado was as angry as the Ambassador and fully prepared to stand up to any pressure the latter might bring to bear on him. Maybe his pension would again be in jeopardy, but this was as much as he could take at that hour of the morning after all that had developed the previous night. The Ambassador was a small man in every sense of the word and Mado felt like giving him a good thump up the knickers.

'Moreover Dr Petrov has not defected,' the Ambassador continued. 'He has brought nothing with him and he states he is not prepared to reveal any secrets he may happen to know. He does not intend to betray his country in any way. He simply wants not to go back.'

'Bully for the West.'

'Mr Mado,' the Ambassador said curtly, 'I'm afraid your behaviour will have to be the subject of an inquiry. I'm not in the habit of being addressed in this manner, and in my own Embassy.'

'You asked me what I was doing at Marides' party. I was doing my job. As for my behaviour, Ambassador, or your opinion of it —I am nominally attached to your staff but I am not in any way subject to your control. And you know it. My brief, about which you were fully informed, is that I can call on you and the Embassy staff for any assistance I need. So let's get ourselves straight. I need and require your help now in this very delicate matter. If I don't get it, you may find your own conduct the subject of inquiry. And if you choose to regard that as blackmail or a threat —that's exactly what it is. I can make life much more difficult for you than you can for me.'

The Ambassador was appalled, his neck a turkey red. There goes the pension again, Mado said to himself, but there was no holding him now.

'Just stop behaving like a Maltese Prime Minister and let me get on with what I was sent here to do. Dr Petrov—and what may follow on—is more important to the West than your job or mine. I'll deal with him now and I shall have an urgent cypher to send as soon as I've seen him.'

He strode out of the room. The military attaché, a regular soldier for whom Mado had a considerable respect, was waiting in the corridor and together they went along to see Dr Petrov.

'I couldn't help hearing . . .' the military attaché began.

'Yes,' Mado cut in, 'but never mind that now. Who else has seen Petrov?'

'Except for the duty officer, only myself.'

'Do you speak Russian?'

'I'm studying it but I haven't yet passed my exam. So I said as little as possible.'

'Good.'

Dr Petrov was in a high state of anxiety. As soon as Mado entered the room, he all but ran across and clasped Mado's right hand with both of his.

He was shaking with fear and there was almost no trace of the arrogant, world-famous Russian scientist.

'I see you took me at my word,' Mado said in Russian. 'Sit down, Dr Petrov, and we'll have a talk.'

'I am afraid for Helen.'

'Yes,' Mado said briskly, 'you have reason to be. Did she know you were going to defect?'

'I have not defected. I have only asked for asylum.'

'We'll deal with that in a moment. Did she know what you were going to do?'

'No.'

'Then have you got her address here in Athens?'

'Of course.'

'Write it down and say—you use French to each other, don't you? Say in French "Please obey any instructions the bearer of this note may give you" and sign it. Better sign it Smootchi—then she'll know it's authentic.'

Dr Petrov looked at him in amazement.

'You know all that?'

Mado stared at him coldly. The whisky-drinking, easy-going man of the previous night had changed completely and he calculated that this alone was adding to Dr Petrov's confusion. The force of personality facing the great oceanographer was considerable.

'Come along, Dr Petrov. We haven't much time. In fact it's probably too late already.'

While Petrov was writing out a shaky message in French, Mado tried to decide on the best course of action to adopt. Should he go himself, or send the military attaché? Or should he risk using Andrea Eckersley? If he or the military attaché with their diplomatic immunity were seen trying to nobble Helen Stanopoulos, there would be further charges of provocation and this would give the Greek security forces any justification they felt they needed to get into the act. From then on the future was unpredictable. He picked up the phone and asked for the Hotel Grande Bretagne.

'Miss Eckersley, please.'

He could hear the phone ringing but there was no reply. Either Andrea was in a deep sleep, which was understandable, or she was not in her room—which was also understandable. He put down the phone and turned to the military attaché.

'I think you'd better cope with this as discreetly as you can.'

He took the little note Petrov had written in execrable French and passed it across.

'Bring her here if you can without attracting attention. I'll have a short, sharp session with the brave Doctor.'

Now everything began to happen at once. That same morning Padstow in London had just got into his extremely private eyrie, which could be reached from the Cabinet offices without going out into Whitehall, when he was handed one of the shortest Top Secret and Most Immediate cyphers he had ever received in his life. It simply said 'Help!' and was signed Mado. Within half an hour Padstow was en route to Athens but not before the Foreign Office had caught him with an equally urgent dispatch from H.M. Ambassador in Athens: 'Request immediate recall Mado plus cancellation diplomatic privilege. Necessary withdraw recognition. Report follows.'

'I'll see the Foreign Secretary,' his Chief said, 'but it may already have got out of hand.'

'Yes sir,' Padstow said, visualizing Mado's pug-like face, 'I'm very much afraid it has.'

In Athens, Voznitsky had not been to bed all night. He and Irina had just returned to the block of flats, known to Western diplomats as the Red Compound, where those Russian diplomats who did not live in the Embassy itself were housed, when he was informed that Dr Petrov had given his guide and companion the slip by the simple expedient of asking him to go back for a brief-case he had left in Marides' house and then driving off in the car himself. A little later the man who watched the British Embassy for them had reported that Dr Petrov had driven up, left the car and gone inside. From then on the die was cast. Voznitsky got his Ambassador to put in an immediate protest of provocation in the accepted form, accusing Mado, and he had then set about the urgent task of securing or in some way of neutralizing Helen Stanopoulos. This was not quite as easy as it looked.

Whatever the world thinks of the present regime in Greece, the Colonels' control of the country is absolute. Things work and the life, in outward appearance at least, is stable. As in any dictatorship, such stability depends upon a well-paid network of informers and a hypersensitive fear of the police. From the point of view of the KGB Greece is a very different bowl of bortsch from sloppy old England where anything goes and diplomats are assumed still to be gentlemen, albeit with foreign accents, who abide by the rules—at any rate until the abuses become so flagrant that a wholesale removal job becomes imperative. In Greece any-thing goes nowhere in this respect. Voznitsky, therefore, found it very difficult to operate in a clandestine way outside the strict bounds of protocol.

Later that morning the Russian Ambassador, accompanied by Voznitsky, called on the Greek Minister for Foreign Affairs who was regrettably indisposed, and they were then seen by a high official who turned out to be none other than Christos Marides, the millionaire's only son by his first wife. Christos, dark, good-looking and vicious, had been noted in KGB files as someone to be very careful about but he was also polite to the point of suavity and both cool and competent.

'I will certainly see that what you have told me, Ambassador, is passed on at once to the appropriate quarters but I must observe that Dr Petrov's secretary does happen to be a Greek subject working in Greece and therefore entirely free to do as she chooses. Greece, I need hardly remind you, is a democracy and the liberty of the subject remains absolute under the law. What-ever arrangements Dr Petrov may or may not have had with his secretary, whatever papers she takes or does not take home with her when she goes back to her flat at night are no concern of the Greek government unless a charge of theft is to be preferred and presumably such a charge, if there are grounds for it, would originate with the United Nations and be dealt with by the police.'

'I consider your attitude unco-operative,' the Ambassador said.

A bland smile spread gently over the Greek's face. He was very much his father's son, Voznitsky thought, and determined there and then that he would have to tackle Marides himself.

'I'm so sorry you feel that way, Ambassador. I am only trying to help.'

'Can you at least inform us of the whereabouts of Miss Stanopoulos?'

'Ah!' said Christos Marides, studying his well-manicured nails, 'now that would be a matter for the Missing Persons Bureau and inquiries can only be made there by a relative. . . .'

From the way he fell silent, the Ambassador and Voznitsky thought he might perhaps have something else to suggest but after a pause nothing further appeared to be forthcoming.

'Very well,' the Ambassador said, getting up. 'I shall report to my government the unfriendly attitude of the Greek authorities in this small matter of co-operation for which we are asking.'

Christos Marides showed them politely to the door and then on and out into the hall: 'And I shall report to my government the great pleasure it has been to receive your visit this morning and to assist you to the full limit of the regulations. Your Excellency is no doubt aware of the fairly lengthy list of matters in Moscow in which our government has long been seeking assistance. If by chance the list has been mislaid, I will be most pleased to furnish you with a copy. Thank you so much for your call, Ambassador, and you, Colonel Voznitsky . . . I look forward to meeting you again socially as we did last night at my father's party, which I hope you enjoyed.'

With a little smile on his lips, he watched them get into their car and drive off. Then returning to his office, he told his secretary to get his father on the private line.

It would have made no difference had Christos Marides chosen to be more helpful. Helen Stanopoulos had disappeared. At least she had gone from the flat which she shared with two other secretaries in Queen Sophia Street, as the British military attaché had discovered to his dismay.

'I'm so sorry, Major Schofield,' said the shiny self-appreciative Greek security officer who met him at the door, 'but Miss Stanopoulos is no longer here.'

He spoke excellent English. Since he also knew the British military attaché's name, Schofield took the Greek security presence there to be no accident. The next remark, however, startled him: 'Indeed, we are looking for Miss Stanopoulos ourselves. Did you wish to see her for any official Embassy reason?'

'No,' Schofield said, quickly avoiding that particular trap, 'it was purely private.'

'At seven in the morning, Major? How delightfully eccentric! But then you diplomats with your diplomatic immunity can do as you please, can you not?'

The studied sarcasm was almost too much for Schofield to bear. His work naturally brought him into contact with members of the Greek police and he detested each and every one he met.

'That is right,' he said with equally studied politeness, 'we need answer no questions and we cannot be arrested—even for the crime of visiting a person's flat at seven in the morning.'

With a curt nod, he turned on his heels and walked down the stairs to his car. As he got in, he noticed two other cars waiting nearby filled with thick-looking men in dark glasses, very obviously trying to give the impression that they were there by accident. Those are not your friendly neighbourhood police in their Panda cars, Schofield said to himself, thinking ruefully of the quiet Surrey town in which he lived in England, those are the gentlemen from Boubolina Street, fresh from their midnight tortures. Mentally he spat in their faces as he passed.

CHAPTER FOUR

'WELL, WHERE IS SHE THEN?' Marides snapped down the phone to his son, 'surely your people know?'

'We shall find her, of course,' Christos said at the other end, 'but for the moment she's simply disappeared.'

'Then the longer she stays disappeared, the better for all of us —at any rate until Dr Petrov is out of the way.'

'I'll let you know as soon as we get a line on it.'

Marides put down the phone and glared at Elissa.

'First your son by Tarnham: now this. I shall never get away to Pekin.'

'I suppose it's my fault in some extraordinary way,' Elissa said, pouring oil on the flames. 'Anyway she's always been exceptionally rude to me, that girl. So far as I am concerned, she can stay away.'

'Her father would wring her neck and now, maybe, I'll do it for him. This is where I need Mournier.'

He began walking up and down in a rage. Mournier had been his lieutenant but had met a violent end when the Tarnham connection had been liquidated.

'Thank God you haven't got Mournier. Or do you enjoy having people shot?'

'It's always better to shoot first,' Marides said, and meant it. It appalled Elissa that she had married someone who looked on the taking of life as casually as that. But whenever she had had it out with him, Marides had always observed that she would never understand the Greeks. On that basis she did not care if she did.

'What are you doing about Mark? Or shall I go to the British Embassy after all?'

'I told Voznitsky last night. He said it would be arranged.'

'Perhaps they'll expect something from you—over Petrov and Helen.'

'What can I give them? Helen's disappeared and Petrov's at the British Embassy.'

'Is that why Mado was here?'

'It wouldn't surprise me. Or they may be after a bigger fish.'

'Who?'

'You'll have to work that one out for yourself,' Marides said, 'last time it was you and me.'

She stared thoughtfully at the hard little man she had married, the embodiment of the tough compact fighter who never gave up and yet who had surprised her so often with his innate tenderness and a sudden capacity for gentleness. He was not what the English call a 'nice' man, but he had once told her with an understanding smile that she was civilizing him.

407

'But I'll put your money in trust,' he added, 'before the process goes too far. Otherwise you might find yourself a pauper.'

He was unique and she was constantly astonished at how much she enjoyed him. 'Don't involve yourself too deeply,' she said, 'I've had enough violence in my life.'

He looked at her incredulously.

'You ask me to get your son back from the Russians. You think they do things for love? Chivalry—that's out in 1917. Gentleness they never had. Huh!' he snorted contemptuously, 'you English! The Russians understand only two things—intrigue and force. You think you can do business with them on any other basis?'

'All right, Pan, spare me the lecture. I don't want you in danger, that's all.'

'You English!' he said, but there was a twinkle in his eye, 'you want the sun to rise in the west.'

'It does,' Elissa said.

Padstow and one of his top interrogators reached Athens in the afternoon and went straight to the Embassy.

'The Russians have demanded access,' Mado said, when the interrogator and Schofield had gone off together to see Petrov.

'Well, that's standard practice.'

'And the great oceanographer says he doesn't intend to talk.'

'Perhaps he will when he settles down.'

'And he wants his Helen.'

'Well, it doesn't look as though he's going to get her.'

Padstow considered the situation for a moment or so.

'What's the next move?'

'I've asked for a frigate from Cyprus—by invitation of the Greeks, of course, on ordinary NATO business. Just in case we have to get him out of Greece in a hurry. I've no idea how long the Greeks will play ball. At present they're turning a blind eye, or we should have heard all about it by now. I imagine it suits them to string it along in that way whilst the Trade Fair is on. But you never know with the Greeks, especially if the CIA gets into the act. Also once the Press latch on to it, anything can happen. By the way, George, the Ambassador wants you removed. You've got a hornet's nest buzzing round your head in Whitehall. How did you manage so much in so short a time?'

Mado told him what had happened.

'You'd better try an apology,' Padstow said, 'and I'll tell His Excellency you'll be disciplined when you get back to England.'

'I'll complain to the Union,' Mado said, but did as Padstow suggested so that the position was 'technically' adjusted.

'I'd like to recommend that Ambassador for another posting,' Mado commented when it was over, 'somewhere down in the Antarctic would do—don't we have an Embassy near Cape Horn?'

Padstow smiled but there was no stopping George Mado once he had started.

'Now I have one for you, Mr Padstow,' he went on, 'what's all this about Andrea Eckersley? Why didn't you let me in on that?'

Padstow laughed. 'I wanted to see how long it would take you to find out. I see the arthritis hasn't set in.'

'Great! Any other little test you'd like me to pass? Perhaps in return you can tell me if she's on some other assignment I don't know about.'

'Why?'

'Because your glamorous Miss Eckersley also seems to have disappeared. The Grande Bretagne say she never came back last night.'

Padstow thought about it for a moment or two, but gave nothing away. He did not seem to Mado to be unduly disturbed.

'With that coloured hair,' he said, 'I don't think she'll be lost for long. Helen Stanopoulos is a much more serious problem.'

Mado wondered what he was holding back. Perhaps nothing at all. But still. . . .

'Man, like it looks you don't trust good old reliable Mado in the way you once did.'

'No, George, it isn't that. Only until things clarify a little, Rule No. 1 applies and the less you know of the whole the better.'

'Thanks,' Mado said grimly, 'you mean they might nobble me in spite of what I think you called "my protective notoriety" in London?'

But Padstow turned the subject: 'I think you ought to take a trip out to Vouliagmeni and see how the Marides household is bearing up.'

Almost as soon as he left the Embassy, Mado knew he was being trailed. A small nondescript Volkswagen started up with a man and a girl in it and kept two cars behind the hired Simca Mado drove himself. He had been at the game so long, he could have shaken off his watchers without any difficulty at all but now he was curious.

He therefore drove as if he had noticed nothing out of the ordinary and made his way to Constitution Square, parked the car and then walked into the Grande Bretagne Hotel without looking back. Once inside the hotel he collected the key of his room and discovered that the man had followed him in but showed no signs of continuing on to the lift with him.

He checked Andrea Eckersley's room, still with negative results. But she was Padstow's headache now—and good luck with it, he thought. He had expected to be followed to his room or at least to receive a phone call. But nothing happened. He presumed his watcher was still down below and although he could easily have got out of the hotel by the service staircase, he decided to discover what it was all about and went down again to the hall, pausing until he was quite sure he had been seen and then continuing on into the bar. The man followed and when Mado ordered a Scotch, came up beside him and said to the barman in Greek, 'Make it two doubles.'

'All right,' Mado said, 'who are you and what's it all about?'

'Don't you remember last night?' the man said in passable English.

'I don't think we've met. I have a fairly clear idea of everyone I talked to at the party. I don't recall talking to you.'

'In spite of all that Glenlivet you drank?'

The hard cynical look came back to Mando's face.

'No more guessing games, sport. I have a busy day. What's your thing?'

'Let's say I'm one of the staff at Vouliagmeni, Mr Mado. I want to offer you a deal.'

The man's vague familiarity came into clear focus when Mado visualized him in a white waiter's jacket and black bow tie. This one could have been one of the many who had replenished his glass from time to time through that long, long evening.

'Okay,' Mado said, 'that's what I'm here for. To make friends and influence people.'

'We are holding Helen Stanopoulos and we think you might be interested in having her back.'

'Who's we?'

'The people I work with.'

'Obviously, but who are you?'

'Let's say we're just another band of urban guerrillas.'

'You're very strong on the "Let's say" bit. Let's say who exactly you are.'

But the man only shook his head and smiled.

'Very well. Whose side are you on?'

'Our own.'

'Fair enough. Ask a silly question . . . okay, so what's the proposition?'

'We'll trade you Helen Stanopoulos for six of our men in prison.'

'Here in Greece?'

'Here in Greece.'

'You evidently know a lot about me,' Mado said, 'so you must be aware that I haven't a hope in hell of honouring such an agreement even if I made it.'

'You'll honour it, Mr Mado, because as a precautionary measure our London friends will take your wife Anna and your child into "protective custody". Do you get my point?'

Mado had to admire the skill with which this approach had been made.

Anna's instinct had been right. He should never have come to Greece.

'I have no powers of persuasion over the regime here,' Mado said, 'and you know it. You're asking me the impossible.'

'Nothing is impossible if you decide to try.'

'And what if I fail?'

'Then you may never see your wife and child again.'

It was incredible—totally incredible—and yet on this early evening of a hot summer's day in Athens, Mado had no option but to believe it. The bar was beginning to fill up. It would not be too difficult to escape. Mado considered simply walking away from the man and out into Constitution Square. Then he glanced at him again. The man was smiling in the sly, knowing way of the city Greek. His right hand was in his pocket which bulged in an all too familiar way. The man saw that he understood and shook his head.

'You were thinking of walking out or perhaps of suggesting we

411

go to the nearest police station, Mr Mado? You would never make it with a hole through your genitals.'

'Hm!' Mado said, 'I think we'd better have another drink.'

'Endax,' the man said, 'but don't try any tricks, will you? I have something else to show you as well.'

With the speed of a conjuror, he produced from his breast pocket with his other hand the sinister-looking identity card of the Greek state security police.

It seemed to be game and set.

'Of course you'll have to make up you own mind, Mr Mado, on how much of this is true and how much is false. I may really be an officer in the Greek police or I may have stolen or forged the card. I may be one of Mr Marides' staff or perhaps I was simply hired for the night in view of the size of the party. There are a lot of things you will have to take on trust.'

'You wouldn't shoot a man with diplomatic immunity in a public bar in the centre of Athens.'

'How do you know? You're not in England now. I don't think you'll risk it, Mr Mado. You'd find out too late. The gun I have in my pocket is a very quiet one. Suitable for hijackers in aircraft, low velocity—get the point? All I need to do is knock over this jug and glasses on the bar as a diversion, and no one will hear the shot. As you know, a bullet in the crutch would be very painful and could possibly be fatal. There is no diplomatic immunity which would protect you against that.'

'All right,' Mado said, 'you needn't labour the point. But how do I know you've got Helen Stanopoulos?'

'What ring was she wearing last night?'

'A silver one shaped like a serpent.'

The man put away the identity card and produced the ring from his left pocket.

'And in case you don't believe me about your wife and child in London, perhaps this will convince you.'

Away went the ring and out of his breast pocket came a slim diary which he flicked open with one hand, his right hand all the time kept steady on what Mado presumed to be the gun.

'You live at 54 Carnegie Street, SW19, and your wife buys her groceries at . . .'

'All right, all right,' Mado said, 'what do you want me to do?'

'There is only one person who can ask the authorities to release the people we want and that is Mr Panayotis Marides. You will put it to him. Here is the list.'

Once again his left hand went into his pocket and produced a typewritten list of six names which he handed to Mado.

'He'd laugh in my face.'

'Helen Stanopoulos is his niece. In Greece family connections are very important indeed.'

'All right,' Mado said, 'I was on my way to see him anyway.'

'Don't try and warn your wife in London. It will only make things happen which you might not like.'

'Do I have your word that she and the child will not be touched if I pull off this thing?'

For the first time the man looked surprised.

'You'd value my word of honour?'

'I haven't much option, have I? But in point of fact, yes.'

'You have my word of honour, Mr Mado.'

Mado finished his drink and prepared to pay but his companion made a sign to the barman and no bill was forthcoming.

'A name might help—and where you want to meet me again.'

'Don't worry about that. We'll keep in touch with you. The name is Nikos.'

'Nikolaides?'

The man raised his eyebrows and paused for a moment before answering, 'So Helen told you all that too?'

Mado nodded. 'You're not quite the man I expected.'

'I don't think Helen is quite the girl you think she is. But then she's a Marides.'

'Did she know you were there last night?'

Mado worked back in his mind to the scene on the terrace when she had filled him in about her life. He realized that she was more devious than her innocence suggested, but she had spun him that yarn about the boy-friend who had fallen by the wayside, the drug scene bit, the 'I don't want him hurt' cry from the heart—and if all the time Nikos Nikolaides had been to her knowledge but a few feet away, then she must also be a very good actress, and he would have to think it out all over again.

So he was relieved when Nikolaides said: 'No, she did not know I was there. She didn't expect me to be there and I kept out of her way. In a house that size and with the number of people at that party, it was not too difficult a task.'

'You simply picked her up on the way home?'

'Endax,' Nikolaides said, 'and she was very surprised and distressed. However, we are looking after her well. She will survive.'

'Did you also pick up Miss Andrea Eckersley—the red-haired English journalist?'

But Nikos Nikolaides merely smiled: 'I think you had better be on your way, Mr Mado. Panayotis Marides is still trying to get off to Pekin.'

Mado was not the only man to try for a private talk with Marides that day. Voznitsky, too, wanted urgently to see his host of the night before and when he was unable to fix up an appointment on the telephone, decided to go out to Vouliagmeni himself. He had good reason for this. Dr Petrov's defection could cost him his career. Without warning he had been plunged into the most serious and urgent crisis of his life. Others might harbour illusions about the consequences of a defection. Voznitsky had none. He and he alone would be blamed.

He had had no sleep. The Embassy seemed to him an antheap on which boiling water had just been poured and not the least of his problems would be to disguise as best he could the utter panic he felt. Moreover he was not at all sure of the help he could ask of Marides nor of what he would receive. His excuse for the meeting, however, was that he had heard from Moscow that Mark Tarnham was on his way to Athens accompanied by Ivan Karai. Voznitsky knew what that would mean. Karai would have full investigational powers, every single person and every file in the Embassy would be sifted from top to bottom and he, Voznitsky, would shortly afterwards be heading back to Russia in disgrace.

Yet there was still a chance. Conceivably the British might yield up their unexpected visitor, provided the Greek authorities would bring some pressure to bear. If only access to Petrov could be obtained, Voznitsky felt reasonably sure he could talk him into returning to the fold under promise of a free pardon and no reprisals.

Voznitsky knew only too well the real value of such promises but this would not prevent him offering Petrov the Kremlin itself on a freehold basis provided only that he would agree to come back. The other and equally urgent task was to find and neutralize Helen Stanopoulos. That girl, he suspected, had experience almost as extensive and valuable to the enemy as Dr Petrov himself. In any case it would be necessary to interrogate her and to find out the extent of her knowledge before Voznitsky could have any hope of clearing his own yard-arm.

Voznitsky was not a happy man. Dedicated and indoctrinated as he had been since boyhood, he had now had enough experience of life in capitalist countries to make comparisons. He had also acquired a taste for some of the goodies which the Western way of life provided. This extended well beyond purely material things. In an appalling moment of self-analysis, Voznitsky had realized that the quality of person he had come to know and like was altogether superior in the enemy world.

He was a lonely man. Well, he told himself, there were a lot of lonely men in Russia, who felt as he did, not a few of them in labour camps. Perhaps this very private sense of longing could be explained away as a lingering end product of his aristocratic forbears about which only he now knew.

Whatever the reason—and the exact cause had no importance— Voznitsky had discovered that there were people in the West who, in their own snobbish-decadent phrase, 'talked the same language'. He had met men and women who understood. Friendship had been offered in a way it would never have been in Russia and Voznitsky had once been crying drunk for three days after facing the inescapable fact that to accept such freely given friendship and understanding was—or would very soon be— the end of his belief in communism and the Russian way of life. Once that step was taken there could be no going back.

Irina did not share the same instincts and ideas. She was not a bad person—even allowing for the spiritually destructive work which the KGB forced her to do—but she thought, felt and lived as if this were the only life she had ever or would ever experience and that the only valid truths were those which were self-evidently physical or could be scientifically proved in a material-mental sense. So far as he could tell, she was totally undisturbed by things of the spirit. She had been taught that God was a bourgeois invention and had been used throughout the ages to keep the toiling masses in slavery—or at best to palliate their dreadful living conditions.

Nothing in her experience had persuaded her otherwise. The world as you saw it, and there was nothing else. When younger she had had a certain animal kindness and she had proved herself a good and loving mother. He was fond of her and he shared her genuine distress at being forced to leave their beloved Boris behind in Moscow. She had a heart.

But heart or no heart, survival was what mattered in Russia. He had no illusions about what she would do if he were to fall from grace. She would cut herself free. She would save herself and Boris, if need be, by denouncing 'her Alexei'. He did not blame her for this. That is how it was and he would do exactly the same. Or would he? As he drove out of the Marides estate, a foretaste of self-sacrifice seemed to present itself for consideration. But he put this quickly away from his thoughts. The fall was not yet certain. Indeed it might never happen at all.

Marides was not available when he arrived but Elissa had him shown in. He did not know whether to take this as accidental or intentional. Marides might well have been there and merely have had other things to do, or be watching them from another room. Elissa received him in the great drawing-room of the house where she had been writing letters at the sort of escritoire which would have been in a museum in Russia. There was an air of royalty in the room which Voznitsky distrusted and yet found fascinating. How was this impression achieved? Where was the palpable fear you felt in the socialist countries? No Russian woman that he knew could look so cool and distinguished, not only blending into but enhancing the background against which she had been set.

'I'm afraid my husband is in Crete, Mr Voznitsky.'

This was a blow and despite his training, Alexei could not prevent a trace of it showing.

'When will he be back?'

'This evening, I hope. Perhaps I can help you instead?'

There was no warmth in her voice. He could not tell if she knew his real job or was merely greeting him as the assistant commercial attaché she had previously met. In any case her dislike was apparent. She looked magnificent, he thought, for a woman of forty. She had the good bones and the breeding of an aristocrat. The firm mouth, the tawny hair—not as red as that girl reporter's —but a sort of clear chestnut, the fine level teeth, the freckled skin and the grey-green eyes—no wonder Marides had undergone all that he had done to get her as his wife, whilst the Tarnham connection was being resolved. Alexei had met her first husband, the late Paul Tarnham, a couple of times. Now that he looked at Elissa, he could not understand how Tarnham could possibly have abandoned such a woman—even for the greater glory of communism.

'Please,' he faltered, 'it's very difficult. I do not really know.'

This was true. He did not know—and had no means of finding out what he needed to know.

'Why don't you sit down, Mr Voznitsky? Would you care for a drink?'

'I think I drank quite enough in your house last night. I hope you received the flowers this morning. It was a wonderful party.'

'Thank you,' Elissa said, 'that was very polite of you.'

In point of fact she had no idea whether he or anyone else had sent flowers that day. Nor did she give it a thought. The social secretary took care of that. This was just as well since, in the hurly-burly of Petrov's defection, the Ambassador had forgotten to order the flowers and Voznitsky had had other things to do so had not checked up. He found her cold inspection of himself embarrassing and this grew worse when she played one of his own trump cards so that the hand he was hoping to use became even further weakened.

'When is my son arriving in Athens, Mr Voznitsky? And why was he abducted to Moscow?'

This was a tricky question. It was a matter Alexei had intended to dodge but it had been sprung on him before he was ready.

'He should be here by midday tomorrow. I'm afraid I don't know what you mean by "abducted". Your son was invited to spend a few days in Moscow as an honoured guest and as a tribute to his late father.'

The picture he had formed of the great lady received a partial obliteration in what she said next. It also made an appropriate answer extremely difficult.

'Don't give me that shit, Mr Voznitsky,' Elissa said, every word steeped in acid, 'I know perfectly well what happened, and so do you.' She paused and stared him straight in the eyes, 'Why?'

He glared back at her, trying as hard as he could to find the right thing to say. But the humanity in both of them got in the way. Moreover there was a trace of irony in her eyes which suggested that it did not matter very much what he said—the facts would remain as they were.

'I can't tell you,' he said.

'You mean you can't make it up quickly enough.'

'If you like.'

'Well, thank God, you're human at least.'

And then Alexei Voznitsky, Colonel First Grade in the KGB Order of Lenin, Star of This, That and the Other, Chief Gauleiter of the Russian sphere of influence in Greece, said something he would never have believed possible, something of which he would have been incapable until the present disastrous situation had broken over his head.

'I don't know what to do,' he said with a grim set to his mouth, 'I'm lost—lost in the great forest.'

'Good heavens!' Elissa said and rang the bell, 'pull yourself together, Colonel.' And then when a servant answered the bell, 'Bring two large Scotch on the rocks.'

When the servant had gone, Elissa said: 'In all my experience of dealing with you people, I've never had such a statement made to me—never once. What were you hoping my husband would do for you?'

'I need to see Dr Petrov. He has lost his head.'

'And you're intelligent enough to know you're going to lose yours.'

'It's possible. It's not likely—but possible. It is scarcely my fault.'

'That's the last thing that matters. You'll be blamed.'

'Not if I can get him back.'

He found himself being studied attentively again by those cool, questioning eyes.

'How can you make yourself do such a job?' she asked, 'a sensitive, intelligent man like yourself?'

He managed to achieve a tiny smile. He was a strong, good-looking, powerful man with unwavering eyes, who had trained himself to act as if everything he said was sincere. He was a past master in the ultimate swindle but the fact that he knew this in his being made his next remark all but grotesque.

'It's my karma,' he said.

She laughed outright but there was very little jollity in it.

'Then there's no hope at all. A Colonel in the KGB who thinks he has karma . . .'

The drinks were brought in, together with a slip of paper for

418

Elissa. She looked at this and then said to the servant: 'Ask him to wait.'

When the servant had gone, Voznitsky said: 'If you reveal anything of what I've just said, I'll deny every word.'

'And who do you think will care? Why throw yourself on my mercy in this crude and clumsy way? You can't honestly imagine I'm going to help? I've seen what it's like in your communist paradise. I know. Surely by now your people must have appreciated that I'm not and never have been on your side? I loathe and detest what you do and everything you stand for.'

'That is not our information,' Voznitsky said with a stony face. Then, after a pause: 'But, please, I was only talking to you as one human being to another.'

'You do presume, Colonel, don't you?' She mimicked him, 'One human being to another indeed! What sort of treatment would you be handing out if our roles were reversed? You know the answer very well indeed. There would be no mercy from you. Then why presume on me? When have *you* ever helped anyone in *your* life?'

'That is only known to myself and God.'

'Then God help you now,' Elissa said curtly and rang the bell, 'because I doubt very much if anyone else is going to.'

He thought she was asking him to leave when the servant appeared but instead a further shock was in store.

'Ask Mr Mado to come in now,' Elissa said, and then when the servant had gone, 'you may well stiffen up, Colonel, Mr Mado knows what the inside of the Lubyanka is like; he may be able to give you a wrinkle or two on the way to behave.'

'I do not wish to meet the spy Mado.'

'Then you are at liberty to go,' Elissa said, getting to her feet. 'You asked yourself here. You have only to go through that door. I will tell my husband of your visit and if you will write down what you would like him to do, I will see that he considers your request. In the meantime I await the safe arrival of my son, Mark, for which we hold you totally responsible as the senior KGB officer here in Greece. And I warn you, Colonel—should Mark's arrival be delayed, my husband will make things even hotter for you than they are at present. He has a certain power with your people, as I think you know. He won't hesitate to use it.'

The door opened and George Mado was ushered in.

419

CHAPTER FIVE

MADO PAUSED for a second or two as the door closed behind him.

With his mind full of what had just happened at the Grande Bretagne, worried about Anna and the child and trying to contrive how he could best get Marides to do as he wanted, he had certainly not expected to find Voznitsky there. He glanced first at Elissa and then at the Russian. He needed to work very fast indeed and for a moment or so could think of nothing to say. Then Elissa came to his rescue.

'I don't know if you met Mr Voznitsky last night, Mr Mado?' She waved a vague introduction with her right hand.

'How do you do, Colonel?' Mado said, seizing the initiative. 'No, we didn't meet last night. We simply admired each other from a distance.'

Neither he nor Voznitsky offered to shake hands. Voznitsky conceded him the briefest of nods, at which Mado smiled. Now that Mado had taken the advantage of speaking first, he pressed on ahead.

'Although I have the impression—I can't think why—that the Colonel doesn't think very highly of me. Odd, isn't it? The more so since I have a high regard for him.'

'Are you trying to provoke me, Mr Mado?'

'Here we go again,' Mado said with a contemptuous smile. 'Provocation! It's a great word. You know . . .' he switched to Elissa, 'there are some days when you can't remark on the sun shining in the sky without a charge of provocation from the Russian Embassy. No, Colonel, why should I bother to provoke you? You have enough troubles of your own and no doubt that's why you're here.' He turned again to Elissa, 'I gather Pan is in Crete?'

'Yes,' Elissa said, 'but I expect him back at any moment. As you know, he's trying to get away to Pekin.'

'Please,' said Voznitsky, 'I think I will return when Mr Marides has come back.'

'Why not wait a little longer, Colonel,' Elissa said with an imperious undertone in the voice, 'now that I've brought you and Mr Mado together, I'm sure you have mutual interests you might care to discuss.'

'I don't think so,' Voznitsky said. He appeared to be very cold and correct, but from Mado's previous experience of the KGB and the terror structure on which it is run, he had no doubt the Russian was in a fine old tiz underneath.

'Come, come, Colonel,' Mado said, 'we are on neutral ground. Neither Mrs Tarnham—I beg your pardon, Mrs Marides—nor I are trying to trap you in any way.'

He looked Voznitsky straight in the eyes: 'I won't say we could ever be friends. However, there might be the possibility of a deal.'

'You have great impudence, Mr Mado.'

'We have Dr Petrov.'

'I don't know what you're talking about.'

This was too much even for Elissa: 'Don't be ridiculous, Colonel. Or I shall talk about karma. Mr Mado is being strictly accurate when he says there may be the possibility of a deal.'

'Depending, of course, on what the Colonel has to offer,' Mado put in.

All this time the two men studied each other completely unemotionally as if they were poker players assessing the odds.

'I have no plenipotentiary powers,' Voznitsky said in the end, 'and I do not mean to be rude,' he went on in a slightly more gentle voice, 'but I do not suppose Mr Mado has either.'

'Correct. But we're talking tactics, not strategy, Colonel. I'm sure we understand each other behind it all—the realities of our respective situations, if you like. Equally I have no doubt that both of us have the power to honour any local arrangements we may agree.'

Voznitsky said nothing. He had never been in a comparable situation before. Moreover he was finding it difficult to maintain his apparent contempt for the spy, Mado. To his private embarrassment he liked the man and was forced to respect his nerve. There were no such characters in the circles in which Voznitsky had passed his life. This in its tiny way merely added to his inner distress, and he cautioned himself to be doubly careful not to show any trace of such feelings to either of the other two.

'You say you have Dr Petrov, Mr Mado, but for how long? We are in Greece, not London, England. We are both visitors in

421

a foreign country. It is the Greek state security police that matter here in Athens. Or am I teaching my grandmother to suck eggs?'

'Your grammar is excellent,' Mado said, 'and mine's dead.'

'Pardon?'

'Not at all. I beg yours.'

Then, seeing that the Russian did not fully understand, he went on: 'Sorry—just a poor schoolboy joke. Yes, Colonel, we do know about the Greek Gestapo. We don't woo it to the extent which you and the CIA do with your immense resources, but we are equally aware of its power. And we are not entirely without friends where it matters.'

This was getting them nowhere. Voznitsky paused for a moment or so and then decided on taking a risk.

'You say you have Dr Petrov. Can you then arrange access?'

'Ah!' said Mado, 'the light is beginning to dawn. Well, now, Colonel, you know how the English behave over these things. If someone asks us for political asylum, we invariably grant it to begin with so that the man in question is in protective custody until the facts are known. Protective of the person concerned—and also to see that our good offices are not abused. After all you may be sending us the great doctor as an agent for yourselves. He may not be defecting at all—you may simply be planting him in our midst. We usually have no objection to "access", as well you know, but we leave it to the character concerned. If Dr Petrov agrees to see you, I've no doubt it can be arranged. Now—what can you offer in return?'

'What do you want?'

'Ah!' said Mado, smiling with his mouth but not his eyes, 'this is getting to be like the fairy-tale about the three wishes.'

Mado lapsed into silence. Presumably, Voznitsky assumed, he was playing for time. Both men looked steadily at each other without saying a word but as if carrying on some private dialogue. Both were aware that Elissa continued to watch them with a degree of impatience. This increased the pressure which both felt and to which both reacted in their different ways. The tension became almost unbearable, but still neither man spoke. Eventually Mado broke the pause, having evidently come to a conclusion which Voznitsky assumed centred upon himself.

'I have a notion we understand each other, Colonel Voznitsky,' Mado said in a calm, deliberate voice. 'We are both men of experience and I imagine you would agree that sometimes it is wiser not to put things into words.'

Voznitsky remained rock still. The implication was obvious. It was himself they were after. It almost took his breath away and his first instinct was to lash out in anger. But the intense training he had undergone over the years now stood him in good stead.

He did not indicate by so much as a flicker of an eyelid that he understood what Mado was saying.

'In other words, Mr Mado, you wish to take what Americans call a "rain check" on your own demand?'

'You could put it that way.'

Voznitsky shrugged his shoulders and turned away: 'If that is what you want.'

'Shall we shake hands on that?' Mado said quietly.

'On what, Mr Mado?'

'On our understanding of each other, shall we say?'

Again Voznitsky shrugged his shoulders: 'I do not know what you are trying to commit me to—but if that is all you intend . . . very well.'

The two men shook hands in a crisp, military way and at this point Elissa brought the encounter to an end. She had clearly suffered their presence long enough. She moved slightly towards the door, saying to Voznitsky who followed her: 'I'm so sorry you have to go, Colonel. I will get my husband to call you as soon as he returns. In the meantime you will let me know when my son is expected at the airport, won't you?' She turned and stared coolly at him, 'I am sure you and I understand each other too.'

She saw him to the front door of the house. As soon as he stepped outside, his car drove up and after he had gone she walked slowly back to the drawing-room, where Mado had remained by the doors to the terrace staring out at the deep blue sea.

'I'd better go back to the Embassy, too,' he said

'I think Pan would like to see you first. I'll call him.'

Mado grinned. This was more like the Marides he knew.

'He never went to Crete? He was here all the time?'

She smiled in a cat-like way.

'He returned about ten minutes before Voznitsky arrived. He

didn't want to get involved until he had more information at his fingertips.'

'I have some very hot information indeed,' Mado said, thinking back to his meeting with Nikos Nikolaides in the bar of the Grande Bretagne, 'but I also need to get back to the British Embassy fast.'

'All right, Mr Mado, I'll. . . .'

'Look, Mrs Marides, stop putting me in my place. You and I have known each other a considerable time. I know you don't particularly like me. . . .'

'You're quite wrong there.'

'But surely if Pan calls me George, you could manage a little less formality.'

'I'm sorry, George,' she said, with an unexpectedly warm smile, 'it's all my fault. Perhaps you don't realize how shy I am. You know, if you marry someone like Pan and take on all this . . .' she indicated the house with a wave of the hand, 'jealous relatives, a son by the first wife who would quite gladly see you dead . . . well, you know my background and my circumstances. . . .'

'Okay, doll, I'm sorry to dot the i's and cross the t's but I think you may have me in the wrong perspective, too. You think I've only one idea in my head where women are concerned.'

'That's pretty well so, isn't it?'

'It's only part of the truth. Of course I'll lay any attractive bird who shows willing, even if it's only by the flutter of an eyelid—but there are other things as well. I have a young wife and a very new child. They mean as much to me as . . .'

'My family means to me,' Elissa said. 'Yes, George, I know. I'm sorry we didn't have this out and settled before.'

They smiled at each other.

'You're not such a skinny, stuck-up bitch after all.'

'And you're not just the elderly lecher I used to think you.'

'What's going on?' Marides said, striding into the room, 'you making the pass at my wife, you failed spy, you . . . ?'

Although Mado was a good two inches taller, Marides thundered up like an irate bull, picked up Mado by his lapels and held him in such a way that it was clear he could have thrown him across the room if he chose. He held him like this for a moment or so and then put him down with a short laugh.

'I don't-a trust you with my grandmother of ninety-two.'

'Yes,' Mado said, straightening himself and wondering who would have come off better had there actually been a fight, 'I went through the grandma bit with our Russian friend.'

'What are you going to do with Petrov?'

'I don't know. It's out of my hands.'

'You know where my niece, Helen, is?'

'No, but I know who's got her.'

'Ah!'

Marides stopped dead in his tracks and for a moment or so froze into a complete stillness.

'Who is holding her?' he asked in a low voice.

The almost instant transformation from raging bull into humming dynamo struck Mado as extraordinary even though he had witnessed it many times before. Marides was dangerous when violent, lethal when he was quiet and still.

'I was approached by someone called Nikos Nikolaides.'

'Yach!'

'You know him?'

'Nikos—no. Nikolaides is the code name for the current urban guerrillas. They operate under cover names. Like in Ulster: like the Tupomaros in Uruguay. What do they want?'

'Six of their people released by the Greeks. He told me only you could get it done.'

'Ay! ay! ay!' Marides sighed and for the first time in his life Mado felt a twinge of pity for the millionaire.

'It was coupled with a threat to me.'

'Why you?'

'I supposed they thought you might listen to me.'

'And what was the threat?'

'To Anna and my daughter in London. That's why I must get back to the British Embassy as soon as possible.'

'You take it seriously?' Marides asked, his hooded eyes brooding over the scene like a vulture.

'Wouldn't you? This is a kidnap-hijacking age. It's all too easy in an open society.'

'Yes,' Marides agreed, 'and it's not too difficult here in Greece.'

'This Nikos was one of your waiters last night.'

Marides said nothing, his mind apparently on other things.

'I need Mournier,' he said eventually and then with a sharp look at Mado, 'you'd better take his place.'

'I can't. But thanks for the offer. I'm working for someone else and I have a pension on the end.'

'Yach! pensions . . . you work for me, you don't need a pension.'

'I can see that, Pan. You mean I wouldn't live to enjoy it.'

'No, I do not mean that. I'll look after you and your family.'

'He will, you know,' Elissa put in.

'I'm not a killer like Mournier.'

'I'll find you a man for that.'

'You'll have me in the Lubyanka again.'

'It's an occupational risk. Anyway, I'm finishing with Russia.'

'I don't fancy the Pekin equivalent. Look, Pan, you know I can't opt out of my British commitments in a five-minute conversation.'

'Leave that to me.'

'I was going to work for you before—and you know what happened then.'

Marides made that little backward jerk of the head with a click of the tongue—the negative ογι sign—which is peculiarly Greek.

'That Mournier was a jealous man. Afraid for his job. Well—he had reason to be. He wanted to take me over. Me!'

He gave a short contemptuous laugh: 'You don't-a have such ambitions. Only one thing, George Mado, I catch you making a pass at my wife and. . . .'

He drew his finger across his throat.

'Oh! we're just good friends,' Mado said, 'as of five minutes ago. She doesn't fancy me.'

'I'll talk to your people in London.'

'I'll think it over.'

'Oh! no you won't. Yes or no now.'

Mado held the pause for as long as he dared. Then with a little shake of the head and a glance at Elissa, he said: 'Not until I'm released from my present commitments.'

Marides' mouth set in a hard firm line.

'You think I'll hold open the offer?'

'If you won't then we're all of us wasting our time.'

To the surprise of both Elissa and Mado, Marides looked across at his wife with raised eyebrows.

'You think I should wait?'

'Wait,' Elissa said as if the outcome had never been in doubt. Marides turned his baleful look on Mado and nodded.

426

'You see who takes the decisions around here now? All right, George, you'd better get back to the Embassy. I've a lot to do.'

'Like putting off your trip to Pekin?'

'Call me in two hours' time,' Marides said, 'and let me have that list of six names you've got in your hand.'

Mado handed over the piece of paper given him in the Grande Bretagne bar. Then with a smile at Elissa, he left.

The news about Dr Petrov broke via a French paper the following morning. The item was brief and to the point. One of the world's most celebrated oceanographers had disappeared from Athens. The Russians had disclaimed any knowledge of Dr Petrov and referred inquirers to the United Nations who at first denied Dr Petrov's existence, then that he had come to Athens at all, then that he had disappeared and finally, as a last resort, referred callers back to the Russian Embassy. The Greek authorities had no comment to make.

In a matter of hours, specialized members of the world press homed in on Athens. Andrea Eckersley's editor in London thought that her presence there might well put the paper ahead of the crowd and waited impatiently for her story to arrive. It was unlike her Little Ladyship—her label when things went wrong—not to come up with something bizarre. When several deadlines had come and gone, however, a phone call to the paper's local man in Athens revealed that Andrea, too, like Dr Petrov had disappeared off the scene. After one or two sharp remarks about the reliability of ladies with red hair, the group's top Kremlinologist hurriedly flew to Athens. But by the time he arrived, other developments behind the scenes had already taken place.

The Royal Naval frigate, which Padstow had requested, had arrived in Piraeus 'on a normal courtesy visit' and a party of officials from the British Embassy, all with diplomatic privilege and all conveyed in official Embassy cars, had visited the ship. Amongst these was someone well shielded from casual eyes but who looked like Dr Petrov. Technically Greek security could have 'cut out' any of this visiting party at the point where they left the Embassy cars at the foot of the gangway leading up to the British warship. At that point anyone without diplomatic immunity was for a few moments on Greek soil and therefore unprotected by the international umbrella.

But when the cortège of cars drove up to the ship, Greek security police proved to be conspicuous by their absence. To all outward appearances the position was simple. A British warship had arrived in the port on a friendly visit and some of the local Embassy staff had gone on board for a drink.

'However, any idea that the Greeks are unaware of what's going on,' Padstow said to the military attaché, when the transfer operation had apparently been successfully completed, 'is pure mythology—and mythology began with the Greeks.'

This, indeed, was true.

'He's thought to be on board HMS *Jasmine*,' Christos Marides said to his father, when he arrived for dinner that night, 'and the Nix have got Andrea Eckersley as well.'

'Who's she?' Marides growled.

'The red-haired journalist who was here the other night,' Elissa put in, 'the one who's going to do your profile for her paper. We had a letter from the editor—remember? And she wanted to take photographs of your party.'

'What's the interest in her?'

Elissa said nothing. The introduction Padstow had provided was entirely private to herself. She might tell Pan about it later on, if by then he had not already guessed. She was certainly giving nothing away in the presence of Christos, who in any case answered the question.

'She probably has an intelligence assignment,' Christos said, 'in addition to her role as a journalist.' He shrugged his shoulders, 'though not a very important one, I imagine. At any rate she's of little interest to us. She has never attacked the regime. She's no Lady Fleming.'

'Then why should the Nikolaides bother?'

'They may want something from the British press.'

'Yach!' Marides said, evidently dismissing it from his mind, 'so how do we get Helen back?'

Now it was Christos who fell silent. He was like his father, Elissa thought, he could drop a mask over himself in a Middle Eastern way which made his thoughts—indeed his whole self—impenetrable to ordinary European eyes. How much did he know? Was he, perhaps, half in with the Nikolaides? He was high up in the Greek Foreign Office—and his father was Panayotis Marides—so naturally his face fitted in with the regime. Or did it? She could not possibly guess.

All she did know for certain was that behind the smiling eyes, the easy glistening charm and the warm, polished manners, lurked an enemy. She did not know why. He would inherit as much of the Marides empire as he could possibly need or want. He was the Crown Prince and she merely the Dowager Queen, to be taken care of later on by a discretionary trust. So it was not —at any rate primarily—to do with money. Why then did she dislike him so much—and feel instinctively that this antagonism was amply reciprocated? Why was she afraid, at times, even to be in the same room?

Marides took out the list of names given him by Mado, and passed it over to his son.

'I know none of these people. Would it hurt *o kyrios* Lamda to set them free?'

O kyrios Lamda—Mr L—was the way Marides referred to a certain Lycopoulos who was currently the man in the regime with the power to make the Minister of Justice and the Head of the Security Police do as he wished. On the basis that all dictatorships are run sooner or later by those who control the secret police and their files, Mr L was, at that time in Greece, the quiet, unknown, rarely seen man with the essence of power in his hands.

Christos shrugged his shoulders: 'I can ask him,' he said. 'I have the number of his private account in Zurich into which you could pay direct. I suppose these people could always be re-arrested unless they went underground straight away.'

'How much would he want?'

Christos made an upward gesture of the eyebrows and clucked his tongue.

'It's more likely to be a percentage of the Pekin deal.'

An expression of acute pain passed over Marides' face. It made Elissa smile and she went over and put an arm round his shoulders, aware as she did so of the distaste she was giving to Christos.

'She's your niece, Pan,' she said ironically, 'and it's only money.'

She thought he was going to explode and for a second or so wondered if she had gone too far.

Then unexpectedly he laughed.

'All right, Christos,' Marides said, 'you do the preliminaries and I'll talk to Mr L tomorrow. What do the Nix want for—what's her name? Miss Ackity?'

'I don't know. I'm not directly in touch—obviously. I doubt I could find that out without prejudice to my own position.'

But Elissa noticed that he was careful to look away as he said this so that his eyes could not be seen.

'Why do you ask?' Christos demanded.

'I'll have her back as well. She's here for one of the Sundays, isn't she?'

Marides waited for a reaction from Christos and Elissa. He had the crafty look of a merchant in the *souk* about to dispose of a dubious jewel.

'My niece's life story could cost a newspaper a sizable sum of money. Of course,' he added, 'it will be worth it in Fleet Street terms—so perhaps everyone will make money in the end.'

CHAPTER SIX

WITHIN A FEW HOURS of Dr Petrov's supposed arrival on board, HMS *Jasmine* was ordered to sail from Piraeus 'for an unknown destination'. A team of highly sophisticated interrogators from British Intelligence had been flown out to Athens and some of these also went on board the warship.

'You'd better get down there as well,' Padstow said to Mado in the British Embassy, 'you're certainly a familiar face to the Greek security forces.'

'Don't you think I'd be more useful here? What about the Nevsky Prospekt—Voznitsky, I mean?'

'Well . . .' Padstow hesitated, 'it's difficult to assess. I'll get you back as soon as I can. I don't think that'll come to a head yet.'

'And Helen Stanopoulos?'

'I'll keep in touch with Marides. I've asked London for special protection over the next few days for your Anna and the child. I'll get someone to chat her up so that she'll know what's happening and won't be afraid.'

'She'll be scared all right,' Mado said grimly, 'and angry as well. You tricked me with this assignment, John, you've a lot of responsibility for what's happened.'

'Don't kid yourself,' Padstow said, with an attempt at lightness, 'you're having a whale of a time.'

'Marides wants me to work for him?'

'Why don't you, George?'

He smiled at the pug-faced man who was, in fact, far more valuable to the firm than the establishment was prepared to admit. 'You'd make a lot more money than you would with us.'

'I had a desk job and a pension. Now look what you've done.'

'You were bored to distraction.'

'I'm getting too old for this sort of thing.'

'Nonsense,' Padstow said impatiently, 'you're just entering your prime. Off you go now with your bag of red herrings.'

Mado thought about this for a moment or so.

'What if Petrov still won't talk?'

'You know the answer to that, George, as well as I do. The Russians can have him back. However—with our friend Voznitsky in mind—perhaps not quite yet. The inquisitor is due to arrive tomorrow.' He visualized the scene and laughed, 'Mr Ivan Karai is a very very nasty piece of work. Voznitsky isn't going to have a nice time at all. That should console you when you start to feel seasick on board HMS *Jasmine*.'

'So be it,' Mado said, going to the door, 'at least HM ships still carry duty-free Scotch.'

It was just as well, from Padstow's point of view, that Mado had disappeared temporarily off the scene since a few hours after HMS *Jasmine* had sailed, an ominous message came through from London. Mrs Mado and her child were not at home. A neighbour had seen milk bottles collecting outside the door and the local police had broken in. There was evidence of a hasty departure and the phone had been knocked off its hook. The Nix, it could only be presumed, had effective associates in London.

At much the same time Marides received a phone call giving him forty-eight hours to secure the release of the six whose names he had already placed in front of Mr L. Otherwise Helen Stanopoulos and Andrea Eckersley would both be executed when the deadline expired. The tension began to build up.

'Your son by Tarnham is supposed to arrive tomorrow morning at midday,' Marides said sourly to Elissa, 'and I've postponed my visit to Pekin.'

431

'Did you see Mr L?'

'I saw Mr L to the extent of a million Swiss francs. But it's not as easy as that. Mr L has to carry other people with him on this. Accidents can always take place: not least of all to Mr L himself. He's very much aware of the dangers.'

'If you live by intimidation,' Elissa said, looking hard at her husband, 'blackmail becomes an operational risk.'

'What kind of talk is that? Are you addressing a meeting?' Marides said contemptuously. 'All business in this part of the world relies on intimidation and blackmail—at any rate to a certain degree.'

'And you call a million Swiss francs a certain degree?'

'It's recoverable,' Marides said, 'the life of my niece is not— once it's been taken.'

'When is Mr L going to act?'

Marides shrugged his shoulders. Normally when he was in such a mood, Elissa would have left him alone. Now she could not free herself of the anxiety in the air.

'Do you really trust Christos?' she blurted out, realizing from the glare she received that this was precisely the sort of question he did not like her to ask.

'What's wrong with you, Lissy? Why suggest a thing like that? Do you trust your own son?'

'My son is fifteen. Yours holds a somewhat different position.'

'Yach!' said Marides, 'I trust myself, that's all. And sometimes I have doubts about me.'

Padstow had been right, when commenting to Mado that Voznitsky was not having a nice time at all. Predictably Moscow was furious about the Petrov defection and the silent, internally applied terror began. Karai made it clear when he arrived that a full inquisition had been ordered and that he himself had plenary powers. The fact that Karai was junior in rank to Voznitsky and treated him with the polite deference a Resident expects to receive, only made the realities of the situation more deeply sinister in their implications to Voznitsky's experienced mind.

However, he was still as of now the Resident, still the local Czar, whatever the threat. It had taken him several sleepless nights to recover from his meeting with Mado. The realization of where he stood in the British scale of values, compared even with someone of the calibre of Dr Petrov, was not in itself remarkable. What was disturbing—and this nagged at him like a sore—was the insolent suggestion that he himself might be 'ripe'.

Mado had not put it into words but the message had come through all the same and the shock had stayed with him like an ache in the bones. The other factor which these days never left him for long was the magnetism Elissa exercised on his waking thoughts. It was absurd, it was hopeless, worse—it was fraught with unnecessary dangers—but the emotion could not be suppressed. He reflected ruefully that he was like a schoolboy suffering his first experience of romantic love.

She and her daughter Lucy had come to the airport to meet the Romanian plane from Bucharest on which her son, chaperoned by Karai, arrived at Athens. As Voznitsky watched her getting out of the Marides' Rolls-Royce in the cornflower blue dress which so suited her, and walking so elegantly into the airport, he once again found himself astonished that the defector Tarnham could have abandoned such a woman.

'We kept our promise, you see,' he remarked, as they waited for Mark Tarnham to clear the formalities.

'We should all have been better off if there'd been no promise to keep,' Elissa replied. 'I wish your people would simply leave me and my son alone.'

When Mark came through the barrier almost running, he seemed to be bursting with enthusiasm. Elissa had not seen him so animated since those carefree childhood days before Paul Tarnham had left them and had so ploughed up their lives.

'It was absolutely super,' he said, after kissing his mother and giving his younger sister a perfunctory nod. 'It's been the best trip I've ever had my whole life. This is Mr Karai, Mother.'

'How do you do?' Elissa said formally. She did not offer her hand.

Mr Karai brought his glistening charm to bear and said quickly: 'I hope you've forgiven us, Mrs—Marides. But it has been such a pleasure to show your son something of our great city of Moscow and to make him aware of the esteem in which his father is held by the Russian people.'

Elissa stared at him with an icy contempt which would have withered anyone less armour-plated than a high official of the KGB. Then she turned away and walked towards the car.

433

'Come along, Mark,' she said, 'you and I are going to have a talk.'

Lucy made a face at her brother whose ebullience drained away like air out of a balloon. Mark shot a furtive look at Karai, from whose face the smile had also begun to fade, and at Voznitsky, whom he had not met. He then followed his mother with the despondency of a dog caught romping away on its own.

'Welcome to Greece,' Voznitsky said to Karai, who returned him a cold, ironic smile.

'That remains to be seen, comrade Colonel,' Karai said, 'let us go to the Embassy straightaway.'

The deal by which Helen Stanopoulos and Andrea Eckersley would be set free in return for the release of six of the Nikolaides then in prison, depended—as Marides had forecast—on a number of factors not under the direct control either of Marides or of Lycopoulos. The paramount one was secrecy.

Mr L, though all powerful, had nominally to work through others, since the regime was at pains to play down the dictatorship aspects of the current scene and Marides, on his side, had no wish to encourage further blackmail attempts.

Marides seemed always to be angry these days. He stormed into the British Embassy and demanded a meeting with Padstow, whom he knew to be in Athens. Half the people he asked did not even know of Mr Padstow's existence and when he eventually reached the military attaché, Schofield said: 'He's gone out to Vouliagmeni to see you, sir.'

Schofield was privately appalled at the way a man like Marides could break all the security rules in the Embassy, marching in and demanding to see anyone he chose.

'Yach!' Marides said and turned on his heel.

'Er, excuse me, sir, did you have a pass to get in?'

But Marides had already gone.

'This is going to help us a lot,' he said when he reached home and found Padstow with Elissa. Marides threw down one of the English Sunday papers in which there was an article headed 'In with the Nix' by Andrea Eckersley.

'Have you any idea how that was got through?'

'None whatever.'

Padstow had seen the article before coming out to Vouliagmeni.

He, too, was appalled to read how Andrea Eckersley had been 'kidnapped on my way back to Athens after attending one of Panayotis Marides' old Hollywood-style parties'; and how she had then been held incommunicado by the Nikolaides whilst a ransom was negotiated for herself, and the release of important members of the Greek Democratic movement agreed in return for the life of 'the Greek secretary, or Dr Petrov's *petite amie*.'

Andrea had evidently been in communication with Helen Stanopoulos. Indeed from the way the article read, there seemed little doubt that they were held together.

'Our captors tell us in a completely factual way that if a deal is not speedily agreed, we will both be executed. I have no reason to disbelieve this. I therefore asked permission to write what may prove to be my last article for this paper . . . the Nikolaides I have met are no ordinary gang of thugs. They are educated, intelligent, middle-class Greeks determined upon restoring democracy to the Colonels' paradise. They are also, so far as I can see, completely ruthless and one hundred per cent effective. Helen Stanopoulos and I are merely the trading tokens of the moment and, as one of our jailers sardonically remarked "In Northern Ireland today this would not even get into the papers". There is no doubt we are into an age when human hostages are shopped around like Green Shield stamps.'

This theme was developed in the well-known Andrea Eckersley manner. Unquestionably the article was authentic. Equally certain was the embarrassment it would cause.

'Just another bunch of Palestinians,' Marides growled. 'They want it all ways—the money, the power, the publicity. Take all, give nothing and above all boast. I had it fixed until this. Now we shall have to start all over again.'

For a moment or so nothing was said. All three of them tried individually to assess the possibilities.

'What would be the effect of Dr Petrov's return from limbo? I mean—suppose he decided to have second thoughts?'

Marides stared at him.

'How possible is that?'

'I think the Russians will be given access. He seems disposed to meet them. But I want the offer of this to be handled first by Voznitsky. I'll have Mado back here tomorrow.'

'As a matter of interest—from where?'

435

Padstow hesitated.

'I shall find out in the end, Marides went on, 'so you might just as well tell me now.'

'Gibraltar,' Padstow said, 'it's the nearest place unquestionably British.'

'You owe me a thousand drachma,' Marides said to Elissa, 'that's where I said they'd take him.'

'It doesn't sound as if Dr Petrov is being co-operative,' Elissa remarked.

'He's not,' Padstow said. 'All he wants is his Helen.'

'It's proving an expensive taste,' Marides said, 'for everyone else.'

Mado duly returned to Athens, as Padstow had arranged. They met at the airport and together went to the Embassy.

'Fly RAF,' Mado said. 'It's so healthy and quick, but you do miss the pretty hostesses. Now, John, I've one or two bones to pick with you.'

'I know, George, but don't pick them yet.'

'All right,' Mado said grudgingly. 'How's your pretty defector?'

'Obstinate. He's got the full double think going. He won't budge from his original line. He hasn't "defected"—he just wants to stay with his Helen. He's not betraying his country and he's not going to talk.'

'What's the next move?'

'London has reassessed him,' Padstow said, 'and he's come out of it with a somewhat lower rating. Also he's now prepared to discuss his problems with someone from his own Embassy. I want you to offer that one to Voznitsky.'

'How?'

'Marides has agreed the use of his house as before—if that's the way you want to play it—so why don't you get it set up from here and then go on out to Vouliagmeni? Or perhaps you can do it on the phone?'

'You give me the easiest assignments. Who's the next one I nobble? Breshnev?'

'You speak Russian, George, you're the only one who can pull it off with Voznitsky. You're already halfway there. I think he trusts you.'

He paused and looked at him hard: 'I'm desperately sorry I've no good news about Anna but there's a red alert on that one now in London. Everything that can be done is being done.'

'Don't give me that government spokesman stuff. I'd rather go back and find them myself.'

'How? What can you do that isn't already being done?'

'It's my wife and child.'

'I know,' Padstow said, 'I understand.'

'Bully for you,' Mado said. 'That helps a lot. I haven't slept for two nights.'

In fact Padstow had never seen him in such a state.

'You don't catch me this way again,' Mado went on sourly and picked up the phone. 'Get me the Russian Embassy. I want to speak to the assistant commercial attaché, Mr Voznitsky.'

Whilst Mado was waiting to be put through, Padstow said: 'By the way, Marides thinks that the Petrov scene is taking place in Gibraltar.'

'Who gave him that idea?' Mado said, his hand over the phone.

'I did. It's the nearest place unquestionably British and it's where Marides thought we would take him.'

A glint of a smile came through the tiredness in Mado's eyes. 'What made you pick on the Rock?'

'I've noticed Marides doesn't always know what he lets you think he knows. So I played on his deviousness. Cyprus was too obvious. Malta's too busy being independent—so I settled for Gibraltar; which seems to have been exactly his own train of thought.'

'Well, Master John, you're certainly learning fast.'

'I knew you'd be proud of me, George, even all that time ago in Beirut.'

But Mado gestured him into silence and said in Russian into the phone, 'Good afternoon, Colonel. This is your friendly British spy, George Mado. I suggest we meet where we met before at your very earliest convenience. You won't find it a waste of time.' He put down the phone.

'That wasn't Voznitsky,' he said, 'but it will be interesting to see if he turns up.'

'He'll bring Karai.'

'An added pleasure to look forward to. . . . Reach into your bottom drawer, sport, and produce me a Scotch. I suppose we can call on the RAF for some more transport, can't we?'

437

Padstow nodded: 'You think Voznitsky will trust you to that extent?'

Mado shrugged his shoulders: 'He'll soon be desperate. If he isn't already.' He paused in thought. 'Of course they can always make their own travel arrangements, if that's what they want. It's up to them. What our friend isn't going to pass up, though, is the chance of a confrontation with Dr Petrov. That's the only valid way he has left of clearing his yard-arm.'

They were just leaving for Vouliagmeni when the door opened and the military attaché brought in Andrea Eckersley. She looked distraught and dishevelled, as if she had been sleeping in her clothes, but there was still some sparky fire in the eyes.

'Is this where I get a bath?' she said, flopping into a chair, 'if so, just wheel it in. And I could do with a drink as well.'

Padstow produced another Scotch from his bottom drawer.

'Where did you find her?' he asked the military attaché.

'I didn't. She just turned up.'

'You could put it that way,' Andrea said, 'aren't you going to ask me if I'm all right?' And then, before anyone could speak, 'Well, I am, thank you very much.'

She took a long drink and suddenly began to cry.

'Don't pay any attention,' she said, like a general addressing an army, 'it's the effect of not being shut up in an airless cupboard any more.'

The three men watched her in silence.

'I'd come over and comfort you,' Mado said, 'except you'd misunderstand.'

This made her laugh and she tossed her head in the old defiant way.

'I'm much better than I look,' she said. 'All I need is a dainty dress and I'm ready for the garden party.'

'Who else knows you've escaped?'

She shrugged her shoulders. 'I didn't escape. They took me out in the country last night. They said I'd be shot . . . and I believed them. Instead they dumped me halfway to Delphi. That's why the taxi here cost rather a lot.'

'What about Helen Stanopoulos?'

'I don't know. She's their trump. Me they just wanted to frighten. They succeeded in that.'

438

She laughed rather shakily but the whisky was taking effect and she seemed to be regaining her composure with every moment that passed.

'You were together?'

She nodded.

'I think they only grabbed me because I saw her picked up so they wanted to shut my mouth.'

'Why did you do that article?'

'I had to. At gun point.'

'Hm!' Mado said, 'something doesn't add up.' He shifted his gaze from Andrea to Padstow, who raised his eyebrows slightly and said nothing.

'What's upsetting you?' Andrea said with a guarded look. She was suddenly made aware of a hard, professional inspection, tinged with possible hostility, which the three men were beaming towards her.

'It's all a little too pat,' Mado said. 'You happen to see Helen Stanopoulos picked up in the middle of the night after the Marides party, you happen to be picked up yourself, you do a highly questionable article for a world-famous Sunday newspaper . . .'

'For which I work.'

'And which blows into smithereens any secret negotiations then in progress.'

Andrea sat up, put down her glass and said angrily· 'Are you accusing me, George Mado? If so, of what? What *is* this—an interrogation?'

'All George said was that it struck him as a little too plausible,' Padstow remarked in what Mado knew to be a deceptively relaxed way. Mado had a long-standing prejudice against upper-class public schoolboys and the way they carried on, but there were times when that casual style could achieve results he doubted could be obtained in any other way.

'Like maybe you have friends in London with contacts here in Greece,' Mado said.

Andrea stood up and seemed to shake herself into a blaze of anger. 'How else does a journalist work? What's going on around here? Of course I have contacts. Who hasn't?'

'Do you suppose your contacts could find out where my wife and child could have been taken in London?'

439

Andrea stopped dead.

'What's that? Have they seized them as well?'

'You didn't know?'

'Do I look as though I knew it? Jesus Christ, what do you think I am? Some sort of double agent? You think I spend a week in a stinking cupboard under threat of being taken out and shot to have you start accusing me of *that*?'

'Okay, gorgeous,' Mado said with a glint at Padstow, 'you're clear with me.'

'Huh!' she said, 'since when has that mattered? And who are you anyway other than some pseudo-hippie with dated ideas on the way women react to your non-existent sexual charm?'

'Well!' Mado said, going across and putting his hands on her shoulders, 'I should keep that in for the column next week.'

He was about to embrace her when she gave him a stinging slap on the face.

'And that's for your column next week,' she said, 'don't you try that stuff on me, Mr Mado.'

Padstow smiled broadly. The military attaché looked startled and then reverted to the deadpan expression he adopted when well out of his depth. Andrea turned away.

'I'm going back to the Grande Bretagne to have a bath and clean up.'

'And then come out to Vouliagmeni,' Mado said, apparently unmoved, 'I need you to work on Marides.'

She looked sharply at Padstow.

'Yes?' she said.

'Yes, please, Andrea,' Padstow said.

'Well, tell your lecherous friend to keep his hands off me at a time like this.'

She stopped, looked at Mado and then went over and kissed him.

'It's all right, you grotty little man, I could get to be quite fond of you if I don't try too hard.'

She walked to the door and then said to Padstow: 'I have someone in London might just be able to help find Anna and the child.'

'Ah!' said Padstow, toying with a paper-knife.

'But I'll have to do it personally, if he's there. He doesn't like the telephone.'

'Oh! yes?' Padstow said. The slight inflection in the voice demanded an explanation.

Andrea hesitated and then went on quickly: 'On account of the drug scene. He's a dealer . . . with interesting contacts.'

They all thought about this for a while.

'What do you want me to do?' Padstow asked, 'book some seats on an aircraft?'

'Marides has an executive jet,' Mado said. 'We might persuade him into a package deal. Come along, gorgeous, are you really set on that bath? Or can you delay it?'

'I need a bath more than anything else in the world,' Andrea said. 'Let's be on our way.'

On leaving the Embassy for the Grande Bretagne they were followed, but in a casual way which Mado took to be merely routine, not of the kind likely to lead to another incident in the bar. At the desk, when they picked up the keys of their rooms, the clerk asked Andrea if she had had an enjoyable trip, so someone must have put over a cover story on the hotel. Her absence appeared otherwise to have been unremarked.

'Yes,' she said, 'I consulted the oracle at Delphi—a very successful experience.'

Clearly the clerk had been better informed than his innocent question suggested. However, that too could be taken as normal. Receptionists at first-class international hotels acquire a facility with the oblique and this after all was Athens. Moreover—as Mado well knew—holders of press cards do not excite suspicion if they unexpectedly stay away for a night or two. They went up to her room.

'Help yourself to a Scotch,' Andrea said, 'and chat me up with the news.'

'You could always make it as a stripper,' Mado observed, as she tore off her shirt and jeans and walked naked to the bath. 'You have some magnificent equipment stacking up there.'

She soaped herself all over, shampooed her hair and then lay in the bath, looking at him perched on the end, a Scotch in his hand.

'This is the nice part of the job,' Mado said, appreciating her splendid proportions and the unaffected smile she gave him. 'However, you'd better know what's been going on down here in the midden since you've been away.'

441

He gave her a résumé of what had happened in the Grande Bretagne bar and also of his meeting with Voznitsky out at Vouliagmeni.

'If Voznitsky meets you . . .'

'He'll come.'

'What are you going to offer and what do you want?'

'It's very simple really,' Mado said. 'Should Petrov really decide to defect, then inevitably Voznitsky's career is at best damaged and at worst kaput. Maybe he won't he disgraced, since even the KGB allows for bad luck, and our friend must have done exceptionally well to have reached Resident status in a Western country—but once the tumult and the shouting are over, there's likely to be a nasty blotch on the record. In the end it's the man on the spot who picks up the blame. So the Grade I dacha, the promotion to General and all the fringe benefits will be delayed, put in doubt or possibly scrubbed out for ever.'

'So he might end his days pottering about like Kruschev?'

'If he's lucky. On the other hand if he can persuade the great Doctor to see sense—I mean Soviet sense—then the blotch becomes something of a halo and he certainly has the complete answer to Ivan Karai. That one goes inquisiting back to Moscow to arrange a proper welcome for Dr Petrov.'

She got out of the bath, dried herself and put on clean jeans. Mado helped himself to another drink and watched her reflectively as she dressed. He thought it was very friendly of her to receive him in this way, although it clearly pleased her to behave as she did. But like her as he did, he still found himself wondering if there might be an ulterior motive in the way she was handling him.

'I'm sorry I misjudged you to begin with, Andrea. You're quite a girl—literally and metaphorically.'

'Well, thank you, George Mado. I'm glad we understand each other at last.'

'Why do you think they let you out?'

She paused and looked up into the distance for a second or two.

'I'm more use to them out and about and writing than stuffed away in a cupboard weeing myself with fear.'

'Who are you really working for?'

'My paper. You know that.'

'And who else?'

'You'll have to work that out for yourself—if that's what's worrying you.'

'You're a better newspaper woman than I thought,' Mado said. 'I'm not asking you to give away your sources.'

'Oh! yes you are. That's what you've been up to since we first met. It's okay by me and one of these days I might let you in a bit more. But don't try and winkle it out of me by going round the corner and laying little traps.'

'Answer me one question, though. Do you really think your friend in London can find Anna for me when all the rest of us have failed with all the resources we can call on?'

'You've spent a lifetime in security and you ask a simple question like that?'

'Yes. Yes I do.'

Mado visualized some of the action MI5, the Special Branch, the CIA and the KGB could respectively lay on when they chose to go into high gear.

'Then ask yourself what freemasonry can cut right across, through, up and down your intelligence scene—without any of you really knowing.'

'The Roman Catholic Church.'

'Not bad. A near miss,' Andrea said, leading the way out of her room. She looked as fresh as a daffodil and even Mado with every instinct negative found the sexuality disturbing. 'However, you're wrong—or rather, a little out of date.'

'All right, then, what?'

'Drugs.'

He thought about this as they left the hotel and walked to their car. He made no comment and asked no further question. When they were safely on the way to Vouliagmeni, Andrea said: 'You've never pushed drugs, have you?'

'No,' Mado said firmly, 'certainly not.'

'The drug scene defeats the lot of you professionals. I could deal, if I wanted to, in Buckingham Palace or the Kremlin—you name the place and I'd find the man I needed in a matter of hours, sometimes minutes. It's worldwide. It's the super-state of today. I'll find your Anna for you, if she's still in one piece.'

'They owe you a favour?'

'I don't answer that sort of question. I'm doing you one,

though. Let's get Marides to help us out with some fast transport.'

They drove on to Vouliagmeni, followed at a distance as before. Parked near the front door of the great white house was a CD car with a turnip-headed chauffeur studiously looking neither to the right nor left.

'He's here,' Mado said, 'and I wonder who else.'

As they entered the house, Marides was standing by the main staircase in the hall, talking to Lars Sweeney, one of the American lawyers he employed in his oil business and whom Mado knew to be also connected with the CIA. They had met during the liquidation of the Tarnham connection. Indeed Lars Sweeney's activities had played a considerable part in bringing the Greek multi-millionaire to the point of actually asking Elissa to marry him. Since those events, Sweeney had prudently kept out of the way.

Like Mado, he had an acute eye for the opposite sex, and this double-edged quality called for strong self-control, especially when one's employer was a man as passionate as Marides. Mado saw the process flash up and then disappear like lightning as he walked in with Andrea, and this made him smile. Outwardly neither man gave any sign of recognition of the other.

'You go and talk to Elissa upstairs in the blue room,' Marides said to Andrea, when the introductions had been made, 'and Mr Voznitsky is waiting for you, George, in the drawing-room.'

'Is he alone?'

'No. He has Karai with him.'

'And the news on Helen?'

Marides made a slight negative gesture: 'Deal with our Russian friends first,' he said and turned back to Sweeney. Mado continued on to the drawing-room where Voznitsky, his face the colour of putty, stood stiffly by the big french windows on to the terrace, whilst Karai leant with an appearance of nonchalant disdain against the balustrade. A glance at the two told Mado all he needed to know about the interrelationship and the power structure. It was refreshing to meet such tormentors from a position of strength and in his mind's eye he remembered flashes from very different meetings in very different places.

'Good afternoon, Colonel,' Mado said, walking across and proffering his hand, 'I see you've brought a friend.'

444

Voznitsky shook hands as if Mado were infected. Karai walked towards them with the sort of smile Mado had seen on the faces of East End gang leaders. He affected a pungent scent and moved as carefully as a cat on the prowl.

'This is Mr Karai,' Voznitsky said, 'who is visiting Athens for the Trade Fair.'

Karai did not offer to shake hands. Like Voznitsky he gave Mado the impression of being in the presence of a bad smell, and it crossed Mado's mind that he might be asphyxiating himself with his own after-shave.

'Well, Mr Mado,' Karai said in English, 'what have you got to say to us?'

'To you, nothing,' Mado snapped back in Russian, 'so I suggest you keep walking and wait in your car. Colonel Voznitsky and I will not detain you for long.'

There was a moment of paralysis as the two KGB men digested this statement.

'I would prefer Mr Karai to hear what you have to say.'

Mado pursed his lips and did not immediately reply.

'Then it's been rather a wasted trip for both of us,' Mado said after a lengthy pause and then began walking away. Voznitsky nodded curtly at Karai who raised his eyebrows and left the room without a word and without a further glance at Mado.

'All right,' Voznitsky said when they were alone, 'now that we've met that condition, what is this about?'

'I'm prepared to offer you—and only you—access to Dr Petrov who is himself willing to talk to you.'

'No Helen Stanopoulos?'

'No Helen Stanopoulos.'

'Where?'

'You will have to put yourself in our hands for that.'

'It's not here in Athens?'

'You know that already.'

The two men stared at each other like mutually opposed frontier guards at a time of strained relations.

'You're fully protected by your diplomatic status, Colonel. You have nothing to lose.'

'Why are you making this offer to me?'

'Because you are the man concerned. I'm sure neither of us

need go into detail and I'm equally sure that we understand each other very well.'

'Then I do not comprehend what it is you are expecting from me.'

Mado cocked his head slightly to one side and smiled.

'The British are far more generous than you give us credit for being. Shall we say we expect nothing in return? Let's see what happens as the result of your meeting with Dr Petrov. After all, Colonel, you are still the Resident here—still the man in charge.'

At that moment a tremendous explosion coming from the direction of the hall first shook the entire house and was then followed by the sound of collapsing masonry. The centre wall began crumbling in a great cloud of rubble and dust and the ceiling fell in, a huge chunk of it striking Mado on the shoulder and knocking him to the ground. The rumble continued for several seconds and it became obvious that a bomb had destroyed the centre of the house. Voznitsky, who was untouched, recovered from the initial shock and helped Mado up from the floor.

'Are you all right?' he asked.

'I think so,' Mado said, dusting himself off, 'we'd better see what's happened outside.'

They picked their way over the mess to where the hall had been. Somewhere under the rubble there were people crying for help. Karai and the Embassy driver came running in from the outside and, as the dust settled down, it became clear that most of the middle part of the first floor had collapsed in what at first sight seemed to be like the bottom end of a landslide.

CHAPTER SEVEN

THE DESTRUCTION of the Palazzo Marides made the front pages of every great newspaper in the Western world. Nameless soldiers and civilians were daily shot in Ulster or Vietnam, but this had become routine. The attempted assassination of a multi-million-aire, the blowing up of his house and the unknown motives behind it shredded into pieces the fabric of secrecy with which Marides had surrounded his current affairs. It attracted not only on to him and his household but on to Greece and its regime the full glare of world publicity.

Rumours accelerated after the Greek army had finished excavating the rubble and had taken three of Marides' staff, Lars Sweeney, Elissa and the two children together with Andrea to hospital, suffering from shock and a variety of broken limbs, but had found no trace of Marides himself.

The essentials of a first-class mystery, therefore, presented themselves. Almost anything Marides did these days became instant news. This was not only because he was enormously rich and successful but also there were unanswered questions concerning his life and affairs. Was it only love or could there be a more subtle reason for his marriage to the ex-wife of the most celebrated British defector since Philby? Was it purely coincidental that the person whom the world's press were unable to find and who appeared to be the prime cause of a counter defection in the person of Dr Petrov, was none other than Marides' niece?

This blaze of publicity did not suit the Greek authorities at all. Until the outrage at Marides' house, the Greek security service had kept very much in the background. This was standard practice. The Greeks had everything to gain and very little to lose by allowing the British, the Americans and the Russians to make Athens the sort of foyer for the interchange of intelligence that Lisbon had been in the second world war.

But this hospitality depended, like Swiss banking, on a system of hermetic secrecy. The world's press was now milling about Athens to a degree and in sufficient numbers to bring highly unwelcome attention on matters the Greeks wished to keep to themselves.

'No doubt they're seizing this opportunity of servicing the equipment in Boubolina Street and taking a few days leave,' Schofield remarked to Mado and to Padstow as they awaited the arrival of Colonel Voznitsky. The cover plan had worked well. Even the Greeks, who knew almost everything else, had been fooled into thinking that Dr Petrov had been smuggled out of the country in a British man-of-war when all the time he had remained incommunicado and under interrogation in the British Embassy in Athens.

There was a sound reason for this. Petrov himself had maintained from the start that he was only asking for asylum because of Helen Stanopoulos. He did not wish to discuss his work or the

447

allied subjects on which he was a world expert. That would be disloyal to Soviet Russia and was therefore unthinkable. But, if he persisted, why should the British bother with him at the expense of a further worsening of relations with Russia? A man on the run is one thing, a man who merely wants to stay with his girl-friend and does not have the right kind of visa is another.

'Doctor Petrov will have to learn some of the hard facts of life if he really wants to stay in the West,' Padstow had written in his report, 'but our task would be easier if Miss Stanopoulos could be ransomed or otherwise produced and brought to the Embassy for a discussion with the Doctor.'

It was the day after the explosion and Voznitsky had been invited to come to the Embassy and be prepared to travel on. Coincidentally units of the American Sixth Fleet were anchored in Piraeus harbour and so was another British frigate which had come overnight from Cyprus. Smoke screens at different levels had thus been laid. But still no news of Anna and the child in London had come in, nor of Helen Stanopoulos in Athens. Now that Marides himself had also disappeared, confusion seemed complete to the three men in the military attaché's room, as they sat drinking cups of unpleasant coffee brought in by Schofield's secretary.

'What's the current state of the casualty list?' Padstow asked. He had been keeping a careful eye on Mado, whom he thought to be near breaking point.

'Elissa and Andrea have broken legs, the children got away with facial cuts and bruises, Lars Sweeney has internal injuries and is still unconscious, and one of the servants died two hours ago,' Mado said. 'And if anyone's interested, I have a bruise the size of Piccadilly Circus on my left shoulder.'

'Have we any idea where Marides might be?'

Mado shook his head.

'The only person who might give us a clue is Sweeney, who was with him in the hall when I entered the house, and Sweeney, as I said, isn't in too good shape.'

'I think I'll send you back to London tonight, George. I don't see that there's much more for you here.'

I thought you wanted me around for the Nevsky Prospekt?'

'Yes, George, I do. But you're obviously so worried about Anna, I don't think there's much point in keeping you hanging about in your present condition.'

'Oh! well,' Mado said, hardening his mouth, 'I don't suppose I'd be any better off in London. Her little Ladyship had the bright idea of invoking some big wheel in the drug scene but I always thought that was a far-out idea and anyway if Andrea's in hospital she can scarcely do much on a long-distance basis. If the Special Branch on a red alert can't find my wife, I don't suppose there's much I can do. I'll stick around here.'

'I'm very sorry, George.'

'Thanks! I only hope it never happens to you,' Mado said and walked to the window looking out on the Embassy garden with its beautifully kept lawn. The peace and quiet seemed to counterpoint the stress bearing down on all of them at that time.

'Do we have anything new on why the explosion took place at all? And who was behind it?'

Neither of the other two rose to this and eventually Mado turned back from his study of the garden and said: 'I have nothing to go on but it wouldn't surprise me if Christos Marides was somewhere in that.'

'Yes,' Padstow agreed, 'that had occurred to me, too. He's certainly very shifty about Elissa.'

'Colonel Voznitsky is here,' the secretary said, coming into the office. Schofield and Mado followed her out to the hall. Voznitsky was standing stiff and erect near to the watchful Embassy guard, trying, as it seemed to Mado, not to breathe too much of the tainted British Embassy air. They greeted each other formally.

'Have you brought your overnight things?' Mado asked.

'Yes. They are in the car. I would also like Mr Karai to be present if that could be agreed. He, too, is in the car.'

'Ah! yes,' Mado said, 'Mr Karai. . . .'

It was clear from the way Voznitsky had spoken that he was under orders to state this request. It was also clear to Mado that if the attempt to make Dr Petrov think again were to succeed, it would detract from the kudos Voznitsky could legitimately claim for his persuasive powers. Mado came to a quick decision.

'I'm sorry,' he said, 'it is only you whom Dr Petrov wishes to see.'

'Very well, but please note that I have made an official request.'

'Of course,' Mado said, 'please come this way.'

He thought he detected an almost visible relief on Voznitsky's face at the turning down of the request. The military attaché told the guard—who was an ex-Royal Marine—to keep an eye on the Russian Embassy car outside and then caught up with the other two.

'So he was here all the time,' Voznitsky said as they entered the storeroom which had been adapted to accommodate Dr Petrov, and for the first time smiled at Mado.

'We British can be damned sharp at times,' Mado said, affecting his nineteen-twenties upper-class voice which Voznitsky was not quite sure how to interpret. From then on, however, they spoke in Russian so that the linguistics were not on Mado's side. Yet to get a smile, he reflected, could be counted as some sort of achievement in the circumstances.

Dr Petrov was in a highly emotional state. The interview, which was openly tape-recorded, began in a formal way. Mado asked Dr Petrov to identify himself and to state whether he was there of his own free will or held by force. Once it was established to Voznitsky's satisfaction that, if Dr Petrov chose, he could walk out of the Embassy there and then, a more relaxed atmosphere came about. Then the confessional began.

Although both Schofield and Mado had read reports of other defectors on whom at one stage or another the KGB persuasive technique had been brought to bear, neither of them had previously been present at such a confrontation. Mado himself had been interrogated several times and in depth by the Russians—once when he had been blown originally as the result of the Tarnham affair and again after he had been kidnapped in Beirut during Operation Powder Train and abducted to Moscow. But Mado had been a professional agent. Dr Petrov was nothing of the sort.

None of Mado's experiences bore the slightest resemblance of this calm, understanding, dignified discussion now taking place in the bowels of the British Embassy in Athens between the world-famous Dr Petrov and the local KGB Resident. It was one of the unwritten rules of the game that once access to a defector had been given, the host side would bring no persuasive power to bear on the defector either to stay or to return.

Even so Mado found it difficult not to jump in when Voznitsky voiced some particularly unbelievable promise. It was like watching a child teetering on the edge of a high building and not reaching out a hand to prevent a fall. But Petrov was an indoctrinated Russian professional man with no ability to strike a line of his own, with no comprehension of the real meaning—or the responsibilities of independence. He was putty in the hands of a skilful manipulator such as Voznitsky.

Moreover he was heartily sick of being out on a limb. Emotionally crippled by his obsession for Helen Stanopoulos, he believed or appeared to believe everything that this high, sympathetic and trustable officer of the state security was telling him. Mado watched the process with a kind of detached fascination.

'Wisdom and wit are little seen,' Mado murmured to Schofield at one point, 'but folly's at full length.'

'I beg your pardon?'

'I was merely quoting some eighteenth-century poet.'

'Ah! . . . yes.'

'He was actually referring to an art exhibition where Beau Nash's picture had been placed at full length between the busts of Sir Isaac Newton and Mr Pope,' Mado said, and then seeing that he was making but little sense to the British military mind, went on with a glance at Voznitsky: 'Forget it. What odds would you give on Arsenal?'

'Odds on, I'm afraid.'

'Then see if you can raise a little Embassy Scotch. We shall all be needing it.'

But it was to be some time before they could decently relax over a drink. As he left the room, Schofield found his secretary about to come in.

'Mr Padstow would like to see you at once,' she said, 'and I don't think we'll be having dinner tonight.'

'Why not?' he said as he walked out.

'I'd say you'll have too much to do,' she answered enigmatically and went back to her room. These young secretaries were getting very saucy and independent, Schofield thought, as he made his way upstairs. Perhaps it was contact with the practical side of intelligence—or merely having an old ram like Mado groping his way round the place. That side of things was not on the curriculum at Sandhurst, and Schofield, like his predecessor, could not wait to get back to some active soldiering even if it meant Belfast.

Padstow was standing by the window looking at the garden as Mado had done, when Schofield entered the room. As soon as the door was closed, Padstow said: 'How is it going?'

The question took the military attaché slightly by surprise. He had expected a panic of some kind, not just a request for a progress report.

'I think Voznitsky will persuade him to go back. My Russian isn't all that good but I gather Mado thinks so too. Was there something else you wanted to see me about?'

Schofield considered himself more experienced than this young civilian whose very presence in the Embassy was supposed, on orders from London, to be secret. He slightly resented Padstow's status and power, though he did not admit this consciously even to himself. However, the next remark put all professional jealousy out of his head.

'I've just been rung up by Marides,' Padstow said.

'He's alive! How did he manage to escape?'

Padstow shrugged his shoulders.

'He didn't waste time telling me that sort of thing. I don't even know if he's still in Greece. What he rang up to say was that we may expect Helen Stanopoulos to be delivered here at any moment.'

'Good heavens.'

'Addressed to George Mado. I only hope not as a corpse.'

'Why here? Why the British Embassy?'

'I don't know. I suppose because it's secure.'

He saw that the military attaché was not following his train of thought, so he went on: 'Marides makes a great play of his British passport—which he got through the back door in Cyprus a long time ago. Naturally he takes advantage of his Greek and Panamanian passports as well whenever it suits him. However, in times of stress he has the nice old-fashioned idea that somehow or other it's safer to be British. Regimes may come and go, bombs may explode, but the British Embassy will somehow or other always be there.'

'Well, of course he's quite right: we will be,' the military attaché said and there was no joky tone in his voice.

'Yes,' Padstow went on, 'if Helen Stanopoulos does show up, it's likely to alter the scoreboard on Petrov. I'll warn the ambassador —and that's going to help our popularity here: would you express the news privately to George? I think we ought to ease Voznitsky out of it as soon as we can.' He paused for a moment, trying to work out the implications and then added: 'Preferably before Petrov comes to a final decision.'

'I'll get down right away and pass on the gen to Mado,' Schofield said and left the room.

However, events overtook them all. Before Padstow could alert the Embassy hierarchy—the Ambassador being out on a visit and the Counsellor not available—and while Schofield was passing across to Mado a piece of paper which simply said: 'Helen Stanopoulos being brought to Embassy. Padstow suggests V asked to exit', a taxi had driven up to the front door and from it emerged, under the watchful eye of Karai and the Russian Embassy driver, the pale, limp figure of Helen Stanopoulos.

Immediately she was out, the door slammed and the taxi drove quickly away. She was alone and appeared only just able to stand. At first sight she looked either drunk or drugged and as she tottered into the Embassy hall, the guard rushed forward to prevent her falling to the ground. She was bloodless in colour and seemed scarcely able to talk, only just managing to ask in slurred tones if she was at the British Embassy.

'Yes, miss,' said the guard, whose twenty-one years in the Marines had taught him to support heavier bodies than this before, 'you're fair and square on British soil, miss.'

'Mister Mado,' the girl said with a quivery smile and then collapsed in his arms, apparently losing consciousness.

The guard, helped by a receptionist, got her to a seat and while this was in progress the Ambassador and one of the First Secretaries arrived. His Excellency had no wish for his Embassy to be used as a resting-place for sick or inebriated girls.

'What's going on?' he asked with a frown, but as no one could tell him, he passed on, ordering the First Secretary to find out what it was all about.

'She's asking for Mr Mado, sir,' the guard said and at that moment Karai entered from the porch and, with an easy smile, walked up to the group.

'Perhaps I can help?' he said in English. 'I think this is the lady who was brought by a taxi to the wrong address. We have been expecting her at the Russian Embassy. I have a car outside and can easily put things right.'

Without waiting for a reply, he leant over Helen Stanopoulos and tried to hoist her to her feet.

'I don't know who you are,' the First Secretary said, 'but thank you, we'll attend to this matter ourselves.'

'Ivan Karai—my credentials,' Karai said imperiously, producing a small wallet from his pocket.

'Thank you,' the First Secretary said, without looking at them. 'Have you an appointment, Mr Karai?'

'We were informed that the taxi had gone to the wrong Embassy,' Karai said glibly, 'so I have come to pick up this lady and take her to the right address.'

'Excuse me, sir,' said the guard, 'but wasn't you waiting for the other Russian gentleman, sir? The one who's with the military attaché?'

There was a slight pause. Helen Stanopoulos remained inert and unconscious in the chair and at that moment Padstow appeared. He quickly took in the scene and then said to the guard: 'Escort Mr Karai to his car.'

In silence but with a nasty frown Karai turned on his heel and made for the door.

'See him *into* his car,' Padstow said as the guard hesitated near to the door.

The two men then left the Embassy.

'What's going on?' the First Secretary said somewhat querulously, 'and who are you?'

'Help me to get this girl somewhere less public,' Padstow said curtly, 'and we'd better call in a doctor we can trust. God knows what they've put into her to make her like this.'

They carried her into Schofield's room.

'The Embassy doctor is Greek,' the First Secretary said. 'He's very discreet and reliable. Who is this girl?'

'I suppose there'll be a naval surgeon on board the frigate in Piraeus, won't there? Could you ask the naval attaché if he could come here at once?'

'Now look here,' the First Secretary said, bridling, 'I don't know what's going on. . . .'

At that moment the Ambassador's secretary came in with a message she obviously enjoyed delivering to Padstow.

'The Ambassador would like to see you in his room right away.'

Having delivered the message, she waited. Padstow was going to have to satisfy British bureaucracy in addition to the other problems he faced. He swore silently to himself. During the pause which followed, the First Secretary said: 'I still don't know who you are.'

But there was a slightly more friendly and questioning tone in his voice, and since the timing had now become critical, Pad-stow took a risk. This was another of those moments of crisis when the outcome depended on the goodwill and persuasion of strangers.

'I haven't time to explain,' he said, 'but would you go down to the second storeroom in the basement and ask the military attaché to come up here at once. I'll see His Excellency in the meantime.'

The First Secretary hesitated, looked at the Ambassador's secretary from whom he got no help and then set off on his mission with the pained expression of a cleric in a cathedral close to whom someone has made a sporty remark about the Virgin Mary. Padstow went in to the Ambassador, seething with impatience and before he could say a word, found himself at the receiving end of a tirade.

'I don't know what you people are up to,' the Ambassador said, 'but this has got to stop. I'm not having my Embassy used one moment longer as a sort of Harrods' waiting-room. I've been summoned to the Greek Foreign Office to receive an official complaint. You can guess as well as I can what it's about.'

'No, sir, I can't. So far as I know we've done nothing offensive to the Greeks.'

'Who's that young woman in the hall?'

'Her name is Helen Stanopoulos. She is Doctor Petrov's secretary. She is also Marides' niece.'

'It struck me she was drunk. What's she doing in my Embassy?'

'I don't know,' Padstow said grittily. 'Perhaps you could ask Mr Marides. It's cost him a million Swiss francs to get her here.'

'What's that? How do you know that?'

A scathing retort rose in Padstow's mind but he controlled himself and went on: 'And the KGB have just made one of their cruder attempts to take her out of your Embassy and into theirs.'

'Here?'

Padstow felt like telling him to belt up or wring himself out. However, he was part of the mechanism which had to be used, like it or not. He was the Ambassador for better or for worse.

'Now if you'll excuse me, sir. . . .'

To Padstow's surprise, and for no reason he could discern, His Excellency suddenly thawed, rather in the manner of a self-important judge who decides he may have overdone it and that it is time he wooed the jury.

'You must find us a pain in the neck, Mr Padstow.'

'Well . . .' said Padstow. A pain in the arse is what you should have said, you pompous oaf.

'I know this is no time for apologia but I wish you people would sometimes consider the man on the spot. This sort of thing doesn't make life easy, you know, especially when you have to put up with someone like Mado.'

'If it wasn't for Mado . . .' Padstow began and then thought better of it. 'I'm sorry, sir, but I think the sooner I get back to what's going on, the better.'

'Very well,' the Ambassador said. 'I'll be leaving for the Ministry of Foreign Affairs in ten minutes' time. If you've news for me before I go, be sure I'm properly briefed.'

'Can I ask the naval attaché to get us a doctor from the frigate in Piraeus?'

'To attend a Greek girl in the British Embassy? I don't think that's a good idea. Suppose she dies on our hands?'

'She won't die,' Padstow said, an ironic twist to his mouth, 'that would be the easy way out.'

Down in the second storeroom in the basement, Mado had already decided that enough pressure had been put on Dr Petrov when the news about Helen Stanopoulos arrived. He tried to assess the effect it would have. Smootchi had long forgotten what it was like to be proud, impatient and arrogant. The confessional had reduced him to jelly, and Mado felt something akin to compassion as he witnessed the deadliness of this self-destructive process.

It did not seem to matter whether it was operated by the Church or the KGB. It had all been done in a soft voice with gentle, suggestive words. Mado could not but admire his adversary.

Voznitsky had induced the guilt into Dr Petrov and then the poison had gone racing round the veins as if he had been bitten by a snake.

But it could all be put right, Voznitsky said. Academician Petrov had made a small error in thinking—that was all. Once he came back, it would be overlooked. He could resume his life and his status as before. No one would know about his few days' folly in Greece. There might be a small inquiry on his return to Moscow but this would be a formality—simply to straighten the record. Everything would be all right and on that Voznitsky gave his word of honour as an officer of the KGB.

'Your time is nearly up,' Mado said to Voznitsky in English.

'For all of us,' Voznitsky replied with a wry smile. Now that he was really in action, he exhibited an extraordinary self-confidence. The resemblance to a priest, quietly exercising the authority of his faith, was remarkable.

'A sense of humour is a dangerous attribute,' Mado remarked casually.

'Exactly. If our friend here had had one, I shouldn't be sitting here now.'

Mado presumed that by talking in such a way, Voznitsky was either acting from bravado or taking a calculated risk. It was true that Dr Petrov's English was the minimal required to read scientific documents. It was unlikely to extend to conversational nuance. Indeed from the way he gazed from Voznitsky to Mado and back again, it was clear that he did not understand. He was like a lost dog trying to pick up a human reaction he could interpret. Nevertheless it struck Mado as a strange remark for a Russian interrogator to make in the present circumstances.

'And the outcome?' Mado asked, looking hard at Voznitsky.

'It was never really in doubt.'

'I wonder,' Mado said and decided not to let him get away with it as easily as that.

'Have you come to a decision, Dr Petrov?' he asked in Russian.

Dr Petrov went through his by now familiar routine of twitching his eyebrows, coughing and slightly shrugging his shoulders.

'I shall leave with Colonel Voznitsky.'

'Would it help to discuss it first with Helen?'

This had a bomb effect. Voznitsky tautened and Petrov almost leapt out of his skin.

'She's been found? Where is she? When can I see her?'

'I think that can be arranged.'

'Comrade Petrov,' Voznitsky said, 'remember what we've just been discussing.'

'Come, come, Colonel,' Mado said in English, 'I'm sure *your* sense of humour is more than skin deep.'

Voznitsky flashed him an angry look and then smiled.

457

'Are you certain you can do as you say?' he said in English, 'otherwise you are only provoking difficulties.'

Schofield who had left the room earlier on and had then come back, now whispered a question into Mado's ear.

'Yes,' Mado said, whereupon Schofield again left the room.

'I can deliver,' Mado went on to Voznitsky in English. The Russian reacted with a barely disguised sneer.

'My information is that a meeting with the girl is unlikely ever to be possible.'

'Where is she?' Dr Petrov mumbled in Russian, 'where is she?'

Great tears were rolling down his cheeks in a lugubrious way which was both pathetic and ridiculous.

'*Ever* to be possible?' Mado said to Voznitsky. 'That's a big statement.'

'But not made without reason, Mr Mado.'

'In other words,' Mado went on, leading him further and further into the trap, 'you have the lady under your control.'

'I did not say that.'

There was a pause as they looked at each other.

'Of course adjustments are always possible.'

'Yes,' Mado said, enjoying himself, 'you can say that again.'

At that moment Schofield opened the door and ushered in Helen Stanopoulos. She still looked pale and frightened, but at least she was now conscious and able to walk in a normal way. Dr Petrov emitted a sort of animal groan and stumbled across to embrace her. Voznitsky froze into a statue-like immobility, watched closely by Mado and the military attaché.

For a few moments while Petrov and his love exchanged more or less meaningless phrases of relief and pleasure at seeing each other again, Mado kept quiet, wondering if the ransoming of Helen Stanopoulos also meant that Anna and the baby would be released in London. Of course, he thought bitterly, that was only his personal life—a by-product of little importance. But there was no time to indulge himself in this way for long. The drama in progress in the basement of the British Embassy would have to be speedily concluded and Mado realized he must keep the initiative.

'Well, Colonel,' he said to Voznitsky, 'did I not tell you we could deliver? Somewhere along the line your information must be at fault.'

Voznitsky inclined his head stiffly in acknowledgement. He was in a considerable turmoil, but none of this showed except for a sharp anxious look in the eyes. In fact he was completely at a loss. He had been taken by surprise, let down by his subordinates as usual. He would institute a little private terror of his own when he got back to the Embassy. In the meantime what was he now to do?

He felt a disgust in the pit of his stomach. Although he had just put up a virtuoso performance with this sentimental fool of a Dr Petrov, he could draw no satisfaction from it. He knew what would happen to Petrov when he got back to Russia. This working cynicism, for so long part of his daily life, a part he had once relished as a member of the élite, now made him almost physically sick. He became aware of being closely studied by Mado and he therefore stared back.

'You're wondering where she's been these last few days.'

'Yes.'

'So am I.'

Why was this British ex-spy being so co-operative and helpful? What sort of trap was being laid for him now? A sudden desire to be done with it all struck him with overwhelming force, so much so that to Mado's evident surprise, he sat down and in a rather clumsy way got out his handkerchief and wiped his face.

'Are you all right, Colonel?' Mado asked.

He nodded but looked away.

'Well, I could do with a drink,' Mado said, 'suppose we go upstairs—you and I—and leave Dr Petrov and his secretary together for a few moments? They'll be perfectly safe.'

Voznitsky hesitated, still on the watch for an obvious trap. Contrary to all his instinct and training, he was forced to admit to himself that he warmed towards this British spy with his pushed-in face. Indeed he not only liked him but trusted him. Once again he became aware that Mado was studying him quizzically. He managed a rather frozen smile, wondering why he felt as odd as he did. 'I accept your invitation,' he said in a formal way.

'I suggest you use the naval attaché's room,' Schofield said as they went upstairs. 'Ginger's down at Piræus so you'll be undisturbed.'

It was important to keep Padstow out of it at this juncture.

'Look in on the lovebirds,' Mado said, 'and tell Mr P where I am.'

CHAPTER EIGHT

WHEN THEY HAD helped themselves to the naval attaché's Scotch and had settled down with Mado behind the desk and Voznitsky in the comfortable visitor's chair, an atmosphere of anticipation filled the room. Like the military attaché's office, the one they were in had an agreeable view of the superbly kept Embassy lawn and garden. They might have been two leisured gentlemen in an eighteenth-century English country house, but the feeling in the air was more like that of a theatre or television studio just before the show begins.

Voznitsky thought ruefully of the contrast this deeply civilized décor made with the Soviet embassies he had known. One such embassy in which he had served had been unkindly but aptly described as an oasis of darkness in a sea of light. Once again he was compelled to admit privately to himself that it was the spirit which mattered, the spirit which gave this place its life and which so basically disturbed him.

Even though it was now a complex of government offices, the British Embassy in Athens still retained some of the elegance of the great private house which it had once been. The comparison with the furtive soullessness of his own Soviet premises filled with their ill-arranged and unloved ex-bourgeois furniture, their cracked mirrors, their seedy propaganda magazines in the waiting-room and the general imprint of prison fear, undermined yet further the wavering loyalty which was all he had left. In that sense he knew himself to be more at risk than ever he had been before, and he wondered in passing how much of this might be apparent to Mado.

He did not have long to wait.

'I'm going to take a chance,' Mado said and then paused as if searching for the right words, 'I'm going to level with you.'

'I'm not sure what that means,' Voznitsky said and Mado then explained in Russian that he was going to lay his cards—or at any rate some of his cards—on the table in a spirit of trust.

'What are you expecting from me, Mr Mado?'

'Everything, I suppose,' Mado said, looking at the bronze bust of Nelson on the naval attaché's desk. And then with a shrug of his shoulders, 'Or nothing. Usually it's nothing in the experience of both of us.'

'I suggest you stop talking in riddles and come to the point.'

Mado laughed.

'I've never known a Russian yet who prefers the direct approach. But just as you like. . . .'

There was another pause.

'I think I can guess what the question is going to be,' Voznitsky said, 'so perhaps it would be just as well if we approached it obliquely.'

'You see? At least it proves what I said. You're certainly a Russian.'

Again there was a pause.

'It doesn't look as if I'm going to get a lot of help from you,' Mado went on at last, 'so let me start going out on a limb. Then when I've gone far enough, you can saw off the branch.'

Voznitsky smiled. 'That allegory I understand.'

'Let me sort out the pieces and tell you what I see as the state of play,' Mado said. 'To begin with I think you're a unique and very unhappy man. You're successful but you have a great deal —a very great deal on your conscience. This has never worried you very much in the past because your life has been spent in the company of similarly-minded spiritual cretins.'

Voznitsky realized he was being insulted but the detail escaped him. Mado saw this and checked himself.

'I'm sorry,' he said, 'but I sometimes get carried away.'

'You're trying to get me to defect, aren't you, Mr Mado?'

Mado stared at him hard, holding the pause as it seemed to Voznitsky for ever.

'But of course,' he said in a quiet voice, 'and insulting your brother officers of the KGB isn't going to help. I see that and I'm sorry. However, what I've just said is true. You are within sight of the highest range of jobs in the largest private army in the world. I salute your success. However, since you've been the Resident here in Greece, you've been finding, to your great dismay, that your heart isn't in it any more. You're an aristocrat and your life has been spent with the serfs.'

At the mention of the word 'aristocrat', Voznitsky again became completely still and as watchful as an Afghan sentry on the Khyber Pass.

461

'What makes you say I'm an aristocrat? Or are you simply insulting me as well as my brother officers?'

'I'm not insulting you at all,' Mado said, 'the very opposite in fact. I don't carry it around with me, but we do have a very full dossier on your great-grandfather, grandfather, father and yourself. So far as the first two are concerned we had that information before 1917 when so many records in Russia got so conveniently lost. I'm not shooting a line and I'm not trying to scare you but we do have a very detailed file on you, your wife and your relatives. We know what sort of man you are. We know most of the shameful tricks you've played. We have a long list of the people you've had shot or otherwise put away. If you were a German Nazi, you would not be alive and of course, in a sense, you have been a Nazi in spirit the whole of your adult life. Your latest victim is down below there in the storeroom kissing a fond farewell to what little he knows of a free and fulfilling life. Poor old sod! You put it over on him, didn't you, Colonel, with your very best expertise? I must say I admired your technique—and so will the wretched Petrov when you've got him safely locked away in one of your psychiatric hospitals—*if* he's allowed to stay alive. However . . .'

Mado poured out more Scotch for both of them and lit another cigarette: 'As I said before, you're a very unhappy man. You've begun to question yourself and that's a dangerous course of action to take. Add to that the fact that your wife spies on you and when she isn't doing that bores you to distraction . . . so you are generally disgusted with the life you have so far led. In addition you've acquired a full range of Western tastes. You even have friends—not a luxury recommended for high officers of the KGB. You've discovered you're a human being, too, like the rest of us. It all tots up to one devastating conclusion you can no longer avoid. It's simple and it stares you in the face. If you could devise some way of getting your son out of Soviet Russia, you wouldn't think twice about doing a Petrov yourself.'

Voznitsky sat very still, hardly seeming to breathe. He was mildly surprised at the accuracy of Mado's knowledge but this he could understand. He realized that the Britisher was not talking in an aggressive or provocative way. He was simply stating the facts as Voznitsky would be doing himself were the roles reversed. The extraordinary thing was that instead of resenting it, he felt almost relieved. He had just applied a similar process to the man

Mado described as his 'victim' and he had seen the relief flush across the old fool's face when at last it was out and the nagging, gnawing, guilt-generating secrets had been brought into the open and at least partially exorcized.

'Only one thing, in fact, holds you back,' Mado went on, 'and even of that you're beginning to be somewhat ashamed. You'd come over now—just as you are—did you not happen to have a high sense of duty—and that's the only reason you're not out of your mind.'

'I supose I should be grateful,' Voznitsky said, 'to have one good quality admitted by this public prosecutor you seem to have become.'

Mado stiffened his approach. This was no genial chat. He had Voznitsky where he wanted him for the moment. It would be fatal to let him relax.

'Look, sport, don't interrupt me when I'm belting it out. I'm still going out on this limb. No one has yet handed you a saw. And I can get very mean and disagreeable at the drop of a hat.'

'You're surely not threatening me, are you? That would be too absurd.'

'No, no, no,' Mado said, a lightly sarcastic tone in his voice, 'no threats. Not with shiny Karai out there in the car park. Who needs blackmail when you have a man like Karai in the compound?'

'It could be that you're getting carried away again,' Voznitsky remarked in a calm voice. 'Mr Karai is merely doing his job.'

'Okay, but you're not exactly enjoying his visit.'

'He will disappear from the scene when Petrov returns to Russia.'

'And that's what Dr Petrov is going to do?'

'Oh yes, Mr Mado, I don't think there's much doubt about it.'

'I wouldn't be too sure now that he's seen Helen Stanopoulos again.'

Voznitsky twisted his mouth into some sort of smile: 'I thought you British had a sense of fair play? Was it fair to bring her in at the moment you did?'

'I'd been listening to the promises you were putting over on Petrov.'

'Well,' said Voznitsky, managing to suppress the anger he felt, 'your introduction of that particular problem will not work to your advantage. We shall require her to go to Russia as well. She knows too much of Dr Petrov's work.'

463

'And if she decides not to go?'

'My dear Mr Mado,' Voznitsky said, assuming a familiarity which somehow or other did not ring true, 'you ask strangely innocent questions for a man of your experience.'

'You mean she might have to be eliminated from the scene?'

'If you were in my position, Mr Mado, I wonder how you would react?'

'Yes,' Mado said after a reflective pause, 'you're a jolly lot of thugs and murderers, you KGB.'

'Insulting us—as we said before—isn't going to advance your cause in any way.'

'Look, sport, let me make myself clear. I'm not advancing a cause. I'm doing a job. . . .'

'As I am, too.'

'I carry out orders. In this case I was told to make you an offer. It's a very simple and pleasant one to make. I'm giving you the chance of opting out of it all. Whether you take it or not matters to you but not to me. Personally I couldn't care less. My only private feelings are those of disgust. Disgust and surprise that you've put up with it as long as you have. If you don't lay hold of this lifeline I'm throwing you, I shan't lose any sleep. I haven't got at least fifteen murdered men on my conscience. You're the guy with the answering to do. And you're no Karai. You don't relish what they force you to do. What's more you're intelligent enough to know that you're very unlikely to get a second chance like this. Once your present posting is over, you won't be leaving Russia again. They'll kick you upstairs, as we say in my country, when they give out the titles and take away the power. You'll be neutered and put out to grass. Don't tell me you haven't read your *1984*. So you have some quick thinking to do.'

'You're not coolly suggesting that I should defect here and now?'

'Why not? What better chance will you have?' He held Voznitsky's eyes in a cold, steady gaze. 'What *other* chance will you have? And if you pass it up, you'll never know, will you? Your life will have gone through and you'll end up as an old piece of machinery—an old car in a scrapyard—your service usefully done but with no profit whatever to your eternal soul, if you admit to such a thing . . . as I think perhaps you do.'

It was incredible. Voznitsky felt himself gulping in an attempt to suppress the emotions surging up to his throat.

'I can scarcely believe my ears,' he said in the end, and lapsed into silence. A bluebottle buzzed angrily against the window-pane and with unconscious symbolism Mado got up and let it out. Then he sat down again and stared at Voznitsky with what seemed to the Russian to be a calculated smile. Around them in the immediate vicinity the daily routine of a busy Western embassy continued on its normal course. Occasionally the naval attaché's secretary put her head round the door to see that her two visitors were not getting up to any mischief. A messenger brought some files and dumped them into the In basket in a casual way which would certainly not have taken place in Voznitsky's office. From time to time the sound of distant traffic penetrated the room and outside the afternoon sun beat down with a merciless glare.

'How long have you been approaching this point?' Voznitsky asked. The 'aristocratic' virus was doing its work. Mado shrugged his shoulders as if the question had no relevance.

'How would you answer such a question yourself? I'm merely the guy who puts you the proposition.'

'And what would you do if I happened to say yes?'

'Ah!' said Mado, rubbing the bridge of his nose, 'you'd have to say yes to find out.'

'I think *you* will find out that my Ambassador will shortly be calling on yours to complain that I am being held here by force. What then?'

'You would have to confront him—and your mate, Karai—and tell him you weren't.'

'And suppose I claim that I was?'

'I think we should survive,' Mado said, with an ironic smile.

'All right,' Voznitsky said, getting to his feet, 'this has gone on long enough. I am now going to leave your Embassy and I shall take Dr Petrov and Miss Stanopoulos with me.'

Mado, too, got to his feet and went to the door which he opened to allow Voznitsky to go through first.

'You may certainly take Dr Petrov with you if he wishes to go. We have yet to find out what Miss Stanopoulos wants to do with her life—but I don't imagine our friend Marides has ransomed the lady at a high cost just so that you can calmly abduct her to Russia.'

'So you would hold her here by force?'

'Force seems to loom large in your thinking,' Mado said, as they made their way down to the basement, 'but you know as I do the rules of this dreary game we both have to play. So be a good chap and don't provoke us too far yourself. Otherwise you'll be pushing your luck.'

Schofield was evidently glad to see them return. Dr Petrov and Helen Stanopoulos were sitting on two chairs in the corner holding hands like lovers in a park.

'Mr P would like to see you,' Schofield said to Mado, 'but he leaves the timing to you.'

'Lucky old me,' Mado said, looking hard at Dr Petrov and his secretary. 'I get all the nice decisions to take. How are you feeling?' he went on to Helen.

She compressed her lips and gave him a watery smile.

'Not very well.'

'Colonel Voznitsky is leaving,' Mado turned to Dr Petrov. 'He wants you both to go with him to the Russian Embassy.'

They looked at Voznitsky who stood near erect and formidable near to the door. It struck Mado that they had the dejected look of cattle walking up the ramp into a slaughterhouse and so far as Dr Petrov was concerned, exhibiting the same level of intelligence.

'You are both free to do as you please. You are both here in the British Embassy by your own choice and though I've no doubt whatever that your uncle would want you to stay here, Helen—at any rate until your mind is clear—I repeat the decision is yours.'

There was a pause. Here in this basement room lit only by artificial light, the sunlight, the embassy garden and the outside world seemed difficult even to imagine. Voznitsky said nothing. His presence was threat enough. Then slowly Dr Petrov got to his feet, and addressed himself to Voznitsky in Russian.

'You say that facilities can be provided for my secretary to accompany me to Russia?'

'I shall be delighted to arrange it. There will be no difficulties whatever. In fact it is really your duty to go.'

'Well, Helen. . . ?' Petrov said. Helen Stanopoulos gazed at him with her dark sad eyes. Then slowly she shook her head.

'I'm staying here . . . perhaps a little later. . . .'

'You need not commit yourself to stay in our country,' Voznitsky said, 'you may accompany Dr Petrov as a visitor and leave when you please.'

It was on the tip of Mado's tongue to remark that if she believed that she would believe the world to be square, but he kept quiet waiting to see what she would say.

'No, thank you,' she said. 'I am not going to Russia.'

'Very well,' Voznitsky said, as if dismissing a squad on a parade ground, 'you can always change your mind. All you need to do is ask for a visa. Come along then, Dr Petrov,' he went on in Russian, 'we are expecting you to dinner tonight. My wife, as you know, makes a very good bortsch.'

'*Ne vas pas, ne vas pas,*' Helen cried in a low voice, 'I can't stand it if you go.'

She threw herself into his arms, watched impassively by Schofield, Mado and Voznitsky. With sudden and unexpected roughness, Dr Petrov pushed her away and then went over to the door.

'You stay with the girl,' Mado said to Schofield and led the way up to the Embassy hall and out into the porch. As soon as they appeared the Russian Embassy car drove up. There was no sign of Karai. As Dr Petrov got into the car, Voznitsky—somewhat to Mado's surprise—offered his hand.

'Thank you,' he said, 'I hope we shall meet again.'

'I hope so, too,' Mado said, shaking his hand and seeing him into the car, 'my wife makes a terrible bortsch but I expect we can rustle up an egg—if I can find my wife, that is.'

'I think you'll discover she's at home in London and none the worse for the little holiday she took. Why not call her up now? Before the crisis breaks here.'

'What crisis?'

Voznitsky smiled in a foxy way.

'You don't suppose the Nikolaides will be content with blowing up a millionaire's house, do you, Mr Mado?'

'There are other treats in store?'

'Don't let your people deprive you of your diplomatic immunity,' Voznitsky said, 'in some situations it may be all you have left.'

Then, with a wave of his hand, the car drove out of the Embassy grounds.

Dr Vakelopoulos, the Embassy doctor, was a discreet man who looked after a number of embassies but who continued to hold down his job thanks to the close rapport he maintained with the

467

security police. Because of this, his presence became a mixed blessing, his embassy clients feeling that the Hippocratic oath inevitably got itself a little bent in the process. It was inadvisable to leave him alone in a foreign embassy and now that he was examining Helen, the military attaché told his secretary to be there throughout.

She had been right—they were going to be a little too busy to have dinner together that night.

Mado seized this break in the action to put a call through to London, in the meanwhile analysing the situation with Padstow.

'I don't think I did all that well,' Mado said, 'I took Colonel V by surprise—perhaps too much so.'

Padstow had been leafing through the considerable Voznitsky file. He was fully aware of the gamble they had taken and of how little they might have to show for it at the end.

'He was expecting some sort of approach. There's always a risk with the timing and I asked you to dive in when you did. Anyway I've no complaints. A Resident is a valuable catch but if it doesn't work, it doesn't work and that's all there is to it.'

They worked back over the sequence of events they had been through in the last few days.

'I think Colonel V has a connection with the Nikolaides which we don't know about.'

'That's very likely.'

'Or he was bluffing about Helen Stanopoulos.'

'I don't think he was bluffing,' Padstow said. 'The Colonel has good underground contacts with Greek security. He'll get what help he needs in pressurizing the girl. In spite of the price paid, in spite of being Marides' niece, I wouldn't rate her chances of survival as high. She knows too much.'

The telephone rang.

'Your call to London, Mr Mado,' the operator said, and to Mado's astonishment and relief, he heard Anna's voice at the other end of the line.

'Are you all right?' he almost shouted.

'We're both all right,' Anna said.

'What happened? Where have you been?'

'We were taken somewhere in the country—several hours in a car. Where, I don't know—but we're all right. When are you coming back?'

'Just as soon as I can,' Mado said. 'You were quite right—I should never have come out here.'

'Well, make it soon. I don't want another experience of that kind.'

'Were you treated all right?'

'It wasn't exactly a rest cure. But physically we're all right. We've now got police protection twenty-four hours of the day. It's a little late but it's comforting all the same.'

'Don't worry,' Mado said, 'your British police are wonderful.'

A very rude word in her native Czech impinged on his ear.

'I can tell you're all right,' Mado said, 'I'll be back as soon as I can.'

He put down the phone. A wave of relief engulfed him so that for a moment or so he felt unable to speak. Padstow poured him out an extra large Scotch.

'You can go tonight if you like,' he said, 'the Ambassador will be delighted, I'm sure.'

Mado took a long drink and stared out of the window at the Embassy garden. There was a gentle wind and above the trees the matchless blue of the Greek sky shimmered in the heat. The clarity of the light and air never ceased to astonish him and now that he knew Anna and his child to be safe, at least for the moment, he felt like taking a few hours off and going for a swim. Gradually, however, as he mastered his feelings and the Scotch took its effect, the old gambler's taste for danger returned. Padstow watched him with a smile and kept his peace.

'I said a little while back I was getting too old for this sort of thing,' Mado said eventually, 'however, I'm not too far gone not to see this thing through. I'll stick around a little longer—and His Excellency can lump it.'

'Good,' Padstow said, 'that was what I was hoping you'd say.'

CHAPTER NINE

THE BRITISH AMBASSADOR returned from the Greek Ministry of Foreign Affairs in a rare old rage which he vented at the first opportunity on Padstow. When the summons into the ambassadorial presence came, Mado said: 'I'll bet you a drachma the

469

first thing he says is "I don't know what you people think you're doing. . . ." '

Padstow frowned. 'Us people are getting brassed off with always being put on the mat simply for doing our job.'

'Gird your loins, sport,' Mado said. 'His Excellency has some other shocks coming his way. Tell him good old reliable Mado is working on the time-bomb in the basement. That'll cheer him up.'

'What time-bomb in the basement?'

'Helen Stanopoulos. Marides didn't have her sent here for fun. I'm going to have a talk with the lady as soon as Dr Vakelopoulos is through examining her. We may not have too much time.'

'I take your point,' Padstow said and went in to see the Ambassador.

'Now look here, Mr Padstow,' His Excellency said, and from the expression on his lined 'official' face, Padstow knew he had lost the bet he had just been offered by Mado. 'I don't know what you people think this Embassy is but these irregular activities have got to be brought under control. I'm not having any more of it— I don't care how many personal letters you produce from the Foreign Secretary or anyone else. I've had an unpleasant and completely needless interview with the Greek Foreign Minister and I don't intend another. The Greek authorities have been very patient with us so far, but that won't continue for ever.'

'Patient—with us?' Padstow could scarcely believe his ears.

'Of course the Greeks are fully aware of the Petrov business,' the Ambassador continued, 'and, as I was forced to agree, obliged us by in no way interfering when matters reached a delicate point.'

'With respect, sir,' Padstow put in, trying not to overdo the acid, 'it suited their book not to interfere whilst the East European Trade Fair was on.'

The Ambassador did not like being interrupted. He shifted impatiently from buttock to buttock.

'Are you trying to teach me my business, Mr Padstow?'

The Ambassador glared at him with such intense dislike that Padstow made no reply.

'I am fully cognisant of the fact that your immediate chief reports directly to the Prime Minister. I realize that you are not a civil servant—nor is your Mr Mado—and that you use your constitutional position, if that is the way to put it, to suit your secret purposes. I accept the legitimacy of that. However, there is nothing in the regulations applicable to me which says that I have to enjoy your presence in my Embassy and I assure you I do not. I am also the man responsible on the spot. You come and go like fairies in the night ['Whoever told him we were queer?' Padstow said afterwards to Mado]. You suit yourselves. And you leave us to pick up the pieces and clear up the mess.'

'What pieces and what mess?'

'Well . . .' the Ambassador said, with a rather too obvious attempt to control his annoyance, 'you haven't done too well with Dr Petrov, have you? I gather he decided not to defect after all.'

'That was always his privilege. There are other equally important matters at stake.'

'The British Embassy does not exist to give sleazy little foreign dissidents the opportunity to pleasure their secretaries,' the Ambassador said. 'Nor is there any welcome here for the girl in question who, I would remind you, is a Greek citizen in her own country. That young woman is not to be given asylum here. The Greek Foreign Minister was insistent on that. They want her out of here in double quick time—and I see no reason for not complying with their wishes.'

This was a little too much even for Padstow. He decided to fight back. Disdain and exasperation were not a monopoly of the higher members of the diplomatic service. He, too, had been to Harrow.

'I was given to understand, sir, that we could look to your Excellency for all the help and support we would obviously need on our extremely delicate mission. I'm afraid the Prime Minister —through my immediate chief, as you have observed—will have to be told that things are not quite as we expected in Athens.'

'What do you mean by that?'

'Helen Stanopoulos was kidnapped, threatened with death, expensively ransomed and brought to the British Embassy because this is the one place in Athens where she might be thought to be safe. You are now proposing to show her the door.'

'Well?'

'Which is the equivalent of signing her death warrant. Why? Because the Colonels have shown a touch of steel to a foreign Ambassador?'

His Excellency was appalled. He rose slowly to his feet.

'I beg your pardon, Mr Padstow?'

'As you say, Ambassador, I am not a civil servant and as Mr Mado observed to you before we are only unwelcome visitors in your Embassy. To adapt the Duke of Wellington's famous remark: "I don't know what your Embassy does to the Greeks, but it certainly puts the fear of God into me".'

The Ambassador looked as though he might be having a heart attack.

'Luckily for all of us,' Padstow went on, 'we can call on a little more co-operation from the CIA. It's not what I want but unless you can see your way to helping us to a greater extent than you have so far, I shall be forced to arrange for Miss Stanopoulos, Mr Mado and myself to transfer to the American Embassy forthwith.'

He waited for a second or two to see if there were any signs of a change but none were forthcoming.

He therefore excused himself correctly, turned on his heel and left the room.

The Ambassador sat down, overcome by shock, and then rang for his secretary.

'I shall have a pressing report for the Foreign Secretary,' he said, 'which had better go off to London tonight.'

But again events overtook them. No sooner had Padstow returned to the military attaché's office, than the naval attaché, a young Post Captain with flaming red hair and the inevitable nickname, put his head round the door.

'You'd both better come and drink some of my duty free,' he said, 'I've a piece of news which may interest the cloak and dagger department.'

As they walked along the corridor, Mado said to Padstow: 'Dr Vakelopoulos wants to remove Helen S to hospital for observation.'

'That will certainly suit His Excellency,' Padstow remarked and quickly put Mado in the picture as to what had just transpired.

'Unfortunately she refuses to go.'

'Why?'

'A little understandable Greek mistrust. She seems to think they'll "get" her once she's no longer under British protection.'

'What does Dr Vakelopoulos say is wrong with her?'

'He doesn't know, or he won't say.'

'How is she—in your opinion?'

'Schofield's secretary says she seems to be quite all right. What-ever was put into her is obviously wearing off. As she and Dr Vakelopoulos talked in Greek, though, the secretary doesn't know what was really said. The doctor has gone, saying he'll send an ambulance for her. Apparently this produced an outbreak of the οχι's with a great shaking of the head.'

'I suppose she could claim political asylum, though that's the last thing the Ambassador wants.'

By this time they were in the naval attaché's room, where Ginger deftly supplied them with drink.

'His Excellency may well have to stiffen up to another situa-tion,' the naval attaché said, 'the Trade Fair ends tonight and the word is about that the Greeks are cleaning out the stables. We all know what that means. A precautionary rounding up of any pos-sible suspect—left-wing, liberal or urban guerrilla. The Nix can always be blamed. Then comes the administration of treatment where necessary in Boubolina Street and another wave of police terror to discourage any dissidents who may still be around.'

'Where did you learn all this?'

'From my American friends. The Sixth Fleet is a great comfort in times of trouble. But that's not what I got you along for. I have a message for you from Panayotis Marides.'

'You've seen him yourself? Where is he?'

'On board one of his ships in Piræus, a ship flying the Red Ensign,' the naval attaché said with a smile.

'You did see him yourself?'

'He asked me to visit him—all perfectly legitimate, you see, for the British naval attaché to go aboard a British ship. When I asked him why he was there, he said, "Well, you can't trust the Greeks, can you?".'

'That's Pan all right,' Mado said with a chuckle, 'what's the message? What's on his mind?'

'He wants you to get his wife out of that hospital and into the British Embassy. He added that you should take Miss Eckersley along as well.'

'Why?'

'Because of what I said earlier on. The Colonels are cooking up something, and life's going to be tricky in Athens for the next few days.'

473

Padstow and Mado considered the implications of this and then
Padstow said: 'Did he mention his son?'

'No. But I gather from my American friends that Christos
Marides has had a sudden posting away from Athens.'

'Do you know where?'

The naval attaché smiled: 'I believe there was some emergency
in the Greek Embassy in Moscow which he was required to take
care of.'

'Or, in plain English, to get him out of the way.'

'How was Marides?' Mado asked.

'I don't know him as well as you do,' the naval attaché replied,
'he seemed to be chafing at his bit. He told me he still intends going to Pekin as soon as he can get away. I had the impression,
though, that he was waiting for something to happen. What, I
don't know. Naturally he needs to find out who planted that bomb
in his house . . . and whether he was really the target . . . if he
doesn't already know.'

'He'll know,' Mado said. 'It's the remedial action that's keeping
him here.'

'We have some remedial action to take ourselves,' Padstow said.
'I'll get Helen Stanopoulos over to our American friends. You'd
better go out to the hospital and collect Elissa and Andrea.'

'Since when has there been an Embassy ambulance?' Mado
asked sourly. 'How can I do that if they can't even walk?'

'You'll think of a way, George,' Padstow said. And then with a
questioning glance at the naval attaché, 'Perhaps the Royal Navy
could sail in to your help?'

'I have a car with CD plates,' Ginger said with a glint of pleasure
in his eye, 'let's be on our way.'

The naval attaché had been right in his prognosis of the general
situation. As every service and press attaché in every major Embassy was soon to discover, the Greek dictatorship had decided on
a show of strength. Not that the Colonels were insecure. Not that
there was any threat to the regime. The reasons were mixed.

As Andrea Eckersley had written in one of her earlier features,
the Colonels were highly successful in their running of Greece.
The country was prosperous. Law and order in its outward form
prevailed. Freaks and drop-outs were prevented at the frontiers
from dropping in or had their hair cut and their wallets examined

before being allowed to spend their money in the cradle of democracy. As under Mussolini, the trains ran more or less on time. As under Hitler, you did not argue with anyone in uniform. As under Stalin, you kept a cautious eye on the friendly stranger next to you in the bar, especially if he showed a tendency to sympathize with any criticisms you might be making of present-day life in Greece.

Why then were the road blocks suddenly manned, the uniformed police roving the streets in force, identity papers being spot checked, police cars and military vehicles rushing about Athens in a self-important way and the checking of travellers at airports and frontiers so clearly intensified? Tension was being openly and visibly stepped up by a display of force.

'Keep your diplomatic immunity,' Voznitsky had said as his parting words to Mado. 'In some situations it may be all you have left.'

Mado thought about this as he drove out to the coast hospital where the victims of the Marides house bombing had been taken, the red-haired Royal Naval captain obviously enjoying the freedom the CD plates on his car bestowed.

'Did Marides let you into any secrets as to what all this is about?' Mado asked as they passed through yet another road block, manned by arrogant-looking Greek security forces. The naval attaché shook his head.

'There has to be a display from time to time. It's part of the game. All bully boys like to show off, whether's it's picketing the docks in England or tarting about like this lot here. Dictators can't live in silence for long . . . and they are the masters now. My guess is simply that there's a power struggle going on behind the scenes. Some new manipulator has gone to work. No doubt he wanted to get rid of Marides first.'

'He's such an old hand at dealing with that particular ploy,' Mado said, 'he's almost indestructible. Who do you think is behind the present gymnastics?'

'The Nix,' said the naval attaché, 'they're the only real threat the Colonels admit to themselves. And why? Because some of the top Greek brass is in with the Nikolaides behind the scenes; because the Nix are highly organized; because they work on personal trust, they don't write things down, they avoid the telephone, they act on a nod of understanding and they take money and help from all sides without promising anything in return. They run a sort of *samizdat* of Greece. Like communists will do anything to discredit capitalism, these people act in dozens of different ways to bring down the regime. And the Colonels remain uneasy because the Nix very often know what goes on from the inside. No one is completely sure who the inside boys really are.'

'You're well informed,' Mado said.

'Well, the game began with naval intelligence, didn't it?' the captain said crisply. 'However, I don't vent that sort of remark in the Embassy. There I'm just a naval clot with ideas above his station. I can tell you, George Mado, in this appointment I've been patronized by experts.'

'I wish your Ambassador . . .' Mado began and then thought better of it. 'I suppose the little chap is just doing the best job he can by his own lights, pompous though he is.'

'Ah well, the diplomatic knows very well indeed how to be a law unto itself. That's the establishment attitude which so niggles my military colleague, Schofield. But he's more involved in it than I am. Luckily I still have a certain independence, subject of course to the Naval Discipline Act. But the Foreign Service is taking a long, long time to recover from Philby and that first husband of the lady we're going to see. Tarnham did their mandarin complex no good at all. Old pursemouth doesn't like to be reminded of that.'

'You don't seem to think very highly of our country's diplomatic representative.'

'It's a little matter of guts,' the naval attaché observed, 'and especially of not passing the buck in the Whitehall way.'

'All right,' Mado said, 'now I'll take you up on that. We've been thrown out—or rather we've just thrown ourselves out of the Athens Embassy. Now, looking at this lot . . .' he jerked his head at yet another group of ugly-looking security police who were leaning on a motorist they had stopped for interrogation, 'the timing couldn't be worse. Padstow and I need a home. The CIA can—and may have to—help us out at the American Embassy. Personally I fancy something a little more British and secure.'

The naval attaché smiled.

'Well, well, well,' he said, 'now isn't it a stroke of luck that the captain of that frigate in Piræus just happens to be a friend of mine.'

Mado showed his appreciation and pressed on: 'And suppose—

just suppose I had some guests—some embarrassing guests I wanted taking care of. . . .'

'A Greek girl?'

'Or the wife of a Greek multi-millionaire—a well-known woman journalist—possibly even a Colonel in the KGB.'

'You need a wholesaler, not a ship,' Ginger said, 'however I think you'll find that hospitality on board HM ships is much the same as it ever was. After all a captain of a ship is the captain of a ship. It's his judgment on the spot which really matters. The "reasons in writing" come later. It's the now that counts.'

'It's the now that matters now,' Mado agreed as they drove into the hospital grounds and negotiated yet another security check from the Greek police.

'Here is a full detailed statement of your abduction by agents of the British security forces; your confinement against your will in an underground prison cell in the British Embassy; your ill-treatment, starvation and torture, both mental and physical, together with the names of the perpetrators of this crime against human rights, notably that of the ex-spy Mado. . . .'

Ivan Karai smiled at the morose expression on Dr Petrov's face.

They were in one of the interrogation rooms of the Russian Embassy, watched by Voznitsky, the proceedings as usual being recorded on tape.

'But . . .' Dr Petrov began and then stopped. He was taking a long time to accept or even to realize the hard facts of his new situation. 'That was not quite what happened,' he went on lamely.

'It is how you described it under interrogation last night,' Karai said grittily, still with that KGB smile Voznitsky knew so well and which now more than ever sickened him in the stomach. 'I should advise you to sign, Dr Petrov,' Karai went on in his smooth, friendly way. 'The matter is then adjusted so far as Athens is concerned.'

'They treated me very well,' Petrov mumbled, 'I went there of my own free will.'

'I'm afraid I didn't catch that last remark,' Karai's voice took on a sudden, steely tone. 'If you wish to add to your formal statement for the record, I must ask you to speak up in a loud, clear voice.'

'When are you arranging for my secretary to rejoin me?' Petrov

477

said, toying with his pen but still not signing. The fool, Voznitsky thought, he still thinks of himself as the great Doctor Petrov, a power in the land. There would not be many secretaries around for him when he returned to Moscow.

'She will follow us to Moscow,' Karai said, dropping back into the syrupy tones he had used so far. 'No doubt as soon as Comrade Voznitsky has again brought his persuasive powers to bear. I congratulate you on the good sense you have so far shown, Doctor Petrov, in co-operating as you have. Now, however, time is getting short. We have a plane to catch, you and I. So if you would kindly sign that report which you have made without pressure of any kind, then, as I say, the matter is adjusted so far as Athens is concerned.'

'There will be other interrogations in Moscow?'

'Come, come, comrade, you cannot expect me to speak for the authorities in Moscow. I've no doubt you'll be asked certain questions as a result of your actions. That is natural enough. But, like this, it will be a mere formality.'

Voznitsky turned away and lit a cigarette. He felt physically sick and for a moment or two thought he was going to vomit. It was not that he could honestly express much sympathy for Dr Petrov, whose puerile lechery had brought its inevitable reward. He did not care a fig for the wobbly old fool. What was now causing him such nausea was the KGB process itself, the stench of hypocrisy in which he had lived all his life and the glimpses of dignity, honour and reasonable human behaviour he had been vouchsafed during his time in Greece.

Now in this room which, like the storeroom in the British Embassy, admitted no light of day and with its ironbound grille could only be seen as the prison cell it was, memories of Elissa, Marides and even Mado, the ex-spy he had come to respect, rose in his mind like a cloud of ignitable gas from some jungle swamp. One match was all it needed, Voznitsky thought as he inhaled deeply, one match could blow it all up.

'Very well,' Dr Petrov said with a heavy sigh, 'I sign.'

He did so and as Karai took the document from him, the smile faded from his face.

'You will remain here until we are ready to go.'

'But . . . what about my papers? I have to pack. There are people I should thank. I have to say my good-byes.'

'All that is taken care of,' Karai said briskly. 'Your papers and clothes have all been collected. Explanations for your sudden departure have been made. In any case the Press, which made such a fuss about your attempted defection, will see to it that your return to the Soviet Union—of your own free will—is adequately publicized. Well, Colonel,' he said over his shoulder as he went to the door, 'if you have no more questions to ask, let us leave Dr Petrov to order his thoughts.'

They left the room and nodded at the waiting guard. As they walked down the corridor, they heard the familiar sound of a key turning in a lock. Part of the music of my life, Voznitsky thought, as he followed Karai into the Ambassador's room.

'Now for the girl,' Karai said with the wary look of a tiger about to pounce.

'Yes,' Voznitsky said, 'that you will leave to me, Major Karai. You have two hours before your plane leaves for Prague.'

As the naval attaché and Mado were conducted to the private wing in which the Marides victims had been put, there could be no doubt of the tension in the air. There were even uniformed police or soldiers inside the hospital, pacing the corridors in pairs or leaning with an affectation of nonchalance against the doorposts of wards which for some reason it had been found expedient to lock.

'Spend your holidays in the carefree atmosphere of Greece,' Mado remarked to his new friend Ginger. 'Even this hospital pongs of prison.'

Elissa had a large pleasant room and in one corner the boy and girl were playing Scrabble. It seemed to Mado that Tarnham's luckless children spent their lives hanging about waiting-rooms, shielded, often inadequately, from the consequences of their father's defection and yet paying for it all the same. He was sorry for them. He had detested the father and in the early stages this had extended to the mother. Now that so much had happened since the original event, however, he found himself in a bizarre way fond of Elissa and protective of her and of the children.

She lay there in bed, looking delectable even to Mado's very different tastes. Her left leg was in plaster but the enforced rest in bed had taken the worried, strained look off her face. Or

479

perhaps it was that, physically trapped, she had forced herself to accept the imposed relaxation with a wary humour.

'How nice of you to come,' she said, as if welcoming them to a garden party.

'You've met Captain Ericson, our naval attaché, haven't you?' Mado said. 'In any case Pan knows him and asked us to come and get you out of here.'

'I know. He told me on the phone. Things must be in a very bad way if he can't come himself.'

'The place is crawling with police. So is Athens. They must be celebrating the end of the Trade Fair and the return to a normal life. And all those nasty communists will have gone back to their own countries.'

Elissa smiled. 'With nice fat deals in their pockets done in back rooms with members of the regime.' She gestured with her hand as if brushing the whole tawdry business aside and then went on: 'I think I'll take the children home to England for a while. Since the house was destroyed, Greece seems to me an even more uneasy place than it was before.'

'Have you any idea who was behind the attack?'

'I think I can guess.'

Mado looked her straight in the eyes, 'But hasn't he had another posting?'

She nodded.

'However, his chief and his friends remain. So Pan is lying low out of caution. I think he must have identified the root of the trouble. That's why he wants me out of here and why I want my-self to go back to England for a while.'

'How are the other victims?'

'The children, as you can see, are all right. The Americans have taken Lars Sweeney.'

'What Americans?'

'A naval ambulance from the Sixth Fleet came yesterday to take him aboard the flagship. He's going to need a long convalescence.'

'What about Andrea Eckersley?'

Elissa smiled. 'Can't you guess? She discharged herself yesterday just before all this police protection arrived.'

'I thought she'd broken a leg like you.'

'No. It was her arm. She looked in here before she left. I think she persuaded a young doctor to help get her out—well, he looked as if he might have been a doctor. She said to tell you, George, that as you'd obviously forgotten her existence, she had decided to remove herself before other interested parties got at her again. She said her shuttlecock days were over and you'd next hear all about it in the columns of the *Sunday Expectorator.*'

'Which arm was broken—the writing one?' Mado asked. 'Andrea can look after herself. You're the one who obviously needs some help. How soon can you be ready to move?'

'In about ten minutes,' Elissa said, 'but you may—we may have a little trouble with the staff.'

CHAPTER TEN

DUSK WAS SETTLING over an Athenian day in which inner and outward confusion had slopped over the scene like storm water over marshy land. To unspecialized eyes the show of force which the Greek authorities were making remained discreet. It was high summer. Athens still bulged with tourists and the dictatorship had by now become expert in applying pressure only—or more or less only—where it suited the purposes of the moment.

The tourist board and the business community of Athens had long been anxious—indeed at times desperately anxious—to improve the tarnished image of Greece as a free country where the life was all the time improving in quality and where any political restrictions could be depicted as purely temporary but necessary measures to achieve specific ends.

Secrecy, of course, remained an essential cloak over what really went on at any particular time and when that cloak had to be drawn aside, as in the current show of force, it was done as tactfully as possible so far as foreigners were concerned.

Outwardly, therefore, in the streets of Athens there was overt control but no paralysis. Traffic bustled about more or less as usual. Certainly identity checks were being carried out but no one was manhandled. No one was hindered from goofing at the Parthenon nor from swigging ouzo in the cafés of Constitution Square.

In so far as foreign embassies were concerned, the daily routine had gone on without interruption. Appointments were made and kept, people came and went and, in the British Embassy, no visitors and few of the staff were aware of the strange events connected with Dr Petrov, nor of the carry-over effects on a white-faced Greek girl now sitting unhappily in the leather armchair in the military attaché's office.

By now the ordinary working day had come to an end. No one remained in the Embassy except the duty officer, the guard and the few officials wishing to dispose of their paperwork after hours. Even these drifted away in ones or twos until only Padstow, Schofield and Helen Stanopoulos were left. Outside in the darkening garden, a little evening breeze moved in the trees: otherwise the Embassy had been put to bed in its normal way.

'You want to get rid of me, don't you?' Helen said to Padstow and Schofield. 'Why?'

'Because you are a Greek girl working in Greece for the United Nations. Because you have recently been the secretary of a controversial Russian specialist. Because your uncle is embroiled in Greek politics, and local urban guerrillas have just used you as a bargaining counter. All that adds up to an embarrassment to us or to any foreign embassy,' Schofield said. 'And now that you have refused the ambulance Dr Vakelopoulos sent, there are bound to be repercussions.'

'You say my uncle had me ransomed and sent here: then why doesn't he come here and collect me himself?'

'He may be in danger himself. Not maybe but obviously is,' Padstow said, looking down on the colour dying out of the hibiscus and bougainvillaea in the Embassy garden. In spite of the quiet evening, he felt a growing unease as if some jungle animal were prowling in the undergrowth out of sight but nevertheless very much present.

It had been on just such an evening some years before that Rupert Eynsham had been shot, an early by-product of the Tarnham connection, and now the wheel had turned once more—or was it a spiral and not a wheel? Not that it mattered. Tension, not philosophy, dominated him now. He turned back from the window as Helen Stanopoulos spoke after a pause.

'My uncle has led a dangerous life, but he is a man the Colonels respect and admire. He is powerful and rich.'

'Then why are you so afraid?' Padstow asked gently.

'I am not my uncle. I'm just me.'

'But you can't stay in the British Embassy the rest of your life.'

You're not even a Hungarian cardinal,' Padstow said with an unsuccessful attempt at a lighter touch. As the evening deepened into darkness so did this feeling of nervous pressure, of some great unknown danger looming over their heads.

'I don't know what to do,' Helen said simply, staring at her feet.

'It's about time we heard from Mado and Ericson,' Padstow remarked to the military attaché, and at that moment Mado walked into the room, taking the stage so to speak, and reopening their connection with the outside world.

'What are you glowering about?' Padstow said.

'I've a lot to glower about, I suppose,' Mado replied and gave a brief smile at Schofield, who, in an almost automatic reflex, poured him a sizable Scotch. Then Mado turned on Helen and gave her a clinical look.

'I'm glad *you're* still here at any rate,' he said. 'Are you all right?'

She nodded in a glum way. Mado took the drink from Schofield and then walked to the window to stare down into the garden which was now a dark, shapeless mass.

'Well, George, you're certainly building up the anticipation. We're all of us agog. Where is Elissa? And if it comes to that— where's the white hope of the Sunday press?'

'Andrea got away and out of it before we arrived,' Mado said. 'Elissa and her children are being held in the hospital by force. There's an armed guard on them all. They refused—after a little tapping of revolvers—to let us remove them into our CD car.'

'Where's Ginger?' Schofield remarked.

'He dropped me here and then went on to see Marides.'

'What's your interpretation?' Padstow asked. Mado shrugged his shoulders and paused before answering.

'The simple one would be Greek red tape—which is certainly in it anyway. The officer in charge told us that Mrs Marides and her children were being kept where they were for their own safety. He obviously believed what he had been told. Those were his orders and I don't think he knew much more about it than that. Conceivably it's true and justifiable. The name Marides certainly carries its usual impressive weight. The security officer was in awe of it and was only doing what he was told. He quite evidently felt awkward and afraid but there could be no getting round him— diplomatic status or not. There she was and there she stays.

Frankly I think they're after Marides himself. We're into yet another of the Colonels' internal razzamatazzas. Marides and his son
are both deeply committed . . . not necessarily on the same side.'

'A sort of local King Lear situation?'

Mado nodded.

'Except that Pan will never let himself be caught like the hoary
old king. He has a high sense of self-preservation. What would
you say to that, Helen?' Then, without waiting for her to answer,
went on: 'Marides is more than a match for the Colonels en masse
—or en Mafia if you like—just so long as he stays alive.'

He paused and then, watched by Padstow and Schofield, walked
over to Helen and perched himself on the arm of the chair next to
her.

'I have a feeling you could help us very much more than you
have so far,' he said, 'of your own free will.'

He looked at her hard so that she turned away uncomfortably.

'Without ideological pressures—even if you are any one of the
dozen different breeds of communist—which I somehow doubt.'

'Why should I help you?' she said with an irritated toss of the
head. Mado shot an amused glance at Padstow who was studying
the Greek girl intensely.

'You Greeks really have *hutzpah*, haven't you? I'll tell you,
Helen Stanopoulos, why you should help us—because you're sitting safe and sound in the British Embassy where no one is going
to do you any harm. Because if we throw you out, as our Ambassador has told us to do, there are two things likely to happen to you.
One is that you will be abducted all over again by your Russian
friends and the other is that you will be tactfully and quietly
killed. You want to bet on it?'

He paused, expecting a reaction, but rather surprisingly none
was forthcoming.

'You know too much, you've made a proper fool of yourself and
of all of us by your affair with Dr Petrov. Now that he's let you
down . . .'

'He hasn't let me down.'

'I don't see him around. If he really loved you, wouldn't he have
stayed?'

'That's not fair. He . . . he didn't want to be disloyal to his
country.'

'All right, Helen. We're not writing the front page of a newspaper. Let's say he's not disloyal. But you love him—why don't you follow him to Russia?'

'I very well might.'

'Knowing what is likely to happen to you there if you did?'

'Yes,' she said, looking down at the floor. 'Even though I am very afraid.'

'Your ex-boy-friend Nikos—if that's his name, but you know who I mean—he's the key to it all, isn't he? He's the one the KGB pays, he's the one who can talk—softly or loudly—to Mr L or whichever of the Colonels' gang is currently playing the Heinrich Himmler part. He's the one who organized your abduction and your subsequent release—the one who put it over to me in the Grande Bretagne bar. He's the one we really have to deal with, isn't that so?'

'I think so,' she said, 'but I'm really not sure.'

'What does Nikos and his—what do the nickerboys want?'

'I don't know.'

'I think you can make an informed and intelligent guess. They've got Mr Lycopoulos his million Swiss francs. They've had their six comrades released. What are they after now?'

'I really don't know,' Helen said and at that moment the telephone rang. Since they were in the military attaché's office, Schofield, on a nod from Padstow, picked up the phone.

'Of course—put him through,' he said and then identified himself to the caller at the other end. 'Yes, it's Dick speaking . . . WHAT? . . . Good Lord . . . what are you going to do? Sorry, that's a silly question . . . I know . . . well, thanks for the call. I'll drop round and see you later on.'

He put down the phone.

'I think I must ask you to wait next door, Miss Stanopoulos,' he said, 'I have something to discuss here in private.'

She got up and followed him into the naval attaché's room where, after he had given the room and the desk a brief security check, he left her and then returned to the others.

'That was my opposite number in the American Embassy,' he said. 'Two of the Soviet cypher clerks have defected. They went to the American Embassy and asked for political asylum. As you know, the Russians never let out any of their key Embassy staff alone—there's always one watching the other—well, this time the pair of them, the watcher and the watched, have done it together.

485

My colleague thought it might be of interest to us with the current problems we have.'

'I'd whistle,' Mado said, 'if I could find the breath.'

'Colonel Voznitsky really isn't having a nice time at all, is he?' Padstow said with a huge grin. 'My heart bleeds for the KGB.'

'What happens now?' Schofield asked, as if talking to himself.

'It could do the trick,' Mado said, sucking on a tooth reflectively. 'Voznitsky can possibly survive not getting that Greek lovebird to follow Dr Petrov to Moscow: but two more defections by vital Embassy personnel . . . I think that signals his instant recall.'

'And if that happens, he might just decide to make the break.'

'The point is do we wait for him or do we go out and get him?' Mado asked and immediately regretted it.

Padstow smiled at him: 'I think you might go and get him, George.'

'Thanks. Just walk into the Russian Embassy and ask him to follow me out? *How* do I get him?'

'Just go and get him, Georgey,' Padstow said. 'You have your diplomatic immunity and all that lovely charm.'

'You mean it, don't you?' Mado said incredulously. 'You think I'll do anything to get myself in shtuck, don't you? Well—this time —no!'

'It's what you came here to do.'

'There's that little matter of provocation—remember?'

'As we're not personæ gratæ in our own embassy,' Padstow said, 'I think we can drop that one out of the top twenty.'

Almost as if they had been overheard, the duty officer knocked and entered the room. He hesitated a moment, wondering whether to speak in front of them all and then said to Padstow: 'I've just had a phone call from the Ambassador. His Excellency asked if Miss Stanopoulos was still in the Embassy and if so I was to ask you why?'

'And what did you say?'

'I told him she left five minutes ago.'

'Thank you,' Padstow said. 'It's very good of you to front for us in that way.'

'But she did leave five minutes ago.'

'What?'

The three intelligence officers froze and concentrated an abrasive, disbelieving stare on the duty officer.

'She simply walked out. I thought you knew . . . I mean . . .'

The duty officer faltered into a numbed silence. He had only been in the Foreign Service a couple of years and this was his first foreign posting. The military attaché, Padstow and Mado looked at him so intently that he felt like a piece of cellophane melting in a fire. A total silence took possession of the room.

'You don't get a lot for a million Swiss francs these days, do you?' Mado remarked casually. The funny side of it struck him so that he had to turn away to hide a smile.

'I . . . I didn't know,' the duty officer stammered. 'Wasn't she free to leave?'

'Oh yes,' Padstow said, 'free as the air. After all this is British soil. We don't have a KGB. We don't hold anyone by force . . . Christ Almighty,' he said and then realizing it was pointless, went on: 'well, I'm glad you set the Ambassador's mind at rest. Thank you.'

He nodded a dismissal and the duty officer left in a crestfallen way.

'Any more Scotch in that bottle of yours?' Mado asked Schofield. 'It's turning a little chilly for August, isn't it?'

If the Soviet Embassy, on Dr Petrov's departure, had been like an ant-heap on which boiling water had been poured, it now resembled a town facing the lava stream from an erupting volcano. The whole building became fear-haunted to the point of a paralysing panic.

No one knew what would happen next but it was certainly not going to be 'kulturny'. Voznitsky had had the building sealed. No one could leave even for normal rest and recreation until further orders. He had already applied the first investigation process ordered by the regulations. The defectors' immediate superior was under arrest. The news had been immediately passed to Moscow since the two cypher clerks had taken with them the current key codes to an important part of the system.

Voznitsky had just finished briefing his Ambassador for the calls he would have to make on the Greek Ministry of Foreign Affairs and the American Embassy, when Mado rang up.

'You're a very difficult man to get through to,' Mado said in Russian, knowing that everything said would be recorded.

'What do you want, Mr Mado?'

'I wondered if you were free for a drink.'

'I'm sorry. I'm not available.'

'Even if I have some interesting news of Helen Stanopoulos?'

'What news?'

'You would hardly expect me to tell you on the phone.'

'I can see you for a minute or two if you come to the Embassy.'

'Thank you, Colonel. My last visit to Russian soil turned out unhappily. I shall be in my room at the Grande Bretagne in half an hour's time. I shall hope to see you there.'

Voznitsky put down the phone and looked at the picture of Lenin which faced his desk. He had always secretly detested the crafty look on the little father's vole-like face. Now he found it almost unbearable and it was all he could do not to get up and turn the picture to the wall. It was just as well, however, that he resisted the temptation since a moment or two later his wife came into the room.

'I have not been able to contact Nikos Nikolaides,' she said in the military tone of voice she used when on duty. 'He did not attend the rendezvous.'

'See if you can produce some more good news,' he said sourly, 'then we can open the champagne.'

'You talk like a Western decadent,' Irina said, unable to keep out of her voice the haughty power which he knew she possessed. It was an unwelcome reminder that he, too, was under observation twenty-four hours of the day. Such softness as she had ever exhibited in the privacy of their home was totally absent now in the KGB officer whose job was to watch and report on her husband. Voznitsky's stomach heaved as he looked at his wife.

'It's high time we went back to Moscow,' she said, an unexpected break in her voice, 'this kind of life is not for us, Alexei. It results in what is happening now—and that is not good for either of us, and least of all for Boris.'

Suddenly and to his distress and embarrassment, she began to cry. She stood quite still in front of his desk in the correct stance a subordinate should adopt in the presence of a senior officer—even if that officer were her husband—and the tears coursed down her face. He got up and put his arms round her thick, sturdy shoulders.

'Don't cry,' he said, 'it has all happened before and it will do so again. It is not our fault. How can it possibly be our fault?'

'We should never have come to Greece,' she cried, 'it was all a mistake. We are better off in Russia, Alexei. Ask for us to go back as soon as we can.'

'I don't suppose that will be necessary,' he remarked dryly and nodded at her to go, 'I should think we will be recalled just as soon as Karai or some other ambitious young tiger can be sent back to Athens.'

Not that George Mado set off for his assignment in any benign frame of mind. Although neither could know it, both Mado and Voznitsky stood in a somewhat similar relationship to their respective establishments. A few minutes before Mado left the British Embassy an urgent Top Secret telegram had been handed to Padstow by the duty officer. It was from his chief in London.

'Strongest representations have been made by Ambassador Athens requiring cessation all special operations forthwith plus withdrawal diplomatic privilege Mado stop Had Petrov co-operated pressure could have been resisted stop However in default positive results Operation Resident must now be regarded as cancelled stop All personnel return London earliest.'

'A great message of good will,' Mado commented as he drained the last drop of Schofield's Scotch and prepared to leave for the centre of Athens. 'The General addressed his troops on the eve of battle,' he declaimed, striking a Napoleonic stance, 'and told them not to worry too much about the enemy, they would all be shot in the back in any event.'

He had decided to walk. This would irritate the car-borne trackers put on to follow him and it would also generate a certain local uncertainty as to what he was minded to do. He knew he would be followed, and he also knew that Schofield would be following the followers. Picturing this somewhat ludicrous process as he walked gave him a brief exhilaration and made him smile. There was very little else to amuse him in the prospect before him.

Mado did not hurry. What was there to hurry for? If Voznitsky had decided to defect, he would do so now without further pressure from Mado. He could wait. If he were only trying to find out some news about Helen Stanopoulos, then the aggravation this would provoke could well be delayed. Mado felt an old familiar calmness steal over him as he walked. This was always an indica-

489

tion of danger in the offing. Exactly what danger he did not know nor did he attempt to analyse the form it might take. Mado had been too long in espionage not to appreciate how comparatively unimportant were the lives of individual operators. He had survived so often in similar circumstances only by the grace of God. Now he had the full fatalistic approach to what remained of his life. He wondered if Voznitsky had reached the same point of understanding. Not that it mattered. *Que sarà, sarà.*

He collected the key of his room at the Grande Bretagne and went upstairs. Everything appeared to be in order. The few papers in his brief-case had again been sorted through and inspected for the umpteenth time but as they contained nothing of value, this was, if anything, an indication of normality without sinister overtones.

He walked over to the window and looked down on the centre of Athens. It struck him that there were fewer people than usual bustling about Constitution Square but no doubt the news of the current security blitz had been spread about. Such rumours ran round the Greek capital like quicksilver and were always acted upon. The Greeks had become expert at going to ground when trouble seemed in the offing and to know what was happening slightly ahead of the arrival of a security squad might well be the difference between survival and the usual treatment. The Greeks were no fools, Mado thought, as he watched a youth dodging an identity check whilst a girl-friend distracted attention. They had learnt a thing or two from the Turks in five hundred years.

'Well, Mr Mado, are you enjoying your stay in Athens?'

He spun round to find himself being addressed by a complete stranger who had either entered the room noiselessly or had been there, in hiding, when Mado himself had arrived. The man was heavily built and affected dark glasses so that his eyes were invisible. He moved, in the way Mado had trained himself to move, with an easy stealth so that 'cat-like' was an apt rather than a merely trite description of the stranger. He was expensively dressed and his thick sensual lips gave him a cruel, sardonic expression. Not a nice man, Mado thought, to find in your room uninvited at a time like this.

'Who are you? And why are you here?'

'I am Mr Lamda,' the stranger said and smiled as the effect of this sank in. Mr L's smile was one of the nastiest Mado had seen in years. 'As no doubt you know, I am the one who usually asks the questions.'

His English was excellent and as if reading his thoughts, the Greek went on: 'You are wondering how I speak such good English, Mr Mado. I will tell you. My mother was English and I went to an English school.'

Mr L was clearly enjoying himself and his attitude reminded Mado of Panayotis Marides whenever he chose to be in one of his cruelly playful moods.

'I know who you are,' Mado said and stared back at the dark glasses. He supposed that the chief of the Greek Gestapo wore such glasses in order to increase the fear his appearance induced.

'Why are you here?' he went on as Mr L did not seem disposed to talk.

'I have one or two matters to settle in a quiet place. What better than in the room of a visiting diplomat in the Grande Bretagne?'

'Matters to settle with me?'

The smile broadened: 'No, Mr Mado, you can relax. You were sent here as "bait" were you not? Well, I am a fisherman, too. It is the people coming to see you who interest me.'

'People? I'm only expecting one man.'

'There may be a bonus.'

'All right, Mr Lamda,' Mado said cheerfully. 'Would you care for a Scotch before the curtain goes up or shall we order our drinks for the interval?'

'Thank you. I neither drink nor smoke.'

'Lucky old you,' Mado said, helping himself to a drink, 'and I bet you've a tidy little nest-egg put away as a result. Like a million Swiss francs, for example.'

Mr L showed no sign of reacting to this. He sat down delicately in an armchair and peered, stared or glared through his dark glasses at Mado. It was impossible to gauge what was going on in his mind.

'Ah! yes, money,' he said, 'and what is your interest, Mr Mado, in following the occupation you do?'

'I've been asked that question a number of times in a number of different ways.'

'Try answering it then.'

There was a soft, soft threat in the voice. Mado did not reply.

'Isn't it primarily money?'

491

'Yes,' Mado said, watching the other acutely. 'We all need money. Why do you ask?'

'I am a student of psychology.'

Mado suddenly realized that Mr L had a small gun in his hand. He had not seen him take it out of his pocket and he was not threatening Mado. He simply had it in his hand, resting on his knee as if it were the most natural thing in the world.

'I'm surprised Mr Lycopoulos finds it necessary to go about armed.'

'You have several surprises in store, Mr Mado.'

'But surely your presence here means that there are security guards festooned round the place?'

'Sometimes I prefer to work by myself.'

The telephone rang and the hall desk informed Mado that he had a visitor.

'Send him up.'

'I will wait in your bathroom,' Mr L said, putting away the gun, getting up and going across the room in one continuous movement.

'I'll be sure to shout if I need any help,' Mado said with an attempt at a joke. He felt more coldly in danger than ever before, without knowing why. Whilst waiting for Colonel Voznitsky to arrive, he tried to work out the real reason for the presence of Mr L and in what way it could affect the proceedings. What was he doing there at all? And why had he made a display of being armed?

A shiver went down his spine as the door opened and instead of Voznitsky whom he had expected, Andrea and Nikos Nikolaides walked into the room.

CHAPTER ELEVEN

IT STRUCK MADO AT ONCE that although Andrea appeared to be carrying on in a normal way, she must nevertheless be there under some form of duress.

'Surprise, surprise!' Mado said, glancing quickly at the Greek's right hand to see if he, too, was armed, and then at the smiling face.

'You would expect me to be, wouldn't you, Mr Mado?'

'What can I do for you now?'

But it was Andrea Eckersley who answered: Colonel Voznitsky is on his way here. Nikos wants a word with him too. That's why I brought him along. He helped me get out of that hospital yesterday.'

'I think Colonel Voznitsky is expecting to find me alone.'

'The Colonel is used to quick alterations of plan,' Nikos said.

'None the less, if it's all the same with you,' Mado said, 'I would like to talk to the Colonel all by myself. Perhaps you could wait in Miss Eckersley's room next door—or in the bathroom.' He turned away to suppress a smile. It was a nice idea to put them all in together.

However, events moved too quickly for any of them. The door opened and Voznitsky walked into the room, stopping dead in his tracks on seeing the young Greek guerrilla leader. Then he turned to go out.

'No, no, no,' Nikos said, 'now that you're here, you must stay.'

Voznitsky paid no attention but continued to the door.

When he had his hand on it and was about to open it, Mado said:

'He has a gun, Colonel.'

'No doubt,' Voznitsky said contemptuously, 'but he won't use it here.'

He had scarcely finished speaking when Nikos put a shot into the door a few inches away from his hand. He had been telling the truth, Mado thought, in the Grande Bretagne bar—the low-calibre pistol made very little noise and was obviously an effective close-range weapon.

Voznitsky turned in a dry rage: 'How dare you?'

'How dare *you* not honour your side of the bargain?' Nikos said, equally coldly. 'You owe us a great deal of money.'

'You did not deliver.'

'Mr L is no longer around. He has been taken care of. Tonight he will be officially replaced as head of special security by one of us—with the regime's concurrence. What else were you expecting us to deliver?'

'You tricked us over Helen Stanopoulos. You traded her to the British.'

'That was where Mr Marides wanted her sent.'

There was a slight pause and Mado said: 'But surely, Colonel, that is why you are here now?'

Voznitsky turned and looked Mado straight in the eyes: 'No, Mr Mado. I am not here to find out anything about Helen Stanopoulos. I have no need to. She has come to the Soviet Embassy of her own free will and has asked for a visa. She wants to join Dr Petrov in Moscow and so, of course, arrangements are being made. No, Mr Mado ... I have come here to see you.'

'Ah!' said Mado and smiled with his eyes. 'I understand.'

There was a pause, during which Mado digested the news. There could be only one conclusion to draw. Voznitsky was about to make the big jump.

In the event the Resident's decision looked so simple that all the complications which had previously hedged it in now lay scattered about in bits. But if it were as simple as it now appeared, why had Voznitsky not gone straight to the British Embassy? Why risk it a moment longer on so-called 'neutral' ground? Once again warning bells began to ring in Mado's mind.

'In the meantime where is the money you contracted to pay us?' Nikos went on relentlessly. His gun still covered the Russian.

'You have already been paid.'

'Only fifty per cent. Come, come, Colonel—don't waste my time. We know the money is there. Only the transfer form needs to be signed. You don't really think you could shortchange us on a matter of this size, do you?'

'It will be paid tomorrow when Mr L's disappearance is definitely confirmed.'

'Yach!' Nikos said, 'you are playing with words. If *I* tell you Mr L has gone, you know quite well it is true. You already accept that we really control Athens, Colonel. You know that I have only to give the order and you yourself will disappear from the scene until the matter is settled ... or you could disappear for ever.'

That, no doubt, was what the Colonel intended to do in another sense, Mado thought ironically, as he now watched the intimidation process being applied to someone expertly accustomed to handing it out himself.

'Why are you threatening me?' Voznitsky said. 'I don't carry the transfer form around in my pocket. Also you did not come to the rendezvous as arranged: you could have had the transfer then.'

494

'That is merely a stupid lie,' Nikos said.

'We asked you to *eliminate* Mr Lamda,' Voznitsky said.

'Your people must have checked that he has disappeared. He is no longer around.'

'A temporary disappearance is not the same as elimination,' Voznitsky said. 'Proof is required before the final payment is made.'

'Proof? What proof? Do you want a sight of his scalp?'

Once again Mado tried to cool it: 'But surely that doesn't concern you any more, does it, Colonel?'

Before he could answer, the door was flung open and Marides strode into the room, stopping abruptly as he took in the scene. Almost lazily Nikos ordered him in Greek to put up his hands.

'I don't carry a gun,' Marides said with the greatest contempt. 'What is all this play-acting about?'

'No play-acting,' Nikos said, gesturing with the gun. 'Simply a trap—and you've walked into it. You should never have left your ship.'

Marides laughed in that dangerously mirthless way Mado knew so well.

'You're not seriously trying to put this over on *me*, are you?' he said. 'You failed when you blew up my house, you don't imagine . . .'

'I should do as he says, Pan,' Mado remarked quietly. 'He's a very trigger-happy young man.'

'And you keep out of it,' Nikos snapped to Mado. 'Your part in this matter is over.'

He signalled to Marides with his gun and, with a look of incredulity on his face, Marides raised his short, thick arms above his head.

'You must be crazy,' he muttered.

'Not at all,' Nikos said with a smile, 'you came here expecting to find Mr Lycopoulos but Mr L has already been removed from office. By tonight the rest of his particular clique will have been disposed of and we shall then control the situation outwardly as we now do behind the scenes.'

Nobody moved in the room. Now everyone realized that although Nikos Nikolaides might well be foolhardy—perhaps even mad—he certainly meant what he said and had the means in his right hand of imposing his will.

Mado glanced at Andrea and tried by a jerk of his head to get her to go to the bathroom, but this signal was intercepted by Nikos, who said sharply: 'No one moves. Everyone stays where they are.' Then with a brief look at Mado he added: 'And you can join the others over there with your arms above your head.'

'I might spill my whisky.'

'No funny jokes,' Nikos said curtly.

'My jokes never are funny,' Mado said and moved across as ordered. Out of the corner of his eye he saw the bathroom door open. Nikos had his back to this door and was watching Mado move across when everything seemed to happen at once.

On a sudden impulse Mado hurled his whisky glass hard at the guerrilla's head. This missed but shattered a mirror on the wall behind. At the same time Nikos fired at Mado, grazing his inner thigh, but a moment later himself crumpled up and fell to the floor, having been shot three times through the spine by Mr. L.

Voznitsky decided to get out as quickly as he could, and wrenched open the door but found himself gripped in a tight bear hug by Marides.

'Stay a little longer,' Marides said and with a quick jab swept his legs from under him so that Voznitsky fell to his knees. 'You've some questions to answer.'

'In any case,' Mr L said, calmly walking across to look at the dead guerrilla leader, 'you wouldn't get far.'

The room now began to fill up with security police. Andrea, who had been crouching for cover beside the bed, came across to where Mado had fallen and helped to get him up on the sofa. His leg was bleeding but it was only a flesh wound on the top inner groin, the bullet having missed its vital mark by a couple of inches.

'Are you badly hurt?' she asked.

'I don't think so. Not where it matters. Get some towels from the bathroom and bind up my leg, would you?'

Very much shaken, Andrea did as she was asked. In the meantime Mr L had gone over to Voznitsky and ordered him to stand up.

'Your diplomatic immunity is not going to help you now,' Mr L remarked. 'I intend having a full report from you in your own words of every transaction you made or were planning to make with this young man—especially my own removal. I think we can help you make this report at police headquarters and I'm sure you know what I mean by that.'

He nodded at two of the security police, who dragged Voznitsky to his feet and took him out of the room. Then Mr Lamda walked over to Mado, whose wound was being bound up by Andrea and Marides. When this was done, Mr L continued his apparently sightless gaze at Mado.

'Your help was vital and Greece will thank you for it,' he said with acid politeness, well aware of the way this remark would be received.

'I don't collect medals,' Mado said, 'at any rate not from people like you. I just like staying alive.'

He broke off to watch two policemen carry out the dead Nikos. Then he looked over to see where Andrea had gone. She was now sitting on the bed trying to control a fit of shivering which had overcome her. Mr L watched them both through his dark glasses, an impassively calculating expression on his face. Mado had to remind himself consciously that Mr L had just killed a man in front of his eyes. Anything could happen in Greece these days.

'However, I think it would be advisable for you to stay away from Greece, Mr Mado, even if you do change your employment.' Mr L glanced at Marides as he said this, but Marides was adjusting his tie and brushing off his suit. 'It is none of your business how we run things in Greece. I know you came here for a different purpose and then found yourself involved. Nevertheless you will not be a welcome visitor here for some little time.'

'Is that how Greece thanks me for my "vital help"?' Mado stared back at the dark glasses and, as always, attacked when he thought he had the advantage. 'How about trading me the Colonel,' he said, 'once you've got your report. Then we can call it quits. You give me Colonel Voznitsky, preferably not too badly shopworn, and I'll stay away from your country for as long as you like.'

'You certainly live up to your reputation of nerve,' Mr L said coolly, 'or perhaps I should say impertinence.'

'What are you going to do with the Colonel, then? When you've finished your personal vendetta?'

'That will be for the military tribunal to decide. Probably give him back to the Russians. They know how to deal with people who fail.'

'You can't brush aside his diplomatic status just like that.'

Mr Lycopoulos smiled and made a little chewing movement with his lips.

'Can't we?' he said. 'I think you'll find that we can. Mistakes are always being made . . . and of course apologies can always be given at a later date. In any case we shall have a very full admission of the facts—which the KGB may well wish to suppress—and that will be enough. But you are right in one respect,' he shot another glance at Marides, 'there will be reprisals on our own diplomats in Moscow. I'm afraid Christos may find things a little difficult for him there. After all, he and Nikos Nikolaides were close associates, were they not, Panayotis?'

'I know nothing of that,' Marides said curtly. He had finished repairing his appearance and was now intending to get on with his ordinary life without further delay. 'I take it I can now collect my wife from the hospital without further obstruction?'

'Of course, of course. Everything is normal again.'

'What about my offer?' Mado said, struggling to sit up in a more comfortable position. Marides came over to help Andrea move him so that the three formed a group in opposition to Mr Lamda who stood by the door, the last of the security police having left.

'You're not serious, Mr Mado?' Mr L said with a laugh that sounded more like a cough.

'As I said earlier on, no one ever laughs at my jokes. However, I do want Colonel Voznitsky and I want him in mint condition.'

'Mr Mado—your Colonel Voznitsky and that young man they've just carried out plotted together to eliminate me and Mr Marides from the scene here in Greece. They blew up Mr Marides' house. . . .'

'But Colonel Voznitsky was there with me at the time. He could scarcely plot to blow himself up.'

'That was unforeseen—and naturally unintended. Accidents happen in every plan. But they were going to murder Mr Marides and me. They failed. What would you yourself do if you were in my shoes?'

'I'd take those ridiculous dark glasses off for a start,' Mado said, 'so that my beautiful eyes could be seen. Just because you happen to be the number one torturer and murderer here in Greece is no reason to go around dressed like a Tonton Macoute nor to take such umbrage when someone does back to you what you've been doing to hundreds of your victims since you crawled into power.'

'That kind of talk will get you nowhere, Mr Mado. In fact it could even be dangerous.'

'Listen, sport, I very nearly lost my life—or at any rate some valuable marbles—a few moments ago. I certainly didn't do it to keep you in blinies. To me there's one word for you and your lot—revolting. However, we needn't go into that just now. I came to this marvellous country of yours to get Colonel Voznitsky and get him I did. Now—how about stopping the process down in your filthy police headquarters and letting me take Colonel Voznitsky away from Greece . . . without reprisals or any further fuss?'

'Incredible!' Mr Lamda said. 'Simply incredible!'

Andrea had now recovered sufficiently from the shock to enable her to speak without too much shaking and shivering. She straightened up and faced Mr L.

'Why don't you do as Mr Mado suggests?' she said. 'Pick up that phone and stop the brutality before it really begins.'

'I advise you to keep well out of this, Miss Eckersley.'

A slightly tremulous look crossed her face and for a second or two Mado thought this had shut her up. He was wrong.

'On the contrary I'm going to get further in. You're supposed to be a man who understands deals, Mr Lamda, so now here's one from me. You've just killed the guerrillas' chief of staff, if that's the way to describe him. But you know—and I know—we all of us know that the movement itself goes on. Tomorrow another Nikos will be found. You and your associates will again be under threat. In the end you'll have civil war here as you had it after the second world war—as we have it in Ulster.'

'There will be no civil war because nobody wants it. As in Spain, Miss Eckersley, one civil war is enough. The Greek people demand a peaceful and prosperous life. We give it them. We know what we are doing. We also know when foreign agitators get into the act and that's when we take the necessary precautions.'

'Mr Lamda or Lycopoulos or whatever your name is,' Andrea said imperiously, 'I've just seen you kill one man and send another to be tortured. The Sunday after I get back to England your life story—with full documentation—will be published by my paper.'

Mr L appeared to be quite unmoved.

'I am already the arch devil so far as the British press is concerned. I can stand another attack. Are you sure you have the documentation you talk about?'

'Oh! yes.'

'I think you may find it missing when you next look through your papers, Miss Eckersley. And your paper might find a libel suit very expensive.'

'My duplicates are already in a bank in London,' Andrea said, without turning a hair. 'The story itself won't take me long to write up.'

'If you get back to London yourself, that is.'

Now it was Andrea's turn to surprise the Greek with a short contemptuous laugh: 'I don't think you'll touch me, Mr Lycopoulos. Herr Entdecken wouldn't like it at all—and then you'd have an unwelcome interruption in your essential supplies, in the one market where you really clean up.'

A silence followed on the mention of Herr Entdecken's name. It meant nothing to Mado but then he knew little of the international drug scene. Herr Entdecken evidently carried a lot of weight with Mr L.

Marides, who had been watching this exchange with growing impatience, now took charge.

'You're both wasting time trying to blackmail each other. I suggest you turn over Colonel Voznitsky to the British as Mr Mado has asked and Miss Eckersley will write something else for her paper on her return to London.'

Mr L turned his dark glasses on the Greek millionaire and for a while said nothing.

'Provided there's a cash adjustment,' he said in the end.

'No,' Marides said firmly, no cash adjustment. You've got your million Swiss francs for my niece, who has now decided that love conquers even Siberia. Any cash adjustment from now on comes from the other direction. And don't threaten me—or my businesses here in Greece,' he went on before Mr Lamda could open his mouth. 'If I have any more provocation from you and your associates, I pack it all up overnight—and I never come back. You'll be left with some valuable hardware but that's about all. Greece and I have done very well for and with each other. I think your friends would want that state of affairs to continue as it is.'

No one spoke and no one moved. Mado found his eyes returning to the spot where Nikos had fallen to the floor. He was heartily sick of it all. No matter what Padstow might offer, he would never take another assignment like this again. His thoughts went back over all they had been through in the last couple of weeks. To be within sight of success and now to find the result at the mercy of some kind of macabre auction—in which all could be lost if their bid did not succeed—struck him as cruelly ironic.

'Very well,' Mr Lycopoulos said, opening the door, 'enough is enough.' He nodded at Mado and at Andrea. 'I want you both out of the country by midnight tonight. You will write nothing about me in your paper, Miss Eckersley, and Colonel Voznitsky will be delivered to the British Embassy in an hour's time. Of course,' he added as he went through the door, 'since in Greece everyone is free to do as they like, your Russian Colonel may not wish to defect after all—and as you pointed out, he has diplomatic immunity . . . so it will be up to him, will it not?'

After the door had closed behind Mr L there was a lengthy pause while each of them thought out what had just been agreed and what was now likely to happen.

'Thanks, Pan,' Mado said, 'it all depended on you.'

Marides looked at him and unexpectedly smiled.

'I'll get Doctor Spiro to examine your leg. Next time, George, you'll be working for me.'

'Hm!' Mado said, 'you're not supposed to take advantage of a wounded man.'

'Will that creature do as he says?' Andrea asked. Marides nodded abruptly.

'He is totally corrupt. He enjoys both money and power. He'll honour the deal. And so must you,' he added with a sudden warning note in his voice and a sharp look at Andrea. The enigmatic smile had gone from his face and he was again the tough, hard man the world understood him to be.

'It's too good a story to lose,' Andrea pleaded, 'what am I going to tell my editor?'

'However, lose it you will—or you may find Herr Entdecken getting nasty with *you*.'

'You mean it?' Andrea said, playing it unexpectedly soft.

'Ask George whether I mean what I say—and what happens when people don't toe the line.'

501

Then, without allowing her to comment, he went on sharply: 'I'm now going to collect Elissa and the children. I'll have the 707 ready for six o'clock tonight. We'll be in London by ten. You can tell Mr Padstow he can bring his new Russian friend if he wants ... and I shall expect a knighthood in due course.'

He walked to the door. 'I must find out who they'll be sending as the next Resident to Greece.'

'Why not Ivan Karai?'

'Why not indeed?' Marides said, 'it's an ideal piece of casting.'

>>> If you've enjoyed this book and would like to discover more great vintage crime and thriller titles, as well as the most exciting crime and thriller authors writing today, visit: >>>

The Murder Room
Where Criminal Minds Meet

themurderroom.com